Also by Fazil Iskander

The Goatibex Constellation
Sandro of Chegem

THE GOSPEL
ACCORDING TO
CHEGEM

THE GOSPEL ACCORDING TO CHEGEM

Being the Further Adventures of
SANDRO OF CHEGEM

FAZIL ISKANDER

*Translated from the Russian
by Susan Brownsberger*

AN ARDIS BOOK

VINTAGE BOOKS
A DIVISION OF
RANDOM HOUSE   NEW YORK

Library of Congress Cataloging in Publication Data

Iskander, Fazil.
The Gospel according to Chegem.

"An Ardis book."
Translation of: Sandro iz Chegema.
Continues: Sandro of Chegem.
"Published in the United States by Random House, Inc.,
New York, and simultaneously in Canada by Random House
of Canada Limited, Toronto"—T.p. verso.
I. Title.
PG3482.S5S213   1984   891.73'44   83-40378
ISBN 0-394-72377-5

FOREWORD

The Gospel According to Chegem carries forward into the 1970s Fazil Iskander's epic narrative about the tiny Caucasian nation of Abkhazia and its larger-than-life inhabitants. The first part of this collocation of semi-independent tales, Sandro of Chegem, *was published in the United States last year. Iskander's foreword to his book, originally printed in that volume, is reproduced below.*

I began writing *Sandro of Chegem* as a comic piece, a gentle parody of the picaresque novel. The concept gradually became more complicated, overgrown with details; I tried to break away to the wide-open spaces of pure humor, but I couldn't do it. This is one more proof of the old saying that the writer merely follows a voice, which dictates the manuscript to him. . . .

I have wanted the images of the people I portray in these chapters to reveal the might and beauty of the moral sky under which the people of Chegem lived. The history of a clan, the history of the village of Chegem, the history of Abkhazia, and all the rest of the world as it is seen from Chegemian heights— that is the concept of the book, in broad outline.

Increasingly, as the book developed, my inspiration has been the poetry in the life of the people. That is what matters.

Kenguria is a fictitious district in eastern Abkhazia.

Enduria is an even more fictitious district in even more eastern Abkhazia.

The Endurskies are the mystery of ethnic prejudice.

Every people perceives its own way of life as the greatest one of all. This perception seems to reflect a nation's instinct of self-preservation: Why should I imitate another people's way of life if mine is the greatest? Hence ethnic prejudice; it is inevitable, for the time being. To pretend that it did not exist would be cowardly and vulgar. Ironic mockery of another people's way of life is the most peaceful form of ethnic prejudice. That is all I make of it. In portraying that irony, and in speaking ironically about it, I have tried to be true to life and true to the natural principles of equality among nations.

Following the traditions of classical Russian literature, which revealed the value of the inner life of the so-called little man, I have attempted to reveal, to the best of my abilities, the significance of the epic existence of the little nation.

In my childhood I caught fleeting glimpses of the patriarchal village life of Abkhazia and fell in love with it forever. Have I perhaps idealized a vanishing life? Perhaps. A man cannot help ennobling what he loves. We may not recognize it, but in idealizing a vanishing way of life we are presenting a bill to the future. We are saying, "Here is what we are losing; what are you going to give us in exchange?"

Let the future think on that, if it is capable of thinking at all.

—FAZIL ISKANDER

ACKNOWLEDGMENTS

Many people have been very generous of their time in answering my questions and commenting on my manuscript. I thank them all—most especially Professor Michael Connolly of Boston College and my friend Rima Zolina.

—SUSAN BROWNSBERGER

CONTENTS

THE GOSPEL
ACCORDING TO
CHEGEM

UNCLE SANDRO
AND THE END
OF THE GOATIBEX

U NCLE SANDRO and I were walking toward an old mansion that now houses one of our glorious agencies, where the most worthy people are rewarded with decorations and medals, and others—also worthy but less eminent—with certificates of merit and citations.

I too had once received a certificate of merit here. That was after a ten-day festival of Abkhazian art, though I didn't enter the festival myself, merely covered it for our thrice-renowned newspaper, *Red Subtropics*. Evidently I did a pretty good job of covering it, because they nominated me for honors along with the top entrants in the festival. And not only nominated me but gave me the certificate.

On the other hand, to be perfectly honest, I think the truth is that they would have coughed up a medal for me, if my write-up on the festival—even just the key passages—had been more brilliant. But, as the saying goes, you don't shake your fist when the fight is over. So there's no point feeling bad about it, especially since even the certificate, which had an exceptionally handsome gold border, caused some awkwardness.

What happened was that it got stolen by one of our fellow Chegemians, namely Kunta. He arrived in Mukhus to sell nuts, sold them, and then came over to spend the night with us. My mother, wishing to boast of my career achievements, found nothing better to show him than this certificate.

Evidently it made an indelible impression on him, though we didn't realize it. That night he slept in the same room with me, and I remember he tossed and turned for a long time. When I asked what was troubling him, he made no reply, or rather, countered with a question of his own: "What's the shortcut from your house to the bus?"

"Why take a shortcut?" I said, still ignorant of his plot. "Turn at the corner, and it brings you right out to the station—"

"I'd rather take a shortcut," he sighed, and fell silent.

Then, a week later, another relative from the village came to visit us, and my mother, wishing to boast of my career achievements, rushed for the certificate. That was when it all came to light. At once I remembered his sighs, his tossing and turning, the fact that he had left the house at daybreak without even having any tea, and of course his fantasy of taking a shortcut to the bus. This fantasy, absurd under urban conditions, was actually an expression of his subconscious fear of being overtaken by a posse.

None of this is meant to imply that I was now on my way to receive another award. On the contrary, my affairs had recently taken such a bad turn that I had been forced to enlist Uncle Sandro's help in a little escapade in the hope of strengthening my position at the newspaper.

That was why we were approaching the mansion. Uncle Sandro was holding in his hand an airline bag with the inscription "Air France." From within it came an occasional hollow drumming, or to be exact, the thump of the impatient tail of a flame-colored spaniel against the inside of the bag.

What we had to do was to swap the spaniel for a certain top-secret document of an economic nature, which I would carry with me as my ace in the hole. In an emergency I would present it—or, to be quite safe, a copy of it—to Avtandil Avtandilovich.

The document contained a secret order concerning goatibexes. It dealt with the clandestine (so as not to cause talk among the people) resettlement of the goatibexes from the various kolkhozes to one state livestock farm.

The resettlement was prompted by a mysterious disease widespread among the goatibexes. The unfortunate animals had developed foot rot. Apparently their genetic structure had proved unstable, an event largely foreseen, incidentally, by those who had doubted the viability of the new animal.

So, we were approaching this mansion, which housed, in addition to the agency that issued awards to worthy people, the Agriculture Administration and a number of other lesser offices.

This airy, handsome building, obviously of prerevolutionary origin, was crowned by a brightly silvered dome, reminiscent of the dome of an Orthodox church—although the red flag streaming over the dome at once exposed the inappropriateness of this simile.

Now the flag was barely fluttering, as if overcome with the heat, and it might have been likened to an ideological fan, indolently waving away a miasma of hostile ideas as if they were a swarm of midges, hovering importunately, though not too dangerously, over the silver-helmeted head of a watchfully dozing fairy-tale knight.

When we drew even with the entrance to the mansion, Uncle Sandro stopped suddenly, so that the skirts of his lightweight cherkeska flared open to reveal trim legs tightly buttoned into soft boots. He stopped and with the hand unencumbered by Air France drew an invisible line from the mansion's entrance across the width of the sidewalk.

"Don't you notice anything?" he asked archly.

"No," I said, surveying the bare sidewalk with its solitary urn at the edge of the pavement.

From the bag came a hollow drumbeat.

"He feels his master nearby," Uncle Sandro said. Running his eyes over the sidewalk he added, "There used to be a marble walkway from the entrance right out to the street."

It was true—I remembered that when I passed by here as a child I could never refrain from hopping around on the colored chess squares of this marble parquet. I even used to imagine that the mansion's inhabitants could play chess looking out the windows, if they had an attendant below to move the pieces. In the end, I even thought of a way they could manage without an attendant, by simply using a long bamboo pole like the ones used to pick fruit from trees. All they had to do was attach a hook to the end of the bamboo pole and a ring to each chess piece.

I think this odd, inappropriate fantasy was prompted by the fact that the other kids and I had just learned to play chess, and wherever I went I was on the lookout for a game.

"Where did it go?" I asked Uncle Sandro, meaning the marble walk. I sensed that he was waiting patiently for my question.

"The former leaders filched it," Uncle Sandro replied, his big blue eyes expressing a complex grief: he grieved half for the marble squares, half for the former leaders, regretting that their cupidity—which had incidentally affected even the fate of these slabs—had reduced them to the status of "former."

"What did they want them for?" I asked, placing no great faith in this odd story.

"Their fireplaces," Uncle Sandro said confidently. "Rich people are building fireplaces in their houses now, the way they did before the revolution. And you can't get colored marble anywhere now. Especially marble from czarist times; it never wears out."

For some reason I began to feel very bad about the walkway. After all, I had sometimes hopped around here as a child, although I never did get to play chess.

"I used to come to this house back before the revolution," Uncle Sandro said thoughtfully, "and again under Lakoba . . ."

"How do you mean?" I asked, anticipating something interesting.

From the bag there came again the hollow drumming of the dog's resilient tail.

"Let's go," Uncle Sandro said, gesturing toward the entrance. "I'll tell you later."

He turned and walked through the doorway. I followed him. Downstairs in the vestibule there was a glassed-in booth that looked like a hothouse and was obviously of later origin than the mansion itself. A man peered out at us with the exaggerated perplexity with which all men, especially administrators, peer out from behind glass. This may be why every man who peers at you from behind glass seems to look like an administrator.

His first impulse was to try and stop us, but then he evidently recognized Uncle Sandro and let us through with a nod. Uncle Sandro led me up a broad marble staircase, and his trim figure in the cherkeska on this staircase lent a ghostly quality to the whole scene. And yet, for moments at a time, this ghostly quality became so real that all concept of place and time would disappear, and reality itself (especially as embodied in the Air France bag, or in its lightly quivering contents) became fantastical and therefore ghostly.

I kept thinking Uncle Sandro would turn around, clasp the spaniel (extracted from the bag) to his breast, and sing the dying aria of a sovereign prince; or perhaps some men would come running from somewhere upstairs, seize us by our not-so-white little hands, and either seat us at a banquet table spread wholly with heavy roast ox haunches or else drag us into some feudal chimney-corner and crush us there on the quiet, after stopping our mouths with the classic gold-embroidered turban. (Perhaps embroidered in the same gold as the border on my stolen certificate?)

The ghostliness of reality was intensified by the sight of a heavy (good Lord!) golden rug or curtain hanging all along the wall over the staircase. I reached out to touch it but jerked back my hand at once when I felt the cold of the wall: the curtain, with all its folds and pompoms, had been painted on the wall. This was something new. It had not been there when I received my certificate two years before.

Halfway up the first flight of the marble staircase, Uncle Sandro stopped and pointed his toe at a step that had a fist-sized chip in its edge.

"Before the revolution," Uncle Sandro said, "I once rode my horse up these stairs, galloped through all the rooms, and rode down . . . And here," he went on, setting his foot in the gouge as if, in touching his foot to the mark left by his horse's hoof, he brought close the days of his youth and caressed them in memory, "the horse's hind foot slipped and gouged the stairs."

"What were you doing here?" I asked, involuntarily lowering my voice, because sounds reverberated here as they do in a church or a bathhouse, that is, in places for ablution of the soul or the body.

"Before the revolution I used to come here to see the famous tobacco merchant Kolya Zarhidis," Uncle Sandro said. "He lived here . . ."

"And after the revolution?" I asked still more softly, because from downstairs in his hothouse the administrator was again peering up at us in surprise.

"And after the revolution," Uncle Sandro said, finally lowering his own voice, "I'll tell you later."

But what had brought us here, why did I need this secret document about the resettlement of the goatibexes?

The problem was that quite recently, following a critique of the goatibexation of agriculture, a sociological study of our goatibex had appeared in one of the Moscow magazines. Although it came out only after the article criticizing goatibexation, and we should have known enough to expect further attacks, the goatibex study was perceived in local circles as a very painful blow, a completely unexpected injustice.

By the way, absolutely no one suffered after the official critique except, of course, the goatibex. Or rather, the goatibex *per se* didn't suffer at all, just its name, which totally disappeared from the pages of the newspapers. Since we have every reason to believe that the goatibexes themselves did not have the slightest conception of their fame—although they might well have suspected something, considering all the fuss that was made over them—of course there was no way they could take notice of, or offense at, the disappearance of their name and portraits from the pages of the newspapers.

In point of fact, the only one who suffered was Platon Samsonovich, the first to advocate the goatibex: he was demoted. Even he recovered quickly from this blow, diverted by the tempting idea of attracting tourists to some newly discovered stalactite caves.

After the first official critique of the goatibex, the sign over the Watering Place of the Goatibex, a soft-drink pavilion, was easily corrected to read "Watering Place of the Ibex." By that time, a new restaurant had sprung up next to the pavilion, on the picturesque ruins of the ancient fortress, and it too, without much imagination, had been named Watering Place of the Goatibex.

Now, when the pavilion had to undergo a slight change of name, the restaurant manager suddenly felt a surge of boldness and creative imagination and gave his restaurant the name Hellas, as if to remove it at one stroke beyond the range of ideological storms. His total break with the goatibex may also have been prompted by the circumstance that the restaurant had until recently been adorned by a local artist's celebrated painting, "Goatibex on Svanian Tower."

Thus, what occurred after the official critique of goatibexation was a comparatively peaceful reorganization, the resorption of a not too malignant tumor. The newspaper printed a self-critical article, the gist of which was, "Dear Moscow: You mean you don't like goatibexation? Very well, we shall halt it."

And halt it they did, as I have already said. Then this sociological study suddenly came out. Avtandil Avtandilovich turned gloomy. And he wasn't the only one. There were a lot of phone calls back and forth among the powerful officials of our land in those days, and even more frequent exchanges of remarks as they gathered in small, sadly cozy circles. In the evening they strolled along the embankment just as sadly, pulling long faces like children, looking jealously into the faces of their acquaintances to determine whether their expression was one of sufficient patriotic sorrow. If some official forgot himself and a smile or a cheery expression flitted across his face, it was instantly noted from afar, and his sorrowing colleagues nodded significantly to one another: What can you say about him, he's obviously not one of us . . .

It was anticipated that following this sociological study the Moscow newspaper would come back to the question of goatibexation, the more harshly to condemn all its adherents. In order to forestall at least part of this criticism, the Abkhazian leadership commissioned the district organizations, among them our editorial staff, to check around carefully and see whether any traces of the campaign lingered on in the names of individual enterprises, in posters, brochures, or other graphic adjuncts to the campaign. As careful inquiry showed, the spirit of the goatibex had by this time totally vanished from the mental habit of our land, unless you count a few dozen pamphlets entitled *The Livestock Technician's Handbook*, gathering dust in a Kengur bookshop, and a plaster goatibex found in the possession of a Kengur private photographer.

The copies of *The Livestock Technician's Handbook*, which contained guidelines for the care of goatibexes (as if the poor livestock technician didn't have enough to worry about!) were dealt with in a trice. The same cannot be said of the plaster goatibex.

Its owner balked and would not give up his goatibex, pleading that ever since the critique of goatibexation the vacationers had been especially eager to be photographed beside it—and children and liquored-up men, even astride it. When threatened with confiscation of the plaster goatibex, he replied that those days were over, he would complain to Moscow. This, of course, was something the city soviet had not counted on.

In the end, wiser heads prevailed and a compromise was found. The photographer was allowed to keep the goatibex's body but ordered to replace its horns with those of a deer. He ostensibly gave his consent, but this, it turns out, was a cover for perfidy.

There did appear over the goatibex's body quite a decent pair of branched horns, having nothing in common with goatibex horns, which curve up like a well-trained Cossack mustache. The net effect was that of a very strange animal, thickset, undersized, with a disproportionately large head, and suddenly (what on earth!) crowned with langorous, heavily branched horns.

By way of reward for making this concession, the city soviet allowed him to set up shop in a sector of the park beside the sea, where it was richest in clients.

But it seems that when he removed the permanently riveted horns from his goatibex, he set into its head two iron pipes, threaded on the inside, and then equipped the goatibex horns, as well as the deer horns, with matching screws of the same diameter.

So the usual seaside crowd comes strolling along and sees the usual seaside photographer, photographing deer-lovers beside his somewhat strange, perhaps, but in any case quite legal, deer.

But now a young man detaches himself from a small group of friends, who are ostensibly out for a careless stroll. He approaches the photographer, whispers something in his ear, and the photographer nods his assent. The young man nods to his acquaintances, they pose beside the deer, but the photographer, instead of snapping the picture, for some reason rummages in his kit and comes up with a strange object wrapped in burlap.

The rest takes only a few seconds. A few strong twists, and the dancing little deer-horn tree ends up on the ground. The burlap is carelessly dropped over it. A few more strong twists in the other direction, and the goatibex, furnished with the horns proper to him, favors the lovers of black-market liberal photos with his company.

"No one knows yet who's going to win out," the photographer murmurs, and he snaps several contraband pictures. The young man receives his commission, the lovers of black-market liberal snapshots receive their photographs in due course.

I was told about all this by a fellow Chegemian who works as a policeman here. He had tracked down this photographer in the line of duty, and now he also receives his commission. The photographer wasn't depressed by this; on the contrary, he was emboldened. Now he himself corrupts his usual clients, casually suggesting to them, "With the goatibex or without?"

But that, of course, is beside the point. The point is that the central newspaper did not, as expected, repeat its critique. Now the people who had been involved in promoting the goatibex revived, especially when the Moscow press came out with a critique of the magazine that had criticized goatibexation. Although the magazine was not being criticized for its criticism of goatibexation, some people here in Mukhus took it to mean that the magazine was in trouble and had no business criticizing us. Other people, however, maintained that even in the past the magazine had undergone repeated criticism. And then an issue of far-reaching poignancy was raised in local circles: Could criticism from a criticized magazine be considered real?

No, said some, of course we shouldn't take the criticized magazine's criticism seriously, we've got nothing to worry about, they said. Others, more inclined to dialectics, responded that this was not true: until the magazine was shut down the criticized magazine's criticism was in fact real, regardless of our wishes.

"Why regardless of our wishes?" the first speakers said with rueful indignation. "Aren't we people?"

"Hegel," the more dialectically inclined replied dryly. The very dryness of their reply hinted at the mental unprofitability of more extensive explanations in the given instance, a hint which the spokesmen for the given instance naturally found offensive.

On the whole, people awaited the shutdown of the magazine with great excitement. While they waited, it was criticized several more times, so that their excitement knew no bounds, but still the magazine was not shut down, for some reason.

Worse than that. Like the legendary machine gunner—repeatedly covered by the heavy artillery of criticism, crushed and spattered with dirt and rubble—it suddenly opened fire from under its own debris, forcing its long-eared enemies to stampede, running backwards and kicking the air with their flying hooves as they fled. The newsreels attached a reverse meaning to this flight, that is, depicted it as an attack. The flying hooves, inexplicably kicking rearward, were explained as being due to an excess of daring and the impossibility of kicking forward.

Since the magazine still had not been shut down, the pent-up anger at the sociological study could find no All-Union outlet, and a local outlet had to be found. The question was formulated thus: "Who informed to Moscow about our goatibex? Who crapped in his own nest?"

Although the data on the goatibex had been openly printed in our papers, everyone seemed to think that somebody had secretly informed Moscow about the goatibex, enlisted Moscow's support, and after that the critique had appeared in the Moscow press.

Little by little the circle of suspects narrowed ominously, and despite my protestations closed on me. More precisely, my nerves gave out, and I began to protest somewhat before the circle closed.

With great difficulty I succeeded in proving that the goatibex study had been written not by me, but by another countryman of ours who now lived in Moscow but spent his summers here in Abkhazia.

Their answer to this was that maybe that was so, but I was the only one who could have slipped him the data on the goatibex. I defended myself, but this opinion evidently came from the top, and several people on the newspaper staff stopped saying hello to me, as if gathering momentum for some future conference where they would have to come out against me.

Others bravely continued to say hello to me, but made it plain that this took so much spiritual strength that I must not be surprised if they collapsed under the strain before long.

I was already planning to go to the editor of the newspaper, Avtandil Avtandilovich, and have it out with him myself, when his secretary came into our room—in a fright, as always—and announced that the editor was expecting me in his office in fifteen minutes.

The exasperating uncertainty of it so oppressed me that I went to him almost immediately, without waiting for the appointed time. Avtandil Avtandilovich was sitting at his desk with his eyes half-closed, listening to the action of a new fan, whose powerful blades spun below the ceiling. A stepladder towered in the middle of the office, and on its bottom rung stood an electrician, who looked now at the fan blades, now at Avtandil Avtandilovich's face.

"Feel it?" he asked.

Without opening his eyes, Avtandil Avtandilovich turned his face slightly, as people do when they are trying to catch the stream of cologne from an atomizer over their whole face.

"So-so," Avtandil Avtandilovich said with a sullen expression. "Can't you put it lower?"

With these words he opened his eyes and noticed me.

"Any lower and it won't be stable," the electrician said, still gazing at the spinning fan blades.

"Okay. Fine," Avtandil Avtandilovich said, and with a barely perceptible movement of his hand he pressed a button. The fan stopped.

The electrician picked up his tools, which were lying under the ladder, put them in a bag, folded the ladder, and calmly left the office as if leaving a workshop, tracking white cement dust across the floor. On the floor underneath the fan there remained a carelessly spilled, and then just as carelessly trampled, little sand-dune of cement.

Seating me with a gesture, Avtandil Avtandilovich looked at this disorder for a while with an expression of fastidious pain, as if unsure which was better: to summon the cleaning lady first and then talk with me in a clean office, or to talk with me first and then incidentally order the premises cleaned.

He was silent for a few moments, and I thought the first alternative had triumphed.

"Is it true?" he asked me suddenly, looking me in the eyes with fatherly directness.

"No," I said, striking a harmonious note of filial candor.

"Then why does he write as if he worked here himself?"

It was true: the idiot had written his study in the persona of a young staff writer sincerely striving to understand the point of goatibexation. By introducing this rationale for his search for truth he had undoubtedly brought the pointlessness of the whole goatibex campaign into sharper relief; but by the same token, he put me in jeopardy, because that is exactly what I was at the time—the youngest member of the editorial staff.

I tried to explain this subtlety to Avtandil Avtandilovich—that is, why it was that the author had introduced the young staff writer into his study—but, as always in such cases, too detailed an alibi engenders fresh suspicions.

"Don't try and kid me, you know . . . ," Avtandil Avtandilovich said, after gloomily hearing me out.

"I know," I said, and stopped talking.

"How could he have known about what went on here at the office?" he asked. With a quick squint at the fan, he added, "About certain things—"

"But he's been here," I said. "He even dropped in to see you."

In the summertime a good many distinguished people come here from Moscow on vacation, and they frequently drop in at the editorial office. Obviously Avtandil Avtandilovich would not remember a then little-known sociologist. That was what I was banking on.

"A small fellow, a redhead?" he asked, the fastidious expression returning to his face.

"Yes," I said, although he was not all that small and by no means a redhead.

"All right," Avtandil Avtandilovich said, after reflecting a moment. "How will you prove that it wasn't you who told him, even if you didn't write it?"

"But wouldn't it have been enough for him to go through our files?" I asked.

"But what's in there?" Avtandil Avtandilovich said. "Imagine—two or three articles."

Two or three, indeed! But I was not about to broach that painful subject. An audacious but rather pointed argument occurred to me at that instant, and I hastened to use it before I was waylaid by any reflex of caution.

"If I had meant to harm my own newspaper," I said, "you know what I would have told him about?"

"What?" said Avtandil Avtandilovich, suddenly anxious.

"I would have told him, for example," I continued distinctly, "how the debate with our North Caucasian colleagues went, and how we all participated afterwards in the opening of the Watering Place of the Goatibex, the restaurant now renamed—"

"I know," Avtandil Avtandilovich interrupted hastily. He peered attentively into my eyes to see whether I remembered how the debate went. Perceiving that I did, he added, "Platon Samsonovich took full and total responsibility for the debate, and as for the restaurant . . ."

Here he hesitated and looked into my eyes again, trying to determine whether I remembered the restaurant. Convinced that I well remembered the restaurant too, he added, "As for the restaurant, so what? . . . Scorpions . . . A natural calamity . . ."

"Of course," I said in a conciliatory tone. "But if he'd heard about that, I'm sure you realize he would have had a field day."

"That's true too," Avtandil Avtandilovich agreed, and the shadow of memories of that unforgettable day crossed his face.

"Okay. Go," Avtandil Avtandilovich said. He reached a hand out to the fan button, then suddenly stopped motionless. I went out of the office and only in the secretary's anteroom noticed that I had tramped right through the spilled cement.

As I walked to my office, scenes from that day—whirling, disjointed scraps— flashed before my eyes and disappeared. Some of them, as if having preserved their fragment of sound, screamed and died away before I could make out what they meant.

Madness! How to assemble them?

The debate on the topic "The Goatibex Yesterday, Today, and Tomorrow" was devoted, as its title indicates, to today's achievements and tomorrow's progress in the goatibexation of agriculture. Invited to the debate were, first, our North Caucasian ibexigoat colleagues, and then Abkhazian agriculturists who had already cast their lot with the goatibex, as well as those who were close to doing so if goatibexism should be declared a general trend in livestock breeding in the Caucasus and Transcaucasia.

It should be observed that within our republic there were still some unyielding opponents of goatibexation, who continued to doubt the capabilities of the new animal.

The overall plan outlined by Platon Samsonovich, the head of my department, was as follows:

a) to rout the uncoordinated ranks of our own unbelievers once and for all;

b) on the basis of our successes in the goatibexation of Abkhazia, to establish goatibex as the All-Union name of the new animal once and for all, and reject the North Caucasian name ibexigoat as a manifestation of chauvinistic local patriotism unjustified by scientific indices;

c) to establish our country as the center for All-Union goatibexation in the future, and on this basis receive the subsidies presently anticipated from the Ministry of Agriculture.

Incidentally, a powerful spokesman from the Ministry of Agriculture had arrived two days before the debate and had already been acquainted with two or three of the most picturesque spots in Abkhazia. Our well-known successes in goatibexation were not the only factor in an issue such as the organization of a science center: no small role is played by the beauty, the picturesqueness of the locality where the science center is to be situated, as well as the natives' mild hospitality, which never turns into gastronomic sadism. They have all this in Northern Caucasia, too, of course, but, to compare with us, they would have to artificially recreate the Black Sea and also maintain it at a temperature agreeable to officials from Moscow. Therefore, even before the debate we had the best chance for the subsidy.

The debate itself was timed to coincide with the opening of a new seaside restaurant, picturesquely built into the ruins of the old fortress. The debate was supposed to conclude with a banquet at the new restaurant, to which several of the participants had been invited, specifically, some High Achievers in Agriculture, so that they could meet some High Achievers in Industry and a sprinkling of representatives from the local intelligentsia.

I don't know what the situation was with other representatives of the intelligentsia, but those of us on the editorial staff were hit for fifteen rubles apiece. Several people grumbled, pleading that they could not attend the banquet because of domestic complications, but Avtandil Avtandilovich personally informed them that they were not obliged to attend the banquet, they were only obliged to pay. He reminded them how some of our editorial staff had gone to Northern Caucasia a few years before and how well they had been received there. Moreover, Avtandil Avtandilovich pointed out the sum paid by the trade union of the industrial workers who were to take part in the banquet. The sum proved to be much greater than ours, and that mollified our group somewhat. We all had to fork out, and having done so, we all forgot about our domestic complications and showed up at the banquet as one man.

I am tempted to bypass the debate and go directly to the banquet, but I'll say a few words about it anyway.

It was set for twelve o'clock noon and was supposed to take place at the printers' club. Our small but close-ranked group was led out of the building by Platon Samsonovich, festive in a new (but cheap) suit, with a wide tie and a stiffly starched shirt. I remember he struck me as unpleasantly lumpy, for some reason, though I didn't touch him, of course, and had no intention of doing so.

We had already emerged on the street when he suddenly informed us that the debate had been moved from the printers' club to the tobacco workers' club.

"But what about people coming from out of town?" I asked. My hackles rose at the thought that even I, a literary colleague from his own department, had been told about this at the very last minute.

"Whoever needs to know has been warned," he answered vaguely, and became still more lumpy. I suspected that this treacherous tactic had been devised as an attempt to get rid of certain kolkhoz chairmen and livestock technicians who were still opposed to the goatibex.

When we walked up to the door of the tobacco workers' club, I was startled by the size of the crowd standing at the entrance. Moreover, from their appearance it was evident that they had no connection with either agriculture or the debate. It was the familiar crowd of local pseudohipsters who converge on movie-theater box offices on days when they are showing cowboy films, or mill around for hours in the hotel lobby when a stylish jazz band or a big-city soccer team arrives.

A policeman with a list stood at the door, along with the club manager, who peered into the crowd with hawklike vigilance, plucked people out of it with his glance, and let them through the door.

"What's up, kids?" I asked, as we forced our way to the door. They met my eyes with crafty glances, reluctantly making way.

"That's a hot one—he doesn't know they're going to give away American cigarettes," I heard the ironic remark behind my back.

"They already are," someone else added sorrowfully.

Before I had time to react to this information, I walked through the lobby and saw people running into the conference hall with red cartons of Winstons. I looked around at the snack bar and saw a small crowd straggling away from the counter. Evidently the cigarettes had just run out.

The hall was full. Many people held the red cartons in their hands or clutched them to their breasts; it looked festive and sporty, as if the members of two teams had gathered here, and these red symbols would make it easier for the judges to distinguish one team from the other.

On either side of the hall were several displays with charts and diagrams, in some of which one could recognize very stylized depictions of the goatibex. Thus, one diagram depicted the comparative flow of ordinary feed within one goatibex and of a rational diet within another. The flow of ordinary feed was represented in the form of a black broken line, which apparently passed through the goatibex without any particular benefit, because the flow was traced up to the very last act of ejecting the leftovers, where the broken line rather cleverly changed into a dotted line and poured out from under the goatibex's tail.

The flow of the rational diet was represented in the form of a red line branching out inside the goatibex, encircling the stomach and softly conforming to its curves, as the warm current of the Gulf Stream conforms to the curves of the Scandinavian peninsula on school maps.

The dimensions of the two goatibexes left no doubt as to which form of nourishment was more useful to them. The one on the diet was slightly reminiscent of a mammoth, perhaps partly because of the long sparse tufts of wool drooping from his flanks.

At the back of the empty stage hung a painting by a local artist, "Goatibex on Svanian Tower." I knew that this painting had already been bought by the restaurant where the banquet was to take place today. I gestured to Platon Samsonovich to ask what it was doing here, because he was the one who had helped the artist sell it to the restaurant.

"They'll take it after the debate," he answered distractedly, and began surveying the hall.

Suddenly Avtandil Avtandilovich appeared from the wings at stage right and was met, for some reason, by stormy applause. Not at all fazed by it, he walked to the table on the stage and halted by a carafe of water that stood in the middle of it.

After raising a hand to calm the wave of greetings, which was subsiding anyway, he declared the meeting open and suggested an honorary presidium, to be composed of the spokesman for the Agriculture Ministry (he mentioned his name), the leader of the North Caucasian delegation, a spokesman for the Regional Committee, several kolkhoz chairmen, and Platon Samsonovich. Every name he mentioned was accompanied by the applause of the hall, the sound of the applause being a bit out of the ordinary because some people were showing their approval by clapping on the surface of a cigarette carton.

The moment the applause for the last-named comrade quieted down, the editor of the Kenguria district paper suddenly leaped to his feet and shouted, in the tone of a man who is speaking the truth at risk of his life, "I propose that the presidium include the editor of our Leading Newspaper, Avtandil Avtandilovich!"

The thunder of applause and the outspread hands of Avtandil Avtandilovich: I am totally in your power, do with me as you will.

As soon as the applause quieted down, he requested the comrades he had named to come up on stage. Among them was Uncle Sandro, whom no one had named. Admittedly, he had been standing next to the Regional Committee spokesman, Abesalomon Nartovich, who at the time was collecting people who represented Abkhazia's past. And Uncle Sandro sat beside him in the presidium throughout the entire discussion, looking down—sometimes at me, sitting in the second row—with insolent, unrecognizing eyes.

Before the debate began Avtandil Avtandilovich said a few introductory words to the effect that everyone should express his own thoughts, his own critical observations, as well as any complaints against us, the press, regarding our promotion of this interesting undertaking, which the whole country—and this was safe to say (a nod toward the spokesman from the ministry)—was now watching. When he spoke of making complaints, Abesalomon Nartovich nodded weightily: Don't worry, go ahead and criticize—he's not speaking just for himself, he's coordinated it with me.

After reading a telegram from the minister of agriculture welcoming this interesting undertaking and the participants in the debate, Avtandil Avtandilovich yielded the floor to the main speaker—Platon Samsonovich.

I will not recount Platon Samsonovich's presentation, for one way or another all his thoughts rested on data that had been printed in our newspaper. I can say the same for his North Caucasian opponent, too, who was twice doomed—both by the fact that the debate was taking place on our territory, and by the fact that the warm sea laving the shore of this territory assured it of being the center of goatibexism.

The debate went off so successfully that toward the end its success began to seem too complete. Evidently Platon Samsonovich had gone too far with this change of clubs. There wasn't one man in the hall who would have wished to present a critique of the new animal. An attempt was made to find elements of fundamental criticism in several orators who criticized, let us say, the goatibexes' diet or their insufficient meatiness, or the sluggish growth of their wool.

"So your opinion is that we shouldn't get involved with it?" Avtandil Avtandilovich would ask, in order to liven up the too-placid debate. But the livestock technician or kolkhoz chairman would not walk into this trap; invariably he said that the goatibex in itself was fine, it just didn't grow its meat or its wool fast enough.

The only unplanned turbulence arose during a speech by a colleague from beyond the mountains who was criticizing our name for the goatibex and our diet. Platon Samsonovich was listening to him with a sarcastic little smile, now and then jotting something down on a notepad.

During his speech he was interrupted several times from the floor by our local patriots, and he had rather effectively parried a couple of heckling comments when suddenly a commotion erupted in the back row. Someone had shouted something, but his voice did not carry to the presidium, and the orator on the platform fell silent, with a glance at the chairman of the meeting, Avtandil Avtandilovich. Avtandil Avtandilovich glared threateningly at the back of the hall to make everyone quiet down there and let us hear the comment that had originated in the last row. After a few moments the commotion did quiet down, and there came a loud but completely unexpected cry: "We're opposed to abstract art! We ordinary workers don't understand it!"

"We don't understand it and don't accept it!" The cry was echoed by the ringing voice of a man obviously sitting next to, or very near to, the first. Now the hall resounded with laughter, and Avtandil Avtandilovich, clenching his fists, ordered the orator to continue. The orator continued, the noise gradually died down, and Avtandil Avtandilovich glared threateningly at the last row. After a few minutes his glare faded and he turned toward the orator. As soon as he did, a commotion rose in the hall, and over the commotion a voice rang out more distinctly than ever: "We're opposed to abstract art! We ordinary workers don't understand it!"

"Don't understand it and don't accept it!" the same ringing voice echoed again, as if rejoicing in, and to some degree taking pride in, the reliability of its own failure to understand.

The noise and laughter in the hall had reached somewhat scandalous proportions. Even Abesalomon Nartovich looked up with an attitude of benevolent severity toward the noise. Avtandil Avtandilovich banged the lid of the carafe on the carafe for almost a whole minute. Finally the hall calmed down.

"Comrades," Avtandil Avtandilovich said, addressing the back row, "we agree with you completely . . . But at the present moment we are having a debate here on the goatibexation of agriculture, not on the development of our art."

For the sake of clarity, as he spoke of the goatibexation of agriculture he pointed to the painting that overshadowed the presidium, "Goatibex on Svanian Tower," as if he didn't trust these fellows' hearing and was trying to influence them through a visual image.

His gesture provoked more laughter in the hall, and another commotion arose in the back row. Evidently those who were shouting about art had begun to force their way to the exit, muttering something to those staying behind.

Like everyone else, I jumped up to see who they were, but saw nothing very definite except a few faces looking back as they flitted through the crowd. The pale shadow of the club manager's face also flitted after them.

Some man, evidently an instructor from the Party's city committee, jumped up on stage, ran to Abesalomon Nartovich, and began whispering something in his ear. When he finished, he disappeared. Abesalomon Nartovich suddenly began cleaning, with his finger, the ear into which the man had whispered. There was no way of knowing whether the whisper had dirtied his ear or whether the whisper had indicated to him that his ear was dirty.

Avtandil Avtandilovich followed this procedure attentively, as if trying to guess which was the cause that had made Abesalomon Nartovich go after his ear. Whether he would have guessed or not is unknown, because, after Abesalomon Nartovich cleaned his ear, he himself leaned over to Avtandil Avtandilovich, who was already leaning toward him, showing by a respectful nod that he agreed in advance with everything that Abesalomon Nartovich would say to him. As he listened to Abesalomon Nartovich, he leaned at the precise angle necessary to bring his ear within range of a whisper, without abusing this range for an instant, however, and especially without leaning so far toward him as to express a rude intimacy.

After nodding again in agreement, he moved his head away and then aggressively bent over Platon Samsonovich and began saying something to him, nodding toward the depths of the hall. Apparently the subject was these opponents of abstract art. Platon Samsonovich undertook to explain something to him and even demonstrated something with his hands, as if trying to explain what had happened as being due to the floor plan of the tobacco workers' club.

Incidentally, I decided at first that the strange reaction from these fellows— who were slightly plastered, I thought—had been caused partly by "Goatibex on Svanian Tower," although there was nothing abstract about it, of course, and partly by the numerous charts and diagrams hanging on the walls.

But I later learned that a debate against abstract art was supposed to be held in this club at the same time. These fellows had showed up for that debate, not knowing that it had been switched to the printers' club through the efforts of Platon Samsonovich.

When the debate was over, its organizers clustered together and discussed its pleasant details as they moved slowly toward the seashore. Next to Abesalomon Nartovich, but lagging just slightly behind, as if to express a modest respect for the leadership, walked Uncle Sandro. In my capacity as a close acquaintance, I walked over to him, simultaneously keeping an ear out for what the organizers of the debate had to say.

"What are you doing here, Uncle Sandro?" I asked, greeting him.

"He took a fancy to me and here we are, out for a stroll," Uncle Sandro said with a sly nod toward Abesalomon Nartovich.

"There wasn't a single intelligent opponent of the goatibex," Avtandil Avtandilovich was saying with rich annoyance, clicking his tongue in a way that was somehow appetizing, as if the subject were an excellent, just-abandoned banquet table, where there had been everything one's heart desired, only through some misunderstanding they had forgotten to put out the pickled cucumbers.

"The goatibex can't have any intelligent opponent," Platon Samsonovich told him dryly.

Everyone burst out laughing.

"You said it!" Avtandil Avtandilovich continued with still richer annoyance, clicking his tongue. "One good opponent and even Moscow might envy a debate like that."

Everyone looked at the comrade from the ministry. He nodded several times in agreement, not so much to confess Moscow's envy of our debate as to agree that everything had been done right. Suddenly his spectacles flashed unpleasantly in my direction, and I withdrew, after saying good-bye to Uncle Sandro.

My mood was spoiled, for some reason. For some reason it was unpleasant, this spirit of remote enmity that had flashed in my direction in that glance from under the spectacles.

There is a type of person who hates me at first glance, sometimes even violently.

The worst of it is that I don't usually get wind of it, and sometimes I begin to understand someone's true attitude toward me too late. To discover it during a session at table is especially unpleasant, because too much has always already been said; and besides, the very environment of a friendly session at table is unnatural next to hatred and malice.

One time at a birthday party for one of our staff members, when everyone was pleasantly plastered, and after someone at the table—I remember this well—had made some sort of joke, when everyone had laughed loud and long, and I along with everyone else, and Avtandil Avtandilovich along with everyone else, and when everyone had stopped laughing and the conversation momentarily spread out in shallow little rivulets, Avtandil Avtandilovich suddenly leaned over to me and said in my ear, "Why do you always have such an insolent stare?"

"That's how I am," I replied with an involuntary shrug, but inwardly I went cold.

Only then did I realize how he hated me; I had had no idea before. The funny thing was that I learned about it when he was in a very good humor. Right at a moment of boundless good humor, he finally took a notion to find out the cause of what I think was an unacknowledged hatred.

Incidentally, I am absolutely sure that my insolent stare, if I have one, is no more frequent than any other man's. Irritation seeks something external to peg itself to, hence he had convinced himself that I had an insolent stare.

I had never before, by the way, had any personal clashes with the editor; our very faintly recognizable disagreements over the goatibex came to light much later. Up to that time everything had gone smoothly, not counting a certain seemingly microscopic clash which I recalled that night, as I returned home wondering why the editor hated me.

He had called me to his office one day and talked to me benevolently about something, and I had listened to him with a certain unnecessary, exaggerated warmth, as if grateful that here I was, a rather young employee, and the editor was talking to me as he would to a peer. I think this warmth was somehow written on my face (now here's a time when I don't think my eyes could have been called insolent), and any minor baseness on my part lay in the fact that I actually experienced the warmth.

"Incidentally," he remembered suddenly, "when you go on your break, buy me a pack of Kazbeks."

He was about to reach in his pocket for some money, but I stopped him, waved a hand to indicate that he could pay later, when I brought the cigarettes. It's staggering how quick-witted we are sometimes. I think it's some sort of subcortical mind operating here. In me, at least.

I instantly sensed—sensed, not perceived—that there was no way I could buy cigarettes for the editor; this was not a simple request, it was a conscious effort to humiliate me. At the same time, I sensed that I couldn't refuse outright, either; I didn't have it in me to make such a proud mutinous gesture. Hence the wave of the hand with which I had stopped the editor from reaching for his money.

After all, if I took the money I would have to return it; I had no intention of buying him the cigarettes, and if I returned the money, there was no way I could avoid having it out with him. Of course, if I were touchier and more spiteful, I could take the money and then bring it back to him and say with a straight face that I had run all over town and couldn't get cigarettes anywhere—that is, pay back my humiliation with a sophisticated insult.

No; I simply didn't take the money. I warned Platon Samsonovich as to what editorial business would keep me away from the office, and was very late coming back from my break. Of course I realized that when the editor saw I wasn't there, he wouldn't be patient and manfully await my arrival, he would simply send his secretary or chauffeur for cigarettes. Well, if by chance we ran into each other somewhere in the building, I thought, and if he wanted to clarify everything completely, I was prepared to reply that I had simply forgotten to buy him the cigarettes.

Everything went off all right that time, but I remained on the alert, and not in vain. About two months later, he suddenly turned up in our office again (I was alone). He sat down at my desk and began telling about his first editorial assignment, and oddly enough I sensed those treacherous waves of warmth passing through me again. But this time I controlled them.

"Listen, it's awfully hot today," he said suddenly, with this friendly, charming smile. "Let's have a Borzhom, eh?"

And again, the hand in the pocket. Again I stopped him, and he left the office with a light step, calling over his shoulder, "Bring it right in to me!"

I plunged around the office, feeling that I was lost, there was no way I could buy him a Borzhom and no way I could tell him so straight out. Now I was absolutely sure that he still had the same goal—to humiliate me.

I walked out of the building, approached the stand across the street, and asked for Borzhom water, vaguely hoping they wouldn't have any. But they did, and the vendor pulled out a sweating bottle and gestured with it: To go, or open it here?

"Open it," I said, for some reason.

He opened it, I drank off the icy Borzhom and went back to my office. About ten minutes later the secretary came running in—in a fright, as always—and asked, "Where's the Borzhom? Avtandil Avtandilovich is waiting."

"I forgot," I said, like a moron.

"Forgot?" she repeated with horror.

"Forgot," I repeated, and nodded for good measure.

"I can't tell him that, of course, but . . ." She threw up her hands and walked out, pursing her lips.

I don't know how it went or what explanation she gave him, but there were no further friendly conversations between us. Incidentally, all my complications with Avtandil Avtandilovich began with that unfortunate secretary. I noticed that he personally cultivated and sustained this fear of hers. Why should he humiliate me, why should he need this constant fear in his secretary, when she served him devotedly anyway, and besides he could not get along without her and had brought her with him from his previous job?

I think it's just that people who hold a superior position not by right, not by ability, need all this for their own inner self-affirmation, and also as an affirmation of the reality of the life that goes on around them.

A man who for years has been in charge of people writing articles, who has rejected some of these articles, praised others, while himself incapable of writing either the articles he rejects or even those he praises, and while knowing that everyone else knows he is incapable of it—from time to time this man cannot help doubting the reality of what goes on around him.

Is this some kind of a practical joke, all these people pretending to listen to me, submit to me? Isn't there some vast mockery going on around me? Is that so! Now we shall summon employee X, he seems to have some malice lurking in his eyes.

He presses the button. In runs the secretary, and recoils under Avtandil Avtandilovich's chilling gaze. No, they're not mocking me, he thinks, slightly reassured; no one could fake fear like that.

"Summon employee X for me," he says, and he gets X's article out of the file. Fifteen minutes later the employee leaves Avtandil Avtandilovich's office with the article, which yesterday was accepted but today is returned for reworking.

Never mind, let him sweat a bit, thinks Avtandil Avtandilovich, thoroughly reassured. This is what I suppose must happen in his mind; what actually happens, or whether anything at all happens, we'll never know, because he'll never tell.

. . . In short, I returned home in an unpleasant mood because of the hostile glance that the Moscow official had flashed in my direction.

The city lay under a towering, stifling, muggy heat. The leaves of the camphor trees on the main street were sweaty and oily, motionless like the air. And there was only the prospect of a few drinks that evening to lull the soul (as one blows on a burn) with the fresh breeze of forgetfulness . . .

Pain, pain, everywhere pain!

When we arrived at the restaurant, the tables had been pushed together and spread with cold hors d'oeuvres and assorted bottles. On the snow-white tablecloths there met the eye:

The currantlike transparence of red caviar.
The crisp freshness of greens . . .
Black caviar lay glossy on a large flat plate,
like a sexual lubricant for heavy industry.
You'd think people ate it
by sucking at and spitting out the bearings
like olive pits.
The meekness in the poses of the suckling pigs recalled
infanticide in general
and the murder of the czarevich in particular.
The drugstore amber of the cognac bottles,
thickets of them, rising dense at the head of the table,
changing to a mixed forest of wine, vodka, champagne,
with one lone specimen of a cognac bottle
at the opposite end of the table,
as if in token
that this thoroughbred mahogany tree
could, in principle, grow even there, in arid lands
far removed from the big shots.
The fecundity of the tables, though somewhat less noticeably,
also diminished toward that end.
In the air hung the voluptuous Venetian smell of a rotting sea.

Near the readied tables, with an expression of commercial good humor, stood the huge stout restaurant manager, surrounded by a small knot of waiters. For some reason it had been decided to dress the waiters in the national costume, and they were standing around in lightweight cherkeskas with rolled-up sleeves. The ferocious determination on their faces made them look like gunmen or, at best, bodyguards to the restaurant manager's huge body.

Later, when they began waiting on table, it was somehow unsettling and even a little frightening to accept, say, a skewer of *shashlyk* from them or, God forbid, to commission them to open a bottle of champagne.

Either because they were unused to their costumes, or because of all this stupefying festive bustle and the heat before the storm, their eyes bulged dreadfully at every request, their nostrils flared, they breathed officiously in your ear and understood nothing.

I asked one who was standing nearby for a corkscrew, and immediately regretted it. When he saw that I had turned my attention to him, he bent over me rapaciously and shouted in my ear in accented Russian, "What you want, ask for! You are guest! Guest!"

Having deafened me in one ear, he evidently felt he had done his duty, and he bobbed away from me. Furious on behalf of my victimized ear, I turned around and asked for a corkscrew again, gesturing with my hands to help him grasp the purpose of the object I was requesting of him, all the while holding my head in such a position as to hinder his access to my ear.

He heard my shout but paid no attention to my hands. He swiftly bent over me and without a moment's hesitation went for my ear. Instantly overcoming my pathetic attempt to pull away, he shouted again, "Corkscrew! That's called corkscrew! Just a minute!"

At that he straightened up and peered with pained attention into the clouds of tobacco smoke that rose over the table. It seemed to me he was preparing, magicianlike, to pluck a corkscrew out of them. But then he unexpectedly leaned over the table and seized an open bottle standing not far off, set it beside me, and put my unopened bottle where the other had been. Having thus resolved, or in any case removed, the corkscrew problem, he bobbed away from me for good and barked loudly over the tables, "Eat, drink, dear guests!"

I forgot to mention that the musicians were arranged on a huge pile of rubble, a remnant of the fortress wall. At the top sat the drummer; a little below him, the remaining members of the orchestra were arranged on tiny rocky ledges. They gazed at us from their dangerous elevation with the same botanical indifference to risk with which a goat gazes at us when he is suddenly revealed to us (and we to him) from a mountain road, up on a dizzying slope, where, as he gathers a green stalk into his mouth, he looks at us for exactly as long as it takes him to finish gathering in the stalk.

Incidentally, the painting "Goatibex on Svanian Tower" already hung directly over the rubble pile and the musicians. For some reason I was irritated that the painting had overtaken us again. It gave me the feeling that from now on it would always be passing me and coming out to meet me from some elevation.

At the foot of the rubble pile stood an upright piano—thank God they had lacked the imagination, or perhaps the wherewithal, to hoist it to the top. Later, when the pianist was accompanying the musicians and especially the singer—who stood amid the rubble, his concert shoes gleaming—he craned his neck way back and seemed to be nodding to the goatibex: Ready? Let's go!

Our famous singer was naturally conspicuous among the musicians. An Armenian repatriate from Cyprus, he goes by the name of Armenak. Now he was wearing a sumptuous pale green suit, which, since he was tall and thin anyway, made him look especially lanky. His elongated body was crowned by a small dark head with deep eye sockets. The pupils sparkling from their depths emanated the dry heat of a harmless vocal madness.

Incidentally, he was very proud of this suit, which his Uncle Vartan had sent him from France. The local boys had observed that he always got irritated if they asked him where he had bought this suit or had it made. He felt that one fleeting glance at his suit was enough to make it immediately obvious that it was from *over there*. Once they noticed this weakness in him, the boys began inciting their acquaintances to ask him where he had bought his suit, and if they did this three or four times in one night, he went into a rage.

On the whole, I must say, he was notable for the insolence of a vagrant who has long commanded the magnificent landscapes of the Mediterranean at no cost, and the extraordinary voracity of a man who has starved for just as long, or perhaps even longer.

He lived at the hotel year round and was famous also for covering the walls and floor of the bathroom with newspapers when he bathed, out of a pathological fastidiousness. For all that, I must say he had a very good voice and ear, and had mastered the Russian language with the extraordinary quickness characteristic of true adventurers, including Mediterranean ones. Admittedly, he spoke Russian with a Greek and a Turkish accent at the same time, because he had grown up in Cyprus. His coming here he explained by citing the eternal enmity between the Greek and Turkish Cypriots: "They keell eets other, and what's eet to me? I am Armenian."

Abesalomon Nartovich sat down at the head of the table, having seated the Moscow guest at his right and Uncle Sandro to his left. Then, after a slight hesitation, Avtandil Avtandilovich was seated next to the comrade from Moscow, and next to Uncle Sandro the spokesman for the North Caucasian ibexigoats. The latter ended up directly across from Platon Samsonovich, as if even the seating arrangement for dinner reiterated their intransigent scientific opposition.

After this Abesalomon Nartovich waved a hand at the other, lesser, leaders: Figure it out for yourselves, now, and take your seats in the order of your decreasing rank and power. A dozen comparatively petty bosses—that is, spokesmen for the businesses that were presenting their High Achievers in Industry, as well as officials of the city trade union—looked at each other. Stiffly and reluctantly acknowledging the degree of decrease in their rank and power, they gradually figured it out and sat down.

Incidentally, I forgot to mention that sitting next to Platon Samsonovich was the artist who had painted "Goatibex on Svanian Tower," and next to the artist

was Vakhtang Bochua, now director of the art gallery. He had been transferred
to this job in order to pacify the troublesome tribe of artists.

The young High Achievers in Industry occupied the opposite end of the table—
Oh, wide-eyed little fool, diamond-scratch on my soul, you who once bestowed
on me your gentle friendship, what are you doing here?

(Then this fellow showed up who had known her even earlier, and had loved
her earlier. By way of protest, before her mother's very eyes, he drank a vial
of iodine and was taken to the hospital, from which, three days later, he returned
a conquerer.

I was forced to withdraw because I didn't know what he would drink the next
time and because I knew I could never threaten anyone with my own corpse.)

She nodded joyfully to me and her companion greeted me gloomily, as if
threatening to double or triple the dose of iodine if necessary.

(It subsequently became clear, or rather, I came to the conclusion, that he
had acted in alcoholic hysteria. Had her mother had a glass of vodka handy, he
would willingly have drunk that instead of the bottle of iodine . . . However,
none of this meant anything now.)

I had thought they would choose Uncle Sandro as tamada, but everyone began
proposing Avtandil Avtandilovich, and of course he consented. I caught Uncle
Sandro's eye. From his imperturbable stare I understood what he wanted to say:
he wanted to tell me that he, as a real Professional, was accustomed to real
connoisseurs of the table and would not want to lead this motley table of un-
disciplined enthusiasts. He peered at me fixedly until he was convinced that I
had correctly read this thought in his eyes.

Suddenly Abesalomon Nartovich beckoned me over, and I stood up feeling
that this would not end well. I would have to be a bit careful with the comrade
from the ministry: as I approached, he was already flashing his hostile spectacles
at me. And meanwhile, the ingenuous Abesalomon Nartovich was whispering
to him about me, evidently something good, because the hostility of the horn-
rimmed spectacles increased markedly.

The waiter who was stationed behind Abesalomon Nartovich brought a chair
and seated me next to the comrade from the ministry. I felt him shrink with
hatred to keep from touching me, and I myself shrank from brushing against
him.

It seemed that Abesalomon Nartovich and the comrade from the ministry had
been college students together. This, as I now observed, lent their relationship
a tinge of cautious familiarity. Without loosing themselves from the tether of
their current jobs, and without straining at the tether too much, they occasionally
approached the zone of student reminiscences, where they would sniff out some
dried-up story; after expressing flaccid rapture over its fragrance, they returned
to the visible everyday world.

The orchestra began to play the song "High in the mountains the ibex lived . . . ."
and our famous singer, standing on a rocky ledge, sang it in the rhythm of a
tango. He could sing it in all dance rhythms.

"You should push that song," the comrade from the ministry said, seething gently with ambition. "It does a fine job of capturing the aggressive essence."

"We are pushing it," Abesalomon Nartovich agreed, watching the dancers. "They're singing it everywhere . . . They even broadcast it on 'The Lighthouse.' "

"And what do you say?" Without turning around, merely twisting his head on his high thick neck, he trained his spectacles on me.

"Me? Nothing," I said, trying with all my might to be loyal to the goatibex song. Since I could not be loyal to it, however, and my inner censor was concentrating on the formal meaning of my reply, my true attitude lurked in my mildly treacherous tone of voice, which I did not recognize right away. Once I recognized it, it was too late to put another construction on it.

"You must have some opinion of your own," he said, by now seething with restrained fury. I suddenly realized that he had already had a few drinks somewhere else. He wasn't controlling himself well: his fury had overflowed before I could supply him with a cause.

"I did have an opinion," I said, in the tone of a man who would never think of expressing himself before such an important person without an insistent order.

"Then let's hear it," he said, cordially encouraging me, in the hope that I would at last supply him with a cause for his choking fury. "Either you agree or you—"

"I forgot," I said in distress.

"Forgot what?" he asked, flushing purple. Now he turned his whole body to me.

"My opinion," I said, as simply as possible.

I felt a kick under the table. Abesalomon Nartovich was reminding me of his wish not to risk the subsidies.

"Lay off—he's a real shit," Uncle Sandro said to me in Abkhazian, conveying Abesalomon Nartovich's wish more frankly.

For several seconds the spokesman for the ministry and I looked each other in the eye.

No matter how far I back down or give in, I thought fleetingly, he knows perfectly well what any normal person thinks of all these campaigns and the songs praising them. So what is it he needs to find out? To determine the degree of fear people feel before him, to take true aesthetic delight in this fear and secure the use of it in conducting future campaigns—that's what he needs . . .

We looked at each other for several seconds, and suddenly he lowered his eyes. And not only that. At the same time, with a sullen pout, he did the most unexpected thing—but also the most apt, as I later realized. He quietly extended his hand and picked a piece of lint, perhaps a symbolic one, off my shirt. It was a magnificent familial gesture, a gesture acknowledging a blood relationship that extended a hand over any quarrel, a secretly apologetic gesture. A gesture that said: Of course I could get worked up in a quarrel, but when it comes to a real speck of dust (hair, lint) on your shirt, you see, I simply extend my hand and pluck, blow, or flick it off, this pernicious speck of dust.

I had always suspected that that was the law operating here: who blinks first. My suspicions were fully justified. Of course it was risky. But apparently he decided that I had some backbone, that Abesalomon Nartovich had some reason for being nice to me.

Abesalomon Nartovich's liking for me actually stemmed from the fact that I alone knew his secret calling, and it was what I valued in him. He was an entertainer at heart, a true teller of tales, and sometimes he let himself go a little at table, momentarily forgot the unwritten code according to which he had to keep chewing on sawdust in his off-duty conversations.

He was good at telling all sorts of stories from folk life, and during a session at table this gift of his, like any gift, would inexplicably break through in spite of the fact that local ideological circles were not overfond of it.

Sometimes he would tell a story about some cutthroat abrek, complete with juicy details on his way of life, and then add, recollecting his office, "Now, of course, we look on this differently, but for those times he was a hero . . ."

Abesalomon Nartovich began admiring the dancers. The spokesman from the ministry sullenly watched them, too.

Conspicuous in the crowd of dancers was a tall handsome young man from the meat-packing plant. From time to time he spread his columnar legs and swung his partner through with a single toss, accompanying it with the monotonous cry, "Through the legs!"

"They're good dancers," Abesalomon Nartovich said, surveying them with a smile. He even seemed to be following the fate of the frail girl as she flew into the aperture between her partner's columnar legs and successfully flew out again.

"What's good about it," the comrade from the ministry said dubiously. Unexpectedly he added, "The Americans will find their work done for them when they come."

"You, Maksimych," Abesalomon Nartovich pronounced, "are lapsing into pessimism. To put it simply, you're talking rot."

"And you, Nartovich, are too kind," Maksimych replied.

"Let's go to my place, I'll show you my collection of cognacs," Abesalomon Nartovich said, standing up. "Avtandil Avtandilovich is an expert tamada, he'll do everything right."

Now I knew why he had called me over. He had wanted me to go back to his place with them. There, sure of at least Uncle Sandro's neutrality and my full support, he would tell one of his magnificent stories. But now that he had seen the comrade from the ministry skirmishing with me he cut me off, taking the risk of being without his best listener. Well, to hell with him, I thought, although of course it was actually a swinish thing for him to do.

Abesalomon Nartovich left the table with the guest from Moscow and Uncle Sandro and quietly moved toward the exit. The restaurant manager walked ahead, clearing a path for them through the dancers.

Avtandil Avtandilovich gave me a look, and I realized that with Abesalomon Nartovich gone I was impermissibly close to the captain's cabin. I went back to my place, and the space where Abesalomon Nartovich had sat with his friends was not filled in for quite a while, as if the spirit of those who had sat there continued to be marked by a Gap of Honor.

Back in my place, I took a clean wineglass, reached for the cognac, poured the glass almost to the brim, put the bottle down. Then I remembered that I had not tried the caviar (still with the same hurt and sorrow!), reached for the red, spread it on a slice of cucumber after flicking off a funereal piece of ice, distributed a dab of *ajika* on the coarse-grained surface, raised the glass and slowly—so as not to choke and swallow the wrong way, God forbid—drank it off. I realized that otherwise things would go badly for me.

The golden fire spread softly through my body. I could almost feel my nerve ends—frayed by the torture of universal goatibexation—being disconnected. I took a bite of frozen cucumber and caviar.

Gradually getting high, I noticed that Abesalomon Nartovich's departure had stimulated a mad surge of gaiety.

Wine gushed into the glasses, and a hurricane-force downpour fell upon the earth—or more precisely, upon the sea, because only the sea was visible from here. Through the impenetrable darkness, an instantaneous flash of lightning suddenly lighted up the rapaciously curved crests of the waves, which were approaching with the stealthy swiftness of a mighty predator. Some of them, in their youthful ardor, failed to bear their passion to the shore and collapsed in the sea. Streams of rain, curving majestically in the flare of the lightning, fell in the sea.

"Eat, drink, dear guests!" the manager of the restaurant cried, shouting over the storm. His voice not only summoned us to courage in the face of the implacable elements, but also suggested a way of fortifying our courage.

"*Shashlyk* here!" he shouted toward the kitchen. Almost immediately several waiters popped out, each holding in his upraised hand a bundle of smoking meat skewers. They might have been banderilleros attacking a bull, or janissaries breaking into the fortress under cover of the storm.

"Zuleika-Khanum, for you-ou-ou . . . ," Armenak crooned, standing on the rocky ledge.

Gusts of ozone-filled wind kept tugging at his voice as if it were laundry on the line. Sometimes too strong a gust tore off a scrap of melody unheard, swept it away, and flung it on the shore.

Sometimes, on the contrary, it was as if the wind had shoved back into his singing mouth a part of the song already sung. Armenak, tensing, would knock it out of his throat with the next scrap of melody, and for several moments the air jangled with scraps of melody, jammed together and straining in different directions like chained dogs.

Now and then he managed to anticipate an onrushing gust of wind. Without ceasing to sing, he leaned toward it slightly and shook his fists in encouragement—Come on, attack!—the way a boxer in the ring summons an overcautious opponent to energetic action. At last, the squall of wind burst into the balcony, but Armenak—ready for it, straining terribly—fractured the oncoming airstream and triumphantly finished the melody.

A new squall—this time of grateful applause—would wash up to him, and he would lean back against the cliff like a boxer resting on the ropes; or, wiping his face with a handkerchief, he would call down insolently, "That's nothing! I was praised by Marshal Voroshilov heemself!"

At one time they had forbidden him to boast about that, but he had gone all the way to Abesalomon Nartovich, who had corroborated the resplendent fact. Then they permitted him to boast of Voroshilov's praise again, deeming this sort of immodesty forgivable in a man who had grown up in the world of bourgeois advertising.

By the way, even I can offer some corroboration of that incident. We were having coffee on the upper deck of the Amra Restaurant, when suddenly the restaurant manager ran the whole length of the deck and disappeared below.

Everyone was very surprised to see him run, especially since he had been lame from birth. Now he was running so fast that his bad leg, unable to keep up with the good one, seemed to stream out in the air behind him. Some people tried to fall in step with him as he ran past, in order to find out what was up, but he brushed them all aside and went hurtling down the spiral staircase.

Many of the people who were drinking coffee were bewildered that he had run off like that and brushed aside their questions. In the good old days his haste might have been stimulated by a surprise inspection. Now, however, when the inspectors not only announced the day and hour of their arrival, but also asked the inspectee whether that day and hour would be convenient for him, his haste was hard to understand.

About twenty minutes had gone by when the prettiest waitress, who worked on the upper deck of the restaurant, was called below. Then she reappeared and ordered ten cups of coffee from the coffee chef.

"Make it good, Khachik," she said. "Voroshilov himself is going to drink your coffee."

"I make it the way I make it," the old coffee chef answered. He began burying little *jezves* full of coffee in the glowing hot sand.

That was when everyone heard about Voroshilov. Correlating the lame manager's headlong flight with the waitress's report, perhaps even with her artless betrayal of a state secret, they realized that it was true.

When she came by, carrying the tray of coffee, they surrounded her and asked whether it was true. Cautiously moving on, she told everyone that it was true, he was so little, and very, very old, but you could recognize him once you knew it was him.

There were four or five of us at the table, and we did not stay to hear what the pretty waitress said. We got ahead of her and went below.

It was a good thing we did, because a few minutes later we wouldn't have seen anything. We went around outside the glass-walled banquet hall to see what was going on inside. But, as the saying goes, they're no fools either, thank God. The glass wall turned out to have been covered with a blind.

Luckily for us, the blind was open just a crack right at the corner, although this was the spot where the captain of our municipal police force stood. He was guarding this unscreened bit of the wall and simultaneously watching over the screened expanse (just in case).

We exchanged a few words with the captain about this and that and the weather, and realized that there would be no great obstacle if we should ask to peek in. And in fact, realizing that we were peaceable people who were politically quite mature and would not do anything silly from behind the glass, he did allow us to peek in.

I did, and spotted Voroshilov and several representatives of the local leadership, including Abesalomon Nartovich. There stood the members of the orchestra, and among them our famous Armenak, although he was not singing right at that moment. The orchestra was playing contemporary music, and a young girl in glasses—Voroshilov's granddaughter, it seems—was jokingly teaching one of our local leaders to dance. Voroshilov stood by the wall and unhurriedly clapped his hands. Well, all right, to be perfectly frank, Abesalomon Nartovich was the one she was teaching to dance. On the whole I don't see anything wrong with that; on the contrary, it was a touching scene. No one was sitting at the table. To all appearances, they had started their dinner a long time ago, perhaps not even here but some place else.

Just then the people who had besieged the waitress, and wasted a lot of time doing so, came crowding out. They began elbowing us and we had to back off. Our amiable captain whispered that we should wait at the exit from the pier, because it was time for Voroshilov to rest, and they would be leaving soon.

We did so. At the exit from the pier on which the restaurant was situated, there was already a small crowd, meekly standing and waiting for Voroshilov. We joined the crowd and could not refrain from boasting that we had already seen Voroshilov, that the old man wasn't much to look at, bright enough; he'd grown old, but if you got a good look it was him.

Presently Voroshilov did come out of the restaurant, along with the representatives of the local leadership. Two of our leaders held Voroshilov by the arms, keeping a severe expression on their faces, thereby letting the crowd know from a distance that no one had any intention of holding any meeting. Moreover, we had a feeling that they were keeping a firm grip on Voroshilov, for fear of ideological unpleasantnesses.

We had a feeling that our leaders were extremely reluctant about this unplanned encounter with the populace. This was not long after the Twenty-second Party Congress, where Khrushchev had excoriated Voroshilov for evincing signs of sympathy toward the Anti-Party Group. Admittedly, Voroshilov had written the congress a repentant letter, in which he totally repudiated his sympathy toward the Anti-Party Group, and had been forgiven.

But in the crowd which now met Voroshilov there were people who, not without reason, viewed the criticism of Voroshilov as a continuation of the policy of unmasking Stalin. In the depth of their souls these people did not in the least approve of unmasking Stalin. Therefore, when Voroshilov was ushered past us, the most impatient of them began to applaud Voroshilov. The applause was rather sparse, but still there was some.

The men holding Voroshilov were much displeased by the applause, and they took an even firmer grip on him. But Voroshilov stopped and freed his arms from them, letting them know that he was still a marshal and responsible for his actions. With a tottering step, caused both by his age and by the wine he had drunk, he went to the people who were applauding and shook their hands.

While he was shaking hands, the men who had been holding him indicated by the expression on their faces that the applause was for the marshal's long-ago services in the Civil War, not for his recent sympathies, which were most likely due to a touch of senility, as was this desire to shake hands with the people applauding. They even frowned slightly as if peering into the glow of the heroic conflagrations of the Civil War.

Incidentally, this was superfluous on the part of the men holding Voroshilov, because those who applauded knew why they did, and those who did not were naturally asking no questions.

Nevertheless, after letting the marshal shake three or four hands, they caught hold of him. He offered no further resistance but got into one of the waiting cars and rode away.

The artist's voice brought me out of my stream of sentimental recollections.

"Won't the painting suffer from the wind?" he asked, looking askance at the painting that hung over the rubble of the stage. The canvas quivered lightly; it seemed the goatibex was angrily coming to life.

"Won't suffer," the manager said, bending close to the artist. "In for good."

"Who's in for good?" the manager of the meat-packing plant asked anxiously.

"Not in that sense," the restaurateur brushed him aside. "Spike is in good and tight."

"Ah-h," said the other, regaining his composure.

"Please," the restaurant manager said, bending down, "I want to have painting over here, 'Seal Playing with Ball,' and here, 'Polar Bear with Cubs on Ice.' "

"Instead of air conditioning, my friend," Vakhtang put in.

Everyone laughed. The manager nearly grinned, but, seeing that the artist was not laughing, he turned serious.

"Sea is air conditioning here," he said pacifically, correcting Vakhtang, "but would be nice for our patrons in the heat—for our patrons."

"All right; I don't duck my responsibility, like some people," the artist said importantly. He poured himself a big drink of cognac and tossed it off.

"I propose a toast to the hit of our fall exhibition!" Vakhtang's voice rang out.

I closed my eyes. Roar of waves, gusts of wind, and gusts of madness.

Whenever an especially big wave rolled under the balcony, it creaked and seemed to heave slightly, like the deck of a ship.

"Once more! *Allaverdy!* 'Song of the Goatibex'!"

> High in the mountains the ibex lived,
> Many a she-ibex sighed for him . . .

"In my opinion, your diet is too low in calcium . . ."

"Bravo, Katsia! Let's ask him to sing '*Allaverdy*'!"

> *Allaverdy* to all topers,
> All high-rolling gamblers,
> All queens of our hearts!
> *Allaverdy! Allaverdy!*

"O, most beauteous of women machinists," Avtandil Avtandilovich's voice rang out, "ornament the bleak life of a toiler of the pen. Sit here, my child!"

"Through the legs!" thundered the voice of the handsome fellow from the meat-packing plant.

Someone shook me by the shoulder. I opened my eyes. A man I did not know thrust into my hands a glass of Borzhom, with pieces of ice floating in it.

"She sent it." He nodded in Avtandil Avtandilovich's direction. I looked over there and saw her. She was sitting beside Avtandil Avtandilovich and winking at me. I slowly sipped the icy Borzhom.

Holding a huge bone, Avtandil Avtandilovich scraped out the marrow, spread it on some bread, and offered it to her. I sat very still, listening.

"Very good for the growing body," Avtandil Avtandilovich rumbled.

"Where am I supposed to grow? I'm already twenty-one," she laughed, and bit into the bread offered by our editor. "Thank you, Avtandil Avtandilovich."

Avtandil Avtandilovich had his head down like an Assyrian bull.

"Very good for the growing body," Avtandil Avtandilovich rumbled, glancing at her. Now he had his head down like an embarrassed, aggressive Assyrian bull.

"Please explain," two dancers said, stopping by the artist, "why the goatibex is standing on top of a silo? What did you mean by that?"

"That's not a silo," the artist said patiently. "That's a Svanian tower—a symbol of enmity among the peoples—but the goatibex is trampling it."

"Oh, so that's it," the young man said. He kept his arm around his girl the whole time he was listening.

"But you said—" the girl said, and they danced slowly away, if you can call those barely rhythmicized embraces dancing.

"Incidentally, our ibexigoats assimilate silage magnificently," said the colleague from the other side of the mountains.

"If the goatibex is forced to go hungry, he'll even gnaw on boards," Platon Samsonovich parried.

I felt myself beginning to sober up and had another drink.

"I'd swear by my mother, Comrade Sergo did time in this prison!" came an unexpected voice, apparently that of a trade union leader. I listened, but his voice was drowned by a wave breaking on the shore.

"We'll have to ask Comrade Bochua!"

"Old-timers here in Mukhus remember . . . Here, back at the beginning of . . ." (A wave, and a peal of thunder as well, completely cut off whatever it was the old-timers in Mukhus remembered.)

"Rock! Rock!"

"Let's boogie, Klavushka!"

"Armenak stole my girl . . . What'll we do to him?"

"Depends what kind of girl!"

"My dear Vakhtang, is it true that Comrade Sergo did time here?"

"I can't hear you, say it again!"

"That girl was too much! Man, could she drink! She was a parachutist from Kiev. He was still singing at the Amra then. Soon as she heard him she went ape. Shit if I didn't invite him to the table, on principle. Well, never mind— the Greek colonels didn't get him, but I will!"

"Absolutely true, my friend. His cell was right on this spot, where we're sitting."

"We sit here eating and drinking, but they suffered here."

"That was why they suffered, my friend—so that we could enjoy life."

"It's not her, Slavik. Screw her and her parachute too. It's the principle of the thing . . ."

"Forgive me for butting in, my dear Vakhtang, but Comrade Sergo's cell was in the other wing, we keep our wine cellar there now."

" . . . They come back homesick for Lake Sevan, but then they stay here with us on the Black Sea . . ."

"Let them stay, they're not bothering anyone!"

"Let them stay, of course, but it's the principle of the thing, Slavik . . . If you're homesick . . ."

"I propose we organize an excursion to Comrade Sergo's cell!"

"Rock! Rock!"

"Through the legs!"

In a flare of lightning from the hellish darkness of the night, white-foamed waves and waves of madness on the veranda. Lightning from the sky and pathetic flashes from our news photographer recording the festivities. The downpour suddenly ceased, and the music ceased, too. I looked around.

The musicians had abandoned their high place and were sitting at a table eating. Armenak ate a little apart from the others, surrounded by a twittering flock of worshippers. Rather, he allowed himself to be fed. From a large platter that held the meat from at least five skewers, the girl sitting beside him took a forkful of meat and directed it into Armenak's sweet-voiced mouth. Over the bristling starch of the napkin, a thin proud little face. In his hand a piece of bread, which he held with two fingers through a paper napkin.

Individual portions of meat bulged now in one cheek, now in the other. Strong knots of muscle, the breathtaking danger of the swallowing motion, the gentle adoring eyes of the worshippers watching him.

"What you got good here ees girls. Russian girls are world-tsampion girls."

"Really, Armenak darling—only the girls?"

With a martyred swallow, Armenak freed his overstuffed mouth. "Boys world tsampion too," he laughed.

"Scorpion!" came a man's sudden shout, accompanied by the heart-stopping shriek of a woman. Everyone jumped up from the table, knocking over chairs, and dashed toward the shout.

I jumped up too and pushed my way through the crowd surrounding the source of the cry. Right at the railing over the sea, facing out toward the water, stood the same girl who had approached the artist with her boyfriend. The young man stood next to her, white as a sheet, holding a writhing scorpion impaled on a fork. In his fury he was shaking the fork in front of the manager's mountainously looming torso. His gestures made it clear that the scorpion had fallen from somewhere up above and landed on his girl's dress.

"We'll look into it, my dear fellow, we'll look into it," the manager repeated, glancing first at the ceiling, then at the girl. "Would you like me to take you home in my car?"

"Another one! Another one!" came a sudden shout from the thick of the crowd, and people scattered in all directions.

"Scorpions! Invasion of scorpions!"

I recoiled against a table, and just at that moment, with a sickening swish, as it seemed to me (although how could I have heard a swish in that din?), a scorpion plopped onto the table beside me. I took a bottle and squashed it. To my disgust, it stuck to the bottle, and I threw the bottle over the railing.

Uproar, screams, a crashing din. Hysterical laughter, provoked by a drunken couple who took refuge from the scorpions under an umbrella and launched into a dance, singing, "Who's afraid of the scorpion, the scorpion, the scorpion?"

Everyone looked at Armenak, who was standing on the table with a plate in his hand. When he had drawn everyone's attention to him, he silently extended the plate in various directions, holding it in his outstretched hand as if demonstrating his readiness to accept on the plate any scorpion that might fall from the ceiling. When no scorpion fell, he pulled the plate toward him with a flourish and started to thread chunks of meat on a fork and put them in his mouth, turning from side to side so that everyone could see him. By the emphatically furious working of his jaws he was declaring the danger over and summoning us to follow his example and carry on with the feast.

"Hey guys, last bus!" someone shouted, and the High Achievers of Industry began to throng toward the exit, some of them picking up their girls, and some, their girls and bottles of wine.

"Now ees not dandzerous! Dandzerous is *Martios! Aprilios!* Where there ees *r!*" Armenak shouted, pacing along the tables. "Now ees *Augustos!*"

Finally the janissaries standing around the manager caught the point of Armenak's kind appeals—in any case, that August was not a spring month and there was no *r* in its name. They began running around the tables, spearing the fallen scorpions on skewers and shaking them over the wooden railing.

Outside, a car door slammed and the car sped off at police speed. I realized that this was Avtandil Avtandilovich. I quickly scanned the tables, anticipating that she would be gone. She was. I was seized with a feeling of emptiness and indifference.

When he heard the roar of Avtandil Avtandilovich's departing car, the restaurant manager began beating his brow again. When he noticed this, Armenak, still holding the plate in his hand, walked to the edge of the table and began angrily comforting the manager.

"What deed you do? Nothing! Nature!"

I shut my eyes, and for a while I felt the balcony rising and falling.

When I opened my eyes, the restaurant was nearly empty. I went out on the rain-freshened street. Two cars stood by the entrance to the restaurant. In the first of them sat Armenak. A grimace of scornful anger distorted his profile. He was still seething from his argument with the crowd.

"*Skorpios*," he muttered. "May *skorpios* f--k your mother."

The musicians were bustling around behind him but he did not once turn to look at them, even though a girlish twitter floated forward from time to time. Carefully, with economical use of the space, the musicians were packing girls and instruments into the cars. I have been to all sorts of banquets, and the musicians always drive away with girls, even when they didn't know a single one of them before.

The cars started, the girls shrieked joyfully, and once again I glimpsed the stern profile of Armenak, who was still mentally taming the crowd.

Suddenly, in the headlights of the first car and the headlights of the second, I glimpsed her face, lazily shielded from the light by a bare arm. She was holding something in her upraised hand—I could not immediately tell what. Only when her face flashed again, and the beam of light from the second car picked up her bare feet and went out, did I understand that she was holding her shoes. He was standing beside her, shifting a bottle of cognac from one pocket to another.

Spraying mustachelike fountains of water, the cars crossed the stream formed by the torrential rain.

With no thought at all, feeling only a wild joy that she hadn't left with Avtandil Avtandilovich (that could only have occurred to a drunken mind; besides, he would never indulge himself so publicly!), I ran to her and grabbed her hand. Suddenly she sprang away as if I had handed her the baton in a relay race. We ran straight ahead, our feet slapping over the warm night water, and were already across the street when we heard his cry: "Wait! We'll work something out!"

I knew he wouldn't be able to keep up, because he could never bring himself to throw the bottle away, and we ran and ran—stopping for an instant to catch our breath, snatch a fugitive kiss the way one drinks off whatever is overflowing the brim—and ran on again.

Break away, for once in my life, and snatch forgetfulness, snatch it even at the cost of blood, and to hell with everything! But now, run and keep running!

Run down the boulevard, through the flabbily sagging, lashing oleander branches, run, choking with laughter, remembering how carefully he ran so as not to break the bottle, run again and stop and press myself to this gentle, fragrant, laughing, white-toothed, crazy mouth—remember it this way!

Run from the unexpected shrill of the night watchman asleep right on the dock of a seaside shop, who was brought back to his duties by the sound of our footsteps and perhaps for that reason gave an especially long, angry shrill on his whistle, which threw us into a fresh paroxysm of laughter.

. . . The suburban shore, the crunch of gravel, the creak of sand, whispers, rustling . . . And the damp booming of the water, long, like a daydream, and the tangy air effervescent from the nearness of the surf.

Before dawn, the distant roll of thunder at the first signs of satiation, a belch from the resting sky.

Pain, pain, everywhere pain!

The next day the restaurant was closed for repair (incidentally, the piano ended up in the sea, for some reason). It was a month before they opened it again, this time without any fanfare.

Some people attributed the invasion of scorpions to the fact that the designers of the restaurant building had not allowed for strong wind, during which streams of water would be deflected onto one of the outer walls of the fortress adjoining the balcony. Because of this mistake, they said, the water got into the scorpion nests.

Others said that the gutter system had nothing to do with it; even before, evidently, the scorpions used to go into the deeper, inner parts of the fortress during a heavy downpour. This time they crawled out here with no suspicion of what was happening, and when they suddenly found themselves in a storm of electricity and music, they were stupefied by this excessive dose of civilization and began plopping down, landing now on the banquet tables, now on the people—but without meaning any harm.

During the repairs, all the exposed parts of the fortress walls were coated with some sort of hard, in any case obviously scorpion-proof, varnish. Of the fate of the scorpions immured in this part of the fortress, nothing is known to the storyteller. We can only conjecture.

Most likely they ended their lives in suicide (which is typical of scorpions), unless they thought to dig themselves a tunnel (which is obviously atypical of them, but typical of the prisoners of idyllic bygone times, the golden age of the tirelessly developing science of prison construction).

Now, just a year after this banquet, Avtandil Avtandilovich was telling me that there had been nothing or next to nothing in the newspaper about the goatibex. After our conversation I dropped by the municipal library and asked the reference librarian to give me a list of all the articles on the goatibex printed in our paper.

The librarian, a young fellow evidently just out of college—I hadn't seen him here before—went up to the second floor of the library, where the bibliographic office was. I stayed downstairs in the reading room and stood at the checkout desk, chatting with a girl I knew who worked there. Soon the librarian returned and handed me a card on which were neatly entered the title and date of the first story on the goatibex, as well as the date on which we reprinted the Moscow article criticizing the goatibexation of agriculture.

"That's all?"

He hesitated and spread his hands in a lovably awkward gesture. He had such a pure, almost girlish face, and he obviously had not yet learned to lie without qualms.

"What do you need?"

"I need all the issues of our newspaper that mention the goatibex."

"But what for?" he asked, sensing that he was infringing on my natural right, and therefore dreadfully unsure of himself.

People in the reading room began listening to us.

"The thing is, you have to have special access to those materials," he said, lowering his voice to diminish the overtones of hypocrisy.

"Since when?" My heart stood still.

"I don't know," with a sigh of relief, "I'm new here myself . . ."

"Don't you see," I said to him, "I'm on the staff of the paper . . ."

"I'll go ask the director . . ."

As soon as he left, I turned swiftly to the girl standing at the checkout and said to her, "Please—the files of *Red Subtropics* for the last three years."

"Right away," she nodded, and went back into the stacks. A moment later she came out lugging the files. I put them on one of the farthest tables of the reading room and came back to the chimney corner where the reference librarian had his little desk. He returned and stood by his desk to report with doleful severity, "The director said that he had no orders regarding journalists."

He continued to stand by his desk, as though sympathizing with me over this disagreeable news.

"Well, okay," I consented, with feigned resignation.

"Unfortunately, there's nothing more I can do to help you," the boy said, spreading his hands awkwardly. It struck me that he had expected me to be more stubborn and was now somewhat disillusioned.

I walked over to my place and sat down. When I began to leaf through the file, I stumbled across the first story on the goatibex almost immediately. The issue containing the story had been torn out of the file for some reason and simply stuck back in.

But I couldn't get any farther than that, for some reason. As carefully as I went through the files for the three years, I couldn't turn up one piece on the goatibex. What the hell, I thought—after all, the first big piece on the goatibex was carried about a week after the first report. I began going through the file again, this time looking attentively at the dates.

And suddenly the truth was revealed in all its policemanlike simplicity: they'd torn them out! They had torn all the issues out of all the files, left only the first story and the last Moscow article, and consequently the references they had given me were exactly right! Now I knew why the issue with the first story had been torn out and stuck back in the file. They had torn it out by mistake, and then stuck it in again. They did have method in their madness, I thought, carrying back the shambly heap of castrated files.

Meanwhile, my situation at the newspaper was apparently deteriorating. I saw it in the faces of the staff. It was becoming more and more noticeable that saying hello to me cost them a lot of civil effort, if not civic courage.

One day there was an emergency staff meeting. When he turned on the fan, Avtandil Avtandilovich threw me a reproachful glance, as if to say, "Is this what you wanted?"

I understood that something was about to happen. And in fact, a few minutes later Avtandil Avtandilovich started talking about that accursed sociological study on the goatibex again. (It seems that one of the Moscow papers had run another article that day, criticizing the magazine that had printed the study.) He called it slanderous, even though he confessed that our newspaper had erred in publishing the several pieces on the goatibex.

"Yes," he was saying, "the central press has severely pointed this out to us. And rightly so, comrades! We fully accept this criticism!" Here he threw a glance at the fan, functioning smoothly on the ceiling. "But those," he continued, pointedly avoiding my eye, "who has slandered us himself" (my soul sank straight to my stomach—I noticed an ominous contradiction between the plural form of the demonstrative pronoun and the singular of the following verb) "or assisted others in slander will answer for his slander when the time comes."

Now several of our staff writers began to cast glances at me, obviously saying: You see what a position you've put yourself in, you see how hard it will be for us to say hello to you now?

I tried to cheer them on with my answering glances: Hang in there, all is not lost.

But they averted their eyes distractedly, letting me know that they would not accept my good cheer because its origins were too uncertain.

Right after this meeting I was sitting in my office, gloomily reflecting on my situation, when the phone rang. It was a fellow Chegemian, grandson of the famous hunter Tendel. He worked in the agriculture administration.

"How are things?" he asked, in a voice filled with secret exultation.

"Bad," I told him, and I gave him the gist of it briefly. We shared a hometown bond that did not go too deep.

"That's just what I'm calling about," he said in Abkhazian, and then, in Abkhazian, warned me not to switch to Russian.

"I have some news," he went on, "it's kingdom come! I'll meet you right after work!"

I could hardly wait for the day to end. We met, and he did in fact relate some surprising news. It seems the agriculture administration had had a top-secret conference on the goatibex, at which they had passed a decree to round up all the goatibexes and secretly transport them to a certain state livestock farm, because their hooves had begun to rot.

"Why secretly?" I asked.

"You know why—so that the populace won't get riled up," he replied. It was totally unclear why the rotting of the goatibex's hooves (or the transport of goatibexes with rotting hooves) should cause even scattered outbursts of dissatisfaction among the populace.

Although I begged him to show me the text of the decree, he flatly refused.

"How could I," he replied. "We hectographed a hundred copies. We're going to circulate them to the kolkhozes. Stamped top secret."

"A long decree?" I asked, although in point of fact the size of the decree did not matter at all.

"No," he said, "one page. If you get in a jam you can mention it, but don't do it right away, only after three or four days—"

"Why?" Another mystery.

"We'll have had time to distribute it," he said, smiling a strange smile. "That will mean it was leaked by some kolkhoz, not by us . . ."

"Ah-h," I said.

As always at our infrequent meetings, he invited me to go hunting with him the next Sunday. I replied that I was not in a mood for hunting.

"Have you heard about my spaniel?" he asked joyfully. "He's not a dog—he's a person!"

Tendel's grandson, even though he had come down from the mountains and become a clerk in the ministry of agriculture, had not ceased to be Tendel's grandson. As a matter of fact, on close inspection, all his activities might be said to boil down to guaranteeing the conditions for present-day hunting.

People say he's an expert hunter, but that is hard for me to judge because I'm no hunter myself, although I have gone hunting with him.

Once he invited me on a pigeon hunt. This was about the end of September. We left Mukhus at dawn, and in the Gudauta district we parked the car by the road and climbed up to the top of a picturesque hill covered with drying cornstalks and a sparse, glossy scattering of eggplants.

We stood for a while on top of the hill, and I admired the vast curvature of the sea, faintly crimsoned from the east and still lost in a blue-gray haze in the west. I did not see any reason for the pigeons to fly right over us and therefore did not believe that they would.

Nevertheless, they flew over twice. Both times I failed even to raise my gun. He succeeded in both raising his gun and getting off a couple of shots, but even he did not succeed in killing anything. The wild pigeons had flown over with the speed of a swift.

On the way back, not the least embarrassed by his failure, he picked a dozen ears of corn, added about as many hefty eggplants, and having thus substituted for his hunter's bag its vegetarian equivalent, he stowed it all in the trunk in a businesslike manner and we started back. Along the way he told me about the splendor of government hunts, to which he was admitted as an expert huntsman. He frequently brought Uncle Sandro along as another expert huntsman, although I think Uncle Sandro revealed his own talents somewhat later, during the hunters' feasts.

. . . Anyway, despite my best efforts to persuade him, he would not consent to hand over a copy of the decree. He refused even to display it from a distance. Of course, I could mention the fact that it existed, but since they had classified it as secret, they could and would deny its existence.

A day later I encountered Uncle Sandro, and I complained to him about Tendel's grandson not wanting to give me a copy of the goatibex decree. We were sitting drinking coffee at the far end of the Amra.

"Try and persuade him," I begged Uncle Sandro.

"Do you need it very badly?" he asked me, turning serious.

"I may lose my job," I said, and I gave him the situation in a nutshell.

"I'll try," Uncle Sandro said, pushing away his demitasse, "though your job hasn't been much use to us."

This was an allusion to the fact that I had not helped him with either the pension, or obtaining the insurance money for the house, or with other, more trivial favors.

On this note we parted. But before Uncle Sandro could meet with Tendel's grandson, the latter called me himself.

"Haven't you heard?" he asked agitatedly.

"No," I said, and for some reason I had the insane thought that the classified goatibexes had run away from the state farm and thereby declassified the decree.

"No greater woe have I known since the day my grandfather died . . .," his voice quavered in the receiver. (Poor Tendel had overeaten at his own centennial celebration and surrendered his soul to God.) ". . . They've stolen my spaniel . . .I beg you, find Uncle Sandro for me, he knows everyone in the city . . . Any amount of money . . . Get him to find the dog . . ."

Two hours later, during the dinner break, I brought them together. After hearing him out attentively, Uncle Sandro pointed at me and said, "You give him the document—I'll find your dog. You don't—I won't look."

"Uncle Sandro, how can I," Tendel's grandson whined. But not for nothing was he a member of the hunting clan, and the quail season was at its height.

"What are you afraid of?" Uncle Sandro said, to finish him off. "The kolkhoz chairmen have long since wiped themselves with your paper. And if there's any trouble he'll say he got it at a kolkhoz."

"Okay," Tendel's grandson agreed bleakly. "Find him as fast as you can . . . If the dognapper takes him out of the city, we'll never find him."

"If the dog's in the city, we'll find him," Uncle Sandro said, and we parted.

The next day he came to me at the newspaper with the jiggling Air France bag in his hand.

"All set," he said. "Call that no-good before his dog messes in my bag."

Platon Samsonovich glanced at the jiggling bag as if he divined a connection between its contents and the epic of the goatibex, by now as distant as his youth.

I telephoned Tendel's grandson.

"Alive and well?" he asked. "Come on over and walk straight through to the men's room!" he shouted in Abkhazian, and hung up.

And now, having climbed the marble staircase, Uncle Sandro and I walked through one of the corridors. After pointing out to me where the men's room was located at the far end of the corridor, he himself stopped at the near end at one of the offices, where he said he had a little business to take care of.

"Make your swap and come by for me," he said, handing me the quivering Air France bag.

I started down the corridor past the offices. Some of the doors were upholstered in leatherette; beside them, the ordinary doors, covered only with gray paint, looked like orphans done out of their birthright. Like any institutional corridor, this one logically ended in a toilet, and that is where I went.

A few minutes later I heard footsteps in the corridor, the door to the men's room flew open, but the man who walked in was someone else entirely. From the doorway he walked over to the urinal, his rear end yawking like a horse's spleen. Heavy and flabby, he stood for a long time grunting at the urinal, attending to the processes taking place in his bladder. From time to time he looked back at me with an expression of pained attention, as if including me, too, in the array of obstacles hindering him from exercising the indisputable right to an adequate consummation of his metabolism. Every time he gave me that pained backward look, I twitched the bag a little closer against my leg, to show that I was trying to influence his bodily processes as little as possible. During one of his backward looks, his eyes lighted on the bag for an instant, as if realizing what this gesture of mine might mean, and then, not realizing after all, they seemed to say, "I've got trouble enough as it is, and now there's something wiggling in his bag . . ."

Without looking at me, but at the same time radiating dissatisfaction with me and everything about me, he walked past me and out into the corridor.

A few minutes later footsteps again sounded in the corridor, and before I guessed that it was Tendel's grandson, the bag emitted a soft joyful yelp and began quivering in my hand. But the steps went on past us, then faded away. After a few minutes they again sounded in the corridor and stopped indecisively outside our door.

"Are you there?" he asked.

"Yes," I said. Simultaneously emitting a still more joyful yelp, the Air France lurched and bounded upward in my hand.

"Come out, fast!" he hissed in Abkhazian. I opened the door a crack.

"Next door!" he hissed. Almost before I knew what was happening, I found myself in the next room. This was also a men's room but obviously a poorer one: a pungent smell of bleach powder, rust streaks on the leaky urinals, an ownerless stream of water from the faulty faucet on the washstand.

He walked in.

"Did anyone see you?" he asked, anxiously indicating the first men's room.

"No," I said, feeling that I'd better calm him down.

"I forgot to warn you," he said, already absorbed in the contents of my bag and therefore blurting out his explanation as if in passing, "that one's for department heads and senior deputies . . . Ah, my precious! You know me!" He reached for the bag, which was yelping and rocking toward him, but at that point I reminded him, "First the decree."

Still reaching for the bag with one hand, with the other he fished a piece of paper from his inside coat pocket and held it out to me, jerking his chin toward the toilet stall: "Read it in there."

I handed him the bag and shut myself in the stall. It was what I needed. I had no doubt at all as to the authenticity of the document. I suddenly felt well and happy. Say what you like, the power of the paper is obviously still strong in every one of us.

While I glanced over the secret document, I could hear a smacking of kisses and the yelping of a joy-crazed spaniel on the other side of the stall door.

Having satisfied his first rush of love, Tendel's grandson recalled that he was still an employee of the agriculture administration. He reinstalled the dog (who was extremely displeased at this, incidentally) in the Air France bag, after a hard time closing the zipper. The dog's body kept bursting out, and he had to stuff it in bit by bit.

"I'll take him home now," he said. Signaling me not to follow him right away, he went out of the men's room, humming a little song.

A moment later, I walked down the corridor and opened the door to the office where Uncle Sandro had gone. It was the State Purchasing Agency. Uncle Sandro was sitting beside the desk with his back to me.

Behind the desk sat a middle-aged man, very neat, correct, benevolent, with hair like a silver fox. Catching sight of me, he smiled at me without interrupting his conversation, yet indicating that my visit was noted and I was invited to take a seat on one of the chairs that lined the wall. I continued to stand, so as not to prolong Uncle Sandro's stay here.

While he talked with Uncle Sandro, part of his mouth smiled at me from time to time, indicating that he had not forgotten my presence, as though asking my forgiveness that he could not attend to me immediately.

He spoke softly, but as the conversation flowed into the shallows, the murmur of his voice became a distinct babble: "My dear Sandro Khabugovich," I heard, "we'll be airing this issue again . . . Of course, it's only temporary, a temporary freeze on purchases from private parties . . . But just next Tuesday Georgy Bagratovich will be back from Tbilisi, and the possibility cannot be ruled out that he'll be bringing us additional instructions from Tariel Luarsabovich. I'll give you Georgy Bagratovich's phone number and my own, but don't call him. In any case, call me first, before calling him, and I, in my turn, will make a note on my calendar to have a preliminary consultation . . ."

So saying, with evident satisfaction, he folded a piece of paper, tore it precisely in half, carefully and with no less satisfaction traced out the promised telephone numbers, made a note on his calendar not to forget to have a consultation.

Then he set the calendar back in its place, put the pen in a wooden mug with several others—colorful, probably equally harmless ink arrows sticking up as if from a quiver—and for some reason shook the mug to make the arrows stick up in a more picturesque curve. Obviously pleased that this had come off at first try, he proffered to Uncle Sandro the paper with the phone numbers.

Now he transferred his cordiality to me, reminding me that he had not forgotten my presence for a moment and was now ready to devote his full attention to me.

"No," I said, ashamed of my ingratitude, "I'm waiting for him."

"Ah, for him," he repeated knowingly. He nodded in farewell, smiling again, this time as if at his own awkward slow-wittedness, in fact, his own simple-mindedness, which was, however, frankly speaking, caused by his zeal to serve.

We left the office. That type of official is well known to me. Such men are encountered in several sectors of our government, sectors which have fully or almost fully succeeded in breaking their living bond with life.

A man sits in his office—his wages keep coming. He is incapable of doing anything, but naturally he doesn't feel like saying so openly, confessing that he gets paid for doing nothing. Besides, it didn't happen overnight.

The gradual withering away of a sector intensifies the outward activity of the man who works there. When you come to him with some sort of request, he joyfully devotes himself to you—writes notes, makes phone calls, consults— and in the end it becomes clear that there is nothing he can do.

But after all his trouble you are not disillusioned in him, you even experience a quiet, mystical delight before the perfection of his handiwork. In some people this quiet delight develops into a quiet horror. It isn't easy, you know, after the man's lengthy, gentle, halfhearted efforts to push your request through, to learn that the thing was doomed from the very beginning and that from the very beginning he knew this perfectly well. After all, it's as if you are watching— perhaps from behind glass, but with your own eyes—watching an operation of many hours' duration which a surgeon is performing on someone dear to you, and suddenly you learn that the patient died before the operation even began, and he was operated on only because according to the Plan he had been slated for an operation and the supplies appropriate to the operation had been issued, which then had to be used, and what really staggers you is that they did not begrudge your dear one anesthesia—anesthesia! This is the last straw: it's the anesthesia, as if they had injected part of it under your own skin, that plunges you into a quiet reverential trembling . . .

But here my stream of thought was interrupted by Uncle Sandro's muttering. We were already descending the marble staircase.

"May the jackasses of Chegem have you," he was muttering, "as many times as you'll help me with your phone numbers."

His words, as always, returned me to a healthy sensation of reality. For all the oddity of the equation he had suggested, for all the complexity of the balance between the activity of Chegem jackasses and the quality of the help that had been offered, his words contained not the slightest tinge of mysticism.

After we descended the staircase, I looked again at the administrator in the bell jar. He sat drooping his head, a bit like a human embryo in the womb or a fantastic stalk crowned by a drooping tendril. As he sat in his hothouse he seemed to be carefully hearkening to his own growth process.

Nonetheless, by rapping on the glass, Uncle Sandro forced him to turn his attention to our departure. At the same time, by nodding in farewell, he thanked him for having let us into the building without any trouble. The nod was a bit exaggerated, I think in anticipation of his future needs in this building.

"So how did it happen that you galloped around here on a horse?" I asked when we left the mansion and started down a quiet lane planted in bay laurel trees.

"To tell you in peace," Uncle Sandro said archly, touching his mustache, "we'll have to go sit somewhere at a modest little table."

"It's a deal," I said. I decided to stop in at the newspaper on the way and think up some pretext for sitting a while with Uncle Sandro in some cozy chimney corner—of which, incidentally, there are fewer and fewer left in our part of the world.

We turned into a street that led straight to the sea. At the last moment, as we turned out of the lane, Uncle Sandro put out his hand and picked a few bay leaves. He rubbed them in his palm and sniffed them. He seemed to be cleansing and preparing his olfactory organs for the session at table.

"This government," he said suddenly, dusting off his hands, in the habitual tone of a man who has sampled all the governments in the world and is ready to try still others, "doesn't always do the right thing either."

"What do you mean?" I asked.

"They've stopped taking bay leaf from the populace. I have two hundred kilograms, I can't even give them away."

"What does the government have to do with it?" I asked, guessing what he had been talking about in the office of that splendid purring fox with the silver hair.

"They've reached an agreement with the Turks. They're buying bay leaf from them now."

I had heard this story many times. It was impossible to refute, even in the local press, because of the way things are done here: to confess that these rumors existed meant confessing that they had some importance, and to confess their importance meant confessing they had at least a little truth. This is a vicious circle. When the bureaucracy defends itself, it covers up everything that can be covered, including its own eyes.

"Who told you?" I asked, just in case.

"That's what people say. Sure it's true. We used to be able to hand it over to the government every year and get money for it. Now they don't take it. Why buy bay leaf from the Turks, when we've got plenty of our own? I want to write to Khrushchit . . . What do you think, would they seize the letter?''

"Who," I asked blankly, "the Turks?"

"Why the Turks? Our own people!"

"But why would they seize it?"

"To keep us from displaying dissatisfaction . . . But they say it'll get there if you mail it in Sochi. Or if you're acquainted with any pilots, they can drop it in the mailbox in Moscow."

"I don't really know," I said, a little bemused by his illegal alternatives for communicating with Moscow.

We agreed that he would wait for me by the newspaper building until I came back out. I was already at the doorway when I felt the cherished document in my pocket and remembered: "Uncle Sandro, where did you find his dog?"

He was standing solidly by the newspaper's display board, examining the photographs. At my question, he turned around, threw a cursory glance at the passersby, and said quietly, "I found him where I hid him."

Some historians are true to the social truth, others to the historical. If you ask me which is better, I will reply in the words of Comrade Stalin: "They're both worse."

Thus, to be true to the social and the historical truth simultaneously, I must say that Uncle Sandro's account of the marble walkway has not been fully corroborated, though it hasn't been fully refuted either. An engineer from the city soviet (possibly Uncle Sandro will count him an Endursky) has said that they didn't filch the marble walkway for their fireplaces, they just spread asphalt over it when they repaired the sidewalk.

It goes without saying that I myself have made no attempt, with a crowbar or any other instrument, to break up the asphalt and check whether the walkway is intact, in view of its immediate proximity to the government building and the consequent possibility of someone's putting too broad an interpretation on my actions.

So the question is still open. I don't even know which is worse—to spread a colored marble walkway with asphalt or to filch it for fireplaces. Perhaps I would have preferred the latter, for at least in that case the beauty of the slabs would be acknowledged. Then again, there is always a possibility that that is just what happened.

THE SHEPHERD MAKHAZ

HE HAD SEVEN DAUGHTERS and not a single son. He very much wanted to have a son, to whom he could leave the farm and the livestock, and who would be a continuation of him, the shepherd Makhaz, in future life, when Makhaz was no longer in this world.

After each daughter he waited for a son, tried to beget a son, but only daughters were born to him. After the fourth he ceased to believe, in the depths of his soul, that he could have a son. He was only mildly curious to see how his wife's next delivery would end, although even now, against all reason, against his will, he still had a glimmer of hope: Suppose he got lucky?

But he was not lucky. Seven times, one after another, came daughters, seven herculean daughters were borne by his tireless wife Masha. The eldest was already married to the miller's son, and the youngest was not yet in school, although she could already shake the peach sapling hard enough to bring down its fruit when she wanted some.

After the seventh girl he reconciled himself to the fact that he would not have a son. Up on high, evidently, He who decides what kind of corn harvest there must be this year, whose cow the bear must choose from the herd and kill, what part of the village the storm cloud must pass over, full of death-dealing hail like a sack of stones, and exactly when this sack must break—in short, He who decides all this had made a note to Himself up there in the heavenly book that the shepherd Makhaz must not be allowed to beget a boy, and had appointed one of His servant angels to see to this.

Although the Chegemians had explained to him time and again their theory of the progenitive form—that there are some women who carry within them two progenitive forms, a boy's and a girl's, while there are some who have only one progenitive form and it keeps on turning out only boys or only girls—he, the shepherd Makhaz, considered all that a silly superstition. When the conversation came around to this topic, he always smiled scornfully and jerked his chin toward the sky: "It's all in His hands . . . If He wants, a woman will even give birth to a bear cub."

Makhaz was a peaceable, taciturn man; he lived mainly on the kolkhoz livestock farm, far from other people. He was not home much. Once or twice all summer he would come down from the alpine meadows to have a good wash and change his clothes, do a few things around the farm, and then—back to the mountains.

In the spring and fall he was there more often. In the spring he plowed and planted his private field, and in the fall he harvested the corn and the grapes, made the wine, which was drunk mainly by his wife's numerous guests, whom he could not stand; he was forced to put up with them in view of his wife's indomitable enthusiasm for life and hospitality.

If any of the kolkhoz authorities or his neighbors offended him, he never found it in him to answer the insult immediately. He would dourly retire into himself, and his resentment would break out many days later, sometimes in a completely unexpected place.

One time in the alpine meadows, for example, one of the goats got up on too steep a cliff, from which she might have fallen to her death. Without a moment's hesitation he scrambled up the cliff and grabbed her foot with one hand. But with the other hand he beat the struggling and uncomprehending goat unmercifully, which endangered not only the goat's life but also his own.

This punishment was a response to an order from the kolkhoz management to collect from the shepherds the price of any livestock that perished from elemental forces. What had prompted the order was that too many of the livestock were dying in the summer pastures. In summer in the alpine meadows, far from all authorities, the shepherds often slaughtered an animal for themselves, writing it off later to natural disaster. So the order was fair with respect to the shepherds who abused their trust, but it was unfair with respect to Makhaz, who never engaged in such practices. Thus, in beating up the goat that had grazed in too risky a spot, he was unburdening his heart, even entering into polemics with the kolkhoz management.

Four years ago his wife had sent their daughter Mayana—the second eldest, after the one who had gotten married—to the city, so that she could finish her education at the Abkhazian high school. In Chegem there was only a seven-year school.

Although Makhaz himself was opposed to this trip—he felt that seven years of study were quite enough for a girl—he had to yield to his wife's insistence.

They outfitted the powerfully built girl as best they could, gave her the red plywood suitcase that Aunt Masha herself had carried when she moved to Chegem, and sent her to the city.

Although Makhaz's sister lived in the city, they lodged the girl with a distant relative of Aunt Masha's, who worked in a store and was practically ready to burst, he was so prosperous. That was what Aunt Masha said of him.

There was also a boardinghouse in the city, for young people like this from distant villages, but Aunt Masha felt that to put the girl in a boardinghouse in a city where she had a relative bursting with prosperity would be a mortal insult not only to him, but to all Aunt Masha's relatives.

As for that, the relative had never laid eyes on Mayana and would somehow have survived if she had lived on her own in Mukhus. Nevertheless, this handsome little man, who was very adept at managing his affairs, cheerfully and willingly took his distant cousin into his house.

Shaliko—for that was his name—began making advances to her almost immediately, brazenly passing off his attentions as displays of a suddenly kindled sense of kinship. He liked this powerfully built highland girl. Unfortunately, Mayana also liked him, although she did not realize it.

For a long time she had had in her mind's eye an image of the herculean hero she would one day encounter and fall in love with for life. So she attached no importance to the advances of the clown puppet, as she called him.

One time in the city she encountered a dozen or so young men of heroic size. Her heart stood still in her breast, she thought she had met some of her future bridegroom's tribe. She even thought that one of these young men might turn out to be her future bridegroom. Faint with agitation, she followed them, trying to be inconspicuous, and soon they came to the municipal basketball court. When she saw them taking the ball away from each other like children and realized that they were not a single tribe of heroes, she was disillusioned with them and went home.

Shaliko's wife quite often went to visit her relatives in the country: now for a wedding, now for a funeral, now to call on the sick. At such times she asked Mayana to watch the children, which Mayana did skillfully and willingly, because she had been trained to take care of her own little sisters at home.

Mayana conscientiously fed the children and put them to bed—there were two of them—while condescendingly brushing off her diminutive uncle when he badgered her.

"You're so little," she said sometimes, putting aside a book or a paper to peer at him as he hovered over her trying to steal a kiss or put an arm around her.

"The little cornstalk has a big ear," he would say gaily.

"Not always," Mayana would correct him, after thinking a moment and completely missing his off-color joke.

At this point he would begin to laugh for some reason, and Mayana, embarrassed, found that with her embarrassment came a sensation of pleasure.

"Watch out!" She shook her fist at him. "If you try anything I'll break your skull."

In reply, to show that he fully recognized his own weakness, he put up his hands like someone in the movies. Poor thing, Mayana thought, aware that her superiority over him in physical strength was no joke.

But what had to happen happened. That night, taking advantage of his wife's absence (she had gone to a fortieth-day memorial feast for a dead relative), he climbed into bed with Mayana. At first Mayana repulsed him easily, saying over and over, "Pretty sly, aren't you now . . . Lord, what a sly one . . . What's the little devil think he's up to . . ."

Why, I can strangle him with one arm if I have to, she thought, meanwhile clasping him forcefully to her with that same arm, thereby, she thought, showing how she would strangle him if she had to.

Poor Mayana did not know that nature is not to be trifled with. But no wonder she did not understand this, for she herself was a part of nature.

An hour later, having paid for her virginity with a tuft of hair she tore out of his head, the unstrangled relative went off to his own room. Mayana wept; wept, and submitted to her new fate.

Shaliko's wife continued to visit her relatives from time to time . . .

Four months later poor Mayana quit school and suddenly returned home, carrying the red plywood suitcase in her hand and the child of this terrible deceiver in her belly.

Aunt Masha somehow managed to hush up the story, and poor Mayana, after crying her eyes out, came to understand that she must give up hope for her hero. A year later, at her mother's insistence, she married quite an old man who lived in a neighboring village. Aunt Masha called him not an old man but a venerable one.

The venerable man was getting on for seventy, and according to rumors that the Chegemians spread, citing reliable sources—according to these rumors, on their wedding night Mayana broke two of her venerable husband's ribs, which never did heal properly as long as he lived.

What is more, if we are to believe Chegem rumors, the old man rose to the occasion, because, even as a man with broken ribs, at least he succeeded in begetting two more children, if, as the Chegemians hypothesized, he had succeeded in begetting the first child before his ribs got cracked. All in all, three children were born to him. Of these, as the Chegemians noted, the first was a girl, and the other two turned out to be boys.

Reverberations of these rumors reached Mayana's father. He listened to them, correlating them with his own experience, and decided that from up on high the old man had been rewarded with boys because of the courage he had displayed. It could not have been easy at his age, and with broken ribs at that, to subdue a girl as powerful as his Mayana.

Aunt Masha thought her husband knew nothing of what had happened to Mayana. So she thought for a while, at least—until one time when he was sitting before the fire in his wet clothes, with clouds of steam rising from him, and he suddenly muttered something that he had been thinking ceaselessly for many days and many nights.

"Had to take it out on a wretched old man . . . If you were going to break anyone's ribs, it should have been someone in the city."

Aunt Masha sighed heavily and said nothing. They never returned to the subject, either directly or indirectly.

Incidentally, when Mayana got married, the city relative secretly sent a present for her, through other people: new shoes, a length of wool coating, and a thousand rubles cash.

Say what you like, it was a rich gift, and Aunt Masha (keeping it secret from her husband, which was easy to do) forwarded it to her daughter. The daughter accepted nothing, returning a message to her mother that the shoes were too small for her, and she would not take the present in any case.

Three years went by. Mayana successfully bore her babies, and the Chegemians subsided, or at any rate ceased to speculate on the state of Mayana's old husband's ribs.

By this time Aunt Masha had developed a plan for Khikur, the next younger daughter after Mayana: she would be sent to a bookkeeping school in the city. The kolkhoz chairman himself had given her the idea by saying that he had pulled strings at the district committee to arrange a slot in the program, so that he could send a Chegemian.

When rumors of this reached the kolkhoz stock farm, Makhaz left without saying a word to anyone. He came down the upper Chegem road, skirted his own house, and descended into Sabid's Hollow. At the foot of the Prayer Tree he took an oath to drink the blood of anyone who, in the city or any place else, made an attempt on his daughter Khikur.

Having taken this oath, he felt better, and looked in at home on his way back to the stock farm. He not only felt better, he could hardly contain the secret exultation that gripped his soul. When his wife told him about her ideas for Khikur, he replied, "I don't care if you send her to the devil in hell . . . I've just been to the Prayer Tree and taken an oath to drink the blood of anyone who makes an attempt on my daughter."

"Hopefully no one will," Aunt Masha replied. "And besides she's going to live in the dormitory, even if we do have a villainous relative bursting with prosperity."

So Aunt Masha's next daughter went away, the still more powerful and blooming Khikur. She started the bookkeeping program, studied hard, lived in the dormitory, but her heart, her highland maiden's heart (no one suspected this) burned with a furious thirst for revenge. She had been a little girl when she was stung by the rumor of what had happened to Mayana. Without ever once indicating to any of the grown-ups that she knew what had happened, she had suffered and given birth to an idea for a just revenge.

Poor Mayana was too kind and trusting, and the villain had deceived her. Oh, if only Khikur had been in her place, she would have showed him! She'd have wrung his neck like a chicken!

Khikur studied hard in her courses, and in her free time strolled around the city, hoping to encounter her sister's seducer at last and somehow take revenge on him.

She remembered what he looked like from the time when Mayana had studied in the city. Khikur had come to the bazaar with her father to sell walnuts; they had spent two days in the city and had seen their jolly relative several times.

Now that she had arrived to study in the city, she thought she would surely meet the villain somewhere. But several months had already passed, and he hadn't crossed her path. It was surprising to her that he hadn't. She was waiting for this meeting in order to take revenge on him, although she herself had no clear idea how she would do it.

First of all she had to meet him somehow. She began strolling up and down the street where he worked. Once he walked past her with a comrade. He did not notice her, or did not recognize her. That provoked her further; she began strolling up and down the street more often. Once, when he was walking toward her, playing with a bunch of keys to the store, they bumped into each other and he recognized her.

"Say, aren't you Mayana's little sister?" he asked in surprise, not at all embarrassed, she noticed.

"Might be," Khikur replied, sarcastically, she thought.

"My, how you've grown," he said, surveying her luxuriantly blooming flesh with satisfaction.

"Some grow upward, some down into the earth," she replied, alluding to his perfidy.

"You're a bold one!" he said, continuing to survey her.

"I'm no Mayana," she replied with an ominous hint, but he pretended not to understand.

"Mayana was pretty, too," he said pacifically. "Thank goodness she's married now . . . getting along . . . How's your father?"

"He took an oath before the Prayer Tree," Khikur replied severely, "to drink the blood of anyone who made an attempt on me."

She sensed that here in the city, with cars speeding by and big buildings towering overhead, her father's oath sounded unconvincing.

"Who'd touch a girl like you!" he cried gleefully. "You could kill anyone you wanted to yourself, I bet!"

"If he made an attempt," Khikur replied importantly, and he burst out laughing.

He invited her to stop by, and a few days later she went to their house. She had decided that this was necessary for her future revenge. His wife was very glad to see her. Remembering Mayana, she kept saying how surprised she had been when she left so suddenly, from which Khikur concluded that she knew nothing of what had happened to her sister. Aren't you the sly one, Khikur thought, gazing at her relative as he flitted gaily about.

She began visiting their house. Khikur decided to let him approach a little closer. Then when it became clear that he was making an attempt on her virginity, she would kill him, or better yet, maim him for life. Now whenever Shaliko's wife was going anywhere, she herself invited Khikur to look after the children, and Khikur came and spent the night, not forgetting her plot for an instant.

Khikur fed the children, put them to bed—now there were three of them—and kept thinking of the revenge that lay ahead and trying to choose the most awesome and merciless method.

She still could not decide at just what stage of his advances she would be fully justified in breaking his skull, smothering him, or maiming him for life. So far, he had not done anything more than kiss her, and Khikur did not consider this enough reason to smother a man, say, or to break his back so that he would be a hunchback. At night, mulling over this method of revenge, she smiled sarcastically as she pictured it: small to begin with, he would barely stick up over the counter of his store once he was a hunchback.

Meanwhile, Shaliko was waiting for her to become accustomed to his kisses, waiting for his caresses to arouse in her a responsive spark of sensuality.

He felt no remorse over Mayana's fate. He decided that everything had ended happily, he had given Mayana a fine present, and if she had married an older man that was their own business, plenty of village girls married old men.

Finally there came a night when they were again alone in the house, and each of them secretly resolved that this was the night it would all happen. After putting his children to bed, Khikur did not sit down to her books, but went off to bed, alertly listening to the sounds of the house.

He did not come for a long time, and she decided he was waiting for the children to fall sound asleep. Or was he waiting for her to fall asleep? Well, let him wait! About an hour later he put out the light, took off his shoes, and stole quietly into her room. Khikur lay without moving.

She was suddenly aware that she feared his indecisiveness. He stood at the door and looked at the bed, where Khikur lay rigid with fear that he would take fright and leave.

She sensed within her the strength and the ability to carry out her plan. She was only afraid that the children would wake up and start crying if they heard anything. Now she made a final resolve that she would smother the accursed seducer by stuffing the pillow over his face.

He went softly over to the bed and sat down beside her. I'll flatten him with the pillow, Khikur thought, quietly exulting, I'll mash him under the pillow till he stops squirming.

He had already bent over her and had cautiously begun kissing her, but she kept on pretending to be asleep, lest she scare him away, and he became bolder and bolder. She lay rigidly waiting for the moment when she must fling herself on him and flatten him with the pillow, but for an instant, when she gave heed to his caress, she had let something go, and now she could not catch what she had let go, could not make up her mind, could not do anything, because a sweet weakness enveloped her body and soul.

Her virginity did not cost Shaliko even the tuft of hair that Mayana had once torn from his head. He fell asleep then and there, and Khikur wept, wept with her face buried in the pillow with which she had meant to smother her sister's seducer. Now he was sleeping with his mouth open, and she could have done anything she wanted to him, but she understood that now it was no use, it was stupid and too late and . . . pathetic . . . So Khikur did not succeed in avenging her sister.

Time passed, and Shaliko's wife continued to go and visit her relatives in the country.

About three months after that fateful night, Makhaz was plowing his field. It was getting near noon, and the plowman had an ear cocked toward the house: any minute now his wife would be calling him to dinner, and besides it was time to rest the oxen.

Raising his head for a moment to wipe the sweat from his face, he suddenly saw his daughter Khikur, with the blasted red suitcase in her hand, walking down the road to the house alongside the wattle fence. Why is she suddenly back, Makhaz thought, sensing trouble. The girl's face was dark and portended no good.

"What is it?" he shouted when she drew abreast of him on the other side of the fence.

The girl looked darkly at her father and walked on without saying anything. She was wearing a wool coat made from the material that had once been sent for Mayana. And she looked exactly the way Mayana had, coming back from the city with that same suitcase in her hand. Staggered by his conjecture, Makhaz stood motionless for several minutes.

"You're going to run out of old men!" he shouted after his daughter, who had disappeared. Then he urged on the oxen. "*Or! Khee!* Wolfbait!"

He decided not to spare the oxen, to finish plowing the field. He knew that his hour had come. He finished the field, drove the oxen into the yard, and went into the kitchen, where his tearstained daughter was sitting by the fire with her mother. When he walked in, his daughter fell silent.

"Pour for your father," her mother said, and began setting the table. The other children came running in from the main house and took their places at the table, from biggest to littlest. Makhaz sat down at the head of the table. For the first course they had hot cornmeal mush with lima beans and sauerkraut; for the second course, yogurt. Makhaz felt nothing now except an unreasoning irritation at the red suitcase, which stood in his line of vision on the other side of the fire. All the misfortunes of his life seemed to be linked with that red suitcase.

"There's one thing surprises me," he said, jerking his chin toward the suitcase. "We've gotten old since it first showed up here, but we can't wear it out."

Aunt Masha stood up and silently put the suitcase away in the main house. When he had eaten, Makhaz washed his hands again and rinsed his mouth. Khikur poured for him. After washing his hands, he took a mug of water and went behind the house, where a big whetstone lay. He pulled his long shepherd's knife from the sheath hanging at his belt, poured water on the whetstone, and began sharpening his knife. The knife was sharp as it was, but he decided to sharpen it to the very limit. When the knife got so that it would shave the hair from his arm like a razor, he drew the blade over his hardened palm several times and put it in the sheath.

Then he went into the main house, changed his clothes, strapped on his leg-wrappings, and exchanged his homemade rawhide moccasins for city ankle boots. Then he put on a quilted jacket and slapped his pockets to be sure he had everything. His glance fell on a decanter of *chacha* standing on the mantel. Next to it stood a few shot glasses. He stuck one of them into his pocket.

He went into the kitchen, where his wife and daughter were still sitting by the fire. When they saw him they fell silent again.

"Why bother to whisper, girls?" he said. Turning to Khikur, he added, "He?"

"Who else," the girl answered, hanging her head.

"Did he know about my oath?" Makhaz asked.

"I told him myself," Khikur sighed.

"Did you!" Makhaz said in surprise.

"Listen to me," he went on, still addressing his daughter and making it clear that he was addressing her, "take the oxen to the Big House . . . If I don't come back, have one of my brothers plant my field . . . Toward evening drive the goats to the stock farm, tell them I've gone away on business, have them put someone else in charge of them."

He went out to the yard without saying good-bye to anyone and walked toward the wicket gate. His kolkhoz goats were grazing on the steep slope between his yard and the upper Chegem road. He did not even glance at them.

"Wait!" Aunt Masha cried, and ran after him a few steps. He did not look back and did not slow down.

"Don't do anything bad," she said, stopping helplessly in the middle of the yard.

For the first time in her life she felt she did not have the power over him she used to, had no power at all. And for the first time in her life she felt respect for him, which she had never known.

"Don't do anything worse," he replied, without looking back. Kicking open the gate, he went out of the yard and started up the path along the wattle fence that enclosed his field.

People in the Big House saw him go by, but no one except his old mother, who was sitting on the veranda, paid any attention to him. She asked the others to hail him, find out where he was off to in such a hurry, but no one bothered: as if it could matter where the man was going!

Although his old mother had the worst eyesight of them all, she could tell by his decisive, uncharacteristic gait that he was planning to do something decisive, uncharacteristic of him. From her life experience she knew that when a man was trying to do something decisive, uncharacteristic of him, it most often ended in blood. She became anxious for her son.

Makhaz left Chegem and started down the steep path that led to the Kodor.

As soon as he came out on the slope, the roar of the river struck his ears. Far below lay the delta of the Kodor, all its branches gleaming with a muted luster.

His glance swept over the valley revealed below, with the delta of the river running to the sea, and he sighed, as if he felt for the first time the power of his fateful duty and, simultaneously, the end of the free life just now revealed to him in the farewell beauty of the expanse that unfolded before him.

He descended quickly, with a shepherd's light step. A dry stream of fine little pebbles tumbled after him and struck his legs as if to drive him forward.

The steep path reminded him of something that he had never actually forgotten, or rather, that was always with him, even if he was not thinking about it.

Many years ago, when he was working as a guide in a geological party, the chief of the party had sent him to Kengur to meet his wife, who was coming from Leningrad to join him.

On that long-ago early morning, he stood in the crowd on the dock waiting to meet the steamship, holding by the bridles two saddled horses. The chief's wife recognized him immediately. She waved right from the gangplank and ran over to him. Her husband must have told her beforehand that she would be met by a man with horses.

When she ran up to him, dazzling him with the whiteness of her face and her blinding smile, he was so flustered that he wanted to jump on his horse and gallop away, but he contained himself. Removing his felt cap, he merely shook the hand she offered, long and awkwardly.

Then they both started to laugh at his discomfiture, and he felt at ease, completely at ease. He helped her mount her horse, and she jumped into the saddle, sitting astride it like a man. Her skirt, on the side where he was helping her mount, rode up a little on her leg, baring a knee as round and soft as a baby's cheek. His head spun, and he pressed his face to that cool knee and kissed it.

"Why, you silly!" she said, and with her hand she moved his head away from her knee. But in touching his head in order to push it away, for the tiniest instant, with a light motion of her palm, she caressed it. He jumped on his horse, struck it with his whip, and made it rear.

He was twenty-five years old, and it was the first time in his life he had kissed a woman.

For three years, with breaks over the winter months, he served as a guide under her husband, picked up a few words of Russian, and every time he saw her was a holiday for him. He never tried to get anything from her, because she was the wife of another man, and such a remarkable man at that.

What impressed Makhaz about this man was that he was not at all like most city folks. In particular, he was not like city folks who had recently left the village, and who quickly—surprisingly quickly after becoming city folks—became disused to manual labor, to overcoming all that a man who spends his life under the open sky must overcome.

Before meeting this man, Makhaz had believed that every learned man, starting with those who could read only letters and numbers, moved away from manual labor in exact proportion to his degree of learning. That was why they became learned, he believed, from all those wretched clerks on up: precisely in order to get away from manual labor and life under the open sky.

But this learned man was completely different. He could spend seven or eight hours in the saddle, could drive his horse across a mountain stream, build a fire in the wettest weather, and sleep covered up with a burka, or the Russian way, in a sleeping bag.

Looking at this man, Makhaz was persuaded that things were not all so simple, and learning was not necessarily prompted by a desire to avoid manual labor, but could be a consequence of higher aspirations too. Because of this he felt great respect for him and, without knowing it himself, loved his wife with the purest, most romantic love.

In three years they finished their work in the mountains around Chegem and went away to Tkvarcheli, where their main base was. Almost a year before their departure he began thinking what he might give the chief's wife so that she and her husband would remember him for a long time. In the forest that year he encountered a red bear, very rare in our part of the world. He killed it, dried its flame-colored hide, and gave it to them in farewell.

Later he went to Tkvarcheli from time to time and visited them, bringing with him a skin of wine, or walnuts, or smoked meat, which she had tasted here for the first time and taken a great liking to.

When he left them, they gave him presents, too, in the highland tradition of friendship. Once his friend even gave him a double-barreled shotgun. Later, when he married Masha and the babies started to come, she gave them clothes, dress material, or city sweets. Makhaz's wife was not jealous of her; on the contrary, she was always encouraging him to go there. And if they slaughtered an animal at home she would say, "You should take your Russian relatives their share."

When the plague of '37 began, Makhaz realized immediately that his friend would not escape and suggested that he hide in Upper Svanetia, where no one would find him. For some reason his friend merely chuckled in response to Makhaz's serious talk on this subject and said that such a thing couldn't happen, they wouldn't take him.

It's amazing the way learned people sometimes don't understand simple things. A month after they last talked about this, he learned that his friend had been taken. After pining for several months, his wife went home to Leningrad with her little daughter.

In a year the rotten time came to an end, and they stopped seizing people, but they did not release the ones they had taken. He should have waited out the year in the mountains, and he would have come back to his family safe and sound. Makhaz understood that his friend had been hampered by false pride (he was ashamed to hide), and besides, Makhaz felt, he had not believed anyone could hide from them. But Makhaz knew perfectly well that it was possible to hide from them, the way some abreks had hidden, and not only the abreks.

Yes, they were good people, God grant them health, if they were still alive.

Three years had gone by since she left. The first year she had sent him several letters, in which she wrote that everything was all right at home, but her husband was still in prison, and her efforts on his behalf were of no avail so far. Then the correspondence died, and he did not know what had happened to her or whether her husband was alive.

Yes, about twenty years had passed since he went to meet the chief's wife, and much had changed since then. He himself had taken a wife and produced a brood of girl babies, and his eldest daughter had married in the accepted manner, and two of his girls had been defiled by a son of a bitch, and now he was on his way to the city to wash away their dishonor.

A lot of time had passed since then, and he still remembered as if it were yesterday that bright day in his life. There had been good days both before that day and after, but never such a happy one.

Makhaz came down to the village of Naa, which nestled by the Kodor. He walked out to the river, but the ferryman was not there. The ferryman's house was situated farther down the river, about a hundred meters from the crossing. Makhaz looked toward the house and saw the ferryman plowing his field. The shepherd whistled piercingly several times, the ferryman stopped his oxen, turned around, and raised a hand to indicate that he had seen Makhaz.

Not far from the crossing was the village cemetery. Makhaz saw an old wolfhound walk by on her way over there. On the second try, the dog jumped the wooden fence surrounding one of the graves and disappeared behind it.

He knew that this was the grave of a local hunter who had died two years before. He had heard about this dog, which since her master's death had lived on his grave. At first she would not leave the grave at all, night or day, so that the hunter's relatives had been forced to bring her food here. Now the dog came home two or three times a day to eat and returned to her master's grave as if guarding it.

Makhaz had also had a remarkable wolfhound in his time. Once the dog had saved his life. It had happened like this. In the woods beyond Sabid's Hollow, Makhaz discovered a lot of bear tracks at the foot of a wild pear tree. Evidently a bear was coming here to enjoy the pears; Makhaz decided to set a trap here, and did so.

Ten days later he was tending his flock close to this spot and decided to check his trap. He set off with his dog. Leading to the foot of the wild pear there was a narrow footpath through thickets of fern the height of a man, overgrown with brambles.

He went first, and the dog followed. About ten paces from the pear tree the dog let out a growl and tried to push ahead, but he did not let her past him. In a few seconds, just as he reached the end of the path, the bear suddenly loomed before him, standing on its hind feet. The bear was just a step away, so close he could smell its stinking breath, and there was nothing he could do, he could neither unsling his gun nor back off. Instinctively he ducked forward under the bear. The bear struck him with its paw, the blow landed on the butt of the gun. The force of the blow knocked the wind out of Makhaz, and he was waiting for the next one, when he was suddenly aware that the bear had growled and given up.

Makhaz looked up and saw the bear down on all fours, and the dog hanging from it, gripping its throat. A few seconds later the huge bear crashed to the ground, with the growling dog still holding it by the throat. The bear was dead.

Makhaz sat down on the ground to collect himself. He called the dog, but she was still holding the bear by the throat and only growled in reply. Makhaz noticed that the bear had dug a huge pit beside the trap. Its hind foot was caught in the trap. The bear must have been starving and tried to get roots from the ground.

With trembling fingers Makhaz rolled a cigarette and lit up. He called the dog again, and this time she came to him, but she was still very aroused, because after sitting beside him for a few moments, she went back to the bear's body and with a growl sank her teeth in its throat, in the same place where she had held it before. The dog seemed to want to make sure once more that it was she who had strangled it.

Makhaz had never heard of a dog strangling a bear. This bear must have been greatly weakened by hunger and its futile efforts to break loose from the trap. Of course, if its paw had not landed on the butt of the gun, it still had the strength to mutilate him with two or three blows or dispatch him to the next world. But what a dog, to jump fearlessly on the shoulders of an infuriated bear standing on its hind legs!

While he waited for the ferryman, he was joined by two local peasants who were crossing to the other shore. The ferryman arrived, and they all got into the ferry. The ferryman pushed off from shore with the boathook, and the ferry started off against the current, fitfully jerking forward.

On learning that Makhaz was going to the city, the ferryman asked him to bring him back a new padlock. Makhaz replied that he was afraid his business in the city might detain him for a long time.

"What kind of business?" the ferryman asked. They were already in the middle of the river, and the roar of the river drowned their voices.

"A small thing," Makhaz shouted back, "but a lot of trouble!"

The ferryman did not try to ask him anything more. The ferry bumped against the opposite shore, Makhaz paid the ferryman and jumped to the ground.

Ages ago, when his sister married a fellow from Mukhus, he, Makhaz, had traveled along with the bridal party. They rode down to the crossing and discovered the ferry lying at the other shore, and the ferryman nowhere to be found. Makhaz got down off his horse and climbed the post to which the steel cable that spanned the river was fastened. Ignoring the cries of the bridal party—his sister especially cried out—he fearlessly crossed the Kodor hand over hand, jumped to the ground on the far side, pushed the ferry off, and rode back to the other shore. His hands hurt for a whole month afterward, chafed by the steel cable.

That fellow, his sister's husband, had also been taken in '37. At the time he had suggested to him, just as he had to his friend, that he hide in the forest and wait out the rotten time. He had not wanted to hide either, and now Makhaz's sister was left alone in the city with three children on her hands. Of course her family helped her, and besides she worked at the hospital as an attendant, but it wasn't easy alone in the city with three children. He should have waited out the rotten time, and a year later he would have come out of the forest all safe and sound and returned to his family. But now it was too late, there was no point even thinking about it . . .

When Makhaz came out at the village of Anastasovka, the bus to Mukhus was already filling up with passengers. He bought a ticket, climbed on the bus, and took his seat. All the way to Mukhus he wondered whether he should drop in and see his sister before taking care of his business, or whether he shouldn't. In the end he concluded that he shouldn't burden his sister with this needless encounter. She would have enough to endure when he had taken care of his business.

From the bus stop in Mukhus he started straight for the store where Shaliko worked. The store was on a corner, and for that reason he could watch it from a distance. He stopped about thirty meters away from the store and settled down to watch. Several times he caught glimpses of Shaliko behind the counter. Shaliko was the manager of the store. Makhaz knew that the manager usually stayed on after the store closed, either to count the receipts or to attend to other business.

He decided to meet with him in that interval, when the salesmen would have left and he would still be there. If he should leave along with the salesmen, Makhaz would have to go to his house and settle accounts with him there. That would be rather unpleasant, because the wife and children were there. He was sure that he would find a way of being left alone with him, but it would still be unpleasant.

From passersby he learned that it was still over an hour before the store closed, but he decided not to go anywhere, to wait right here. Anything could happen . . . What if they took it into their heads to close their store early.

Shaliko could not understand why he had been in a bad mood all day, when things were going better than ever. The day before yesterday he had received a fifty-gallon barrel of honey, which he and his senior salesman had opened early yesterday morning. After taking out ten gallons of honey, they had poured an equal quantity of water into the barrel. After that they had spent a whole hour stirring the thick heavy mixture until the water was completely blended into the honey.

Then what? For two days they did a lively trade in honey, stupid customers stood in line for it and had nothing but praise for it. And wouldn't you know, today, when the honey in the big barrel was gone and he ordered them to sell the pure honey, the ten gallons taken from the barrel, it was this honey that some customer found fault with, saying it tasted bitter.

This undeserved complaint once more suggested to Shaliko that you had to fleece the customer, only you had to do it skillfully.

The junior salesman must have caught on when they began selling honey from the reserved barrel. Shaliko had not initiated him into this operation, in order not to have to share with him: he was still young, let him do the scutwork for a while.

But he must have caught on, because he went around pouting all day, and Shaliko thought that this was what was spoiling his mood. Shaliko could not decide: should he stop the man's mouth with a pair of thirty-ruble bills, or was it worth demeaning himself? It's not worth it, he decided finally; let him do as much scutwork as I did, and then he'll come into his share.

The former manager of this store had been arrested a year ago, when Shaliko was the senior salesman. A surprise inspection of the store had revealed a sack of uninvoiced sugar, which had been forwarded to them secretly, through trusted accomplices, from a candy factory.

Shaliko was at the market at the time, and someone there managed to warn him that there was about to be an inspection at his store and he should tell his manager about it. But Shaliko deliberately failed to hurry back to the store. When he got there an hour later, they were in the middle of the inspection, which revealed the uninvoiced sugar.

The manager took full responsiblity in court, and the other salesmen were not touched. A short time later Shaliko was appointed as the new manager.

He felt some remorse over betraying the manager but consoled himself with the thought that the manager had been drinking so much lately, and behaving so incautiously, that he would have landed in jail anyway sooner or later, and might have taken them all with him.

Twice this year he had given five hundred rubles to his former manager's wife, who had been left with two children. She said that she had written her husband about it and he would never forget the help that Shaliko had given his former manager.

That was how Shaliko's affairs stood that day, as the shepherd lay in wait for him, stationed not far from the store.

Incidentally, he had learned still another bit of good news that day, which for a while had triumphed over his flickerings of bad feeling. When he dropped by the market, he had bumped into another store manager, and the latter, bending close to him, had whispered slyly, "Our monk has cracked."

"You're kidding!" Shaliko said in surprise.

"It's true!" his colleague nodded to him.

He related that the new inspector, who had been working with them for about two months and whom everyone feared because he did not take bribes, had complained to a mutual acquaintance that he was insulted at the way people at the market were treating him. It emerged that he was not taking bribes because he was afraid of tangling with the wrong kind of people, and they weren't giving him any, fearing that he was the kind that didn't take bribes. This misunderstanding, it seems, had been successfully resolved.

Everything went as it should, and now, at the end of the day, as he sat in the stockroom counting the day's receipts, which he was planning to put in the bank, he thought: Here's the thing that'll stop any mouth and any hole.

He put the money in a special bag, but before he had time to seal it he heard the cautious creak of the door opening. His first thought was that one of the salesmen had come back for something he had forgotten at the store. Then when he saw an unfamiliar figure in the doorway, he thought it was a robber and put his hand on the heavy sealing tongs, which were lying on the desk where he sat. The unfamiliar figure continued to stand in the doorway. After a moment he recognized it as the shepherd Makhaz and turned pale.

"Well be you," he greeted him, in Abkhazian, and stood up.

"Well be you, too," the shepherd replied. Shutting the door behind him, he came into the stockroom and looked around. He wondered briefly where would be the most convenient place to do it. Seeing to his left an iron sink with a water faucet, he decided that that was where it should be done.

The minute Shaliko saw Khikur's father, he recalled what had been spoiling his mood all day. That morning he had dropped by the dormitory where the girl lived, and the housemother had told him that Khikur had left for her village early in the morning, taking her red suitcase. The housemother said this as darkly as if she knew all about his relationship with his kinswoman.

And he had had such hopes for tonight: his wife was going to the country and had asked him to tell Khikur to feed the children and put them to bed.

Shaliko had sensed that Khikur's sudden departure meant trouble. And it had been spoiling his mood ever since morning. Later in the day he had forgotten just what had spoiled it, but the mood stayed with him.

Could she really have gotten pregnant and gone off to the country without saying anything to him, just like her sister? Damned savages! Here in the city it could all have been arranged so that everything would be kept dark.

Never mind; whatever you do, don't lose courage, he told himself, and thought: It's a good thing I didn't get the money bag sealed. He didn't have much money of his own in his pocket.

"Sit down," he suggested to his guest respectfully. Pointing to a chair on the far side of the desk, he thought to himself: I'll give him a thousand rubles and that'll put the lid on it.

Makhaz did not sit down, and this was a bad sign. Seeing that the shepherd was not sitting down, Shaliko did not dare sit down either.

"So what brings you to us?" he asked, as hospitably as he could, plucking up his courage.

He thought feverishly: Evidently the shepherd knows all about Khikur, but does he know about Mayana? Sometimes, in thinking about it before, he used to decide: Probably he knows, since they married a blooming young girl to an old man. Other times he thought: Maybe he doesn't know; after all, he's always with his goats, and Aunt Masha could have accomplished all that behind her husband's back.

"Didn't Khikur tell you?" the shepherd asked.

Shaliko thought that the father meant the girl ought to have spoken with him before leaving. But she had never spoken with him about anything like that. If he's asking about Khikur, he thought with relief, it means he doesn't know anything about Mayana.

"No, she didn't tell me anything," he replied with complete sincerity, because she really hadn't told him anything.

"Didn't she tell you I'd taken an oath: If this happened once more I'd drink the blood of the one who did it?" Makhaz asked.

Once more! The words echoed in Shaliko's head. Then he knows about Mayana! He decided to hand over to the shepherd all the day's receipts. There were eighteen hundred rubles lying in the bag. He recalled once more, with relief, that he had not yet sealed the money, as if this little piece of lead, like a bullet, decided whether he would live or not live.

He gave the money bag a slight push toward his visitor, as if cautiously indicating the direction in which their further conversation should develop. Then he looked at the shepherd, but Makhaz's face remained impenetrable.

Suddenly he perceived that money would get him nowhere. This face had no crack into which he could thrust money, these ears were incapable of being bewitched by the rustle of these bills.

All the same, he quelled this premonition of evil and said, glancing at the money bag, "Perhaps you need money . . . Who doesn't . . . For the farm . . ."

The shepherd paid no more attention to his words than if Shaliko had scratched himself. After waiting a few seconds, he asked again with patient stubbornness, "Didn't she tell you?"

If Shaliko had been dealing with a man like the ones he usually dealt with, he would have begun trying to get out of it, demanding evidence, and in the end he would have gotten out of it. But he recognized that the man before him was altogether different, and a petty lie could only worsen his position.

"She did tell me once," he sighed, "but after all, I didn't force her—"

"Say you offer a child poisoned candy, that's not force either, is it?" Makhaz asked. It was obvious that the shepherd had thought out what to say.

"Sorry," Shaliko said, hanging his head. He did indeed feel sorry and he was consciously acting out the feeling, because his senses told him that this was now the only way he could deflect the retribution of this savage.

"Ha!" the shepherd said. Without looking, he reached for his knife, unsheathed it, and thrust the blade skyward. "Tell that to Him."

"What?" Shaliko asked, stupefied. He could not believe his eyes. "You want to take my blood?"

"I didn't swear to take it, I swore to drink it," the shepherd corrected him, referring to the oath as to a document that must not be tampered with.

Now he was looking at Shaliko without hostility, and that was what terrified Shaliko most. A peasant looks without hostility at a sheep destined for slaughter.

Shaliko felt his insides turning numb with fear, although he was not a coward. His muscles refused to obey. He squinted at the heavy sealing tongs and thought he could throw them at him or hit him with them. It was a limp, hollow thought; he knew that he was incapable of resisting now.

Ten steps away from where they stood was the street, and cars could be heard going up and down it. Each time, at the instant he heard the sound of an approaching car, Shaliko's heart leapt with a dim hope, as if the car must stop in front of his store, as if people would get out and save him from this terrible man.

Each time, the car went on by, and with a soundless cry of despair his soul rushed after it, fell behind, and returned here, to listen again to the voices of people walking past the store on the sidewalk, to the sound of other cars approaching.

Strangely, he placed almost no hope in the people walking past the store. He placed his hopes in the car that would suddenly stop at his store, and then something would happen such that the shepherd would dare not touch him. His hopes reached out with mystical intuition to a car, to something technical, that is, to the thing that lay farthest from this shepherd and whose very existence annihilated the shepherd's ancient beliefs, his savage ideas and superstitions.

At moments he felt like screaming at the top of his lungs, pelting the shepherd with bottles from the cartons that stood behind him, but a little common sense suggested to him that if he raised a racket he would die sooner. Despite all, he had a glimmer of hope that the shepherd was trying to scare him but would not kill him.

"Come out from behind the desk," the shepherd said.

"Why?" Shaliko asked, his thickened tongue barely turning in his mouth.

"You have to," the shepherd said. Sensing that the fellow's mind had stopped working right, he went to him and lightly pushed him over to the sink. It can't be, it can't be, Shaliko thought, he's going to give me a thrashing and let me go.

"Bend down," the shepherd ordered, and Shaliko obediently bent over the sink as if he were planning to wash his face.

At the same instant, he felt the shepherd lean the full weight of his body against him from behind and press against him with such force that he thought the edge of the sink was about to cut into his belly. He felt an extraordinary pain in his belly, which was crushed against the edge of the sink, but out of this pain a joyful thought sprang to his consciousness: since the shepherd was hurting him this much, he was not going to kill him. When the shepherd seized him by the forelock and bent his head back with terrible force, still more forcefully pressing against his body, out of the pain there again sprang the joyful surmise that since he was hurting him this much, he was not going to kill him.

At the instant Makhaz slashed his throat with the knife, he did not feel the pain, because the pain he was already experiencing was worse. He only had time to feel surprised that there was water gurgling and gushing from the faucet, although the shepherd hadn't turned it on. He felt nothing more, although his body went on living for another few minutes.

Makhaz had pressed him against the sink with all his might because he knew that any living creature, no matter how benumbed by the fear of death, makes incredible efforts to leap away from it at the last moment. At these moments even a goat kid finds within itself such strength that a grown man must tense all his muscles to hold on to it.

When the blood gushing from the slit throat had almost stopped, he threw the knife into the sink. Carefully, so as not to stain his pocket, he reached in and took out the shot glass. Still holding Shaliko's body up by the hair with his left hand, he set the shot glass under the stream of blood, as if it were the straw of a still.

After collecting half a glassful, he raised it to his lips, blew away the lint that clung to it from his pocket, and then carefully drained it in two gulps. He set the glass in the sink and, after waiting for the blood to stop completely, carefully laid the body on the floor.

He went back to the sink and turned the water on hard. The sink filled with a pink, foamy mixture of blood and water. Gradually the mixture began to have more and more water in it, it grew lighter and finally became completely clear. The shot glass sparkled, thoroughly washed, and the knife was clean without a single spot.

He turned off the water, sheathed the knife, and dropped the glass into his pocket. He looked around the stockroom and saw an old raincoat hanging on the wall. He took it down and covered the dead man with it. He noticed that the raincoat was too big for Shaliko. Then it's not his, he thought, one of the store employees'. Actually the raincoat had belonged to the former manager. He had forgotten it here when the police took him away right after the inspection.

As he drew up the raincoat, Makhaz paused, lost in admiration of Shaliko's face, which was now calm and handsome, by its own blood purified of its own foul life.

He thought that if everything had been decent, he would not have refused such a son-in-law, in spite of his being small. No, he would not have refused, he would even have considered it an honor. But there was no point thinking about it now.

He glanced around looking for the padlock and found it hanging on the wall near the door. He glanced around once more, searched the desk top with his eyes, but did not see the key to the padlock anywhere. It occurred to him that the key might be in Shaliko's pocket. He did not feel like rummaging through the dead man's pockets. To his mind there was something impure in that. Taking the padlock he went out of the store, shut the door, and hung the padlock on it, turned so that from the outside it appeared to be locked.

He went out in the street and looked around. Two seedy-looking men, who had spread a simple picnic on the store's outdoor display table, were drinking vodka, munching smoked horse mackerel and bread. They did not appear to be in any great hurry.

He did not like to go off and leave two suspicious men here by the unlocked store. They might enter the store and rob it. Besides, he thought they might defile the body by rummaging in its pockets and moving it around any old way. That prospect may have bothered him more than the possibility of the store's being robbed.

He hurried off to turn himself in as quickly as he could, so that the authorities would come here to seal the store and take the body to the relatives.

The policeman was nowhere to be seen. He knew that the city was full of them, but right now, for some reason, not a single one crossed his path. He recalled that he had seen a policeman near the entrance to the city's botanical garden.

He hurried in that direction. He felt his feet growing lighter with every step, and his head began to ring as if he had had a slug of first-shot. Can you really get drunk on human blood? he thought. No, he corrected himself, this is a sign that I have carried out my duty, and the Lord has lightened my soul. His, too, he thought; the Lord has forgiven his sins now, and his soul may be hurrying to his native village, feeling purified. If so, he thought, his soul will soon be where it belongs. Shaliko was a native of Eshery, quite near the city.

Makhaz turned the corner and saw a policeman coming toward him. He could tell by looking that the policeman was Russian. He would much rather an Abkhazian policeman had approached, or, if not an Abkhazian, a Mingrelian. But he had no choice, and he tensed his mind to make it bring the right Russian words to his tongue.

He went up to him with a light step—prancing, as it seemed to the policeman. "My cut amaster astore," he informed him.

The policeman decided that this was a tipsy peasant. He had just come off duty and was on his way home, and he was thoroughly reluctant to get involved.

"Go home," the policeman replied sternly, and walked on. Makhaz stopped, amazed at the policeman's indifference. He stood still for a moment and then caught up with him.

"My cut amaster astore!" he shouted insistently.

"You make a row and I'll arrest you," the policeman said impressively, and waggled a finger under his nose.

"Yes, yes, arrest!" the shepherd confirmed joyfully. He had been quite unable to think of this important word, and here the policeman himself had supplied it to him.

"You killed someone?" the policeman asked, with interest.

"Killed," the shepherd confirmed sorrowfully. He spoke the word sorrowfully, not because he felt repentant, but because he wanted to show the policeman that he properly understood the sad significance of it.

". . . Cut throat: hrr, hrr," he added, just as sorrowfully, "amaster astore . . ."

"Why?" the policeman asked, beginning to understand a little and noticing the tip of the knife sheath at his side, sticking out from under his quilted jacket.

"Did bad thing," Makhaz explained painstakingly. "My took oath: who does bad thing—my drinks blood. My drank blood amaster astore."

Makhaz took the shot glass from his pocket and showed it to the policeman as a final convincing proof that he was telling the truth. But the policeman, who had almost believed him, began to doubt his sobriety again when he saw the shot glass.

"Go home," he told him. "Get on the bus and go—"

"Go—can't!" shouted the exasperated shepherd. He had tried so hard to hammer it home to the policeman what he had done, and now they seemed to be back where he had started from.

". . . *Chada! Chada!* (Jackass! Jackass!)," he added in Abkhazian, to get it off his chest, and switched back to Russian. "My cut amaster astore . . . I swear to God, this jackass will force me to commit a crime," he added in Abkhazian, sick to death of the policeman's obtuseness.

He thought that what he had said to the policeman had been said with such total clarity that it was impossible to misunderstand. How very unclear the Russian language was, he thought; an Abkhazian would have understood him at the first word.

"Okay, let's go," the policeman said, and turned back toward the city police station. The shepherd walked beside him with a light step. If he really did kill someone, the policeman thought, I'll be cited for my vigilance.

Makhaz, now that he felt he was being dealt with correctly and would be arrested, began to display anxiety regarding the slain man's body.

"Amaster astore dead," he said after a pause.

"You killed him?" the policeman asked him.

"My killed," he affirmed offhandedly, so that the policeman would not dwell on this already explained question. "Dead at night rat eat—bad. People shamed—bad. Tell to home: take dead amaster astore. Night—can't: rat spoil . . ."

"We'll get it cleared up in a minute," the policeman said. They were already entering the yard of the police station.

The policeman led him into the building and handed him over to the lieutenant on duty, explaining to him what he had understood of the shepherd's story. The lieutenant summoned an Abkhazian policeman, and the shepherd told him everything as it had happened, explaining that he was avenging his daughters. Why his daughters needed avenging he made no move to explain, but the policeman guessed anyway.

Fifteen minutes later the police car pulled up to the store. They opened it and satisfied themselves that everything the shepherd had said was true. They frisked Makhaz and took away the shot glass and the belt, with the shepherd's knife in its sheath.

"Have they sent the dead man home?" Makhaz asked when he saw the Abkhazian policeman.

"Don't worry about him, everything's in order," the Abkhazian policeman answered, to ease his mind. He did not try to explain that quite a few formalities remained to be taken care of before the body could be handed over to the relatives.

The policeman who had brought the shepherd in, now that he was sure he really had committed a crime, was sorry he had not told the lieutenant that he had detained the criminal himself. It now seemed to him that this peasant had immediately struck him as suspicious-looking; he was just about to detain him when the fellow came up to him.

They led Makhaz to a detention cell and locked the door behind him. He immediately lay down on the bunk, covered his face with his felt cap, and began to think.

At last I have fulfilled my duty, he thought, freed my soul by avenging both my daughters. He felt that now, by fulfilling his highest duty as a man, he had proved his right to a son. Too bad he wouldn't have his wife near him for a long time, to see if he was right. He thought that if they didn't kill him and he didn't get too old for this sort of thing in prison, then he might have a son in either ten or fifteen years, depending on how long they gave him.

That his wife Masha would not get too old for this sort of thing, he was sure. He was sure that his wife would never willingly, of her own accord, get too old for this sort of thing. But he was not worried about her honor. He knew that he had now defended his daughters' honor and his own in such a way that nothing could ever stain them. Especially if he was killed. He knew that if the court decided that he must be killed, and they killed him, this would be yet another water for his daughters' honor; it would wash their honor clean for life, no matter how long they lived.

He fell asleep and dreamed of his far-off youth, the Kenguria port, where he held two horses by the reins as he waited for the big steamship to come in from Novorossisk.

And there were a great many gaily dressed people waving handkerchiefs from the dock, and a great many gaily dressed people waving handkerchiefs from the steamship as it slowly came alongside the dock.

And the young wife whom he had never seen ran up to him, blinding him with her bright face and radiant smile. He helped her mount the horse, and a knee round and soft as a baby's cheek was bared, and, unable to restrain himself, he kissed that knee. And from above, from up on the horse, the woman tousled his hair and said to him the sweetest thing he had heard from a woman or ever in this world:

"Why, you silly!"

And he was happy in his dream and yet in his dream he was piercingly sad, knowing that it was a dream, and sooner or later the dream must end.

ABDUCTION
OR
THE ENDURSKY ENIGMA

O N THAT WARM OCTOBER DAY, fairly late in the afternoon, three young men stood beside the enormous trunk of a chestnut tree, whose crown was tinged with gold by the sun and the leisurely Abkhazian fall.

There was a mild tang in the air, perhaps from last year's carpet of leaves gently decaying on the ground, or from drying blueberries not stripped by people or pecked clean by the birds, or from tree sap fermenting in the mighty trunks of the mixed forest.

That mild tang reminded all three men of the smell of Isabella wine at fall wedding feasts—which seems quite plausible if we consider the reason why the young men had concealed themselves at the foot of the enormous chestnut tree.

But in order to establish with absolute precision the true array of smells the young men were inhaling at that hour, we have had to hold a seance with the spirit of our remarkable writer Ivan Bunin, whose gifted nostrils were no less keen than the nostrils of a nobleman's hound, and the breadth of whose intellectual interests defied all comparison.

Among other things, we had almost forgotten to mention that four horses had been tied to the branches in a stand of young alder, twenty meters uphill from the thick chestnut tree. Since they had been tied there quite some time ago, the above-mentioned smells were commingled with the smell of fresh horse dung—a fact which our famous author's spirit kept sternly pointing to, by the way, but we were too obtuse to see what he meant at first.

So three young men, two in black cherkeskas and one in white (you're wrong, it's not Uncle Sandro in white; he never did have a white cherkeska), have concealed themselves at the foot of the chestnut tree, four horses are tied in a stand of young alder, and the reader can guess for himself that this is an abduction.

But who are the other two men? One of them is a buddy of Uncle Sandro's named Aslan. He's the one sporting the white cherkeska. Despite the recent October Revolution, Aslan does not hide his noble lineage; on the contrary, he stresses it by every possible means, including his snowy cherkeska. What Aslan fears above all is that someone might think he feared his lineage.

Typically for the customs of our part of the world, although the new Soviet regime had removed the members of his class from high office—those who held such office—it did not continue to persecute them, as was done in Russia, but looked at them from afar with a valedictory respect.

True, the new Soviet regime looked at them with that expression only on occasions when its face could not be seen from the direction of Moscow. But since Abkhazia was hard to see from Moscow in those days—not only because of the natural barrier of the Caucasus Mountains but also because of poorly developed communications—the local authorities almost always, except on revolutionary holidays, looked at their former aristocrats with a valedictory respect.

Abkhazia's distinctive national psychology has, along with its faults, one indisputable virtue: an almost complete absence of servility, and hence of churlishness.

By grace of their peculiar national traditions, the Abkhazians, in contrast to many peoples, had hardly known class isolation. It was an ordinary phenomenon for children of the nobility to be raised in peasant families—not breast-fed, but raised to the age of ten or twelve.

Nationwide race meets, wedding feasts, funerals, and assemblies, moreover, all drew people of different classes quite frequently to the ethnic mystery of ritual, where the peasant, on meeting a nobleman, usually conversed with him respectfully but without the slightest nuance of any loss of personal dignity.

By grace of traditions imbibed with his mother's milk, therefore, the Abkhazian peasant, even when he became a Bolshevik revolutionary, was utterly unable to violate the established relationships.

A conquering serf naturally becomes a churl. A conquered churl easily makes the transition to servility. But the man who has not known servility cannot immediately become a churl. A certain historical interval is required.

That is why Aslan continues to pride himself on his noble lineage and sports a snowy cherkeska. Next to Aslan stands the jolly cutthroat Temyr, who regularly performs the dirty but honorable work of abduction. Incidentally, the rolled-up sleeves of his cherkeska, which bare his strong hairy arms, are direct testimony that the work of abduction is precisely that—work. Now and again a fleeting smile crosses the jolly cutthroat Temyr's round face in anticipation of an event that we will relate in these pages without delay.

What is remarkable about this scene? The remarkable thing is that Uncle Sandro's face, for perhaps the first and last time in his life, bears the stamp of Hamletism.

What has happened? Whence this expression of irresolution, ambivalence, introspection?

Let's start with the bare facts. Uncle Sandro's friend, namely Aslan, has been preparing to abduct a bride. Granted, under the circumstances we would naturally expect to find irresolution, ambivalence, joy, sorrow on the face of Uncle Sandro's friend. But why are all these contradictory feelings, which are characteristic of normal men when they are about to get married, expressed not on Aslan's face (which, incidentally, looks vacant and calm), but on that of Uncle Sandro, who is so resolute under all of life's circumstances?

The trouble is that Uncle Sandro is in love with his friend's bride, and by all indications she is in love with him too. Tonight she must become his friend's wife, and he, Uncle Sandro, not only cannot stand in the way, he is forced to help his friend.

But why? Why is he in such a fix? Because for all his celebrated guile Uncle Sandro cannot break the laws of friendship, even for the sake of his flaming passion.

Aslan, who lived in the village of Atary, had invited Uncle Sandro to stay at his house, with the idea that Uncle Sandro would help him arrange meetings with the girl he liked and then take part in abducting her.

In such situations, young people who like one another try to arrange meetings in some neutral house having family ties with neither side, neither the secret groom's nor the secret bride's.

To just such a house Aslan brought Uncle Sandro, having told his bride beforehand about Uncle Sandro's still young but already legendary life, full of jolly adventures and dangerous (mainly to his stomach) dinner-table feats.

Aslan and Uncle Sandro came to this house for a whole month, off and on, to meet Aslan's secret bride, who also came there with her girl friends.

On the very first day, Uncle Sandro fell in love with this sweet-faced girl. He might somehow have withstood the sweetness of her face, but her dimpled cheeks played a fateful role. Uncle Sandro was completely unprepared to meet a girl whose every smile brought dizzying dimples to her cheeks. Every time she smiled, Uncle Sandro's soul split in half and fell into these two little traps, and had no desire in the world to climb out.

There is also the possibility that a small but in this case conclusive role was played by the girl's name—a Russian name, then rare in our part of the world—which we won't reveal for the time being.

As everyone knows, a woman's name, especially if it bears the stamp of an alien tribe, has an added sensual coloration that many men find captivating.

Now we come back to the dimples, thereby perhaps expressing (as the well-known doctrine alleges) our own secret affinity for them.

The trouble was that Uncle Sandro's experience in love—the high point of which, without question, had been the princess famed for her loving heart—had somehow failed to include dimpled cheeks. Perhaps dimpled cheeks are generally uncharacteristic of highland women (the princess was a highlander), perhaps they express a certain genetic placidity characteristic of hereditary lowlanders.

We don't know. At any rate, the village in question was situated down in a hollow.

Until meeting this girl Uncle Sandro had never attached any importance to dimples, these tiny hollows, tiny craters, sweet tiny traps of feminine nature.

He may not even have noticed them. In those days, in our part of the world, the most highly prized marks of feminine beauty were thick eyebrows, large eyes, and long hair. The aesthetic menu of those years as reflected in song, tale, and legend featured no such dish as "dimpled cheeks."

But it is interesting to note that the highest feminine attribute was considered to be the degree of lightness with which a woman served her household and especially her guests. To this day, when appraising some woman or girl, Abkhazians in general and Chegemians in particular prize this quality above all.

The highest exemplar of womanhood is the woman who not only performs all her duties well—that's not enough for our exacting taste-testers of feminine charm—but also performs them with joy, even with gratitude that people have given her occasion, or better yet many occasions, to do something for them.

"Her face is pretty enough," the Chegemians will say of a woman, "but what's the use—she's a lead-bottom."

So much for beauty. A total loss.

Or the other way around, in speaking of another woman: "She's not much to look at—but she *flies!*"

This rapt finding utterly strips away any natural imperfections in the woman's appearance and opens wide the beauty of her winged soul. The elemental humanity of this approach delights me. Your nose is too long? No need for an operation. Step lively, and you'll grow prettier in flight! But we digress. We must get back to those fateful dimples (suppressing a certain irritation), because we haven't exhausted their role in the story yet.

On the sweet face of Aslan's bride, then, Uncle Sandro saw for the first time, or noticed for the first time, those delicate little depressions. Bravo to the unknown sculptor!

Again, Uncle Sandro might even have grown used to those two dimples somehow and betrayed his passion to no one in the world . . . But one day Aslan's bride came to this meeting place legalized by an abundance of men-friends and girl friends (a strange, belated echo of the illegal prerevolutionary Bolshevik May Day gatherings)—well, she came in a dress that revealed her neck, and Uncle Sandro was overwhelmed.

Where the girl's delicate neck began its blossoming growth above her apparently no less blossoming body, there was yet another dimple, which proved the most ruinous for Uncle Sandro's heart.

"How many has she got!" Uncle Sandro cried (to himself), enveloped in the flames of love-madness. That Uncle Sandro's love was mad can be considered medical fact, because it did not confine itself to a general delight in the abundance of dimples but demanded that Uncle Sandro forthwith establish an exact count of them. Pedantry, as everyone knows, is always a sign of madness.

Frankly, it was no easy task. Uncle Sandro tried to make his love-madness
see reason; he impressed upon it that the idea of establishing the number of
dimples on the body of his friend's bride was both ignoble and unbecoming,
and ultimately dangerous. But love-madness answered him, "For friendship's
sake you are sacrificing your very great love. For your love's sake, then, can't
you do one tiny thing, fulfill its one small whim? Just establish the number of
dimples on her apparently (what do you think?) blossoming body!"

Well, what can you say to love-madness? Uncle Sandro found no convincing
argument in favor of modesty. Yes, dear reader, you and I would have found
one, but Uncle Sandro did not. That's because he lives to live, while we live
to admire his life. These are simply two different professions, and sometimes
I'm sad to think which is the more interesting.

So Uncle Sandro found no convincing argument in favor of modesty. "Yes,
yes," he told himself, "I renounce my love for a girl who is obviously giving
me signs of her favor. I renounce happiness because I don't want to take it away
from my friend. But in saying farewell to love, can't I allow my love-madness
this small whim?"

And he did allow himself this small whim. Uncle Sandro knew that on very
hot days the girls of the village went to bathe in the forest, where spring water
flowed down a rocky hillside through a wide wooden trough. The Abkhazian
name for this ancient folk-style shower is *achichkhaley*. To our ear the word
conveys not only the babble of water flowing from a height, but also the pulsing
irregularity of the spurting stream.

Here the village girls bathed on hot days. When getting ready to bathe, they
usually posted a patrol on the forest path that passed near the spot. Two girls
watched the path in both directions to guard against accidental, though unlikely,
passersby.

But someone as sly as Uncle Sandro needed little imagination to outwit them.
Poor Prince Oldenburgsky! If he had known the uses to which Uncle Sandro
would put his excellent Zeiss binoculars, he might have abstained from his gift.
How paradoxical are the gifts of the world's great! Let us recall that the prince
had given these binoculars to Uncle Sandro precisely as a reward for his sharp-
sightedness, which, however, Uncle Sandro had grossly exaggerated.

It was an easy matter to find, within a hundred meters or so of the artificial
waterfall, a tree from which he could get a view of the wide wooden trough
with the white-foamed stream crashing down it. And one hot day, only because
he was under the sway of love-madness, Uncle Sandro sat on a limb of the beech
tree and carried out his little crime.

No, no—we won't follow him and spy through Prince Oldenburgsky's binoculars! We won't even specify whether Uncle Sandro lowered his binoculars
when the other girls ran out of the hazelnut bushes with their hair flying and
dashed bravely under the majestically lashing, spurting falls, as the hard cold
streams of water parted the streams of hair, breaking over the young shoulders,
icing those flushed shoulders and scattering generously to drum on huge, trem-

ulous, primitive butterbur leaves that greedily seized the deflected droplets, until the girls ran out from under the waterfall tormented to a sweet daze, pricked by thousands of silvery needles—laughing, wet, shrieking!

We will merely note that the binoculars not only brought close the figure of the bathing girl, they invariably amplified her shrieks, as if they contained a hidden sound-detecting device. For some reason Uncle Sandro insisted on this point, perhaps partly in an effort to explain why he was so drawn to his torridly close and shrieking beloved that he nearly fell off the limb of the beech tree.

O youth, intoxicated by the stern craftsmanship of Zeiss lens-grinders! Uncle Sandro miraculously held on to the limb and said in later years that this was a sign from God, though he didn't guess it at the time.

His arms and legs trembling, Uncle Sandro climbed down from the tree and quietly took the long way home to Aslan, who had so incautiously involved him in the matter of his marriage. This supposedly small whim on the part of love-madness had proved in fact to be its most subtle tactical maneuver. Now Uncle Sandro was ready. But what about his beloved?

A sweet, pure girl who had never loved, she naturally interpreted her liking and respect for Aslan as love. Her liking for him was quite explainable, because Aslan was attractive enough, even though he grossly exaggerated the influence of his own charms. And her respect was prompted by the fact that Aslan was the scion of highborn parents, whereas his bride was a simple peasant girl.

Perhaps precisely for this reason, she did not understand that now, after the revolution, she must be deemed highborn, according to Marx's laws. Conversely, Aslan must be deemed to have been tossed out on the trash pile of History.

Admittedly, it is hard to imagine that this young man of well-bred appearance had crawled from the trash pile of History, dusted himself off without leaving so much as a speck on his snowy cherkeska, and begun to court the sweet-faced peasant girl.

It is much easier to imagine what would have happened to a provincial theoretician of proletarian philosophy if he had met Aslan and tried to convince him that he belonged on the trash pile of History. It would have been a big mistake, in this case, to consider the silver dagger that hung at his narrow waist a purely ornamental appurtenance to the national costume.

Our poor theoretician would have stood a chance of survival only because of the extraordinary difficulty of hammering home to the rustic young feudal lord what the trash pile of History was. To Aslan (and here we agree with him completely), the concept would have been as senseless as the bathroom of God.

Anyway, Aslan's bride was even farther removed than he was from all these subtleties. For this reason she waited calmly and gaily to marry her bridegroom. But suddenly Uncle Sandro appeared. When she caught sight of Uncle Sandro, who had been praised repeatedly by her well-born bridegroom, the girl's mind was thrown into a state that Stendhal would have termed favorable for the crystallization of feeling.

If we are to believe Stendhal's biographers, women loved him little, or at any rate less than he would have liked. Be that as it may, the astounding Frenchman created a "Theory of Love." He dreamed of winning a favorite woman as he would a brilliant chess game. A fantastical task, but what faith in the power of reason!

Anyway, the curiosity kindled in the mind of Aslan's bride by her bridegroom's tales was fully vindicated. Uncle Sandro really was good-looking, jolly, and resolute. It is hardly surprising that the young people fell in love with each other. During that month they not only fell in love with each other, they managed to declare their love to each other.

The simple-hearted girl—who, let us stress, was bound to her secret bridegroom by no formal tie—suggested that they honestly confess all to Aslan. But Uncle Sandro rejected this straightforward plan. He was not born for straightforward plans. He was born for the straightforward execution of fantastical plans.

Uncle Sandro felt that such a confession would be a deadly insult to the laws of friendship and, no less importantly, to the whole of Aslan's distinguished clan. Although Aslan's parents would at first have perceived their scion's marriage to a simple peasant girl as a distasteful breach of custom, the possibility that a simple peasant girl might refuse their son for Uncle Sandro would have been an unforgivable insult.

"No," Uncle Sandro said resolutely to his beloved, "that's impossible. I can't insult my friend by confessing our love. I'll think of something that will make him repudiate you himself. I swear by the Prayer Tree of the village of Chegem, I'll think of something!"

"Then think quickly," the sweet girl said, "or it will be too late."

"Trust me in everything!" Uncle Sandro exclaimed ardently, although—or perhaps precisely because—he himself was sure of nothing as yet.

"I trust you," said Uncle Sandro's beloved, rejoicing in his ardor and for this reason, of course, involuntarily forming delicate (this is the last time I'll mention them) dimples on her cheeks.

Uncle Sandro began to think, but this time, despite his keen intellect, nothing came to him. He couldn't take the classical road, that is, slander the girl. For one thing, as we might suppose, there were reasons of decency. For another— and this was more to the point—he couldn't marry a girl whom he himself had slandered.

Every night Uncle Sandro's mind churned with a multitude of schemes whose impracticability was inevitably revealed with the sun's first morning rays.

Meanwhile, all unsuspecting, Aslan carried on as usual with his preparations for marriage. Apart from being convinced of his own irresistibility, he felt that his marriage would confer happiness and social elevation on a simple peasant girl.

The day set for the abduction was approaching, and Uncle Sandro still hadn't thought of anything. A distant relative of Aslan's in a neighboring village had already been informed that on such-and-such a day, or rather night, Aslan would gallop up to his house with a stolen bride.

On the eve of the fateful day the jolly cutthroat Temyr was summoned from the village of Ankhara to carry out the dirty but respectable work of the abduction. And meanwhile Uncle Sandro had found no way of inspiring Aslan to repudiate his bride voluntarily.

If ever anyone believed in his lucky star it was Uncle Sandro, yet he was still very worried. The night before the abduction he was so very worried that even Aslan noticed it.

"Listen, Sandro," he told him, "you're as worried as if you were the one getting married, not me."

"I feel bad for your parents," Uncle Sandro sighed. "It will be such a blow to them . . . First the Bolsheviks seize power, and now their son marries a peasant girl . . ."

They were lying in their beds in Aslan's room. From the next room came the peaceful snores of the cutthroat Temyr.

"They'll reconcile themselves somehow," Aslan assured him, displaying the traditional insouciance of the nobility, thanks to which, in large measure, they had lost power. A few minutes later Uncle Sandro realized from Aslan's breathing that his insouciance was by no means feigned.

And the next day they stood at the foot of the mighty chestnut tree overlooking the village road, at a point where a path forked off toward one of the settlements.

It was all arranged. Three girls from this settlement, among them Aslan's bride, would be coming home from the Sunday games in the village center. The jolly cutthroat Temyr would leap out on the path and grab one of them, she would struggle in his grip for the sake of appearances, and a few minutes later she would turn up at her bridegroom's side and they would all dash away to the house where they were expected.

Any minute now the girls would appear on the road, and Uncle Sandro still hadn't thought of anything. Is it any wonder that on this occasion Uncle Sandro's usually resolute face bore the stamp of an ego-alien Hamletism?

And now the girls appeared! Two of them were chattering gaily, sharing their memories of the Sunday games, while Aslan's bride, the girl who was also Uncle Sandro's beloved, walked beside them with mournful countenance, unable to bear this double burden. When her delicate sad profile flashed by on the road, everything turned over inside Uncle Sandro.

"Which one?" whispered the jolly cutthroat Temyr. He licked his lips in anticipation of his sweet labor.

"The one on the side nearest to us," Aslan answered quietly. The little path that led to the settlement dipped down into an elder thicket, and the girls disappeared.

Hugging the ground like a beast of prey, Temyr set off through the azalea bushes in order to surprise the girls by leaping out on the path in front of them. Ten minutes later came heartrending screams. Suddenly, crashing through the bushes like a bear, Temyr reappeared at the chestnut tree with a girl over his shoulder. She was screaming nonstop and hammering at his face with her free hand. Aslan froze open-mouthed . . .

"Wrong one! Wrong one!" Aslan cried when he recovered himself.

"What do you mean, wrong one?" bawled the cutthroat, who could not have been called jolly now. Dropping his unsubdued captive and wiping a hand across his bloodied cheek, he added, "You said the one on the side nearest to us!"

"Wrong one! Wrong one!" Aslan cried again. "They must have swapped places."

"Why the hell didn't you tell me!" Temyr bawled, turning to the girl. "You've scratched up my whole cheek!"

Dissheveled, her eyes burning with hatred, the girl stood there gnashing her teeth and pugnaciously glaring around. Despite the fact that Uncle Sandro was busy with mind-boggling calculations and felt that the clock had just about run out on him, to use a contemporary expression—despite all this he had time to notice that she was pretty. He even recalled that he had seen her somewhere, but he could not remember where.

"Did you ask me?" the girl cried. She planted her hands on her hips and even took a step toward Temyr. "You had it coming, you monster! I'm sorry I didn't scratch your eyes out!"

"All right, go along," Aslan said. "And you, run and get mine! But not the one in the red sweater, the other one!"

Temyr rustled off through the azalea bushes and suddenly turned back. "What if they swap sweaters?"

"That can't happen," Aslan shouted. "She's mad about me!"

Temyr disappeared in the bushes.

"Why are you standing here? Go on!" Aslan waved a hand to indicate to the mistakenly stolen girl that she was free. Upset over the false start of the abduction, he was irritably straightening the skirts of his cherkeska, peering at it as if trying to see whether the failure had stained its snowy surface.

"I'm not going anywhere!" the girl cried audaciously, eyeing Aslan and Uncle Sandro as if sizing them up. Again Uncle Sandro had the tormenting recollection that he had seen her somewhere, but he simply could not remember where. The main thing was, she had been wearing something else. For some reason this was important, that she had been wearing something else. But what? Ah, that's what—nothing!

Prince Oldenburgsky's binoculars, which hung around his neck and had jostled his chest at an abrupt movement, had reminded him of this. And now we are convinced that Uncle Sandro hadn't always lowered the binoculars when someone other than his beloved appeared in his view. Once, at any rate, he had not succeeded in lowering them.

"What do you mean, you're not going?" Aslan asked crossly, but also distractedly, because he had an ear cocked for what was supposed to happen on the path and nothing seemed to be happening down there.

"I'm not going, that's all!" the girl cried, tidying her hair and casting burning glances at Aslan from under her brow. "You disgraced me in the eyes of my girl friends, and now you abandon me? It won't work!"

"Who disgraced you?" Aslan bawled, his ear still cocked to the path. He was surprised that there was nothing to be heard. "You can see it was a mistake!"

"You kidnapped me, you have to marry me," the girl retorted. "Or else my brothers will shoot you down like quail!"

She finished tidying her braids and planted her hands on her hips again.

"You want both of us?" Aslan said savagely, because there was still nothing to be heard from the path below.

"Why both?" the girl replied with unheard-of audacity. "One's plenty!"

"Will you listen to that!" Aslan said, turning to Uncle Sandro. As if taking belated cognizance of the social changes underway in the land he added, "They've gotten out of hand!"

With that he adjusted the silver dagger hanging at his waist, but the warlike gesture did not appear to produce the requisite impression on the girl. She kept shifting her burning gaze back and forth from Uncle Sandro to Aslan, trying to divine in each of them the bridegroom-to-be and guileful deceiver who was seeking a way to escape from her.

Now, at precisely this moment, Uncle Sandro's mind instantaneously drew up a brilliant solution to his unsolvable problem! Like true artists and scientists, who torment themselves a long time over a creative riddle and then suddenly find the solution in their sleep or in a seemingly accidental coupling of words or events, Uncle Sandro recognized with inspired clarity what to do.

"The girl is right," Uncle Sandro said firmly. "One of us has to marry her."

"Not me, at any rate," Aslan replied, his ear still cocked to the path. By now he felt highly irritated. While the cutthroat Temyr fussed around with this first captive, who had suddenly styled herself a bride, the girls had evidently walked way ahead or given him the slip completely.

"We'll see," Uncle Sandro said. "At any rate, she's a good-looking girl, believe me . . ."

"I don't argue with that; she's a good-looking girl," Aslan agreed, beginning to recognize the danger that hung over him. He knew that if her brothers, who were even more audacious than she, got wind that someone had lightly abducted and abandoned her, the affair could end in blood. They would not look into his origins, especially in times like these. But even in the past very few had delved into genealogy in such a situation.

Aslan was struck that Sandro liked the girl. It would be amusing, he thought, to bring home two brides today. It would be our way, the Caucasian way, the noble way. Thus he had abducted a bride with the help of a friend, and, lest the friend be bored, he had seized her girlfriend too!

"Well," Aslan said, winking at Uncle Sandro, "our Shazina's as pretty and shapely as a little roe deer . . ."

"That's true," Uncle Sandro agreed, and here the azalea bushes snapped and the jolly cutthroat Temyr appeared with Aslan's sweet bride draped over his shoulders wearing a look of doom, "but I have something sad to tell you, Aslan . . ."

"What now?" Aslan asked anxiously, and he started toward his bride. But Uncle Sandro blocked his way.

"Now this here's a modest girl, I can tell!" the jolly cutthroat shouted. Setting down Aslan's bride, who sadly bowed her head, he started to mop the streaming sweat from his face.

"Go off to one side, I have to ask her something," Uncle Sandro said. Temyr walked off, gingerly feeling his cheek, which was still bleeding a little where Shazina had scratched it.

"Still here, you ragged cat?" he shouted when he caught sight of her.

"I'm not going anywhere!" she answered. "And if you disgrace me, my brothers will shoot you down like quail!"

"Let her stay." Aslan winked at the jolly cutthroat. "I have a plan!"

"You don't mean to marry them both, like a Turk?" Temyr asked, now mopping his face and neck with a big kerchief.

"I have a better idea," Aslan answered with a mysterious smile and a nod toward Uncle Sandro.

Meanwhile Uncle Sandro was putting his own brilliant plan into action.

"Listen closely," Uncle Sandro told his beloved, "here's my idea. You'll tell him you have some Endursky relatives. Stick to your story no matter what, and the rest will take care of itself."

"All right," said the slightly dazed girl who was Uncle Sandro's beloved, even though still Aslan's bride, "I'll say my grandmother on my mother's side is an Endursky."

"Doesn't matter which side," Uncle Sandro explained hastily. "The main thing is, stick to your story!"

"What's all the whispering?" Aslan shouted. "Someone could come along any minute!"

"I have something important to tell you," Uncle Sandro pronounced. With the gloomy expression of a messenger of woe, he went to Aslan and drew him aside.

"What's this, an assembly?" Aslan muttered, sensing that something disagreeable lay ahead and realizing he couldn't wriggle out of it.

Uncle Sandro gave him the sad news. He said he had heard a rumor yesterday that Aslan's bride's grandmother on her mother's side was an Endursky. Since he hadn't been able to ask her yesterday and verify this for himself, he had been worried all night, though he'd said nothing to Aslan so as not to upset him in case the rumor should not be confirmed. But now, unfortunately, she herself had confirmed it.

"You have killed me without a knife," Aslan wailed softly. "A peasant, and an Endursky too! Now my father, mother, brothers, sisters are lost to me forever!"

"I know," Uncle Sandro said, and added firmly, "I will save you!"

"Save me!" Aslan's face lighted up. "I'll give you anything you want!"

"You'll bring one ox to our house," said Uncle Sandro, who still had a weakness for oxen.

"Two oxen!" Aslan exclaimed.

"No, one's enough," Uncle Sandro protested modestly.

"But how will you save me?" Aslan exclaimed.

"I will marry her," Uncle Sandro said solemnly, like a man taking upon himself the fulfillment of a difficult duty.

"You?" said Aslan, taken aback.

"Yes, me," said Sandro. "My father is a simple man, and he won't bother to find out what she has for relatives on her mother's side."

"But will she consent?" Aslan exclaimed. "She loves me. How will I ever look her in the eye?"

"I'll take care of everything," Uncle Sandro said. "Besides, she's guilty before you."

"Of what?" Aslan brightened up, very much wanting her to be guilty before him.

"If she intended to marry a blue-blooded man like you," Uncle Sandro said importantly, "she should have warned you that she had an Endursky admixture."

"That's true too," Aslan agreed, "but after all, I never asked her. It never entered my head! But are you sure she'll consent to marry you?"

"I'll try and persuade her," Uncle Sandro said. "After all, she's got no place to hide now . . ."

"I did praise you to her very highly," Aslan reassured him. "But for God's sake, Sandro, spare me from having to talk to her. I'd be terribly ashamed!"

"I'll handle everything," Uncle Sandro said.

"But where will you take her?" Aslan asked. "You aren't ready to get married!" What he meant was that according to Abkhazian custom the bride-groom who has abducted a bride does not take her straight to his own house.

"To your relatives," Uncle Sandro said simply. "We're both getting married, I to your former bride and you to this—what's her name?"

"Shazina?!" Aslan said, once more taken aback. He looked around at Shazina, who was watching them vigilantly, and then glanced at his snowy cherkeska as if asking its advice.

"Yes," Uncle Sandro said relentlessly. "In the first place she's a beautiful girl. In the second place, we'll disgrace her if we abduct her and don't marry her. And in the third place, your relatives are expecting you with a bride, and it will look as if you've put them out of pocket to get your friend married. You'll be a laughingstock."

"Oh-oh!" Aslan said, and he clutched his head. "I forgot all about them . . . If I don't get married, people will say I couldn't abduct the girl."

"That's the trouble," Uncle Sandro agreed.

"It will stain my honor," Aslan said, and he surveyed his snowy cherkeska again.

"That's the trouble," Uncle Sandro agreed again.

"But I feel very awkward," Aslan said, suddenly thoughtful, "marrying my bride's friend with her watching."

"Never mind," Uncle Sandro said. "Your bride too will marry your friend with you watching."

"How's that?" Aslan flared.

"By your own wish," Uncle Sandro reminded him.

"Yes." Aslan subsided. "By my own wish."

"Listen," he said, suddenly struck, "what if Shazina has an Endursky admixture too? Then I'd do better to marry my own girl."

Uncle Sandro took fright.

"Your luck couldn't be that bad!" he exclaimed. "I'll find out right now!"

Feeling his body break into a cold sweat of anxiety, Uncle Sandro walked up to Shazina. To force his own beloved to confess herself an Endursky when she was an Abkhazian, and then persuade someone else's girl, if she had an Endursky admixture, to pass herself off as a pureblooded Abkhazian, was too much even for Uncle Sandro.

"Listen here," Uncle Sandro said softly when he walked up to the girl, "just tell the truth. Are there any Endurskies in your family?"

"Endurskies!" the girl shrilled. Her eyes hurled two lightning bolts into Uncle Sandro's eyes. "Will you look what a devilish trick they're using to get rid of me! Why, my brothers will shoot you down like quail just for *thinking* so!"

"That's that," Uncle Sandro said. "You're getting married!"

"To whom?" blazed the self-styled bride with quite appropriate curiosity.

"Aslan," Uncle Sandro said. "Not another word!"

"Aslan?" the girl said, slightly taken aback. "Didn't he and Katya have—"

"They did not!" Uncle Sandro interrupted, feeling a rush of jealousy. "They did not and could not!"

Uncle Sandro went to his beloved and told her that she was no longer Aslan's bride but his. Whatever she did, keep control of herself. No joy. A light, decorous, but inobtrusive mourning. Uncle Sandro's beloved, although she understood almost nothing, nodded to him and hung her head.

"Oh, Katya, Katya!" said Aslan, who was watching them from a distance and sensed that Uncle Sandro had persuaded her. "Why didn't you tell me the truth to begin with?"

"You didn't ask me," Katya replied, unable to raise her eyes.

"Too late for regrets, it's all settled!" Uncle Sandro boomed. "To the horses!"

"Swear by Allah that you don't have an Endursky admixture!" Aslan begged for the last time, peering at his new bride. He also seemed to be apologizing to the old one, by pointing out the reason why he couldn't help dropping her.

"An Endursky admixture?" Shazina exclaimed in exasperation. "Don't make me laugh! Why, my brothers—"

"We've heard about your brothers," Uncle Sandro said. "Hurry up, let's be on the way!"

"A miracle!" exclaimed the jolly cutthroat Temyr. "Who'd have thought the little minx could snag a fellow like this!"

"But we only have four horses," Aslan remembered as he led the way to the alders where the horses were tied.

"The little minx wanted to get married so bad," the jolly cutthroat said, "I bet she'd run along beside the horse!"

"Run along beside!" Shazina exclaimed again. "Why, my brothers—"

"Don't call her that," Aslan said in a conciliatory manner. "You know whose bride she is now—"

"I guess we've figured it out," Temyr said, and he touched his scratched cheek.

"Aslan and I will ride my horse," Uncle Sandro said. "She can handle both of us!"

They seated the girls on the horses. Aslan displayed noble tact in helping Katya mount the horse that had a woman's saddle. That is, although he had changed the content of the original plot (we're thinking of the change of brides), he left the logistics intact—Katya was supposed to ride this horse, and she did. But the man's saddle suited Shazina's character exactly right.

Uncle Sandro hospitably yielded his own saddle to Aslan and took a seat behind him on the back of his skewbald courser.

"If I'd known you were both getting married," the jolly cutthroat said, "I'd have dragged off the third girl for myself!"

"Too late," Uncle Sandro responded from behind his friend's white cherkeska. "Besides, Shazina has spoiled you for your wedding portrait."

They rode single file down the dense forest path, Temyr in the lead. With the handle of his quirt he sometimes pulled back the silkvine-entwined beech, alder, and chestnut branches overhanging the path and let the others pass.

Through the mighty, brambly forest, then through patterned fern pampases that hobbled the horses, and back into the green, moist gloom of a forest interlaced with all its branches and roots, enmeshed in all its vines, choking on its own furious abundance, and parting as unexpectedly as a sigh near a noisy little river with several bright, humbly bowed willows on its bank, as if to hint at the possibility of a Christian principle in the tempestuous kingdom of the heathen forest.

That hint, we imagine, was lost on the cavalcade. Shouting and cracking their quirts, the young men drove the horses into the stream and the horses walked across, jibbing now and again, looking askance at each other, tossing their manes, snorting, clicking their hooves, slipping on the stones of the bottom, stumbling and angrily jerking, and then the girls cried out, the young men laughed, and with a whoop they quirted the horses up the steep bank overgrown with buckthorn and tamarisk.

Uncle Sandro felt an unbearable gaiety bubbling up inside him, but he made a mighty effort to control himself so that Aslan would guess nothing. Now and again Aslan glanced at his former bride, then shifted his gaze to his new-fledged one, sometimes as if he didn't understand where she'd come from. Then he would study her, trying to get used to his new situation.

But when the path was lined with especially thorny bushes or the horses went into the water, he forgot about both brides, totally preoccupied with the fear of snagging or water-spotting his snowy cherkeska.

Now and again Shazina turned around to her bridegroom and for some reason burst out laughing. Her audacity surprised Uncle Sandro, who thought she was laughing as she recalled the details of this whole incident. His surprise soon gave way to angry astonishment, however, when it became clear that she was actually turning around to laugh at the extraordinary speckles (will you look at that!) on his famous dappled courser, his pride and joy!

Hardly had Uncle Sandro recovered from this unheard-of audacity when Shazina suggested aloud that her brothers would die before they'd ride on a long-tailed skewbald snake like that.

Uncle Sandro wanted to send her back, on foot, but he was checked by the fear that if he did, Aslan would revert to the original version of his wedding plans.

But evidently there was no limit to her audacity. Halfway home to Aslan's relatives, Uncle Sandro's horse began lagging slightly behind. She was having a little trouble after all with her double burden. Here again Shazina could not refrain from an audacious comment.

"Faster," she said, turning around to her bridegroom, "or my brothers will overtake us—"

"Let your brothers light a candle to God for having rid them of you!" shouted the cutthroat Temyr.

"Her brothers," said Aslan, warily standing up for his bride, "are valiant, respected lads."

"They take after her," the jolly cutthroat persisted. *"She* abducted *you!* Truth to tell, it's you we should put on the horse with the woman's saddle!"

"Friends," Aslan warned, "just don't joke like this in the house we're going to. They might not see it as a joke, and they'd take offense on my behalf."

Everyone agreed to that, and the rest of the way, as long as it was light enough to see, Aslan kept glancing at his bride, trying to get used to her and slowly begin falling in love with her.

In the night the cavalcade arrived at the house where they were expected. Their hosts, of course, were very surprised that the friends had brought home two brides. But, in keeping with the laws of hospitality, they hid their consternation by taking the opposite tack—they expressed surprise that their third companion had arrived without a bride.

The guests and their friends sat at the festive table almost till morning. At first, the long mark left on the jolly cutthroat's cheek by Shazina's fingernail was passed off as a vague hint that certain complications had arisen during the abduction, but gradually, as glass after glass was downed, this vague hint became a transparent one that Temyr's cheek had been grazed by a bullet from their pursuers. The curious tried to ascertain precisely which bride it was whose pursuers had hit Temyr.

"Must have been Shazina's brothers," the jolly cutthroat answered. "They're the ones that especially raved . . . ."

"There's one thing I can't understand," Aslan asked Katya, choosing an opportune moment. "When Temyr grabbed Shazina, why didn't you tell him he'd made a mistake?"

"How could a girl speak up?" Katya answered in all sincerity. "You might have changed your mind, something might have happened . . ."

"That's true too," Aslan agreed. But then he asked, still watching her closely, "Well, are you pleased to be marrying Sandro?"

Uncle Sandro gave her a swift kick under the table: Get a grip on yourself.

"You said yourself that he was good," Katya said, perhaps covertly explaining why she had fallen in love.

"Yes, of course, I said so myself," Aslan reiterated firmly.

The newlyweds stayed in this hospitable house for ten days. Every morning, for some reason, when they emerged from their rooms and met on the veranda, Aslan peered searchingly into the eyes of his former bride. The possibility cannot be excluded that he was still seeking in her eyes, and not finding, any trace of a light decent mourning.

Twice in those ten days his young wife washed his snowy cherkeska. The jolly cutthroat Temyr joked about it, saying that in the very near future Shazina would dye his cherkeska so she wouldn't have to wash it so often—dye it red, most likely, to blend in with the new era.

"Never," Aslan answered, unable to accept such a future even in jest.

But now, as is customary, the young husbands' relatives arrived and took them home to their villages.

Two weddings were celebrated in the two houses, this time independently of each other. Three weeks after his wedding Uncle Sandro saw Aslan come riding up to the Big House, leading a fine red ox on a rope. The snowy cherkeska gleamed triumphantly. Uncle Sandro was glad to see his guest and even felt certain pangs of conscience over the gift, but he could not refuse it now.

The distinguished guest met an excellent reception in Uncle Sandro's house, and sweet Katya simply flew, doing her utmost to entertain her former bridegroom.

"You haven't let her dye your cherkeska," Uncle Sandro said, recalling the cutthroat Temyr's joke.

"Impossible," Aslan said proudly, as if to imply that an Abkhazian nobleman still had control not only in the family but in Abkhazia itself.

When Uncle Sandro and Aslan were left alone, the latter made an unexpected confession.

"I must tell you, Sandro," Aslan began, "that I had some doubt as to your honesty. And now I want to confess to you. I thought it was very strange the way things turned out. I decided you had set it all up—the cutthroat Temyr dragging off Shazina, and my bride suddenly turning up with an Endursky admixture. Despite my anger and resentment, I decided to sit down and figure it all out before taking revenge for the insult to my honor and the honor of my clan. This is how I reasoned: If you had set it up for Temyr to grab Shazina— who was in love with me, of course—I'd never learn the truth from her. But then why, I thought, did she scratch Temyr's cheek so hard? And this is how I answered my own question: So that it would all look like the truth.

"All right, then, I thought, if Sandro lied that Katya had a grandmother of Endursky descent, he couldn't come up with a substitute grandmother! I found out where she lived, went to Enduria, and convinced myself it was all true. Yes, you were a real friend, and it was the devil that gave me evil thoughts.''

"What's true?'' Uncle Sandro was taken aback.

"That she's of Endursky descent," Aslan said.

"Endursky?'' Uncle Sandro cried.

"What, didn't you know?'' Now Aslan was taken aback.

But Uncle Sandro had already gained control of himself.

"Endursky, but on her mother's side, not her father's!'' Uncle Sandro exclaimed.

"That's what I mean,'' Aslan said soothingly. "On her father's side everything's in order . . . I'll always remember that you saved me . . . My parents have old-fashioned ideas, or else I'd never have repudiated Katya . . . But I don't think Endurishness should bother anyone in the new life.''

"No, of course not,'' Uncle Sandro agreed, mentally regretting that he had refused the second ox. "I think the new life itself is inclined to Endurishness.''

"That's what my parents think, too,'' Aslan agreed importantly. "So don't be downhearted. It's all for the best . . .''

The next day Sandro and his young wife saw Aslan off on his homeward journey. Uncle Sandro, as is customary when seeing off a respected guest, held the stirrup for him, and at the same time, as is customary among the hospitable Abkhazians, tried to persuade him to stay and visit a while longer. But the toe of Aslan's soft boot slipped into the waiting stirrup. He said good-bye to the newlyweds, rode out of the open gate, and trotted off toward home. So ended the story of Uncle Sandro's wedding.

I heard about it on the same kind of caressing fall day, albeit fifty years later. We were sitting in his yard on an ibex skin in the shade of a fig tree, sipping from cut-glass tumblers of cold, mildly tangy *ayran*—a blend of yogurt and water.

Now and again as he told the story, Uncle Sandro lifted to his nose a huge golden quince that looked like a lion's face. In sniffing the mighty fruit's subtle aroma, he seemed to be using the smell to bring close the days of his youth, as he had once used Prince Oldenburgsky's binoculars to bring close the bathing girls.

From time to time Aunt Katya emerged from the vegetable garden carrying a small wicker basket filled with beans in the pod or violet eggplants. The eggplants she took to the kitchen, but the beans she scattered on the veranda floor to dry.

Whenever she passed, Aunt Katya gave us a condescending smile, as if to show that Uncle Sandro's story shouldn't be taken all that seriously, though you could listen if you had nothing better to do. The discussion of dimpled cheeks, and more especially the episode involving the binoculars, Uncle Sandro conveyed with care lest Aunt Katya hear.

"So that's how she tricked me into marrying her, and as you see, I live with her to this day,'' he concluded his story, ignoring the fact that Aunt Katya was approaching us with another basketful of beans. She heard Uncle Sandro's remark. Although this was obviously not the first nor even the tenth time she had heard it, she stopped when she got to us, set the basket on the ground, and looked at Uncle Sandro resentfully.

"Why 'tricked,' you and your shameless eyes?" Aunt Katya said with a certain weary obstinacy.

"And wasn't it a trick?" Uncle Sandro said, brightly pouncing on her words. "I told you, 'Say you're an Endursky.' And what did you say?"

"I said, 'All right, I'll say my grandmother on my mother's side is an Endursky.' What kind of a trick is that, you and your shameless eyes?"

"There's the Endursky character!" Uncle Sandro exclaimed. It seemed to me he was admiring both his wife's stubbornness (a rare trait, native to Endursky women exclusively) and her total humorlessness (also a rare quality, native to Endurskies of both sexes), which, however, offered him endless possibilities for displaying his own sense of humor. "All these years, and she's still stuck in the same groove! Goathead—I figured I'd invented your Endurishness! If you'd told me, 'Yes, I really do have an Endursky admixture,' I still don't know whether I'd have married you or not."

"Tell me, how are the Endurskies worse than you?" Aunt Katya asked, again with a certain weary obstinacy. "They're a hundred times better than you. They drink less, and—"

"Drink less!" Uncle Sandro repeated sarcastically. "They can't drink, that's why they drink less—"

"Endurskies try for their families, for their homes, for their dear ones," Aunt Katya cooed, lost in a dream of Endurian domesticity. But then she came to and added plaintively, "And you?"

"Here's where your Endurian stupidity shows up," Uncle Sandro answered. "To this day you have no idea how important it is for people's lives that they should eat and drink gaily, intelligently, without hurrying, and listen to my stories, and sometimes contribute something themselves, if they have anything to contribute—"

"You forget how old you are," Aunt Katya sighed hopelessly.

"Harping away!" Uncle Sandro said with a wave of his hand. Turning to me, he added, "No, I'll tell you honestly. My wife's too nice for an Endursky. She's lived with me for over fifty years, and so far—knock on wood!—she hasn't poisoned me."

"I wonder who the Endurskies have poisoned?" Aunt Katya asked challengingly. She had started to pick up her basket, but now she put it back down on the ground.

"You'd better ask who they haven't poisoned," Uncle Sandro said. He lifted the quince and sniffed it attentively, as if suspicious it had been poisoned by Endurskies. No, apparently they hadn't gotten around to it. He lowered his quince-hand to the ibex skin and turned to me: "The Endurskies have dealt in poisons since time immemorial. They're so sly about using poisons that no prosecutor has ever trapped them.

"For example, you're visiting an Endursky, and at the time he has an enemy in that village or the next one. And the Endursky tells you, 'Listen, there's a nice fellow lives here. He's heard lots of good things about you. Drop in on him, humor him, he'll have you to dinner. Just don't say I sent you, because he'd be embarrassed. Stop at his house as if night had overtaken you here.'

"So you trustingly go to this man, rejoicing that people know about your good deeds, when you didn't think anyone knew about you. Sometimes you've even thought maybe you didn't have very many good deeds. But no, it turns out you have enough good deeds, and kind people know about you.

"So you trustingly go to this man, thinking you'll make him happy and have dinner with him. You get there and the poor fellow has you to dinner, because there's no place to hide—a guest. But the Endursky who sent you there has already given you a poison, and it will take effect in twenty-four hours. Having eaten your genial host's dinner, you lie down in his bed and die.

"Next day the police and the doctors are all over the place, they find out you were poisoned, and they put your poor host in prison for having poisoned a totally innocent man. That's how the Endurskies sometimes dispatch their enemies. The interesting thing is, he's got nothing against you personally, he's only thinking about his enemy. It never enters his head that you'll die."

"But," I laughed, "suppose you promised to go to this man and then didn't go?"

"No problem!" Uncle Sandro waved a hand. "He'll send someone else another time! And it never even enters his head that you'll die an innocent death—"

"Don't listen to the old fool!" Aunt Katya said, as if angry at herself for having listened spellbound. She resolutely picked up the basket and left, remarking, "Sooner or later they'll arrest him for his tongue. And rightly so. It's just that it's shameful . . ."

She went up on the veranda. Uncle Sandro glanced after her with good-natured irony (he really did love her, the old deceiver!), sniffed the quince again, and said, "I should have reversed the binoculars before I looked at her, but, fool that I am, I brought her close. You should always look at an Endursky through reversed binoculars, keep far away from him. And there was a sign from God in the fact that I nearly fell out of the tree, but I didn't understand Him. God was shouting to me, 'Watch out—an Endursky!' But I didn't understand Him at the time, and now what? Now it's too late . . ."

"Uncle Sandro," I asked, "what do you think of women in general?"

"There's one thing you can say to any woman and never be wrong," Uncle Sandro replied offhandedly, his mind obviously still on the Endurskies: " 'With a character like that, you might have been prettier . . .' But the Endurskies— they're something else again . . ."

Uncle Sandro smoothed his mustache, obviously pleased to have added a few more strokes to the psychological image of the Endurskies that he never tired of creating. He fell into a thoughtful silence.

I sipped the tangy coolness of *ayran* from my glass and weighed Uncle Sandro's aphorism. To my mind it was just plain good. I wondered whether I should pass it off among my friends as my own impromptu remark . . . Or save it for the next chapter of the novel on Uncle Sandro's life? After some hesitation I concluded that I shouldn't go blabbing it. Somebody would steal it, and then I couldn't prove I was first with it. I'm always having to restrict myself this way for the sake of art, and what does it get me?

From the veranda I could hear the rustle of bean pods; Aunt Katya was picking them over, still grumbling off and on. A swallow flew twittering through a veranda window, obliquely slashed the length of the house (she did it in less time than it takes to tell), and flew out another window. What need was there for her to fly into the veranda and fly back out? None; sheer mischief. But this is a mark of life, her ecstatic painting in the air. It justifies all.

The sun was warm but not scorching. In the thick green foliage of gnarled mandarin trees gleamed the gold of ripening oranges. From here on the hill I could see suburban houses surrounded by fruit trees. Conspicuous among them were the persimmon trees, leafless now, their branches studded with crimson fruit.

"Uncle Sandro," I asked, deciding to show him my gratitude for the aphorism, "why do I keep hearing our folks call the Endurskies parachutists?"

"It's so," Uncle Sandro said, coming to life. "They're dropping them on us now by parachute."

"Who is?" I asked.

"No one knows, but it's a hostile government," Uncle Sandro replied firmly.

"Surely you can't believe," I said, "that despite border guards, radar installations, and all manner of equipment, foreign planes could fly over our territory and drop parachutists?"

"Why should I believe, when I know for sure," Uncle Sandro replied. "Alpine shepherds keep finding parachutes in the mountains. How many thousands of those parachutes are rotting in impassable forests? By the way, they say it's good material. Doesn't wear out."

"Have you seen one of these shepherds?"

"No," Uncle Sandro said. "Who do you think I am, a kolkhoz chairman? And besides, he wouldn't even show the parachute to the chairman, or else he'd have to give it to the police. Excellent foreign material. Nice for a summer suit, or it'll do for a mattress, or you can make a tent out of it—it's waterproof."

"Uncle Sandro," I said calmly and firmly, "it's absolutely impossible."

"Mm-hm," Uncle Sandro said, and he lifted the quince to his face. "You'll believe it when an Endursky lands smack on your head . . . But he's not fool enough to do that . . ."

"Well, how could it be possible?" My voice was beginning to rise a little. "Weren't there Endurskies living around here before they had airplanes?"

"So what?" Uncle Sandro replied imperturbably, and he sniffed the quince again. "They didn't have planes, but they had parachutes—"

"But how could they have parachutes when they didn't have planes?" I exclaimed, trying to get at his logic.

"You interpret everything straight, like a stick," Uncle Sandro said. Laying the quince on the ibex skin, he continued, "Every era has its own parachute. You laugh when I say the Endurskies have bound us hand and foot. But I'll make you a bet. On your way back to the city you'll be going by the Government Building, where all our ministries are. Pick any floor and walk past ten offices in a row. If eight of them don't have Endurskies in them, I'll stand you and any of your friends to a good dinner and take an oath not to talk about Endurskies ever again."

"Are you serious?" I asked, appalled by the turn the conversation had taken. His conjectures about Endurskies had never been supported by figures, and now all of a sudden he had appealed directly to statistics.

"Of course," Uncle Sandro said. He lifted the lion-faced quince and sniffed it as an aesthete sniffs a rose. "But if you lose, you'll stand me to a restaurant dinner and confess before all my friends that you've been a blind calf and all your life Uncle Sandro has been thrusting you to the teats of truth."

"It's a deal!" I agreed—and then I remembered what he had told me the week before.

The new secretary of the Georgian Central Committee, Shevarnadze, had launched a campaign against bribe-takers and embezzlers of every sort. The rumor was abroad in our city, as in all other cities of Georgia and Abkhazia, that it was now extremely dangerous to carouse in the restaurants, because investigative agents went there in disguise to establish who, exactly, was having a spree on stolen money.

The week before, touching on this topic in conversation with me, Uncle Sandro had said that he'd never enter a restaurant now, even if someone threw his cap into one. This remark implied that he had some tie to the underground life of the local bigwigs, although I knew for a fact that he had no ties to them whatever. He sat at their tables, drank their drinks, but he was never admitted to their affairs. That I knew for a fact. Now, in connection with our bet, I reminded him of his pronouncement about the cap thrown into the restaurant.

"You misunderstood me," Uncle Sandro said. "The men who watch the restaurant-goers are looking to see who pays the bill. And in this case, I'm sure that the one who pays the bill is going to be you."

"All right, we'll see," I said. I told Uncle Sandro good-bye and started to leave. I was on my way down the path that led to the wicket gate when I heard his booming voice from behind the mandarin orange bushes:

"When you make the reservation tell him Uncle Sandro will be at the table, or else he'll palm off a bad wine on you . . . he's an Endursky!"

Twenty minutes later I was at the Government Building. I hesitated for a minute by the entrance. I was very nervous. I had not expected myself to be so nervous. I didn't know what floor to choose for an unbiased experiment. For some reason I settled on the third. It struck me as being the freest from the play of chance.

Taking the stairs two or three at a time, I bounded up to the third floor. Before me lay a vast corridor, with people walking lazily past carrying floppy, fluttering papers.

I started down the corridor, counted off ten offices on the right (for some reason it had to be the right), threw open the door to the last one, and stopped on the threshold.

Behind the desk sat a balding Endursky, no longer young. When I opened the door he looked at me with an inimitable expression of wan perplexity. Only an Endursky can look at you like that, and then only if you're a stranger.

I hastily shut the door and headed for the next office. I shoved open the door and was immediately blasted in the face by loud Endurian talk. Behind the desk sat an Endursky, and two other Endurskies stood beside it. All three were talking, and all three stopped in midsentence as soon as I appeared in the doorway, as if they were hatching a conspiracy. All three stared at me in silence.

The blood rushed to my head in a mighty geyser of panic. I flung open door after door, and just as in a terrible dream about school, when you dream that the examiner has turned away from the desk and is talking to someone, and you're going through the question cards looking for a lucky one, but every card has unfamiliar questions, and you keep looking for a lucky card, though by now you're pining for the first one, which was easier than the rest after all, and the lucky one still hasn't turned up, and the examiner is just about to turn back to his desk, and you'll lose your chance to select a card, and you've already forgotten where the first one was, the one that was easier than the rest, and by the cunning smile on the face of the examiner, who has now swung slightly around to you and is finishing up what he was saying to someone else, but you realize that he's smiling at what you're doing, and suddenly you guess that he knew all this in advance, that he intentionally turned away in order to humiliate you more fully—just like that, I . . .

Just like that I opened eight doors, and in each of the eight offices sat an Endursky. In despair I opened the ninth door. There proved to be a very young Endursky in the office, and he looked at me very benevolently. I rushed over to him and stopped dead by the desk. Sitting behind the desk, he watched me mildly and attentively.

"Excuse me," I said, "I want to ask you a question."

"Go right ahead," he replied, smiling shyly and thereby seeming to take a part of my nervousness upon himself.

"Are you Endurian?" I asked. Perhaps I was too direct, or perhaps the very tone of my voice begged him not to be Endurian, or at least to renounce Endurishness.

The young man looked suddenly sad. Then, impotently pressing his palms to his chest, he stood up, bowed his head as if in partial confession of its guilt, and said, "Yes . . . Why? Can't I be Endurian?"

"Yes! Yes!" I shouted. "Come now, of course you can! Rule, Enduria, rule!"

At that I leaped out of the office. Without ceasing to mutter "Rule, Enduria, rule!" I raced down from the third floor and lunged outdoors.

I woke up in an open-air café by the sea, where to calm my soul I ordered myself two cups of Turkish coffee. I was shaken by the fact that Uncle Sandro had proved right. After the first cup, however, when I had calmed down a little and cooled off in the sea breeze, I suddenly realized that there were indisputable Endurskies in only two of the offices—the one where people were talking loudly in Endurian and stopped short when I opened the door, and the one where the young man bowed his head in a partial confession of its guilt. My frightened imagination had sketched the rest. I was even more shaken by this second discovery than by the first. Then I too was susceptible to this mystique?

Now I understood how it had happened. At first I had been absolutely sure that Uncle Sandro's claim was crazy. But at the bottom of my heart I wanted a fantastical reality to triumph, not the squalid reality of daily life; I wanted life to be deeper, more mysterious. That was why I had given the improbable mystique a head start, as it were, by identifying the owner of the first office as an Endursky. But when Endurskies turned up in the second office, and stopped in midsentence so suddenly and hostilely when I opened the door, the idea was instantly crystallized. It's very unpleasant to have people look at you and stop in midsentence.

However . . . It would be easier to stand Uncle Sandro to dinner than to repeat the experiment now.

I was interested to note that three of the guests Uncle Sandro brought to the restaurant turned out to be Endurskies. He had met them before and engaged them in ideological duels. And now two of the Endurskies spent almost the whole evening arguing with Uncle Sandro, quite academically by the way, in an effort to prove that they, the Endurskies, were less guileful than Abkhazians. Uncle Sandro argued the reverse.

"The bad thing is that you folks deal in poisons," one of the Endurskies began, and suddenly he expounded a version of the text very close to the canonical one, if Uncle Sandro's is the only text to be taken as such. I looked at Uncle Sandro, but he was not in the least embarrassed. He refuted my skepticism with a cold, firm gaze, as if giving me an order: "Don't believe it! The tautology is imaginary."

Incidentally, the third Endursky had nothing to say, for some reason. He sipped at his wine and listened to the others argue. I asked him what he thought about the argument.

"He's right," the Endursky said unexpectedly, with a nod toward Uncle Sandro. His eyes were sad.

I felt terribly sorry for him. Not knowing how to comfort him, I took from the platter the biggest trout—so delicately grilled that you could still see the virginal golden speckles on its skin—and transferred it to his plate.

"It's all nonsense," I said, and slapped him lightly on his stooped back, encouraging it to straighten up. "Pay no attention. Eat!"

His back did not heed my encouraging slap; on the contrary, it stiffened, insisting on its stoop. Nevertheless, the sad Endursky went to work on the trout, stooping to it in a lonely way.

(At this point some reader may grab me hastily by the arm and say, "Not true! In what restaurant in Abkhazia can you order trout in this day and age?" I answer, "Almost any, but only if you're in the company of Uncle Sandro.")

Anyway, the evening went off pretty well, especially since besides the main topic we had others that were entertaining enough. Our guests took their leave after midnight, and I walked part of the way home with Uncle Sandro. I remembered the sad-eyed Endursky and asked what he thought of him.

"An Endursky who confesses the guile of Endurskies," Uncle Sandro said instructively, "is the most guileful Endursky of all. By confessing the Endurskies' guile he puts us in a good mood, and then our good mood makes it all the easier for him to achieve his Endurish goals."

On this note Uncle Sandro and I parted. Incidentally, even without Uncle Sandro people in our city will say anything about the Endurskies. Two or three times a year the city is filled with rumors that the Endurskies have seized power in Moscow. How they seized it, why they seized it, and most importantly who let them seize it—none of that is known. Everyone knows only one thing: the Endurskies have seized power in Moscow.

On these occasions it is said that one of the Endurskies' first reforms, to be effected in the near future, will be to proclaim all the peoples of our country Endurskies, albeit with a designation of their aboriginal hue, as for example: Russian Endurskies, Ukrainian Endurskies, Estonian Endurskies, Georgian Endurskies, Armenian Endurskies, Jewish Endurskies, and so on. The Endurskies themselves will be called "Endurian Endurskies," with the modest explanatory note, "native population." Native population of what, however, is not indicated: exactly which district or republic or country? Or the globe? This ominous reticence is what frightens our folks most of all.

"So they're the native population? Then we're newcomers?"

"So it seems," your companion sighs.

Rumors of an Endursky power-seizure usually last about a week. Any attempt to inquire of the Endurskies themselves usually leads nowhere.

"Why no," the Endursky answers evasively. "People are always exaggerating . . ."

Our folks sometimes rush to interrogate Muscovites who have just arrived here on vacation. But they don't really know anything either, although for that matter they don't much bother to hide their fear of being seized by someone.

"So long as it's not the Chinese," the Muscovites say.

All these rumors are spread mainly by the endurgentsia. I think it's time to explain what that is. Long ago our intelligentsia was stratified into two parts. The smaller part has heroically remained an intelligentsia in the old Russian sense of the word, but the greater part of it has become an endurgentsia.

Within the endurgentsia itself, three types can be discerned: the liberal endurgentsia, the patriotic endurgentsia, and the governing endurgentsia.

The *liberal endurgentsia* usually do their work poorly, presuming that by doing poor work in their own sphere they are doing good work toward a dem-

ocratic future. They interpret democracy as the complete subjection of everyone
else to their own way of thinking.

At home among their own kind, or when visiting among their own kind, they
always criticize the government for not moving toward a parliament.

Gazing upon the vastnesses of their beautiful homeland, they often become
despondent when they think of the huge volume of work to be done when the
liberalization comes.

In the presence of a bribe, however, they are easily cheered up and will carry
out with precision any task entrusted to them. They'll take their bribes in one
form or the other, but prefer them in the other. They take under color of a fund-
raiser to support the struggle for democracy.

The *patriotic endurgentsia* and its local ethnic offshoots: just as their fathers
and grandfathers made a career out of internationalism, these people make a
career out of patriotism. The patriotic ideology exists within the old ideology
like a privilege-store coupon within the general monetary system.

They usually do their work poorly and know their professions poorly, deeming
the acquisition of knowledge, which often involves the use of foreign sources,
to be incompatible, in principle, with love for their homeland. They are elegiacal
in their recollections of the golden thirties, as well as the silver forties. They
often criticize the government for having degenerated into a parliamentary gabfest.
This does not prevent them from occasionally advising the government that those
who are trying to send people to Siberia should be sent to Siberia.

The patriotic endurgentsia consider it their duty to blame all of the country's
misfortunes on members of other ethnic groups. They love to pass off this habit
of theirs as a manifestation of their guileless straightforwardness.

Gazing ecstatically upon the vastnesses of their beautiful homeland, they end
by growing despondent when they recall how many non-Russians have made
themselves comfortable there. In the presence of a bribe, however, they are
quickly cheered up and will carry out tolerably well any task entrusted to them.
They'll take their bribes in one form or the other, but they prefer the one. They
take under the pretext of a collection for the altar of the fatherland. Judging by
the size of the bribes, the altar is in sad shape.

The *governing endurgentsia:* They do their work poorly, believing that it takes
so much strength to love the government that any serious work is out of the
question. The governing endurgentsia, too, sometimes criticize the government,
because it doesn't notice their lonely love and doesn't promote them fast enough
to positions of leadership.

They hate the endurgentsia of the other two categories, but they're a little
afraid of the patriotic ones and sometimes yield something to them in the fear
that otherwise they'll take everything. Deeming their frame of mind to be a state
secret, they never get into conversation with foreigners, merely smile at them
with the apologetic smile of a deaf-mute.

Gazing upon the vastnesses of their beautiful homeland, they sometimes become despondent when they think how many dissidents can hide in such a huge

territory. In the presence of a bribe, however, they are easily consoled and will carry out with some precision any task entrusted to them. They'll take equally in the one form or the other. They take under color of aid to eternally struggling Viet Nam.

Their favorite pastime is to tell—and show, if they have a map handy—how many foreign governments could be fitted into the vastnesses of their beautiful homeland.

But it's time we returned to our subject. While the rumor of an Endursky power-seizure in Moscow lasts, people usually take any chance occurrence as a secret sign.

For example, they're all sitting around their televisions, watching people see some minister off. Well, as everybody knows, when ministers go away somewhere they kiss the other ministers. That's the way it's done here—soccer players, hockey players, government ministers, they all kiss each other on television.

So here are the ministers kissing, and suddenly, in the crowd of people seeing him off, some third-ranking, totally unknown leader smiles slyly in the background. Now the people sitting around their televisions let out a roar like a stadium when someone gets a goal.

"Him! Him!" they shout as one man. "It's all in his hands!"

The interesting thing is that several days later, when everybody is convinced that nothing has happened, and the country is moving smoothly along on its former course, the rumors are not fully canceled.

"It must have fallen through somehow," our folks say. "But now we'll never know what it was . . ."

One time the central newspaper reviled a certain conductor. Big deal, they revile a conductor, who cares. But a week later, when the same newspaper, without a word about his previous errors, reported that he was giving concerts in America with great success, Mukhusites were thrown into an incredible uproar. Such a thing had never happened! For ease of comparison, since many thoughtless people had ripped up or thrown away the issue of the newspaper that reviled the conductor, entrepreneurs began selling it for ten rubles a copy and it became impossible to get.

Mukhusites contrasted the two notices and came to the conclusion that the Endurskies had established full control over the government. By reporting favorably on the conductor's concerts, in defiance of the earlier report, they were demonstrating that they had now turned everything topsy-turvy, everything would now be backward.

As usual, our folks went around peering into the faces of the local Endurskies to determine how they intended to behave, now that they had been so extraordinarily elevated.

But the Endurskies behaved with enigmatic self-control, which optimists interpreted as a promise of loyalty to us and pessimists interpreted as a temporary ruse connected with the shift of their main forces to the attack on the Russians.

In a word, people around here are always waiting for something. Although it's a long time since you yourself have waited for anything, and you try to prove to others that there's nothing to wait for, still, you too unwittingly begin to wait, so that when the others' time of waiting is over you can remind them that you were right in saying there was nothing to wait for. But since the others' time of waiting is never over, it turns out that you're waiting along with everyone else, that everyone around here is always waiting for something.

In point of fact, that's not a bad thing. It would be dreadful if people weren't waiting for anything. Humble thyself, proud man, live your life and meekly (or stormily, like my countrymen) wait for something.

But this is getting sad. So it goes—you begin with laughter and end in tears . . .

Why is the voice of gaiety stilled? O Russia, answer me! She doesn't answer. Uncle Sandro, answer me! Sometimes he does.

HARLAMPO
AND DESPINA

I FEEL THAT THE TIME has come to tell of Harlampo's great love for Despina.
Harlampo, old Khabug's shepherd, was betrothed to Despina. They were from
the same village, from Anastasovka.

Despina Iordanidi was the daughter of a prosperous peasant, who by local
standards was counted an aristocrat. Harlampo was the son of a poor peasant,
and although Despina's father had allowed them to become betrothed, he refused
to give his daughter in marriage until Harlampo should start a home and farm
of his own. That was the tragedy of their love.

Harlampo had nine brothers and sisters left at home. He was his father's
eldest son. After him came a whole string of sisters, for whom husbands must
be found and dowries laid by. So Harlampo sent all his earnings to his family,
and there was no way he could start his own farm. Without it, Despina's
father refused to give him his daughter. Having been unable to dissuade
her outright from marrying Harlampo, the father apparently hoped she
would tire of waiting for her bridegroom and marry some other, more solvent
Greek.

But Despina proved to be a devoted and patient bride. Seven years she waited
for her bridegroom, and what happened in the eighth year is the story we will
tell in these pages.

All those years, as he waited for the chance to marry his bride, Harlampo
never forgot that Despina's father, her *patera,* had insulted his house, Harlampo
himself, and ultimately Despina.

"O, patera," he said through clenched teeth several times a day, for no apparent reason, and it was clear that the flame of resentment raged undying in his soul.

"O, patera?!" he said sometimes in angry amazement, raising his eyes to heaven, and that could be taken to mean: "Father in Heaven, is he really a father?!"

Two or three times a year Despina came to visit her bridegroom. She would appear at the Big House in the company of a thin, spry old lady in a black sateen dress. Auntie Chrysoula, although she sometimes made a rather naive effort to disguise her role, was there to guard her niece's virginity.

Auntie Chrysoula, Despina's father's sister, had never had a family of her own. She had practically raised Despina, and she doted on her. Despina apparently loved her aunt, too; otherwise it would be hard to explain how she endured her endless sermons without ever blowing up. Auntie Chrysoula often repeated with pride that she had reared Despina on double-yolked eggs exclusively.

That could have been true, to look at her niece. Despina was a strong, sunshiny girl with broad hips and a pleasant, extraordinarily white face. The whiteness of her face was a point of pride to her, to Auntie Chrysoula, and to Harlampo. He listened with an expression of morose satisfaction whenever any of the Chegemians marveled at her extraordinarily white face, which was oddly incongruous with her strong brown peasant hands.

Despina's long chestnut braids swung at her hips when she walked, and on her head she always wore a dark blue kerchief. When she went out in the sun, the kerchief covered up her face almost like a chador. Her eyes were the same dark blue as her kerchief, and for some reason, since she never took off the kerchief, it seemed to me that her eyes were gradually getting bluer from constantly reflecting the color of the kerchief.

So, if Despina forgot and went out in the sun for a moment without pulling the kerchief over her face, Auntie Chrysoula immediately hailed her.

"Despina!"

With a habitual, deft gesture, Despina would pull the kerchief down over her face. Auntie Chrysoula, and perhaps Despina's other relatives too, apparently viewed a common suntan as a partial loss of chastity.

Despina and her aunt were received very respectfully in old Khabug's house, undoubtedly on orders straight from him.

Usually, if there were no guests in the house, we all took our places at the long, low Abkhazian table, with old Khabug always sitting in state at the head of it. But if there were guests, the adult men, presided over by Grandfather, sat at an ordinary table (a Russian one, to the Chegemian way of thinking). Harlampo was never seated at that table on such occasions. He was put at the little low table with us—the children, teenagers, and women (the women of the household, of course).

Although this ritual went unchanged for many years, Harlampo was always painfully aware that he was not seated with the guests. This was obvious from the expression on his face. In an apparent effort to mollify him, my Aunt Noutsa kept slipping him the tastiest morsels from the guest table.

Harlampo ate everything she gave him, of course, but made a display of taking no personal pleasure in it. This was obvious from the guarded, disdainful working of his jaws, from a sort of forcible swallowing motion. At times I even thought he somehow halted the action of his salivary glands. His face said: Yes, yes, I shoved down everything you gave me, but I didn't taste it, I couldn't and don't want to.

But when Despina and Auntie Chrysoula arrived to visit Harlampo, old Khabug seated him with them at the guest table, while all the rest of us were put at the usual one.

In these hours we could tell that Harlampo's soul exulted, although outwardly he remained morose and guarded as always. From there behind the high table he sometimes glanced at us with an odd expression, as if trying to imagine what a man feels like when they put him at a little low table. Then he would turn away, unable to imagine it.

From time to time he would cast a glance at his bride and Auntie Chrysoula, trying to impress on them that here he was, sitting with Grandpa Khabug, he wasn't actually just a hired shepherd in this house, he was practically a member of the family.

Old Khabug ignored all these subtleties. He had his own policy, which could be interpreted thus: I receive your guests with highest respect because I know that it's useful for your relationship with your bride. As for the fact that I don't seat you at the high table with my own guests, that is a matter of my customs, and I don't care if it makes you suffer.

Auntie Chrysoula and Despina would stay at the Big House for a week, sometimes two. In the evening the young people of Chegem would gather in the kitchen or on the veranda, and Despina chattered happily with them in Russian or Turkish, now and then laughing out loud at the Chegem boys' jokes, which invariably brought her a rebuke from Auntie Chrysoula.

"Ken drepese, Despina! (Shame on you, Despina!)" she said, and added something more in Greek. To judge by her lip-movements, she was indicating the decent limits on how far an aristocratic girl—*aristokratiko koritsi*—could open her lips while laughing. Despina hastily covered her mouth with her big brown hand, but a few minutes later she would forget herself and go off into peals of laughter again.

Sometimes even if Despina wasn't laughing, merely talking too vivaciously with one of the Chegem boys, Auntie Chrysoula would rebuke her again.

"Despina!" Auntie Chrysoula warned. Turning to Aunt Noutsa, she would say that Despina had gotten completely out of hand here in Chegem, she'd been unbalanced by her meeting with Harlampo. Back in Anastasovka, she said, Despina didn't speak to strangers, and many people took her to be mute.

"What a nice girl," strangers often said if they came to Anastasovka. "Such a shame she's mute."

Again Despina went off into peals of laughter, and again Auntie Chrysoula snapped in a voice full of reproach, *"Ken drepese, Despina!"*

Harlampo watched Despina with calm, morose adoration, and it was clear that in his conception all the goings on were quite natural, this was the only way for an *aristokratiko koritsi* to behave.

Sometimes when Harlampo came home with the goats he brought a big load of firewood on his shoulder. He would dump it by the kitchen wall with an unvarying, emphatic thunder of domesticity (he could obviously have let it down more gently), and Aunt Noutsa, wherever she was at the time, would respond to the thunder with a grateful echo: "Our provider is back!"

Just as Harlampo emphasized his thunder of domesticity by dumping the firewood, to make his arrival audible all over the house, so Aunt Noutsa used a loud voice to hurl her exaggerated gratitude to Harlampo.

When Auntie Chrysoula and Despina were staying at the Big House, Harlampo raised this thunder of domesticity to its uppermost limit. He didn't just dump the firewood in his usual fashion, without bending down; he didn't even set foot on the kitchen veranda now, merely went up to it and hurled the heavy load across to the kitchen wall with a strong shoulder-thrust.

Afterward, Harlampo usually looked around and caught Auntie Chrysoula's eye, as if she were a transmitting station through which to send his undying, morose reproach to Despina's father.

"O, patera!" he said sometimes, the words boiling out of him.

"Despina," Auntie Chrysoula said softly, somewhat oppressed by Harlampo's thunder of domesticity, the justice of his reproach, and perhaps her own role as a transmitting station, "pour for Harlampo."

Despina quickly went to the kitchen and came out carrying soap and a pitcher of water, with a towel flung over her shoulder. Harlampo pulled off his shirt, and though he kept his undershirt on, it bared his powerful naked arms and mighty shoulders.

The sight of Harlampo half naked returned Auntie Chrysoula to anxious reality. It was as if her momentary oppression had never been. She left her place on the veranda adjoining the main house to come and stand right by Despina, who was pouring the water for Harlampo.

Auntie Chrysoula fixed her eyes on them, and under her gaze they stood rooted to the spot in an effort to emphasize their physical separation. Their very effort had a sculptural force that laid bare their secret reciprocal drive, causing Auntie Chrysoula a certain vague uneasiness.

Now, supervising as Despina poured water for Harlampo, watching the crystal stream flow from the pitcher held in the girl's strong, chastely upraised hand, Auntie Chrysoula felt an incipient agitation as the stream grew shorter—that is, as Despina approached her pitcher-hand to the back of Harlampo's neck or his proffered arm.

"Despina!" came Auntie Chrysoula's cautionary voice, and the girl raised her pitcher-hand again.

When he had washed, Harlampo straightened up and reached for the towel that hung on the girl's shoulder. With his slow-motion reach (Look how I'm controlling myself), as well as his graphically displayed thumb and forefinger, he made it convincingly clear in advance that his intention of taking hold of the end of the towel was purely functional.

Even so, Auntie Chrysoula did not feel it superfluous to warn of the approaching danger: "Despina!"

Needless to say, all during Despina's stay at the Big House Auntie Chrysoula never let her niece out of sight. There could be no question of Despina and Harlampo's retiring to the garden or going off to visit the neighbors. Sometimes Harlampo took them with him to the forest, where he went to graze the goats. Auntie Chrysoula would come back with her lips stained like a little girl's with blueberry, blackberry, or cherry-laurel juice.

I should mention that Auntie Chrysoula was conspicuous for her appetite, which was unusual not only for an aristocratic old lady but even for an ordinary old lady. We simply couldn't imagine where it all went, considering that she was quite withered and little.

But Auntie Chrysoula not only loved to eat, she had a great fondness for homemade spirits. Again, she could drink a sizable amount, considering that even though spry and not *very* old she was still an old lady. She could easily put away five or six drinks.

The Chegem boys made a point of playing the good host to her, with the idea of making her fall asleep and leave Despina and Harlampo alone together. But Auntie Chrysoula never got so drunk as to go to bed, she merely went all soft and said emotional things to her niece, laying her head on Despina's shoulder.

Sweet Despina didn't scold her auntie at all; on the contrary, she pitied her. She kept kissing the dark, softly wrinkled little face pressed to her young shoulder, and saying caressing things. Auntie Chrysoula babbled something in reply. This cooing exchange, with its rhythmic pauses and repetitions and Auntie Chrysoula's sighs, somehow became intelligible of itself, as if they were speaking Russian or Abkhazian.

"Chrysoula's a silly, Chrysoula's had a drop too much . . ."

"Despina, forgive your silly old lady . . ."

"Chrysoula's a silly little thing, Soula's had a drop too much . . ."

"Despina, forgive your little old lady . . ."

The Chegem boys, who knew the long, woeful story of Harlampo's love, often suggested that he find a convenient occasion and possess Despina. Then her father would have no place to hide, he would finally let her get married, without waiting for Harlampo to start his farm.

They even suggested that if Auntie Chrysoula wouldn't leave them alone together he should give her the slip in the forest, do his deed, and then come back to her. But first, someone specified, Harlampo should take a bell off one of the goats and hang it on her neck so she wouldn't get lost in the forest.

No, someone else corrected him, the bell wouldn't help, because Auntie

Chrysoula would just come running after, jangling the bell not a step behind them. The best way, he elaborated, was to tie her to a tree with good strong vines. Only he mustn't be gone too long or the mosquitoes would eat her alive.

No, someone else argued, once you've made up your mind to something like this you don't want to hurry it. But, to keep the mosquitoes from eating Auntie Chrysoula alive, after tying her to the tree he should build a little fire beside her and toss on some rotted wood scraps to make it good and smoky.

Harlampo listened to all this advice with morose attention, without the shadow of a smile, and rejected it with a shake of his head.

"Despina's no ordinary girl," he said. *"Despina aristokratissa."*

Shaking his head significantly, he let them know that even if you could marry an ordinary girl by this method, you couldn't an aristocrat.

Even though Harlampo's reply made it clear that he did not intend to marry Despina by this means, every time he came home from the forest with Despina and Auntie Chrysoula, driving the goats ahead of him, the Chegem boys looked at him questioningly from afar and waved in wordless inquiry: Did you get anywhere?

Harlampo caught their questioning looks from afar and firmly shook his head again to show that he had no intention of using such guile to possess the girl he loved. This may have been his pride showing through, buried though it was under an avalanche of humiliations—his conviction that in the end, having waited so long, he would receive by legal means what belonged to him by right of love.

(When recalling Harlampo's countenance, and especially that gaze of his, I often used to feel that I had encountered something similar at other times in my life. But for a long time I couldn't think exactly what it was. Now at last I remember. Yes, just like Harlampo, our intelligentsia turn that gaze on people who propose using force to possess Democracy—who is also Greek, like Despina. And just like Harlampo, our intelligentsia invariably and firmly shake their heads, to let us know that only by legal means will they secure what belongs to them by right of love.)

The interesting thing is that even when returning from the forest with a big bundle of firewood on his shoulder, propped up by the *tsalda* ax on his other shoulder, and even though the weight forced him to walk with his head down, still, when Harlampo saw the Chegem boys he waited patiently for their wordless inquiry and took the trouble to raise his face a little and firmly shake his head, though the gesture was impeded by the firewood sticking up over his shoulder— yes, still, overcoming this impediment, he let them clearly know that they had waited in vain.

The interest the Chegem boys took in his love story must not have seemed importunate to him; his mighty passion, locked in hopelessness, must have needed the support of well-wishers, or at least spectators.

Auntie Chrysoula's constant watch over Despina's chastity was the object of all kinds of joking and needling from the inhabitants of the Big House and their guests.

For example, if they were all sitting on the veranda in the evening and Harlampo was in the kitchen, someone would quietly ask Despina to do her a favor and fetch something from the kitchen: the scissors, perhaps, or some knitting, or wool, or a spindle. As if she had overheard the request accidentally, Auntie Chrysoula usually managed to jump up before Despina and run to the kitchen.

If they did succeed in sending Despina off without Auntie Chrysoula's noticing, she responded in various ways depending on the circumstances. I should mention that Auntie Chrysoula was an incredible chatterbox. In this connection the inhabitants of the Big House observed that if it wasn't one thing it was the other—her mouth had to be working.

"Give her something to nibble on and she might shut up," someone would say in Abkhazian when she had everyone dizzy with her jabbering.

So, sometimes when she was deep in conversation, Auntie Chrysoula really did let Despina out of sight. When she collected herself, however, and realized that she had seen her niece a few moments before, she calmly got up and went to the kitchen as if she needed something there herself.

If she noticed that Despina had gone off somewhere but Harlampo and all the young people visiting the Big House were sitting in their places, she tolerated her absence a fairly long time. Now the inhabitants of the Big House, or its guests, intentionally tried to provoke her anxiety by asking where Despina had disappeared to.

"Anh!" said Auntie Chrysoula, and she brushed them aside: I don't know and I don't want to know.

But if, on noticing Despina's absence, Auntie Chrysoula recalled that she had been deep in conversation and had let her out of sight for ten minutes, let's say, and Harlampo or one of the other young men had also disappeared, then she forgot all camouflage.

"Despina!" she screamed, and she jumped up as if trying, by means of her voice, even before she reached the kitchen, to restrain Despina from the fatal step.

Admiring the diversity and wealth of Auntie Chrysoula's tactics in guarding Despina's innocence was a favorite pastime of the Big House.

Sometimes Despina disappeared to the kitchen when Auntie Chrysoula knew perfectly well that Harlampo was there, but for some reason she showed no uneasiness. This stratagem, which Auntie Chrysoula thought of as very shrewd, afforded the inhabitants of the Big House especially subtle merriment.

"Chrysoula," someone would say, with a significant nod toward the kitchen, "aren't Harlampo and Despina in there?"

"Anh!" Auntie Chrysoula would wave a hand. "Bride and bridegroom!"

A little more time would pass, and with great anxiety they would again remind Auntie Chrysoula of Despina and Harlampo's indecently prolonged sojourn in the kitchen.

"Anh," Auntie Chrysoula would say with a wave of her hand, adding in Russian, "Who gives a doom!"

What was the explanation for Auntie Chrysoula's insouciance? Auntie Chrysoula knew for a fact that old Khabug was in the kitchen just then, but she thought the others didn't know it.

Harlampo and Grandpa Khabug slept in the kitchen at night. Despina and Auntie Chrysoula were put in the best room, the main hall. Although it had two beds and two couches, Auntie Chrysoula had refused once and for all to sleep in a separate bed. She slept with Despina. They did not lie in the bed head to foot but with their heads at the same end. My cousins (they slept in that same room, but there is always a possibility that the irreverent little girls exaggerated) claimed that when Auntie Chrysoula got into bed she wound Despina's long braid around her hand so that she couldn't run away to Harlampo in the night.

The same little cousins claimed that Auntie Chrysoula said "Despina!" several times a night in her sleep. Still in her sleep, she jerked her hand to feel the weight of Despina's head, to make sure she hadn't run away to Harlampo after voluntarily cutting off her own braid.

Late one afternoon, someone succeeded in sending Despina to the spring for water just at a time when Harlampo was there grazing the goats, although Auntie Chrysoula didn't know it. She thought he had gone to Sabid's Hollow as usual. Actually, he had; but he had also agreed to help Uncle Isa split shingle near the spring, and he had driven his goats over there via the hollow.

All the residents of the Big House and their nearest neighbors—everyone but old Khabug, whom no one initiated into these schemes, of course—waited with curiosity to see how it would all end.

Despina was obviously taking too long, and it was clear that she had met Harlampo. Despite everyone's best efforts to distract Auntie Chrysoula, she became uneasy after a while and went outdoors calling, "Despina! Despina!"

Despina answered. Loudly reproaching her, Auntie Chrysoula started across the barnyard to meet her. Just as she went out the gate, the flock appeared on the path that led to the spring. In back of the flock came Despina, with the big jug on her shoulder, and Harlampo paced solemnly beside her. Auntie Chrysoula wrung her hands and ran to meet them.

"*Ken drepese, Despina! Ken drepese, Despina!*" she screamed, pointing at Harlampo, whose morose expression was meant to impress on Auntie Chrysoula that although her suspicions humiliated him he would endure even this, as he endured all for the sake of his great love. Bracing the jug with one hand, Despina gesticulated vigorously with the other, right in Auntie Chrysoula's face. Her gestures made it plain that she had met Harlampo completely by chance; at the same time, by repeatedly jabbing her hand at the jug, she seemed to be pointing out that nothing could happen in the presence of such a witness as a big copper jug. Apparently she was insisting that she had met Harlampo on the way up from the spring with the jug and had had no choice but to keep on going beside him.

Now Auntie Chrysoula's attack fell upon Harlampo. Her gestures made it plain that if he accidentally met his bride face to face on the road, he was supposed to hurry on ahead with the goats (she pointed, to show how he should do it) or drop back (and again she pointed, to show how he should do it).

Harlampo said something in reply, and by now they were entering the barnyard. To judge by his tone of voice his reply was imbued with guarded dignity, and the gist of it was probably that he had no reason to run away from his bride, especially when he encountered her on the road with a jug on her shoulder. So saying, he thrust his own shoulder forward as if stooped under the weight of a jug, apparently insisting on the total absurdity of the proposition that a girl could engage in amorous intrigues beneath such a weight.

As he replied to Auntie Chrysoula's attacks, Harlampo morosely sought the eyes of the Chegem boys, who looked at him questioningly from the veranda and waved in wordless inquiry: Well, did you finally have some success?

Still fending off Auntie Chrysoula's attacks, Harlampo looked at them morosely and indicated with a firm shake of his head that nothing of the sort had happened, nor could it ever.

In short, Auntie Chrysoula watched Despina tirelessly, all the while finding most unexpected occasions to bring her within the bounds of aristocratic behavior. Despina had only to start petting a big Caucasian sheepdog that had run up on the veranda, let's say, and Auntie Chrysoula would check her, apparently finding the male principle too obviously expressed in the dog's appearance.

"Despina," she said, and explained something. To judge by the fact that she was pointing at the cat, which was dozing peacefully on the veranda railing, one could surmise that an *aristokratiko koritsi,* even if betrothed to the shepherd Harlampo, must not play with a sheepdog, although she might confidently pet a cat or even take it in her arms.

The young Chegemians who dropped by the Big House enjoyed stealing glances at Despina. My cousin Chunka—a sharp-tongued jokester, tall, thin, and lithe as a walnut switch—even flirted with her a little, so far as that was possible under Auntie Chrysoula's vigilant eye.

Chunka was the grandson of Grandpa Khabug's brother. He and his sister Lilisha lived in our yard in their own house, although he spent most of his time with us in the Big House. His father and mother were long dead. The Chegemian custom is to spoil orphans, and of all my various cousins and young uncles he was the most spoiled.

Although he noticed the attention they paid Despina, Harlampo was not jealous but seemed to morosely encourage their advances, which were really quite innocent. He obviously felt that this was how it had to be; young Chegemians lucky enough to spend time in the company of an aristocratic girl couldn't help trying to make advances to her.

One time Chunka brought a big wooden bowl full of plums and set it at Despina's feet as she sat on the veranda with the other women. The girl gave Chunka a grateful smile, reached for a big lilac plum, and was just about to bite into it when Auntie Chrysoula grabbed the fruit away from her.

"Despina!" she ejaculated. Quickly wiping the plum on the hem of her dress, she began to explain something to her.

The gist of it, apparently, was that before a girl of her status could bite into a plum she mustn't fail to wipe off the dust, even if there was nothing else handy but her auntie's hem. Wiping the plums one by one on the hem of her dress, she handed them to Despina—not forgetting some for herself, of course.

But the delicacy that Auntie Chrysoula loved best of all was figs. Two large fig trees grew in the kitchen garden. One was a fig of the white variety, the other black. Auntie Chrysoula especially loved the black figs.

One time Despina and Chunka climbed the black fig tree. Despina removed her sandals and tried to go first, but Auntie Chrysoula stopped her, sent Chunka up first, and launched into a rapid jabbering. Apparently she was explaining that an aristocratic girl, when climbing a tree with a strange man, always lets him go first.

Chunka and Despina climbed the tree, stood on different branches, and began picking figs, now eating one themselves, now throwing one to us. Chunka also managed to collect some in a basket.

Chunka was the only one who threw me any figs, and it was mainly Despina who threw to Auntie Chrysoula. But Chunka often threw to her, too, because Auntie Chrysoula was really wild about black figs. Forgetting her lineage (or perhaps even without forgetting), she ate the figs with remarkable speed, not even bothering to peel them.

The figs kept plopping into her hands, and considering her advanced age it was amazing how adroitly she caught them, never missing a one. Sometimes an overripe fig splatted on her hands, but that didn't faze her in the least, she just slurped the sweet gooey mess right into her mouth.

"I'm going to work one miracle in my lifetime," Chunka said in Abkhazian, with a rustle of leaves as he reached for a branch and carefully bent it down. "When Auntie Chrysoula dies, I'm going down to Anastasovka with a pail of black figs. I'll walk over to the coffin and put a fig to her lips. And then, to the horror of the Greeks around her, she'll open her maw and eat the fig. Next she'll sit up, and without getting out of the coffin she'll empty the whole pail—unless of course the Greeks collect their wits and shoot me for bringing the glutton back to life."

While Chunka was saying this and bending the branch down to reach a fig, Auntie Chrysoula, who of course didn't understand a word, kept her devoted eyes fixed on him, being very interested in the fate of precisely that fig.

Sometimes Chunka purposely threw her several figs in a row, perhaps to see her pick them up off the ground and eat them, or perhaps to silence her, if only for as long as it would take her to eat the figs.

A sharp-tongued jokester himself, he may have been a little jealous of the never-silent Auntie Chrysoula. Besides, she hindered him from getting something going with Despina. But when he threw her several figs at almost the same time, Auntie Chrysoula mobilized instantly to spread her long-suffering aristocratic hem under the flying figs, and in they plopped.

"There's one thing I can't understand," Chunka would say then in Abkhazian.

"Why the hell did I bring a basket, with this old woman dogging our footsteps?"

When a fig landed in my hands, Auntie Chrysoula glanced it over with a melancholy eye. If my fig seemed especially big and ripe, and it almost always did, she complained to Despina that she wasn't getting her fair share.

While she ate the figs, Auntie Chrysoula kept up a constant patter.

"Despina!" she cried, and raised her hand to point out a ripe fig that Despina couldn't seem to see although it was right close to her. Finally, after turning back the lop-eared, leathery leaves, Despina reached the desired fig. Trying not to squish it, she picked it and threw it to Auntie Chrysoula.

"Despina! Despina!" she screamed when the girl stepped on too narrow a branch.

"Des-pi-na!" she called severely when the branch the girl was standing on proved higher than the one Chunka was standing on. She would jabber away, pointedly smoothing her own skirt, obviously to remind her that an *aristokratiko koritsi,* when in the same tree with a strange man, must not climb so high that the strange man can look at her from below.

Despina said something in reply, pointing to the branch Chunka was standing on and calling her auntie's attention to the fact that the strange man's sight-line from that branch could do no damage to her modesty.

"Despina!" Auntie Chrysoula cried in distress, staggered by her naiveté. Apparently proposing that Despina should learn to look ahead a little, she gestured to show how easily Chunka could jump from his branch to hers if he took a mind to.

"Lord!" prayed Chunka. "Isn't she ever going to shut up? Listen—pull up a good big beanpole, sneak up behind her, and give her a good conk on the noggin! She won't croak, of course, but she might shut up for half an hour and I could throw something into the basket. Only a dolt like me could climb a fig tree with a basket when that trencherman is standing under the tree and won't shut up for a minute."

Incidentally, while Despina was answering Auntie Chrysoula, throwing figs to her, and eating them herself, she also found time to banter with Chunka, flashing her dark blue eyes. They talked back and forth in Russian, and Auntie Chrysoula rebuked Despina several times for speaking Russian, which was unintelligible to her, instead of speaking Turkish, which was intelligible to all. Auntie Chrysoula could not grasp the fact that by now the young people of our polyglot villages found it easiest to speak Russian.

"Go home—vodka, vodka!" Chunka yelled to her in Russian.

No such luck. Auntie Chrysoula started jabbering an indignant reply to him in Greek, forgetting that Chunka did not understand Greek. The words "Vodka! Vodka!" cropped up several times in her jabbering, and it was clear that if, like many aristocratic old ladies, she was fond of having a glass or two, it still didn't mean she'd leave her favorite niece to the whim of fate here in the tree.

"This is a circus!" Chunka yelled. "Now she's made me a Greek!"

Chunka climbed to another branch with his basket. Down below, I moved over to make it easier for him to throw figs to me. Auntie Chrysoula looked at me, distraught. Aware that Chunka would now have trouble getting figs to her, and yet reluctant to reveal her dependence on him, she took a couple of steps toward me. We were to understand that she had just happened to move over, without any purpose.

Now, right behind me loomed the menace of a lush clump of nettles. As he threw me a fig, Chunka noticed it and yelled to me in Abkhazian, "What have you decided to do, flog her with nettles? Nettles will only make her raise a howl to all Chegem. I told you—conk her on the noggin with a good stout beanpole! You said you wanted to go on a bear hunt. This'll be a try-out for you. Though maybe you're right. Maybe that's backwards. Maybe we should try you out first on a she-bear, and then turn you loose on this unbelievable old woman."

Suddenly Chunka reached for a huge, ripe fig with a red open maw. He picked it carefully, hailed Despina, then kissed the fig and lobbed it to her. Despina caught it adroitly and gave Chunka a dazzling smile. Steadying herself by lightly leaning back against the tree trunk, she began to peel the fig with her thumb and forefinger.

Auntie Chrysoula, who saw all this, was struck dumb with indignation. In the stillness, for some time, the peelings could be heard falling plop! plop! plop! on the broad fig leaves. By the time Auntie Chrysoula recovered, Despina had put the sweet pulp in her mouth.

"Despina!" Auntie Chrysoula screeched, and she started jabbering faster and faster, apparently explaining to her that an aristocratic girl, when in the same tree with a strange man, cannot accept the fruits of the tree from him, especially a fruit defiled by his kiss. She lifted her fingers to her lips to show how very disgusting that kiss was.

Despina made her some sort of answer; to judge by her hand-movements, she was demonstrating that she had peeled the fig before eating it and had thus neutralized the effect of the defiling kiss.

"Despina!" Auntie Chrysoula shouted in despair, and she flung her arms wide, jabbering something that appeared to mean, Why did you have to eat the fig at all?

"I know a way to make this old woman shut up!" Chunka shouted. He reached for a fig, picked it, and threw it into the basket. "I'll take the basket and jump out of the tree onto her head. Even then, I'll get a broken neck, but she'll just dust herself off and start picking up the figs that have fallen out of my basket."

As she chewed the fig, Despina made some sort of answer to Auntie Chrysoula; to judge by her hand-movements and her glances at the branch where Chunka stood, she was saying that the fig had been thrown without her approval and she had had no choice but to catch it and eat it.

"Despina!" Auntie Chrysoula cried, as if refusing to recognize the very possibility of being so ignorant of the simplest laws of etiquette. Then she started jabbering afresh, ceaselessly moving her hands to illustrate her words, so that it was easy to tell what she meant. She meant that even after catching the defiled fig, Despina could have remedied the situation honorably, simply by throwing the fig to her, Auntie Chrysoula.

In the dappled light, her face illumined by the sun, Despina looked down at Auntie Chrysoula from the height of her branch with clear blue eyes, as if she herself marveled at the simplicity of the remedy and regretted that it hadn't occurred to her in time. She was still chewing distractedly on the defiled fig; I think Auntie Chrysoula found this especially irritating. She waved her arm and started jabbering again, and I thought I distinctly heard the beginning of the phrase, "Stop that, please."

"You bonked her with a beanpole, and she didn't even feel it?" Chunka said without looking down. He made his way to the end of the limb, now and again testing its sturdiness with bouncy movements of his feet, while hanging on to an upper branch with one hand. When he could feel that the limb probably wouldn't hold any farther, he stopped, found a twig to hang the basket on, and looked around in search of ripe figs, then continued his thought: "I knew it. The only thing that can shut this old woman up is my shotgun. But I'll have to pull both triggers at once, and with both barrels stuck in her mouth. Otherwise it'll be pointless—if she's even one meter away from the gun, the bullets will be so horrified by the old woman they'll fly off in different directions."

Suddenly Despina climbed from her branch to a higher one and disappeared in the thick foliage of the fig tree. Auntie Chrysoula looked up and waited silently for several seconds, expecting her to lean out of the foliage and throw her a fig. But for some reason Despina did not lean out of the foliage, and Chunka climbed over to the same branch. Before disappearing in the thick foliage, he impudently hung the basket on a twig, as if making no effort to hide the fact that the fig-picking was now over and something quite different had begun. It all happened in a few seconds; if they had prearranged it, we hadn't noticed from down below.

"Despina!" Auntie Chrysoula cried in horror.

No answer.

"Despina!"

Again, silence.

Auntie Chrysoula glanced around, obviously trying to find out whether there were any chance witnesses to this disgrace. Her glance fell on me. She looked quickly into my eyes, trying to anticipate me in case I attempted to put on a feigned expression. Deciding that she had anticipated me, she tried to find out whether I understood the meaning of what was happening. Establishing that unfortunately I did understand, she wanted to determine whether I could at least keep my mouth shut if the worst should happen. Unable to determine this and not wishing to waste precious seconds on me and vexed over those already wasted, she ran howling to the tree and peered up the trunk, trying to discover the vanished couple. But she could not discover them. Then she suddenly looked down, and her gaze lighted on Despina's sandals. She stared at them distractedly for several seconds, as if Despina had been carried off to the sky and it was decidedly unclear what to do now with her sandals.

Then, as if shaking off the hypnotic spell that had riveted her gaze to the sandals, she began running around the tree, shouting and wailing, trying to find a break in the foliage of the crown through which she might see them. Her tone of voice could only mean that if they thought they'd hidden from her they had another think coming—she had discovered them long ago. But since she kept running from place to place the whole time, it was clear that she didn't see them after all.

After two or three minutes, Despina's laughter and Chunka's guffaw rang out from the thick foliage.

"Despina!" Auntie Chrysoula screamed with hysterical reproach, nevertheless rejoicing that she was at least alive.

At long last Despina parted the leaves, and her laughing face looked out, illumined by the sun. Auntie Chrysoula, one hand pressed to her heart, reproached her for a long time.

Now Chunka's laughing face looked out of the foliage. He reached for a fig, picked it, and tossed it to me, shouting, "Since you didn't stun her with the beanpole, for Allah's sake tell her I'm no hawk, to carry a girl off from a tree like a chicken!"

Although Auntie Chrysoula did not cease to reproach Despina and Chunka, when Chunka's fig plopped into my hands she couldn't refrain from looking to see if it was any good.

Despina picked a fig and drew her arm back to show that she intended to toss it to her auntie. Auntie Chrysoula started jabbering with renewed force and waving both arms to show that she wasn't about to accept a fig from her after such perfidious behavior. But Despina tossed the fig. As if against her will Auntie Chrysoula caught it, and as if against her will put it in her mouth, still reproaching her niece.

Chunka leaned out of the foliage again, reached for a good fig, picked it, and smilingly drew his arm back to show that he intended to toss it to Auntie Chrysoula. Auntie Chrysoula wagged her head, flailed her arms, and started jabbering as if anew, even though she had never ceased to jabber. Her whole appearance indicated that here was someone from whom she would never again accept another fig.

"God grant me as many years of life as you'll accept figs from me," Chunka said, and he tossed her the fig.

As if reluctantly (since it was in flight), Auntie Chrysoula caught the fig and, as if reluctantly (since it was in her hands), put it in her mouth.

"I swear by the Prayer Tree," Chunka yelled in Abkhazian, "no one on God's green earth can outtalk, outeat, or even outdrink this old woman! Maybe Uncle Sandro could outdrink her, but she'll talk him to death first and then she'll outdrink him!"

Auntie Chrysoula gradually regained her composure, or rather, switched to the jabbering-frequency she had been at before Despina and Chunka hid in the crown of the fig tree.

The last rebuke she gave them (not in general, but in the tree) was when they were climbing down. Chunka was about to go ahead of Despina, but Auntie Chrysoula stopped him and ordered him to let her go first. The ensuing explanation could be interpreted to mean that if an *aristokratiko koritsi* lets a strange man go first when climbing up a tree, then the strange man, on the contrary, must let her go first when climbing down. That's how it's done.

Gently, though rather heavily, Despina jumped down from the tree. Picking up her sandals, she looked around and found a green islet of grass, went over to it and carefully wiped the soles of her bare feet, then put her sandals on. Watching her, Auntie Chrysoula nodded slightly in approval: in this situation, at least, Despina herself knew what to do and acted the way girls of her status acted.

As a token of complete reconciliation, when Chunka jumped down from the tree he held out the basket of figs for Auntie Chrysoula to choose the ripest ones. For several agonizing seconds Auntie Chrysoula struggled with herself, glancing first at the basket, then reproachfully at Chunka, then still more reproachfully at Despina, trying to emphasize that the main burden of guilt was actually hers, since she had been first to hide in the crown of the fig tree.

She even turned a penetrating gaze on me, trying to see whether this disgraceful episode had slipped my mind. To oblige her I nodded my head, meaning that it had. Then Auntie Chrysoula's gaze expressed bewilderment, as if asking how I could understand the meaning of her gaze if this disgraceful episode had really slipped my mind?

After that she reached out to the basket and, letting us know that she wouldn't be too long choosing, pulled out three figs. She showed the laughing Chunka that she had pulled out only three figs, as if to let him recognize the modesty she had displayed. Then as a small reward for her modesty she pulled out one more fig.

Auntie Chrysoula adored black figs.

Uncle Sandro, who was always on the lookout for someone to do a little of his work for him, ignored their lineage on one of these visits and hired both Despina and Auntie Chrysoula to weed his corn. Aunt Noutsa tried to dissuade him, reminding him that they were guests and it was awkward to utilize them for such heavy work. But Uncle Sandro didn't bat an eye.

"In contrast to our folks," he said brusquely, as if sacrificing national sensibility in the name of truth, "the Greeks don't like to sit on their hands."

Despina and Auntie Chrysoula readily agreed to help him, however, especially since Uncle Sandro promised them seventy-five pounds of corn, albeit from the new crop. Evidently aristocrats, too, aren't always above picking up a little extra.

They worked in his field for three or four days. Not far away from them was Uncle Sandro, also taking a few swings with his hoe.

Sometimes the Chegemians stopped by Uncle Sandro's field, astonished that Despina was hoeing corn with her face almost completely veiled by the blue kerchief.

"Is she a Persian, maybe?" they guessed, shrugging their shoulders.

When Harlampo drove the flock past Uncle Sandro's field, he too would stop and listen to the Chegemians' astonished comments on Despina's veiled face. Gazing at his bride with morose satisfaction, he explained this oddity to the Chegemians.

"Despina's not a Persian," he said. Cocking a finger and grinning at the Chegemians' naiveté, he added, *"Despina aristokratissa."*

He wanted to tell the Chegemians that an aristocratic girl wouldn't hoe corn with her face exposed, like an ordinary peasant woman, but would always cover it completely this way, leaving just an eye-slit, so that her face would stay pure and white.

After standing there a while, Harlampo drove the goats into a hazelnut thicket so that they could start grazing without him. Vaulting the wattle fence, he went and took the hoe from Auntie Chrysoula.

Harlampo may have begun to hoe with the idea of showing Auntie Chrysoula what a hard-working husband her niece would have. But gradually he worked himself into a frenzy, into the self-oblivion of labor, while Despina bent low over her hoe and tried to keep up with him.

Clods of earth positively flew from under Harlampo's hoe, they piled up around the roots of the corn, the chopped weeds wilted under the upturned dirt, pillars of dust flared up under his feet, while he kept swinging the hoe, without stopping for even an instant to catch his breath, changed hands only occasionally as he went along, jerked his head to shake the sweat from his face and went on hoeing, sometimes turning toward Despina to help her finish her strip and then moving ahead again, step by step. And Despina tried to keep up with him, working her hoe with fine, quick strokes.

Uncle Sandro, meanwhile, still taking a few swings with his hoe, glanced with sad reproach at the amazed Chegemians, as if to remind them that all his life he had been trying to teach them to work just like that, but alas, they hadn't learned very much.

The ecstasy of their labor grew more and more intense. It even became somewhat excessive from Auntie Chrysoula's point of view, although she did feel a cautious admiration.

"Despina," she enunciated from time to time, as if suggesting that they ease up a little.

Watching this self-oblivious pair, one Chegem Freudian suddenly declared, "They've gone wild with their hoes! I daresay it's not Sandro's field they're doing so zealously—they think they're doing it with each other!"

"Bull's eye!" several Chegemians standing nearby chorused in agreement. It was obviously a load off their minds: they realized at once that there was no need to kill themselves working, no need to envy this sublimated love play.

Incidentally, when I recall Chegemian pronouncements of this sort and compare them with quotations that I have come across from books by the Viennese conjurer, I am impressed by the abundance of coincidences. Since the Chegemians cannot be suspected of having read Sigmund Freud, I have reached the inescapable conclusion that he once made his way to Chegem in the guise of a distinguished foreigner, wrote down all manner of tales and sayings, and published them under his own name, brazenly omitting mention of their source.

Over the years, I think, the world has taken advantage of my countrymen's illiteracy to squander Chegemian ideas, the way the ancient Romans ruthlessly felled Abkhazian boxwood. I have arrived just in time to gather what's left, but much is irretrievably lost.

Take the theory of surplus value, for instance. In point of fact, this is a Chegemian idea. No, I don't deny that Marx discovered it on his own. He could hardly have been to Chegem, even if Engels—as always, poor fellow—assumed the expense of the trip.

But the theory was also discovered, without any prompting, by an illiterate Chegem peasant named Kamug, whom many Chegemians took for a madman, though not a threat to human life.

(It doesn't bother us, as the saying goes, that this mad world takes many geniuses for madmen. Some geniuses are reconciled to it, so long as they're left alone. What bothers us is that this mad world, in implementing its mad notions of justice and balance, often declares madmen to be geniuses. It reckons up how many geniuses have been declared mad and declares exactly that many madmen to be geniuses. Many geniuses are aghast to realize that madmen will be declared geniuses according to their number. In their pity for mankind they often hide their genius and die of drink. But this is a very large subject and we won't get into it here.)

Our nice Chegemian didn't quite escape the mad ways of this world either. Yes, the Chegemians considered the genius Kamug a madman, of course, although to their credit it must be stated that they have never in all their history declared a madman to be a genius. That is a plus for my Chegemians.

Kamug had the following habit. Every time he started to shell his corn in preparation for going to the mill, he first broke each ear in two, then took half the broken ears to his cornfield and buried them in the ground. All his life, whenever people asked why he did it, he took the trouble to explain his great discovery to them.

"From one kernel," Kamug would say, "you can get one good ear of corn, on the average. One ear, on the average, has two hundred kernels of corn. A hundred kernels from each ear are enough to cover the outlay for maintenance of the plow, hoes, and sickles, for consumption by the plowman and his family, and for seed. To whom, then, do the remaining hundred kernels belong? To the earth. She worked for your harvest, she earned half of it, and you must return to her what belongs to her."

And he invariably returned to the earth half of the ears he picked. His wife suffered greatly from this. One time, against his wish, she even began to dig up the broken ears, clean them somehow, and feed them to the chickens on the sly. When Kamug found out about it he went into an incredible rage, especially since his wife wouldn't confess how long she'd been doing it and he didn't know how much he owed the earth.

In short, he beat his wife unmercifully, which by Abkhazian standards is considered very disgraceful, and threw her out of the house, which does not adorn an Abkhazian either but is considered more tolerable. You might say that Kamug's behavior toward his wife exhibited in elemental, rudimentary form the idea of the dictatorship of the proletariat, standing guard over the interests of the toiling earth.

The next time around, poor Kamug had a lot of trouble finding a wife. Being an honest man, when he went courting he explained to his future wife's relatives why and how he would divide the corn harvest with his field. At the same time he tried to infect them by his example, admittedly without result.

"From one kernel," Kamug would say, launching into an explanation of his theory, and the relatives of the woman he was courting would begin to glower, or say a cowardly yes-yes, or cut off the negotiations forthwith, depending on their temperament and their assessment of the degree of danger in his madness.

Sometimes Kamug courted widows or spinsters whom the relatives were very eager to have off their hands. In an effort to somehow mitigate, ennoble, his version of the allocation of the corn harvest, they implied to him that they interpreted his theory as an unfamiliar but essentially good Chegemian custom— bringing sacrifice to a fertility god.

But with great candor (which, incidentally, was characteristic of other bearers of this idea at a certain stage), Kamug rejected their version and said that he pursued only one goal, to return to the earth what she had fairly earned. At last he was successful in courting a widow with many children. Her father, apparently in token of his distaste for the theory, ordered this message to be relayed to his future son-in-law: "Half the harvest has already been reaped from her. Let him try and reap the other half."

When she felt at home in Kamug's house, his new wife decided to amend his theory. Though apparently not devoid of a certain slyness, her reasoning remained unintelligible to the Chegemians.

"If you've decided to destroy half the crop," she told her husband, "why dig it under? Just scatter it on the field . . ."

They say Kamug looked at her and tapped his forehead expressively.

"You're even stupider than the other wife, I see," he said. "She at least took the corn that the earth had earned and fed it to the chickens, but you want to feed it to those loudmouth jays. Not on your life!"

The new wife meddled no more with his theory, but the wild boars did: they happened to dig down to the corn that the earth had earned. Kamug lived in a rather secluded spot, near the forest. Incidentally, that's where great ideas always arise—in seclusion.

The wild boars began visiting his field at night more and more often. Each time now, Kamug buried deeper and deeper the corn that the earth had earned. But the wild boars dug down to it even so, with their long, unclean snouts.

Kamug began burying the corn in various different parts of his field, but they found it even so. Then Kamug began burying the corn in small portions all over his land so that the boars wouldn't get all of it, the earth would get some share.

But late that winter the wild boars, those dry-land sharks of the Chegem forests, dug up the whole of Kamug's farm in their search for corn. (Incidentally, doesn't the Russian word *ryt'*, "to dig," come from the word *rylo*, "snout," i.e, that which digs? How fertile Chegem is: the slightest contact with it leads to incidental small discoveries, even in Russian philology.)

When they saw Kamug's land all dug up by the wild boars, the Chegemians assessed the event according to their own lights.

"Now he won't even have to plow," they said. "He's not all that crazy, Kamug's not."

Kamug was very offended to hear this. Determined to prove his complete lack of self-interest, he took up his gun and began keeping watch over his land at night. By the next spring he had killed fifteen boars.

As a true Abkhazian, even though he was the discoverer of a universal idea, Kamug did not eat pork. Taking the slain boar by the tail, he would drag it over to the fence and send word to the local Chegem Endurskies. They came and bought his kill for a laughably low price.

"I accept money only for my powder, bullets, and vigil," Kamug said.

"That's the weirdest thing of all," the Chegemians reasoned. "No matter what plague lands on us, it works out to the Endurskies' advantage."

When he was worn out from his nocturnal vigils, Kamug sometimes got his wife to spell him keeping watch. But now the Chegem elders rose up in arms. They could not reconcile themselves to this violation of Abkhazian custom.

"By our law a woman defiles a weapon," they said, "and a weapon dishonors a woman. Doesn't he know that?"

Especially since the sharp-eyed hunter Tendel had brought back unprecedented news the year before, after a visit to the city.

"It's kingdom come!" he shouted as he entered Chegem, and he told what he had seen.

He had been walking around the city in the evening and had noticed near a certain store an old lady with a gun in her hands, and with eyeglasses on her nose besides, guarding the store. An old lady with a gun in her hands guarding a store, and in spectacles besides—it staggered the Chegemians' imagination.

Many Chegemians went to the city on purpose to look at the amazing old lady. They stood near her for hours, pitying her and marveling that an elderly woman should be treated so barbarically.

"May I live to mourn the men who have exposed you to public disgrace," said some.

"Poor woman," said others, "instead of spending time with her grandchildren she's guarding a government store with a gun in her hands and eyeglasses on her nose."

"What's come over the Russians?" one of the Chegemians said, throwing up his hands. "Who's cast the evil eye on them, that they're putting their own mothers out to guard stores?"

"They were always like that," some skeptic said.

An older man shook his head. "No, we remember them being quite different. Somebody's hexing them."

"Not the Endurskies—?"

"Nah, the Endurskies won't go after anyone else till they've destroyed us."

The poor old lady, who kept a vigilant eye on these incomprehensible nocturnal delegations of Chegemians, broke down one time and blew a whistle to summon a policeman.

The Chegemians were staggered: "A tin whistle on her neck, too!" Though not at all disturbed that she had whistled for help, they were more appalled than ever at the number of objects on her person that were incompatible with the appearance of a respectable elderly woman: gun, eyeglasses, a tin whistle.

"Whistle all you like," one of the Chegemians said. "Your relatives on the male side have whistled away your old age, may I live to mourn them."

The policeman who responded to her whistle of summons, unhappily for him, proved to be an Abkhazian. Instead of establishing order he had to defend himself against both the Chegemians and the watchwoman.

"Why did you do it to her?" the Chegemians demanded. "What is she, an orphan?"

Trying to explain why the old lady had been put out to guard the store, the policeman said it wasn't because she was an orphan but because a new law now recognized the equality of men and women in the cities. It was beyond the Chegemians to recognize such a ludicrous equality, and they asked in amazement why the policeman, having a weapon and being invested with authority, recognized such a foolish equality.

For her part, the watchwoman tried to find out why the Chegemians were so curious, and demanded decisive action from the policeman.

"They won't rob you," he reassured her. "They've just never seen a woman guard. They're highlanders, a little bit primitive."

One of the Chegemians, who understood a few words of Russian, translated the policeman's remark for the others. Not only were they not offended, they saw the whole scene in the new, true light of its mad comedy.

Roaring with laughter and going over the details of the encounter (what struck them especially funny was the way she had blown her whistle, puffing up her cheeks and keeping her eyeglasses trained on the Chegemians), they went off to spend the night at a relative's.

"We were pitying the poor old lady, marveling at her primitiveness," the Chegemians laughed, "and all the time they thought we were the primitive ones! Ha! Ha! Ha!"

"To put an old lady out for the night with a gun in her hands, eyeglasses on her nose, and a tin whistle on her neck—even an Endursky won't think up anything more primitive than that! Ha! Ha! Ha! Ha!"

"And our own policeman!" they said, remembering the policeman's attempts to explain away this disgrace as some sort of equality between men and women which was recognized by the authorities in the cities.

Not a year had passed since this unprecedented event when there appeared in Chegem itself a man who forced his wife to warn away the wild boars with a gun in her hands. It was intolerable.

"You should buy her some eyeglasses, too, and put her out with the gun like that Russian watchwoman," one of the old men remarked caustically when Kamug entered a room where the elders were sitting.

"And hang a tin whistle on her chest, like on a child," said another.

"Don't you know," added a third, "that by our custom a woman defiles a weapon and a weapon dishonors a woman? Sending a woman out into the night with a gun is the same as sending her out into the night with a strange man. What kind of a husband are you if you send your own wife out into the night with a strange man?"

But now the eldest of the elders checked them with a gesture, authoritative but not insulting, and spoke calm, wise words to Kamug, who bowed his guilty head.

"By our custom, son," he said, "a woman may take a gun in her hands in one case only: if her clan has no men left to avenge spilled blood. Then a woman is a hero, and our people glorify her in song and story. But for an Abkhazian woman to take a gun in her hands and shoot, and shoot at such an infidel animal as the wild pig—such a disgrace we will not tolerate, son. Either forsake the village or leave your wife in peace."

Kamug had to submit. Exhausted by his nocturnal vigils, poor Kamug died before his time. To all intents and purposes he may be called a true martyr to an idea and numbered among the revolutionary saints.

While in no way disputing Marx's primacy, I propose that the law of surplus value be renamed the Marx-Kamug law, just as the law of the conservation of matter is called the Lomonosov-Lavoisier law.

Even at this late date, I think, it would be only fair if the name of our self-taught genius became famous. In the last analysis he deserves it, for his discovery, his sufferings, and his selfless defense of the toiling earth against parasitic boars.

"What's come over the Russians?" the Chegemians used to inquire from time to time—with a sort of perplexity and bitterness, as best I recall.

The question was first voiced, I think, when the Chegemians learned that Lenin had not been buried but had been put on exhibit in a coffin in a special building called the Amausoleum.

To the Chegemians, the committal of a dead man to the earth is such a solemn and obligatory act that their moral sensibility could never make peace with the fact that the dead Lenin had lain for years in a building above ground, instead of lying in the earth and mingling with the earth.

In general, the Chegemians regarded Lenin with a mysterious affection. This feeling may have been partly due to their having first learned of the great man's life only when they heard about his death and the unjust non-committal of his dust to the earth. Until then no one but Uncle Sandro and perhaps two or three other Chegemians had known of Lenin's existence.

That was how the Chegemian myth of Lenin arose, I think. The Chegemians said of him that he had meant to do good but hadn't had time. Exactly what good they didn't specify. Sometimes, feeling ashamed to use his name lightly, and in part wanting to encode it against the evil curiosity of nature's dark forces, they did not mention him by name but said "The One That Meant to Do Good but Didn't Have Time."

In the conception of the Chegemians, whom young people surreptitiously chuckled at in my day, Lenin was the greatest abrek of all times and nations. He became an abrek after his older brother—also a great abrek—was caught and hanged at the order of the czar.

His older brother had not intended to become an abrek. He had intended to become a teacher, like his father. But fate saw fit to arrange otherwise. It seems that in those days Petersburg, like Abkhazia, had nationwide race meets. Lenin's older brother got fascinated by a race and didn't notice that he was standing too far forward from the crowd, blocking Czar Nicholas from riding by to his place of honor to enjoy the races.

Lenin's brother did not mean to insult the czar, but that's how it looked. The czar's men didn't get there in time to clear the way before the czar's horse, and the czar, being the czar, rides to his place of honor without stopping. When Czar Nicholas, dressed in a white cherkeska and mounted on a white horse, rode up to Lenin's brother, and the brother was too fascinated by the racing horsemen to notice him, then in front of the whole nation the czar lashed him with his quirt, which was braided of lion hide, and rode on.

That was how it all began. It seems that Lenin's clan was a very proud one, although the men of the clan had always been teachers or aspired to be teachers. Lenin's brother could not bear to be insulted in front of the nation, even by Czar Nicholas.

Incidentally, by Abkhazian standards the most terrible insult one can inflict on a man is to strike him with a stick or a quirt. Such an insult is washed away by the blood, and only by the blood, of the offender. He struck you with a quirt or a stick—that means he put you on the level of an animal! And what is there to live for if they put you on the level of an animal?

Incidentally, a blow with a quirt or a stick is also considered a grave insult—occasionally leading even to bloodshed—when someone strikes a horse without the permission of the owner. It is especially scandalous if, out of rudeness or native brazenness, someone strikes a horse on which a woman is mounted. Of course, if the woman says nothing and none of the relatives has noticed, there may not be any trouble. But if whoever struck the horse doesn't offer his apologies in time, things may end very badly.

This is what usually happens. A cavalcade of villagers will be riding to another village for a wedding or a funeral. Suddenly a horse on which, let's say, a woman is mounted, balks at crossing a ford, perhaps sensing that the rider lacks self-confidence, perhaps for some other reason.

And now it may happen that in the heat of the moment, without asking permission, the man following behind lashes her horse to make it go into the water. Just at that moment one of her relatives turns around and sees the whole scene in all its barbaric indecency. No, of course he doesn't say anything, to avoid disrupting the social event they are participating in.

But the wrath in the relative's soul has already begun to crystallize, with an almost chemical inevitability. The rider who thoughtlessly struck the horse on which the woman is mounted, however, can still make everything right.

He has only to ride up to the glowering relative and say, "No offence, friend, I didn't mean to lash your horse—"

"Don't mention it!" the relative replies, utterly sincere in his magnanimity. "That's what an animal's for, to be lashed. Put it out of mind! Don't trouble yourself over nothing!"

But we digress. As we were saying, Czar Nicholas lashed Lenin's brother with his quirt, never suspecting what vast historical events would ensue from this instantaneous flare of czarist wrath.

Lenin's brother went off to be an abrek, taking with him two or three trusty comrades who would help him wash away with the czar's blood his public insult. But the gendarmes caught and hanged him along with his comrades.

Lenin, then still a boy, took an oath to avenge the blood of his brother. Had Czar Nicholas been like the Big Mustache, of course, he would have wiped out Lenin's whole clan on the spot, so that there would be no one to take revenge. But Czar Nicholas was a rather kind and overtrusting czar. He didn't think a clan of teachers could be so proud. That was a big mistake.

Lenin went off to be an abrek, he hid for twenty years in the Siberian forests, and all the gendarmes in Russia could do nothing about him. Finally he lay in wait for the czar, killed him, and overturned his regime. According to another version, he only wounded the czar, and the Big Mustache finished him off later. But either way, the czar was no longer able to maintain his regime, and Lenin overturned it.

But his many years in the cold Siberian forests had undermined his health, a fact which the Big Mustache took advantage of. Before his death, though, Lenin did have time to write a paper in which he gave orders to his comrades on what to do when he was gone and how to do it.

The first thing he wrote was, Drive the Big Mustache out of power, because he's a vampire.

The second thing he wrote was, Don't round up the peasants into kolkhozes.

The third thing he wrote was, If you absolutely can't do without kolkhozes, don't touch the Abkhazians, because when an Abkhazian looks at the kolkhoz he wants to lie down and quietly die. But the Abkhazians must be protected, since even though not numerous they are an exceptionally valuable breed of men. They must be protected so that in the future, with the aid of the Abkhazians, gradual improvements can be made in other breeds of men, who though much more numerous are too simple-minded and don't see the beauty of custom and family ties.

The fourth thing he wrote was, In all affairs of state don't forget the Endurskies, keep your eye on them constantly.

When retelling Lenin's testament the Chegemians invariably called their listeners' attention to the indisputable fact that before his death Lenin had been preoccupied above all with the fate of the Abkhazians. After that, how could the Chegemians not love and revere Lenin?

Incidentally, I think the news of Lenin's testament was brought to Chegem by a once-famous Civil War commander, Uncle Fedya, who lived in Chegem first with one host, then with another. He sometimes went on binges of a duration miraculous for Chegem. Since everyone in Chegem drank but there were never any alcoholics, his binges were perceived by the Chegemians as a disease distinctive of Russian dervishes.

"He heard a voice," the Chegemians said. "That's why he abandoned all and came to us."

The Chegemians found this flattering. We will tell Uncle Fedya's story in more detail elsewhere, but he was a quiet, peaceable man who in brandy-making season kept watch by the still for days and never got drunk when on duty.

He really had been a legendary commander in the Civil War, and then after the triumph of the revolution a large-scale economic planner. Unlike many men of his ilk catapulted to administrative posts, he frankly confessed to his superiors that he knew nothing about his job. He was demoted several times, and suddenly one fine day he had a revelation. He understood that there was nothing he could do in peacetime except be a peasant farmer, as he had been in the province of Kursk before the German war.

When he placed this truth beside the rivers of blood he had shed in the Civil War, and the parents and wife cut down by White Cossacks in his native village— he could not bear it.

A mighty tsunami of alcohol caught him up, dragged him all through Russia, swept him over the Caucasian crest. One day the tsunami broke and the Civil War hero woke to find himself in Chegem, with the Order of the Red Banner miraculously spread on his chest.

But more about him elsewhere; here we'll go on with the Chegemian legend of Lenin. Lenin wrote a testament, then, or a Paper, as the Chegemians said, but the Big Mustache stole it and burned it. Lenin, however, being a wise man even though broken by mortal illness, had found time to read it to his relatives.

After Lenin's death the Big Mustache started wiping out his relatives, but they managed to relay the substance of Lenin's paper to other people. The Big Mustache started wiping out great numbers of people, hoping that among them he would get those who had managed to find out about the paper. He wiped out millions and millions of people, but even so, he could not wipe out the news that such a paper had existed.

So they put Lenin's body on exhibit in a little house called the Amausoleum, years and years went by, his bones cried for the earth, but no one committed them to the earth. Such cruel official obstinacy could not but find an intelligible explanation in the Chegemian mind. And it did. The Chegemians decided that the Big Mustache, proud of having triumphed over the greatest abrek, went every night to relish the sight of him lying there dead.

Nevertheless, the Chegemians did not tire of hoping that even the Big Mustache would finally take pity and decide to commit Lenin's unhappy bones to the earth. With a great stubbornness that sometimes verged on despair, the Chegemians waited years and decades for this to happen.

If anyone arrived in Chegem from a city they hadn't been to in a while, or especially if anyone arrived from Russia (as did those who served in the army), the Chegemians invariably asked, "What's the news? The One That Meant to Do Good but Didn't Have Time—are they going to commit him to the earth, or not?"

"No news on that yet," the newcomer would answer.

The Chegemians would let out a sorrowful whistle and shrug their shoulders in perplexity. The many troubles that beset our country they were often inclined to attribute to this great sin, the non-committal to the earth of the dead man's bones, which yearned for the earth.

Not that the Chegemians thought of nothing else day and night, but for many of them the disgrace of a duty unfulfilled was a gall on the soul.

Several Chegemians might be walking to work, their hoes on their shoulders. They're walking along, peacefully talking back and forth about this and that. Suddenly one of them explodes: "Sons of bitches!"

"Who, the Endurskies?" his companions ask, taken aback.

"Them too of course," answers the one who exploded, regaining his composure. "But I meant the ones that aren't burying Lenin."

"They don't ask us . . ."

Or it might be a cozy evening in some Chegemian kitchen. The whole family is gathered in pleasant anticipation of supper. The fire roars gaily on the hearth, the kettle hangs on the hearth-chain, the mistress has pulled it slightly away from the fire and is stirring the cornmeal mush with a spatula. Suddenly she stops the mush-spatula, straightens up, and turns to her family, asking plaintively, "Won't they ever commit to the earth the One That Meant to Do Good but Didn't Have Time?"

"Oh," sighs the eldest of the household, "don't touch our aching tooth. Better go ahead and make your mush."

"Well, they can just sit where they are," the woman exclaims bitterly, taking up the mush-spatula. It's unclear which she means, the thick hide of the rulers or the long-suffering inertness of the people.

Once I was standing in some hazelnut bushes and saw a Chegemian walk by alone on the path, deep in thought. As he drew even with me—of course he didn't see me—he suddenly shrugged his shoulders and spoke aloud.

". . . Dreamed up some sort of Amausoleum . . ."

And he disappeared around a bend in the path, like an apparition.

Or a Chegemian might be standing in a huge chestnut tree to cut a hefty limb. The sultry air rings far and wide with the long, lonely tooock! tooock! tooock! tooock!

Sinking the ax into the timber, he straightens up for a moment to lean back against the trunk and catch his breath. Suddenly, far below, he notices a countryman passing by on the upper Chegem road. By the man's clothes he guesses that he's coming from the city.

"Hey," he shouts at the top of his voice, "you, coming from the city! The One That Meant to Do Good but Didn't Have Time—have they committed him to the earth, or not?"

The passerby looks around, trying to make out where the voice is coming from, aware that it's from somewhere above (from the heavens?). He may not even catch sight of his countryman standing in the tree, but he waves a negative hand and tips his head back to shout, "No-o! No-o!"

The Chegemian spits furiously. "Well, they can just sit where they are!" he says, and who knows which he means—the thick hide of the rulers or the long-suffering inertness of the people. He yanks out the ax, and again comes the inescapable, long, lonely tooock! tooock! tooock! tooock!

Or let's say one of the Chegemians gets sick, lies in bed half the year or more. People come to visit him—his fellow villagers, relatives from other villages. They bring presents, they sit around him, they ask after his health.

"Oh! Oh! Oh!" the sick man groans in reply. "Why ask about me? I'm long dead. I'm like poor Lenin, there's no one to bury me . . ."

Stalin's death and his installation in the mausoleum were perceived by the Chegemians as the beginning of retribution. Right away they began saying that his name and his fame couldn't last long now.

So they weren't at all surprised to learn of Krushchev's famous speech at the Twentieth Congress. They approved of the speech, on the whole, and said, "Good for Khrushchit! But he should have used stronger words for the Big Mustache's vampirism."

And again they marveled at the Russians.

"What's come over the Russians?" they said. "Here in Chegem we knew about the paper Lenin wrote and all the Big Mustache's vampirisms. How is it they didn't know?"

Contrary to the liberal exultation in the land when the coffin with Stalin's body was removed from the mausoleum, the Chegemians were disappointed.

"They should have done it the other way around," they said in despair. "They should have buried Lenin and left that one, and written on the Amausoleum, 'HERE LIES THE VAMPIRE WHO DRANK OUR BLOOD.' Wasn't there anybody to suggest that to them?"

Through all of life's vicissitudes, the Chegemians stubbornly went on waiting for the time when they would commit to the earth, at last, the One Who Meant to Do Good but Didn't Have Time.

But that's enough digressing. Let us tell of Harlampo and Despina, since that's what we undertook to do. I have a feeling that these digressions will be the death of me sooner or later, as poor Kamug's nocturnal vigils were the death of him.

When Despina and Auntie Chrysoula left for Anastasovka, we children and Aunt Noutsa went with Harlampo to see them off, as far as the slope down to the River Kodor.

Before the farewell Auntie Chrysoula set down her basket, which was filled with nuts, *churkhcheli,* and cheeses. Despina held in her hands some live chickens with their feet bound together. For some reason it bothered me a little that she was taking our chickens, when they never laid double-yolked eggs.

The lovers' bitter farewell went on for several minutes.

"Harlampo," Despina said, and her dark blue eyes filled with tears.

"Despina," Harlampo breathed, hollowly, with ominous anguish, and his cheekbones came alive with knots of muscle.

"Harlampo!"

"Despina!" Harlampo said, hollowly, guardedly, with such inner force that the chickens felt it and anxiously began clucking and flapping their wings in Despina's hands.

"Despina," Auntie Chrysoula intervened in this duet, trying, although she was unnerved herself, to comfort her niece, who was wiping away tears with a strong hand that still clutched the chickens.

"Harlampo," Aunt Noutsa said, comforting her shepherd and stroking his broad back.

At length Auntie Chrysoula reached for her basket, and they walked on down. We watched them go. Despina's long, sun-gilded braids quivered at her back, and the blue of her kerchief was visible for quite some time.

"*Ey, gidi dünya!* (Damn this world!)" Harlampo said, in Turkish. He turned and went back to his goats.

"They'd do better not to come at all," Aunt Noutsa sighed. God knows what she had been thinking. All of us—saddened by this farewell, cleansed by it, unconsciously proud, I think, that such a love existed on earth, and unconsciously hoping that we too would some day be worthy of it—went home pitying Harlampo and Despina.

Now we must describe a fantastic love-madness, which the Chegemians ascribed to Harlampo and which was actually a reflection of their own madness.

The reader remembers that the day after Tali's abduction Harlampo got the walnut rabies from eating too many walnuts and chased after her pet nanny goat. He ran as far as the mill, where Gerago, who was even mightier than he, grabbed him, bound him, and immersed him in the stream. There he lay for twenty-four hours with a two-hundred-pound millstone on his belly to counteract the current and thoroughly ground the lightning of madness that had pierced him.

In twenty-four hours the walnut rabies had evaporated, the fevered brain had cooled in the icy water, and the lightning of madness had left his body for the ground. When he was warmed up beside the mill fire, Harlampo regained consciousness and was sent back to the Big House, along with the goat. A Chegemian who had been at the mill followed him at a little distance and discovered nothing remarkable in his behavior—only that the goat sometimes looked back apprehensively.

Harlampo was soon fully recovered, and the Chegemians seemed to have forgotten the incident. But it turned out they had not forgotten. The next year one of the goats in old Khabug's flock was barren. This was a fairly common phenomenon. Unfortunately, the barren goat was the one Harlampo had chased.

"Oh-oh," some of the Chegemians are reported to have said (in later years the Chegemians couldn't recall exactly who had said it first), "it's plain as day why she's gone barren. He's been fooling around with her! He won't let a one of the billy goats near her!"

This discovery soon became the property of all Chegem. The Big House didn't believe the rumor for a minute. Aunt Noutsa, who took the news as a personal insult, had a violent falling out with several women who tried to broach the subject in the tobacco field.

It must be said that many Chegemians received the news humorously, but there were also some who were seriously offended for the honor of the Chegem livestock and, via their stock, for their own honor as well.

They went to the elders of Chegem with the request that Khabug be ordered to banish Harlampo from the village, but the elders got their backs up. The elders demanded testimony from an eyewitness, but no such witness proved to be available. Many Chegemians stared at each other as if amazed that the person they were staring at had hitherto been taken for an eyewitness and now for some reason wasn't confessing.

That didn't faze the Chegemians for long, however. They were convinced that since all Chegem was talking about this, it was inconceivable that there wasn't at least one man who'd seen Harlampo's foolery with his own eyes. Now that the case had reached the elders, it was decided, the elusive eyewitness had turned shy to avoid clouding his relations with old Khabug.

Notwithstanding the madness that gripped Chegem, it must be stated in all fairness that even in this condition the Chegemians proved tactful enough not to confront Harlampo himself with their accusations.

Only the cranky forest warden Omar went absolutely berserk when he learned of the Chegemians' suspicions. Neither the honor of old Khabug's nanny goat nor the honor of the Chegem livestock was of any intrinsic interest to him. But the conviction lodged in his stupid head that Harlampo would not stop at the goat, nor even at goats in general, but was sure to get Omar's mare, who usually grazed in Sabid's Hollow and whose allure Omar held in the highest regard.

"If I see him I'll slice him in two!" he shouted. "Like I sliced the foreigners in the German war!"

Some of Omar's relatives, ashamed of his cranky foolishness, said that he had gotten that way in the Wild Division. A shell had allegedly exploded near him at the front. But old Chegemians, who remembered him well, said that he was even worse before the German war; on the contrary, he had even acquired a little polish in the Wild Division.

Over and over again the forest warden Omar stole down into Sabid's Hollow, burrowed in among the ferns there, and spent hours watching Harlampo's behavior.

Once Chunka and I were eating blueberries in Sabid's Hollow when suddenly Omar appeared below us on the path and started quickly uphill. The cavalry saber dangling at his side kept snagging on the sarsaparilla vines that overhung the path. He was obviously returning from many hours of watching Harlampo.

"Well, did you catch him at it?" Chunka asked. He was mocking Omar, but of course Omar didn't realize it.

Omar turned to us, his face distorted by a grimace of doubt; he spread his hands several times and brought them slowly together, indicating that the issue remained at a stage of mind-boggling confusion.

"He walked past my mare twice," he said darkly, as if he felt sure of the criminality of Harlampo's intentions but at the same time, being a man invested with the power of the law, understood that this was still insufficient cause to slice him in two.

"Did he pass close?" Chunka asked.

"It was about ten meters the first time," Omar said, trying to be exact. "Seven meters the second time."

"See, he's working up to it," Chunka said.

"I'll slice him!" Omar yelled. He went on by, his saber rattling over the rough spots in the stony path. "It beats all—two regimes have appointed me to watch over the forest, but that kinless Greek is forcing me to watch the animals. If I catch him I'll slice him!"

But he never could catch Harlampo, and because of this he was more and more often racked by fits of epileptic fury. Not only couldn't he catch him with his mare, he couldn't even catch him with the goat. His inability to catch him with a four-legged girl friend did not dispel his suspicions, however. On the contrary, it deepened them: in his eyes it turned Harlampo into a craftily disguised pervert and saboteur.

Sometimes in the late afternoon, when Harlampo and his flock returned from Sabid's Hollow, some of the men, who were also returning home after work, would stop to let Harlampo's flock go by, to gawk at him and at the suspect goat, and to gossip.

Some of the women, after work in the tobacco field or the tobacco shed, would also stop, a little apart from the men, and observe Harlampo and his goat with curiosity. Those who didn't know exactly which goat had taken Harlampo's fancy would nudge the others and ask them in an undertone to point her out.

"Will you look what he picked!"

"She's sort of a sad little thing."

"That's just an act."

"She's running ahead of the rest—she's proud of it!"

"No, she's hiding from him!"

"Hide from that vulture? Not likely!"

Silently, with sullen malevolence, the men surveyed the flock and Harlampo himself, and after letting him go by they began to discuss what had happened. In contrast to the women, they did not linger over intimate psychological details but emphasized the social significance of the misfortune that had befallen Chegem.

"If we let it go on like this, the Endurskies will be all over us!"

"As if they weren't already."

"They'll take over completely!"

"And they put him up to it."

"What's in it for them?"

"Same as always—anything to humiliate us."

"If only that confounded father of Despina's would break down and let him marry her!"

"What does he need her for? All the Chegem animals are Despinas to him now."

"He's going to Harlump all our animals!"

"That's just what I notice, every year more and more of our stock are going barren."

"This Greek will put us all in the poorhouse!"

"I can't believe our elders won't order old Khabug to banish him!"

"Our elders walk on tippytoe in front of old Khabug."

"Prove it, they say!"

"What if we get that redbearded picture-taker up here from Mukhus and have him catch a picture of him with his goat?"

"Catch him? Not likely! He knows what he's doing!"

"Can't we get the village soviet to banish him?"

"What do they care? They'll say, 'It doesn't interfere with politics.' "

"Then we've got no one to turn to, it seems?"

"So it seems . . ."

Harlampo walked silently past these malevolently silent Chegemians, glancing at them with morose aloofness and indicating by his glances that he had foreseen even these humiliations, all this had been written long ago in the book of his fate, but for the sake of his great love he would endure even this.

Among these Chegemians, sometimes, were the boys who had proposed earlier that he possess Despina and thereby force her father to let Harlampo marry his daughter. Now they reminded him by their glances that he had been wrong not to take their advice; had he taken their advice there'd be none of this stupid talk. But Harlampo caught these glances, too. As firmly as ever, with a shake of his head, he managed to reply that even now, beleaguered by slander, he did not regret his adamant decision to hold out for a proper wedding to Despina.

Once when Harlampo and I were driving the flock home, Omar leaped out of the fern thicket. Contorted by the fury of his fruitless watch, with a dribble of dried foam at the corners of his lips (the fury must have been accumulating for a long time), twitching all over and twitching at the hilt of his saber, he ran after us, dropping back one minute (he couldn't seem to unsheathe the saber), overtaking us the next. When he finally overtook us with the saber unsheathed, he ran along beside us, jostling Harlampo and showering him with curses.

"Greek spy!" he shouted in Russian. "My horse! I'll cut your head off!"

That sounds funny now, but at the time, I felt my body suddenly weighted by a physiological horror at the closeness of the loathsome, inhuman spectacle of a man being murdered. It was the only time I have seen, close up, the face of someone taking part in a pogrom, though of course I didn't know then what it was called. The most fearsome thing about that face was not the bloodshot eyes nor the dribbles of dried foam at the corners of the lips, but the expression it wore, its absolute conviction of its own natural rightness. Before our very eyes a man had ceased to be a man and was acting out the destiny of one who had ceased to be a man.

Added to the horror that Harlampo might be murdered was my terror for myself, the dread that he wouldn't stop at Harlampo, the awareness that after Harlampo he might slice me too. Somehow it was hard to believe that after murdering Harlampo he would immediately become a man again and cease to act out the destiny of one who had ceased to be a man. I had an ignoble urge to move away—way, way far away—from Harlampo.

Yet I did not move away from him, perhaps because along with all these ignoble fears I felt the beauty—more inspiring with every instant, snatching me away from my fears—of Harlampo's valor.

Yes, for the only time in my life I saw Hellenic valor, I saw a truly Socratic scorn for death, and never in my life have I seen anything more beautiful!

For probably fifty meters, until we reached the Prayer Tree, Omar belched forth curses and jostled Harlampo, brandishing the saber in his face. Sometimes he tried to dart ahead, perhaps to get a better vantage point for slicing him through, or perhaps to halt Harlampo before executing him.

But Harlampo did not halt. He went his way, sometimes shouting to drive on a lagging goat, sometimes pushing aside the saber waving in his face, pushing it aside with no more interest than if it had been an alder branch overhanging the path. Not once did he glance in Omar's direction, not once! But the knot of muscle on the cheekbone that was turned toward me kept swelling and sinking, and from time to time he sorrowfully and proudly nodded his head, letting it be known that he heard all, and up above They too heard all and understood all that Harlampo was suffering!

On the approach to the Prayer Tree Omar dropped behind us, continuing to yell and threaten from afar. I had the sudden momentary thought that he had been checked by the power of the sacred canopy of the Prayer Tree. Harlampo kept on walking behind the goats and threw me a look that I did not fully understand at the time. Only now do I understand that it was a reminder: "Don't forget!"

In my childish sensitivity I spent many nights tormented by the ignobility of my terror and the clear, humiliating awareness that I was incapable of behaving as Harlampo had. At the time I did not understand that only a great dream can generate great courage. Harlampo, of course, had that great dream.

Reverberations of these crazy rumors undoubtedly reached old Khabug, even though in greatly attenuated form. Whenever people started talking about it in the Big House, Aunt Noutsa kept glancing out the door to see if he was around. At the sight of old Khabug, Chegem's fools—and unfortunately Chegem, too, had quite a few of them—did the only thing a fool can do with his folly: manifest it in moderation.

One time, however, one of them could not contain himself. Several Chegemians were standing near the Big House, apparently waiting for Harlampo to go by with his flock. Just then old Khabug appeared on the road. He was carrying on his shoulders a huge bundle of hazelnut branches, feed for the goat kids, and he walked past rustling the mound of fresh hazel leaves, almost concealed by them. Perhaps emboldened by his very concealment, one of the men waiting for Harlampo leaped out in the road and shouted after the departing Khabug, as if Khabug had been diminished by this huge load with its rustling leaves, even bucolicized by it to some extent: "So how much longer do we have to put up with your goat-humper?"

Old Khabug went on walking for several moments in silence, and the mound of hazel leaves quivered rhythmically at his back. Then from under this moving grove came his calm voice: "Don't worry about my nanny goats. Guard your own tails from the mustached billy goat . . ."

Taken aback by the unexpectedness of the reply, the Chegemian stood there for a long time trying to grasp old Khabug's words. When he finally did, he wrung his hands and shouted after him in a tearful voice, "But it's not us keeping him in the Kremlin, it's the Russians!"

In the end, rumors of Harlampo's goat-humping reached Anastasovka, although people in the Big House did not rule out the possibility that Omar had secretly ridden over there and told them all about it.

Late one afternoon Auntie Chrysoula and Despina appeared at the Big House. Even from a distance we could tell by their faces that they knew something. Sweet Despina had grown thin; her dark blue eyes seemed to have faded and now looked much lighter than her kerchief.

Auntie Chrysoula launched into her complaint, but old Khabug checked her and said that we must have supper first and talk about it afterward. Auntie Chrysoula quietly took a seat on a bench by the hearth and sat staring at the fire, leaning on her thin little bird-claw hand and mournfully shaking her head. Despina sat on the couch and sadly turned away when Chunka tried to flirt with her.

All unsuspecting, Harlampo arrived with the flock. He walked into the yard with the firewood on his shoulder and dumped it by the kitchen wall, producing his usual thunder of domesticity. When she heard it Auntie Chrysoula shook her head still more mournfully, as if to say: His thunder of domesticity too was meant to deceive us.

When he came into the kitchen and saw Despina, who hung her head when he came in, and Auntie Chrysoula, who didn't even turn in his direction, he understood that they knew all, and he morosely withdrew into himself.

We sat down to supper almost in silence, and—oh Lord! Auntie Chrysoula barely touched her food.

"The world has turned topsy-turvy," Chunka said in Abkhazian. "Auntie Chrysoula's lost her appetite!"

"You be quiet!" Aunt Noutsa told him loudly, and she thrust a big chunk of cheese into Auntie Chrysoula's steaming mush. She was very agitated and wanted to mollify her somehow.

When we finished, we all washed our hands and took our places at the hearth on the big bench. Harlampo sat down by himself on the couch, looking slightly like a prisoner in the dock.

Auntie Chrysoula began. There was a long Greek conversation, with bitter mutual reproaches, with constant plaintive gestures toward Despina on Auntie Chrysoula's part. I even had the impression there was a mention of double-yolked eggs. From time to time Despina shed a few tears and wiped her blue eyes with the end of the blue scarf.

Harlampo's eyes burned with the somnambulistic fire of despair. His voice became harsher and harsher. Never had he spoken to Auntie Chrysoula in such a voice. This was an uprising of the plebes against the aristocrats!

He presented a catalog of the humiliations he had endured because of the cruel obstinacy of Despina's father, her *patera*. On his fingers, for total clarity, he counted off the years of forced separation from his beloved, and as he counted his voice rose higher and higher.

"Ena! Dio!! Tria!!! Tessara!!!! Pende!!!!!"

Five curled fingers marked the incredible sufferings of five years. But even that was not enough, he had to curl down three more fingers on the other hand. He held the pose for some time, his hands raised, the fingers of one hand curled into a powerful fist, and the other fist nearly ready. Another two years and Harlampo's fists would go after Despina's father and all the other aristocrats of Anastasovka, if there were any others.

(I see Harlampo as clearly as if all this had happened yesterday. And again, I cannot shake a persistent awareness of the likeness between his countenance and that of our intelligentsia. In terms of the historical time scale of their patience, it will be hardly fifty years before they, too, go after their aristocrats!)

Auntie Chrysoula heard out Harlampo's mighty attack with some understanding. She seemed to acknowledge that there were certain grounds for an uprising against the aristocrats.

Undaunted, however, she went on the offensive herself. Sometimes they both turned to Grandpa Khabug, as to a judge—switching to Turkish, although he had a good understanding of Greek. Aunt Noutsa also intervened from time to time, trying to defend Harlampo in her preposterous Turkish. When she especially mangled the words, Chunka clutched his head in horror, indicating that an accent like that was sure to wreck Harlampo's case.

Auntie Chrysoula's indictment boiled down to the fact that Despina's father would want nothing to do with Harlampo now, and no other Greek would want to marry Despina.

"Who's Despina?" Greeks from other villages would ask, according to Auntie Chrysoula.

"Despina," the Greeks of Anastasovka would reply, "is the *aristokratiko koritsi* whose betrothed preferred a nanny goat."

"Ken drepese, Harlampo?" Auntie Chrysoula said, turning to Harlampo. He too seemed to acknowledge, in part, the import of Auntie Chrysoula's argument.

The conversation was long, involved, tangled. It seemed that before appearing at the Big House Auntie Chrysoula had gone incognito to the mill and learned from Gerago about how Harlampo had come running to the mill chasing a goat.

Harlampo and Grandpa Khabug explained to her that his dealings with the goat had been confined to this aimless and harmless scamper.

Why, why, Auntie Chrysoula asked, did he have to run after the goat, when he had a bride waiting for him in Anastasovka, white as snow and innocent as an angel? When she heard these words, Despina shed a few more tears.

Harlampo said it had all happened because he ate too many walnuts and got the walnut rabies. Auntie Chrysoula scornfully denied the very existence of such an illness. She adduced proof. Auntie Chrysoula said that the last time she and Despina had left the Big House for Anastasovka, she'd eaten almost half a basket of walnuts on the way and hadn't gotten any walnut rabies.

"Isn't that true, Despina?" she said, turning to her niece, but it was Chunka who responded.

"Of course it's true!" he exclaimed in Turkish. "Who could doubt it!"

Auntie Chrysoula glanced at him. "No, you didn't see," she said. "Despina saw."

With a sad nod, Despina confirmed Auntie Chrysoula's words. At this point Harlampo apparently decided to break with the aristocrats for good. In Turkish, so that the daring candor of his words would be intelligible to all, he said the reason she hadn't gotten the walnut rabies was that both she and her brother had been crazy anyway since the day they were born: *"Delidür!"*

"Yes," Auntie Chrysoula confirmed, woefully shaking her head, "of course Chrysoula's crazy, if she allowed her innocent little lamb to be betrothed to this *diabolos.*"

"Well, it's not all that far from a lamb to a goat!" Chunka yelled in Abkhazian.

Aunt Noutsa shook a threatening fist at him: "You be quiet, shameless thing!"

Again Despina began to cry soundlessly, again she wiped her blue eyes with the end of her blue scarf.

And now old Khabug spoke. He said that he would set Harlampo up with thirty goats, to be repaid with future work. He said that next to Uncle Sandro's farmstead he had spied out a good piece of land for Harlampo. He proposed to build a house there and hold a wedding this very fall and move the young people in. He said that he and Harlampo would begin preparing the shingle and boards tomorrow.

Slowly Harlampo turned pale, slowly he stood up from the couch. His gaze expressing an unconditional authority over Despina, an authority gained through the sufferings of eight years of waiting, he extended a compelling arm toward old Khabug and said in a compelling voice: "Here is your father, Despina! You have no other father, Despina! *Filise ton patera sou, Despina!* (Kiss your father, Despina!)"

And Despina jumped up, Despina burst into tears, Despina burst out laughing—instantly she was transformed into her old blooming, gay self. She ran to Khabug and bent down, embraced him tenderly and kissed him on both cheeks. Old Khabug carefully pushed her away as if she were an overfilled vessel that threatened to spill on him the water of young happiness, indecent for a man his age.

"Now me, Despinochka!" Chunka yelled in Russian.

Despina glanced at Chunka and broke into a peal of gay laughter. Auntie Chrysoula too was instantly transformed into her old self, and in the same old voice she warned her niece, "Des-pi-na!"

It was such an amazing transformation that everyone burst out laughing.

Five months later Harlampo celebrated his wedding in his new house, and of course the tamada at the wedding was Uncle Sandro. Much wine was drunk at the wedding, many Greek and Abkhazian songs were sung. Chunka danced the *syrtaki* beside Auntie Chrysoula, trying, or pretending to try, to tell how he and Despina had picked figs. Auntie Chrysoula rushed at him in indignation and stopped his mouth. Naturally Auntie Chrysoula outtalked and outate everyone at the wedding, but even so she couldn't outdrink Uncle Sandro.

For complex psychological reasons old Khabug included in the settlement of thirty goats the one suspected of having been the object of Harlampo's special affections. Had he kept her at home, evil tongues would have begun saying that he had done so to avoid mucking up Harlampo's family life.

There is a scene that sticks in my memory, of perhaps the most cloudless family happiness I have ever seen in my life. I am walking, along with several women and the other little boys, from the tobacco field to the tobacco shed. The women have big baskets of tobacco on their shoulders.

Now we pass Harlampo's house. Harlampo is standing in the pen among the goats and holding the horns of the ill-starred nanny goat, who has finally given birth to a kid. Despina, pregnant Despina with a big belly, in a wide flowery dress, with a milk pail in her hand, squats on her haunches by the goat and begins to milk her. Harlampo looks around at us, morose and triumphant, and I feel that Harlampo's moroseness is now a mask shielding his happy life from the evil eye of fate. He gazes at us as if to invite our attention to the strict, classical, natural arrangement—the only one that is or could be—of their figures by the goat.

One of the women takes the trouble to stop and turn to another, carefully, so as to keep the huge basket balanced. "Why's he holding the goat?" she says.

"He'd better," says another woman with an equally huge basket on her shoulder. "The goat's jealous—"

But suddenly she breaks off, subdued perhaps by the powerful, calm streaming of harmony from this idyllic Old Testament scene.

Harlampo holds the goat by the horns, and through the morose mask of his face I feel, truly feel, the irrepressible, triumphant bubbling of his happiness. In my soul dawns the vague intuition that one can arrive at such happiness only through such suffering. When I recall this scene now and recall the amazing feeling of gratitude spreading sweetly in my blood, the gratitude to something unintelligible, life itself perhaps, that I felt then watching Harlampo and Despina, it occurs to me that man has yet another chance at being happy—through the ability to rejoice in someone else's happiness. But grown-ups rarely retain this ability.

Inside of three years Harlampo had three children. The first, a girl, was named Soula in honor of her auntie. Auntie Chrysoula spent days at a time with the children. As for Despina, by now she had become the best tobacco stringer in Chegem, although of course she couldn't compare with Tali. But for an aristocratic young woman who was having a baby a year it was no small accomplishment.

After Despina had her third baby, Auntie Chrysoula came to the Big House and said she was planning to keep watch by Despina's bed for a year. She requested that one of the women of the Big House spell her from time to time. When they asked why she had to watch by Despina's bed, she replied that Harlampo must be kept away from Despina's bed so that she could rest up from being pregnant, if only for a year.

Aunt Noutsa consulted old Shazina: Was it acceptable, according to our customs, to watch not only by the bed of a sick person but also by the bed of a married woman? Shazina replied that this too was acceptable, according to our customs, but only close relatives were permitted to watch, and therefore the inhabitants of the Big House could not stand guard by Despina's bed.

Auntie Chrysoula sighed. "I'll watch alone, while I have the strength," she said.

But if Auntie Chrysoula did keep watch, it was not for long. The Patriotic War broke out, and all the young men of Chegem, including Harlampo, were taken into the army.

Unlike many of our neighbors, unlike poor Chunka, who was killed on the western border early in the war, Harlampo returned home. Yes, he returned, and his life was happy right up until 1948, when he and Despina and the children and Auntie Chrysoula and all the Greeks of the Black Sea coast were deported to Kazakhstan.

. . . A truck by the kolkhoz office. (By this time vehicles had started coming up to Chegem.) The truck bed filled to overflowing with several departing families. The sobbing of the women who are departing and the women who are saying good-bye to them.

Sitting on some logs twenty paces away from the truck are the elders of Chegem, ruffled, estranged, like eagles in a cage. No longer tapping their staves on the ground as usual but sullenly leaning on them, they glance disapprovingly in the direction of the truck, now and then exchanging a few words.

They seem to recognize that they should have stopped what is happening, and though they realize that they are powerless to do anything, they feel oppressed by guilt for their own silence, the defilement of their spiritual authority.

Her face swollen with weeping, Despina keeps jumping down from the truck into the crowd to embrace those she has not had time to say good-bye to. Auntie Chrysoula, in a black dress, stands in the bed of the truck and shouts something unintelligible, raising her thin hand to the heavens. (The Father of Nations was not satisfied with deporting to Siberia thousands of Russian peasant women, whom he was apparently trying out in the role of the Boyarynya Morozova for a painting by a new, as yet unknown Surikov; he found it necessary to try out Auntie Chrysoula in the role as well.)

Two pale, distraught submachine gunners in the truck bed, and on the ground an officer, paler still, his lips quivering as he tries to check the people climbing, screaming, reaching their arms into the truck, the people jumping down to the ground and being reinstalled in the truck.

And over all this howl, over the tear-stained faces, over the reaching arms— the morose, tearless face of Harlampo, with knots of muscle contracting now and again under the skin of his cheeks, with his eyes turned toward the Chegemians. He nods his head as if to remind them of the prophetic meaning of the countenance he has always worn. He seems to be saying: Yes, yes, I foresaw this, and for that reason prepared myself for it all my life with my morose countenance.

. . . The officer, despairing of driving the Chegemians away from the truck, shouted something to the submachine gunners, and they leaped down. Holding the submachine guns before them in horizontal position like barrier gates, they began pressing the crowd back. But since the people in the rear did not move, the crowd was not pressed back, it was pressed together. As if from the very press of the crowd the air thickened with the electricity of compressed anger. The officer, who probably sensed this better than the others, tried to forestall the possible explosion of nervous tension.

The explosion occurred even so. Two teenage boys, an Abkhazian and a Greek, were standing by the truck, embracing. One of the soldiers tried several times to break the Abkhazian boy's hold on his departing friend. But the boys would not let go. Then the soldier, who was probably under nervous tension too, gave the boy a shove with the butt of the submachine gun.

Unluckily, two of the boy's uncles and his older brother were standing right there. All three blazed up at once. The boy's brother and one of the uncles pulled knives, and the second uncle whipped a German Walther from his pocket.

The women set up a wail. Both soldiers backed up against the truck and put their submachine guns forward, while the officer, who was standing next to them, forgot about his own pistol and kept repeating like a record with the needle stuck in the groove, "What are you doing! What are you doing! What are you doing!"

The boy's brother kept trying to pick an opening to go in from the side and knife the soldier who had struck the boy. The first uncle tried to create an opening for him by holding the Walther on the soldier and threatening with it, to distract him. The second uncle, with his knife, threatened the second submachine gunner, who was keeping his gun on the one threatening the first soldier with the Walther. Both sides, without prearrangement, had all at once assigned who should do what.

No one knows how it would all have ended if, in response to the women's screams, realizing that something terrible had happened in the crowd, an elder of Chegem had not gotten up from his place. He planted his staff in the ground, smoothed his white mustache, and started toward the crowd, his face unchanged in its sullen, ruffled estrangement.

He walked at a steady, calm pace, seemingly confident that if what had happened in the crowd could be brought within bounds of reason, then whatever it was it would wait for him. And if what had happened could not be controlled by reason, there was no point hurrying in that case either.

When he walked into the crowd, still ruffled, the people made way and tried to tell him the gist of what had happened. He evidently understood it at once and now merely waved aside the excessive clamor in distaste.

Without a word he walked up to the three men. Instantly determining the degree of danger in each, expecting no resistance and not even weighing the possibility of resistance, he casually snatched the knife from the boy's brother's hand, then the pistol from the first uncle's hand, then the knife from the second uncle's hand. Almost without looking he tossed them all aside like so much scrap iron, the way a peasant tosses over to the fence the stones he pulls from the tilth.

After that he turned to the boy who had been the cause of it all and slapped his head with all his might. The boy's felt cap flew off his head, but he didn't pick it up, he turned and walked through the crowd with his head down, apparently holding back tears of resentment. He simply walked away, without a backward glance.

"You should take away their submachine guns, let's see you do that!" the owner of the Walther shouted excitably. "They're always bullying us!"

An unfriendly clamor rose from the crowd.

"A soldier is a state employee," the elder said, addressing the crowd. "He does what he's told. The Big Mustache must be having another fit of vampirism. In this time we stand in, we have to keep quiet even if they strike us with a stick."

"Oh, the time we stand in!" sighed the crowd.

The elder turned and walked back to his comrades. Their ruffled heads up, they were waiting for him with no outward display of curiosity.

"Into the truck!" the officer yelled at the soldiers. He himself jumped into the cab, trying to get ahead of the crowd. The soldiers sprang up into the truck bed, but the crowd managed to close in around it again.

The truck honked, then moved quietly forward. A howl of farewell went up. The officer stuck his arm out the window and flailed it convulsively to make the people who were staying let go. He continued to flail until they were finally left behind.

. . . Today Greek and Turkish are not heard in our land, and my soul grieves and my ear is bereft. From my childhood I was accustomed to our little Babel. I was accustomed to hearing in the air of my homeland Abkhazian, Russian, Georgian, Mingrelian, Armenian, Greek, Turkish, Endurian (yes, yes, Uncle Sandro, Endurian too!), and now that some accustomed voices have been cast out from this sweet polyphony, from the welling freshness of the song of the peoples, there is no joy to my ear, no ecstasy in the air of my homeland!

. . . Thus Harlampo and Despina disappeared from our lives forever. But they are strong people, and I hope they've put down roots there in the dry Kazakhstan soil, started their own home, their own farm. Very probably they have found something for Auntie Chrysoula to nibble on. I don't think there are any figs in Kazakhstan, though, and Auntie Chrysoula so loved figs, especially the black ones.

Then again, it's been such a long time. Auntie Chrysoula must be dead by now, and I feel sure her bright soul is in the garden of Eden, eating her beloved black figs.

THE FOREMAN
KYAZYM

THREE TIMES DURING the war and the two years after, large sums of money disappeared from the kolkhoz safe in Chegem. Each time, since the only key to the safe was held by the bookkeeper, and the bookkeeper couldn't explain where the money had gone, he went to prison.

The third bookkeeper had been taken into custody a week ago, after the discovery that a hundred thousand rubles had disappeared from the safe. The bookkeeper was sent to Kenguria Prison, and kolkhoz chairman Aslan Ayba came to the Big House to ask the help of Kyazym.

Kyazym was rightly considered to be one of the smartest men in Chegem. Moreover, everyone knew that he had solved several crimes committed in Chegem and neighboring villages, crimes which the Kenguria police had been unable to solve.

In the simple peasant way of life, any gift of a man's, if the significance of the gift be clear and demonstrable, is calmly and unreservedly acknowledged by those around him. In a cultured milieu, by contrast, where the demonstrability of one or another gift seems less evident to the eye—that is, it manifests itself most often in words, and is confirmed or denied also by words—assessments of men are much more muddled and the experts much more often in error.

For example, a good poet would seem to be no less self-evident than a good farmer, yet it is easier to dispute the worth of a good poet's verse than to dispute the gift of a good peasant. The condition of his field or livestock speaks too plainly for itself.

Moreover, the peasant who is a worse farmer than his neighbor would look doubly foolish if he started claiming he was really a better farmer. He would still get from his field a smaller harvest than his neighbor's, and he would lose his fellow villagers' respect as well.

In an intellectual milieu, meanwhile, if an evil thought claims to be richer than a noble thought, a variety of factors may enable it to eclipse the noble one temporarily and gather a greater harvest of recognition. For this reason the temptation to hypocrisy is stronger in a cultured milieu, and the soul has more opportunities for self-corruption.

But for this same reason, the best of the intelligentsia are morally more vigorous than the best of the peasantry, because their souls are constantly being tempered in the struggle with falsehood and demagoguery.

And again for this same reason, most of the peasantry are morally higher than most of the intelligentsia, because most of the intelligentsia claim their own worth at the expense of constant little lies, while most of the peasantry have in effect no reason to lie.

That is why the young kolkhoz chairman Aslan Ayba felt no inhibition about coming to the Big House today to ask the help of the illiterate foreman Kyazym.

Now the two of them sat on the bench by the kitchen hearth and talked about the case. Legs crossed, hands clasping his knee, Kyazym sat and stared at the fire as he listened to the chairman.

"Well, the other two were arrested before my time," the chairman was saying, slapping his quirt on the floor, "and I believed they'd been caught with their hands in the till . . . But I just can't believe my bookkeeper took that kind of money from the till. Poor Chichiko, what could he have hoped for? Maybe he gave it to one of his city relatives—one of them's a petty tradesman—and the relative didn't have time to return it? I've racked my brains, but I can't think it through."

"All these three thefts are the work of one hand," Kyazym said, still staring into the fire. ". . . And since the money has been stolen for a third time, when two bookkeepers are already in prison, we'll be right in thinking that it's the hand of someone else entirely."

"But whose?" The chairman shrugged his shoulders and spanked the quirt on the floor. "The bookkeeper was the only one who ever had the key. I implore you, give this your best thought."

"I will," Kyazym said, rolling a cigarette. When he finished rolling it he leaned over to the fire, which illumined his handsome, close-cropped head, the sunken cheeks and small deep-set eyes. He lifted a burning brand and lit up, squinting against the smoke, then tossed the log back into the fire with a shower of sparks.

A few minutes later they came out of the kitchen, and Kyazym untied the chairman's dark bay stallion, who had been tied to the railing of the kitchen veranda. Holding the impatient horse, he helped the chairman mount.

It was a hot summer day, but the sky was covered with torn, scudding clouds, and the sun kept coming out, going in. Seen from the Chegem heights, the surrounding hills and valleys were spotted with shade and sun like the hide of a mysterious animal.

Kyazym accompanied the chairman to the upper gate of the yard, treading the green grass softly in his rawhide moccasins. Though his gait was light and lazy-looking he easily kept pace with the prancing stallion.

Now they were talking about the new tobacco shed: Kyazym was shingling the roof, with Kunta helping him. He promised the chairman he would have the job done in a week.

Kyazym opened the gate and the stallion went out on the upper Chegem road, his impatient hooves clattering on the stones.

"I ask you as a brother, give it your best thought!" the chairman called back over the clatter of his horse's hooves. He quirted the stallion, who suddenly blazed forth in gleaming scarlet dapples—the sun had looked out from behind the clouds.

"All right," Kyazym said, involuntarily admiring the powerful stallion, who was bearing the clatter away beyond the bend in the road.

That clatter, which reverberated with a sad sweetness in Kyazym's soul, finally faded away, and he shifted his gaze to the beehives that stood along the wattle fence to his left. His big work-hardened hands, according to his habit, were thrust into his Caucasian belt, a pose that pulled the narrow thong out from his body and unintentionally emphasized his extraordinarily sunken belly and bulging chest.

From the yard came the almost unceasing laughter and squeals of children. His younger daughter Zina and another little girl her age, the strapping Katusha, Masha's daughter, were giving his four-year-old son a ride on a sheepskin.

At the rough spots in the green yard the girls tried to jerk the sheepskin out from under the little boy, who sat in state, clutching at tufts of matted wool with his strong little hands. The big black mongrel dog joined in the game too, by barking and trotting after the sheepskin. When the little boy got dumped off, the girls kept on running and pretended not to notice the loss. But now the dog caught up with them. Seizing hold of the sheepskin, growling in fun, he tried to make them stop and pick the boy up.

"Fell off!" little Gulik shouted after them in an irritated voice, as if he were speaking not of himself but of some extraneous object. It was the very constancy of his tone, and the little boy's pose, that struck the girls funny. Dissolving in laughter, they would pretend to suddenly realize that the sheepskin was empty. Each time, for some reason without changing the pose in which he had landed when he flew off the sheepskin, the little boy would angrily look after them from afar, as if to say, What fools—they'll never learn how to give me a ride!

Kyazym, with his cigarette still in his mouth, stood near the beehives and listened attentively, perhaps to the friendly drone of the bees flying in and out or crawling around the entrances, perhaps to the distant song of the women stringing tobacco in the tobacco shed, perhaps to the welling joy in the voices of the children dragging the sheepskin around the yard.

Really he was listening to all of this and at the same time thinking about what had happened to the kolkhoz safe. He felt that the motor had already been switched on, and what he heard and saw around him did not hinder him from thinking calmly. On the contrary, it helped.

Still thinking his own thoughts, he went over to the last hive, spat out his cigarette butt, and bent down. Smoothly, so as not to irritate the bees, he grasped the log in two hands and lifted it. He could tell by the weight of the log that enough honey had accumulated. This was his usual way of determining whether or not it was time to harvest the honey. After a long rainy spell he used the same way of determining whether there was honey in the hive but made a mental allowance for the log's being heavier from the rain.

Now he decided to open the hives. On his way back to the kitchen he was momentarily struck with admiration for the sunlit faces of the barefoot girls dragging the sheepskin, for his little boy solemnly sitting on it. Seeing Kyazym stop a moment to look at them, the dog who had been running after the sheepskin also stopped, as if to ask his master, Does it look too shameful—me, a wise, grown-up dog, having fun with the children?

But now Kyazym shifted his gaze to his red cow, who was standing across the yard with her head drooping dejectedly and a rope of spittle dribbling from her mouth. Ginger hadn't grazed for a whole week now, all she'd had was a thin gruel that Kyazym's wife made for her. She wouldn't let her calf come near, because a huge swelling had formed under her udder. To milk the cow forcibly, someone had to hold her by the horns.

While he watched her the sun went behind a cloud. The green yard immediately went dull, and the welling gaiety of the children's voices seemed to recede into the distance. Kyazym recalled that he had asked four young men of the neighborhood to come over tonight. With their help he was planning to throw the cow and lance the abscess.

The gate slammed at the far end of the yard. It was his wife Noutsa, coming up from the spring with the big copper jug on her shoulder. Thin, lean, bending slightly forward, she crossed the yard with strong and steady steps. He followed her into the kitchen. When she let the jug down from her shoulder with a grunt and stood it by the door, he took a mug from the table, tipped the wet, icy jug, poured himself some water, and slowly drank it.

"When are you going to get to Ginger?" his wife said, struggling to catch her breath. "The poor animal, she and I are both exhausted."

"Tonight," he replied, and went through to the storeroom. There he took down a basin from where it hung on the wall and heaped it with specially dried horse dung that lay in a wooden trough. Then he went back to the kitchen, got a glowing brand from the hearth, and stuck it in the basin. The dung immediately sent up an acrid, odorous smoke. He took from the mantelpiece a curved, double-edged knife for cutting the honeycomb, his wife handed him a big pail, and he went out of the kitchen with the pail in one hand and his bee-smoker in the other.

"Some day those bees are really going to sting you," his wife called after him, but he made no reply. He always opened the hives without any net or gloves.

"Pépé's going to get the honey!" Zina shouted, and she and her cousin abandoned the sheepskin to run after him. ("Pépé" was what the children called him, for some reason.) Little Gulik toddled after them too, trying to keep up, but not letting go of the sheepskin. Only the dog stopped where he was. He sat there now with his big head slightly cocked, for he knew from experience that the master didn't like anyone to come near when he was opening the hives.

Kyazym turned and looked severely at the children, indicating that they were not to follow him. The children stopped. The little boy also stood still, holding on to his sheepskin.

Again Kyazym began the climb up to the hives, and again he heard behind him the swish of the trailing sheepskin. He turned and looked at the children again, silently and severely, through the clouds of smoke rising from the basin. The little boy, still gripping the end of the sheepskin, was out in front now. He was less sensitive to the force of paternal severity than the others, and that was why hc was out in front. But this time the little girls woke to the power of the customs that allowed no one either to approach or to converse near a man who was opening hives. Zina took the little boy by the hand, whispering persuasively to him, and turned him back.

With quiet, smooth steps Kyazym approached the last hive. Careful to avoid any clanking, he set down the pail, lowered the basin, and laid the knife beside them. Acrid horse-dung smoke rose thicker and thicker from the basin. He loved this smell, as he loved everything to do with horses. Yes, everything to do with horses, but it was better not to think about that.

He leaned over the hive, gripped the middle of the upper part of the split log firmly in both hands, and lifted it. Turning it over, he set it on the ground. From the log came the strong scent of fresh honey. The bees began buzzing around him in agitation. He shifted the basin so that the movement of the smoke would force the bees farther away. Smoke rose thicker and thicker from the basin.

The overturned half of the log was nearly filled with even rows of honeycomb, glinting gold and dark brown. He took the knife in his hands and with slow smooth motions began to scrape out the oozing combs. Pleasantly aware of their lightness in his hands, he transferred them to the pail. One bee managed to sting him on the hand and got stuck there, unable to pull out her stinger. He calmly flicked her off with a finger of the other hand and went on working. He removed about half the honeycombs from the log and left the rest as sustenance for the bees. Slowly moving from one hive to the next, he harvested all ten in this manner. The pail was full to the brim with oozing combs, amber and dark brown. Some of them still had half-asphyxiated bees stirring in the cells.

The sun looked out from behind the cloud again and sparkled in the slabs of honeycomb, splitting into tiny suns in the dark brown ones and making the amber ones transparent. Kyazym thrust the knife into the combs, took the pail in one hand and the still-smoking basin in the other, and went over to the fence to dump the remains of the smoking dung in the nettles.

The pain in his badly stung hands reminded him of the cow. He glanced over to where she was standing. The calf came and tried several times to nuzzle at her udder, but she moved away from him each time, and then even drove him away with her horns. Unable to grasp the reason for his mother's irritation, the calf stood there dejectedly for a while. Then he went off to the other calves and began cropping grass.

"Pépé got the honey! Pépé got the honey!" Zina and little Gulik cried simultaneously as he came across the yard. Katusha stood beside them, glowing bashfully. Because she was very big for her age she felt embarrassed to show such open joy at the treat that lay ahead.

They followed him into the kitchen. The little boy was still trailing his sheepskin. The children took their places on the bench by the kitchen hearth. Noutsa handed out iron bowls, then cut off big chunks of honeycomb and plopped one in each bowl.

"*Mash-Allah!* (Abundance!)," she said, and ate a big chunk of honeycomb right from the tip of the knife.

Kyazym glanced at his wife. "Look out you don't swallow the knife," he said.

"Maybe you'd have some?" she asked him, chewing and sucking lustily on the wax.

Kyazym frowned—he did not like sweets.

"Pour for me," he said, and went out on the veranda. His wife brought a pitcher of water out to him, and he carefully soaped the honey off his sticky, bee-stung hands.

Then he smoked for a while, sitting by the fire, listening with pleasure to the children's lip-smacking, their joyful exclamations, their frightened shrieks when they fended off bees that flew into the kitchen in pursuit of the honey. His eyes bright with mocking warmth, Kyazym looked sidelong at the little boy, who had finally dropped his sheepskin and was stuffing chunks of oozing honeycomb into his mouth with both hands.

"I'll be in my room," he told his wife as he got up. "No matter who asks, say I'm not here."

"All right," Noutsa said. Lifting the pail of honey and taking the basin in the other hand, she went to the storeroom, where she hung the basin in its place and transferred the honey to a vat.

Almost till evening Kyazym lay on his couch and thought, occasionally coming out to the kitchen to get a light at the fireplace fire. The cow was still standing motionless by the slat fence; she moved only if the calf came over to her. She would move away, and he would stand near her awhile, then dejectedly go back to the other two calves.

"Get up, the boys are here," his wife said, coming into the room where Kyazym lay.

"Mm-hm," he said. He hiked himself up and sat as if half asleep a few minutes longer, waking from his thoughts. Then he got up and went to the kitchen.

The four young men were happily sitting and talking on the kitchen bench, spooning honeycomb from iron bowls and spitting their chewed wax into the fire. They stood up when they saw him, falling silent in embarrassment, although out of inertia they went on chewing what was left in their mouths. He gestured for them to sit down and go on with their treat. Then he poured a mug of water from the big jug, went out on the veranda, and sat down on a bench by the whetstone. After splashing water on the stone, he pulled his knife from the sheath at his belt and honed it.

"Would you bring some first-shot!" he called to his wife, splashing the rest of the water on the knife blade. His wife brought a half-liter bottle of pink *chacha* from the storeroom. He opened the bottle, which was corked with a whittled-down piece of corncob, and generously doused both sides of the blade with the aromatic grape spirits. Still holding the knife in his hand, he corked the bottle and called to the kitchen, "Get up, sweet-eaters!"

The boys were still chuckling and chewing wax as they came out of the kitchen. Kyazym went out to the yard with them, carrying the knife in one hand and the bottle of *chacha* in the other.

The dog followed along, attracted by the knife in his hand. He thought that Kyazym meant to butcher the cow and he would get a share, as he usually did in such cases.

"Be off!" Kyazym shouted at him, and he stopped in the middle of the yard to watch them from afar.

Kyazym led the way to the cow. She stood by the slat fence, hanging her head and making no effort to drive away the flies that circled over her and crawled around her sad eyes. Kyazym set the bottle down, propping it against the fence, and sank the knife into one of the slats. Then he straightened up and went to stand in front of the cow's head. With his palm he stripped the cluster of flies from around her eyes. Holding her by the horns with one hand, with the other he began to scratch her withers.

"You'll hold her from that side," he told two of the boys, "so that she doesn't crash to the ground. And you two will jerk her off her feet at my signal."

He had selected the two that looked strongest and stationed them beside the cow so that simultaneously, using both hands, one could jerk a hind leg out from under her and the other a foreleg. The other two boys, meanwhile, stationed on the other side, were supposed to catch the cow so that she would land softly on the ground.

At Kyazym's signal the first two boys—who had crouched down and taken a two-handed grip on the hind leg and foreleg on the side of the cow farther away from them—jerked as hard as they could, but the cow remained standing. Several times he gave them the signal, but either they weren't strong enough or they failed to do it simultaneously, because the cow merely lurched and shifted from one foot to the other, but did not fall.

"Here now, back off," Kyazym said. Both the boys who had been crouching straightened up, redfaced not so much from exertion as from shame. He stationed one of them to hold the cow by the horns, and had the other one join the two who were supposed to catch her.

He crouched down, murmuring a caressing refrain, and began to stroke the cow's foreleg and hind leg to relax them.

"Get ready," he said to the boys, avoiding any change in his caressing tone, in order to hide from the cow what he meant to do. His big hands grasped the cow's legs right at the pasterns, and—oof!—with an abrupt and powerful motion he yanked both legs from under the cow. For several seconds, looking as if she had just remembered something, she tried to remain standing on two legs. Then she tipped over, but the boys who stood on the other side caught her and kept her from crashing down.

"What strength!" said one of the ones who had crouched down. "He buried us alive."

"We're children of wartime," the other joked back, "but Kyazym's from czarist times, he grew up on meat . . ."

Yes, Kyazym knew he was still strong, but his heart wasn't worth a damn. After especially heavy work or hard drinking it made its presence too well known. Now he sat on his haunches for several moments, trying to get his breath.

When he did get his breath, he leaned over and began to study the big swelling that had come up right by her udder.

"Hold her," Kyazym said, and he began cautiously pulling on the teats to milk the cow. The cow shuddered at every pull and groaned softly. The milk was pink with blood. When he finished, he reached for the knife, pulled it out, shifted it to his right hand, and began to stroke the swollen spot in an effort to see which way the pus would spurt so that he wouldn't be in its path. He put the knife to the swelling.

"Now hold her as tight as you can! Especially the hind legs!" he ordered the boys.

Two of them held the cow by the hind legs, one by the forelegs, and one by the horns so that she wouldn't get hurt banging her head on the ground.

Kyazym slashed the razor-sharp knife along the swelling. The cow let out a stifled bellow and jerked with all her strength. A fountain of pus gushed from the wound.

"Hold tighter!" Kyazym bawled furiously. He slashed the knife across the swelling again, this time at right angles to the first incision. Now the pus ran mixed with blood.

With both hands Kyazym squeezed the cow's belly around the wound to force out as much blood and pus as possible. The cow groaned like a man. Kyazym took the bottle in his hands, opened it, and—again ordering the boys to hold the cow as tightly as possible—began pouring fiery *chacha* slowly into the wound. The cow kept shuddering, panting noisily, groaning. He poured slowly, taking a long time about it to make the spirits penetrate the open wound as deeply as possible.

"You could at least leave some for us," one of the boys joked. Kyazym left his words unheeded. By Abkhazian standards, the joke was too familiar for someone his age.

They let go of the cow and walked off a few steps. She lay there a while, but then twitched a couple of times, turned over on her belly, got to her feet, and walked off a few steps. Scenting blood, the dog began stalking toward where the cow had lain.

"Be off!" Kyazym shouted at him. The dog recoiled and went off to the middle of the yard, waiting for them to walk away from the cow. But now Kyazym's wife brought a shovelful of hot ashes from the hearth and carefully sprinkled the places where the milk, blood, and pus had spilled.

The next morning Kyazym was wakened by his wife's jubilant voice.

"Ginger's grazing!" she shouted, coming into the room where he lay. Kyazym got up, dressed, and went out on the veranda. The cow was grazing in the middle of the yard. Anyone who looked closely could see that she wasn't cropping the grass so eagerly as an ordinary cow, but still it was a clear sign that she was on the mend.

While Kyazym washed up, the calf came over to her, but this time, without waiting for him to nuzzle at her udder, she briskly walked a few steps away from him and began cropping grass again. The calf stood dejectedly, as if still making an effort to understand what had come over his mother, and then began languidly cropping a little grass.

Kyazym's wife started for the barnyard to milk the goats, a pail and a switch in her hand.

"Don't turn the horse loose!" he called to her, drying himself on the towel. Noutsa looked back. "Where do you mean to go?"

"Where I must," he said, and walked through to the kitchen.

Eighteen years he had lived with his wife. Jealous of all his affairs that were unrelated to the house and farm, she was always attempting to make him give them up. Although she hadn't once succeeded in all those years, she simply would not resign herself or abandon her stubborn but doomed attempts.

He went into the kitchen, shoveled out the live coals still hidden in the ashes, then went to the kitchen veranda and brought back an armload of firewood and dry twigs. After breaking up the twigs, he shoveled the coals together, blew on them, and piled a bunch of the broken twigs on top, then blew up a flame. When it had properly caught, he put on the wood.

Then he went to the storeroom, where a garland of dry tobacco hung on the wall. After pulling out an armful of leaves he returned to the kitchen and sat down astride the bench. Taking from the heap one leaf at a time, he laid it on the bench and smoothed it. The leaf crackled pleasantly under his big hand. When it was good and smooth, he pressed it to the bench with his fingers spread wide, and with the other hand took hold of the stem. Carefully, so as not to injure the leaf, he ripped out the stem, along with all the veins that stuck up between his spread fingers. As he ripped out the stems he stacked the leaves neatly the way one stacks money, and perhaps he took no less pleasure in this than a tradesman neatening up an easy profit, or a lucky gambler. Then he folded over the whole stack (which is another thing often done by people who have money, and not only easy money), unsheathed his knife, and crisply cut through the stack (which totally precludes any similarity, however remote, to the actions of people who have money).

Piling the halves of the stack together with the cut edges even, he began to shave off fine shreds of tobacco. When it was all cut except for a last little clump, which he tossed into the fire along with the stems, he worked the curly tobacco shavings with his hands to fluff them up. Then he pulled his big leather tobacco pouch from his pocket and packed it full.

Like all true smokers he took pleasure in this fuss with the tobacco. He pulled out a sheet of newspaper, tore off a piece for a cigarette paper, softened it in his fingers, sprinkled tobacco on it, rolled it, took a light from the fire, and inhaled with pleasure.

His wife came in with a full pail of milk.

"Time you should wake your lie-abeds," he said as he got to his feet.

"Leave the children alone," Noutsa replied as she strained the milk into a kettle. "Let them sleep till breakfast."

He took a bridle down from the kitchen wall and went outdoors.

"Where do you mean to go?" his wife called after him, her voice condemning his expedition in advance.

"The kolkhoz office," he replied, without stopping.

"What did you lose there?" she called after the trim, tall figure crossing the yard. He made no reply.

Ever since his beloved horse Dolly had been mobilized during the war to deliver military supplies to the pass, and had suddenly come home by herself, deathly tired, with her back raw, and, most importantly—he was absolutely sure of this—with her spirit broken, her racing qualities forever ruined, he had made himself a vow never to raise horses. No one in the world knew how he had suffered over the ruin of his beloved horse, and he made himself a vow never in his life to raise horses again. He sold Dolly, so that the sight of her would not torment his soul.

Yet his friend Bakhut, who was also a horse-lover and guessed something of his feeling, had recently offered him this horse.

"Look," Bakhut said, "if you don't like her, return her, but if you do, buy her . . ."

After that last horse he was afraid to love any horse. He tried to treat this one like an ordinary domestic animal, and he seemed to have succeeded, but there was something not quite right about it. She was a good horse, and as a born horse-lover he should have developed a relationship with her. But the memory of that pain evoked the fear that it would be repeated, and he held himself back. In the depths of his soul this engendered a feeling of guilt toward the horse, and he was sure that the horse herself sensed his unjust indifference toward her, his coldness. Naturally he wouldn't have confessed this to anyone in the world. He was a born horse-lover and had repeatedly taken prizes at race meets before the war, but he was through with that, he thought, forever.

He went to the barnyard, caught and bridled the horse, then led her into the yard and tied her to the kitchen veranda.

"Tell people Nuri's in trouble, he's embezzled money in the city," he said to his wife as he came into the kitchen. "Tell people we have to borrow fifty thousand rubles from someone."

Nuri was Khabug's youngest son. Before the war he had quarreled with his sister's husband. Being an extraordinarily hot-tempered young man, Nuri threw an ax at him, and he bled to death. The affair was successfully hushed up, because no one complained to the authorities, but at a family council Nuri was expelled from his clan and Chegem forever.

But after the war, when old Khabug passed away, when so many friends and relatives did not return home and Nuri himself was gravely wounded, the attitude toward him softened. He began coming to Chegem occasionally from the city, where he lived, and only his sister, who had loved her husband with all her heart, would not forgive him, would not see him or speak to him.

"What are you up to now!" Noutsa exclaimed, turning at her husband's words, the mush spatula motionless in her hand.

"You must," Kyazym said firmly. He finished rolling a cigarette and bent down to thrust it into the coals on the hearth.

"You won't find that kind of money in all of Chegem!" his wife exclaimed.

"I think you'll find somebody has even more," he said with a grin.

"May I dig up the bones of my dead if you'll find that kind of money in all of Chegem!" his wife exclaimed.

"Leave the bones of your dead in peace," he said, "and get on with your mush."

"You'd better tell me what you're up to!" his wife asked again anxiously, and he marveled, as he had so many times, at her stubbornness. Eighteen years, and she invariably asked him what he was up to. In all those years he had never once confessed what he was up to, and yet every time he undertook anything she tried to drag his intentions out of him. But he never confided his intentions to her. Now, especially, he couldn't, because with her skimpy woman's mind she might spoil everything.

"Do as I told you," he pronounced firmly. "You'll find out when the time comes!"

She realized that she wouldn't get anything out of him and stirred the mush with her spatula for some time in silence.

"Watch out you don't get into trouble," she sighed after a moment, and began to sprinkle meal into the mush kettle.

"I don't expect I will," he said.

Noutsa said nothing, but he could tell from the muffled, furious scrape of the mush spatula on the bottom of the kettle that she was holding back irritation.

The children got up. His eldest daughter, seventeen-year-old Riziko, took the jug and went to the spring for water.

"You're bloated with sleep," he said, addressing his elder son Remzik and his daughter Zina, who was rubbing her sleepy, pretty little face.

"Leave the children alone!" his wife said. She was having a hard time turning the thick mush with the spatula.

"Pépé, bring some candy!" the little boy said sternly as he came toddling over the threshold into the kitchen. Seeing the horse tied to the railing of the kitchen veranda, he understood his father was going somewhere and had decided to derive a profit from this fact forthwith. Wordlessly Kyazym glanced at the little boy, his eyes bright with mocking warmth.

"Drive the goats to the bottom of Sabid's Hollow and keep leading them along the stream," he told his elder son, who had sat down on the couch. "The grazing is good there."

"I don't need you to tell me," his son snapped.

"Is that any way to speak to your father?" Noutsa said, turning around to her son.

Kyazym held his peace. Remzik was fifteen, and he was already ashamed that they made him graze the goats. This was the strange and new thing that was slowly but unstoppably coming to Chegem. For some reason they were all ashamed to be goatherds, when their fathers and grandfathers had never been ashamed.

After eating breakfast with his family, Kyazym carried out the leftover mush and began feeding the dog, who had silently waited his hour at the threshold of the kitchen veranda. He threw the mush in small slices so that the dog wouldn't choke out of greed. His black coat gleaming in the sun, his tail wagging gratefully, he caught the prize with a clack of his teeth and swallowed almost instantly, as if choking with pleasure.

Then Kyazym washed his hands and saddled the horse.

"Buy some salt, since you're going," his wife said. She brought out a small sack and tried to strap it to the saddle. But he took the sack from her and stuck it in his pocket. He knew they still had enough salt in the house, but his wife was using this request to bind him to the family, from which, as she thought, he was always trying to break away for the sake of separate men's affairs or Chegem affairs.

He untied the horse, wordlessly threw his light, strong body across the saddle, and trotted across the yard to the upper Chegem road.

Forty minutes later he rode into the village soviet yard. After tying the horse at the hitching rack he mounted to the kolkhoz office. Two accountants, one a young girl and the other a woman his own age, were bent over their desks, clicking away at their abacuses. Their doleful faces still seemed to radiate mourning for the arrested bookkeeper.

"Is he in?" Kyazym asked, with a nod toward the chairman's door.

"Yes," they replied. They had both stood up when he appeared. The older woman's face came alive with the softly reflected glow of a long-ago tenderness. He gestured for them to sit down and walked through to the chairman's office.

This woman, the one his age, had loved Kyazym all her life, although he probably had never guessed. In her youth she had thought him so much smarter and better-looking than herself that she never confided her love to him, nor to anyone else. She thought him worthy of some remarkable girl, and he apparently had one in the village of Atary; there was a pledge between them, so people said. But that girl suddenly married another man, and after many years Kyazym married his present wife. What had happened there she did not know. The years passed, she herself got married, had her children, but her feeling for him did not pass, although the pain did, and she continued to watch his life from afar and worry about him, because she knew that he had a bad heart.

He had been in the chairman's office for twenty minutes now, and both women were surprised not to hear their voices carrying from the office. It was clear that they were talking very softly on purpose. Finally came the scrape of a chair being pushed back, and they heard Kyazym's voice.

"Only no one must know, otherwise everything will fall through—"

"Don't worry, Kyazym!" came the chairman's voice. "This will die between us . . ."

The door opened, and Kyazym and the chairman came into the room where the accountants sat.

"There's a mistake in your report," Kyazym said, giving the girl a derisive look. He said the word "mistake" in Russian: *ashipka*. It had passed easily into the Abkhazian language as a kind of solemn State concept, which didn't sound quite right in translation.

"Is there?" the girl asked, coloring deeply. She knew that he was never mistaken.

"Get busy with your abacus," he said, coming over to her desk.

He knew that she didn't make mistakes on purpose, but it always gave him pleasure to catch literate people in mistakes and correct them. He began to catalogue the jobs done by his work brigade over the last month. While she multiplied the hectares of corn and tobacco weeded, the cord-meters of tobacco leaves strung, he stood over her, each time multiplying faster in his head and naming the figure before she could calculate it on her abacus.

"You got it—smart girl," he would say when she came up with the same figure he had named. If she made a mistake—and sometimes she made mistakes precisely because the chairman was watching and Kyazym was pestering her— he said, "Well, do it over!"

She did it over, and it always came out just as he had said.

"Oh," the chairman sighed, when he finished checking the report, "if somebody in Kengursk had a mind like yours we might accomplish something."

"Aim higher!" the woman Kyazym's age could not refrain from saying.

"Drop it," the chairman said.

A fresh newspaper lay on the girl's desk, and Kyazym recalled that he was running out of paper for cigarettes. Before the war he had always bought his cigarette paper, but for some reason there wasn't any after the war.

"Anything worth knowing?" Kyazym asked the chairman, pointing at the newspaper. He asked this with his usual playful gravity, which the chairman knew well.

"Okay, okay, take it," he said, not wanting Kyazym to expatiate on this subject in front of the office women.

"Not if it's anything you need," Kyazym said. He rolled up the newspaper and put it in his pocket. "It'd be worth its weight in gold if they'd issue it without all these crooked little lines."

"That's enough," the chairman said, trying to cut short a conversation that was already a little unsafe even for Chegem.

"Oh, I don't mean all of them," Kyazym added, "just the ones they send to us bumpkins."

The woman smiled.

"You may be smart, but you talk a lot of nonsense," the chairman observed querulously. Shoving Kyazym gently along, he led him out on the veranda.

Kyazym descended the steps and walked over to his horse. Now he recalled his wife's order, or rather, his little boy's.

"Is the storekeeper in?" he asked. Already grasping the saddle bows, he looked back at the chairman, who was still standing on the steps. The store was located in the same building as the office, but in back.

"He's gone to Kengursk for merchandise," the chairman said.

"Just once I'd like to see his merchandise," Kyazym said, mounting his horse and finding the stirrup with his toe. "All he ever does is go for merchandise."

He started back. The sun went behind a cloud and the huge yard at the village soviet immediately turned dark. But just ahead, within two hundred meters, the clumps of chestnut trees, the road gleaming white with stones, the green of a cornfield, all still held the light of what seemed an especially joyous sun. As if feeling this, as if trying to hurry into the golden strip of light, the horse trotted quickly toward home.

Halfway there, Kyazym turned off and rode up to the house of former kolkhoz chairman Timur Zhvanba, or informally Temyr, as the Abkhazians say it.

"Oh, Temyr!" he shouted, riding up to the gate. A red dog sprang out from under the house, barking, but when she reached the gate she recognized Kyazym. Ashamed that she hadn't recognized him to begin with, she turned her head slightly to one side and gave another few barks, to show that she'd had some other reason for barking.

Timur hardly fed his dog at all; she scrounged in the neighbors' yards and often wandered as far as Kyazym's house. Timur had always been rather stingy, by Chegem standards, and after he finally lost the chairman's job and was pensioned off with the unknown title of Honored Citizen of the Village, he went totally berserk, turned wild and unsociable, became an animal, as the Chegemians said.

He had very much wanted not to lose the chairman's job, had expected that he would at least be given some other job, in Kengursk. But the district committee did not give him any job, because everyone was sick of him. However, knowing and fearing his litigious character (he was quite capable of firing off a letter saying that there were unexterminated Trotskyites entrenched in the Kenguria District Committee), the district committee gave him this unknown but consoling title, Honored Citizen of the Village.

There was always the possibility that the district committee had displayed considerable psychological subtlety in giving him this title. They knew his love for all marks of distinction, and at that time there was only one other man in the whole Kenguria District who held the title of Honored Citizen of the Village. So, if Timur Zhvanba moved to Kengursk in search of a leadership job, even the lowliest, it seemed he would automatically lose the title of Honored Citizen of his abandoned village.

Despite having lived in Chegem for over fifteen years, Timur had never learned how to really run a farm, although from time to time he tried all sorts of crank innovations on his land. Thus, one year he planted half of it in watermelons, although watermelons would not ripen under Chegemian conditions and he had to feed his entire crop to the livestock. Another time he bought up half a hundred mandarin orange seedlings, but they all died off that same winter.

With every year, the Chegemians observed, he became more of an animal and more of a miser. He counted every egg laid by his hen, and if the hen didn't lay, according to the Chegemians, he accused his wife of secretly eating the egg. For a long time now his household had drunk only buttermilk, instead of milk, and, finally, he had married off his daughters disgracefully, by Chegemian standards, without a dowry, not a stitch to their backs. Both his daughters were pretty, however, and made quite good marriages.

Anyway, Timur Zhvanba, with his inborn fear of heights, had always looked a little odd in the mountain village of Chegem, and after losing the chairman's job he looked especially ridiculous, like an urban madman who had somehow landed in a village. In Chegem the role of the village fool had long ago been assigned to Kunta, and he filled it pretty well, so that the Chegemians had no use for Timur.

Although the Chegemians snickered at him, they treated him with some caution. For one thing, despite having lost his job, he still went around in a tussah tunic, as if to hint that his power was not gone, it had taken another form. This gave considerable grounds for far-reaching conjecture. Moreover, despite his generally recognized stupidity, he was distinguished by a considerable capacity for what the Chegemians called shitty tricks.

Thus he tracked down a certain Chegemian who had a secret pen, deep in the forest, where he kept five illegal cows. Timur himself later recounted boastfully how he had become suspicious of the peasant because his sheaves of corn straw, which Chegemians usually stack off the ground, up on some lopped-off tree growing on their land—well, this peasant's suspended stack, as he noticed, was diminishing at a rate incommensurate with the number of domestic animals he had. So he tracked him down and unmasked him. The peasant wasn't touched, of course, but the kolkhoz took the cows.

This incident, as may easily be guessed, had not increased the Chegemians' liking for Timur, because they all tried, with all the means available to them, to preserve their livestock. They never understood and could not understand why this bothered the State. The same goatherd was needed to graze thirty goats as to graze three hundred, and with our evergreen groves the goats had no need of synthetic feed. So what did it matter?

Whoever had decided not to let the peasants breed livestock probably thought that when a peasant lost interest in his own stock he would acquire an interest in the kolkhoz's. But that did not come to pass, nor could it.

Now, at the gate of Timur's house, Kyazym's thoughts returned to him once more. Many times Kyazym had pondered why people who earned their bread under the roofs of offices went to pieces much faster than ordinary peasants when fate dealt them a blow. He had noticed this also in the lives of many Kenguria big shots who lost their jobs.

Thinking it over, he came to the following conclusion. Those who earned their bread under an official roof were always gnawed at by the terror that they would be driven out from under that roof. And when they really were driven out, they no longer had any reserve of strength to preserve their dignity.

Peasants like us, he thought, who earn our bread not under the roofs of offices but under the open sky, never experience that terror. He who works under the sky cannot be driven out from under the sky, because the sky is everywhere, and when fate deals him a blow, he still has a reserve of strength left that hasn't been gnawed away by constant terror.

Our stock is stronger, he thought. But even believing that peasant stock was stronger, more and more often he recognized with dull pain that strong though our peasant stock might be, its strength was not limitless. The corruption of time, rising up from the lowland towns, was reaching Chegem—now secret, now obvious, but most importantly, unstoppable.

Timur's wife emerged from the kitchen and started toward the gate. To look at this grubby, aging woman it was hard to believe that in her youth she had been a teacher and worked with her husband in the Kenguria school. Darting suspicious glances at Kyazym, she came to the gate.

"Is Temyr home?" Kyazym asked, although he knew that he was not.

"He's not here," the mistress said. "Can I give him a message?"

Kyazym hesitated and did not answer. He was attentively surveying the windows of the house. The last window frame on the right had visibly begun to rot. The other frames were intact. I must remember that, he thought.

"Where is Temyr?" Kyazym asked finally, after a deliberate pause.

"He went to Atary," the wife replied. "What message should I give him?"

Kyazym knew that he had gone to Atary.

"When will he be back?" Kyazym asked.

"He promised tonight," the wife answered, alive with anxious curiosity. "What do you need of him?"

"We've got trouble," Kyazym replied reluctantly. "My brother in Kengursk is in a bad fix. If I don't come up with fifty thousand in the next day or two, he'll land in jail. I thought maybe Temyr would lend me—"

"Are you out of your mind?" Timur's wife wrung her hands. "We've never seen that kind of money in our lives!"

"My brother's in trouble," Kyazym repeated pensively. "I thought maybe Temyr would lend, would share—"

"Share?" the mistress repeated in angry astonishment. "May I bury my own children if we have any money at all in the house, let alone fifty thousand!"

"A wife doesn't always know what her husband has," Kyazym said instructively.

"What's there to know?" Timur's wife wrung her hands again. "You must be off your rocker! I'm telling you in Abkhazian—we've never seen that kind of money in our lives!"

"Well, all right," Kyazym said. He turned his horse and added, as if talking to himself now, "But I thought he'd lend, he'd share—"

"Share what, you crazy fool?" Timur's wife screamed after him, but Kyazym, no longer able to distinguish the words of her lengthy curses, was turning onto the upper Chegem road.

Ten minutes later he turned off the upper Chegem road again and climbed up to the old hunter Tendel's house.

Tendel was sitting by the still in the shade of a walnut tree. He was sitting sidewise to the gate and watching the fine stream of alcohol flowing down the straw into the bottle. Now, in profile, his broken hawkish nose was especially noticeable.

"Oh, Tendel!" Kyazym shouted, stopping by the gate.

Tendel jumped up from the bench. A bony old man, agile for his age, he looked at Kyazym from afar, his yellow hawk eyes flashing.

"Dismount, Kyazym, dismount!" Tendel shouted from afar as he approached. "Try my first-shot! It's kingdom come! It'll cut down a bird on the wing—a bird!"

Tendel's voice was so piercing that Kyazym's horse almost bolted at the first sound of it, but he restrained her. The old hunter had obviously been sampling his liquor while he made it.

"I can't," Kyazym said. He checked Tendel, who was trying to fling open the gate under the horse's muzzle. "I'm in a hurry. I wanted to ask, when are you having your party?"

Tendel's grandson had returned from the army, and he was planning to celebrate the event.

"Day after tomorrow," Tendel said. He had adjusted his voice somewhat to his companion's nearness, but his yellow hawk eyes still blazed. "We'd have let you know!"

"Are you thinking of inviting Temyr?"

"How can we help it, may he be struck by lightning! He's a neighbor!"

"Right; invite him, and his wife too!"

"He'd come anyhow, for free eats!" Tendel shrilled, so that the horse tried to bolt again. "If I had my way, I'd invite them to hellfire!"

"Good," Kyazym said, turning his horse, who had been trying to turn her muzzle the whole time anyway. "I may be a little late. Start without me."

"We'd start anyhow!" Tendel shouted. "But Kyazym, dismount, you won't regret it! Try my pear brandy! It'll cut down a bird in flight, *anasını!*"

But Kyazym was already descending to the upper Chegem road.

Kyazym spent the rest of the day, until evening, shingling the roof of the new tobacco shed. Kunta helped him. In the evening, when they finished work, Kyazym arranged with him that they would set out for the forest early tomorrow morning to split shingle. Kunta did not see why they had to split shingle when they still had enough left for several days' work. But, submitting to Kyazym's will as always, he did not contradict—Kyazym knew better.

Kyazym had purposely decided to split shingle both tomorrow and the day after, in order to avoid encountering Temyr before the party at old Tendel's house.

Early in the morning, taking cheese and *churek*, Kyazym went off to the forest with Kunta for the day. He had warned his wife not to say where he was if Temyr should ask for him. When he came home in the evening, pale with fatigue, his wife told him that Temyr had come by and asked for him three times.

She told him about it while she was pouring water from the pitcher and he was washing, his sleeves rolled up on his strong hairy arms and the collar of his sateen shirt turned back.

"Well, what did you tell him?" Kyazym asked, cupping his huge hands under the stream of water.

"I told him you'd gone to the fields," his wife replied.

"What did he say?" Kyazym asked. Without waiting for her reply, he splashed water on his face and noisily scraped his hands over his stubbled cheeks.

"He asked, 'Is it true your brother's in trouble?' "

She handed him the soap, and he soaped his hands and face, then cupped his hands again under the stream of water. Noutsa was in a hurry to tell him the whole story, but she submitted to his rhythm. Again he splashed water on his face, again cupped his hands under the stream, then finally asked, "What did you say?"

"I said, 'It's true!' As you taught me."

"What did he say?"

"He said, 'Why the hell is your husband asking to share? What am I supposed to share?' "

"What did you say?"

"I said, 'How should I know! That's men's business.' "

"Right," Kyazym said approvingly, rubbing his wet hands over his strong neck and prominent Adam's apple. "I see you're a smart girl."

"He came back twice. He said, 'I didn't find him, either at the tobacco fields or at the cornfields.' And I said, 'Maybe he's gone to the office.' And he said, 'Well, I'll catch him there!' I've never told so many lies in my life!"

"You're a smart girl," Kyazym said as he straightened up. "No other word for it."

"There now," Noutsa said, pleased. "For once in your life you've admitted I'm smart."

"Come, come," Kyazym said. Taking the towel from her shoulder, he dried his face and hands.

Handing the towel back to his wife, he went into the kitchen to sit down on the bench in front of the fire and roll a cigarette. He had tired himself out that day, but he was pleased, both by the fact that he had split a lot of shingle with Kunta and by the way Temyr had behaved, and especially by the fact that he had foreseen Temyr's behavior.

"If Temyr comes tomorrow," he told his wife, after a little thought, "tell him I've gone with Kunta to split shingle in Sabid's Hollow."

"I don't understand any of this," Noutsa said in surprise, placing the long, narrow table between the hearth and the bench. "Weren't you splitting shingle above Isa's house?"

"Never mind," Kyazym said, "make it look that way."

"Strike me blind," Noutsa said, taking helpings of steaming cornmeal mush from the kettle and laying them out on the clean-scrubbed table with a slap of the mush spatula, "if I understand any of this. You ought to be ashamed, bamboozling an honored man—even if honored only for his age."

"He's no honored man, he's a son of a bitch," Kyazym said.

"All the same he's the former chairman," Noutsa remarked, taking cheese from a plate and sticking two chunks into each helping of mush, "even if he had no love for our house."

"He's no chairman, he's a son of a bitch," Kyazym said, his eyes bright with mocking warmth: he was watching the little boy clamber into his place beside him. The other children took their places, and Noutsa sat down at the end of the low table.

"So why are you asking him for money?" she asked, energetically nibbling hot mush from her helping.

"That's none of a woman's affair," Kyazym said. Picking the softened cheese out of his mush, he took a languid bite.

In the evening, when he came home pale with fatigue, his *tsalda* ax slung over one shoulder to support the bundle of firewood on the other shoulder, his wife met him with a tirade. She said that Temyr had come again; she had told him her husband was off splitting shingle in Sabid's Hollow, and he had spent half the day ransacking the hollow without finding Kyazym, then returned to the Big House and raised such a hullaballoo that the women had come running from the tobacco shed.

"Everything's going as it should," Kyazym said. "Heat up the water for me, I'll shave and wash."

He stropped his razor and shaved carefully in a little mirror set on the mantelpiece, from time to time applying a hot wet rag to his face and then lathering his cheeks with soap.

"Don't you look handsome, Pépé," his eldest daughter said. "Let me trim your hair, it's getting long in back."

"Oh, all right," he assented, and settled down on the bench by the hearth.

With a snick of the scissors, his daughter began trimming his hair. She always took pleasure in barbering him.

"You're hardly gray at all, Pépé," she chirped, bending over his head, "and you don't have any bald spot."

"Mm-hm," he assented, bowing his head obediently.

"Why don't you grow a mustache, Pépé?" his daughter asked. "You'd look good in a mustache."

"I'll do without," he said, standing up and brushing off his shoulders.

Then he washed in the storeroom, changed to clean underwear, put on a gray wool shirt and new black wool breeches, pulled up his soft Caucasian boots, and fastened on his narrow belt with the knife in its leather sheath. Spreading back the folds of the shirt over his lean belly, he went out to the kitchen.

Then he took his place by the hearth and sat there for a whole hour, smoking and guardedly playing with his Gulik. The little boy sat on the sheepskin, his chubby cheeks softly illumined by the firelight as he leaned forward to build a Tower of Babel out of corncobs. He laid two cobs parallel, laid two more on top of them at right angles, and thus the tower gradually grew, but at some instant it would come crashing down. Breathing heavily in his irritation, the little boy would begin raising it up again. Like all innocents, he failed to understand that the Tower of Babel, being a Tower of Babel, was doomed to come crashing down. This was what Kyazym was thinking about, although not in these words, of course, as he glanced at his little boy and occasionally bent down to straighten a crookedly laid corncob.

Noutsa was already getting supper when he left the house. It was cool, and he shivered a little as he started up to the upper Chegem road. The night was starry and bright. The clouds that had been cutting and recutting the sky for two whole days, without ever being able to cover it, had disappeared.

So ends in nothing, Kyazym thought, any affair too long delayed. There was still no moon, but the white stones of the upper Chegem road glinted in the darkness. The slope above the road was dark with thickets of privet, blackberry, Christ's thorn. In the dark of the bushes, huge gray boulders loomed like the weird ghosts of antediluvian animals. From among them came the song of cicadas.

The language of universal silence and the sorrow of eternity could be divined in the humble ticking of the cicadas, whereas the distant barking of dogs brought to mind the warmth of a man's dwelling, the comfort of life's temporary joy.

It seemed that eternity sorrowed for the comfort of life's temporary joy, which was inaccessible to her, while the comfort of life's temporary joy was sweet to a man's soul by the very inaccessibility of eternal life on this earth.

Kyazym suddenly remembered the first horse he had loved, his famous black pacer, whom he had had in the days of his distant youth. The celebrated horse-lover Daur—he lived in the village of Dzhgerda—had tried over and over again to buy that horse from him. Over and over again Daur had offered Kyazym a handsome price for his horse; then he offered him a handsome price and a good horse into the bargain; but Kyazym, proud of his racehorse, had never consented to sell her.

Then Daur resigned himself and no longer raised the subject with him. But he started dropping in on him frequently at home, and many people said to Kyazym, "Oh-oh, that man's going to walk off with your pacer! It's not for nothing he's taken to visiting you! He's looking things over!"

But Kyazym did not believe the man capable of guile. So his heart told him, even though these flying visits of Daur's did seem a little odd to him: first night found him in Chegem, then a thunderstorm forced him to turn off the road, then it was something else. Things went on this way for about two years.

One time, waking by chance at dawn, Kyazym saw that his guest's bed was empty. They slept in the same room. He decided that Daur had gone outdoors for a call of nature, but quite a lot of time went by and still he didn't come back. Kyazym was alarmed. He got up, dressed hastily, and went out in the yard. As he approached the stable he noticed that the door was half open, and he felt the blood stand still in his body.

He stepped in through the half-open door and stopped dead. Daur was standing by his horse, stroking her long mane, scratching her withers and whispering words of some sort to her, sometimes kissing her on the muzzle. No, this wasn't how a horse thief behaved!

Appalled at what he saw, Kyazym sprang back from the doorway as if he had accidentally caught a pair of lovers in caresses not meant for outside eyes. He himself loved horses, but for a grown man to caress a horse and kiss her muzzle, like a little boy—that he had never heard of.

So this was why Daur had taken to coming over so often, this was why night or bad weather kept finding him in Chegem! His yearning soul was drawn here, it thirsted to see the horse he loved, to touch her, to whisper tender words to her.

Kyazym quietly returned to the house and lay down in his bed. About an hour later Daur came into the room.

In the morning they got up, had breakfast and something to drink, and the guest prepared to leave. Kyazym, naturally, said not a word about what he had seen. When the family came out of the house to see their guest off, and Kyazym's younger brother Makhaz led Daur's horse to the veranda, Kyazym went to the stable, led his pacer out by the bridle, and stood her next to Daur's horse.

"What, did you mean to go somewhere too, Kyazym?" Daur asked.

"No," Kyazym said. He went to Daur's horse and took hold of the saddle girths.

"I've already cinched them," the guest said, not yet grasping the point.

"But I've decided to loosen them," Kyazym grinned. He undid the saddle girths, took the saddle off, and, without a glance at the paling Daur, transferred the saddle to his own horse. Everyone there froze in astonishment. Pale Daur said nothing, but the lash of the quirt that he held in his hand quivered ever so slightly. That was what the family said later, telling about it.

"I'm changing horses," Kyazym said, to break the awkward silence. "I'm a little tired of mine. Yours is no worse . . ."

"Kyazym, even you don't know what you have done," Daur said, and could manage nothing more. He rode away.

Kyazym knew what he had done, and he never regretted parting with his beloved horse. This was nothing like what happened later with Dolly. This was the same as giving a beloved daughter in marriage to a worthy man. And he had given her and never regretted it.

Daur later invited him to his house, of course, gave a big feast in his honor, and presented him with a silver dagger of rare workmanship.

"Kyazym," Daur told him several times at the feast, leaning over to him, "remember that you've comforted my life, and I don't have long to live! But now I have no regrets!"

"May your tongue wither, Daur!" his poor mother cried, the two times that she caught his words. "Why are you killing me!"

But Daur made her no reply. Kyazym did not attach any great importance to his drunken declarations then, even though he knew that blood lay on Daur's clan. Twenty years before, in accordance with the laws of the blood feud, his uncle had killed a member of the Tamba clan. The uncle had been arrested and exiled to Siberia, and he had died there. The uncle had no children; Daur might some day be the victim of an avenger. But on the other hand, the uncle himself had perished, twenty years had passed, and it might be hoped that the Tamba clan had cooled off, satisfied by the death of Daur's uncle.

In such a case it is usual for the clan on which the blood lies to avoid all possible encounters with the clan that has the right to shoot. Clan members do not visit places where their enemies live. When preparing to attend wedding or funeral feasts for people who are not close relatives, they use complex calculations involving remote degrees of kinship to compute the possibility of an avenger's showing up at these gatherings. If the possibility is more or less realistic, they avoid them.

About a year after Kyazym gave his pacer to Daur, Daur passed within ten kilometers of the village where his enemies lived.

When he came to the mill, he decided to get a light at the mill fire. He dismounted and went inside. The mill was running, but the miller was asleep on the bunk.

Daur did not wake him. He bent over to get a light at the fire, and when he turned around to leave, he saw, standing in the doorway with an ax in his hand, the son of the man his uncle had killed. As later became clear, the son had been looking for a lost cow. Finding himself near the mill, and seeing a horse tied there (no, he didn't know whose horse it was), he decided to stop in and ask the traveler whether he'd seen a cow anywhere along the way.

Daur's death was terrible and swift. Wordlessly, with an ax-blow of incredible strength, the avenger cut off his head. The head crashed into the fire and rolled out, and a fountain of sparks showered on the miller.

Half asleep, uncomprehending, the miller sat up with a start and saw standing before him the headless body of a man. Another instant and it too crashed down. The avenger grabbed the severed head, extinguished its smoldering hair, and laid it on the bunk next to the miller, who by this time had gone out of his mind, it seems. He had fallen peacefully asleep to the sound of the millstones and could not bear the transition to this ghastly waking reality.

The avenger did not hide, he told all about it himself. They tried him and sent him to Siberia. He too died there, incidentally, many years later, during the construction of Komsomolsk-on-Amur. The story was long remembered in the Kenguria District. And every time Kyazym recalled it, although nearly thirty years had passed since then, Daur's drunken prophecy rang in his ears:

"Kyazym, you've comforted my life, and I don't have much longer!"

If a son is in his mother's womb when his father is killed, folk wisdom takes it as an omen that his vengeance will be especially savage. So it was this time. Does the fetus, Kyazym wondered, imbibe the poison of the mother's woe?

Wondering about this, he marveled at the wisdom of folk omens and thought with conviction that there was such a thing as fate, and there were people who had a feel for it. Daur was one of these. He had a feel for fate, just as he had for horses.

If there was no fate, why had his steel broken right near the mill? A broken steel had been found in Daur's pocket. Or perhaps, nervous about being so near a dangerous village, he had struck the steel too hard on the flint, and it had broken? And then, ashamed of his nervousness, he had dismounted and gone into the mill? But why had the miller been asleep at precisely that time? If he hadn't been asleep, he might possibly have stood between them. Such things happened. Why had the avenger strayed so far in search of the cow, and why had he come to the mill at precisely that hour?

A man does have a fate, and a clan has a fate, Kyazym thought. From his life experience he knew for certain that there were clans where many people had a good feel for horses. Such was Daur's clan. There were hard-living clans where many people possessed enormous physical strength, although they looked ordinary. Such was the avenger's clan. There were clans where the wise were often born, and there were clans where the sly were often born, and there were clans that were quick off the mark, and there were clans of slow thinkers, and there were clans with many warmhearted people. But those were few; or did they die out faster?

And there are some clans, Kyazym thought—this time mistakenly, with himself in mind—to whom literacy is not given. He himself had never gone to school, because in his day there was no school in Chegem. But now his children were poor students. Although outwardly he mocked them, at the bottom of his heart he suffered this keenly.

. . . As he approached Tendel's house he heard an already disorderly roar of voices, with the piercing voice of the host himself bursting out above it from time to time. Kyazym opened the gate and crossed the yard, surprised and on his guard because the dog had not made her presence known. Right by the house, she shot out from under the stairs joining the kitchen veranda to the main house and charged him almost in silence, with one savage roar. Flinging his right foot out to meet her, he rammed the toe of his boot into her open jaws. The dog let out a howl of pain and sprang back. Now, from afar, she barraged him with hysterical barking. By this time Tendel and his grandson had come running out of the house, shouting.

"What is she, berserk?" Tendel bawled. He grabbed a stick of firewood from the kitchen veranda and hurled it at the dog. The throw proved accurate; the dog let out a howl and disappeared in the darkness.

"Don't tell me she bit you!" Tendel asked, coming up to Kyazym.

Kyazym raised his foot and examined his boot in the strip of light pouring from the wide-open door of the house. It was intact.

"No," Kyazym said. "I'm not all that easy to bite."

"She's out of her head, doesn't recognize her own folks!" Tendel yelled, his eyes flashing as he peered into the darkness where the dog had fled.

Kyazym grinned. "She's trying to see that she gets a bigger share after the party."

When they went into the big room where the celebratory feast was being held, the guests joyfully jumped up to greet him and moved over to make room. Kyazym sat down across from Timur, who kept shooting him spiteful and suspicious glances. His wife, along with the mistress and Tendel's daughter-in-law, was serving the pushed-together tables. Later she took her place at the end of the table, where two more women were sitting. Everything was going as it should.

"The world has turned topsy-turvy," Bakhut shouted from the far end of the table, where he was sitting beside Tendel. "Kezym is late to a drinking party!"

Bakhut was a Mingrelian and pronounced Kyazym's name in his own way. They loved each other, although of course they had never in their lives spoken of it; on the contrary, they needled each other endlessly.

"I'm late," Kyazym said, settling himself comfortably, "because I dropped by Temyr's house. But it turns out he's already here."

"Why did you drop by my house?" Timur asked, looking at him from under his brow with the eyes of a boar at bay.

The mistress set a plate of cornmeal mush in front of Kyazym and spread it with a dollop of *ajika*.

"My wife said you'd been by to see me several times," Kyazym said pacifically, and he picked a chunk of meat from the platter. He touched it to the *ajika,* bit into it without appetite, as always, and began to chew. Chewing lazily, he looked at Timur, and the depths of his small blue eyes held a lurking taunt.

Still strong, his head shaved, Timur sat before him wearing a freshly laundered tussah tunic and the iron-willed expression of power, although he had already lost power and preserved it only on his face. Kyazym could recognize a big shot by that expression in any crowd; what he didn't understand was whether they were chosen for that expression or whether it developed out of their power over people. But in the depths of Timur's dark eyes there was no power, Kyazym saw this clearly. There was a deadly yearning for power, and fear and uncertainty.

"So why have you been hiding from me?" Timur asked quietly. Although he was seething, he controlled himself.

The mistress set a tea-glass before Kyazym and poured wine into it. He had refused the brandy that was alleged to cut down a bird on the wing. Kyazym raised the glass unhurriedly, wished abundance to the house, and drank, then went back to the meat. Timur waited, his shaven head bent forward.

"Why should I hide from you," Kyazym said. He took a bite of meat. "I haven't stolen anything, so that I'd have to hide . . ."

Chewing languidly, he looked at Timur, and the depths of his small blue eyes held a lurking taunt.

"Why the hell did you come to me for money?" Timur asked, seething but controlled. "Where would I get that kind of money?"

In the general uproar their conversation had not yet attracted the attention of the other people at the table.

"If you don't have it, you don't," Kyazym said, laughing with just his eyes. He drank off the wine and set the glass firmly on the table. "I'm not taking it from you by force—"

"But you told my wife I was to share," Timur seethed, and Kyazym noticed that even his shaven head had turned crimson. "What's that supposed to mean?"

"Anything you want," Kyazym replied, his eyes still laughing.

It turned out the sharp-eared old hunter had caught the apparent drift of their conversation after all.

"You've picked a fine one to ask for money!" Tendel yelled from the far end of the table, his hawk eyes flashing. "Temyr's like the chickadee when they told her her droppings were medicine. After that she always tried to go and crap over the sea!"

"Share," Timur grinned darkly, paying no attention to Tendel's yelling. "Where would I get that kind of money—"

"You're surprised I asked you for money," Kyazym said, "but what's really surprising is that you spent two days looking for me to say you didn't have any."

Timur stopped motionless with a joint in his hand. "So what?" he asked, trying not to let himself be outwitted.

"Does a man who has nothing to give," Kyazym said, still jeering with just his eyes, "look for a man who's asked him for money? After all, if a man is asked for money and looks for the man who asked for it, that means he has it and wants to share it."

"I was looking for you, you spawn of a kulak," Temyr seethed quietly, with a might effort to control himself, "to say how very sorry I am that I didn't pack you off to Siberia in 1930!"

Timur was exaggerating his powers in the heat of the moment. Very few people in Abkhazia had been touched during collectivization, and not a single man from Chegem had been exiled. A true popular orator, Nestor Lakoba, president of the Council of People's Commissars of Abkhazia, had won the people over at myriad assemblies; through subtle allegories he had given them to understand that he shared their anxiety, but they must submit in order to save themselves. And the people had grumblingly submitted.

"Yes," Kyazym said, now shaving strips of meat off the bone with a knife and putting them in his mouth, "you missed your chance. Because the key was in your hands then, and now it's in mine."

"What key?" Timur asked, and fear congealed in his eyes. Open-mouthed, motionless, he looked at Kyazym.

"The key to power." Kyazym relaxed the reins a little, still jeering with his blue eyes. "So now it's in my hands."

"Power? Big deal—a foreman," Timur said scornfully. He peered at Kyazym, trying to believe that this was what he had meant, and at the same time feeling the horror of helplessness before the ambiguity of his innuendoes. That ambiguity, the ray of hope that permitted Timur to avoid a direct reply, was worse than if Kyazym had accused him directly of whatever he was winking about with his unbearable laughing eyes.

Meanwhile, some of the people around them were already looking at them, although no one understood what lay behind their conversation.

"Leave that pukeflint alone, Kyazym!" Tendel yelled from the far end of the table, his hawk eyes flashing in their direction again.

Everyone burst out laughing. Tendel sometimes used words that no one understood. The difficulty was that sometimes in ordinary speech he would come out with words from the special hunter's language, intelligible only to the initiated. Other times he unconsciously twisted common words so that they sounded uncommon. That was what had happened this time.

"What's a pukeflint?" they began asking Tendel through their laughter.

"A pukeflint," Tendel explained simply, "is a man who doesn't drink as much as he pukes."

"I'd better sit somewhere else," Timur said, noisily getting to his feet, "or this man will drive me to a crime!"

Kyazym looked at him. "I even know which one, by the count," he said. Laughing with just his eyes, he held up his hand as if ready to count off on his fingers how many crimes Temyr had committed.

Timur lowered his shaven head, muttering something incoherent, and went and sat nearer to Tendel.

"Enough of your bellyaching," the old hunter told him pacifically. "It's a long time since you were dehorned, Temyr, but you keep on trying to butt. Better sit here and listen to my story."

Old Tendel began to tell the tale of how he got married. His wife, still a very lively old lady, was now standing over the table with a clean towel draped on her arm. Eyebrows arched in her effort to get every word, she listened to his story as if it concerned some other woman, not her. A further comic element, which did not go unnoticed by the company at table, was that along with this sincere curiosity about the story, her whole attitude expressed a vigilant preparedness to reply instantly to any covert or open assault her husband might make on the dignity of her clan. This preparedness, as her rather ample experience had shown, was not superfluous.

As Tendel told it, it had happened in the days of his distant youth, when he hadn't yet outgrown folly. Here the guests interrupted his story with friendly laughter, their laughter expressing the conviction that even to this day he hadn't yet outgrown folly. Tendel paid not the slightest attention to the laughter, but his wife beamed with pleasure, nodding gleefully: That's the truth! Who, if not she, would know that he hadn't yet outgrown folly!

Well then, Tendel went on, in those days, when he hadn't yet outgrown folly, he happened to go carousing at a certain house in the village of Kutol. There, after the guests had had a good deal to drink and the dancing began, the host's daughter joined the circle, in a white dress. In token of the remarkable smoothness of her dance, in token of the chaste purity of her glide, one of the neighborhood girls set a bottle of wine on the daughter's head, and she made two turns that way without swaying once. Who knows how many more turns she might have made, but at that point Tendel snapped. Unable to otherwise express his delight in the girl and her art, he drew his Smith & Wesson and shattered the bottle on the girl's head with one shot.

The girl, as Tendel told it, broke off her dance (it would have been strange if she'd continued it, with red wine spilled all over her), but the guests and the host were simply struck dumb by this unheard-of audacity. Tendel himself was the first to come to his senses.

"You may reckon I've 'left a bullet' in your house!" he yelled, his voice probably no less piercing than in his old age. Vaulting the table, he dashed for the exit.

He leaped on his horse, who was standing at the hitching rack. Not to lose time opening the gate, he jumped the wattle fence. Accompanied by the thunder of shots—fortunately not a single bullet touched him—he went galloping into the forest, which was not far from the house.

To "leave a bullet," by Abkhazian custom, means this: When the bridegroom's relatives come to the bride's house to court her, after all has been agreed upon, they leave their hosts a loaded cartridge and fire into the air. The loaded cartridge and the shot in the air most likely symbolize the seriousness of the agreement, the right to a fatal outcome in the event that the agreement is broken by either side.

But for a self-styled bridegroom to leave a bullet, and in such a fashion—that was unheard-of audacity.

But let's get back to Tendel. After galloping about two miles, his horse unexpectedly crashed to the ground. When Tendel extricated his foot from the stirrup and stood up, the horse was dead. Not understanding what the trouble was, Tendel walked around him and suddenly saw that there was a rip nearly a meter long in the horse's belly. When he peered into the wound, Tendel was stunned—it was empty inside. Evidently the horse had cut himself on a stake when they jumped the fence, and his stomach had fallen out.

"Now you tell me," Tendel shouted piercingly, "has anyone ever heard of a horse who saved his master by galloping two miles with his guts fallen out?"

Here the guests began to laugh, saying that the horse could have lost his stomach somewhere along the way, perhaps right near where he had collapsed on the ground.

"No! No!" Tendel shouted. "When I jumped the fence I was aware of something falling plop underneath me, but I was so het up I didn't look back!"

Tendel clucked his tongue, reliving the death of his beloved horse with uncommon vividness, and now he turned his searching hawkish gaze on his wife as if staggered by the inequivalence between the sacrifice and the reward obtained.

His wife cast down her eyes. Suddenly she flicked the towel that lay on her arm and slung it over her shoulder, as if to create for an instant, by the mercy of magic, the illusion of that white dress, and through this magic summon him, as was only proper, to fairness—that is, to the necessity of comparing that horse with that girl, and not with this worn, though lively, old lady.

Tendel looked at her, but either he didn't catch her hint or he attached no importance to it, because he turned his hawkish gaze on the company at table and went on with the story.

As Tendel told it, the parents and brothers of the girl who had taken his fancy (they must have caught her hint after all) swore never to marry their daughter and sister to this crazy cutthroat. Evidently, Tendel went on, they didn't much trust their own house or their own courage (here his wife pricked up her ears, but the insult was insufficiently distinct, and she held her peace), and, knowing his unheard-of audacity, they hid their freak (no, they hadn't caught her hint) with a relative who lived in another village. He was an even more audacious cutthroat.

"To their mind," old Tendel added, after a sarcastic pause.

At this his wife's whole attitude expressed preparedness to repulse the obviously nearing, but as yet insufficiently near, insult to her clan.

"But they," Tendel said, so significantly that now not only his wife but also the guests began waiting with benevolent curiosity for the nearing insult, though Tendel avoided it this time, too, and went on, "didn't know that I alone held this man's secret in my hands."

It seemed that this very relative had killed a constable two years before, and Tendel, alone in all Kenguria, knew about it. Not only did the man not hinder him; on the contrary, he helped him secretly abduct her from his own relatives.

"That's how she turned up in my house," Tendel concluded, "though no one's seen the use of her yet. And now let us drink, my guests, unless I've talked you to death!"

The guests looked at Tendel's wife and roared with gratitude, indicating that the allegation of her useless sojourn in Tendel's house was totally disproved by the abundance of food and drink on the table.

"Every affair has its own key," Kyazym said, "and whoever holds it in his hand is the one it serves."

"Truly spoken, Kyazym!" Tendel shouted. "I held the key to that man in my hands, but they were a pack of fools and didn't know it!"

Tendel's wife had let down her guard somewhat when the marriage story ended and the feast revived. Now she gave a start of surprise, but hastily pulled herself together.

"There's nobody more of a fool than you," she parried, "in your own clan, let alone mine!"

"Quiet! Quiet!" Tendel shouted. "I'm sorry I wasn't drunk enough that night to shoot you in the head!"

When Kyazym made his remark, Temyr lowered his head and didn't raise it once during the rest of the party. Looks like he's ready, Kyazym thought.

Kyazym shifted his gaze to Bakhut. He recalled that Bakhut had fidgeted all through the old hunter's tale, first pushing his *svanka* (which he took off only when he went to bed) to the back of his head, then pulling it down to his eyebrows. This was a sure sign that Bakhut wanted to tell his own famous story. Although nearly everyone at the table had heard it, some of them more than once, Bakhut plainly wanted to tell it again.

"Listen, Tendel," Kyazym said, "you can figure on Bakhut's not going home tonight, unless he tells the story of how he sold his wine."

"No, what for, *katso*," Bakhut protested. "If everyone's heard it, I won't tell it. But if people haven't heard it, that's different."

"Come on, come on, Bakhut," the old hunter shouted, "and afterward I'll add something to what you tell!"

The guests roared with approval, indicating their readiness to drink another glass and listen to Bakhut's story. Bakhut pushed his little Svanian cap to the back of his head, revealing the sparkle in his small, black-olive eyes, and launched into his story.

"*O da*," he began, with a Georgian-Mingrelian expression that means something like "Well then . . ."

"*O da*, I met this Vakhtang the winter before last at a funeral in Anastasovka. And there we made an agreement: I'd give him sixty gallons of wine, and he'd bring me six hundred pounds of corn.

"Three days later he arrives on a cart, this was already late in the afternoon, he's bringing me the corn. I open the gate and lead the cart to the house.

"*O da,* we unload the four sacks and carry them into the kitchen. And then, together with my son, the three of us roll the sixty-gallon barrel out of the cellar, we put the skids in place and roll it onto the cart. Now he was wanting to leave, but, to my own foolish misfortune, I kept him from it. I felt embarrassed—the first time the man's been to my house, and now he's going to leave without having a glass of wine.

" 'Come on,' I say, and I take him to the kitchen, 'taste the wine you've bought. Maybe I've sold you a bitter one.'

"That's supposed to be a joke, we're already in the kitchen.

" 'No,' he says suddenly, 'I won't taste the wine you sold me.'

" 'Why not?' I ask in surprise.

" 'Because,' he says, 'you didn't weigh the corn I brought you, that means you trust me. If you trust me, I trust you too. I won't taste the wine I bought, but yes, please, let's have another wine.'

"*Ooagh!* But I don't have any other wine. Only Isabella. I'd had thirty gallons or so of Kachich, but we'd finished it up a long time ago. Now what to do? We're already in the kitchen, and my wife has set the table, and he's demanding another wine. But I don't have any other wine and I'm ashamed to just send him away. So I say, 'All right, we'll have another wine.'

"*O da,* we sit down to the table and begin to drink. And I see he likes the wine, it goes down well. He praises my wine, I feel good too, so we sit and we drink, and my family all go off to bed. And suddenly he says to me, 'Listen, I liked this wine very much. Let's exchange the wine I bought for this one. All my life I've loved this kind of wine.'

"*Ooagh!* Now what will I tell him? I don't have any other wine. One wine. I hesitated a minute, not knowing what to say, and he took it his own way. He took it to mean I didn't want to sell him this wine.

" 'Don't be shy,' he says. 'If this wine is more expensive, I'll bring you more corn. I don't grudge it at all, for a wine like this!'

" 'Listen,' I say, 'that's not it. I don't have any other wine now.'

"But I see he doesn't believe me and he's beginning to take offense.

" 'Why do you grudge me this wine?' he says. 'If it costs twice as much, I'll give you twice as much!'

" 'Listen,' I say, 'that's not it. Let's go taste the wine I sold you. If it's worse, then you'll be in the right.'

"So we go to the cart in the middle of the night. Thank God there's snow all over, we can see everything. We climb onto the cart, I open the barrel, draw off wine through a tube, decant it into a jar, and give it to him.

"Taste it? Does he ever! But I see he doesn't trust me. Maybe the wine was too cold, maybe that was why he couldn't taste it properly, I still don't know. And he says to me, 'I won't say anything bad about this wine, but I like the other wine better. All my life I've dreamed of a wine like that.'

"*Ooagh!* What will I tell him now? What?!

" 'Listen,' I say, 'I don't have any other wine. I had thirty gallons or so of

Kachich, we finished it up a long time ago. I served you this wine because I felt embarrassed. It's the first time you've been to my house, and I wanted you to drink a glass of wine in my house.'

"No, he doesn't trust me, I see, and he begins to carp.

" 'You mean,' he says, 'you gave me that same wine?'

" 'Yes,' I say, 'I don't have any other.'

" 'Then,' he says, 'let's go weigh all my corn!'

" 'Why?' I say.

" 'Because,' he says, 'you didn't weigh my corn, that means you trust me. But I tasted your wine, it turns out I don't trust you. If I don't trust you, don't you trust me!'

"*Ooagh!* Weigh out six hundred pounds of corn now, in the middle of the night? But my steelyard takes only ten kilos . . .

"So how many batches would I have to weigh out?" Bakhut glanced around the table as if asking the company to enter into his calamitous situation.

"Twenty-eight batches!" Kyazym supplied, laughing.

"Twenty-eight batches! By that time he'd drive me clean out of my mind! And then I got an idea. The stubborn donkey, he wouldn't take this barrel. But I had one more sixty-gallon barrel standing in the cellar. Better to roll that barrel out and this one in, I thought, than to spend half the night messing with his corn.

" 'All right,' I said, 'as you saw, I have one more barrel standing in the cellar. Exactly the same wine that you drank! If you want it—take it!'

" 'Let's have that barrel!' he shouts. 'Don't begrudge a good man your good wine!'

"What to do? This means I have to wake my son. The two of us won't be able to roll the barrel in. But I'm ashamed to wake my son, too. He'll say, Grown-up men do stupid things. But it'll be even worse if I wake my son and then this one tastes the wine and says again, You're giving me the wrong wine. Because it's cold in the cellar, too, and he can't judge the taste of cold wine.

" 'All right,' I said, 'let's go to the cellar. I'll give you that barrel, but first you taste the wine.'

"I had a terrible time finding a candle in the kitchen—I cursed both my wife and this Vakhtang and the funeral we met at. We went to the cellar, I drew off a half-liter jar through the tube again and gave it to him to taste. Taste it? Does he ever!

" 'Oh! Oh! Oh!' he says. 'This is the wine I've dreamed of buying. Call your son!'

"*O da,* I went quietly into the house and woke up my son. He's young, he sleeps soundly. I could hardly wake him. But I couldn't tell him the truth right off, either—I was ashamed, *katso,* ashamed!

" 'The barrel,' I say, 'we have to put it back, son. Help us!'

" 'What've you been doing?' my son grumbles, and he gets dressed in the dark. 'All this time and you couldn't make a deal!'

"We go out in the yard, and the three of us roll the barrel down from the cart and into the cellar. And now we start rolling the other barrel out, and my son doesn't understand a thing.

" 'Papa,' he says in surprise, 'what are you doing? This is the very same wine! You're crazy drunk!'

"And this cursed Vakhtang, that I met at the funeral to my own misfortune—he mocks me too.

" 'Oh, Bakhuti,' he says—he says it just like Kyazym—'why do you teach your son falsehood, and him still so young! I won't say a word against the other wine! But this wine is just to my taste!'

"I see my son's sulking, he's ready to kill us both. Somehow we roll the barrel onto the cart, and my son silently turns and goes away.

"*O da,* I thought this cursed man was finally going to leave. I accompanied the cart to the gate. And suddenly—he's not stopping, is he? He is!

"Only then did I realize that you should never agree to anything at a funeral. Make a business agreement with a man at a funeral, and he'll come to your house and hold your own funeral.

" 'Listen,' he says, 'it turns out I tasted your wine, but you didn't weigh my corn! So you trust me, but I don't trust you? So you're setting yourself up as the more noble man? Not on your life! Let's go, we're weighing my corn!'

"*Ooagh!* By now I'm ready to give him this barrel and give him the corn too, if he'd only leave! But he wouldn't agree, would he!

" 'Listen,' I say, still keeping control of myself, 'wine is one thing, corn is another! If you've drunk two or three liters of my wine, that doesn't mean I have to eat two or three kilos of your corn! Anyway, I can tell by looking how many pounds there are in the sacks!'

" 'No,' he says, 'it turns out you trust me and I don't trust you. Either we weigh my corn, or you take back your wine and I'll take back my corn!'

"That means we have to wake my son again? He'll kill me! But Bakhut wouldn't be Bakhut if he hadn't thought up the idea he thought up.

" 'Listen,' I said, purposely calmly, 'it's late now. We're both tired. You come back tomorrow and we'll weigh the corn.'

" 'No,' he says, 'why come back tomorrow, when I'm here today.'

"Well, now I showed him. To set a madman's mind straight, you have to use his madness.

" 'That means you don't trust me!' I shout at him, from the bottom of my heart. 'You accepted hospitality in my house, and you're afraid to leave the sacks in my house until tomorrow! You think Bakhut's such a beggar he'll dip into your sacks, snaffle off some corn, and tomorrow he'll say they're short? You're spitting on my hospitality!'

"Oh! Oh! Oh! I see him go out like a candle.

" 'Come, come, Bakhuti,' he says, 'calm down, for God's sake, you'll wake your family. (Now he thinks of my family!) You trust me and I trust you. I'll come back tomorrow.'

"So he left. He didn't come back tomorrow, or the day after, thank God, but he sent the barrel back via another man. And since that time I never make any kind of agreement with anybody at a funeral. And I've stopped going to funerals altogether, except funerals for my closest friends and relatives."

Thus Bakhut ended his story.

"I saw him, Bakhut," Tendel shouted, "a month ago—at a funeral!"

"A funeral's the only place you'll meet a man like that," Bakhut said, shoving his *svanka* down over his eyes.

"I said to him," Tendel went on, " 'What happened there with you and Bakhut?' And he says, 'What happened? What happened was, Bakhut got me drunk and slipped me a barrel of Isabella instead of a barrel of Kachich. And why should I go twenty kilometers to buy Isabella? I could have bought Isabella in my own village.' "

"Vayme!" Bakhut said, and he beat his brow comically as if mourning his own death.

"I saw him too, before that!" one of the guests shouted amid the general laughter.

"At another funeral?" Bakhut asked.

"No, a bazaar!" the man went on, shouting over the laughter, perhaps improvising to some extent. "Knowing your story, I asked him, 'What do you think of Bakhut?' And he told me, 'Bakhuti's not a bad man. A hospitable man. As for what happened with the wine—that was my own fault. If you buy wine, first taste it from the barrel you're taking, then drink with the owner as much as you like. But I drank his Kachich first, got all mellow, and then of course I couldn't properly taste the wine that he'd sold me. If he'd put a barrel of yogurt on the cart I'd have taken that too, like the wine. So Bakhuti's not a bad man. But there's one bad thing about him: why does he school his son to speak falsehood? So Bakhuti's not bad, he was a hospitable man. It's a while since I've run into him . . . Has he died, maybe? Then why didn't they invite me to the funeral?' "

"If God exists," Bakhut shouted amid the general laughter, "I'll go to his funeral first!"

After drinking one last glass to the home and hearth of the old hunter Tendel, the guests began to get up from the tables. Timur, picking a convenient moment, went over and said quietly to Kyazym, "Let's talk."

"Fine," Kyazym replied, "only send your wife on ahead."

The moon was shining, and the night was clear and still when they emerged on the upper Chegem road. Bakhut was standing in the road waiting for Kyazym. They lived out the same way.

"Where are you going?" Bakhut asked. He peered attentively at Kyazym, and then just as attentively at Timur.

"We need to talk," Kyazym answered simply.

"Maybe I should wait for you?" Bakhut asked. He sensed something.

"No," Kyazym said, "you go on home, I'll be along soon."

"Well—as you like," Bakhut said, staring after Kyazym, who was walking away with Timur. The tall, lithe figure receded into the distance beside the stocky one with the shaven head. The tussah tunic glimmered whitely for some time.

"What do you want?" Timur asked quietly, with a sidelong look at Kyazym. Now they had the road all to themselves. In the moonlight Timur's round shaven head, with dark spots for eye sockets, seemed a little gruesome.

Suddenly Kyazym remembered, from stories told by people who had been in prison, that prisoners got shaved. Lord, he thought, if everything goes right they won't even have to shave him. But he's gone around with his head shaved all his life; they could have put him away any old year—best at the beginning, seventeen years ago. He already had his head shaved then. The thought flashed through Kyazym's mind and died.

"Get this straight," Kyazym said without looking at Timur. "If my brother weren't threatened with ruin, I'd never have gotten into this. You give me fifty thousand, I save my brother, and we forget the whole thing. As you see, I'm no better than you—and you and I both know what you are."

"First put your cards on the table," Timur said, forcing the words.

"My card's in my pocket," Kyazym replied, and immediately corrected himself. "Your card's in my pocket."

Timur halted on the road and fixed Kyazym with his dark eyes. His round shaven head seemed weird, otherworldly, in the moonlight.

"But no funny business," Kyazym warned sternly, looking at Timur. He thrust his right hand in his pocket, pulled it out, swung it to one side, and opened it. On his palm glinted the key to the safe.

"Where'd you get it?" Timur breathed with difficulty. His paralyzed gaze was fixed on the key, which gleamed dully in Kyazym's hand.

"I told you I'd dropped by your house," Kyazym said, watching Timur attentively.

"Oh!" Timur roared, and with both hands he clutched at Kyazym's hand, trying to snatch the key away from him. He was still a strong man, but Kyazym was stronger.

The soundless struggle lasted for several long seconds. Kyazym could hardly contain his desire to strike the back of Timur's hateful sinewy neck with his left hand when Timur, unable to unclench Kyazym's fingers, began trying to seize his hand in his teeth.

"I told you—no funny business," Kyazym reminded him with disgusted irritation as he swung his hand away from Timur's teeth. Realizing that sooner or later Timur would catch his hand in his jaws, he wrenched Timur's arm so hard that he let out a groan and fell.

Struggling for breath, Kyazym put the key in his pocket.

"Get up, you're a big boy," he said. He picked Timur up and set him on his feet.

Now they stood silently face to face, panting hard. Kyazym was panting harder, though he was younger than Timur.

"How can I be sure you won't inform?" Timur said, trying to breathe evenly.

"I told you," Kyazym replied after a short silence, when he got his breath, "I'm no better than you. How can I inform to the authorities, if I need the money for my brother?"

"Okay, let's go," Timur said, and they started down the road again. Glancing at Timur's round, shaven head, weird in the moonlight, Kyazym thought tensely that the man might still play a trick. Yes, I broke him, Kyazym thought, but even broken he's capable of anything.

They came to the gate of Timur's house.

"See here," Kyazym said, stopping. "It won't do you any good to try and shoot from the house. Bakhut saw me leave with you. You'll end up in prison no matter where you drag my body. And your money will be lost. All of it! And another thing: if you don't come out of the house promptly, I'll figure you've taken the money out the back way to hide it in the forest. I won't wait for you, I'll go to the chairman and give him the key. The Kenguria police will get you before morning."

"No," Timur said, "I'll come out promptly, I have it laid out in thousands. It won't take long to count."

"Smart boy," Kyazym said. "Always lay it out that way."

"All right," Timur proposed, "I'm giving you the money; you return the key to me."

"Nothing doing," Kyazym said.

"Why not?"

"Because two years from now, when it all blows over, I'll open the iron box and take the money myself. That's when I'll return yours to you."

"Sly," Timur said through clenched teeth. "And I trusted you—"

"But no slyer than you," Kyazym said. "You'd have to be, to hide the key when you were chairman yourself, and wait till after the next chairman to take money for the first time. Slick!"

"I found the key by chance in my house," Timur said.

"Save that for the trial," Kyazym said. "But we've decided to do without a trial . . ."

Timur opened the gate, crossed the yard, and mounted to the house. It occurred to Kyazym that there was no harm in securing himself against a shot, in case Timur suddenly took a notion to escape from him after all. He walked away from the gate and stood in the shadow of a cherry-plum that grew near the fence. And if he came out with a gun? Not likely. And if he did anyway? Forty meters to the left of Timur's farmstead was a thick, thorny forest, which descended right to the upper Chegem road. If he does come out with a gun, Kyazym thought, that's where I'll have to run. No, he's not likely to try it, Kyazym thought, keeping his eyes on the house.

Ten minutes later Timur came out of the house. In his hands he held a white bundle. That was all he had. He crossed the yard, peering anxiously from afar at the spot where Kyazym had stood and where he no longer was.

"Hey," he called, looking around. Kyazym came out of the shadow and went to the gate. Timur stood on the other side of the gate, holding the money tied up in a towel. Kyazym took the bundle in his hands, undid the knots, and made sure it was the money.

"Should I count it?" Kyazym asked, although he knew it didn't matter now.

"All fair and aboveboard," Timur said sullenly.

"Or else I'll come back tomorrow, if it's short," Kyazym said.

"I told you—all fair and aboveboard," Timur repeated.

"That's like you," Kyazym said, stuffing the huge bundle into his pocket with difficulty.

When he had walked away from the gate a few steps, Kyazym turned back and said, "Oh, yes . . . Don't beat the dog for letting me into the house. The dog's not to blame—"

"Well, that's up to me!" Timur shouted after him.

As he descended to the upper Chegem road Kyazym thought, What other tricks could Temyr play? He decided that if the howl and cry of a dog being beaten came soon, it would mean Temyr had decided to take out his fury on her. If all was quiet, the possibility could not be ruled out that Temyr had collected himself and would pursue him with a gun. In that case it would be best not to go home but to walk in the opposite direction, to the new chairman's house. But right now he felt too lazy to walk to Aslan's house.

He was almost down to the upper Chegem road when the yelp of a dog being beaten rang out behind him. Kyazym sighed. He had just reached the road when suddenly, from above, from the slope, came the rattle of loose pebbles—a man was descending. Outwitted! It went through his mind like lightning: He had his wife beat the dog, and pursued me himself by way of the forest!

An instant later Kyazym heaved a sigh of relief: Bakhut leaped out on the road. "What were you doing there?" Kyazym asked in surprise.

"I followed you," Bakhut said. "I didn't like the look of him. Possessed. What did he hand you?"

Kyazym realized that Bakhut had watched them from the forest. He told Bakhut everything, then took the bundle from his bulging pocket and handed it to him.

"Give it to the chairman," he said, "and tell him to send someone to Kengursk immediately for the police."

"What about you?" Bakhut asked, stuffing the bundle into his pocket.

"I'm going to bed," Kyazym said. He started off with his light, lazy step, his hands from long habit thrust into his pulled-out thong belt.

Although Kyazym really did feel too lazy to walk to the chairman's house, he had entrusted this affair to Bakhut for quite another reason. However slight the risk that Timur would collect himself and pursue him, it was a risk he did not want to share with Bakhut. Like Kyazym, Bakhut had nothing but the peasant knife at his belt. So there was no way he could help, and Kyazym did not want to share the risk with him.

In the morning, when the kolkhoz chairman arrived at Timur's house with the police and Bakhut, Timur was sufficiently self-possessed to feign angry indignation at first. But the chairman opened his briefcase and let Timur have a look.

When he saw the money wrapped in the towel, Timur turned pale. Even so he did not give up right away. He returned the second half of the money stolen the last time, but said he knew nothing about the rest. Naturally no one believed him. After a three-hour search, all the money was found.

By this time, having heard about the event, many peasants had gathered in Timur's yard. The kolkhoz chairman came out on the veranda several times and yelled at them, trying to make them go to work. But no one left, everyone waited to see how the search would end.

The police had ended the search and were coming out of the house with Timur when the chairman, following behind them, remembered something.

"Wait," he said to Timur, who was already descending the steps amid the murmurs and angry shouts of the people gathered in the yard. "Give me the key to the safe!"

"What key?" Timur turned back. "Your Kyazym stole it from me!"

"No," the chairman said, "he showed you the second key."

Timur stopped dead for an instant, trying to comprehend what the chairman had told him. Suddenly, without a word, he charged into the house. A moment later came a terrible crash from the back room. Not knowing what to think, the chairman and everyone else ran into the house.

Timur was rolling on the floor in the back room, pounding his shaven head on the floor in a savage frenzy, saying over and over, "He tricked me! He tricked me! He tricked me!"

Beside him lay the torn shreds of a large photograph of his father, with splinters of glass and fragments of the frame. As later became clear, the key had been tucked behind this portrait, which hung on the wall.

For several minutes Timur writhed as if in an epileptic fit, until the policemen bound him, and Bakhut, finding a bottle of *chacha* in the house, forced a hefty dose of this Chegemian sedative through Timur's clenched teeth. Timur relaxed, let go of the key that he had clutched in his rigid fist, and then got to his feet.

When Timur Zhvanba came out of the house, escorted by the policemen and the kolkhoz chairman, the peasants crowding the yard began to spit on him. The sister of the first bookkeeper, who had already sat in prison for more than four years, broke loose from the grip of the people restraining her and dug her nails into his face. They could hardly pull her off of him. He himself didn't even resist her, being deep in a somber reverie.

But in Chegem it's a rare event that passes off without its comic episode. So it was with this one. No sooner had the somber procession crossed Timur's big yard than his wife, as if she had just waked up, chased screaming after it.

"Well, now she's going to give him hell for the daughters!" one of the peasants guessed.

"She's a little bit late!" another added as he gazed after Timur's wife, who was still running and screaming.

But when Timur's wife ran up to the procession, she clutched the kolkhoz chairman's arm.

"The towel!" she cried. "My towel!"

"What towel?" The chairman turned back, trying to throw off her hand.

"The one the money was wrapped in!" she screamed. When he realized what she meant, the chairman took the bundle out of his briefcase. Fumblingly, amid the laughter of the Chegemians, or perhaps precisely because of the laughter of the Chegemians, he undid the knots and flung the towel in her face.

"Shows how far Temyr's Enduricized her," the peasants laughed, "that she'd remember a towel at a time like this."

With that Bakhut concluded his account, laughing a little himself. He and Kyazym were sitting in the Big House kitchen, sipping wine by the hearth. Except for Noutsa, everyone else had already gone to bed.

"But tell me this," Bakhut asked, "why did you decide that he was the one stealing the money?"

"Because," Kyazym said, looking at Bakhut with animation, "I realized immediately that all three thefts were the work of one man's hand. And that meant the bookkeepers had nothing to do with it. Then who did? Any other man who got into the office would either have to break the iron box or carry it off. But the thief opened the box. That meant he had a key. A second key. Where did the second key come from? I asked the chairman, who worked in two kolkhozes before this one, how they handled the keys. He said the office usually has two keys to the iron box: the chairman holds one, the bookkeeper holds the other. That meant we had two keys too, I decided. Where to look for the second key? I put aside the bookkeepers, they weren't guilty. That meant one of the former chairmen. And we've had three. The last one couldn't have held the second key, because both bookkeepers went to prison under him, and they'd have been sure to say if there was a second key, but they said nothing of the kind in court. Now we come to the previous chairman. But no one stole any money under him. He works forty kilometers from Chegem now, and it's hard to imagine that he could find out when there'd be money in the iron box and come to the office at night, just at a time when the watchman has been invited to a celebratory table by one of the neighboring houses, as is the custom here. That leaves Temyr. And I stopped at him. He was our first chairman, and if there were two keys in the very beginning, they were there under him. For another thing—and this is the important thing—if he had decided to pretend the key was lost and steal the money, he would have been sure to skip the next chairman. Because then people could still think: I wonder where the second key went? Later on they couldn't have thought of that, they were used to it, a lot of time had gone by."

"But tell me this," Bakhut asked again, after they drank another glass, "what would you have done if he'd kept the key in the same place as the money? He'd have seen through your trick immediately!"

"I thought of that too," Kyazym said. Carefully lifting the wine jug, he poured them each a glass of fragrant Isabella. Illumined by the flame on the hearth, the tumblers of purple wine were translucent, like precious stones.

"That couldn't happen," Kyazym went on with satisfaction. "If a man has knifed a man and robbed him, he'll either throw his knife away or wash it and hide it somewhere. But he'll never hide it in the same place as the stolen money. Because a knife near stolen money is a kind of witness. And what does a murderer want with a witness? But our Temyr had knifed three bookkeepers, you might say, and the key was his knife. He couldn't keep it with the money."

"What if he'd asked you, How did you get into my house?" Bakhut persisted.

"Ha," Kyazym grinned. He crossed his legs and rolled a cigarette. "I didn't spend two days breaking him just to have him ask a lot of questions. But in case he did, I noticed one of his window frames had rotted a little. That evening I secretly shook it, opened it up, then shut it part way and went to Tendel's house. But hc didn't even ask me any questions, because that night I broke him down completely—"

"Why boast," Kyazym's wife said, coming into the kitchen with an armload of laundry. "You should be wondering how he'll get his revenge on you when he comes back."

"That won't be soon," Kyazym said. He and Bakhut drank another glass.

"He'll get ten years," Bakhut said, putting his glass down on the low table.

"I'm sorry for the dog," Kyazym recalled suddenly. "I set him on her—"

"You'd do better to feel sorry for yourself and your family," Noutsa grumbled, raking out coals on the hearth. Shc scooped some up in a special trowel and emptied them into a flatiron. "You'll drink a second day, and then you'll be groaning: It's my heart, my heart . . ."

Kyazym made no reply but continued to talk to Bakhut, switching to Mingrelian so that his wife couldn't meddle. He still hadn't told his friend all the fine points of the affair. Noutsa knew that her husband was off; he'd drink a long time now, most likely all night. He didn't know this yet himself, but she could already tell by his peculiar animation. Kyazym drank rarely, but thoroughly.

Noutsa did all her ironing and then, still grumbling, went off to the main house holding in front of her the big stack of freshly ironed laundry.

She must have been looking in a crystal ball. At dawn, when the birds were already chirping in all the trees on the farm, Kyazym and Bakhut stood in the middle of the yard. They each had a glass in hand, and Kyazym held the jug in his other hand. They were both drunk, but they weren't staggering or passing out. This was the effect of tradition and long training.

The cow was already grazing, greedily cropping the dewy grass as if to make up for all that she hadn't eaten during her illness. The dog was sitting at the threshold of the kitchen veranda and observing his master somewhat morosely, as though he condemned the disagreeable unusualness of what was happening.

With his head tipped way back, Kyazym was now taking a long pull at his glass. The vessel into which the wine was flowing already appeared to be having trouble accommodating the liquid. Kyazym tipped his head back farther and farther, kept pulling and pulling at the glass, as if his pose were an effort to find in himself a space not yet filled with wine.

Bakhut, in contrast to Kyazym, was of medium height and on the heavy side. In a white linen tunic, his Svanian cap pulled down to his black-olive eyes, he was now watching with a certain mischievous slyness to see how Kyazym's competition with the glass would end.

His expression did not go unnoticed by Kyazym. When he had drained his glass, he straightened up and looked at Bakhut, laughing out loud, not just with his eyes as he usually did.

"Do you think I don't know what you were thinking just now?" he said.

"I wasn't thinking anything just now," Bakhut answered, wiping all trace of the mischievous expression from his face.

"Oh, Bakhut," Kyazym said, "you were thinking just now, I bet Kyazym's going to tip over backwards!"

"I wasn't thinking anything of the kind!" Bakhut said.

Kyazym was terribly tickled at the idea that Bakhut had been waiting for him to tip over, and here he hadn't tipped over. But what tickled him even more was that now Bakhut wouldn't confess it for the world.

"For once in your life," Kyazym said, "can't you honestly tell the truth: 'Yes, I was waiting for you to tip over!' "

"I'm telling you honestly," Bakhut said, "I wasn't waiting for you to tip over!"

"Oh, Bakhut! Oh, Bakhut!" Kyazym shook his head. "Just once in your life, why won't you honestly say, 'Yes, I was waiting for you to tip over!' "

Bakhut realized that Kyazym wasn't about to let him off.

"Suppose you did tip over," Bakhut remarked querulously. "There's nothing to fear. Grass."

"Then you *were* waiting for me to tip over!"

"I wasn't waiting for anything, *katso!* But even if you did tip over, there's nothing to fear. Grass!"

"Ah, my fat little friend! Keep in mind, I know all your wiles in advance!"

"You know what you are?" Bakhut said.

"What?" Kyazym asked with interest, raising the jug to Bakhut's glass.

"You're a dry snakeskin," Bakhut said, moving his filled glass away from the pitcher.

"Why?" Kyazym asked with interest, when he had filled his own glass.

"What you eat eats you! What you drink drinks you!" Bakhut declared triumphantly.

"Why does what I drink drink me?" Kyazym asked with interest.

"You've been drinking all night, and where's your belly?" Bakhut asked. He began tugging at the loose thong on Kyazym's sunken belly. "Where did what you drank go to?"

"It went where it must," Kyazym said, stepping back a little under Bakhut's pressure.

"You're a dry snakeskin," Bakhut repeated, savoring his definition and re-joicing that he was now on the offensive. "You're cruel! You've never once taken your children on your lap! If you're an honest man, tell me, have you even once in your life taken a child of yours on your lap?''

"No," Kyazym said, "we're strict with our children. Abkhazians say, 'Take a child on your lap and he'll hang on your mustache.' ''

"That's why I say," Bakhut pressed ahead, "you Abkhazians have cruel laws!''

"Oh, you Endursky!" Kyazym said.

"I'm not an Endursky," Bakhut objected proudly. "I'm a Mingrelian!''

"No, you're an Endursky," Kyazym said, sensing that he could now shift to the offensive. "I alone know that you're an Endursky.''

"No," Bakhut replied proudly, "I'm a Mingrelian. I was born a Mingrelian and I'll die a Mingrelian.''

"No," Kyazym said, "you were born a Mingrelian, but you'll die an Endursky.''

"Your brother Sandro," Bakhut recalled suddenly, "his wife's an Endursky.'' Bakhut's oily little eyes gleamed: Let's see what you say to that.

"My brother Sandro," Kyazym said, "is the biggest Endursky of all!''

This turnabout struck Bakhut as too sudden, and he thought for a while.

"Then you admit," he said, "that your brother Sandro's an Endursky?''

"Of course," Kyazym said. "My brother Sandro's the biggest Endursky in the world. No, the second biggest. The biggest one sits in Moscow.''

"But if your brother Sandro's an Endursky," Bakhut exclaimed gleefully, "that makes you an Endursky too!''

"No," Kyazym said, "I'm not an Endursky. I'm the only non-Endursky in the world. All around there's nothing but Endurskies. From Chegem to Moscow, nothing but Endurskies! I alone am not an Endursky!''

"Oh, don't get on your high horse, Kezym!" Bakhut shouted, flourishing his empty glass in Kyazym's face. "When you drink you always get on your high horse! I hate it when anyone gets on his high horse!''

Uakhole, uakhole, tsodareko . . .

Not listening to him, Kyazym struck up a Mingrelian song, and before Bakhut could change the angry expression on his face he began to sing along as if caught up in the stream of melody. After singing a while, they drank another glass.

"But sometimes it seems to me," Kyazym said, as if the singing had softened his heart, "that I too am an Endursky.''

"Why?" Bakhut asked sympathetically.

"Because," Kyazym said, "there's nobody to ask whether I'm an Endursky or not. All around there's nothing but Endurskies, and they'll never tell you the truth. And to find out whether I've turned into an Endursky or not, there has to be at least one other non-Endursky who'll tell you the truth. But there isn't any second non-Endursky, that's why I sometimes think I too have become an Endursky.''

Now Bakhut realized that Kyazym had tricked him with his feigned humility. "You're up on your high horse again, Kyazym!" he said, closing in for the attack. "I hate it when anyone gets up on his high horse. Big deal—you tricked that fool Temyr! He didn't even have the sense to buy food with the money! The rats ate half of it! You've got no reason to get on your high horse! But whenever you drink you immediately get on your high horse!"

> O rayda Gudisa-khatsa, hey . . .
> O rayda siua rayda,
> O rayda he-ey . . .

Kyazym struck up an Abkhazian song, and Bakhut maintained a sullen silence for some time. Then he gave in and took up the song, still shooting angry glances at Kyazym.

After singing a while, they drank another glass. As Kyazym drank his glass he heard in the stillness the fitful, juicy sound of Ginger tearing at the dewy grass. He found it pleasant. At times, while he drank his glass, the sound drifted over as clearly as if the cow were tearing at the grass right by his ear.

He knew that such a thing happened only after hard drinking. And he thought, That's what hard drinking exists for, to bring near what pleases the soul and make distant what displeases it. As for those who say this is bad, let them invent a way for a man sometimes to be able to make distant from his soul what displeases it and bring near what pleases it. And if they can't invent a way, they can shut up.

In the east, through the branches of the apple tree, the sky had turned faintly pink. A fresh predawn breeze rustled in the leaves of the walnut and apple trees; it seemed to swing the birds' chirping away, along with the branches, and bring it near again.

Two apples fell one after another—bonk! bonk!—from the tree. After a long moment, as if it had been making up its mind whether or not to fall, a third apple followed, obviously bigger—thud!—and all was quiet again. Only the chirping of the birds and the juicy, nearing sound of the grazing cow. The buffalo cow in the barnyard got to her feet, walked to the walnut tree and selected an especially rough spot on its bark, then began swaying rhythmically, scratching her flank. To the chirping of the birds and the juicy sound of tearing grass was added the swishing sound of the buffalo scratching her thick hide: sshhha, ssshhha, ssshhha.

Kyazym knew that this would go on for a long while now. He felt jolly and at ease, he loved Bakhut very much, and therefore he now took a notion to catch him out from another direction.

"Bakhut," Kyazym said, "how many languages do you know?"

"As many as you do," Bakhut replied.

"No," Kyazym said, "you know one less than I do."

"Let's count," Bakhut said. "Say how many you know!"

"I know Abkhazian," Kyazym began, "Mingrelian, Georgian, Turkish, and Greek. That makes five!"

"I, too," Bakhut said, "know five languages. Mingrelian, Georgian, Abkhazian, Turkish, and . . . Russian too."

This was where Kyazym was planning to catch him. Russians do not live in the villages in Abkhazia, and therefore neither of them knew very much Russian. But Bakhut knew even less than Kyazym.

"You mean you know Russian too?" Kyazym asked again.

"Well, I have a peasant's knowledge of it," Bakhut said. He wasn't letting himself get caught. "What I need for the farm, for the bazaar, for the road—I can say all that!"

"Do you remember the time we were selling nuts in Mukhus and you got the toothache and we went to the hospital, and what you said to the doctor there? And keep in mind, the doctor was a woman!"

"You're a real dry snakeskin," Bakhut said. "Twenty years, and he still remembers. I was joking that time."

"Oh, Bakhut," Kyazym said, "can a man joke when he's got the toothache?"

"*I* can. I was joking," Bakhut said, although he already realized that Kyazym wasn't about to let him off.

"Oh, Bakhut," Kyazym said, "you're a dishonest man. What you said to that woman almost made her throw us out. Repeat what you said in Russian that time!"

"Think of it, it's been twenty years," Bakhut said, reminding him of the mitigating circumstance.

"Repeat what you said that time in Russian."

"You're a dry snakeskin," Bakhut said, realizing that Kyazym wasn't about to let him off now.

"Repeat what you said in Russian that time!"

"*Doktor, zhop bolit!* (Doctor, my ass hurts!)" Bakhut repeated, knitting his brows.

"Oh, Bakhut, you shamed me that time," Kyazym said when he got through laughing. "But do you know now, at least, what you should have said?"

"Of course," Bakhut said, and suddenly sensed that he'd forgotten. He knew, but he'd forgotten.

Kyazym understood this immediately.

"Then say it!"

"Okay, that's enough, we'd better have a drink," Bakhut said, playing for time so that he could recall the right sound of the word.

"Oh, Bakhut, you're being wily again!"

It seemed to Bakhut that he had remembered.

"I should have said *Zop bolit*," Bakhut declared, and knew immediately by the expression on Kyazym's face that he was wide of the mark.

Kyazym laughed long and loud, leaning back the way he did when he drank—without falling, of course, although Bakhut wasn't even hoping for that.

"Oh, Bakhut, you'll be the death of me," Kyazym said, wiping his eyes, when he got through laughing.

"Then tell me what I should have said!" Bakhut asked in exasperation, trying at least to derive a profit from his blunder.

"Zub bolit—z-u-u-b!" Kyazym said instructively. *"U-u-u!* Twenty years, and you still can't get it into your head!"

"I haven't had the toothache since," Bakhut said querulously. He added, "What a language—*zop, zup* . . ."

He began trying to remember some way of catching Kyazym out. But at the moment, as ill luck would have it, he couldn't remember a thing. Then he decided to go back to Kyazym's children, whom he had already mentioned.

"You're a dry snakeskin," Bakhut said. "You've never once in your life taken a child of yours on your lap."

"I've drunk too much for a dry snakeskin," Kyazym said.

"You've loved horses better than your children," Bakhut said, sensing that this theme could be further developed. "You've never taken your children on your lap, you've loved horses better—"

"Yes," Kyazym said, "I've taken horses on my lap."

But Bakhut did not accept his joke, he plunged ahead.

"All your life you've loved horses better than your children. You nearly died when your Dolly came home from the pass ruined!"

"As you see, I didn't die," Kyazym said. He disliked being reminded of that.

Bakhut sensed that he had gone too far, but just now he felt terribly sorry for Kyazym's children, who, he thought, had simply never known a fatherly caress.

"You're a dry snakeskin," Bakhut said, sensing that in another minute he would burst into sobs of pity for Kyazym's children. "You've never once in your whole life taken your poor children on your lap—"

"But I know who *you* take on your lap," Kyazym said, unexpectedly shifting to the offensive. Bakhut played around with a little widow who lived not far from his house, but he disliked being reminded of it. He immediately sobered up, so far as possible in his condition, and forgot about Kyazym's children.

"No," Bakhut said dryly, "I don't take anyone on my lap."

He disliked it when Kyazym reminded him about the widow he played around with, because she was two years older than he.

"Don't take a notion to go see her now," Kyazym warned. "What you need now is the big basin. That's all you need. Your wife will put the big basin by the bed for you."

"I don't need a big basin," Bakhut said, knitting his brows. "You're the one that needs the big basin!"

He disliked it when Kyazym reminded him of the widow he played around with. He especially disliked it when Kyazym reminded him of the widow and his wife in the same breath, because she was two years older than he and twelve years older than his wife.

"When you come to the fork," Kyazym said, and for the sake of clarity he set the jug on the ground and began pointing with both hands, "just don't take the path on the left—"

"What are you telling me!" Bakhut flared. "As if I didn't know my way home!"

"When you come to the fork," Kyazym repeated instructively, and he began pointing with both hands again, "don't take the left path. Take the right one— it goes straight to your house. Do you still remember which is your right hand and which is your left?"

"Don't get on your high horse, Kezym," Bakhut interrupted angrily. "When you drink you always get on your high horse! I hate people who get up on their high horse like a dry snakeskin!"

Sharda a-a-mta, shcharda a-a-mta . . .

Kyazym struck up an Abkhazian drinking song, and Bakhut kept silent for a while to show that this time he wouldn't back him up. But he forgot and began to sing along, and then he remembered that he didn't want to sing along, but by now he couldn't spoil the song, and they sang it through to the end. After that they drank another glass.

The dawn was flaming behind the apple tree. The cow, who had been grazing in front of them, was now grazing in back of them, and they could still hear the same juicy, regular sound of tearing grass. The buffalo in the barnyard continued to scratch her flank, standing by the walnut tree, swaying rhythmically.

A great affair, Kyazym thought suddenly, requires a great deal of time, just as the buffalo needs time to scratch her thick hide.

The morning breeze came up again; perhaps awakened by it, the rooster crowed loudly from the fig tree, where the poultry made themselves comfortable for the night. Two hens flew down and started cackling as if to notify him of their safe landing. Apparently convinced, the rooster thudded to the ground in a blaze of scarlet plumage and began loudly summoning the rest of the chickens to follow his example without delay. A bell clanked in the goat pen.

Kyazym and Bakhut were drunk, but they had not lost the thread of reason. At any rate they thought they hadn't.

"You know what," Kyazym said, "I have a feeling you're not going to be able to tell your left hand from your right. That's why I'm going to pour a little wine on your right sleeve now, so that when you come to the fork you'll know which way to go."

With these words he took Bakhut's humbly offered right hand and carefully began pouring wine from the jug onto the cuff of his sleeve. Bakhut watched with interest.

"You don't want much," Kyazym told him instructively, carefully pouring wine on his cuff, "or your wife will think you've killed a man."

"I'll kill you sooner or later, anyway," Bakhut said, and held the other hand out to him. Kyazym mechanically poured wine on the cuff of his other sleeve.

At this point Bakhut's uncontrollable laughter returned Kyazym to reality. He realized that Bakhut had outwitted him.

"Ha! Ha! Ha!" Bakhut laughed, holding out his hands to demonstrate the total impossibility of distinguishing the one sleeve from the other. "Now which way am I supposed to turn?"

"Oh, Bakhut," Kyazym said, "I'm worn out from your deviltry."

"No man has ever yet outwitted Bakhut!" Bakhut said loudly, his red-cuffed arm upraised. Deciding to conclude the encounter on this triumphant note, he handed his glass back to Kyazym.

Bakhut started home, and Kyazym stood still and watched him cross the barnyard. When Bakhut disappeared around the corner of the barnyard, he began to listen—would he forget to slam the gate? That was where the cornfield began, and the cattle might trample it. The gate slammed—he had not forgotten.

Uakhole, uakhole tsodareko . . .

Kyazym sang the words lingeringly, then stopped and listened to the stillness. The roosters of Chegem were crowing with might and main. After several long moments came Bakhut's voice, taking up the song.

Kyazym clinked the glasses together in one hand, picked up the jug, and started toward the house, his gait still light.

A month later, after first being stripped of his title of Honored Citizen of the Village, former kolkhoz chairman Timur Zhvanba was tried and given ten years. The falsely convicted bookkeepers were released. That same year Timur's wife sold her house and moved to a daughter's in Kengursk. So ended the story of the kolkhoz safe robbery.

The office watchman, who had considered it impolite to refuse invitations to celebratory tables at neighboring houses, was dismissed. But the new watchman didn't put up much resistance either, if some neighboring homeowner was seating guests at his table and told his family, "Well now, shout over to the poor fool that's guarding her ladyship. Have him come sit where it's warm and drink a glass or two."

The new watchman, who usually knew about the upcoming session at table and was vigilantly awaiting the summons, would promptly appear at the house, stick his gun somewhere, and take a seat at the table, casually reassuring the guests, who, incidentally, felt no need of his reassurance.

"Nowadays," he would say, alluding to Timur's arrest, "nobody's going to open the iron box. And there's nothing else to take over there, except the chairs."

"Yes," the Chegemians agreed, "as long as the four-legged graze in Chegem, nobody's going to go stealing chairs. Now if the four-legged die out, maybe then they'll get around to the chairs."

"That's the way things are heading," some skeptic usually observed at this point. Pulling his little felt cap down to his eyes, he would spit lustily into the hearth, invariably trying to hit the very middle of the flame. Most of the time, he succeeded.

KEEPER
OF THE MOUNTAINS
OR
THE PEOPLE KNOW
THEIR HEROES

T HE FOUR OF US SAT on the trunk of a felled beech tree and smoked as we waited for a ride. The strong smell of fresh timber hung over the clearing carved out of the forest. Visible to the right, at the end of the clearing, was the wooden building that housed the loggers' little office and a tiny store. Both were closed now.

Near the office towered stacks of pink, freshly barked logs. Huge hulking tree trunks like this were scattered all over the clearing. It looked as if a wave had carried them out of the forest and then receded, leaving the logs where they lay. In actuality, they are dragged out of the forest by tractors, then taken on trucks from here down to the city.

Two heavy trucks, already loaded, stood by the office. Both the truck drivers had gone to a gathering at the home of one of the local Svans. The drivers, who used to be local Svans, now live in the city, and whenever they meet up with their countrymen they are subjected to a jealous checkup at the table.

This lengthy session at table was why we were waiting now, sitting on the trunk of the felled beech. We were not afraid the drivers would get drunk, because meeting a drunken driver on these alpine roads is about as likely as meeting a drunken lunatic on the ledge of a skyscraper. Although on the other hand, if you were to mount watch over the ledges of the skyscrapers (and why not? public-minded pensioners would be glad to take on the job)—if you did mount watch, you might finally turn up a drunken lunatic. In any case, I have never met any drunken drivers here on the mountain roads. Some who were a little tight, maybe, but never drunk.

Sitting on the tree trunk with me were Kotik Shlarba, a lecturer at an agricultural institute; the artist Andrey Tarkilov; and his friend Volodya from Moscow, also an artist.

We had spent a week in the alpine meadows and were now on our way back to the city. Rather, my friends were going to the city, while I planned to go down to a Narzan mineral spring, where I was supposed to meet Uncle Sandro. He and I had arranged this before I left the city.

A relative of Andrey's, who managed a kolkhoz stock farm, had invited us to stay with the shepherds here. Although the manager himself was not around when we got here, we had a wonderful time—perhaps precisely because he wasn't around.

Let me introduce my traveling companions in a few concise lines.

Kotik is a very good guy. That is even more apparent now—since he's begun to deteriorate—than it used to be. He began to deteriorate last year, when they made him head of a department at his institute. Since then he's become somehow more wary, lost some of his spontaneity; or more exactly, he's established stricter control over his spontaneity. All the same, he's a great guy even now, and when he lets go, you completely forget that he's head of a department at his institute, mounting the podium as if to a throne.

In my opinion, if a man is naturally cheerful, intelligent, full of good will, his perspective will not be easily warped by mounting to a podium. It can be, of course, but this takes time, especially in the case of a live wire like Kotik.

Speaking of podiums, there's a likeable architect who told me a funny story about one.

A certain minister of light industry had invited him to refurbish his office in a more up-to-date style. In the minister's light and spacious office, which was filled with heavy postwar furniture, he was struck by two things: the doilies adorning the back of the divan, and a small podium complete with chipped plywood lectern. Such a lectern, according to him, would have been appropriate in the recreation room of a fire station, but not in the office of a minister.

Our inquisitive architect asked the assistant minister where the doilies—obviously hand-embroidered—had come from. To this the assistant replied that the minister's wife had decided, in line with the general liberalization, to warm up the formal bureaucratic atmosphere of her husband's office. Now, he said, sighing ambiguously, the liberalization had ended, but the doilies stayed.

Then my architect friend very cautiously decided to ascertain from the assistant which of the two ideas implicit in his ambiguous sigh he personally supported. To the melancholy surprise of my architect, it turned out that the assistant minister supported both ideas, because both the one and the other were censorious in nature.

Having satisfied his curiosity with regard to the doilies, the architect began loudly expressing bewilderment with regard to the odd little lectern. The assistant minister explained to him that it wasn't usually there at all, but it had been brought in recently because the minister was using it to get ready for a report.

Now my architect friend was even more surprised and asked why the minister needed the lectern, when he could familiarize himself with the report (compiled by his assistant) while seated at his spacious and comfortable desk.

"One's approach to the podium is also important," the assistant said. Changing the subject, he began explaining how to refurbish the window vents in the minister for light industry's office so that they would be no less beautiful than the window vents in the office of another minister for somewhat heavier industry, though not the heaviest.

He explained in great detail how this should be done, whereby he not only surprised but even offended my architect friend, who is famous for his gifted work. As he says, he has been doing these window vents for forty years and knows more about them than either minister of either weight category.

That was what came to mind when we got off on the subject of podiums, a subject that I brought up, but without meaning any harm.

What can I say about Andrey? One look at his paintings—when he succeeds in exhibiting them—and you immediately see that he's got as much talent in him as a good cow has milk in her udder.

He has a scrappy temperament combined with a terrifying shyness, which no one can figure out. Then again, I could make a guess how he came to be so shy, but it would be boring to go into all that. In boxing, the trainer doesn't have to irritate a guy like him during a sparring match. More especially in the ring.

I should note that his shyness sometimes turns into incredible aggressiveness, and then he's impossible to stop. What usually makes him blow up is a display of rudeness, but when he's tight he's so shy that anything may strike him as rude.

Lately he had been looking rather grim, but here in the mountains he had managed to throw off his worries and had brightened noticeably. His grim mood had been caused by the reaction to a painting he had exhibited that spring at the art gallery.

This rather large canvas depicted three men in navy blue mackintoshes, standing by the sea. Visible in the background was a ghostly promontory, with the contours—also ghostly, of course, because of the great distance—of buildings under construction.

One sensed that the artist saw some evil force in the men he portrayed; at the same time, he had invested this portrayal with a degree of mockery, thereby seeming to imply that the evil force embodied in the men was imaginary. Or was evil itself imaginary?

In a word, the viewer's impression of the picture doubled, tripled, and by its very multiplicity seemed to mock him, giving rise to the thought that any single interpretation he made would be incorrect and therefore stupid. In an extreme case, silly.

But did a multiple interpretation promise to be wise? To all appearances, the artist made no such promise to anyone.

Anyway, the picture (to my eye, of course) held a secret, which was softened—or, on the contrary, mocked—by the artist's irony. Thus, one of the three men had part of a shoe heel showing from under his long trouser leg; it slightly resembled a hoof, but again, whether a devil's or a donkey's remained unclear. Possibly both at once: that is, the heel resembled the devilish hoof of a donkey or the donkeyish hoof of a devil.

The second man, although his shoe heel did not resemble a hoof, had his whole leg relaxed in a horsy way (what I have in mind is the way a horse holds its hind leg when resting). His whole leg threatened to sprout a hoof immediately if need be.

The third man, by contrast, had taut legs that culminated in a photographically exact representation of yellow shoes, their laces tied in bows, with sparkling metal tips. His legs were taut and symmetrically spread, toes apart. Although they did not threaten to sprout hooves on either side, and fully disclaimed any notion of further development, something about them was even more unpleasant than the legs of his comrades. The very pose and the facial expression of the first two men had the respectability, the calm assurance as to outcome, that you see in people standing on an escalator. In this instance, one might infer that the escalator was the evolution of the species, only moving in reverse: We're about to come to the artiodactyls, and that's where we'll get off.

Why did this third man's feet, with their magnificent yellow shoes, seem so much worse? At first, with tingles running down my spine, I guessed that the problem was the unnaturally small size of those shoes. Could dwarf legs support that adult torso? And with this question a guess, and more tingles down the spine: Wait! Was this a dead man, propped upright? Then why did he have such a smiling face, full of the joy of life? Good Lord, had these three men swapped heads?

The painting was called "Trio in Blue Mackintoshes." To all questions Andrey gave his habitual frown, or answered that in this work he hadn't been interested in anything but the effect of the color transition from the navy of the mackintoshes to the blue of the smoothly shaven cheeks.

The painting caused quite a sensation, and they finally took it down before the exhibition closed. Everyone in the city had managed to get a look at it, however. In the comment book, more was written about it than about all the rest of the paintings together, even though there were several other good canvases.

Most of the comments inclined to the opinion that the painting depicted three bureaucrats. To tell the truth, I was inclined to think so myself, but I couldn't bring myself to speak to him about it, since I knew he might be offended at such a straightforward interpretation.

Some of the comments, the ones I thought most amusing, I copied into my notebook. Here they are:

" 'Three Mackintoshes': Great! Great! Great!" (There followed three signatures, from which I concluded that three friends had exclaimed their appraisal in unison.)

"Steady as you go!" (Order from a certain landlubber captain, though he signed his name illegibly. For some reason I always found that landlubber captain more irritating than anyone else.)

"It's a good painting, but why are the three men wearing blue mackintoshes?" (Passionate inquiry from a woman.)

Others just put down anything that came to mind. Thus, for example, a spokesman for the people's inspectorate, whose comment provoked a flood of rejoinders: "If the artist has in mind the managers of Consumer Goods Warehouses Nos. 1, 2, & 3, the problem is not that they're strutting around in blue mackintoshes, although that is aptly noted. The problem is that they're selling scarce goods on the black market, everything right down to jersey. And they can't disguise themselves by swapping heads. Permutation of the addends, as the people say, does not change the sum."

"Shame on Consumer Goods Researcher Tsurtsumia!!!" was someone's angry but completely inexplicable rejoinder. One might guess that it had been written under the influence of the preceding entry, but, as subsequently became clear, the matter was more complex.

Here is an entry from a young representative of the working class.

" . . . A good painting, and correct. While the bosses in blue mackintoshes cool off by the sea, the building stands unfinished and will remain unfinished. I immediately recognized the contours of Cape Orange and the boss of our Building and Construction Directorate. He's the one in the middle, only the artist gave him a different head. That was clever. Cut off one head from the hydra of bureaucracy and it will grow another . . ."

Both the signature and the address were traced with polemical clarity.

Here is one last excerpt, from the last entry.

" . . . This is the first time I've attended an exhibition in the provinces, and I'm amazed. In the first place, why does everyone write whatever he likes, comrades? After all, couldn't people who are traveling around in the guise of tourists take advantage of this? Why didn't you think of this yourselves, why do I have to say it, comrades? After all, I'm just vacationing here by chance, although of course it's not chance that I'm at the ministry of heavy industry's sanatorium. In Moscow, for example, at exhibitions nowadays . . ." There followed a description of how things were done nowadays at exhibitions in Moscow, in his opinion; but more on that later. The comrade from heavy industry not only signed his name clearly but indicated his room number at the sanatorium where he was staying, which could have been construed as an invitation for a more detailed consultation.

I should mention that this quote was preceded by a pretty harsh comment on the painting itself. I think all this had some effect on what happened later.

In any case, one fine day the rumor went around at our newspaper that somebody high up did not like Tarkilov's painting; the editor had already ordered someone to do an article on this, and it would appear in the paper as soon as a certain young prince, from a still younger African state, had left Cape Orange.

At first no one could see any connection between the young prince, who was vacationing on Cape Orange at the invitation of the president of Abkhazia, and our exhibition; but our editor, Avtandil Avtandilovich, explained it all to us later.

It seemed the prince had not yet made a final choice between our way and the American way in developing his immature state. Sometimes he vacationed here, sometimes in Florida.

That was one thing. For another, there were reports that he was collecting art. Although no one knew exactly what sort of work he was choosing for his collection, it was suspected that he was a brash young fellow.

Of course, it was unlikely that the prince would seize our local paper first thing on waking up in the morning. Nevertheless, it was not worth the risk, especially since he was planning to go home in a week. Not to mention that there had already been one rather unpleasant incident, from which we seemed to have extricated ourselves without any great loss. Here I take time out and call upon a countryman of mine to recount that incident.

My Countryman's Story

I don't mean to offend anyone, but some of our leaders (local ones, of course) have a bad habit.

The minute a Negro statesman shows up in Abkhazia, he's hardly stepped off the gangplank, so to speak, before they say to him, "Did you know that we have Negroes of our own?"

We really do have several Negro families that have lived in the village of Adzyubzha from time immemorial. Well, so they live there. No one used to pay any attention to it. Even now it's not known how they got here. They've probably been here for centuries. Anyway, no one knows.

But it's not just our Negroes, we don't know much about our own origins either. Speaking of which, back in the mid-thirties our celebrated scholar and writer Dmitry Gulia tried to discover our origins.

Either on the basis of our Negroes in Adzyubzha, or for some other reason, he advanced the hypothesis that the Abkhazians were of Ethiopian origin. Well, he advanced it, but it didn't go over.

For some reason the hypothesis greatly displeased the president of the Council of People's Commissars of Abkhazia, Nestor Lakoba. Despite his deafness Lakoba was a witty man, but this hypothesis displeased him.

"You're an Ethiopian yourself," Lakoba is supposed to have said, jerking his ear trumpet away from his ear. They say he even blew into his ear trumpet, as if rinsing it of an impious sound, at the same time hinting that he had no intention of rinsing it twice of one and the same story. Naturally, no one breathed another word about the story of our Ethiopian origin.

By the way, not long ago when the newspapers bristled with the name of the unfortunate Lumumba, I thought: What if old man Gulia was right? Lumumba is a typically Abkhazian surname. Compare: Agrba, Lakerba, Palba, and then the distant, but familiar, Lumumba.

No sooner had that interesting scientific observation occurred to me than the dark name of Tshombe appeared in the papers. (Just between us, it would be more correct to say Tshomba.) Oddly enough, from the same region, the Congo. From a conscientiously scientific point of view, having acknowledged Lumumba as one of us, I ought to have done the same with Tshomba. But, I ask you, what do we want with this obscurantist, don't we have enough troubles of our own?

I had to grab my own song quite firmly by the throat, as we say, and leave the development of the Ethiopian story until a better time.

Well then, ever since Negro statesmen from native African governments began to appear in our part of the world, our leaders haven't been able to keep from saying whenever they met them, "You know, we have Negroes of our own."

Sometimes they say it during a banquet, when casual conversation on a general subject is called for. Several African statesmen, especially democratic ones, are said to have hastily ripped the napkins from under their chins on hearing such a communication at the height of a banquet, taking it as an invitation to visit their brothers immediately.

"No—eat, drink," our statesman says, recollecting himself. "I was just making conversation."

Making conversation, nothing! He looks at the visiting Negro, remembers ours, and then says he was just making conversation.

Of course, not all visiting Negroes respond to this communication with such familial zeal. The more monarchically inclined Negro statesmen, on hearing something like that, remain silent; or what's worse, they purse their lips rather insolently and reply, "What of it?"

"What do you mean, what of it?" Our comrade is disconcerted but he can't say anything—politics.

By the way, it all began with Roy Royson. That year Roy Royson vacationed in the Crimea. Well, a man takes a vacation—nothing special. So our comrades even got to Roy Royson there in the Crimea and informed him that we've had Negroes living here from time immemorial.

But, they say, the main thing is, ask how they live. "How do they live?" Roy Royson asks. They live so well, our people reply, that if you ask them about the Lynch law, their big eyes bug out and they say what's that, we never heard of such foolishness. You ask about discrimination, and their eyes bug out again, they don't know anything about that either. That's how Negroes live among us, our comrades say.

I'm glad to hear it, Roy Royson replies, although I myself guessed that if Negroes lived in the Soviet Union it would be that way. Apropos, he allegedly promised to stop in Abkhazia, if he had time, and become acquainted with the life of the local Negroes.

Our comrades, of course, were elated. They began racking their brains over how best to receive this remarkable singer, who, according to rumor, can clasp a live dove of peace to his breast and sing the Negro song "Sleep, My Baby" so tenderly that the dove in fact falls asleep in full view of the audience. The celebrated singer looks at the sleeping dove with a smile and, still holding her on his outstretched hand, implores the audience—silently, with just his eyes— not to wake the sleeping bird with applause. But the grateful audience does not agree to that at all, and as the applause becomes an ovation the dove wakes up with a start. She turns her little head in all directions, trying to remember where she is.

And now, realizing that she is among good, simple people, the dove takes off from his hand and flies up under the dome, thereby offering further proof that she's a real dove, not a fake.

The imperialists of all nations cannot forgive him this, his best act, because their singers cannot duplicate it. They tried to calumniate him, claiming that the singer had a narcotic on his breath with which he allegedly put the trusting bird to sleep. But, after exhaustive tests, an authoritative commission convoked by the Red Cross concluded that there was nothing of the sort, unfortunately; Roy Royson influenced this ancient musical bird exclusively by means of his voice. So say people who have access to the international literature on this issue.

Well, so our comrades racked their brains over how best to receive the cel- ebrated singer. From among our Negroes they chose one appropriate to the purpose in all respects: he was prosperous, had a big family, and looked to be in good shape—no weakling. Besides, he had an appointment, foreman of a tobacco-growing brigade.

Everything about the Negro was fine, the only problem was, he didn't have his own car. What to do? Through the Council of Ministers (our local, Abkhazian one, of course) they quickly made official arrangements for a nice new Volga to be presented to this high-achieving collective farmer.

They kept it a complete secret that Roy Royson was supposed to arrive. Why set tongues wagging ahead of time? They dropped a hint—We'll come by some day with a certain lofty guest—but they didn't say who he was.

"With lofty guest or humble," this prosperous Negro replied, getting in beside the ministry chauffeur, "I would have received you anyway, but now I shall be grateful all my life."

"I should think so!" the council of ministers told him. "Go on home now and wait."

It was perfect. You can just picture it: the green little Abkhazian yard with the traditional walnut tree in the middle, the stone house on high pilings, and near the house a nice new Volga with the windows rolled up to keep the chickens out . . . Here, they would say, is our Uncle Tom's cabin, here is his carriage, and here he is himself.

Incidentally, like all the collective farmers in that village, the Negroes are quite prosperous anyway, but our comrades never know when to stop, and at that point in history there was no one to speak out against them.

Anyway, everything was perfect, but the trouble was, Roy Royson didn't come. Either he thought he didn't need to worry about our Negroes, he should worry about his own; or whatever. In point of fact, he hadn't exactly promised anyone, our people had exaggerated.

Anyway, one fine day the newspapers reported that Roy Royson had gone home to America, where, in all probability, he would be persecuted as before.

Our comrades were depressed. What to do? They had made a present of the car, and then he hadn't come. And now, as if in spite, this prosperous Negro and all his black-and-white family, not to mention the children, were racing around like mad in the Volga, and they didn't know a thing about Roy Royson.

I forgot to say that this Negro, like many of our Negroes, was married to an Abkhazian woman. They had been marrying Abkhazians from time immemorial, but the mighty Negro genes always triumphed and stubbornly produced black descendants. True, in recent years, whether under the influence of radiation, or whatever, Negro genes aren't what they used to be, just between us. They misfire. Every once in a while you get a little brown-skinned baby. But the distribution is uneven. They'll be running solidly black, and then you look and a brown one pops up. Or vice versa.

In one family, where the mother was a pure-blooded Abkhazian and the father a Negro, a boy was born, well, completely white, like a goat kid. The baby's father, thinking he was a cuckold, went into a fury. He grabbed his double-barreled shotgun and charged the room where his wife lay with her baby. By the way, she had stayed a rather long time in the hospital after the delivery. Some people said she had complications; others said she was afraid of her husband, she had waited to see if the baby might get darker.

But the baby had no intention of getting darker, so now the husband grabbed his shotgun and charged the room where the wife lay with her baby. But then everyone within reach grabbed him to restrain him from the fateful step. He couldn't even get into the house—he brought the shotgun from the kitchen, but the kitchen, as is customary here, was separate from the house.

"Even if it were true, what's the baby got to do with it?" they shouted to him, twisting his gun-hand behind his back and simultaneously trying to hobble him. Very strong, this Negro was, especially since he felt insulted.

"The baby's got nothing to do with it!" he replied through his teeth. "I'll shoot her like a dog!"

They had decided that since he had grabbed his double-barreled shotgun, he must be planning to kill both of them, which wasn't quite true.

In a word, there was a terrible row. Now the people who had climbed up on the veranda, the better to observe the brawl and keep out of the way of any stray bullet, began to intervene.

"Pass the rope between his legs!" some shouted.

"Stand on his belly!" others advised.

It was all well and good for them to give advice. But the people who had undertaken to tie up the powerful Negro resented it and told them, "Come on down here if you're so smart!"

They kept on shouting advice but made no move to come down. Not in vain did the great Rustaveli once say of such people, "Everyone thinks himself a strategist, seeing the battle from afar."

Meanwhile, the women sat by the new mother and kept a long-playing record going on the record player so she wouldn't hear the fracas. The young mother was patient at first, but finally she couldn't take any more.

"Dear relatives," she said, "go play it in the next room or my milk will sour."

"We'd better turn it off altogether," the women said, and stopped the record.

In general, people in our district don't have much regard for long-playing records, especially operas. Admittedly, they buy them, because they don't cost much.

Now that the women had stopped the record, they were forced to tell the young mother about her husband.

"Let him in, I'll prove it," she said. She quickly tidied up the bed and sat down on it.

The women ran to the yard and told everything.

"Fine," the Negro agreed. He dropped his shotgun and extricated himself from the ropes.

Again a racket went up, because everyone was curious to see how she would prove it to him. By the way, the ones who weren't doing anything, just watching from the veranda, again proved to be in a better position than the ones who were risking their lives to bind the jealous husband. That's justice for you.

So a hundred people crowded into the house, or more. Granted, about ten got into the new mother's room. They kept the rest out.

"Listen from the hall," they told them. "You can hear it all from in there."

But they couldn't hear anything from in there, and they began to suspect that they had been tricked.

"It's so quiet, why isn't there any sound?" they asked each other blankly.

"Because she's not saying anything," came the answer finally, from the one who was standing right by the door and could see.

Silently looking at her husband, the young mother was undoing her baby's swaddlings. The father stood by the door, his eyes blazing like searchlights: We shall see what you prove by this.

Casting off the swaddlings, she displayed the wriggling baby on her hands—with his back up, by the way, though no one understood why. Only the Negro's mother understood, because a mother, dear comrades, is always a mother.

She was an old Negress, respected by all because she had great skill at reading the future in beans. They called her the Fortuneteller. She would toss a handful of beans on the table, then look and look to see how they lay, and calmly read your fortune. By the way, she never concealed anything. Some people got angry at that.

"Pumpkinhead," she would tell them. "All I do is read your fate; be angry at Him who wrote it."

Anyway, this wise woman bent down to the baby and then signaled for her son to approach. The son approached and reluctantly examined the infant's innocent bottom. The baby was twisting in his mother's hands, turning his head, looking up at his own father with a smile.

Seeing that, some women could not restrain themselves and began to sob; the men found the baby's behavior surprising and rather funny. Although it really wasn't funny, because for one thing the baby could feel it was his own father, and for another, it was the first time he had seen a Negro. Up to this point, he had been in the hospital, and the only people who work there are ours, all in white at that—the nurses, and the nursemaids, and the doctors.

"He does seem to have my butt," the stubborn Negro said at last, partially acknowledging his son.

Here his own mother lost patience. With a spryness unlooked-for in a fortune-teller, she hit him on the head with her cane. She always carried this cane, as an old woman respected by all.

"Go now," she said, and he silently left. It turns out Negroes have birthmarks too, though many people don't know this. It seems the baby had a birthmark on the middle of the left buttock, just like the father's.

Now the relatives on both sides lashed out at the impulsive Negro. What if the mark hadn't been there, they said, or suppose it had been in a completely different spot?

The whole thing, many said, was indecent. Nor was it any ornament to the wife, by our standards, that she knew where her husband's birthmark was. True, some people excused her by saying that she might have noticed the birthmark when he was bathing and asked her to scrub his back with the loofa.

Now the old, respected people sat down and began to think how to get out of the situation in such a way that the incident wouldn't shame them before people from other villages. And here's what they came up with.

Their story was that nothing of the sort had happened. It had all been a misunderstanding. The father, in keeping with our ancient custom, when they brought his son home from the hospital, had decided to celebrate the auspicious event by firing his gun.

One of the neighbors, seeing him come out of the kitchen with his gun and knowing that he had an extremely white baby, decided that he was going to shoot, not into the air, but at his wife. And that, they said, was what started the whole scuffle, because they didn't give the father a chance to explain what he was up to. No one believed this, of course, but the relatives told it this way anyhow.

But let's get back to Roy Royson and the prosperous Negro to whom they had given the Volga—fruitlessly, as it turned out. Through the chairman of the kolkhoz, they cautiously began putting pressure on him to return the Volga without any fuss to the Council of Ministers (local, of course) that had given it to him.

The chairman was elated at the council's new decision, because he resented the fact that the foreman was riding around in a new Volga while he, the chairman, had an old Pobeda. He suggested to the council member who called him about it that the Volga be taken away from the foreman and sold to the kolkhoz.

"You persuade him to return it," the comrade from the council replied, "and then we'll see, because Volgas are hard to come by now."

"How can he be persuaded," the chairman replied. "You'd better order him."

"We can't order him," the comrade from the council replied, "because for one thing we gave it to him ourselves, and for another, Africa is awakening."

"Let Africa awaken," the chairman replied, "and we salute her for that, but the Volga has to be taken away, because those people are going to wreck it."

"Have a nice talk with him," the comrade from the council replied, "and then we'll see."

The chairman must not have believed that anything would come of a nice talk, because he did not do as the comrade from the council had asked. He sent for the foreman and told him in great secrecy that the car was going to be taken from him anyway, so before it was too late he'd better exchange it for the chairman's Pobeda, and the chairman would make up the difference in cash on the spot.

To this the prosperous Negro smiled his characteristic dazzling smile and said that he did not need money, he needed the new Volga.

The chairman went back to the comrade from the council and said it was no good being nice. He suggested to the comrade from the council that the foreman and all his relatives should be forbidden to ride around in the Volga, if only temporarily. Apparently counting on taking possession of the car somehow later, he even supplied a way out: "You could do it through Technical Inspection."

"Come, come," the comrade from the council replied, "that's even worse than taking it away altogether."

"Why?" the chairman asked in surprise.

"You know why," the comrade from the council replied, indicating the world map that hung on the wall. "They're awakening. And here we are, forbidding their people to ride around in their own car."

"They carted watermelons to Sochi in that Volga," the chairman complained.

"Never mind," the comrade from the council replied. "Quite a few foreigners vacation in Sochi, let them see and be envious."

"Yes, but he'll ruin it completely." The chairman would not subside. "Pretty soon it'll be worse than my Pobeda."

"A new Volga will never be worse than your Pobeda," replied the comrade from the council, who was beginning to tire of the chairman's intrigues.

The prosperous Negro and all his relatives went right on racing around the country roads like mad in the Volga, and there was nothing the chairman could do but watch this scene with pain.

Once they met face to face on the road to the village. The chairman was limping back from the district center in his little old Pobeda, and the prosperous Negro was speeding over there, or perhaps even beyond it, who knows . . . Drawing abreast, they stopped and looked at each other.

"Lay off," the chairman said, peering in the window. "Even your father doesn't take a step without that car."

"You don't have the power," the prosperous Negro replied, smiling his characteristic dazzling smile, "to take away a government gift . . ."

With that he calmly dragged at his home-rolled cigarette, calmly stuck his hand out the window, and extinguished the butt—extinguished it? he ground it out—on the door of the chairman's car. The chairman gave a low whistle and drove away, hanging his head. He decided that if the Negro was putting out his cigarette on the door of his car, the jig was up—either some lofty guest had already sent a telegram that he was coming, or something else even worse.

There wasn't really any telegram; the prosperous Negro had simply decided it was time to crack the chairman's psyche, which he partially succeeded in doing.

Anyway, the car stayed with him. True, some people say he bought it from the council at the government price, which amounts to getting it free, the way things work here; but others say he didn't pay even a token amount, because they let the gift stand.

After all, we have quite a few sharp people at the top, too. They decided that even though Roy Royson hadn't come, times were such that other African statesmen would be coming, and if so they could make use of the prosperous Negro and his Volga.

So that's how it happened that the young prince—the one who suffered from political Hamletism, in that he still couldn't choose between our way and the American way—was sent, along with his retinue, to see this Negro.

Even now the chairman tried to intrigue against him. When the same comrade called him from the Council of Ministers and said, "Be ready, we're bringing a prince to see the prosperous Negro tomorrow," the chairman balked a little.

He said, Should we bother to bring a prince to this Negro, when we have other, much more interesting Negroes? Thus, for example, he said, we have a Negro who had a son as white as a goat kid, and moreover there was scientific proof that it was his own child.

"So we heard," the comrade from the council replied brusquely. "It has no political significance . . . You'd better see that they don't talk foolishness at the table, and there'd better be women sitting there, too, not just sprawling louts."

"How many women?" the chairman asked.

"Thirty percent, no less," the comrade from the council replied. He hung up, to avoid further intrigues.

The prince was royally received in the Negro's house, of course. He liked everything here very much: our spicy food, and of course our renowned Isabella wine. There was a lot of joking and talking at the table, and they sang our songs. The prince tried to sing along, which was especially touching.

The master of the house laughingly related how he'd heard so much about the arrival of a lofty guest that he'd thought that the guest would be too tall to get through the door; but the guest had not turned out to be all that lofty, although he was nice-looking.

The host's remark was translated to the prince, and he wasn't at all offended, he merely chuckled at the rustic Negro's naive formulation of the issue.

Anyway, everything was fine, but suddenly, when they were getting ready to propose a final toast to world peace, the prince—meaning no harm, as it later turned out—asked the master of the house, "Well, and how do Negroes get along in the Soviet Union?"

"What Negroes?" the host asked with interest.

"What do you mean, what Negroes?" the prince asked in surprise, looking around at the local Negroes sitting at this same table. "You!"

"We aren't Negroes," the host said, smiling his characteristic smile and nodding at the other Negroes. "We're Abkhazians."

"What's this? Are you renouncing—?" The prince began trying to pin him down, still, thank goodness, through an interpreter.

Now several comrades, including the comrade from the council, began to clear their throats, meaning that the host shouldn't say that, he should agree with the prince on all counts. But the host did not react to this at all; rather, he even began to argue, trying to prove his point, albeit in Abkhazian.

The trouble was that one of the people in the prince's escort was strongly suspected of understanding Russian, although he tried to hide the fact. At a previous banquet, when they served him a liter horn, expecting him to say a few heartfelt words and drink it off, he lost his head and allegedly whispered in Russian, "Well, I'll be darned!"

After he drank the horn, they tried to talk to him in Russian, but by then he couldn't say anything in either Russian or African. The next day, when they jokingly reminded him about it, he totally denied that he understood Russian. So it remained completely unclear what he had meant by his remark, or whether he had said anything at all . . .

Anyway, the prosperous Negro would not give in for anything.

"You should've given him a Chayka too, then he'd have said anything you wanted," the chairman said brightly, remembering his hurt feelings.

"An uncalled-for remark," the comrade from the council told him, and the prosperous Negro, especially since he was slightly tight, flew off the handle.

"If our fathers," he said with pride, "refused to admit to Prince Oldenburgsky that they were blackamoors, why should we give in to this African prince?"

Well, of course, no one had any intention of translating his remark to the prince in this raw form. Nevertheless, as our comrades observed, he was not fully satisfied. Yes, he finally drank the toast to world peace, of course, and then they gradually got him calmed down, but none of it should have happened.

Incidentally, it was no accident that the master of the house brought up Prince Oldenburgsky. In fact, that was a true story. Prince Oldenburgsky, the patron of Gagra, when he learned that Abkhazia had its own Negroes, decided to invite them to come and work for him. He wanted to have himself a Negro guard or something.

As is well known, Prince Oldenburgsky imitated Peter the Great in everything, which is why he took a notion to have his own blackamoors. So a spokesman for our Negroes arrived in Gagra and began negotiating with Alexander Petrovich. Alexander Petrovich offered them very good conditions, but our spokesman flatly refused, because the prince suggested that our men serve in their capacity as blackamoors.

"By all means," our spokesman said, "we are ready to work for you on general principles; but we can't do it as blackamoors, because we are Abkhazians.''

Prince Oldenburgsky tried to talk him into it, first one way, then another, but he got nowhere.

"Oh, all right." Alexander Petrovich gave up. "Go on home, if you're so stubborn.''

"On general principles, by all means, dear Prince," our spokesman reminded him once more, by way of farewell, "but we can't do it as blackamoors.''

"No, go on," Alexander Petrovich repeated. "I have plenty of men without you on general principles.''

And here, many years later, was an analogous incident, only now the point had to be proved, not to the celebrated Prince Oldenburgsky, but to a young African prince.

Of course, on one hand, this stubbornness on the part of our Negroes came as an unpleasant surprise to the authorities who accompanied the prince to the village. On the other hand, as Abkhazians—those of them who were Abkhazians—they were gladdened by the devotion of our Negroes.

"How they do love us," they said sentimentally on the way back, swaying on the soft seat, as they recalled the prosperous Negro's eccentric patriotism.

"Yes, but you have to be flexible, too," grumbled the representatives of other ethnic groups, swaying on the same seats. Our leadership is always made up of many nationalities, and this creates exceptional opportunities for the timely prevention of mutual excesses in policy.

Anyway, after this incident with the prince they decided not to run any more risks but to wait till he left. In any case, I realized that even though the article of course could wait, they would certainly withdraw the painting from the exhibition, especially since the prince had not yet visited it.

Just at that time a friend from Moscow came to visit me, and I decided to use the occasion to drop by the exhibition again. Andrey himself was out in the country, painting his tea harvester. It would have been pointless to warn him of the approaching storm. He was finishing the painting, and under such circumstances he always said that only the death of a close friend or relative would be enough to make him stop work. I knew that those were not empty words.

As soon as my friend and I walked into the exhibition hall I felt a sense of anxiety, but for some reason I attached no significance to it. As we crossed the hall I threw out my arm toward the painting, still invisible behind a column, and said something like, We weren't born yesterday . . .

But alas, the painting was not in its place. I glanced swiftly around the hall, but it wasn't anywhere. Now I understood the cause of my anxiety. During the month that the painting had been on exhibit, I had grown used to the hum of a small crowd seething near it all the time. The painting was a little like a stone, dropped (unwittingly, of course) across the calm current of the exhibition. Although the current had not been blocked, and the stone was not trying to block it, still, the babble of white water around the painting was constantly audible in all corners of the exhibition.

Now all was quiet. That was what had aroused my anxiety; but what really staggered me was something else. In place of Andrey's painting hung a completely different one, by a completely different artist, albeit about the same size. It was one of those endless illustrations to Shota Rustaveli's great epic poem, "The Knight in the Tiger Skin." The painting showed three knights—Avtandil, Tariel, and Fridon—holding a businesslike high-level conference on ways of taking the fortress of Kadzheti, which loomed ghostly in the background like the contours of the buildings under construction in Andrey's painting.

Although the knights, in contrast to the blue mackintoshes, were shown half-face, and Tariel had his back completely turned to the viewer, I sensed a primitive charlatanism in the fact that this particular painting had been hung in place of Andrey Tarkilov's. The calculation was clear: If you had heard something about "Trio in Blue Mackintoshes," when you saw those three knights you would decide that you had somehow misheard or misunderstood. What it amounted to was, We do not support bureaucrats and have no intention of supporting them, but knights—why not? Knights, by all means.

I walked over to the administrator who sat by the door, his elbows scornfully propped on a little desk. Everything about him indicated that he resented the size of the desk and considered it unnecessary to hide the fact from anyone at all.

I asked him where Andrey Tarkilov's painting had disappeared to. He looked at me, his eyes still resentful, and said with a brazenry unheard of since 1953 that he knew of no such painting.

I decided not to give up and demanded the comment book in order to prove to him that he was lying, although he knew that perfectly well. He answered that the comment book was full and had therefore been removed. Then I asked where the new one was if the old one was full. He put out a hand and silently pointed to a plywood box standing to the right of the desk, by his feet.

It seemed that from now on comments would be dropped into this box. A stack of paper and a pencil lay on the desk.

"That's how they do it in all the major cities in the land," he said. As subsequently became clear, the bastard was right. I don't know whether it's true in all cities, but I have seen it with my own eyes in one of the major ones. (In all fairness, I should mention that comment books later reappeared. Possibly this was a wise compromise at the expense of a better-considered selection of paintings for exhibition.)

But I didn't know that at the time and started arguing with the administrator. Each trying to frighten the other with his own proximity to the truth, which for some reason implied proximity to the authorities as well, we were already shouting at each other.

At the noise, Vakhtang Bochua, the director of the gallery, descended to us from a booth within the hall, a mock-up of a captain's bridge. He had been transferred to this job some time ago, although he had by no means given up lecturing.

"I give lectures on all my previous topics, minus the goatibex lectures, plus the art lectures," he said to all who erroneously supposed that he had now abandoned his lecturing job.

In his invariable snow-white suit he crossed the room, treading softly as if afraid he might scare away the brawl. His face brightened as he drew near.

"What's all the fuss?" he asked, giving me an encouraging handshake. On learning what the fuss was, he said that the painting had been withdrawn from the exhibition on orders from above. He looked at the ceiling as if searching for the aperture through which the painting had been pulled out.

I looked at the administrator, but he was not at all embarrassed. Spreading his elbows wide on his narrow little desk, he again withdrew into his personal grief.

"If local folks ask," Vakhtang explained, with a jerk of his chin in my direction, "don't say that it wasn't here, say that the artist himself withdrew it to make finishing touches . . . That's his right . . . And to observe the rights of the artist," he muttered—and, suddenly bending over the box, he peered into its slot, as if to acquaint himself with the general mood of the comments, or even their behavior in the box.

There was a pornographic dynamic in his pose, scornfully muted by his proprietary air. Thus, perhaps, does the chief of the sultan's harem guard peer into the inner chambers, observing his sovereign's captivating but guileful wives.

"And to observe the rights of the artist," he muttered, lowering his voice (lest they hear him in the inner chambers), "is our daily duty . . ."

He straightened up, looked at me with an expression of modest importance, then shifted his gaze to the administrator and gave him a slight nod, intimating that he was right to dream, that his dream of a vaster desk top had been noted in proper quarters and was already growing out woody flesh. After this he silently withdrew. Climbing the short ladder to his captain's bridge, he looked at me again, this time not only with modest importance but also with gentle reproach, as if to say, We don't raise a racket here, we don't shout, but we do encourage art, although that is not so simple as it may seem to certain outsiders.

A week later, Andrey and I were standing on one of our main streets when suddenly a black Volga stopped beside us, or rather, after driving about ten meters past us. The man sitting next to the chauffeur beckoned to us with his finger. Incidentally, Andrey—who of course knew by now that his painting had been withdrawn from the exhibition, and that it was causing a sort of secret row—had been trying to see this very man, but he had had no success, and now suddenly here he was, beckoning Andrey with his finger. That means, I thought, we can hope for a light reprimand without serious consequences.

This was a rather major official, by Abkhazian standards of course. Among other things, both in the line of duty and by his own wish he watched over the world of art, considering himself a connoisseur and a patron of the muses, a fantasy which did in some measure accord with reality.

He had a strange, and at the same time a wonderful, habit. He would blow up at one artist or another for excessive naturalism or, on the contrary, for a propensity to abstraction, or whatever, and then invite that same artist to have breakfast or dinner, or even supper, which was especially tempting, because he was not in a hurry then, and the restaurateurs, since they knew him by sight, did their utmost.

It had even been noted by the artists that the worse he castigated them, the better the treats that followed. To be blunt, some took advantage of this, although it was risky business, because occasionally he would revile someone and then forget to treat him.

Once it happened this way. A certain artist, a drab little realist—whom no one usually raised a hand to praise and there was usually no reason to abuse— suddenly decided to distinguish himself.

More accurately, about two years before that he had painted a picture widely acclaimed at the time, "Goatibex on Svanian Tower." It showed a goatibex standing on a Svanian tower with its forefoot slightly raised: perhaps it was planning to take a step, perhaps it was planning to poke its hoof into the tower to prove that it had rotted through.

The painting was repeatedly praised by our newspaper. I recall one paragraph that directed attention to the goatibex's resolutely raised foot, trampling the Svanian tower as a symbol of enmity among the peoples. Later the painting was bought by the newly opened restaurant, Watering Place of the Goatibex. It hung there right up to the time when the goatibexation of agriculture was criticized, whereupon it was removed from the restaurant and reviled in the press—because of that same Svanian tower, by the way, or more accurately, because the tower was incorrectly interpreted. A Svanian tower, it turns out, is by no means a symbol of enmity among the peoples; on the contrary, it is a symbol of a brave people's resistance to foreign aggressors.

I remember he came to us at the editorial office and complained that he had attached no international symbolism to the Svanian tower, he had simply put the goatibex on an old fortress to demonstrate the triumph of the new over the old.

To this our editors replied, then why was he protesting now that he was being abused for the Svanian tower, but when he was praised for it, he didn't protest?

"Who protests when he's being praised?" he asked. His question went unanswered, and the artist was forgotten.

Others forgot about him, but he, it seems, did not forget about himself. Now he decided to try another route to fame. At the next exhibition he showed several strange canvases in the spirit of abstractionism, and he even stood near them the whole time himself, with an expression of haughty modesty.

The artists quickly saw through this pathetic maneuver of his, which was calculated to gain the attention of Abesalomon Nartovich. (Now I've done it.

I've disclosed his name—fictitious, of course.) They saw through him, and among themselves they derided his pseudoabstractions as ineffective.

Abesalomon Nartovich himself, during his visit to the exhibition, walked right past the man's paintings without a glance, out of long habit; besides, the artists had surrounded him in a noisy swarm. But later, after he had inspected the whole exhibition, someone tipped him off to this comrade's ploy. Abesalomon Nartovich was greatly vexed. He castigated him for his hypocrisy, not for artistic errors—hence there was no excuse for developing the topic at a restaurant.

Usually, as he entered the exhibition hall, he stopped at the door to cast a sweeping glance over the exhibition and say with a smile, "We have a sunny land, many artists . . ."

With that, his face and his large impressive figure streamed sunny benevolence. It was as if he said: You see, I've come to you in a good mood, and from here on out it's up to you.

The inspection began. As he made the rounds of the paintings, surrounded by artists, he would look first at a painting, then at its author, trying to determine by the expression on the man's face what his attitude to his own painting was. Not in respect to its artistic worth, of course, but exclusively on the ideological plane. That is, was he being too cheeky, if the painting had a satirical nuance? Had he been carried away by harmful innovations or dangerous alien ideas, which were, however, ludicrous in their insignificance?

Abesalomon Nartovich had three formulas, which determined the degree of censure in his attitude toward an artist's work.

According to the first, he thought the painting was interesting but might be grist for the wrong mill.

According to the second, he thought the painting was not devoid of interest but was certainly grist for the wrong mill.

According to the third, he thought—it's terrifying even to say what he thought. In any case, there could be no question of any mill here, not even a hostile one.

It was most often the first formula that led to a restaurant development of the topic. The second did not exclude it, in principle, while the third—well, not only did it not lead to a restaurant development, it might be the beginning of a development in the exact opposite direction. The only virtue of the third formula was that it had been used rather rarely in recent years.

So, Abesalomon Nartovich would look at a painting attentively, with his eyes screwed up; then, just as attentively but without screwing up his eyes, at the artist himself. Thus several times, back and forth, forth and back, and everything would become clear.

The artists had agreed not to prompt Abesalomon Nartovich in any way, not to anticipate his opinion, so that the voice of fate would be revealed in its pure form. Once Abesalomon Nartovich had declared himself, they could support him or even object, up to a certain limit of course. Since no one knew exactly what the limit was, they usually objected without reaching it.

If Abesalomon Nartovich said of a painting that it was well conceived, but objectively he thought it might be grist for the wrong mill, then someone would usually raise the objection: "Well, after all, Abesalomon Nartovich, that depends on how you look at it."

"Then look at it from where we sit, look at it from the standpoint of today's interests . . ."

Young artists, especially, took advantage of Abesalomon Nartovich's weakness, and the older ones sometimes sinned as well. It's no secret that in order to dine in the luxurious company of a patron of the muses the artists sometimes purposely feigned spiritual doubts. They looked down when he gazed at them, sighed heavily when he screwed up his eyes (as if preparing an instrument) and aimed them at a painting.

"No, my boy, you're a little bit off . . . ," Abesalomon Nartovich would begin. If he had trouble seizing on a critical principle, the artist himself would supply something to this effect: "No, well, I was trying to polemicize with Salvador . . . um . . . Dali, you know, Abesalomon Nartovich, but I must have gotten carried away . . ."

"I see, I see," Abesalomon Nartovich would agree benevolently, "and that's fine, we're all for polemics . . . But why did you supply him with a forum?"

"No, but you see . . ." The artist would hem and haw. "I was trying to do a parody of his method . . ."

"Back to square one!" Abesalomon Nartovich says in surprise. "Go ahead and parody, but why provide a forum? Look what he's doing there!"

Now the artist raises his eyes, as if seeing his own work anew, as if he has suddenly spotted Salvador Dali leaning out like a little devil, ranting and raving from behind his painting as from behind a lectern.

"You think you've ridiculed him?" Abesalomon Nartovich continues. "That's all he needed, to get a forum . . . Now here he is, shouting to the whole exhibition from your painting. You just try and shout from a painting of his! Would he let you in? Like hell he would!"

At moments like this, you could inconspicuously align yourself with the derelict artist by joining him in some retort, in order to make the stream of Abesalomon Nartovich's criticism spread and divide, its two branches encompassing both of you on your islet of barren error.

"All right, let's go have dinner, we can talk there." At last, the longed-for phrase. Abesalomon Nartovich would sometimes give the second opponent a cursory glance and add, "You too."

Things didn't always go that smoothly, of course. Occasionally, Abesalomon Nartovich would spend a long time shifting his gaze from the painting to the artist and back, and everything about him would express agonizing uncertainty. The problem here was that he liked the painting, a fact not in accord with the artist's guilty, downcast countenance. Unable to correlate these two mutually exclusive impressions, he sought an exit, shifting his gaze back and forth from the artist to the painting. The remarkable thing was that once he had a good impression of a painting he stubbornly defended it, despite the artist's suspicious look.

"But in my opinion it's not bad," he would say in an undertone, and look at the artist, trying to buck him up or else understand what was getting him down. The artist maintained a guilty silence or timidly shrugged his shoulders.

Abesalomon Nartovich would throw another energetic glance at the painting, trying to penetrate its inmost essence and find its secret flaws.

"No, it's really not bad," Abesalomon Nartovich would repeat confidently. Still more confidently, as if he had finally overwhelmed his inner critic, as if by his own example he would show the artist the path from doubt to confidence, he added, "It's just a good, strong piece of work."

"What is it, do you think we're against courage?" he would cry suddenly, guessing at the cause of the artist's low spirits.

"It's not that . . ." The artist would hem and haw, not knowing how else to influence Abesalomon Nartovich's critical sensibility.

"Don't be afraid of your own courage," Abesalomon Nartovich lectured joyfully. "You can be sure that we're always for good courage."

Firmly squeezing the artist's arm to signify support for good courage, he walked on, confident that he had restored the artist's inner peace.

There you have him, our patron of the muses, Abesalomon Nartovich, or simply Nartovich, as the artists affectionately call him behind his back. Now that you can more or less picture him, I'll go on with my story about Andrey and his painting "Trio in Blue Mackintoshes."

When the black car, purring softly, stopped a few meters short of the intersection, and Abesalomon Nartovich turned slightly to beckon Andrey with his finger, I said quietly, trying not to move my lips, "Don't forget, you're with me."

Andrey made no answer, and we started quickly for the car. Abesalomon Nartovich was leaning back in the seat. His magnificent big hand stuck out of the car window, resting majestically.

Suddenly my mouth puckered painfully, and I could just feel myself dipping the wing of a chicken *tabaka* into fiery *satsivi* and then putting a tangy piece of cress in my mouth and tossing in a nice wet radish as well (it had to be wet), and I could hear myself answering him, rumbling, "Well, after all, it depends on how you look at it, Abesalomon Nartovich—"

"Then look at it from the standpoint of today's interests," Abesalomon Nartovich would say. With a glance around the neighboring tables, he would add, "All right, let's drink to the correct line."

"With pleasure, Abesalomon Nartovich, with pleasure . . ."

No sooner had that scene flashed through my mind than we were already standing by the car. Abesalomon Nartovich slowly turned his head, looked at Andrey for a few seconds; without turning his head, gave me a cursory glance as if taking cognizance of the bounds of the contaminated area, in case he had to declare a quarantine; looked back at Andrey and slowly spread his hands in a gesture expressing his catastrophic bewilderment.

"Libel," he said, and the car drove off. His hand—which had stuck out of the window slightly and was still sticking out—now dropped, as if in majestic impotence to help an apostate.

"Is that all?" was all I could say, looking after the departing car.

"To be continued elsewhere," Andrey explained grimly. Then he glanced at me with a nervous laugh. "Don't forget, you're with me!"

Very soon afterward, two articles in succession appeared in *Red Subtropics* two days apart. The painting was referred to only as "Trio in Notorious Mackintoshes." It was as if someone had laid a taboo on any mention of the color of the mackintoshes, in order to reduce the painting's potential for public damage.

As soon as the press began panning it, four men turned up who recognized their own likeness in the figures in the painting and brought suit on this basis for personal insult. Incidentally, Tsurtsumia was not among them.

He himself had never insisted that he looked like the figure in the painting, however; others had foisted this resemblance on him. He himself had no comment and did not even come to the exhibition. Admittedly, he sent his wife.

Well then, this quartet lodged their complaint and even hired a lawyer, a local fellow we knew, who later told us all about it. The interesting thing is that one of them tried to get Tsurtsumia to take part in the suit. He went over one evening when Tsurtsumia was relaxing on the veranda of his mansion, with his feet thrust in an ice bucket, as usual, to boost his mental function while considering commercial operations. Tsurtsumia refused to take part, pleading that he could not stand the courts, they were nothing but a spectacle.

Three of the four plaintiffs were residents of our city, and the fourth came from an outlying district. He proved to be a tea-factory manager from Endursk. The tea-factory manager had not even seen the painting, but his relatives had written him about it. They said this, that, and the other, and while you're sitting at your tea factory an artist here has been misrepresenting you. The manager had no comment at first, merely telephoned his relatives to ask who the other two men in the painting were. The relatives replied that they didn't know the others, and asked what he had in mind.

"I've got something in mind, but it's not for the telephone," he told his relatives sadly, and hung up.

What the tea-factory manager had in mind was that all this was the doing of the district committee (as he later told the lawyer), and they were about to ease him out of his job. Since art exhibitions were never held in Endursk, he had apparently decided they were like the satirical display boards arranged in many cities. That was probably why he was interested in the other two figures in the painting; he may have thought they were the managers of other tea factories, and wanted to find out exactly which ones.

It seems that by the time our exhibition opened he had already had six or seven reprimands from the district committee for his machinations with tea. These innocent machinations consisted of the following. Let's say a kolkhoz arrives at the factory to deliver first-quality tea. Suppose they bring ten tons. The factory determines that eight tons meet first-quality standards, but two are second quality. The kolkhoz has no time to argue and knows it would be a losing proposition (they'd find fault with something else); the rejected tea may spoil soon, which would be even worse. So the kolkhoz goes along.

Another kolkhoz, being short on first-quality tea, is glad—for suitable recompense, of course—to transfer these two tons to its own account. In exchange it will hand over the requisite quantity of second-quality tea. This kind of deal had become so common that when representatives of several kolkhozes brought tea, they went ahead and struck the bargain themselves, at their own expense, so to speak. Get such-and-so many tons rejected, they said, but do it so that some of it comes our way, we're people too.

In brief, it's done, but the Party organs do not approve.

"The state doesn't lose anything by it," the tea-factory manager said in self-defense at one of the district committee offices.

"That's why we're warning you, not putting you away," the district committee replied instructively. "Collective farmers are people too . . ."

So the tea-factory manager arrived to sue the artist, and look at the painting while he was at it. But the painting was no longer at the exhibition.

On one hand, this gladdened him, but on the other, it piqued his curiosity. He showed up at Andrey's house to have a look at his portrait, and perhaps find out who the others were while he was at it. Andrey said that he did not know him and would not show him any painting.

"You show me or I'll sue," he threatened Andrey.

Andrey went savage and shoved the tea-factory manager out the door.

"I don't care, you'll show it to me in court!" the latter managed to shout.

At the bar association, where he went to hire a lawyer, he became acquainted with the other three plaintiffs; either they bumped into each other there, or the lawyer introduced them. There was nothing he could do but join up with the trio, especially since they showed him photographs of the painting, admittedly in black and white, but good-sized enlargements nonetheless. Then and there, right on the spot, he recognized himself.

When the lawyer really got into the case (a good guy, everybody knows him), he discovered that it would be hard to prosecute the artist for insulting his countrymen. It turned out all three of the city-dwellers who claimed an insulting likeness actually claimed to look like just one of the three figures in blue mackintoshes.

In itself this coincidence would not have mattered much if the men suffering from the likeness had looked like each other, which does happen in life, of course. But as ill luck would have it the three were completely unlike each other, and at the same time each of them individually looked like one and the same figure in the painting.

"Who'd have guessed he'd stoop to such malice," they said, apropos of that.

The lawyer warned his clients that the artist's defense would certainly capitalize on this perfidious circumstance.

"What can we do?" they asked the lawyer, exasperated at the unexpected obstacle presented by their own appearance. At that, as the lawyer tells it, each of them looked the other two up and down as if they were more to blame for what had happened.

The lawyer said that the best thing would be for two of the three to drop the charge. The third should join forces with the tea-factory manager (fortunately, he looked like the second blue-mackintoshed figure), win over Tsurtsumia (if he looked like the third), and bring a joint suit for insulting three independent persons.

No one could remember what Tsurtsumia looked like. Even the man who had gone to him to suggest that he take part in the suit could not remember.

"Tsurtsumia won't agree to it," he said. "He doesn't like courts in general—"

"How do you mean, he won't agree?" the tea-factory manager said in surprise. "We'll make him."

That evening they went to Tsurtsumia's house. The latter received them sitting on the veranda of his mansion with his feet buried in the ice bucket. He always sat there. After listening to the suggestion about the joint complaint all over again, he asked, "Do you know Sulfidin?"

"That depends," his guests said in surprise. "Sulfidin the medicine, or the gas-station manager's son, the one they call Sulfidin?"

"The medicine," the laconic Tsurtsumia explained. "The one that certain organisms can't stand, you know?"

"We know," the guests said in surprise.

"Well, just as certain organisms can't stand Sulfidin, I can't stand the courts," Tsurtsumia confessed to the sickliness of his own organism.

After that, despite their best efforts to win him over, he firmly stood his ground. True, to soften the refusal he invited the comrades in misfortune, together with their lawyer, to stay for a drink and a bite to eat. They accepted the invitation in the hope of winning Tsurtsumia over during the session at table.

But during the session at table, not only did they fail to win Tsurtsumia over, the whole thing ended in total catastrophe. From working on Tsurtsumia, the three city-dwellers switched to their own problem and began trying to determine which of them would appear in court. They decided that it should be the one who looked most like the figure in the painting. Here it became clear that each of them considered himself least like the figure, which led to mutual jibes and even insults.

At first the lawyer succeeded in rescuing the case by decisively cutting off the whole city group. He said they should all withdraw the charge, he would act through the tea-factory manager, as being the bravest man. (He understood that no matter how much you empty from the purse of a tea-factory manager, you never reach the bottom.)

"I'll take him on in single combat," the tea-factory manager said. Snatching the photographs of the painting, which the others were still holding in their sticky hands, he put them away in his briefcase.

That's what he said, but then he apparently took a dislike to it all, and he began to pout. He pouted and pouted, and then at the end of the evening he up and said that if that's the way it was he wouldn't go to court either, they had lured him to Tsurtsumia's for nothing—although no one had lured him to Tsurtsumia's.

In the end, as the lawyer tells it, they all quarreled and went home, blaming it all on Tsurtsumia. Completely reassured, the tea-factory manager went back to Endursk that very night—forgetting, incidentally, to return the photographs, or perhaps intentionally not returning them, to their rightful owners.

As radio and television commentators justly say, thus does every union created on the basis of a rotten ideology disintegrate. And thus the lawyer spoke of it, once he got over his disappointment at losing the tea-factory manager. I don't know if I mentioned that he's a local fellow; as a shirtless little kid he used to run around the beach with us, and now it's terrifying to think what kind of cases he handles.

The last trace of public indignation over the "Blue Mackintoshes" emerged at a regional builders' conference, where the chief of a certain Building and Erection Directorate said that it was very hard to fulfill the plan when artists, instead of helping the builders, mocked the leadership in front of the workers by representing them as idlers wandering by the sea for days at a time in blue mackintoshes.

At that point, fortunately for Andrey, a certain powerful official exploded and gave the builder a scathing rebuke, pointing out that the painting had appeared at the exhibition only that summer, but this was the third year his building directorate had not fulfilled its plan.

The powerful comrade's speech was interpreted as a stern hint that the uproar surrounding the name of Andrey Tarkilov must cease. The uproar promptly ceased, and Andrey received several good commissions. Subsequently it turned out that the powerful comrade had not intended any such hint, he had simply revealed the true situation, which was plain enough already.

Then, as they say, Andrey hit the jackpot. A month after the uproar over the "Blue Mackintoshes" ceased, Andrey's painting "Tea Harvester at Rest; or, A Sweaty Noonday in Colchis" (this was the one he had painted out in the country) was chosen by a Moscow commission for an All-Union exhibition.

True, on the way to Moscow the commission somehow lost the painting's subtitle, but that was not important now. Several favorable reviews of the painting came out in the central press, but that happened much later, in the winter.

Our own paper, however, gave it a big write-up the minute we learned that Andrey's painting had been picked for the All-Union exhibition, since we had on our hands a guaranteed hint that the uproar over "Three Mackintoshes" must cease.

Avtandil Avtandilovich wanted the write-up to show (and it did!) that he knew how to take a hint, especially if it was stern; besides, just in case, he was protecting himself against any possible reproach for having persecuted a talented artist. That sort of thing has happened too, although rarely.

The write-up was done by a certain stupid but nimble staffer who was able to slant his own views to fit all these complex tasks of Avtandil Avtandilovich's by pretending to lavish praise on an illicit artist, as if one could praise something illicit.

By the way, our public (which is sensitive like nobody else to the whispers of the subconscious and the subtext) immediately noticed that this write-up was longer, by a quarter of a half-page column, than both critical articles together. Moreover, mention was also made of "Trio in Blue Mackintoshes." True, it was mentioned as an unfortunate experiment, but its harmfulness seemed slightly ennobled by the reflected light of later fame. In any case, it was referred to by its own name again, not, as before, as the "Notorious Mackintoshes."

Apart from all this, there may have been another factor involved. It was now the height of summer and no one was wearing mackintoshes, especially navy blue ones; the theme itself seemed to have lost topicality. In any case, the title of the painting was fully and finally rehabilitated.

As everyone knows, under the complex conditions of contemporary life not all truths, even simple ones, can be expressed directly, lest our foreign ill-wishers use them against us. For this reason we are all good at reading (or think we're good at reading) the language of allusions, the nods and winks of typographical signs.

It need hardly be said that the write-up on Andrey's painting was interpreted not only as a bright spot in his personal fate, but also as a phenomenon with far-reaching optimistic implications.

I, of course, did not particularly believe there was any connection between the length of the two critical articles and the last write-up. Nevertheless, just for laughs, I got out the file and compared them. It turned out to be true. Any way you figured it, the write-up was a quarter-column longer than the two critical articles together. Was it by chance? Who knows . . .

The author himself might have fulfilled Avtandil Avtandilovich's secret desire without even suspecting it. If the editor received a write-up just a bit shorter than, or even the same length as, the two critical articles, he might have called in the author and said, "You know, this part here ought to be expanded."

Or if something needed to be cut, well, no one would ever raise any question. In any case, it became clear that Andrey's fall from grace had been forgiven, with encouraging implications for the future. Right after all this, we went off to the mountains.

Now I would like to pause for breath and continue the story in calmer tones. The problem is that I didn't mean to tell about all that, I only meant to share our travel adventures.

But what happened? The minute I took a notion to introduce my traveling companions in a few concise lines, I suspected myself of attempting to cover up the "Blue Mackintoshes" incident. No, I told myself, I'm not trying to cover up the incident, it's just irrelevant here. To prove to myself that I wasn't trying to cover anything up, I decided to present the excerpts from the comment book. Well, and then the rest came tumbling out of its own accord.

My point is that you can't make any promises; tell the story as it wants to be told. What happens to promises, after all? As soon as you promise, let's say, to be blunt about everything, you're immediately attacked by doubts: "Should I? What am I, nastier than everyone else?" And so on.

If you promise to be concise, similar considerations arise. Conciseness is fine, you think, but what if by being concise you miss something really important? And who knows what's really important? Then you resolve to be concise, but not skip anything that might turn out to be really important later. And so, I return to the beginning of my story, in order to move decisively forward, with no backward glances into the past.

After a week's vacation in the mountains, then, after the icy koumiss, after the smoky evening campfires, after long and unsuccessful hunters' rambles over the rocky summits of the passes, we sat on the trunk of the old beech tree and waited for a ride, warming ourselves in the sunshine, now and then exchanging needless, trivial remarks—we had talked ourselves out over the week.

From time to time Svanian loggers walked by. They were on their way home from the forest to their summer camp, which had been set up near the little river. Some had axes on their shoulders, others carried power saws. They greeted us when they got near, then looked us over attentively as they walked by.

I was struck that for some reason they gave me a friendlier greeting than the others. But then when one of them walked around and inspected me from behind, I realized what it was. They were not greeting me so much as my carbine, which stuck up behind my shoulders. Since the others had no weapons, only Andrey had a small caliber rifle, the respectful attention to my person was fully justified.

Finally some men appeared over by the trucks. Two of them climbed on and began cinching up the cables on the logs that lay in the beds. The rest of the men—there were eight in all—gave them advice from below. Judging by the disproportionate loudness of their voices, they had all had quite a bit to drink. In a few minutes two of them detached themselves from the rest and headed toward us.

One of them, the younger, was wearing quilted trousers and an old cowboy shirt with rolled-up sleeves. He was unshaven, stocky, and frankly drunk, which was noticeable from a distance. The other was small and spare. He wore boots, wide breeches, and a tight black tunic, buttoned all the way up. He carried himself stiffly and had a military air about him. In his hand he clasped a shiny little ax, reminiscent of the ones housewives use to chop up meat and bones.

"Hello, comrades," he said in a somewhat plaintive voice, as he and his comrade halted near us. We stood up to meet them and shook hands with both of them. For several moments he inspected us, fighting off waves of drunkenness, his membranous eyelids blinking and knots of muscle pulsing on his spare, taut little face.

A wan greeting like that is usually followed by a demand for documents, but he did not demand anything, merely sat down beside me. Perhaps because of the carbine he considered me the senior member of our group, which was not the case—Kotik was senior in both age and rank.

Snuffling good-naturedly, the other Svan, the one who was frankly drunk, squatted on his haunches in front of us, apparently in order to communicate with everyone at once. He had the heavy bull-like head of a boozer and bulging blue eyes. From time to time his head fell on his chest, and each time he raised it he looked around at us with an unvarying childlike curiosity. Each time he raised his head he seemed surprised all over again, unable to comprehend how we had appeared before him.

"Where would you be from?" the Svan in the black tunic asked in the same plaintive voice, inspecting us all with a sidelong glance.

"We're from the city, and this comrade is from Moscow," Kotik said amiably and distinctly, his voice indicating that his reserves of amiability were boundless.

"What were you doing here?" he asked in plaintive amazement, half-turning. One hand rested on his knee, the other—the one nearer to me—rested on the handle of the little ax. Now it was clear that he was really smashed, but controlling himself with all his might. The most dangerous drunks of all are the ones that try and look sober.

"We were visiting some kolkhoz shepherds, good friends of ours," Kotik said, still just as clearly and peaceably.

"Named for?" Black-Tunic asked suddenly, blinking his membranous birdlike eyelids. Everything became still.

"What does named for mean?" Kotik asked in the stillness.

"Named for means named for," Black-Tunic repeated firmly, inspecting us with a sidelong glance. The second Svan looked at me and made signs to me. I could not understand what he meant by these drunken signs and nods, and I shrugged my shoulders in reply, just in case.

"I don't understand you," Kotik said, insisting on his modest right to answer only clear questions.

"You've got several kolkhozes here in the mountains," Bug-Eyes explained finally, swaying on his haunches. "That's why he's asking named for . . ."

"Oh, the kolkhoz," Kotik said gladly, and looked over at Andrey.

"Mikoyan," Andrey supplied, barely concealing his irritation. The whole incident was beginning to irritate him.

"Correct," Black-Tunic agreed. With the grimace of a man who knows more than he's telling, he added, "Don't be offended, this is necessary—"

"Of course!" Kotik exclaimed.

"And what do you do?" I asked my neighbor.

"I'd be deputy forest warden," he said importantly, and started to unbutton the breast pocket of his tunic.

"Of course, don't bother!" Kotik said, and put out his hand to stop him.

"I forgot my cap back at my comrade's," he said, as his hand suddenly discovered a rather noticeable crease left on his forehead by a cap. It was not clear whether the crease reminded him that he didn't have his service cap, or the mention of his appointment made him remember an essential part of his uniform.

The situation was clearly becoming less tense. Now the deputy forest warden was not leaning on his ax as on the hilt of a sword, he had simply laid it across his lap. Apparently he had relaxed his self-control and become drowsy. He ceased to stroke the crease left on his forehead by the cap. Propping his elbow on his knee, he drooped his head on his palm and dozed.

As if he had been waiting for this instant, the second Svan stepped up his idiotic nodding and winking. Finally I caught on.

"The carbine?" I asked.

"Sell it," he nodded joyfully.

"It's not for sale," I said.

"Then let's deal," he said suddenly, using the city word.

"No," I said, trying not to irritate him. "I can't."

"I'll give you a German submachine gun," he whispered hastily, "because it drives me wild to look at those neat little Russian carbines."

"No," I said, trying not to irritate him.

"Let me see it," he said, and put out a hand. I sighed and unslung the carbine.

"What do you want with a carbine if you have a submachine gun?" I said, trying to elevate his submachine gun at the expense of my carbine.

He worked the bolt and peered into the barrel.

"A submachine gun isn't so convenient for hunting, it's not accurate at long range," he said, and looked up. "Is it loaded?"

"The cartridges are way over there, in my pack," I said firmly. Evidently he sensed this; he aimed at something and clicked the trigger.

"I love these Russian carbines," he said, reluctantly returning the carbine. I took the carbine and slung it on my shoulder. I felt relieved that everything had ended so well.

"How much does it cost to hire a diver?" he said suddenly.

"Why do you need a diver?" I asked.

"I know a lake," he said simply. "There are German weapons at the bottom. I want a diver."

We burst out laughing, and the fellow sank into a reverie again. At that instant, Black-Tunic raised his head and began saying something to his countryman. The Svan who was sitting on his haunches defended himself good-naturedly, glancing in our direction as if we were allies. Black-Tunic gradually wound down and concluded in a tone of petty administrative irritation.

"Don't wag your tongue," he said finally, in Russian, and picked up the ax from his knees.

"I won't even ask," the Svan answered this time. Turning to Kotik, he asked, "Does a diver have the right to come up here?"

"We wouldn't want to deceive you," Kotik replied virtuously, "but we don't know anything about these things."

"What are you saying, *katso!*" Black-Tunic flared. "How could a diver come here? A diver is a state employee. A diver has no right to leave the sea. Who do you think you are—a district committee, a military commissar, a village soviet?''

"I want a diver for one day," the young Svan said, paying not the slightest attention to this stern tirade. "I'd fetch him and take him back myself, like he was a government minister."

The deputy forest warden suddenly attacked from the other direction. "Tell us, what lake are they in?"

"Uh-uh," the young Svan drawled slyly. He waggled a thick finger at the bridge of his nose. "That's my secret. I'm not telling anyone but the diver."

"I'll book you," Black-Tunic said. Sadly shaking his head, he looked at the blade of the ax as if reading on it the relevant article of the law.

"Tell me," I asked him, taking a lighter tone, "what's your little ax for?"

As a matter of fact, I probably wouldn't have asked him about it if I hadn't noticed a sort of metal seal on the butt of the ax. I wanted to know what he actually did with it. Did he mark a dead tree with a blow of the butt, say, or make notches of some sort? Or was it merely a symbol of his authority over the forest?

The moment I said it, his mouth compressed in a determined streak, his birdlike eyelids stopped still. I sensed that I had committed the worst diplomatic blunder of my life. It was as if, during an audience with a king, one were to suddenly flick a finger against his crown and ask, "What's this thing for, old chap?"

He got slowly to his feet, walked a few paces off, and turned around. Pressing the ax to his hip, he screamed suddenly, "Citizens, your documents!"

"Comrade, you misunderstood him," Kotik said. Getting to his feet, he started toward him with an apologetic smile.

"Citizens, your documents!" Black-Tunic screamed again, and even took a step backward lest he permit any personal contact with Kotik. With that he almost stepped on the other Svan. In any case, he knocked him off his haunches, and he sat down on the ground, throwing up his hands in dim bewilderment: Look what the authorities are doing to me! What have I done to deserve this?

Even the Svans over by the trucks heard his voice and fell silent for a few moments.

"Geno," one of them shouted, and evidently asked what was the matter. From the ground, Geno looked up at the small angry figure of the assistant forest warden and said something to the effect that he was a tough customer.

This really was a stupid turn of events. Black-Tunic meant business. I noticed that the knuckles on the fist gripping his ax had turned white.

Of the four of us, only Kotik and Volodya had documents. Volodya was already digging in his pack. Kotik was proffering his document. It was a red booklet—his ID as a lecturer for the Party's regional committee. In difficult situations it usually had a good effect, especially if you focused on the Party's regional committee and didn't pay too much attention to the fact that he was only a lecturer, and untenured at that.

The man in the black tunic held the booklet in his hand for a moment, glanced from the photograph to the original several times, and returned it to its owner. Evidently it had made a good impression on him.

"And they're your escort?" he asked, with a gesture that made us all into a unit.

"Yes, they're my escort," Kotik said with a smile. He put the booklet in his pocket.

The man in the black tunic slowly inspected each member of Kotik's escort. Manifest in this slowness was his respect for his own office. Volodya, standing, held his passport out to him, but he did not take it. Andrey remained seated, sprawling somewhat picturesquely, staring at the assistant forest warden with a half-scornful grin.

"License for the carbine," he said mildly, when his gaze reached me. My heart skipped a beat. I did not have a license for the carbine. I had borrowed it from a relative, the former chicf of the city police.

"I don't have a license," I said.

"You don't?" He batted his membranous eyelids, refusing to understand me.

"The carbine isn't mine," I said. "I borrowed it."

"I've got no way of knowing," he exclaimed, encouraged. "Maybe you did borrow it, maybe you killed someone, maybe you took it from—"

"*I* know," Kotik interrupted. "He borrowed it from his relative, the former chief of the city police."

"These Russian carbines," thc second Svan said, looking up at us, "I love better than anything in the world, I swear by my children."

"I've got no way of knowing. I'm going to confiscate it!" the man in the black tunic cried.

"Come now, comradc," Kotik said pacifically. "How can you, what will we tell his relative when we get back?"

"I've got no way of knowing, especially if it's a *former* chief of police," he said, leaving a little loophole for more extensive information nevertheless.

"One good Russian carbine," the second Svan said enthusiastically, "I respect more than two German submachine guns."

"Don't wag your tongue!" Black-Tunic shouted, to which the other paid not the slightest attention.

"His relative," Kotik said—Andrey writhed at this—"is a man respected in the city, and he will not be pleased to learn that you have confiscated his carbine."

"Ha! Respected!" Black-Tunic exclaimed, and clasped his ax. "If he's respected, why was he fired?"

"He wasn't fired, he retired on his pension," Kotik said.

"I don't care," Black-Tunic said, stiffening again. "I demand that you hand over the carbine for determination of ownership."

"Don't you do it," Andrey said in Abkhazian. "You won't get it back."

"I won't give you the carbine," I said, very firmly because I did not feel firm inside. "It wasn't you who gave it to me."

"I detain you, along with the carbine!" he snapped, and raised his damn ax again. What had possessed me to say that! If I'd kept quiet about his ax, nothing would have happened. I shrugged my shoulders.

The trucks started up and began slowly backing out to the road. The Svans walked behind the trucks as if goading them on.

"It's time for us to go," Andrey said decisively. He stood up.

"Wait," the assistant forest warden ordered, but evidently he had not anticipated such decisiveness.

"Take it easy, Andrey," Kotik snapped in Abkhazian.

"We're going too," Black-Tunic said suddenly. He ran his hand through his hair in some perplexity.

"That's up to you," Andrey said coldly, and walked on. Burly, long-armed, of medium height—just now he looked like a bear cub.

Black-Tunic began asking the young Svan to do something—as we could guess, to fetch the forgotten service cap from the house where they had been feasting. The house, visible from here, stood on the far side of the river, about a twenty-minute walk.

The young Svan was just getting up from the ground. As he straightened up he suddenly clutched his back and let out a loud cry, as if from a sudden attack of lumbago, perhaps brought on by the assistant forest warden's request, perhaps unrelated to it. In either case, the gesture indicated the impracticability of this small request.

We moved toward the trucks. The truck drivers got out and waited for us, along with the other Svans.

"But I'm not taking that gun away." The forest warden gestured more peaceably at Andrey's back. It struck me that the debacle with the service cap had improved his manners somewhat. "Why not? Because a carbine is a military weapon."

"But up here you run after the deer with submachine guns," Andrey said, turning around.

"The minute we discover any, we take them away!" Black-Tunic shouted at him.

"We know who you take them from," Andrey said, without turning around.

"Don't pick a fight, Andrey," Kotik yelled in Abkhazian.

"Screw his mother," Andrey replied, also in Abkhazian, without turning around.

"Hand over the carbine or I'll detain you at the Rural Area Soviet until ownership is established," Black-Tunic said with renewed firmness. Apparently he had already forgotten the debacle with the service cap, or else he was inspired by the proximity of the other Svans. We approached the trucks.

"How can you," Kotik objected quietly, giving him to understand that there was no point in letting this obscene, although possibly accidental, misunderstanding reach the ears of the others. "We won't leave our comrade—"

"That's up to you," Black-Tunic said loudly, as if rejecting by the power of his voice the idea that the misunderstanding was obscene, let alone accidental. "Someone go get the owner of the carbine."

That was the limit! The young Svan, gesturing enthusiastically at my carbine, told the others the gist of the story. Several Svans immediately set up a clamor, addressing Black-Tunic, and it seemed to me their clamor was benevolent in respect to me.

But now Black-Tunic entered into an argument with them, from time to time darting vicious birdlike glances at me, after which he directed the Svans' attention to his ax, which I had allegedly managed to defile by my question. The Svans inspected the ax, seeking hidden traces of defilement.

Of all the Svans, only one tall old man with a twisted mouth (from being hit by lightning, as they explained to me later) gave him immediate support. He darted even more vicious glances at me than Black-Tunic did. This was the owner of the house everyone had just visited.

Later, on the road, I found out why he behaved so viciously toward me. It seems the Svans who live here almost at the edge of the alpine meadows—and he came from one of these few families—have an ancient grudge against our shepherds.

The alpine meadows, to which several of our lowland kolkhozes drive their cattle, are considered disputed territory by these Svans, because they themselves live right here, and the meadows are very convenient for them.

They consider them disputed territory because during the war no one drove cattle here from the kolkhozes, naturally, and after the war, for quite a long time, there were no cattle to drive. By the time the kolkhozes recovered, the Svans had gotten used to thinking of these meadows as their own. The first year the matter almost came to a knife-fight. Now they had reconciled themselves, but the hostility remained.

I mention this in such detail because, if it had not been for this old man, who could not endure the lowland kolkhoz shepherds and their guests, or if he had not been hosting the other Svans all day, the scales might have tipped in my favor. A small but damaging role may also have been played by the lightning bolt that by some mystical chance had once flown into his mouth and perhaps hardened it forever. In any case, he had been host to all my well-wishers, and in the end they subsided and dropped the argument.

True, we were all going the same direction, and this brought us together temporarily. Kotik, to all appearances, was having considerable success working on a huge Svan, one of those who had defended me and then backed down. Kotik got into the same truck with him and shouted to me, "We'll think of something on the way . . ."

They seated me, as an honored criminal, in the first truck; the rest of my friends settled themselves in the second. The two Svans who had first approached us settled themselves on the running boards to the left and the right of the cab. The Russian-carbine enthusiast stood on the left, and the keeper of the mountains—now my keeper too—stood on my side.

When they were seating us, I suggested that he sit in the cab, in the dim hope that this would drive him to a moral impasse. In spite of my efforts at persuasion, he refused with firm dignity to climb into the cab. He was not about to let anyone trap him in mutual magnanimity.

"How could I, you're a guest," he said importantly, letting me know that the observance of custom is a continuation of the observance of law, and vice versa.

I unslung the carbine from my shoulder, climbed into the cab, and took my place, standing the carbine between my feet. I threw off my half-empty pack and pushed it into a corner of the seat.

The truck began to move. Several Svans, led by the old man that had caught the lightning in his mouth, were standing ahead of the truck. My keeper shouted something to the old man, I think he was asking him to look after his service cap until he returned. The old man did not reply, and we drove on.

My situation was complicated by the fact that I had not been planning to go all the way to the city. I had planned to go only as far as the Narzan spring where Uncle Sandro was vacationing. He and I had agreed to meet there, and I meant to spend several days taking the waters in Uncle Sandro's company. The Rural Area Soviet was much farther down than the spring, and even if I managed, with the help of my friends, to get free of my keeper there, it would still be a nuisance to trek back up to the spring in the middle of the night.

We moved slowly through the forest. The sun had not yet set. Its rays gilded the leaves of beeches and chestnuts that had been touched by the early mountain fall, and sparkled on the rustproof green of the firs.

The fresh scent of mildly fermenting leaves flew into the cab from time to time, as if to compensate for the rather fetid stink of *araki* that emanated from my escort whenever the truck jolted and his head poked into the cab.

The truck labored along over the uneven track, rocky in some places, criss-crossed with bare tree roots in others. The enormous weight in back sometimes rocked the body of the truck so hard that I thought it was about to tip over and crush one of the men standing on the running boards. The driver kept braking and shifting gears.

My keeper was obviously exhausted by the rocking and jolting. He looked at me with the beseeching gaze that people have when they feel like vomiting. A couple of times, when I met his eyes, I suggested that he take my place, but he refused, half-closing his membranous eyelids like a dying swan.

His gaze grew more and more beseeching, and I began to cast imploring glances at him, to forgive me for the carbine. At first he did not understand, looking at me in some bewilderment, and helplessly closed his membranous eyelids. Then he did understand and did not forgive.

"See, I'm having a hard enough time as it is, and you're still pestering me," he said with his gaze, and helplessly closed his membranous eyelids.

"Well, what will it cost you? I won't do it again," I nagged with my gaze, after waiting for him to half-open his eyes.

"Well, see, I'm having a hard enough time as it is, and if I break the law, it'll be even harder," he explained to me with his clouded gaze, and helplessly lowered his membranous eyelids.

We emerged from the forest, and the truck started down the road between a deep chasm and the wet wall of a cliff, which had a great many little waterfalls flowing down it in fine misty sprays. When the truck went close to the wall in one place, my keeper looked up for some reason, as if he meant to greet someone up there. But there was no one to greet, and he suddenly leaned back and put his head under a stream of water. After that, every time we came to a sufficiently convenient stream he deftly leaned back and caught it on his head. From there, from under the stream, in a shining gossamer halo of mist, he succeeded in giving me a look that was both sentimental and at the same time perplexed at my surprise.

Refreshed, he shifted the ax from his right hand to his left. With the freed hand, he took a handkerchief from his pocket and began wiping his face and hair.

Holding on to the open window frame with one hand while clutching the ax in the same hand struck me as so inconvenient and even dangerous that I decided to help him.

"Give it to me, I'll hold it," I said, indicating the ax. This was partly the usual criminal craving to return to the scene of the crime, but there was also an element of calculation. By this new impertinence, after I had been sufficiently penalized for the old one, I was proving to him that even the old impertinence had not existed; in any case, there had been no malice aforethought, only a foolish puppyish curiosity.

He stopped wiping his head with his handkerchief and gave me a long, plaintive gaze, swaying and jolting with the truck the whole time but still not letting me out of his field of vision.

Then, still gazing at me, he smoothed a hand over his wet, wispy hair and transferred the ax to his right hand, where it belonged. His gaze seemed to be trying to determine whether he could name a new penalty for a repeated insult.

I began to fidget slightly, but his gaze suddenly became warmer. He seemed to have decided: No, there was no repeated insult, it was foolishness.

"Hand it into the cab," I said.

"Never mind, we're used to this," he replied, and averted his eyes.

"You know," I said, "I can't go as far as the area soviet."

"Why not?" he asked.

"I'm supposed to get off at the spring."

"I'm supposed to get off even sooner," he said.

"Why?" I asked.

"Because my home is sooner," he said. He gave me an expressive look, meaning that the service required sacrifices from him, too, not just from law-breakers.

"Someone's expecting me at the spring," I said. "He'll worry, you know."

"Fine," he replied, after a moment's thought. "You get off at the spring and leave the carbine."

"I could get off anywhere I wanted without the carbine," I said.

"That's true too," he agreed.

"What I wouldn't do for that little carbine," Geno's voice rang out from the other side of the truck. My keeper started.

"Geno lives right near the spring," he said. "He'll tell your comrade that I detained you."

"Don't bother," I said. Uncle Sandro was expecting me, of course, but not at any particular time.

"Tell me his name, he'll go," the keeper insisted.

"Sandro," I said mechanically.

"Sandro, but which Sandro?" the keeper asked in surprise.

"Sandro Chegemsky," I said.

"Sandro Chegemsky?" he repeated, almost frightenedly.

"Yes," I said, growing agitated. I sensed that the name had made an impression on everyone.

"Ooagh!" said the Svan who had been sitting silently between the driver and me. "What relation is he to you?"

"Uncle," I said.

Now all the Svans, including the driver and Geno on the other side, began clamoring back and forth like screaming eagles.

"Is that the Sandro," asked the Svan sitting beside me, "who brought Petro Ioselyani's body home in '27?"

"Yes," I said. I had dimly heard something about that story.

"Petro Ioselyani, the one the sailor killed on the seashore?"

"Yes," I said.

"No one ever avenged poor Petro," the driver sighed, keeping his eyes on the road.

"Twelve men rode to the city to burn the steamship along with the sailor," said the Svan sitting beside me.

"Why didn't they do it?" the driver asked, keeping his eyes on the road.

"They didn't have time," said the Svan sitting beside me. "The steamship put to sea."

"They had time," Geno called. "But they didn't even let them onto the dock."

"How do you know," said the Svan sitting beside me, offended. "You weren't even born."

"My father was with them," Geno said. "Petro was a relative of ours—"

"Don't wag your tongues!" my keeper yelled suddenly, sticking his head into the truck. "No one has the right to burn a steamship—no, or even a tree!"

"You mean," said the Svan sitting beside me, after waiting out the deputy forest warden's explanations, "this is the very same Sandro of Chegem?"

"The very same," I said.

"A handsome old man, has a mustache too?" specified the Svan sitting beside me.

"Yes," I said.

"Last year, when General Klimenko came here to hunt, he escorted him?" my keeper asked, peering at me.

"Yes," I said, trying not to get puffed up. Circumstances were working for us.

"General Klimenko is an excellent general," said the Svan sitting next to me.

"Like a marshal, that's what kind of general," Geno said.

"That was a big hunt," the driver said, keeping his eyes on the road.

"Comrade Sandro is a respected man," Black-Tunic said firmly.

"That goes without saying!" exclaimed the Svan sitting next to me. "They don't just pick someone off the street to escort General Klimenko."

"We know that," my keeper cut him short.

I sensed that my chances had improved. Not that the deputy forest warden's gaze had become more amicable; no, but now he was scrutinizing me more sharply and, with curiosity, discovering weak shoots of virtue under the depraved crust of my soul.

It was already getting dark. The road still went along above the chasm, where a river channel glinted faintly in the depths. The perpendicular cliff wall had been succeeded by chalky scree, showing pale in the dusk.

A truck came into view about a hundred meters ahead. It was parked by the side of the road. Several people were milling around nearby.

"There was an accident there," said the Svan sitting next to me.

"A truck went over?" I asked.

"Tongues," my keeper warned uncertainly.

"A bus," he said, paying no attention to the keeper's warning. "Thank God it was making the last run to the city, there weren't many people."

"Tongues," my keeper put in more severely.

"Were there any survivors?" I asked, lowering my voice.

"One little boy," said the man sitting next to me. "He was thrown clear of the bus and grabbed hold of a tree."

We pulled up to the site of the catastrophe, and the driver stopped. Everyone got out. The second truck had lagged slightly behind. I walked over to the precipice along with everyone else.

Down below by the water lay the bus, crushed like a tin can. One wheel, knocked off by the impact, lay on the other bank of the river.

"That's the tree the boy grabbed hold of," said the Svan who had been sitting next to me in the truck. Right on the precipice, from a crevice in the rocks, rose the rather narrow trunk of a young oak tree with a broad crown that looked like a green parachute.

"Don't, comrades, there's nothing interesting," my keeper yelled, turning around to the second truck. It had just pulled up, and the men were heading for the precipice.

Paying no attention to his warning, they all walked over to the precipice and peered down.

Along the precipice stood little cement posts, so flimsy even to look at that one good kick would demolish any one of them. The brakes had failed and the bus had plunged into the chasm, knocked down these posts like bowling pins. Things like this happen every year around here, and every time I hear about it I'm indignant, I think I'll write somewhere, chew someone out, but then somehow it gets forgotten, slips away.

"Well, how's it going?" Kotik came up to me. "Have you talked him out of it?"

"I think he's coming around," I said.

"I've been working on mine too," he said. "He's over there talking to him."

Black-Tunic was, in fact, standing next to the Svan from the second truck. The latter was saying something. My keeper was listening to him, his head bent. The little ax dangled from his involuntarily lowered hand. The law, it seemed, was exercising its legal right to a vacation.

"Listen, is it true," the big Svan shouted to me, summoning me with a jerk of his chin, "that you're related to Sandro of Chegem?"

"Yes," I said. As I walked over I could feel Andrey's grin at my back.

The big Svan, with one arm around me and the other around my keeper, took several steps, as if inviting us to a peacemaking stroll. I submitted willingly, but the little keeper, even though he did not resist the friendly gesture, stiffened and drew himself up to his full height, emphasizing his independence. The big Svan kept mildly impressing something on him while we strolled around near the trucks; my keeper listened in silence.

"Let's get going," our driver said, and everyone headed back to the trucks.

"Don't do it, *katso*, don't do it," the big Svan said in Russian when we stopped by our truck.

"We'll see!" my keeper said, and cheerfully raised the ax. The Law, it seemed, was now back on duty, this time perhaps in order to hear the mitigating circumstances. The big Svan gave me a reassuring signal—simultaneously smacking his lips and winking a roguish eye—and headed for his truck. The drivers started the trucks, but now Black-Tunic unexpectedly ran over to the third truck and began furiously herding people into it, although they were planning to get in anyhow. The driver had even started the motor and was simply waiting for us to drive by.

The passengers of that truck resisted his prodding; they stopped and argued, like all men who are prodded when they are walking in the right direction anyhow.

Finally, some of them climbed into the back, two settled themselves next to the driver, and the truck started off. Black-Tunic, walking resiliently backward and beckoning with the ax like a ballet sorcerer, guided the truck past us to the wider, unoccupied part of the road.

When the truck drove past, I noticed that the driver, in his effort to avoid bumping our truck, was not looking at the road, and especially not at the keeper with his beckoning motions.

I had not yet boarded the truck, because I had decided to have him sit down this time.

"You sit down now," I said, when he returned to the truck, pleased with the operation he had accomplished.

"Never mind, never mind." He shook his head and for some reason tossed the ax from his right hand to his left, and with the emptied hand pointed me to the cab. It could have been interpreted to mean that this was a personal, off-duty gesture.

"Never mind, we're used to it," he said, yielding.

"No," I objected firmly. "You sit down now."

"You needn't have," he said, and reluctantly climbed into the cab.

I slammed the door after him, stepped up on the running board, and tightly gripped the lower edge of the window frame. The truck started off.

It was rapidly getting dark. When the chalky scree to our right ended, and a steep slope overgrown with forest again hung over the road, it became completely dark.

The driver switched on the headlights. The brakes squealed incessantly. The whole time the motor seemed to be making a physical effort to keep from being speeded up by all its weight and plunging over the precipice. Before each new turn the driver shifted gears, and the truck stopped for an instant as if catching its breath.

Cold damp air kept flooding up from the black chasm. The farther we drove, the more sonorously the river roared at the bottom. Hollow clouds cut up the sky and recut it, but great starry scraps of sky kept opening up here and there. The stars trembled and swayed as if reflected on the surface of running water.

The truck kept listing violently, and I could not get used to it. Each time, I thought it was on the point of tipping over on its side and crushing me against the cliff wall. I would persuade myself that nothing like that could happen. But a few minutes later the truck would list again, and my body would tense, ready to leap away from catastrophe like a grasshopper, although of course there was nowhere to leap. Oddly enough, each new tilt, at the very moment of the tilt, seemed more violent, more dangerous than the last; but then when the truck righted itself, it became clear that this one had been no worse than the others.

It was uncomfortable holding on to the edge of the window frame, and my hands gradually became numb from the strain. My attention was concentrated on staying on the running board.

When the truck went along smoothly, I almost let go, to rest my hands, and then clenched them again with all my might. Besides, I was stiff all over. Only now did I appreciate the deputy forest warden's strength and tenacity.

Incidentally, he had fallen asleep almost immediately as soon as he got in the cab. The second Svan was dozing too.

At first the deputy slept leaning back against the seat, with both hands cradling the ax in his lap like a lullabied baby. Then his head began to slide into the corner of the cab; from there, drooping lower with each jolt, began to slide along the door; then, changing direction, fell out the window a little way and came to rest against my chest.

There was something touching in the trusting defenselessness with which it rested against my chest and slept, breathing peacefully and noisily. His hands still lay in his lap, tenderly cradling the ax. When a jolt made the ax slip off his knees, he pulled it up without ever waking, and reassured himself by lightly chafing his palms on its surface—the way a mother, sleeping next to her baby, will straighten the covers over him without waking up.

I tried not to move, in order not to wake him. Now I was sure that he and I would come to an understanding. My soul quivered with tenderness. I felt like patting his wispy hair, but I was afraid of waking him.

The road got better and better, and the truck no longer swayed so much. But I was finding it harder and harder to support his head leaning against my chest. I couldn't move, and by now I was very numb.

In the end I decided to shift his head to the seat back. I braced my right elbow on the inside of the door, carefully lifted his head in both hands, and, still bracing my elbow on the door, laid his head against the seat back. The head, without waking up, sighed resentfully. Thus do peasants sometimes carefully take a pumpkin in their hands, one that is drooping from the wattle fence, and shift it to a firmer spot, to keep it from breaking off under its own weight.

A few minutes later he suddenly woke up, as if jolted. He opened his eyes part way, and, without shifting position, pricked up his ears as if trying to think how and in what direction reality had changed, if at all, while he slept. His hands clenched slightly on the ax.

"Did you sleep well?" I asked, like a butler.

"Who, me?" he asked in surprise.

"Yes," I said.

"I wasn't asleep," he declared, covering a yawn with his hand. "He's the one that's asleep."

He indicated the Svan sitting beside him, who really was asleep. After that he leaned back against the seat again, precisely duplicating the pose in which he had awakened. He even closed his eyes a little. All this was supposed to mean that he hadn't been asleep, although he might have looked like a man asleep. I don't know why he had to conceal his innocent slumber. In any case, I was distressed. I decided that he was trying to inspire in me the conviction that I was firmly under his control.

A few moments later he suddenly touched the driver's shoulder, and the truck stopped. I sensed that Black-Tunic was planning to get out, and I was suddenly nervous. He indicated to me with a glance that he would not be averse to opening the door of the cab.

I stepped down on the road and stood in a humble pose. I was really very nervous. He opened the door—hunching in a proprietary way, somehow, against the cool of the night—and got out.

I continued to stand in a humble pose, aware that these moments were deciding my fate.

Suddenly I was aware that, almost without looking, with a faint wave of his hand—the ax, I had time to note, was in the other hand—he had directed me to the cab.

Trying not to create any unnecessary commotion, quickly and yet trying to avoid any thievish agility in my quickness, I slipped into the cab. Slipped in sideways, lest the unlucky carbine loom too directly before his eyes. And when I was shutting the door with a steady exultant pull, I had time to notice a most surprising thing. I had time to notice him averting his eyes from the carbine, with inscrutable slyness, as if agreeing—with it, not with me—that they had not seen each other.

He stood there a few seconds longer, waiting for the other truck. Then, illumined and even slightly blinded by its headlights, he waved the ax, giving it the order to stick with us. Our truck started off, and he vanished in the darkness.

"He lives here," said the Svan sitting next to me. He seemed to have waked up. Possibly he had even been waked by my joy.

"Yes, I understood," I nodded, feeling enormous good will toward this fact.

After the physical and nervous tension, it was uncommonly cozy and warm sitting in the cab.

"You know," said my neighbor in the cab, "he's a good fellow, and competent, but he's a little too fond of . . ." Unable to find the right word, he flourished his hand in the air, as if trying to demonstrate the outlines of the negative emanations that came from the warden's post.

"Yes, I understood," I said, feeling enormous good will toward everything, including even these negative emanations.

I told him how my keeper had tried to deny that he had been asleep. The Svan guffawed, the driver started to laugh too, although he could have laughed much earlier, when it all happened. Then again, perhaps he simply hadn't heard us.

"What are you laughing at?" Geno called suddenly from the other side.

The Svan sitting next to me repeated my story with satisfaction, and they both burst out laughing, along with the driver.

"You mean you held his head yourself, and he says he wasn't asleep?" my neighbor asked me, his hands pointing at an imagined head.

"Yes," I said.

"Ha-ha-ha," he laughed again, leaning back.

"Ha-ha-ha," the driver seconded, more reservedly.

"Ha-ha-ha," Geno rumbled from outside.

"I thought," I said, "that Svanian custom considered it a disgrace to sleep in public and that was why he denied it."

I was being sly here, of course, in order to flatter Svanian custom in a roundabout way. If I respected a dubious Svanian custom like that, then you can imagine the respect I would have for true Svanian customs.

"Geno," my neighbor shouted, "he thinks that according to our custom you can't sleep in a truck!"

"Ha-ha-ha-ha!" they all three laughed.

"I was asleep standing here!" Geno shouted.

"Svanian custom," my neighbor said seriously, "forbids you to sleep only if there's a guest in the house."

"Mmm," I nodded.

"Does Russian custom permit that?"

"No," I said, "Russian custom forbids it too."

"Geno," he shouted, "did you hear, Russian custom forbids it too!"

"I heard," Geno called back.

"Ha-ha-ha-ha!" from all three. The eternal irony of mountain-dwellers toward valley-dwellers, I thought.

"People preserve custom to stay strong," he said suddenly, when he stopped laughing, "but why does a great nation need custom? They're strong as it is."

There's something in that, I thought, even though I did not know exactly what.

"By the way, he's from a good family," my neighbor said, going back to the deputy forest warden.

"Yes?" I asked out of politeness, still thinking about what he had said.

"He'd be a Meliani, from a princely line," he said respectfully.

"Yes, a Meliani," the driver confirmed, and shifted gears.

"Yes, yes, a Meliani," Geno called from outside.

A few minutes later Geno said something to the driver, and he braked. They began to argue about something and I sensed—from the benevolent authority with which he spoke and then simply reached out and signaled piercingly several times with the klaxon—that he was moving into the role of hospitable host.

"Let's have it from the truck!" he ordered, and jumped down.

From the cab, I noticed that off to our right there was a house on high pilings, with lighted windows. The door to the house was open, and a woman was standing on the veranda looking in our direction. We got out. After riding so long it was pleasant to stand on the ground.

"You forgot your pack," the driver said. I reached into the cab and pulled out the pack that I had stuffed in the corner. I plumped it up and slung it over my shoulder. The night had grown brighter. To the east, the rim of sky over the mountain was illumined by the rising moon. The clouds had finally stopped still; they stood in mid-sky in an even row, silvered by the still unseen moon.

The woman walked across the yard with a basket in her hand. From the basket came the glint of bottle necks. Geno loudly gave orders. When the second truck arrived, he ordered them to drive it up in such a way that its headlights would light up the radiator of the first one.

Everything else happened in a few moments. He pulled a clean piece of burlap out of the basket and spread it on the radiator. Next he got out a loaf of white bread, opened a big hunting knife, and went to work with a flourish, bending over the radiator with the loaf clasped to his chest. The loaf creaked, thick slices rolled off and dropped on the burlap. Then he pulled from the basket a wheel of cheese. Voluptuously pursing his lips, he quickly shaved strips of oozing cheese onto the bread. Then, just as quickly, he began taking glasses out of the basket. While he was doing that, he gave her some sort of order, and she went swiftly back to the house, even breaking into a trot.

After pulling out three bottles and setting two of them on the fire-breathing table, he began to pour the third, tipping the bottle of cloudy *araki* straight up. The fire of hung-over inspiration lent his motions quickness and a generous symmetry. Before he could finish pouring, his wife ran up with an embarrassed smile and set the missing glasses on the radiator.

Everyone but the driver of the second truck crowded around the radiator. He had raised the hood of his own truck and was peering into the motor.

The prospect of a few drinks, as always, created a spiritual uplift. Everyone had a pleasant sense of mutual satisfaction.

"Well now," the host suggested authoritatively, and he called to the driver of the second truck. The driver refused, without turning around; but after two or three repeated invitations, he wiped his hands on an old rag and reluctantly came over to us.

"I told you," Kotik said, his eyes shining, "that it would come out all right."

"But of course!" said the big Svan, who was standing next to him. He had heard the benevolence in Kotik's words. Trying to do something nice for me himself, he added, "By the way, he comes from a princely line."

"Yes, I know," I said, and in fact I did take a pleasant satisfaction in his princely lineage. "The Meliani."

"Yes, the Meliani," Big Svan confirmed.

"Meliani, Meliani," the others whispered.

We took our glasses in hand. The drivers both took a piece of bread and cheese and began to eat, indicating that they did not plan to drink. Andrey balked, too, and his comrade from Moscow quickly pulled back the hand with which he had reached for a glass.

"What are you doing?" Kotik said quietly to him in Abkhazian. "They'll take offense."

"Please excuse me, fellows," Andrey said, turning to our host. He frowned with awkwardness. "I'm just not feeling too good."

"Drink," our host said, his voice showing that he had no time to go into details right now. Andrey took a glass. The Moscow friend nimbly followed suit.

"Your copycat makes me laugh," Kotik said in Abkhazian. He liked Andrey and was jealous of his Moscow friend.

"Please, leave him alone," Andrey answered. He frowned again.

"A toast!" our host proclaimed, cutting short all extraneous conversation.

"To a successful trip, to our acquaintanceship, to the hope that no one's offended at anyone—especially since the carbine's where it belongs," he added, for clarity.

"No offense, of course," I said, and everyone drank. Trying not to breathe, I drained the glass. Afterward I breathed out inconspicuously several times, so as to have less of the smell left in my mouth. All the same, as soon as I breathed in, I was aware of a smell as if someone had stuffed a whole elder bush into my mouth. It's that kind of drink, there's no help for it.

But, perhaps precisely for that reason, I immediately felt like eating, and the bread and cheese seemed very tasty. The host poured a second round. Both drivers took a piece of bread and cheese and went off to the other truck. Geno curtly said something to his wife; she went to the house and was back in a moment with two bottles.

"What for?" Kotik said, although his eyes had an oily glitter. The cheese was rich, and eating it with bread after that poison was pure delight. The bread was apparently something the truck drivers brought up from the city.

We raised a second glass.

"To the master of this house, to the wonderful Svanian hospitality, to the eternal hosts of these eternal mountains!" Kotik said, and drank his glass.

"Thanks, friend!" Big Svan said, and drank.

"Thanks in the name of the eternal hosts and the eternal mountains," the second Svan said, and drank.

"*Gmadlob*," the host said in Georgian, and drank.

Andrey's comrade waited until Andrey raised his glass to his mouth. Then, convinced that there was no other place for the glass to go, he drank his. Everyone drank, and everyone felt a still stronger yen for rich Svanian cheese and white bread.

Meanwhile, the full moon had appeared over these eternal mountains. Somewhat embarrassed to have caught us at this repast, she began to rise in the sky— like a certain acquaintance of mine, who, if he fails to find a seat anywhere with his own friends, shows up armed with his embarrassed smile.

"You want to go that way," Geno said, and nodded in the direction of the river. Over there beyond the river, on a gentle slope, was the Narzan town: the shanties, cabins, and tents of a makeshift peasant resort. Somewhere in the middle of the little town a campfire was winking.

We drank another glass. The good thing about *araki* is that it makes any snack seem divine. First you drink to make the food divine, and that makes even the *araki* better—but never divine.

"Say," said the Svan that had sat next to me, suddenly remembering, "is it true that the famous Endursky tamada Bichiko burst when he tried to outdrink Sandro Chegemsky?"

"So I've heard," I said. "Only it's kind of hard to believe a man could burst."

"Oh, but he could," Big Svan corroborated.

"What does Sandro himself say?" asked the Svan that had sat next to me.

"I know that story, I can tell it," Kotik said.

"Uncle Sandro says," I began, suddenly inspired and not realizing that I was getting high, "when they got up to twelve glasses and Bichiko drained them and sent them around the circle—"

"But there wasn't a single man who could drink them," Kotik put in, "except Uncle Sandro."

"Some people drank six or seven glasses," I specified, trying to recapture some detail of the story that was getting away, "but Uncle Sandro drank ten glasses."

"He had only two glasses to go," Kotik specified for some reason.

Suddenly I forgot a small point—what, strictly speaking, had prevented Uncle Sandro from drinking those two glasses? I stopped, aware that an awkward silence was developing.

"Very interesting," Geno said, pouring *araki* in the glasses.

"Don't forget about the music," Kotik reminded me. Good going, Kotik!

"That was the whole point—the music!" I said joyfully, and remembered everything.

"What's music got to do with it?" Big Svan said, and pulled his glass over to him.

"Subtle politics," said the Svan that had sat next to me, and he too pulled his glass over to him. Suddenly I forgot everything again; I must have had too much excitement with the keeper of the forests.

"Uncle Sandro had two glasses to go," Kotik interrupted, delighted that I had forgotten what came next, "and he could feel what he had drunk standing in his throat, he just didn't have room to drink any more—"

"That happens when you drink too much," Big Svan corroborated.

"Worse things can happen," Geno said.

"And then they struck up the music!" I suddenly remembered everything.

"Bichiko's favorite *lezginka*," Kotik chimed in, "and Bichiko flung himself into the dance. He took one turn and suddenly there was a noise like a drum had burst. He fell down and died. Something inside him burst."

"There's some subtle politics here," repeated the Svan (the one that sometime long, long ago had sat with me in a truck, and another Svan had tried to take my carbine away). "Your Sandro had probably made some deal with the musicians."

"Quite possibly," Kotik said.

"In general, when you drink a lot, you shouldn't dance," Big Svan said edifyingly.

"Let us raise these glasses," Geno said, "especially since we don't plan to dance . . ."

We drank another glass, and then another. Geno wanted to send his wife for a fresh bottle, but Big Svan and Kotik put up determined resistance, with the tacit approval of the wife.

We all said good-bye, and my friends got into the trucks with their fellow travelers. The motors started, and while the second truck was backing out to the road, Geno unexpectedly whipped a pistol out of his pocket and fired several farewell shots in the air. Glad shouts rang out from the trucks.

Geno's wife waved a hand in the direction of the house and shouted angrily at her husband. From some elusive intonation, I understood what she shouted.

"The children—you'll wake the children!" she shouted.

"Could I show you the way?" Geno said, putting the pistol away in his pocket. "Or perhaps you'd stay with us?"

"Thanks, I'll be off," I said. We gave each other a brotherly kiss and I offered my hand to his wife. She shifted the basket awkwardly from her right hand to her left and, overcome with shyness, held out her hand.

I crossed the road. The silver moon shone high in the sky, covering the river bed and the Narzan town on the other side with a sorcerer's light. Moonlight makes the earth more barren, clears away superfluous objects, prepares us for life in the next world, where we will not have many of the things that are dear to our hearts but torment us in this world.

The campfire still burned on the other side, and I was sure people were still sitting around it and listening to instructive tales from Uncle Sandro's life.

"The diver! I ask you as a brother!" Geno shouted.

"All right," I said, and looked back. His wife was crossing the yard like a quick, light shadow. He was still standing by the gate.

"Write to the area soviet, they'll give me the message!" Geno shouted.

"All right," I said, "if I can arrange it . . ."

"For Geno Ioselyani—don't forget!" he shouted.

I waved and started down to the river. After riding so long and standing so long in one place, walking was pleasant and easy. My mind was clear and pure, and I don't think there was anything but the nearing roar of the river to disturb its quiet.

. . . Jumping ahead, I must admit that I never did send a diver to the mountains. Occasionally—at night, for some reason—I used to remember my promise and feel ashamed. But the problem was that I didn't know a single diver. And making arrangements with a diver I didn't know for him to go and do a job in the mountains struck me as a shady and implausible proposition. Down by the sea the whole thing looks somewhat fantastic, just as our lowland life does when you remember it somewhere in the mountains, at the level of the alpine meadows.

UNCLE SANDRO
AND THE
SLAVE KHAZARAT

I HEARD THIS STORY from Uncle Sandro as we sat at a table under the awning on the upper deck of the Amra Restaurant. I'm repeating myself, I think, mentioning the upper deck of this restaurant too often. But there's no help for it, we have so few cozy spots left in our city, especially ones where in the heat of summer you can sit peacefully in the cool sea breeze and listen to the splat and plunk of children's bodies hurtling into the water from the diving tower, listen to their wet, soul-refreshing voices, and contemplate the yachts, sometimes with colored sails wind-filled to the curve of a round fruit or body, as in their leaning flight (like a dream of the Tower of Pisa) they plane smooth the soft surface of the bay.

Incidentally, about the Tower of Pisa. Seeing it in all manner of art albums and amateur snapshots always used to provoke me to unaccountable irritation, which for some reason I had to conceal. I myself don't keep albums like that, and especially have never had an opportunity to photograph it myself. So people were always displaying it to me in one form or another, and every time they did I was supposed to marvel gratefully at its idiotic lean.

But how far can you fall with falling down? The way I see it, if you're the Tower of Pisa, then either collapse, at long last, or straighten up! Otherwise, what an inspiring example of steadiness for all cockeyed souls and cockeyed ideas!

I have a recurrent nightmare, admittedly extremely infrequent, but always the same. I seem to have been taken to Italy and tied securely in a spot where I am forced to contemplate the Tower of Pisa day and night, driven to round-the-clock rage by its senseless lean and knowing for sure that it will last my lifetime, it won't collapse while I'm around.

This nightmare is made worse by the fact that some Italian—probably Luigi Longo, though for some reason he won't admit it—brings me a plate of spaghetti three times a day and feeds me, blocking the Tower of Pisa with his back and simultaneously lecturing me on Eurocommunism. I feel so uncomfortable listening to him that I can hardly restrain myself from a desire to shout, "Amigo Longo, go away—better the Tower of Pisa!"

In my dream I speak Italian very well; I say nothing, however, because the unfamiliar spaghetti strikes me as very tasty. With each spoonful I persuade myself, "Just one more, and then I'll tell the whole truth!"

And because I don't say it to him and don't have the willpower to refuse the next spoonful, I feel a further humiliation, which somehow doesn't spoil my appetite but makes it even keener.

I am forced to hear my lecturer to the end, to the last string of spaghetti, but even then, after the last spoonful, some kind of honesty or a remnant of honesty prevents me from telling him what I think. Had I sacrificed even one spoonful of spaghetti I might still have told him the whole truth, but now it's impossible, I'm ashamed, I was unable to sacrifice anything.

He leaves, and now the cockeyed tower reappears from behind his back. I recently learned from friends that a Polish engineer had developed and even implemented a scheme for straightening the Tower of Pisa. It takes a Pole, of course, to come up with a scheme like that. In Poland, of course, everything has long since been straightened out, and his yearning to straighten things out had to be redirected to the Tower of Pisa.

A thought has just occurred to me: What if the lean of the Tower of Pisa used to be a sign indicating the degree to which all earthly life diverges from the divine plan, and now we're deprived of even this illusory reference point? Or thus: What if in actuality the poor Tower of Pisa used to stand aright, while beneath it our earth and all our earthly affairs were out of whack?

So, we're on the upper deck of the Amra Restaurant. *Dramatis personae:* Uncle Sandro, Prince Emukhvari, my cousin Kemal, the photographer Khachik, and I.

Purpose of the meeting? Ordinarily I needn't have answered such a probing question, because we needn't have had any purpose. But this time we did.

The thing was that my cousin Kemal—formerly an army pilot, now a peaceful air traffic controller at the Mukhus airport—had been detained by a motor vehicle inspector while driving, to put it mildly, under the influence.

I've seen him behind the wheel in this condition several times, and never once have his precise army-pilot reflexes or his powerful nervous system let him down.

Several times I've been with him when motor vehicle inspectors have stopped him, suspecting trouble in the car more because of the immoderate hilarity in the back seat than because of any violation.

Usually in such cases, without looking at the inspector, and meanwhile displaying his Napoleonic profile for effect, especially since a profile doesn't give off winy smells—well, in such cases he thrusts at him, without looking, not his driver's license but his ID as free-lance correspondent for the journal "Soviet Police."

The ID produces a magical effect. But this time it couldn't work. This was at night, and he was alone in the car. And when he's had a few drinks and is driving alone in the car at night, his precise ex-army-pilot reflexes are inconspicuously joined by the reflex, displaced in time, of a night bombardier: he thinks that the war isn't over yet and he's on his way to bomb Königsberg, which has long since risen from its ruins and has inconspicuously softened the Gothic angularity of its name in Soviet transcription to become Kaliningrad.

In Stalinist times he could have gotten ten years for this one delayed reflex of his. But in our miraculous time he was merely stopped by the motor vehicle inspector, because, in keeping with his delayed reflex, he was trying to squeeze an airplane's speed out of his Zhiguli.

Kemal braked. He meant to wait patiently until the inspector walked over and then show him his ID as free-lance correspondent for "Soviet Police." But after he braked, he fell soundly asleep at the wheel, so soundly that he was wakened only in the morning, at the motor vehicle inspectorate.

But by then the Chief of Motor Vehicle Inspection of Abkhazia had entered the game. While the violator slept a model report had been filed, making an example of him. When he woke up, still full of his indestructible equanimity, and tried to display his magic ID, the chief had the pride not to back down.

They took Kemal's license away for nearly six months. In so doing they mockingly left him his ID as free-lance correspondent for "Soviet Police," which had lost all meaning as the game now stood. Being a man extremely lazy about walking, however, he couldn't possibly resign himself to such a punishment.

At this point we turned to Uncle Sandro for help. Uncle Sandro brought him together with Prince Emukhvari. Prince Emukhvari had worked in the recent past as the director of the municipal photography studio, but by this time he had gone all out, as athletes say, and opened his own private photography office.

Kemal had known the prince before, of course. But Kemal was a man who had spent a good part of his life in central Russia, where, if there were any aristocrats left, they displayed not the slightest desire to approach the military airfields in which, or near which, his life had passed. Though if they had displayed any such strange desire, who would have let them approach?

So, as a man who had spent his best years in our glorious mother country, and being an extremely phlegmatic man with a certain conservatism in his response to life impressions, he had decided that the influence of the aristocracy was long dead in the land, and he attached no importance to his acquaintanceship with the prince.

And now Uncle Sandro, as a favorite of life herself, pointed out to him the excessive abstractness of his understanding of the laws of history.

The chief of the motor vehicle inspectorate proved to be an emigrant from a village where a distant relative of our prince had reigned before the revolution. Evidently he had reigned well, because even that sort of kinship proved sufficient. The matter was quickly put right.

A word or two about Kemal's phlegmatism, because I might forget about it later. He certainly is phlegmatic, but the rumors about his phlegmatism are highly exaggerated. Thus my sister, for example, tells the story that when he telephones, especially in the morning, she recognizes that it's Kemal by the long mooing sounds on the line. She claims she says to him, "Collect your thoughts, Kemalchik, and meanwhile I'll make myself some coffee."

She has time, she claims, to boil up the coffee and take it off the fire while he collects his thoughts, and sometimes even to fry an egg. But she can certainly make Turkish coffee while he collects his thoughts.

Certainly he's phlegmatic, but if you stoke him properly he becomes a pretty good storyteller. I have a vague intuition he's going to start talking in this narrative of ours, not soon, but he will, near the end. So let's be patient. In general when dealing with Kemal, one must be patient above all.

. . . Ah, how well I remember the first time he came to our house after the war! Then still a trim, gallant officer, he arrived with a chubby, jolly, joking wife and a sad little pale blue volume of Yesenin's poetry.

I already knew Yesenin's poetry, of course, but—to see it published, to hold that little volume in my hands! The book was interpreted at the time as a pale smile of convalescence from a seriously ill Russia.

I remember the sustained laughter of his joking wife and his own occasional rumbling guffaws when I, then a ninth-grader, read him my own *Confession*, which I had written immediately after reading Tolstoy's *Confession*. I had been stunned by it, or rather, not so much stunned by the book itself as amazed by the certainty it revealed to me that I had no less grounds for confessing.

Kemal found himself a job at one of our airfields. Then something went wrong between him and his joking wife, and they got a divorce. His wife went off to Moscow, and Kemal married again, this time for good. By now it had become clear that I was wrong about the volume of Yesenin. What had seemed to be a smile of convalescence was nothing but a tyrant's squeamish supplement to our spiritual prison-slop on the occasion of the Great Victory over Germany.

After the Twentieth Congress, when there was a rush to find the Abkhazian intelligentsia, it became clear that they had been almost totally annihilated by Beria, and the national culture would have to be restarted, as it were. Kemal was abruptly yanked from the airfield and appointed an editor at the local publishing house. In a few years he rose to the rank of editor in chief. He was sufficiently well read for this, his taste wasn't bad, and he had a nice feel for the Abkhazian language.

Several times he clashed with top-ranking writers, and I warned him that it would end badly.

"Limit your task," I told him—by then I was a cub reporter—"to assisting talented young writers. Don't bother the talentless rabble in the top ranks or they'll gobble you up."

He looked at me with his big dark ox-eyes as if I were a madman who had suggested putting an untrained person at the controls of a plane merely because the person had rank. And that was his mistake.

About a year later he wrote a detailed review of a book by a certain ranking writer, proving that the book was without talent. The writer wasn't very surprised by his review at first, thinking that the reviewer's hand was being moved by a powerful opposing group. In the provinces, and perhaps not only in the provinces, there are always two opposing groups in a regime.

Only when he established a year later that Kemal wasn't even acquainted with the opposing group did the top-ranking writer fly into a fit of rage. But when he recovered and pulled himself together, he systematically set his intriguing toadies on Kemal. For two years, thanks to the mighty phlegmatism of his character, Kemal beat off their intrigues, brushed them aside as a bear does bees. Then he gave up, however, and lumbered off toward the airport, where, since he had gained weight and lost take-off speed by now, he got a job as an air traffic controller.

And since he works there to this day, we will return to our plot, that is, our expedition to the Amra Restaurant (upper deck) after Prince Emukhvari's successful dynastic pressure on the incompletely Marxist psyche of the chief of motor vehicle inspection.

I may be giving the impression that Kemal had taken us all for a treat. But that's a completely false impression. Kemal is so constituted that anyone who does him a favor considers it a further pleasure to treat him as well.

His charm is that special. What is the secret of it? I think we have to go back to the Tower of Pisa. In contrast to that tower—which we really did recall by chance and are now supposedly returning to by chance—Kemal's very figure, powerful and low to the ground, along with his calm, level voice and peals of laughter that bare two rows of strong teeth, produces an impression of exceptional steadiness, stability, a well-adjusted center-of-gravity position.

There's a disease of the age, I think, which psychiatrists haven't yet discovered and which I have just discovered and named the "Tower of Pisa Complex." I request that Soviet science be recorded as having primacy in this question.

Contemporary man senses the instability of all that happens around him. He has a feeling that everything ought to collapse and for some reason everything is holding up. The life around him oppresses him with a dual oppression, i.e., both the fact that everything ought to collapse and the fact that everything is still holding up.

When a man with the Pisa complex meets Kemal, he senses that there still exist in this world phenomena and people that are stable, strong, solid. And the man is temporarily released from the oppression of his Pisa complex; he rests in Kemal's shade, and naturally tries to prolong his rest.

So we were on our way to the Amra Restaurant, when right by the entrance we encountered the photographer Khachik, whom I didn't yet know. On seeing the prince he crossly finished up with his clients and rushed to embrace him with the joy of a servant boy encountering his beloved master after a long separation. Khachik was so small that he seemed to have grown old without emerging from adolescence and thereby preserved the right to playfulness.

And of course he came upstairs to the restaurant with us and wouldn't let anyone else pay, including Kemal, if of course it had occurred to Kemal to try and pay.

Several times during the session at table Khachik raised eloquent toasts to his former director and said that in forty years he hadn't had another such director, either before or since this one.

Prince Emukhvari chuckled condescendingly. In his smoke-colored glasses he resembled an Italian actor of the neorealistic era, playing the role of a Hollywood actor who finds himself in an Italian town where he is remembered and loved for his old movies.

I tried to ascertain from Khachik what made him love the prince/director so, but Khachik glanced at me with angry surprise, waved a hand toward the prince, and shouted, "A crystal soul! Plain! Plain!"

When the prince was away from the table Khachik did say, in an apparent effort to shake off my questions, "In five years of work, not once, not from one photographer, did the prince ask for money! He got what he should! But he didn't ask! A plain man! Other directors, you can't get back to the studio at night before they shake you down: Money! But he's a plain man! Not once did he ask! A crystal soul!"

Uncle Sandro made this comment on his words:

"The man who has had everything and then lost everything still feels, for forty years more, as if he had everything. But the man who has been a beggar and then gotten rich still feels, for forty years more, as if he were a beggar."

No doubt Uncle Sandro is right. Plainness is the indisputable consequence of an awareness of inner worth. Not surprisingly, this awareness is more often, though not always, characteristic of people of aristocratic descent. A petit bourgeois is never plain, and this is the consequence of his awareness of an inner lack of worth. But if, thanks to having some special gift, he outgrows that awareness, he is plain and natural, like Chekhov.

But to get back to our companions at table. It all began with Turkish coffee and a bottle of Armenian cognac, and then, well, things went as usual. During the session Khachik photographed us about ten times from various angles, on one necessary condition, that the prince be at the center of the picture. Sometimes he had the coffee chef Hakop-Agha join us.

This tall old man—his face a deep brown, as if cured by the coffee fumes and his long wanderings through the Near East, from where he had been repatriated—would sit down at our table from time to time and turn the conversation toward the Armenians. His fervent Armenian patriotism was touching and comic. From what he said it appeared that the Armenians were a terrible nation because they didn't want to do anything good for Armenians. His bitter grievances against the Armenians usually began with Tigran the Second and ended with Tigran Petrosian, who from his point of view had flippantly frittered away the chess crown. This seemingly illiterate old man knew the history of Armenia like the biography of a neighbor down the street.

He sat down at our table now, listening absently to the conversation in order to collect his thoughts and speak up at the next pause.

"Now take the Ararat soccer team," Hakop-Agha began, when the pause came. "The coach they got now is a real *götferan* (bugger). Armenians will never be champion with coach like that. He took Papazian and put him in at halfback. But Papazian, when was he ever halfback? Papazian was born forward and will die forward. But he put him in at halfback. Why? Because up-and-coming Marobian arrived on the field. Fine, yes, put up-and-coming Marobian in Papazian's slot, but why make Papazian halfback? Shift Papazian to right wing, he hits just as hard from either right or left. And put right wing in at halfback or say, 'Go home, Leninakan!' because he's no good no matter what position he plays. Can you believe he didn't have the sense to see this himself? I wrote to him, but will that *götferan* listen to me? He didn't even answer. That's how Armenians wreck each other."

Still grumbling at the coach, Hakop-Agha collected the empty coffee cups, put them on a tray, and went off behind the counter.

During the session at table the conversation turned to the celebrated brothers Emukhvari, country relatives of the prince. The affair had begun with a blood feud. Three Emukhvari brothers, desperate fellows, had kept the Kenguria police in fear for about seven years, until they were all killed. This was in the late twenties and early thirties. Later, at the political trials of '37, they were remembered, for some reason, and were posthumously cited at these trials as English spies.

"But how could those village princes have been English spies," Uncle Sandro said, "when they didn't even know where England was?"

The prince smiled and nodded his head in agreement. And now, in connection with the affair of the brothers Emukhvari, Uncle Sandro told his story.

You think I always defend Abkhazians and criticize Endurskies (he began, smoothing his mustache), but that's not true. Like Hakop-Agha, I suffer in my soul for our people. And that's why I say—before, in olden times, there was no little foolishness among Abkhazians, and because of it our people suffered. There's no less foolishness among the Abkhazians now, only these days it takes a different form.

Before, the chief foolishness was the blood feud. Several clans totally annihilated each other because of it. No, I'm not against the blood feud, when necessary. It was useful. Why? Because a man who plotted evil against another man knew that the man he plotted evil against didn't end with himself. His relatives would avenge him. And that stopped many an evil affair, because they knew—a man didn't end with himself.

But I'm ashamed even to say what silly things sometimes started a blood feud. Above Chegem, three kilometers from our house, lived the fine Batalba family. This was about fifty years before I was born. And this family was friends with the Chichba clan of the village of Kutol. The two families were friends and loved each other like close relatives.

Every year when the Chichbas drove their stock to the alpine pastures they stopped with their highland friends on the way, caroused there for several days, had some fun, and then drove their stock on up into the mountains. There was abundance, it was that kind of time.

So once they stopped at their friends' house and they had a guest with them. He was sick with malaria, and they were taking him to the alpine meadows so that he'd get strong and be rid of his disease. That was the custom then.

So they stopped with the Batalbas, Batalba slaughtered an ox, and they caroused for two days. When they got ready to leave, the host packed their donkey with two good ox haunches.

The eldest of the Chichbas was greatly displeased at this, he was a strict old man. But he said nothing and rode off with his folks, drove the flock up into the mountains. Now, why was he displeased? Because by our custom (they observed it then, who remembers it now?) when you have a fine guest and you've slaughtered something for him and you've all dined on what you've slaughtered, you mustn't give a gift for the road from what you've already slaughtered. You have to slaughter something specially as a gift for the road. That was the custom.

The Batalbas made a mistake here, of course. Because they treated the Chichbas like close relatives and gave them two ox haunches from an ox they'd already dined on. They forgot that the Chichbas had their guest with them. He kept silent, of course, but he couldn't help knowing that these two haunches were from the already slaughtered ox that they had dined on. And the Chichbas, especially the eldest, were ashamed in front of the guest because of these haunches from the ox that they'd already dined on.

So they're riding up into the mountains, driving hundreds of sheep and goats ahead of them, and the eldest Chichba keeps silent for a long time, but at last he breaks down.

"Those Batalbas!" he says. "Seems they don't count us as people! Tossed us the leftovers from their table as if we were beggars! But they'll be sorry!"

The guest tried to soothe him, of course, but he nursed the grievance. And that's how the trouble started. The Batalbas, by the way, suspected nothing, because in those days there were no rumors and nobody said anything to them, poor fellows. They were thinking, We received our guests well, saw them off well. Well indeed! But they knew nothing—there were no rumors yet among the Abkhazians.

So the members of these families met again at a certain feast. And now a young Batalba made another mistake. When the singing began, they gathered the best singers together in one place. The way it worked out, this young Batalba ended up next to the old Chichba who already considered himself insulted, and now the young Batalba started singing right next to him. That was a mistake, of course.

The young man should have asked the old Chichba, "My singing's not bothering you, is it? Perhaps I should move a little farther away?"

Then the old man would have answered him, most likely, "Go ahead and sing, sonny. If only we'd nothing worse than singing to bother us."

That's what people usually say. But this young Batalba didn't say anything, because he didn't know about the old insult, and anyway he'd been drinking and he counted this old man as his close relative.

Each mistake separately could still have been tolerated, obviously, but the two mistakes together hit the old man like an atom bomb.

"Why are you singing in my ear!" the old man yelled. "You Batalbas, I see, just don't count us as people!"

With these words he drew his dagger and killed the youth on the spot. Now, of course, screaming, an uproar, the women. They quashed it somehow, but could a thing like that stay quashed for long? Two days later the youth's father killed the old man.

That's how the trouble started. Isn't that foolishness? In such a situation, either you turn up respected old people from both villages and they gather the best representatives of both clans and reconcile them; or one of the clans gives up and swarms from its native village like bees from the hive and moves somewhere far away. Or they annihilate each other.

The way it worked out, all that was left of the Batalbas were four brothers and their mother. And there were four brothers and their mother left in the Chichba family too. But the youngest Chichba brother was still little and weak—he was thirteen. And neither family had any close relatives. Only very distant ones.

They had lived like that for about ten years now. No one had touched anyone, and many people decided that perhaps with the aid of old men they would finally settle the matter between themselves.

Now, by the way, it was the Batalbas' turn to shoot. And suddenly that summer Adamyr, the most savage, most courageous of the Batalbas, went off to the summer pastures with the stock, and the other three brothers stayed home. This may have been a sign that the Batalbas wanted peace: Here we've sent our strongest man to the alpine meadows, we want peace, we don't fear for our house.

But the Chichbas took it differently. Their nerves gave out. Rather than wait for our enemies to shoot, they decided, let's take advantage of the fact that Adamyr has gone to the summer pastures. Let's kill these three brothers, then kill Adamyr, and at long last start to live in peace.

And that's what they did. They suddenly attacked the Batalbas' house, killed the three brothers, and stole all the stock that were left at home. And one of the Chichbas, the boldest, started for the mountains, in order to get there ahead of the messenger of woe and kill Adamyr.

But Adamyr, meanwhile, had left the shepherds and gone hunting for ibex. He stayed there up in the glaciers for two days. The Chichba lay in wait for him a whole day, not understanding why he wasn't among the other shepherds. Toward evening he walked up to the shanties where the shepherds lived and asked them where their comrade had disappeared to.

The shepherds sensed trouble, of course, but they didn't know what had happened down below. They told the Chichba that Adamyr had gone through the pass to visit a Circassian buddy of his and wouldn't be back for a week. There was nothing the Chichba could do, and he went back down, into Abkhazia. Never mind, he thought, there's four of us brothers, and now just one of him.

The next day, at noon, here comes the messenger of woe and tells the shepherds what a terrible misfortune has happened down below. While the shepherds are thinking how to prepare Adamyr, he himself comes in sight on the mountain and starts down toward the shanties.

With an ibex on his shoulders, he's coming down toward the shanties like an ibex himself, and he shouts from the distance, Why aren't you coming to meet me? He's happy over his successful hunt, doesn't know what awaits him. Now he's near the shanties, thirty meters away, the shepherds are slowly walking to meet him, he's shouting and doesn't understand why the shepherds aren't running. Usually, in such a situation, people help the successful hunter. But they aren't running to him.

Suddenly he spots the Chegemian among them and senses that the shepherds aren't happy to see him. He stops about ten meters away and looks at the man who's climbed up from Chegem, he senses something terrible and feels afraid. Finally he throws the ibex off his shoulders and asks, "What's happened at home?"

The messenger of woe tells him about the atrocity, and the shepherds say that one of the Chichbas came and asked for him.

"Tell them," Adamyr says to the messenger of woe, "that in two days' time, when I have avenged my brothers, I will come to mourn them. If I don't come, then mourn me too, along with them!"

He loaded his gun right where he was, turned around, stepped over the killed ibex, and started down. He covered the three-day trip in twenty-four hours, overtook the Chichba who had come after him. He killed him, hoisted him to his shoulders like the ibex, and covered another ten kilometers to the nearest house. He shouted for the owner to preserve the body from defilement until the relatives should come, then laid it at the gate and went on.

By dawn he had arrived at the Chichbas' house and set the cowshed on fire. When the cows started to bellow, trying to escape the flames, the brothers came running out of the house. Adamyr killed the two older ones but he didn't kill the youngest, who was still just a boy. He bound his hands and told the mother, "Your sons annihilated my brothers. I will not kill your last son, but all his life he shall be my slave. Complain to the authorities and I'll kill him on the spot—then let them do as they please."

So, when he had avenged his brothers, he drove the poor little boy to his brothers' graves and mourned them, holding in one hand the rope to which the boy was tied. And he pledged his word to his brothers that he would keep the last Chichba as a slave until he died. The boy's name was Khazarat.

People marveled at this event. Some praised Adamyr for not killing the boy, some were angry that he wanted to make him a slave, while some said that he had taken this decision in the heat of the moment and would later cool off and let the boy go.

But he didn't let him go; he kept him about twenty years on a chain in the barn, as a slave. Our old men in Chegem were very displeased at this, but they could do nothing with him. He was such a fierce man, so wild. If he'd lived right in Chegem they would have driven him out of the village, of course, but he lived at a distance and obeyed nobody. They merely informed him that he was not to appear in Chegem.

In those days the authorities paid little attention to this sort of thing. If a feudist in a lowland village killed his enemy and didn't go away into the forest, they arrested him. If he did go away into the forest, they didn't even look for him—although if someone killed a policeman or a clerk, they spared no effort to find the killer and punish him. But here, Khazarat's poor mother was still afraid that Adamyr would kill him, and she complained to no one.

Although he went courting several times Adamyr never did get married, because the Abkhazians were ashamed to give him their daughters.

"How can you give him your daughter?" they reasoned. "Come to your daughter's and there's the slave. What do I want with that?"

They lived like this for many years, and then Adamyr's mother died, and the two were left together—Adamyr and his slave Khazarat.

Several times a year Khazarat's poor mother visited her son, brought him *khachapuri,* roast chickens, wine. Adamyr permitted her all this. He also permitted her to cut Khazarat's hair and beard once a year, and three times a year permitted her to bathe him. And so the mother would come to her son, sit by him a day or two, weep, and go away.

Now, when I turned eighteen, I decided to free Khazarat. A man always wants to free slaves when he's young. Despite my youth I was already very wily. But how to free him! Adamyr went nowhere for more than a day. And when he did go away, the dogs wouldn't let anyone near the house.

So I made friends with Adamyr, keeping it secret from my family. If Father found out about it, he'd throw me out of the house. He didn't count Adamyr as a person at all. Our Abkhazians knew that slavery existed; sometimes the Turks attacked and led people away into slavery. But for an Abkhazian to keep a slave himself—that was unknown.

I gradually made friends with Adamyr by pretending that I was interested in hunting, but I didn't ask about the slave. He was a rare hunter, had no notion of fatigue or fear.

He and I had been out hunting several times now, the dogs were used to me, and he was too, because even though he was a savage man it was dull for him being always alone.

And one time before the hunt he says to me, "I'll feed the dogs, and you feed my slave."

"All right," I say, as if I'm not interested in Khazarat.

He gives me a kettle of milk and a half a loaf of churek.

"Don't I need the spoon?" I say.

"What spoon," he yells. "Pour the milk in his trough and throw the churek!"

So at long last I walk into this barn. In the corner, sitting on some corn straw, I see a man. He's dressed in rags, with a beard down to his waist, and his eyes glow like two coals. Terrifying. Next to him I see a long trough, and a stone is placed under the trough at this end. So it's slanted toward him. From this I gathered that Adamyr didn't go too near him either. I'd already heard that Khazarat had attacked him once when he came too near, but Adamyr had managed to pull a knife and stab him. Khazarat's wound had healed rapidly, like a dog's, but since then Adamyr had been more careful. He used to tell people about that himself.

I poured the milk into the trough for Khazarat and told him, "Catch the churek!"

I told him that because I didn't like the idea of throwing a man's bread on the ground, and of course I was afraid to go near.

I threw the bread. Clap! He caught it in midair, and now I heard his chain rattle. He had a thick chain fastened to his leg.

He started eating the churek and sometimes bent down to the trough to gulp milk. This was horrible to see, and I made a final resolve to free him. It was especially horrible to see how he gulped the milk, chewed the churek, and sometimes looked at me with burning eyes, but felt no shame that all this was happening in my presence. He was used to it. A person gets used to everything.

All this went on for several months. I always had my eye out for a chance to arrange Khazarat's escape. I was both afraid that Adamyr might find out about it and afraid that my folks might find out I was going to Adamyr's.

By now Adamyr was used to me, and every time we went hunting he'd say, "I'll feed the dogs, and you feed my slave."

And I would feed him. Adamyr gave him the same food that he ate himself. Only in a horrible form. He poured the milk and yogurt into the trough, and if he slaughtered a four-legged animal he threw him a hunk of raw meat. Several blocks of rock salt, the kind we give cattle, lay beside him.

Nowadays, I've heard, certain educated fools eat their meat raw. They think it's good for you. But people have boiled and roasted their meat for thousands of years, wouldn't they have had the sense to eat it raw if it were good for you?

Now, what did Khazarat do? He did just two things. He ground corn, turned the millstones by hand. They lay next to him. His arms were powerful from doing this. And he also wove baskets. Adamyr himself brought him the wicker. Adamyr sold the baskets to the Greeks in Anastasovka, because the Chegemians wouldn't take anything from him.

In a few months Khazarat got used to me. Although his eyes always glowed like coals, I knew he wouldn't touch me, and I used to come near him. He hadn't lost his mind and he conversed like a man.

Once I met his poor mother, and that made me want to free him even worse. She spread out a towel on the corn straw, laid chicken and *khachapuri* on it, set out a bottle of wine and two glasses.

He and I ate together, although to tell the truth it was very unpleasant for me.

How could it be pleasant to eat, when the pit where he took care of his bodily functions was nearby? Admittedly, next to the pit there was a wooden shovel, with which he kept it covered. But it was still unpleasant. But for his mother's sake I sat down to eat with him. And his poor mother, all the while I sat next to him his poor mother kept stroking my back and saying in a sweet voice, "Come often to my Khazarat, we've fallen on such misfortune, son. He's dull here, poor boy . . . Come nice and often, son . . ."

Adamyr was at the other end of the barn planing a hoe-handle at the time. It seems he heard her words.

"I'm dull, too, without my brothers," he said, not looking at us, still planing the hoe-handle with his knife.

"Ah, fate," the old lady sighed when she heard Adamyr. And I suddenly sensed that I was sorry for them all. That happens when you're young. I was sorry for Khazarat and sorry for Adamyr and most of all sorry for this old lady.

I felt especially sorry for her when I saw her that day washing and patching Adamyr's clothes. She was trying to oblige him so that he'd soften toward her son. But he was past changing in any way.

One time out hunting Adamyr told me, "Some people think I keep a slave for pleasure. But it's not easy to keep a slave, there's no pleasure from him. Sometimes I wake up at night with the fear that he's escaped, although I know in my mind that he couldn't. It's impossible to grind through the chain with the millstone in one night. I've tried it. And I'll always notice by day if he's been grinding the chain by night. And if he did grind through it, where would he go? The barn is locked. And if he got out of the barn, the dogs would tear him apart.

"But even so I can't stand it. I take a candle, I open the door to the barn and look. He's asleep. In all the times I've checked, he's never waked up. Sleeps that soundly. But I wake up every night. So who's worse off—him or me?"

"Then let him go," I said, "and you'll feel better."

"No," he says, "I pledged my word at my brothers' grave. Only death will remove the chain from him, and from me the oath made to my brothers."

Well, so I was watching closely, keeping my eye out for a way to free Khazarat. The barn he was chained in was made of chestnut. There was a big lock on the door, and the key was always in Adamyr's pocket. But now and then he used to go away for the day or the night. And this is what I decided: I would make a tunnel, cut his chain with a file, lead him out so that the dogs wouldn't tear him to pieces, and set him free. Later, when Adamyr returned, if he raged, I would suggest to him that Khazarat's mother had probably brought him a file in the *khachapuri,* and he'd made the tunnel himself with his wooden shovel and somehow beaten off the dogs. Of course I knew Adamyr wouldn't touch Khazarat's mother.

That's what I'd decided, and one time out hunting Adamyr said to me himself, "Listen, Sandro, come over tomorrow night and feed the dogs. I have to go to Atary tomorrow, I'll be back the next morning."

"All right," I said.

So the next day I could hardly wait for nighttime. My folks all had supper

and went to bed. Then I quietly got up, took a lantern from the kitchen, and a
file, and went to Adamyr's house.

I went, but I was terrified. I was afraid of Adamyr. I was afraid maybe he
suspected something of my plans and had hidden somewhere, waiting. I decided
to search his house before starting the tunnel. If he was home and asked why I
had come so late, I would say I'd remembered that the dogs hadn't been fed.

The dogs scented man from half a kilometer away and ran barking out to meet
me, but when they recognized me they stopped barking. I went into Adamyr's
yard, took a good look around, then went into the kitchen, from there into the
storeroom, then searched all the rooms, but he wasn't in the house.

Then I went through to the barnyard and saw his three cows lying there. I
went into the cowshed, held the lantern up high and saw that it was empty. Then
I went back to the kitchen, got the churek that I planned to feed to the dogs,
but I made no move to feed them. I stuffed both pockets with pieces of churek.
I did this so that I could give the churek to Khazarat. So that when we came
out of the barn and the dogs began to attack, he could throw the churek to them
and it would placate the dogs a little.

Then I went back to the storeroom and took a grape-harvesting basket down
from the wall. Going out to the veranda with the basket and lantern, I picked
up Adamyr's shovel and started for the barn where Khazarat sat.

Now—what's the basket for? A grape basket. It's long and narrow, so that
later, when I'm digging the passage, I can haul all the dirt into the barn.

If I didn't haul the dirt into the barn, Adamyr would guess that someone
helped Khazarat from outside. And because of it he might kill me.

I stood the lantern on the ground and began to dig at the exact spot where the
chain was fastened on the inside of the barn. I dug and dug, and I was surprised
that Khazarat didn't wake up. He really is a sound sleeper, I thought. Finally,
though, he did wake up.

"Who are you?" he asks, and I hear him move in the corn straw.

"It's me, Sandro," I say.

"What do you want?"

"I'll dig through," I say. "You'll find out then."

An hour later I parted the corn straw with my hand, carefully stood the lantern
up, and crawled out into the barn.

Khazarat's sitting there and I see his eyes burning like an owl's.

"Here's a file," I say. "We'll file through the chain and you'll go free."

"No." He shakes his head. "Adamyr will just track me down with his dogs."

"He won't track you down," I say. "You'll go to another village during the
night, and he'll lose the trail there."

"No," he says, "I'm not used to walking any more. I won't be able to walk
far. And near here, he and his dogs will just catch me."

"He won't catch you," I say. "But if you're afraid to go alone, I'll go with
you as far as Dzhgerdy and hide you there with some relatives of ours. Then
I'll return home, and you'll go where you want."

"No," he says, "I don't want to."

"Then what can we do?" I say.

He thinks and thinks, and his eyes burn—terrifying.

"If you want to help me," he says finally, "bring me two meters of chain. We'll join it to this chain, and I don't need anything more."

"Why do you need that?" I ask.

"I'll do a little walking at night and get used to it. And then you'll help me escape."

"But he checks your chain," I say. "He told me so himself."

"No," he says, "the first fifteen years he checked it, but he doesn't any more."

Hard as I tried to persuade him to make his escape now, he wouldn't agree. And then I decided to do what he asked.

"Bring an ax," he said, "to close the links."

So I practically ran home, in the dead of night. I crept into our barn. From an old winepress with all sorts of junk lying in it I got a chain, about the length he'd asked for. I went back, got Adamyr's ax on the kitchen veranda, and crawled into the barn. While I was on the way he had filed through his chain and cut slits in the links on either side. I was even surprised how quickly he'd done it all. He had powerful arms from the hand mill.

He took my chain, inserted it in the links on either side, and laid these links on the millstone, then closed the ends of them so there'd be nothing to see.

"I don't need anything more," he says. "Go! I'll let you know when my legs get strong."

"Maybe I should leave you the file?" I say.

"No," he says, "I don't need anything more. That's all. That's all! Go! Just trample the dirt down well on the other side so the master won't notice anything."

So I took the ax and the lantern and carefully crawled up outside. Then as quickly as I could I piled the dirt in the hole and then trampled it down well, so there'd be nothing to notice. The dogs were milling around near me, but, I thought, dogs can't talk, thank God. And now I remembered I had the churek in my pockets, and I threw it to the dogs.

With the lantern I took one last good look around the spot where I'd dug and saw that there was nothing to notice, then shook all the dirt off the shovel and carried it back, along with the ax and the basket. I put everything where it had been, the way it had been. I extinguished the lantern and went home at a run. No one had noticed anything at home either, thank God.

So time went by, and meanwhile I was a little afraid to go to Adamyr's myself. Two or three weeks went by. Once my brother Makhaz—he had passed not far from Adamyr's farmstead with the goats that day—he said, "Adamyr's dogs were howling all day today."

"That's happened before," my folks said. "Sometimes he goes out hunting with one dog, and the others are bored."

So we forgot about it. But a week later we heard a woman screaming, somewhere up above, and the screaming was coming closer to our house. Everyone at home went outdoors, but no one could understand it at all.

The woman's screaming signified woe. But it was coming straight from the mountain over the upper Chegem road, and no one lived there. Father and I and my two brothers, Kyazym and Makhaz, climbed quickly up toward the woman's voice. In about fifteen minutes we encountered Khazarat's mother. Her cheeks were torn, she was walking without any path, through the thorns, she saw nothing. She looked at us but couldn't say a word, just pointed in the direction of Adamyr's house.

We went running over there. I didn't know what to think, but still I kept glancing at Kyazym, because he'd brought along his rifle. We ran into the yard, and for some reason the dogs were nowhere to be seen or heard.

I was the first to open the barn. The door was just pulled to. And here's what we saw. Adamyr lay dead, on his back, and his face was horrible from the suffering he had been through before he died. His neck was all dark blue spots and his head was twisted like a dead chicken's.

And Khazarat lay on the corn straw, he had folded his arms on his chest, and his face was calm, calm as a saint's. He was so thin that Father slipped the chain off his leg, it no longer held. And then suddenly I remembered Adamyr's words:

"Only death will take the chain from him, and from me the oath made to my brothers."

It had turned out just as he said.

"Evidently," my father said, "Adamyr forgot and went too near Khazarat. And Khazarat jumped on him and strangled him. And then he died of starvation himself, because there was no one to give him his food."

I alone knew why it had happened. But of course I didn't say a word to anyone. My father, incidentally, may he rest in peace, was a real farmer. Nowadays there are none like him at all. Despite the atrocity we had seen, he recognized his chain! He suddenly picked it up in one hand, and I saw him looking and looking in the light—there was a narrow window without glass— he just couldn't understand. He wanted to lift the chain higher to get a good look, but the chain was fastened, wouldn't reach. He got mad, and it was funny to me, despite the horror beside us. Then he tossed it aside and shrugged his shoulders.

All of a sudden, from outside, came the sound of gunshots.

We ran out and we saw Kyazym, he was standing by the barnyard and shooting Adamyr's dogs. One after another he killed six dogs. It seems the dogs had gone mad with hunger and attacked their own cow in the pen, torn her to pieces and eaten her. And then they had killed the other two cows, though by now they couldn't eat them. Thus one savage act gives rise to another savagery, and that savagery gives rise to a third savagery.

Khazarat's poor mother was escorted to her village, along with the body of her son. The unfortunate Adamyr was committed to the earth too, beside his brothers, and with that his clan ended, the once large, hospitable house completely died out. Later even the house and barn were gradually pulled apart and stolen by somebody, most likely Endurskies.

Since then I've thought a lot about Khazarat. Why didn't he go away with me that night, I wondered. And I realized what the trouble was. He was afraid that if he left he wouldn't be able to get revenge. And he deceived me about forgetting how to walk. He could walk, but, knowing that Adamyr was always armed and the dogs could follow his trail, he didn't want to take the risk.

He wanted to lengthen the chain and suddenly leap on Adamyr and strangle him with his powerful hands, and he thought of nothing else. He had no thought that he'd die of starvation, had no thought that he wouldn't be able to free himself, he had one thought only—to get revenge for his humiliation. And then I realized something. A slave doesn't want freedom, as people think. A slave wants one thing—to get revenge, to trample the man who has trampled him.

". . . There you have it, my friends: a slave wants only to get revenge, but certain stupid people think he wants freedom, and a lot has happened because of this mistake," Uncle Sandro concluded sententiously. He smoothed his mustache with far-reaching innuendo.

Kemal roared with laughter, but the prince nodded significantly in my direction as if to say, Learn wisdom from Uncle Sandro.

"And those poor Emukhvari princes' being accused as English spies," Uncle Sandro added, "that's just folly. They didn't even know there was such a country as England. But I was in England in the thirties with Pantsulaya's ensemble. They took us around, and I noticed that England wasn't a bad country. I noticed excellent pastures there, but for some reason there weren't any sheep. But England's no good for goats. A goat likes briar patches, it likes bushes, but a sheep likes clear pastures. I can't understand why they don't raise sheep."

"They do," I said, to mollify Uncle Sandro.

"Ah-h." Uncle Sandro nodded with satisfaction. "Then they listened to me. Twenty years ago an English writer named Priestley came over here. Ever hear of him?"

"Yes," I said.

"Read him?"

"Yes," I said.

"Well?"

"He's okay, Uncle Sandro," I said. "Nothing special."

Uncle Sandro started laughing, a laugh that I didn't quite like.

"I've noticed before," Uncle Sandro said, "these people who write have a strange way about them, they'll never say a good word for another. Now when I danced in the ensemble, I always acknowledged that Pata Pataraya was the leading dancer, though in fact I already danced better than he did . . . But that's beside the point.

"This Priestley got an excellent reception here back then. They showed him the best sanatorium, showed him the sprightliest long-lived person, the richest kolkhoz, and of course they introduced him to me.

"I was tamada at the table. He sat next to me, or rather, a lady interpreter sat between us. And he and I got into a conversation. I told him then that I'd been to England and seen good pastures there, but I hadn't seen any sheep. I suggested to him that English farmers should raise sheep."

"What did he say?" I asked.

"He said, 'All right, I'll tell them,' " Uncle Sandro replied. "So it turns out he did. And he also said this: 'I'll tell the farmers about the sheep,' he says, 'but we have too many sheep in Parliament as it is.'

"So, he was criticizing his government. Then I understood why he was getting such a good reception here. Now I ask you: If you found yourself in a foreign country, could you say, even about a regional committee, that it had goats on it? Keeping in mind that goats are smarter than sheep."

"No," I said.

"So there," Uncle Sandro said.

The prince smiled, and Kemal roared with laughter. Khachik leaped up from the table and recorded this scene from one knee.

We drank another round. Hakop-Agha brought fresh coffee, and when he took the cups off the tray and picked it up, the tray glinted in the sun like a shield. Sitting down at the table, Hakop-Agha laid the tray on his lap and steadied it with his hands; from time to time he tapped it with a fingernail, cocking his ear to the soft chime.

Kemal usually frequented other dens of vice and so did not know Hakop-Agha well. I wanted him to hear a story of his, already a classic in local circles, the story of Tigrankert.

"Hakop-Agha," I said, "I've wondered for a long time. Why did Tigran the Second, after building the great city of Tigrankert, allow it to be burned and sacked by the Roman barbarians? Surely he could have defended it?"

While I was asking Hakop-Agha he nodded woefully, letting us know that the question couldn't help but occur to anybody in his right mind.

"Ah, Tigrankert," Hakop-Agha sighed, "all dahst and eshes . . . It was most beautiful city in the East. And fountains it had beeg as trees. And trees it had on whose brenches set Pershian bird by name of peacock. And walking along streets it had deerss who lowered their eyes when seeing men, jahst like real Armenian gurlss. And why? All dahst and eshes.

"Maybe Tigrankert better than Rome and Babylon, but we don't find out now, becauss no photos then. This heppen in year 69 B.C., and if Khachik had live then he would be jobless or porter. Photography, they don't know what is.

"But do we talk about Khachik? No, we talk about Tigran Second. When this Roman *götferan* Lucullus surround Tigrankert, Tigran take almost hees whole army and leave the city. Tigran-*djan*, why you do?

"Thees was the great king's great mistake. Tigrankert had strong wall, Tigrankert had excellent water, such *soğuk-su* you no drink in one gulp, and Tigrankert had provisions for tree years and tree mahnthsl And why? All dahst and eshes!

"Tigran-*djan,* you could have defend the great city, but first you had to drive out all the Greek *götferan*s, because they turn out be traitors. Greeks, what they care about Armenians? And the devils they open the gates in the night, and Roman soldiers burn everything, and all thet's left of city is dahst and eshes.

"But while they surround it, what Tigran do? I am shame, even, to say what he do. He send detachment, they break into city, but what he bring out? Armenian nation, yes? No! Armenian women and children, yes? No! He bring out hees harem, hees whoreses, thet's what he bring out! I am shame, even, for great king!

"Ah, Tigran, why you beeld Tigrankert, and if you beeld, why you geev to Roman *götferan*s to burn? All dahst and eshes!"

While Hakop-Agha was giving us the history of Tigrankert's downfall, a customer came over wanting to ask for coffee, but Khachik checked him with a gesture. The customer stood motionless at Hakop-Agha's back, listening in surprise.

"Now ask!" Khachik said when Hakop-Agha fell silent, staring mournfully into the too-far distance where the great Tigrankert flourished in peace, with its fountains big as trees, deer shy as girls, and Greeks lurking within the city as within a Trojan horse.

"Would it be possible to have two coffees?" the man asked, no longer very sure he had come to the right place.

"Yes, possible," Hakop-Agha said, standing up and putting the empty cups on the tray. "Everything possible now."

After talking a little about Hakop-Agha's amusing foibles, we returned to Uncle Sandro's story about Khazarat. Uncle Sandro's version of the reason why Khazarat had refused to leave with him was disputed by Kemal.

"I think," Kemal said, taking a sip of coffee and glancing at Uncle Sandro with his dark eyes, "your Khazarat got so used to his barn, over those twenty years, that he was simply afraid of open space—though of course he also dreamed of getting revenge on Adamyr. The nature of fear is altogether surprising and unaccountable.

"I remember in'44 we were based at an airfield in East Prussia. One time I went for a walk outside of our little town with my friend Alyosha Starostin. He and I were buddies all through the war. A magnificent pilot and an excellent comrade. We saw eye to eye on books. He and I were the readingest pilots in the regiment, though of course we liked to drink and didn't miss a chance with the girls. But we saw eye to eye on books, and that fall we were crazy about Yesenin. Both of us had notebooks written all over with poems of his.

"Well, so the weather was beautiful, we went out for a walk, and we were going through some small German villages. The houses were handsome, but there weren't any people, they'd nearly all fled. In one village we stopped at this tidy little two-story house, because it had a rowan tree growing by it, all covered with red berry-clusters.

"I can see it now, Alyosha bent down the rowan with a fresh, crisp snap, his

Russian soul couldn't resist, and he was all fresh and crisp himself, with his belts and his youth—he still is, in my mind's eye—he broke off two branches and let go of the little tree.

"He offered one branch to me, and we stood there with the branches, nibbling off the rowanberries and discussing where the farmhands lived if all these were manor houses.

"Suddenly the door of the house opened, and an old man came out and called us: *'Russe,* come in, *Russe,* come in!'

"We'd been warned to be on the lookout for guerrillas, but we didn't frigging believe in any German guerrillas. And besides, where would you get guerrillas in a land where every tree is tended like a bride.

" 'Want to?'

" 'Let's go.'

"So the old man took us into the house. We climbed upstairs and walked into a room. I looked and there were two women in the room—one just a girl, about eighteen, and the other obviously a *jungfrau,* about twenty-five. Right from the start I had my eye on the older one, I liked her. But for appearance's sake—I knew my buddy inside out—I said to him, 'You choose. Which one do you like?'

" 'First dibs on the young one!' he says.

" 'It's a deal!'

"They were glad to see us too, I saw—they came to life.

" 'Coffee, coffee,' says the *jungfrau.*

" *'Ja, ja,'* I say.

"That means yes in German.

"So she made coffee for us. I must admit it was frigging crappy coffee, maybe they made it from oak sawdust. But what did we care about the coffee? Young, charming girls—ready for anything, I saw. And the old man wasn't opposed, of course. They were afraid of our army, and to secure the friendship of two officers meant to protect themselves from all the rest.

"Anyway, we sat there a while, and I said, *'Abend, Konservy, Schnaps, Brot, Schokolade.'*

" 'Oh!' Both of them lighted up. *'Danke, danke.'*

"They'd been starving, of course. So we came back that night, brought liquor, canned goods, sausage, bread, chocolate. We sat, had supper, drank. It turned out the old man had been a prisoner of ours in the First World War and spoke a little Russian. But he would have done better not to talk at all. He kept getting tangled up, wanting to explain everything. What the frig did we want with his explanations? And he kept trying to prove he was antifascist. They'd all turned antifascist now, so that it was hard to see whom we'd been fighting all that time.

"The girls were a different story, they picked up on everything right away . . . Alyosha and I had a good deal to drink, our young ladies also got a bit high, and we started dancing to the phonograph. Every record had *Nur für Deutsche* written on it—that means 'For Germans only.' When I put the record on, I deliberately asked, *'Nur für Deutsche?'*

"They both laughed: *'Nein! Nein!'*

"Well, since it was *nein,* we started dancing. Finally the old man got drunk, and by now he was talking such blather that even his nieces had ceased to understand. He was their uncle. And we'd been sick of him even before, so we were glad when my *jungfrau* led him downstairs to put him to bed.

"Now we're alone. We're drinking, dancing, in a word, feeling mellow. Well, I give my German girl a little hug and ask, *'Nur für Deutsche?'*

" 'Rascal, rascal,' she laughs, *'Russisch* rascal!'

" *'Nein,'* I say, *'Kavkazisch* rascal.'

" *'O, schönste Kaukas!'* she says.

"Alyosha and I stayed the night in the two upstairs rooms. That was the beginning of our romance, which lasted about two months, with breaks for combat missions of course. Once or twice the guys from the airfield service thought of horning in on us, but they soon sized up the situation and backed off. The guys in our own unit got the picture from the beginning.

"So one time we came to see our girls. Mine was named Katrin—I called her Katya—and the young one was named Greta."

Here Uncle Sandro interrupted Kemal.

"You've gone altogether Russian," he said. "Why do you speak your woman's name in my presence?"

"What's wrong?" Kemal asked.

"How stupid can you be," Uncle Sandro said. "You know that's my wife's name. You should have changed it, if you were bent on telling the story in my presence."

"Well, okay," Kemal guffawed, "I won't say her name any more."

"Dumbbell," Uncle Sandro said, "now that you've said it there's no place to hide, go on with the story."

"Well then," Kemal went on, with a glance at Uncle Sandro, his eyes still laughing, "one time we're spending the night with our girlfriends as usual. About three in the morning I wake up and go outside for a call of nature.

"Suddenly I hear a motorcycle drive up and stop, and two men—I can tell by their footsteps—go up into the house.

"Hell, I thought, now we've been caught, like idiots! My pistol's under my pillow, and I'm standing out back of the house in my shorts, undershirt, and slippers. Hard to imagine a stupider situation. And besides I was a little fuzzy. We'd knocked back a few for the night, of course. So, I thought, we laughed to ourselves when they talked to us about watchfulness and guerrillas, and now what—we're up against it! Surely our girlfriends weren't traitors? No, I couldn't believe it! I liked my . . . what's-her-name . . ."

"Say her name! Say her name, why hide now!" Uncle Sandro put in.

"Yes," Kemal went on, "I liked my Katya, and she liked me, I could feel it, and the other two were just plain crazy about each other. Then had the antifascist betrayed us? I couldn't abandon my comrade and I didn't want to fall into the hands of the Germans—ha! ha!—literally naked!

"Well, okay, I thought, here goes! I poked my head out in the street. Nobody.

A German motorcycle with a sidecar standing there. I went to the door, I heard voices, but I couldn't make anything out.

"All I could tell was, the voices were coming from where my comrade slept. I decided to go up and slip into my room while they were in with Alyosha. The main thing was, I had to get to the pistols. But of course I realized it was curtains for us if the girls had betrayed us, because if they had, mine must have given them the pistol first thing. But I had no choice, I quietly opened the door and quickly climbed the stairs.

"Suddenly I heard Russian talk, coming from Alyosha's room! First off I went limp with relief. I stood there on the stairs, happily listening to the Russian talk, without grasping what it was about. A good thirty seconds went by before I woke up and began to catch the tone. I heard this very harsh voice. Aha, I thought, a patrol. Well, you won't scare us with patrols. I walked into the room. My Katya's standing in the middle of the room, pale, in her nightgown, and she says softly, *'Russisch komandieren, russisch komandieren . . .'*

"At that point I opened the door and shouted across the landing in a loud voice, 'What happened, Alyosha?'

" 'So you're not alone here!' says the voice. Then the door flies open, and a major appears on the landing, and behind him a private.

" 'Disgraceful!' says the major, and turns to Alyosha—he's standing in his room already dressed. 'Why didn't you say you weren't alone here?'

"The poor guy stammered some reply. Evidently he'd decided to at least protect me, if he'd been caught himself.

" 'Kindly get dressed!' the major ordered.

"This major was a drone from headquarters, I saw. At the front, we could spot at one glance a man who hadn't seen action, even if he had medals down to his belly button.

"And my Alyosha, a very brave flier who had been four times wounded and had twice landed burning aircraft, I saw that he was trembling in front of this shit.

"Now, you know it's hard to get my blood up, but at this point I went psycho.

" 'Comrade Major,' I said in a steely voice, 'please leave the premises immediately!'

"He was flustered, I saw, but still keeping up a front. He glanced behind him, realized that Alyosha was a senior lieutenant, but the way I was dressed you couldn't tell a frigging thing.

" 'Your rank?' he asks.

"I turned around, walked over to the bed, pulled my pistol from under the pillow, and went back to the door.

" 'Here's my rank!' I say.

" 'Drop the act,' he answers. 'This is not '41!'

" 'You bet it's not,' I said, 'no thanks to your ass in headquarters!'

" 'I shall be forced to report all this to your unit,' he says, and goes down the stairs. The private follows him.

" 'Go ahead and report,' I say. 'What else are you good for!'

"They went out. There was a silence. The motorcycle started up with a roar and faded away.

" 'You were very rude to him,' Alyosha says. 'Now they'll haul us in.'

" 'Don't worry,' I say. 'You and I know our chiefs well enough. Big deal—we spent the night with some German girls—'

" 'But you threatened him with a pistol,' he says. 'You realize what he can make this sound like.'

" 'And we'll say he's lying,' I answer. 'We'll say he wanted to stay with the women himself and that's what sparked the whole thing. What was he doing racing around on a motorcycle at three in the morning?'

" 'Sure, that's the line we have to take now,' Alyosha says. 'But you shouldn't have been insolent with him.'

"I realized he felt awkward now in front of his Gretochka. They hadn't understood the words, of course, but all was clear even without words: I'd thrown out the major who had made him get dressed.

"To ease the situation I poured some drinks, and we sat down at the table. The sisters started jabbering. Little Greta kept glancing at me with shining eyes, and a dark lock of hair kept falling over her forehead. Damn, she was pretty!

"Anyway, we had a little drink and went back to our rooms.

" *'Major—Gestapo?'* Katya asked me.

" *'Nein, nein,'* I said.

"That's all we needed! But I saw she didn't believe me.

"A day later we flew a combat mission. I landed safely, had supper in the mess hall with my crew. Then I went over to Alyosha—for some reason he was sitting alone—and I said, 'Let's rest up, and we'll go see our girls tomorrow with renewed strength.'

"I saw him hesitate.

" 'You know, Kemal,' he says, 'we have to end this.'

" 'Why end it?' I ask.

" 'They'll haul us in. We'll never get back alive.'

" 'What are you afraid of?' I say. 'If he did squeal on us, you can't change anything now.'

" 'No,' he says, 'that's it. I pass.'

" 'Well, do what you want,' I say, 'but I'm going. What should I tell Greta if she asks about you?'

" 'Tell her whatever you want,' he answers, and he downs his fruit compote in one gulp, like vodka, and goes to his room.

"He always took rank too seriously. He used to stand at attention and listen to instructions as if his life depended on them. I often kidded him about it.

" 'You're a wild southerner,' he'd laugh in reply, 'but we Russians know in our bones what the big shots are.'

"Well, that night I went to our little German girls'. On the way I wondered what to tell them. Okay, I decided, I'll say he's sick. Maybe he'll change his mind.

"I arrived. My girl came running. But Greta stood absolutely still, except that the dark lock falling over her eyes seemed to grow even darker.

" 'Alyosha?' she breathed at last.

" '*Krank*,' I say. 'Alyosha *krank*.'

"Sick, that means.

" '*Krank oder tot?*' she asks severely, and she looks searchingly into my eyes. She thinks he's been killed and I'm afraid to tell her.

" '*Nein, nein,*' I say. '*Grippe*,'

" '*O*,' she beams, '*das ist nichts*.'

"Well, again we sat, drank, ate, danced a little. Several times my Katya gave me the high sign to dance with her sister. I did, and I saw how she faded out one minute, sparked up in a smile the next. She was ashamed she missed him so much. No question, the girl was head over heels in love with him.

"The minute we were left alone, my Katya looked at me with her profound blue eyes and asked, 'The major?'

"Well, how could I lie to her, when the whole truth was in her wise eyes. I shrugged.

" 'Poor Greta,' she says, I've forgotten now how it went in German.

" '*Er liebt*,' I say. '*Er liebt Greta!*'

" '*Ja, ja,*' she says, and adds something, from which I gathered that he loved, but fear was stronger.

" '*Major—papier?*' she asks, and she points a hand as if to say, He wrote a denunciation. The Germans understand all about that.

"I shrugged again, then pointed to the door and said, '*Er ist krank . . .*' He's sick, that means—"

"Just tell it in Russian!" Uncle Sandro interrupted him. "Why must you croak at us with your caw! caw! caw!"

"I remember it better this way," Kemal said, looking at Uncle Sandro with his imperturbable ox eyes.

"Oh all right, go on," Uncle Sandro said, apparently recalling that if Kemal stopped talking now, it would take too much fuel to stoke him up again.

"Yes, m-m-m . . . ," Kemal mooed, but pretty soon he found the track of the story and moved on.

"Anyway, I was still hoping he'd change his mind. The next day I met him and I didn't recognize him. He had sprouted a black cloud overnight.

" 'What's the matter?' I asked.

" 'Nothing,' he says, 'I didn't sleep, that's all. How's Greta?'

" 'Waiting for you,' I say. 'I told her you were sick.'

" 'Did she believe you?'

" 'She did, yes,' I say, 'but her sister suspects.'

" 'It's better to make a clean break,' he says. 'I can't marry her anyway, why drag it out.'

" 'That's dumb,' I say, 'nobody expects you to marry her. But so long as we're here, so long as we're alive, why not keep on meeting?'

" 'You won't understand,' he says. 'To you this is ordinary front-line whoring, but I'm in love for the first time.'

"At this point I went into a rage.

" 'The shakes,' I said, 'should be named by their own name, and it's no use putting on an act.'

"So we turned a little cool toward one another. I visited our girl friends a couple of times and kept on lying to Greta, but I sensed she didn't believe me, and she was wasting away. I felt sorry for her, and this came between Katya and me.

"I felt sorry for him, too. He had withdrawn into himself, he went around looking positively black. Meanwhile, they hadn't hauled us in. I thought, The major's turned out better than we expected. A couple of days later I went to Alyosha.

" 'Listen,' I said, 'you see the major's turned out better than we thought. If he hasn't squealed by now, then it's blown over. But I can see you're out of sorts. You'll get yourself killed in a mood like this!'

" 'What of it,' he says. 'Were the men that we've lost any worse than you and I?'

"Well, I thought, he really is in a bad way! But I didn't let on. We didn't like that kind of talk at the front. If a pilot starts acting sad and mopey, next thing you know he goes down.

" 'Of course not,' I said, 'but the war's almost over. It's dumb to die through your own fault.'

"Suddenly he frowned, as if from unbearable pain, and he said, 'By the way, you don't have to lie any more about my being sick. I think I saw her in town today, and she saw me.'

" 'Stop the foolishness,' I said. 'Let's go over tonight. She's all withered up like a little plant.'

" 'No,' he says, 'I won't go.'

"By now he was blocked by pride and all that kind of thing. He was a very proud guy and gave no quarter to anyone in the air, but he got the shakes in front of the big shots. It's a typically Russian disease, though of course the Russians aren't the only ones who get it.

"So that night I came to see the girls again, with all sorts of food and drink. I climbed upstairs and paid no attention to the fact that the big mirror that used to stand in the front hall was gone. I walked into the room where we usually had our good times, and I saw both sisters come rushing at me. But my Katya was in a frenzy, and Greta's little face was just flaming with joy. It flashed through my mind that Alyosha had come after all, during the day, without me.

" '*Major ist Dieb!*' Katya cries—that is, he's a thief—and she points to the room. 'Major grab! *Alles* grab!'

" '*Ja, ja,*' Greta adds ecstatically, pointing to the bare room—no Viennese chairs, no divan, no cupboard, no tapestry on the wall, only the table. '*Major ist Dieb! Major ist nicht Gestapo! Sage Alyosha! Sage Alyosha!*'

"That means, Tell Alyosha.

" 'Zis is disgracious!' the old man shouts. 'Grab home of antifaschistik!'

"That sounds funny now, but back then, for the first time, I felt the blood in my veins thicken and stop from shame. A lot of men robbed, of course, and we knew that perfectly well. But it's one thing when somebody somewhere gets robbed, and another thing when you know the people and besides have a bond with a woman who's been counting on your protection. Never in my life have I experienced such shame.

"But the worst of it was Greta—beaming all over, her eyes sparkling, I couldn't look at her. She'd decided that since the major had cleaned out their house he couldn't be from the NKVD, and in that case Alyosha had nothing to fear. How could I explain to her that things were more complicated, even though the major really was just a staff officer.

"Then that was why he'd been racing around on a motorcycle at three in the morning: he was looking to see what was where. That was the only reason he hadn't squealed on us.

"I told Greta that I'd tell Alyosha all about it, and lied to the old man that I'd complain about the major. I had to comfort them somehow. The girls brought out some crooked stools from somewhere, we had supper, and I did some hard drinking with the old man.

"The next day I told Alyosha everything, and I saw him perk up a bit.

" 'All right,' he says, 'let's go say good-bye tomorrow. I think we're going to be redeployed some day soon.'

"But we didn't get to say good-bye to our girls. We were redeployed that very night. The new airfield was two hundred kilometers from that little town.

"Alyosha still looked bad, and I couldn't shake a presentiment that he was bound to die. Word of honor, I breathed a sigh of relief the day he got wounded. It was a light wound, and shortly afterward he was sent to a hospital in Russia.

"This time we were living in a small city. Once I came out of a café with some guys and we were waiting by the entrance for a comrade who was still inside.

" 'Kemal,' says one of the guys, 'that girl has her eye on you.'

"I turned around, I looked, there was a German girl standing fifteen paces away, attractive, and she really was smiling at me. Clearly, it was me she was smiling at. I was a little tight, of course, and I smiled back at her, like a fool, and went over to introduce myself.

"Good Lord, but it was Katya! Why hadn't I recognized her! She was wearing a hat and coat, and I had never seen her that way. It turned out she'd been looking for me!

"Well, I told the guys good-bye and went back into the café.

" 'How's Greta?' I asked.

" 'Oh, Greta traurig,' she sighed, and she shook her head.

"I explained to her that Alyosha had been wounded and sent back behind the lines. We spent the night at the apartment of the woman she was staying with.

She cried several times in the night, she kept sighing, and said over and over, '*Schicksal* . . .'

"Fate, that means. I sensed she wanted to say something but couldn't bring herself to it. In the morning, when we got up, she said she was pregnant. She looked at me from under her brows with her attentive, wise eyes and asked, '*Kinder?*'

"Well, what could I answer her? How could I explain to her that this was a trifle more complicated than throwing the major out!

" '*Nein,*' I snapped, and she hung her head.

"We parted that same day, and I never saw her again. But I saw Alyosha thirty years later in Novgorod, at a reunion for veterans of our regiment.

"All of us, veterans arriving from all corners of the country, were staying at the same hotel, where there was to be a banquet that night, presided over by our former regimental commander, now a general. All this time I had known nothing of Alyosha, I didn't even know if he was alive.

"After moving into my room, I went down to the administrator and asked him, had Alexey Starostin arrived? He looked in his book and nodded: yes, he had, he was in room such-and-such.

"I went up to see him, about two hours before the banquet. I looked—balls of fire, what time does to us! How would I ever have recognized this man, now grown bald like me, as that handsome airman, young as a chime in faraway '44, who broke off Prussian rowan branches with red berry clusters! He looks at me and of course he doesn't recognize me: What does this bald fatso want from me? I roared with laughter, and now he recognized me.

" '*Ah-h-h,*' he says, 'Kemal! All that's left of you is your toothy maw!'

"Well, we embraced, we kissed, and I took him to my room. I had brought a good Isabella with me. We sat, drank, reminisced about bygone days. And of course we reminisced about our German girls.

" '*Ah, Gretochka!*' he says with a sigh. 'You can't even imagine what that meant to me! You can't imagine, Kemal! Afterward I was demobilized, got married, flew passenger planes, I have two grown children, like you. Now I'm an air traffic control chief, I have the respect of the district committee and my comrades, but whenever I stop to think, I feel amazed. Do you remember Yesenin? *My life, or have I dreamed you!*

" 'My life seems to have ended there in East Prussia, at the age of twenty-four and all the rest is a sort of weird, drawn-out epilogue! Do you understand this, Kemal?'

"And what do you know—my poor Alyosha was moved to tears. Well, I comforted him, of course, and now he was suddenly in a hurry to get to the banquet.

" 'Come off it, Alyosha,' I said. 'Let's have an hour or so together. They'll be there all night now, and nobody's going to take our seats.'

" 'Oh, no, Kemal,' he says, 'let's go. The general's going to open the gala reception at twenty hundred. I'm embarrassed, let's go!'

"Well, what could I say to him? We went. That's the kind of man he was. But he was a first class pilot. In the air, he wasn't afraid of a frigging thing."

With this Kemal concluded his story and looked around the company, slowly shifting his gaze from one to another.

"Thank God he's done," Uncle Sandro said. "Any more and we'd all be talking German!"

Everyone burst out laughing. The prince poured a round of cognac and said, "He hasn't gotten all that far ahead of you, even in his job."

"No," Kemal said. "Air traffic control chief, he hasn't been any special success."

"He shouldn't have left that girl until they were transferred to another place," Uncle Sandro said. After a moment's thought he added, "But did you understand why he consented to come and say good-bye to her the last time?"

"It was clear why," Kemal replied. "He realized that the major hadn't squealed, so no one was watching us."

"Dumbbell," Uncle Sandro replied, matching his tone, "I have to explain your own story to you. When he consented to go and say good-bye to his girl, he already knew you were going to be transferred to another place that same night."

"No," Kemal laughed, "things like that were held in strict secrecy."

"What do you mean no, when it's yes!" Uncle Sandro protested. "I know better! He hung around the big shots, and somebody told him on the quiet."

"Leave the man alone!" the prince intervened, raising his glass. "He's been punished by fate as it is, poor fellow. We'd better drink to Kemal, who has treated us to a good story from the front."

"Some people treat you to one thing, Kemal to a story," Uncle Sandro said, making it more precise, with a mocking glance at Kemal. "He takes the story right out of his uncle's mouth. Only ca-aw! That's all we get!"

"But I'm sorry for that man," little Khachik said. "Poor man, he loved . . . That's why he cried . . . If he deedn't love, he wouldn't cry . . ."

"Why, no." Kemal started to object, but suddenly he paused, stuck his finger in his ear, and began cleaning it with undisguised enjoyment. Kemal's motions recalled those of a man churning butter, or a plumber clearing a stopped-up washbasin with his plunger.

Frowning with pleasure, Kemal cleaned his ear in this manner for rather a long time, completely detached from those present, which for some reason offended those present. Uncle Sandro gazed at him with silent reproach, as if detecting in his actions a nuance of Freudian indecency, which although not clearly identified as yet by the Abkhazian consciousness was already grossly irritating.

"What do you mean, no?" Uncle Sandro exclaimed, his patience finally at an end.

Kemal very calmly pulled his finger from his ear and inspected the tip of it as if gauging the quality of the churned butter. Apparently he was dissatisfied with the quality, because a grimace of disgusted bewilderment appeared on his face, obviously caused by the distressing discrepancy between the pleasure of the churning process itself and its downright beggarly result. Still wearing this expression, he pulled a handkerchief from his pocket with the other hand, wiped his finger with it, stuck the handkerchief in his pocket, and finished the sentence as if nothing had happened:

" . . . He was a little woozy from the Isabella, that's all, he hit it too hard . . ."

Like any man who has been enamored of many women, Kemal did not attach great importance to them.

"Hakop-Agha," Khachik cried, "another round of coffee, please."

"Coming right up," Hakop-Agha answered, glancing in our direction from behind the counter on which his big brazier was set up with hot sand for making Turkish coffee.

"Excuse me, please," Khachik said, turning to me, "you're the youngest one here. They have delivered some watermelons over there. Fetch two watermelons—I want to take photo, 'Prince with Watermelons.' "

"All right now," the prince said, "we'll manage without watermelons."

"Come on, come on," Kemal interceded for Khachik. "That's a good idea. The prince with watermelons, and us with the prince."

At the far end of the restaurant deck, as though it weren't even part of the restaurant, they were selling watermelons. Ever since childhood, for some reason, I have had the fantasy that a watermelon contained the idea of the sea. Perhaps the wavy stripes on its surface were reminiscent of the sea? Perhaps the coincidence in time—the festiveness of swimming in the sea and the festiveness of eating watermelons, often on shore within sight of the sea? Or the vastness of the sea and the lavishness of the watermelon? Or lots of water in both the one and the other?

Children and teenagers, bronzed by the sun and raising a ceaseless racket, crowded the three platforms of the diving tower. Those who had already dived shouted from the water, and those who stood on the diving platforms shouted to those already floundering in the sea.

Some dove dashingly, with a running start. Others dithered at the edge of the platform; they kept glancing over their shoulders to be sure they didn't get shoved, or trying to excuse their irresoluteness by the fear that they would get shoved.

The children's tanned bodies hurtled steadily into the water—plain dives, sailor dives, now and then a swan dive. The short plunking sound of a body entering the water correctly, and the long splatting sound of an inaccurate landing, with an aftersound of feet finishing the splat. Let's stand a while, admire, listen: plunk! plunk! splat! splat! aftersplat! plunk!

I too used to come here, in our prewar childhood. There was a completely different diving tower here then: it was crowned with a billiard room, and the bravest of the kids used to shinny up to the roof of the billiard room and dive from there.

Peering into those faraway years, I see those kids, but I don't see myself among them. Too bad, but I don't. I don't see myself on the third, the highest, platform either.

No one was admitted here, to the confines of the Dynamo Boat Club—the "Dynamka," as we called it—except those who attended the diving and swimming programs.

But over half the kids weren't in any program and got here from below, by crawling along the beams as far as the swimming docks, and then from there up an iron ladder and to the tower. That was how I got here too.

But it was rather tedious to scramble the eighty meters out from shore along the pilings and the rusted iron crossbeams with their occasional jagged edges. So I sometimes stood for hours near the entrance to the boat club, which was guarded by a corpulent and elderly woman, as she then seemed to me.

The reason I waited there was that a fellow from our street visited the billiard room nearly every day. He was twenty, and his name was Vakhtang. But almost everyone, both adults and children, caressingly and lovingly called him Vakhtik.

When he finished playing billiards, he left the confines of the boat club with a businesslike, festive gait that seemed to signify: I have just concluded a very necessary and very pleasant piece of business and will now undertake another no less necessary and no less pleasant piece of business. At these moments I tried to stand in such a way that he would notice me immediately, and he always did. Having noticed me, he would smile and say something to the woman who guarded the passage. Blooming at his smile, she would let me in.

Sometimes when I was waiting for him he would come rushing up from somewhere behind me, and I would suddenly feel his kind hand rest caressingly on my head or squeeze it in his five fingers like a watermelon, with joking strength, in which case I always tried to smile at him to show that it didn't hurt a bit. We would walk past the guard without stopping. Blooming at his smile, she would come alive sufficiently to recognize me.

What always especially surprised me was the heavy dullness of her nonrecognition when he wasn't there. Not that I asked to go in; but I stood near her, and she might have remembered that I was I, and let me in. Well, all right, I assented mentally, she doesn't have to let me in, but at least she has to recognize me. No, she never did.

The instant Vakhtang appeared, the instant he put his hand on my head, the woman came alive as if she had switched on the lamp of memory, and she included me now in a brief glance of recognition.

For some reason I have remembered him forever as he was in summer, only in summer, though I saw him in all seasons of the year. In the sky-blue silk shirt that he wore untucked, in white slacks and white canvas shoes, he strides festively along the wooden planking of the pier, and his shirt now flutters loosely, now flares out with a fine shudder in the sea breeze and suddenly, for an instant, clings to his trim strong body.

And I see his good face—so I perceived it then, but it really was—with its seemingly strong-willed chin. But I understood even then that his strong-willed chin was laughing at the very idea of a strong-willed chin, because the sum-total of him was not a striving to achieve something. The sum-total of him was the embodiment of happiness achieved, or achievable in five minutes: he would merely go out through the passage, and there, already waiting for him, would be a girl, or more often girls.

"*Sor*ry, girls, I was de*tained!*" he would say on such occasions. As he flung up his arm he would glance briefly at his watch—which was dashingly flipped down onto his hand—and laugh unrestrainedly, laugh along with the girls, as if he had meant his remark to parody the lifestyle of busy people.

It was interesting that Vakhtang and his friends, who played billiards at the boat club for days on end, almost never went swimming. I had the feeling that, for them, this was a stage already passed. But one hot day the whole gang suddenly came roiling out of their billiard room, threw off their dandyish clothes, and turned out to be trim, muscular, strong young men.

They sported uproariously, like splendid animals of an unknown breed, now doing a swan dive off the platform, now a somersault, front or back, now taking a tall stance at the edge of the springboard and piercing the water vertically. They must all have been athletes in some previous life.

Then, in the water, they played tag. They dove adroitly, hiding from each other, and that was the first time I saw Vakhtang swim on his back deep under water in order to watch the boy who had dived after him.

With powerful rocket kicks, each one enveloping him in a bubbling silver of foam, he went ever farther and farther away into the deep of the greenish water, and then disappeared.

The boy who had been chasing him bobbed up to the surface and looked around, treading water, in an effort not to miss Vakhtang when he should pop out of the deep. Even so, after a long moment Vakhtang surfaced behind his back with a cry of "Alley-oop!" and slapped on his neck a handful of sand brought up from the bottom.

Legend had it that Vakhtang, on a bet, had once dived into the sea from the billiard room window. It was one thing to dive off the flat roof, where you had a slight running start, but from here you might not make it to the water. You might easily slam down on the wooden planking of the pier. It's quite possible that he really did dive from the billiard room window; he was brave with an easy, musical bravery.

Vakhtang and his friends splashed gaily around the boat club, and then, as if without prearrangement but in obedience to some instinct, the whole flock went swimming out to the open sea, returned, and one after another pulled themselves up by the handrails with their muscular arms, slapped each other, shook them-selves off, snorted, hopped on one foot and wagged their heads to dash the water from their ears, and then, with loud laughter, grabbing their clothes as if late for billiards the way one is late for a train, they went running up, their heels thudding loudly on the steep wooden stairs.

Where are they? They are silent, gone, their good times and carouses over, but that is how I remember them still—the idols of our prewar gilded youth, in whose neat heads, with the fancy trim at the back of the neck, there shimmered like a mirage the image of Douglas Fairbanks!

Vakhtang's family hadn't lived on our street for very long. It was in my time that their small, elegant house was built, in my time that the living fence of wild trifoliate orange grew up, in my time that the little cottage sprang up next to the main house, joined to it by a common veranda.

"For the young couple . . . when Vakhtik gets married,"—a scrap of conversation between his father and one of the neighbors.

It was in my time that they put up the swing with the two sky-blue cradles in their garden.

"When Vakhtik has children . . ."

The three of them lived together, the father, mother, and son. By the standards of the residents of our street they were rich people. Good rich people. Vakhtang's father was director of some sort of trade organization. We knew nothing more about him. But we had no need to know anything more, and anyway that was beside the point.

On Sundays, or after work, donning a sort of doctor's smock and some spectacles, Vakhtang's father would putter in his little garden. He tied rose stems to stakes, stood on a stepladder to lop off superfluous branches from the fruit trees and withered vines from the grapes. Although Vakhtang's father was a Georgian, that is, a local man, for some reason he seemed like a foreigner to me at such moments.

On weekdays, father and son often encountered each other in the street. The father would be returning from work, while the son would be on his way out to carouse. By this hour the residents of our street had poured out on their little balconies, porches, benches. As if at a silent film, because the words weren't audible, they would watch the father-son encounter with enjoyment.

To judge by their poses, the father was attempting to stop the son and cautiously ascertain where and how he planned to spend the evening. The son, who kept edging away and simultaneously bending toward his father with ironic respect— one guessed that part of the son's irony had to do with the father's cautious attempts to penetrate the secrets of how he spent his time—seemed to be saying to him: Now, Papa, can you really stop a man when he's planning to plunge into the festival of life?

At length they would part; the father would look after him with a smile, and the son would turn to wave and walk on. Interestingly, the son never asked his father for money during these encounters. But everyone knew that in any group Vakhtang paid more promptly and more generously than anyone else. Clearly, in their house the idea that money must be hidden from the son could never even occur to anyone. Clearly, this was why the father worked, so that the son could throw money around handsomely.

Having released his son, the father walked on at his benign, unhurried gait, with a weary smile and a kindly greeting for all the residents of the street. As he walked he fanned the faces of the residents of our street with the breeze of adoration.

"He could've come in a car, like a people's commissar . . ."

"He doesn't want to—a plain man."

"No, he has heart trouble, that's why he walks."

"He's not a man, he's gold . . ."

There were probably people on our street who envied or disliked this family, but I didn't know any. If there were, they hid their envy and dislike from others. All I remember is a universal love for this family, conversations about their generosity and wealth. Thus my comrade Khristyu's older brother, who helped his father finish Vakhtang's house, told fabulous stories of the way the workmen were fed at Vakhtang's. The lavishness and variety of the food were staggering.

"What did it cost for the bread alone!" he said. "Take it like this and it squeezes crust to crust like an accordion. Let go and it breathes till you eat it!"

On our street, of course, the Rich Tailor was also counted a rather prosperous man. But in the Rich Tailor's life one sensed too vividly the crude candor of primary accumulation.

This was different. Vakhtang's parents had apparently been rich for quite some time, and in any case they obviously weren't striving for wealth. To the residents of our street this family was an ideal, a showcase of achieved happiness. And they were grateful to the family for the simple fact that they could peep into the showcase.

All of them, no doubt, or almost all, strove for this or a similar happiness in life. And all of them, to one degree or another, were beaten and frayed by life, and in the end they resigned themselves in their sheltering houses or tiny communal apartments. Admiring Vakhtang's family's handsome house, the garden, the happy life, they were grateful to the family if only for the fact that their own dream was not a mirage, it was a correct dream, they had simply been unlucky. At least *these* people were lucky, at least they allowed the neighbors to admire their happiness. But not only were the neighbors allowed to admire their happiness, they also came in for a goodly share in its abundance.

Sometimes late in the evening, if my aunt and I were returning from the last movie show, we would see Vakhtang's father and mother, invariably sitting on handsome chairs by the gate and waiting for their son.

Between them they usually had a thin-legged little table, on which we dimly discerned the green of a bottle of Borzhom and the appetizing black contours of several slices of watermelon in a tall compote.

Taking a slice of watermelon in hand and bending over slightly lest he spatter himself, Vakhtang's father sometimes ate watermelon as he talked back and forth with my aunt. But what I noticed was the *way* he ate. He was the only man I had ever seen who ate watermelon languidly. And it was utterly obvious that the whole thing was honest, no pretense! So that was what it meant to be rich! Rich people were those who could eat watermelon languidly.

As a rule, on these occasions, my aunt always started talking to them in Georgian, although both she and they knew Russian perfectly well. From this one realized, then, that it was customary to talk to rich people in their own language. After talking and laughing with them a while, Auntie walked on more spiritedly than was her rule, though even as a rule her high heels tapped along quite spiritedly. From this one gathered, then, that association with rich people, even through language, raised one's spirits. And one also divined that the surge of fresh strength called forth by intercourse with the rich must be gratefully demonstrated to them, then and there. Thus they lived on our street, and it seemed there would be no end to this abundance. And suddenly one day everything fell apart! Vakhtang was accidentally shot to death by a comrade while hunting.

I remember his face in the coffin, embittered by monstrous injustice, woeful and offended, as if all of a sudden someone had rudely shoved him—who had been convinced that he was created for happiness—into this unpleasant, this cruel, this irremediable fate.

And at the last moment, when he slammed into this fate, he had been forever embittered toward those who, after making his whole previous life an unbroken string of bright, happy, totally untroubled days, had now so suddenly, so cruelly, gotten back at him for his cloudless youth.

By his cruelly embittered face he seemed to mean: Had I known they'd get back at me like this for my cloudless youth, I would have consented to take life's bitterness in small doses my whole life long, not this way, all at once. But no one asked me . . .

The faces of the residents of our street, who came to say good-bye to the deceased, expressed sincere sympathy but also a certain surprise and even disenchantment. Their faces seemed to say: So you, too, can have such terrible woe! Then why bamboozle us into thinking that you were special, that you were happy!

For some reason it was not Vakhtang's mother who overwhelmed me with the excess of her grief, although she wept and screamed ceaselessly, but his father. Paralyzed, he sat by the coffin and from time to time laid a hand on his son's forehead with a sort of soul-shattering simplicity, as if his son had come down sick and he wanted to feel his temperature. After lightly chafing his son's forehead, his trembling palm would suddenly become quiet, as if assured that the temperature was not dangerous, his son had fallen asleep.

The father did not live even till Vakhtang's fortieth-day memorial; he died of rupture of the heart, as people said then. It seemed his soul had rushed to catch up with his beloved son while it still could. At the time, in my childishly well-rounded logic, I fancied that Vakhtang's mother too must soon die, to complete the image of devastation.

But she didn't die, not in one year or in two. She lived on in this desolation, standing at the gate in a black mourning dress. The years passed and still she stood at the gate, sometimes calling loudly back and forth with neighbors down the street and again falling silent, stood by the hopelessly dust-covered trifoliate orange bushes that now hedged God knows what. Even today she stands at her gate, as she has for years, for decades, and waits for an answer to her wordless question: Why?

But there is no answer. Or perhaps—who knows—fate does give an answer, which has turned her into an obscenely fat, frowzy old woman. Life, it's not the cruelty of your lessons that scares us, what scares us is their enigmatic reticence!

I am telling this story because it was then—as a little boy standing by the coffin, perhaps transfixed for the first time by the sadness of Ecclesiastes, whom I didn't know—that I became dimly and yet powerfully aware of the tragic error that had always been embedded in the life of this family.

I realized that you couldn't live this way, and I had the hope that there was still time ahead and I would guess how you could live. Like a little capitalist, I dreamed even then of investing my life in an enterprise that would never, never go broke.

With the years I came to realize that a thing so fragile as human life can have worthwhile meaning only if bound to something indisputably stable that in no way depends on chance. Only by making it a part of that stability, though a very small part, can one live without glancing over one's shoulder, and sleep calmly on the most anxious nights.

With the years my thirst for a love bond with something stable has grown stronger, my very concept of the substance of stability has grown more precise, and this, I think, has delivered me from many forms of vanity, though not from all, of course.

Now, it seems, I have reached the source of my revulsion toward every instability, every manifestation of Pisaism. I think it's a sin not to strive for stability.

From one stability to another, higher, stability a man climbs, as by steps, to the highest stability. But this, I have only just realized, is what from time immemorial men have called the firmament. A good, strong word!

We are humanly free from inner and outer slavery only in proportion as we have delightedly bound ourselves to the indestructible Stability, the eternal Firmament.

Scraps of these scenes and these thoughts flashed through my mind while I was choosing among the heaped watermelons, and I chose two big ones that struck me as indisputable embodiments of the stability and plenitude of vital forces.

From the sea came the clamor of swimming children, and I felt like chucking a couple of watermelons their way. Alas, I was too sober to do it, and the gesture struck me as excessively rhetorical.

So it goes—whenever it occurs to us to do a good deed, we feel we're too sober for it, but on the very rare occasion when we're consulted for wise advice, it turns out to be precisely the moment we can't talk straight.

I picked up the watermelons and returned to my companions. Hakop-Agha had already brought the coffee. He sat lost in thought, his chin resting on his palm.

"Now we'll take picture, 'Prince with Watermelon,' " Khachik said when I laid the watermelons on the table.

"Khachik, that's enough, for God's sake," the prince protested.

But he who loves is implacable.

"I know when it's enough," Khachik said. Positioning us near the prince, he ordered him to lay his hands on the watermelon and snapped the shutter several times.

We drank our coffee, and Kemal began cutting the watermelon.

The watermelon split open with a loud crack, anticipating the knife as the ice cracks and gives way before the prow of an icecutter. Seeds popped out of the cleft. The crack of the watermelon anticipating the movement of the knife, and the seeds snapping out of the cleft, testified to the solid ripeness of our watermelon. This proved to be true. We drank another round, and with it ate watermelon.

"Now take Mikoyan," Hakop-Agha said. "When Khrushchev lost power and new ones had not come in, was one moment when he could take power . . . Take it, yes? One year, two, he don't need more. Do something good for Armenia, yes? And then geev back to Russians. He deed not take, deed not want . . ."

"You Armenians can be proud of Mikoyan," the prince said. "There's not a man in the government who's been in power longer than he was."

"Listen," Hakop-Agha objected crossly, "I don't need any blah-blah conference! What good hees power do us, if he do nahthing for Armenia? He tried for himself, he tried for his own family . . ."

Grumbling mildly, Hakop-Agha collected the cups on the tray and went back to his station.

"When he found out I was an air traffic controller," Kemal said, glancing after the departing coffee chef with a smile, "he asked me to watch the planes flying from Yerevan with special attention. He said Armenian pilots talked too much at the controls, he didn't trust them . . ."

"The nation that has Hakop-Agha," Uncle Sandro said, "will never perish!"

"The nation that has Uncle Sandro," the prince said, "will never perish either."

"Do *they* understand that," Uncle Sandro said, with a nod toward Kemal and me, probably as being not the best representatives of the nation.

"What should nations do that don't have you?" Kemal asked, and looked around the table.

Silence reigned. It was decidedly unclear what nations that had neither Hakop-Agha nor Uncle Sandro should do.

"All of us will die," Khachik suddenly shouted, "even the prince will die, only photos will be left! But a nation, any nation, is like this sea, and the sea will never perish!"

We drank a last glass, finished the watermelon, then got up and went to the counter to say good-bye to Hakop-Agha.

"You remember what I told you?" he asked Kemal, sprinkling sugar into *jezve*s of coffee and peering at him anxiously for a moment.

"I remember," Kemal replied.

"Remember always," Hakop-Agha said firmly. He thrust half a dozen *jezve*s into the sand brazier and began moving the handles, snugging the copper dippers of coffee deeper into the hot sand.

We started downstairs. It occurred to me that Hakop-Agha himself would never perish. His exacting love for the Armenians bothered no one, and no one could ever take this love away from him. He had bound himself to a stable cause and was therefore invincible.

About a month later I happened to encounter Khachik on the seaside boulevard. I wanted to take him to a restaurant and treat him, in gratitude for the photos. The prince had passed some of them on to Kemal, and Kemal to me.

But Khachik didn't recognize me, and since he was already quite cross with some slow-witted clients, whom he was posing near a cactus bed—he kept jostling a big man closer to a mighty cactus, while the man looked back fearfully, afraid of running into it, and with good reason—I made no move to explain where we had met.

Exactly like the woman who had stood at the entrance to the Dynamo Boat Club, he had seen us only because we were illumined by the light of his beloved Prince Emukhvari, I realized. I was already ten paces away when I suddenly had a mischievous impulse to switch that light on.

I glanced back. Little Khachik was again jostling his big, pudgy, plaster-monument client closer to the toothy cactus, while the client modestly balked as if insisting on compliance with accident-prevention procedures. The women, the monument's companions, watched the skirmish in silence, without expressing sympathy for either side.

"A crystal soul!" I shouted. "Plain, plain!" Khachik abandoned the man forthwith and looked back at me. The man profited by his freedom to take a small step forward.

"Ah-h-h-h!" Khachik shouted, beaming all over with the joy of recognition. "Why deedn't you say right off! This *götferan*'s got me all rattled! That was good time we had! Where's the prince? If you see him, let's do it again! You said right: A crystal soul! Plain! Plain!"

I walked on without waiting to see how Khachik's struggle with his unyielding client would end. I was sure Khachik would win.

THREE PRINCES
CAROUSE IN A GREEN
LITTLE YARD

W E CAME ROLLING INTO this isolated Abkhazian village in three cars, for a reason that has now completely slipped my mind. Most likely there wasn't any reason. One of our party had been invited to visit a relative, and he simply picked us up along the way.

There were about eight of us. Or something on that order, I don't remember exactly. What does it matter, anyway? Briefly, there were more than five but fewer than ten of us. In any case, it wasn't a crowd. What a memory—I'm getting ready to tell a story about people I caroused with, but I can't remember how many of them there were. Oh, I'll probably remember them all as I go along, but at the moment I just can't call them to mind.

I have a feeling I'm about to begin confessing my weaknesses. A tried and true device. It's what I built my literary career on. I thought the device had exhausted itself by now, but evidently not. It turns out to be altogether inexhaustible. The reader likes it when he feels a little smarter than the author. He experiences a surprising rush of energy, merriment, and, in the long run, gratitude to the author. The author, in turn, likes it when he succeeds in pulling the reader's leg a little. He too feels merry. This way, we cheer each other up and the evening's gone before you know it.

There's one thing that astounds me: how it is that I've lived quite an orderly life, orderly by our standards, and reached maturity without remembering a single date, a single number, a single telephone, a single address, or the name of a single big shot (except for Abesalomon Nartovich, with whom life has repeatedly brought me together).

As for dates, I do seem to remember that the Patriotic War with Napoleon was in 1812. And the Patriotic War with Hitler began in 1941. Further, of course, I remember that the October Revolution was in 1917. That's all—I don't remember any more dates.

This may seem like affectation or blasphemy, but I rarely remember what year I'm living in. Yes, I always remember what country I'm living in. But I never remember what year it is. When the postwoman brings me a money order and I have to fill out the form, I'm always forced to ask her what day of the month it is and what year. Sometimes it's awkward. Granted, I always tip them, and they're usually glad to answer my question. But sometimes a new one comes. You ask her this silly question, and she doesn't know yet that you're going to tip her, and she answers your question rather primly. But there's no help for it, that's the way my mind is laid out.

I've even come up with a theory that rather convincingly explains my lack of memory. My theory is that different people's minds are differently laid out. In some people's minds the stockrooms occupy a lot of space, while the machine shop occupies a rather modest amount of space. In other people's minds—like mine, supposedly—the machine shop spreads out of control and crowds out the stockrooms. I think it's quite a sound theory.

I just had a thought: What if my theory about my lack of memory is an attempt to poeticize ordinary sclerosis? No, I disagree. I still have a pretty good memory for real poetry and a few other things agreeable to my soul.

But the most likely explanation is this: My mind is the last bastion of defense against civilization. Even now it is belching up and hurling away the importunate bearers of civilization.

In the bastion of my mind, the last dozen Chegemians (only in my mind are there any left, it seems) are defending it against unclean spirits with forked antennae, who are swarming from all sides, clambering up, crawling into all the cracks. And I cheer on the heroic defenders with might and main.

"Hit 'em, boys!" I shout. "The Endurskies have sent them down on us! Pour boiling cornmeal over them! Smash their skulls with a corn mallet! Skewer them with a crowbar! Poke them in the face with a burning brand plucked from the fire! Lash them with the kettle chain!"

They tell me that civilization is inevitable, therefore you have to like it. But death is inevitable, too—do I therefore have to like it? However, I'll come back to that.

Now that we know what the real problem is, and we're feeling a little calmer, let's go on. As for any kind of table, map, diagram, schedule—all that stuff is complete chaos for me. Not the slightest possibility of mutual insight. For example, I've never had the strength to use the suburban train schedule. It's enough to drive you mad, there are so many numbers going across and up and down; and among all these hundreds of numbers you have to find the one and only number that signifies the time your train leaves.

I'd rather stand a whole hour beside the schedule, waiting for a man with a gentle expression to come up, and such a man can be a long time coming, but still, when he does come, I in turn will put on a weak-sighted expression and ask him, "Would you please tell me when such-and-such train leaves . . . I can't make it out myself because my eyes are bad . . ."

As for any kind of diagram or chart, or that thing called a "development curve"—all that stuff is totally absurd. Yes, I hate all your "development"—precisely because it's always curved and crooked!

Or a route map, let's say. On tours abroad, the foreign guides intentionally hand out maps every day, and our naive tourists pounce on them because they're free. My thought is: Numskulls, what do you want with those maps? You'll be taken wherever you're supposed to go anyway, won't you?

They don't realize that these same guides later go back and report, "These Soviet tourists, they aren't tourists at all. All but one of them are spies—you should see the way they pounce on the maps."

The bourgeoisie then builds its propaganda on that. Now I ask you: Who is better "developed" politically, I or they? Who should get to go abroad more often—I or they?

It sometimes seems to me that the common sense I inherited from my Chegemian forebears protects my mind from unnecessary and even harmful knowledge. When you come right down to it, what does it matter what year you're living in, if you know for a fact that time stopped long ago in your country and is not going anywhere?

This characteristic of my mind, its complete freedom from worldly and scholastic nonsense, permits me to concentrate my intellectual efforts on the most vital and overriding problems. I have already made a number of outstanding discoveries with respect to these problems and will probably make more (unless, of course, they stop me).

There are certain rather well-informed people who notice the isolated shortcomings that still exist in our country and think: What if we crowd the Bolsheviks a little, with the idea that we'll stop crowding them in the future, when we've eliminated these deficiences? To people like that I say, "Watch out, boys! That's not only foolish, it's worse than foolish—it's dangerous. Don't you know that the Bolsheviks dreadfully dislike it when anyone crowds them?"

Now I reveal to these people one of my great discoveries. I alone have grasped what all our social and economic troubles stem from. They all stem from the fact that out in the provinces, and to some extent even at the center, our leaders lack a sense of humor.

It all began with Lenin. The great Lenin, as he confessed to Gorky (this is described in Gorky's reminiscences, and even our censorship did not strike it out), lacked a sense of humor. With characteristic frankness, Lenin confessed to Gorky that while he appreciated other people's humor, he himself, unfortunately, was humorless. But owing to his genius, Lenin partially compensated for his deficiency in humor through his magnificent work as an organizer.

After Lenin, unfortunately, the Bolsheviks, although they did not possess his genius, decided to follow his lead with respect to humor. That was a major blunder. They appointed their most unsmiling man to be the country's leader, in the mistaken belief that the most unsmiling man was the most earnest one. This is what revealed the tragedy in the lack of a sense of humor. Yes, he did smile into his mustache with satisfaction, but only later, after 1937. Some Party members clutched their heads when they realized exactly which of life's phenomena made him smile, but it was too late.

I propose that all the resources of the press and of verbal persuasion should be mobilized to develop a sense of humor in leaders at all levels all over the country. This truly heroic undertaking probably will not be accomplished without sacrifices at first.

They (or we? no, better they), the humorists, will probably be persecuted at first, and some of them even put in prison camp. But even there, they (or we? no, better they) must not lose their sense of humor, they must tirelessly foster it in the investigators, prosecutors, guards, and other persons invested with power. They must behave like the Party members arrested by Stalin, who, even in the most terrible Siberian camps, continued their furious, intransigent arguments on the strategy and tactics of the world proletariat.

And we, the humorists who remain at large (or they? no, we!), must not lose courage for a moment; night and day we must spread humor throughout the land. We must establish departments of humor in all the institutes of higher education and even in the highest Party School. At the highest Party School, Arkady Raikin could be appointed head of the humor department, if, of course, he's a member of the Party, which in itself would not be devoid of humor.

Humor must penetrate all meetings, all conferences, all plenary sessions, all congresses. No, don't take me too literally, the working sessions won't be abolished. But all the reports at the congresses, for example, will be shot through with humor. The delegates will wait with impatience to see what sort of *chochmeh* the representative from Odessa will bring, and others will try and guess what the speaker from Yerevan will say. Everyone is cheerful, Kosygin smiles as if his economic reform had been accepted. And why not? It's quite possible— under humorous conditions they will certainly accept it, Comrade Kosygin!

Under humorous conditions an excellent mood prevails in the land, everyone is equal and everyone has an equal right to laugh and be laughed at. The Party laughs at the intelligentsia, the intelligentsia laughs at the Party, and the workers laugh looking at the both of them. Socialism, gentlemen, is a good joke!

When, at last, humor possesses the Party and the Party possesses humor, we'll get rid of all the shortcomings of our social and economic life with an airy laugh.

"Watch out!" I tell myself. Won't my discussion of humor lead to a certain dangerous loss of sense of humor?

In that case I immediately take back my words. Or even better, I lay my cards on the table. These pages were actually written with the approval of the highest courts, in order to detect people who by smiling, or especially by laughing, reveal their dialectical unreliability.

No, I shouldn't do this. I keep feeling myself getting carried away, and I can't stop. I must get hold of myself immediately and return forthwith to the strict framework of the plot.

And so . . . We came rolling into this isolated Abkhazian village in three cars, for a reason that has now completely slipped my mind. Most likely there wasn't any reason. One of our party had been invited to visit a relative, and he simply picked us up along the way.

There were approximately eight of us. And by the way, we wouldn't have had that discussion about humor if I had known exactly how many of us there were. Judge for yourselves, now, whether an inexact knowledge of his subject is fruitful for an author under certain circumstances, or whether it leads him to shattering ideological lapses.

Our party itself had taken shape accidentally. I was on my way from Gagra to Mukhus to see a comrade whom I had helped to extricate from a very bad situation. Pushed into a fight, he had been forced to kill a man, for which he had been sentenced to twelve years in a strict-regime camp.

He had already served about two years when I wrote—and published, which was much harder to do—an article about this incident, in which I was able to prove that he had inflicted his fatal blow on the man while defending himself against the no less fatal blows being inflicted on him by two men.

After publication of this article, the case was reviewed and he was released from prison. I heard via the grapevine that the slain man's father, an old criminal, was threatening to ''rub out'' both me and his son's recently released involuntary murderer. The man's threats made no great impression on me—he had never seen me, we lived in different cities, and I did not believe he would try to seek me out.

The single precaution I decided to maintain was to avoid going to the town where the old man lived. This was not hard to do, although several of my relatives, whom I was not averse to seeing, lived in the same town. But if I didn't see them I wouldn't die of yearning. In any case, I tried to keep the old man in mind, so that nothing would accidentally bring me to that town.

And here I was, riding to Mukhus to see my friend who had been released from prison. When my taxi reached the outskirts of the city, an oncoming car honked at us, and my driver stopped. I saw my old comrade climb out of the other car. On that day, at that hour, he and a friend of his were on their way to Gagra to see me. Neither he nor I had agreed on a day to meet. How did we both get the idea of rushing toward each other at precisely that time?

My comrade and I embraced. Standing by the side of the road, he and his friend and I began to discuss the virtues and shortcomings of the neighborhood restaurants.

Just now, knocking out these lines on the typewriter, I remembered that I have already described this meeting—and the whole sad episode with my friend that preceded it—in another story, where I credited my own good deed to my hero. And here I've returned to this deed. What's going on? Am I drawn to my own good deed, like a criminal to the scene of the crime? Or am I sorry I credited it to my hero?

Yes; life—my life at any rate—is so poor in good deeds that I have unintentionally framed this plot in such a way as to spotlight my own modest exploit.

Strange is the life of the writer, that is, the observer of life. Who invented this office? Why do I find myself in this office? I have a feeling that some fine day somebody's going to show up and say for all to hear, "Dismiss him from the office of observer of life. Not only is he incapable of observing life when you put her to graze in the green pastures of our ideology—he doesn't see what's going on right under his nose."

Having a premonition that this will come sooner or later, I confess in advance: Yes, I really am a very unobservant person. Here is a rather amusing example of my poor powers of observation.

When I was a student, I made the acquaintance of a certain bewitching girl and we became friends. Before me, she had been in love with some unknown soccer player from her city, and his memory was constantly with her. I tried to soften the bitterness of her recollections with the balm of tender kisses, and I seem to have succeeded.

At any rate, she let me know that if this kept up she might be able to forget her soccer player. I patiently waited for the time when she would finally forget about her soccer player, but she continued to tell stories about him. As soon as there was a pause in her stories, I filled it with a kiss. I tried to extend the pauses in her stories with kisses, and she rather graciously allowed me to do this.

Admittedly, after waiting out the kiss, she got back to her soccer player. She unerringly picked up her story from the point where I had interrupted her. I kept waiting for her to lose her place so that I could take bolder action, but she did not lose her place and continued to tell about her soccer player. I didn't grow impatient, because I liked her very much and kissing her seemed to me an enormous achievement. She and I met this way for about two months, and I was satisfied with life and fate.

In those days I had a friend who lived across the hall from me in the dormitory. He had been initiated into my affairs of the heart and the mournful story of her soccer player.

Once I dropped by his room and found my girl friend standing by the hot plate, frying a cutlet for my friend. At first I was quite badly disconcerted, not having expected to encounter her there at all. Then an easy and noble explanation for her appearance in my friend's room occurred to me. Of course—she was on her way to my room. Seeing her, he had intercepted her and forced her to fry cutlets for him.

That was typical of him; he had a certain inclination to take advantage of the people around him. I remembered all that in an instant and even felt a sudden platonic pride in my girlfriend's culinary talents. A certain shadow of envy, because I had never taken advantage of those talents myself, also flashed through my mind. But I reassured myself with the thought that she was in for a whole lifetime of frying cutlets for me.

Now thoroughly reassured, and invited to their table besides, I had a good time over dinner and then, suspecting nothing, went out for a walk with her.

She began telling about her soccer player again, and this time I noticed in her story a more pessimistic note than usual. She expressed doubt that anyone would ever take the place of this unlucky first love. I need hardly say that I assured her of the reverse.

Two weeks went by, in the course of which the three of us were together several times, before I guessed that a fundamental realignment of the *dramatis personae* had taken place.

I was appalled at what had happened. The scabby experience of mankind had taught me nothing. I could not imagine that such a thing was possible between friends. My own experience pointed to something else entirely. When I was a schoolboy, two of my friends and I had fallen in love with the same girl. All three of us helped one another declare our love to her. Although she rejected each of us in turn, our friendship did not disintegrate. We very much wanted her to give at least one of us a break. But since the breaks were against us, there was no help for it, and we were comforted by our own friendship.

(The impossibility of realizing one's most amazing—as a rule, his first—love. Apparently it has been planned that way from on high. What would a man do, after attaining happiness? In unrequited love, fate lets us sniff at happiness; then, flinging it into the unattainable distance, she says, as to a dog, "Fetch!" And we try to find it. That is the path of spiritual growth.)

. . . It worked out quite differently this time. It seemed he had fallen in love with her at the very beginning and had hidden it from me. It seemed he had been buying her a box of chocolates every day for about two months. If he didn't find her in her room, he left the candy under her pillow. So that if she had been out for a while, when she came back to the room she went straight to her pillow, moved it aside, and got the box. If there was no box, she said, "So he hasn't come yet?"

At first she laughed (her roommates said) as she ate the candy and treated her girl friends. Then her provincial soul wavered, and she decided to show her gratitude for the candy with tender friendship.

That's what I think. Besides, against the background of those daily chocolates, I probably made a rather unfavorable impression. Although I had given her several modest student suppers with beer, to which she had taken a liking since the days of the soccer player, these efforts must have struck her as penury.

Probably a reappraisal of values took place in her pretty little head. She must have reasoned thus: This one kisses me and treats me once in a while to his pathetic Zhigulyovskoe beer. That one doesn't kiss me yet but already treats me, and daily at that, to a box of chocolates. And what will happen when he starts to kiss me?

Anyway, realizing that the scales were obviously tipped in his favor, I quietly withdrew and started living an independent life. I made no explanation either to him or to her. The idea of entering into any negotiation was terribly unpleasant, and they, thank God, did not try to explain themselves to me.

If I accidentally encountered them on the street or at the institute, I greeted them with reserve and walked on. In reply to my nod, she looked at me with an expression of easy melancholy, as though trying to comfort me, as though impressing it on me that I was greatly mistaken if I thought her new situation freed her from the burden of recollections of the wonderful soccer player.

He greeted me quite differently. He greeted me as if raptly listening to the music of the highest spheres, thus letting me know that it was utterly impossible for him, in his condition, to get involved in petty, earthly, human relationships.

This went on for about a month. Then one day he dropped in and said that he was inviting me to dine with them in his room. I consented, although I very much wanted not to go. I was afraid that if I refused I would have to have it out with him. And I didn't want to have it out with him at all. Here was a man I'd been friends with for two years, how could I say to his face that he was a bastard? It wasn't that he got the girl, that happens often enough in life. After all, I had known about the candy he was giving her, long before her soul wavered. I had to pretend that nothing had happened—this suited both sides. Incidentally, I confess to a still greater sin. Even when I already knew that an acquaintance had done something base, I never could help shaking his hand if he offered it, or responding to his nod. Sometimes, in rare instances, I could tell him what I thought of him, but I couldn't help shaking the hand he offered.

Often, after shaking such a hand, I developed an incredible desire to strip the skin from my own sullied palm. Once the feeling lasted for two days. Does that mean I felt the sinfulness of such a handshake? Yes, and despite all I shook the hands of similar people again later.

After "The Goatibex" came out, my own *Red Subtropics* gave it a devastating review. It was a direct call to shed the author's blood. In addition to all my other sins, the review accused me of insulting the national honor.

The man who wrote the review, and the people standing behind him, obviously expected the call to bloodshed to be picked up by the central press. Their expectation was not entirely unfounded. Someone on the staff of our most important press organ later told me that the question had been discussed, but people inclined to moderation had triumphed. They didn't touch the story.

When I read the review I flew into a rage that lasted two hours. I paced the room, and my whole angry monologue against the reviewer can be fitted into one sentence: Why? Why should you, Goldinov, defend the honor of Abkhazians against me, an Abkhazian?

Then I gave up on the whole thing, but I was still very angry at the reviewer, especially since I knew him well. Several years later, I went to Mukhus and accidentally bumped into him on the street. Smiling mischievously, he offered his hand and I . . . and I . . . and I . . . shook it.

Let's try to explore the question calmly. People might say to me, "After all, if you don't shake hands with a man who has done something base, it won't kill him. But he'll find it very disagreeable, and it may keep him from a shabby act the next time."

That may or may not be so. Undoubtedly there is a possibility that the humiliation will lead him to repentance and self-purification. But it is also possible that not shaking his hand will lead a man who has behaved vilely to still greater desperation and a still greater inclination to behave vilely.

What should we do, then? Shake the hand that has done something base, or not shake it? Who thought up this idiotic custom of shaking hands, anyway? Maybe we should abolish it? Or, if it's too late to do that, we should introduce several types of handshake, signifying: I approve of your existence on earth, I do not completely approve, or I completely disapprove.

No, I have to get back to myself. Why do I shake the offered hand despite all, knowing it is the hand of a man who has behaved vilely? The main reason, of course, is that I am constitutionally unable to be an agent of chastisement. I can't, that's all. I don't justify myself, but neither do I utterly condemn myself.

Now let's examine the psychology of people who are brave enough not to notice the offered hand. Among them, of course, are some who are simply honest people with a strong nervous system; their hand, by not moving to meet the offered hand, clearly demonstrates their disapproval of vile behavior.

It's so. That happens. But, unfortunately, most people who condemn evil in that manner act out of completely different motives. Because of our profession, we have a pretty good insight into the background of these motives. The background is this: You have done something vile (sold out, let's say), while I've been struggling with all my might to keep from doing something vile. So am I supposed to shake your hand? Take that—I won't shake it! Let everyone see that I haven't done anything vile; let me substitute that small advantage, at least, for the big one of which I modestly but ardently dream.

Let us try to examine this question on the philosophical plane. There appear to be two types of psychology, two attitudes toward evil. One type of person, noticing evil, strives to deal with it on the spot, so as to restore the harmony of the universe. The other, seeing a manifestation of evil, is aware of its infinite interconnections with universal evil and loses heart at the realization that if he chops off one branch of evil, another, or even many, will grow in its place.

The first says, "Well, what of it—we'll keep chopping them off!"

The second says, "No, that's not right. We have to take a longer path. We have to dig to the roots and extirpate the tree of evil whole."

The first: "But that would take the efforts of a hundred generations!"

The second: "Even if it takes thousands! There's no other way."

The first: "We must force man to be man!"

The second: "We must humanize man, and then he himself will become man."

Of course, my discussion is a bit lame. No, I don't mean to deny the usefulness of those who are occupied exclusively with chopping off the branches. They too are necessary, we'll keep a certain number of those people, but we'll put our main effort into digging up the roots.

On the whole, those branch-choppers—that is, people who war directly with evil—are a rather strange tribe. Sometimes you're standing in line, waiting for your turn. People keep bypassing the line and barging into the shop. Of course you have the fleeting thought that it would be nice to station yourself there by the shop and establish order, to make the line move faster. But a sort of spiritual laziness holds you back, and besides you have to reckon with the possibility of getting punched in the nose. You fall to thinking deep thoughts about how to organize the retail trade so that there wouldn't be any lines at all. Sometimes an amazing scheme will come to you, but you are aware that you don't have what it takes to push it through the appropriate channels.

Sighing heavily, you continue to wait your turn, and brazen upstarts keep on barging into the shop from all sides. Well, okay, you decide to yourself; big deal, I'll spend an extra half-hour or hour standing here.

Suddenly a forceful man steps out of line, stations himself by the shop, and lets nobody in. The line moves faster, and no one even punches him in the nose, he looks so forceful and independent. There *are* real men on earth, you think, and I myself am a doormat. Suddenly a great idea comes to you: you must tell this forceful man about your excellent scheme to eliminate lines. He and he alone will push that scheme past all obstacles and put it into effect! But your inspiration dies at the clear realization that this forceful man will not bother with your scheme, he finds it much pleasanter establishing order here, in view of the crowd. He would even find it somewhat undesirable to live in a situation where he didn't have to establish order in view of the crowd.

The fateful impossibility of coupling an excellent scheme with the actions of a forceful man—isn't that the tragedy of world history?

Sometimes a forceful man like that will stand by the shop, fending off smart alecks, just until the moment his turn comes. Then, followed by the gaze of the crowd, he buys his groceries and departs, as if saying, "I don't need any flowers, any thanks—your silent adoration is enough for me."

It's so. That happens. But sometimes this forceful man fends off the smart alecks for a while and then suddenly, without waiting for his own turn, thrusts some money at the saleswoman, takes his groceries, and departs with rapid steps, as if startled by some thought, which has just now struck him and which requires him to drop everything and walk toward this thought.

And here's the interesting thing. The saleswoman knows he didn't wait his turn, the line knows he got his groceries too soon, and yet everyone is sure that that's only right, he was supposed to have some profit from his timely heroism. The people in line look after him with a long gaze, excusing his behavior and yet at the same time yearning a little for a selfless idol, as though understanding that they themselves are not quite worthy of such an idol.

But I'm getting bogged down. Meanwhile, the man who has done something vile stands with patiently extended hand, and I can't decide: Should I shake it, or not?

There now—I've done it. Afterward I feel disgust for myself and for my own palm. Yet, despite all, I did shake the hand. Does that mean that if I hadn't I would have felt even worse? Am I choosing the lesser of two evils? Why is it the lesser?

Because by not shaking his hand I totally deny that this is a man standing before me, not an animal. Such a punishment is out of proportion to his mis-demeanor, isn't it? What else can I do? Yet could it be that by shaking his hand I confess my complicity in the vile deed the man has committed? Undoubtedly there's truth in that. After all, before doing his vile deed, subconsciously or even consciously he pictured all his friends and relations and sensed that, on the whole, all of them would most likely swallow the vile deed. Since he reached that decision, does it mean we gave him some reason to hope his vile deed would get by, does it mean there was something kindred in us? Of course we weren't the chief culprits, but it was we who gave reason to hope that the vile deed would get by; and now, by not offering him our hand, we are putting all the blame on him, although part of the blame belongs to us. But again, by shaking his hand we fully vindicate his hope that the vile deed will get by. No; we should have been such that he would not dare do anything vile. That's where the truth lies! But after all, should we ever be like that? By not shaking his hand, we show everyone that henceforth we will be such that no one will dare do anything vile; yet he may exclaim, "That's not fair! Why must you start with me? I might not have dared do anything vile if I'd known you were going to punish people, starting with me!"

Good Lord, what to do? It's wrong to offer your hand, and wrong not to offer your hand! Could this be a question without an answer? Could every flight from human society be caused by the impossibility of answering it? Isn't that the idea behind hermitage? Run, run, to a cave, to a monastery, where you won't have to shake anyone's hand!

Could that be the reason Leo Tolstoy ran from Yasnaya Polyana? They're coming from all over the world. A famous writer. A count. Russian hospitality. He has to shake their hands. Talk to them. He, the great psychologist, sees how many dirty dogs there are among these guests. But Sofya Andreevna rejoices and understands nothing. And the explosion of the final decision: Run! Run!

And I run from this question to my traitors, who were charming in their clarity, though the reader has probably forgotten all about them.

I'll have to remind you briefly. In general, when talking with the reader it's best to be brief and loud, as with a deaf person. I can be loud, but not always brief.

I'll remind you, then. In my student days I had a girl, but my friend stole her from me. He seduced her with chocolates. I refused to quarrel with them, partly out of false pride. I had to pretend that nothing had happened. As the song goes:

The platoon did not notice the loss of a man.

That's what I had to pretend. Then this friend of mine invited me to his room to have dinner with them. I wanted terribly not to go, but I had to, to avoid having it out with him. And this is the point where I was distracted to that damned hand.

When I entered the room, she was cooking potatoes on the hot plate. I said hello to her and sat down on a chair. She told him to go get some beer. He reluctantly consented, put on his jacket, and left. I didn't know what to talk about, but she knew. She began in a roundabout way, that is, with her soccer player, although I had not the slightest reason to endure her recollections of him.

She soon made it clear that she missed her soccer player worse than ever. She soon made it clear that she wanted to come back and try, together with me, to overcome her recollections of first love.

But I no longer wanted her back. I didn't want to help her forget her soccer player, although, to be frank, I still liked her. Anyway, I did not hold up my end of the conversation. I only understood that nothing had come of the candy siege.

(The tenacious gaze of the benefactor, the distraction of the beneficiary.)

Suddenly the door flew open and there stood my friend and traitor (after a quarter of a century, I still have trouble combining those words), looking at us with wide eyes. We had not heard his footsteps. He had obviously sneaked up to the door to surprise us in villainous kisses. When he realized that there was no question of any kisses, he happily set the beer bottles on the table. But I already knew the poor guy had nothing to be happy about.

That turned out to be the case. She soon started showing up at the institute in the company of a Hungarian student. To all appearances the romance developed swiftly. She greeted me now without any allusion to the soccer player. The Hungarians, they don't like to stand on ceremony. But then, we didn't stand on ceremony with them either.

That was the end of the story. I never thought I'd remember her. Apparently the sand-grain of pain that lodged in my soul grew out this dubious pearl.

(Establish a clinic where writers can have shots to obtain artificial pearls.)

What made me remember all that? Oh yes—we were talking about being observant. It is clear from that story that I'm a very unobservant person. But I want to say a couple of words in my own defense.

In point of fact, there are no unobservant people. It's just that the people who are considered unobservant are observing some object invisible to us. The most dangerous thing about them is that we never know exactly what they're observing at any given time. Therefore, my friendly advice to everyone is, Avoid playing base tricks and relying on your acquaintances to be unobservant. They may unmask you when you least expect it.

. . . Oh, the chronic uncleanliness of the human race! I am ashamed to turn away from you, yet I lack the tact to endure your stinking breath!

This summer one of our archeologists showed me a bundle of arrows he had found in an alpine cave. By his calculation the arrows were about a thousand years old. I spent a long time examining this priceless gift from our distant ancestor, this well-preserved but slightly shriveled bouquet of death. Especially well preserved were the tips of the arrows, the ideological warheads, so to speak: heart-shaped, rhomboid, sickle-shaped, claw-shaped, toothed . . . What inventive variety of form, with strict unity of content—the propagandist's dream. Looking at those arrows, I felt an uncontrollable urge to vomit on the history of mankind.

To survive, man has too long found it more important to develop versatility of mind than the divine energy of shame. Thus evolved a large-browed mongrel with a puny heart muscle, thus was created the evil autonomy of mind, the orgy of dim-witted civilization, which neither listens to nor hears the anxious cries of culture and which is only now, at the edge of the abyss, waking up a little, dazedly viewing the Earth's tormented terrain.

What is the remedy? Culture must get ahead of civilization and lead the human race. Is it possible? Let us not be downcast. Don Quixotes of the world, to your horses!

How would we live, if the celebrated Spanish caballero on his heroic horse did not come into view from time to time on our roads, enveloping us in encouraging clouds of dust, wearing an expression of majestic importance and infinite confidence in the triumph of good, and ride onward?

Here he has stopped at the kiosk. After handing a coin to the saleswoman, he takes the crumpled helmet from his sweaty head, then stoops for the mug and drinks Russian kvass.

Let us take advantage of his breather, as this little boy is doing, thrusting an apple core into the horse's mouth. See how splendid is this knobby balding skull. What? Among the many bumps, you don't see the bump of wisdom? But don't you know that one bump received for indomitable faith is worth ten bumps of wisdom? And all his bumps were received for indomitable faith!

How greedily his lips are applied to the cooling liquid, how distinctly his knightly Adam's apple moves in his throat; how freely his thin frame reclines, dressed in the dusty, shabby armor; how carelessly relaxed is the foot resting in the stirrup! And every rip in his old cloak is proud of itself, is happy over its coming reward—a patch sewn on by the caressing fingers of Dulcinea. And the larger the rip, the happier it is, because the longer will Dulcinea's fingers fuss over it!

But the main thing is his eyes! Look into his eyes! They are focused now on the mug of kvass with a purposeful fascination, as if they see in it the first oasis of the coming happiness. Yes, the dream is just as real as this mug of kvass, and just as satisfying to the soul as this drink to the parched throat.

Now, having drunk his fill, he rides on. The little boy, guessing something, looks after him for a long time. Good-bye, great caballero! But tell me, can it be that he too is sprung from our weakling race? Yes, he too! Then the race is still good for something? Yes, it turns out it is! Then tenderness, self-sacrifice, trust, goodness, courage—these are not empty names? No, I swear by all four of his horse's hooves, unworn by the world's banality—they are not empty names!

. . . But I have strayed too far from my plot. I can't get it going. My plot is spinning its wheels like Russian history. All the same, we will get it going and move on, for the only form of power we have accepted on earth is power over the word.

And so, I dismissed my taxi (if the reader recalls, I arrived in a taxi), and my comrade and his friend and I, standing by the side of the road, unhurriedly discussed the virtues and the shortcomings of neighborhood restaurants. That is a splendid pastime, isn't it—to stand at the side of the road beside a waiting car and unhurriedly discuss the virtues and shortcomings of neighborhood restaurants?

While we were occupied with this, a black Volga stopped beside us and the monumental face of Abesalomon Nartovich looked out. The last and highest office he had held was as president of the local Council of Ministers. Now he had been dismissed from that office, and he was working as director of a scientific stockbreeding institute. But Abesalomon Nartovich's face, especially in a car, looked just as if he still headed the local Council of Ministers. Abesalomon Nartovich got out of the car and meticulously greeted everyone, as if elevating the people he greeted, by inertia, to his own former ministerial level.

Two more people got out with him. One of them was Uncle Sandro. There seems to be no need to introduce him. Looking at him, I became aware that I was good and sick of him. I even said to him mentally, "I'm sick of you, Uncle Sandro. I have a feeling I'm going to catch it because of you . . ."

Wouldn't you know—the old devil got wind of my timid rebellion.

"Was there something you wanted to tell me?" he asked me challengingly.

"No, no, Uncle Sandro," I said, lowering my eyes.

Abesalomon Nartovich's second traveling companion—tall, well-built, handsome, all crispy-fresh—proved to be a cosmonaut. He cheerfully shook hands with everyone as if investing in his handshake the excess strength he had accumulated in his time off from the cosmos.

Abesalomon Nartovich seemed to have chosen these two men as traveling companions in order to demonstrate two historical periods of our life. He seemed to be saying: Here is the best that was created by our past (Uncle Sandro), and here is the best that has been created by our present (the cosmonaut), and here am I, bringing them peacefully together. That's how it looked.

I have always liked Abesalomon Nartovich for his talent as a storyteller and entertainer. When he was a high official, he was always forced to disguise this talent, though he never quite succeeded in doing so. He liked me too, I think; he couldn't help but see in me an appreciative listener. Any man with an artistic vein can't help but value his admirers. So, what he valued in me, I think, was my admiration for his gift, which he could not develop on account of his official position. Not to its full measure, at any rate.

Yes, I have always liked Abesalomon Nartovich, but it would be inaccurate to say that I liked him only for his yarns. I liked him for those and for the fact that he always harbored a potential for the most paradoxical behavior. Thus, while still at the very height of his career, he said to a certain acquaintance of mine, "No one from our family has ever died a natural death."

That confession was made by a man at the pinnacle of his power. Men who hold such power may sometimes muse on the possibility of their own fall, but in any case they don't confess it to anyone. On the contrary, from top to bottom their main occupation is always to stress the unshakability of their power.

The question may arise, Didn't Abesalomon Nartovich, during his reign (as he himself once referred to it), take presents? If the question actually does arise, as an honest historian I will have to answer in the affirmative. Many people have talked about that, and, as is typical of Abesalomon Nartovich, he himself did not make much effort to conceal it.

Once after a big drinking party with the local artists, he took us home to his place, where he played the Georgian song "Suliko" twice in succession on two different pianos. There was also a harpsichord in the dining room, if I didn't dream it in my cups. That there were two pianos in the room is definitely true. This follows even from the brief dialogue I had with him there.

"Abesalomon Nartovich," I asked, "what do you want with two instruments?"

"They were presents," he replied, shrugging his shoulders in distress. "It's awkward to refuse . . ."

Another time, grumbling good-naturedly, he said of a certain kolkhoz chairman that he had put on airs and had stopped bringing gifts.

The end of the Khruschev era proved to be the end of Abesalomon Nartovich as well. The secretary of the Central Committee of Georgia, Mzhavanadze, in order to lighten his ship, which was quite overloaded with sins, did not defend Abesalomon Nartovich, but gave him to his enemies to be torn to pieces.

Admittedly, Abesalomon Nartovich got quite a respectable retirement. He became the director of the scientific research institute. Not far from the city, surrounded by bay laurels, elephant palms, citrus groves, he lived at his institute like a Roman senator in disgrace on his estate.

I met him here, for the first time after his retirement, and asked him how and why Mzhavanadze had turned his back on him at the decisive hour, the same Mzhavanadze who had been such a fatherly patron to him under Khrushchev. With a gesture inimitable in its antique grandeur, Abesalomon Nartovich bent down a laurel branch, sniffing it and simultaneously crowning himself with it, as if symbolically restoring his past position. Then he released the branch with a swish and sighed, "Senile cowardice . . ."

I must say the disgrace was not a bolt from the blue for Abesalomon Nartovich. Several years before losing his post, he had defended a dissertation in Moscow and earned a Ph.D. in biological sciences. His defense went off brilliantly. True, there was one amusing hitch.

The story goes that during his defense he was asked the question, "What is a cell, in your opinion?"

"What kind of cell do you have in mind?" Abesalomon Nartovich said, with an exactitude that brought the hall to life.

Thus, in becoming director of an institute, Abesalomon Nartovich was actually falling back on a well-prepared position. Since becoming director of the stock-breeding institute, he had published several books. The most interesting of them was *Songbirds of Abkhazia*. It seems that Abesalomon Nartovich had long cherished a weakness for songbirds. He studied them tirelessly. In our day such a sentimental weakness could hardly be encouraged in a high official. Abesalomon Nartovich must have known this. But, even knowing that it could ruin his career, he continued—deep underground, it must be supposed—to study the songbirds of Abkhazia. Yes, this is quite an informative book, even though it bears no relationship to the program at his institute.

But Abesalomon Nartovich would not have been Abesalomon Nartovich if, in writing a book about the songbirds of Abkhazia, he had failed to insert something that would make a specialist's eyes start from his head, while a man who knew Abesalomon Nartovich would merely smile or throw up his hands. Thus, among the songbirds of Abkhazia he inserted the parrot. Hereby, I have just recalled, he brought to spiritual fruition a dream of Prince Oldenburgsky's. The prince, during his stay in Gagra, really did attempt to release Angolan parrots in our forest, though they were quickly pecked to death by the native hawks.

Anyway, no one knows why parrots turned up among the birds of Abkhazia, let alone the songbirds. I can just see Abesalomon Nartovich's imposing figure, taking off over the earth with unexpected ease and neatly doing a double salto!

Since there is no word for parrot in Abkhazian, Abesalomon Nartovich promptly devised an Abkhazian name for it, a rather clever one at that. In reverse translation it's something like "chatterbox." Now, don't you think there's something touching about this man?

Dear Abesalomon Nartovich, if what I write now ever comes to the eyes of a reader, many people may think I'm unmasking you. But that would be a very great error. In point of fact, I love Abesalomon Nartovich, with a somewhat strange love perhaps, but I do love him.

Seriously, there is an element of amorality, or rather premorality, in a writer's love for the model on whom he bases a character. The writer invariably experiences an access of tenderness when he encounters in life a unique model. Apparently the striving for the unique is in the nature of artistic creation, otherwise this worship of the unique cannot be explained. The premorality lies in the fact that it makes practically no difference to the writer, at the moment he encounters a unique model, what sort of uniqueness it is—high or low. For the writer, morality lies in communicating the true features of the unique model with all the precision available to him, not trying to pass off the low for the high or, vice versa, the high for the low. And the more unique a unique thing is, the more the writer loves it. This evidently reflects his as yet unacknowledged gratitude to it for making his work easier. That is, the less he has to add in order to complete the image, the more grateful the writer is for the model's proximity to his own ideal.

And if the high and the low are combined in one man? Then the uniqueness of the image lies precisely in this capricious combination, and the writer itches to preserve it without fail.

Naive people think that the great Gogol grieved as he created images of Russian freaks. I maintain that in describing Nozdrev, Plyushkin, and Sobakevich, Gogol experienced the highest creative and human joy. When he woke up and saw that he had created a parade of freaks, he was somewhat taken aback and flustered, of course. But in creating them he experienced only joy.

It is time to abandon lofty topics, however, and try, despite all, to get the plot moving. So, we are still standing at the side of the road—by now in the company of Abesalomon Nartovich—and still discussing the virtues and short-comings of nearby restaurants. Incidentally, Abesalomon Nartovich had devoted particular attention to the construction of these restaurants when he was in power. To him we are obliged for the restaurant in the Eshery Gorge, where a moist coolness reigns on the hottest day; to him we are obliged for the restaurant on the ruins of the old fortress, on the summit of Mount Mukhus, and many others. He not only expedited the construction of these restaurants, he also took care that they were furnished with paintings by local artists.

As he discussed the virtues and shortcomings of local restaurants with us, Abesalomon Nartovich kept glancing at passing cars. Some of them braked at his glance. He greeted the drivers and sent them on with a careless wave of his hand, indicating that as things stood at the moment he did not need the people in those particular cars.

Incidentally, I feel closer to the man who goes on slavishly serving a deposed idol than to the one who immediately starts being churlish toward him. The first man at least displays a certain sense of responsibility for his past slavery, he seems ashamed to switch to a new condition immediately, he seems to sense that he doesn't deserve it yet. Whereas the second man, by taking revenge for his past slavishness through rudeness, reveals that he is ready to serve a new idol.

At length Abesalomon Nartovich stopped a car that turned out to be carrying, as he had brilliantly divined, the very man who ended up taking us to the village. First he got out of the car and introduced himself to everyone. Then, after hearing us discuss the virtues and shortcomings of neighborhood restaurants, he made his suggestion.

"Listen," he said, "why do you have to choose a restaurant? I have a relative expecting me in the country; he'll give us a better time than any restaurant. Shall we go?"

Everyone agreed to go to the country.

"Only let's drop by my place at the institute," Abesalomon Nartovich said. "We'll pick up some feijoa."

It seems the cosmonaut's wife, who was vacationing with him at the army's sanatorium, suffered from some kind of illness that feijoa was good for. At Abesalomon Nartovich's institute there is a fine orchard, where, among other exotics, there is a grove of feijoa trees. (Myrtle family; tart-sweet prolate fruits, green or yellow in color, if you must know.)

We distributed ourselves among the cars and drove to Abesalomon Nartovich's institute. At last, our party had shaken down into final form, and for precision-lovers we can now count how many of us there were. I, and the comrade I had helped to get out of prison, and his friend, makes three. Incidentally, my comrade soured at the sight of a man who had been such a big shot as Abesalomon Nartovich. He didn't say two words all day. Apparently, in addition to all its other charms, prison also causes a man to develop an incompatibility complex in relation to the authorities. Perhaps I was wrong to bring my comrade into this narrative? He's the hero of a completely different piece. But no—he'll be needed at the end.

Anyway, you can finish the count for yourselves. It will come to eight, if you don't forget Abesalomon Nartovich's chauffeur. What did I say at the very beginning? I said there were eight of us. Some people may think that I set this up in order to boast of something, I don't know what. Of course not. From the standpoint of literary plausibility, it would have been more correct for me to be slightly mistaken.

The cars drove onto the grounds of the institute, passed a small citrus grove, and stopped by a two-story building under a canopy of laurel and camphor trees.

Everyone but the chauffeur got out of the cars, climbed up to the second floor, passed through the waiting room where a young secretary sat at a desk, and went into Abesalomon Nartovich's office. He sat down at his desk and seated us on the numerous chairs that lined the walls of his office. Then, assuming a managerial expression, he pressed a button.

The secretary came in, giving us somewhat suspicious sidelong looks, her wandering smile expressing a certain sexual irony. I don't know who it was meant for. Perhaps Abesalomon Nartovich himself. If that's the case, we can only exclaim *o tempora, o mores!* Even in the recent past, at the pinnacle of his career, Abesalomon Nartovich had been famed as a legendary lover. According to rumor (spread by enemies? or supporters?), he had frequently had to interrupt a meeting of the Council of Ministers (local, of course) and withdraw with his current favorite to a special room. The hushed ministers would wait out the access of amatory dalliance like an inevitable and awesome natural phenomenon or an epileptic seizure.

Meanwhile, the secretary continued to stand, inspecting us with a wandering smile, at the same time hunching in embarrassment, lifting one shoulder in a lonely way, even drawing back slightly, as if she anticipated indecent propositions and was stating, through her physical appearance, that she was not quite ready to comply with them. Showing through these varied sensual masks, softly but urgently, was the secret brazenness of a young woman remembering her off-duty power over a boss who was somewhat tastelessly got up to look young. Or so I imagined, at any rate.

"Have a crate of feijoa put in my car for our cosmonaut, and bring fruit for the guests," Abesalomon Nartovich ordered in an excessively strict voice, trying, or so I imagined, to override the impression made by her secret brazenness.

Recognizing the cosmonaut with rapture, the secretary disappeared. Abesalomon Nartovich drew from his desk a copy of his book *Songbirds of Abkhazia*, inscribed it to the cosmonaut, and began recounting certain virtues of these birds.

I kept waiting to hear what he would say when he got to the parrot, but he did not get to the parrot, because the secretary returned with two ornate compotes filled with apples, pears, and grapes.

With a cool sweat condensing on the fruit, and the grape clusters languidly trailing, the compotes were planted on the desk. Abesalomon Nartovich interrupted his account, clapped the book shut, and handed it to the cosmonaut. The latter clasped it to his breast as if vowing to take it with him on his very next trip into space.

"Did they put the feijoa in the trunk?" Abesalomon Nartovich asked.

"Yes," the secretary said, without removing her enraptured gaze from the magnificent cosmonaut. Her gaze expressed an almost ritualistic readiness to tear off all her clothes right on the spot, like a priestess, at the very first signal from her idol. It embarrassed almost everyone, including Abesalomon Nartovich. I say almost, because it did not embarrass the cosmonaut. Not understanding her appeal, he gave her a cursory glance from the height of his excellent posture— a distant, sterile, galactic glance.

"Sample the fruits of our orchard," Abesalomon Nartovich said, still trying to stress his full control over what was happening.

Everyone reached for a piece of fruit. The cosmonaut took an exemplary red-cheeked apple and with gleaming teeth took an exemplary mighty bite.

"Now I should like to offer you," Abesalomon Nartovich said ceremonially, "a soft drink made from my own recipe . . . Nadya, bring the glasses."

Finding no response to her priestesslike appeal, the secretary had wilted. Now the irony on her face acquired an absolutely universal character, embracing everyone in the office. She turned and walked out of the office, openly mocking us with her swaying hips. Abesalomon Nartovich looked after her somewhat dispiritedly and then glanced at us, as if appealing to us not to attach too much importance to her scornfully swaying hips. Not without a certain despondency, we agreed to swallow this insult.

"The famous Logidze carried the secret of his soft drinks to the grave," Abesalomon Nartovich said. "To the extent of my modest abilities, I am trying to create a drink of equivalent worth."

Interesting, I thought; does anyone in this country tend to his own affairs? Nevertheless, the mighty breadth of Abesalomon Nartovich's character left room for hope that he was not a complete stranger to the affairs of his own institute.

At this point Uncle Sandro took the floor and told a short story about his own encounter with the famous Logidze.

It seems that Logidze made the best soft drinks in the world. His lemon fizz was so fine that the Shah of Persia couldn't live a day without it. Cases of Logidze Lemon Fizz were dispatched to Baku, went from there by sea to Persia, and then by caravan all the way to Teheran.

But in the early thirties Logidze's relations with Beria deteriorated badly. Beria apparently tried to find out the secret of the soft drinks from him, but Logidze would not reveal it. Despite Beria's intrigues, the old man bravely preserved his secret. And Beria couldn't do anything to him because he didn't know how Stalin felt about it. He merely exiled him from Tbilisi. Logidze moved to Mukhus. Here he worked at a soft drink factory, still making his excellent beverages, but did not reveal their secret to anyone.

Nestor Apollonovich Lakoba decided to wrest this secret from him, whatever the cost, so that future generations of the Soviet people could enjoy the amazing drink. This ticklish business Lakoba entrusted to Uncle Sandro. He advised him to shake the old man up, but in such a way that he didn't shake the soul out of him along with the secret of the drink.

Having picked up the keys to his apartment beforehand, and having learned that the old man would be alone in the house that night, Uncle Sandro concealed his face with a mask, armed himself with a pistol, and went to his house. He turned on the light and approached the head of the old man's bed.

The old man woke up, but he did not take fright on seeing a masked man standing over him with pistol in hand and was not even flustered. And that, as Uncle Sandro told it, made him feel flustered himself. He simply had not allowed for the fact that by this time old man Logidze's spirit had been splendidly tempered by the long intrigues of Lavrenty Beria.

"More of Beria's little tricks?" he asked, settling back in the bed.

"No," Uncle Sandro said, "but you have to reveal—"

"The secret of Logidze water?" the old man asked scornfully. Taking a cigarette from the chair that stood at the head of the bed, he struck a match and lit up. "Remember this: there isn't any Logidze secret."

"What do you mean, there isn't?" Uncle Sandro asked in surprise.

"There just isn't," the old man said, inhaling. He waved at Uncle Sandro's pistol. "Put it away, or it'll go off by accident . . . No, there isn't any Logidze secret; there's love for the work and knowledge of the work."

"How do you mean?" Uncle Sandro asked, putting the pistol in his pocket.

"Do you know how your cornmeal mush is made?" the old man asked.

"I do," Uncle Sandro replied.

"Does each and every housewife know how to make cornmeal mush?" the old man asked.

"Each and every one," Uncle Sandro replied.

"And there's no secret to it?" the old man asked.

"There's no secret," Uncle Sandro replied.

"Then why are there some housewives who make cornmeal mush that's a real treat, while others aren't very good at it?" the old man asked.

"Some are better at it, and some aren't," Uncle Sandro replied, trying not to let himself get confused.

"But don't those who are worse at it know everything that those who are better at it know?" the old man went on. "Or do they have some sort of secret?"

"No," Uncle Sandro said. "How could there be a secret, everyone knows how to make cornmeal mush."

"Then why," the old man asked, "are some first-rate at making it, others a little worse, and still others thoroughly bad?"

"I don't know," Uncle Sandro admitted at last.

"Because there's talent and love in the world," the old man said, "which your bosses won't ever understand. A woman in whom talent and love are combined makes cornmeal mush better than the others. Love teaches her to choose fresh meal at the bazaar, to sift it well, and talent helps her correctly grasp the relation of the fire to what is being cooked on the fire."

"Then what should we do?" Uncle Sandro said.

"Just respect talent," the old man replied, "and when I'm gone there'll be people who will make soft drinks no worse than I do."

"But I'm supposed to find out the Logidze secret," Uncle Sandro said, reminding him that he was also in a subordinate position.

"You need a document?" the old man asked.

"Yes," Uncle Sandro said.

"All right," the old man agreed. He got up out of bed and went to the desk. Taking a piece of paper, he dipped the pen in the inkwell, wrote something on the paper, waved it in the air to dry, and held it out to Uncle Sandro.

"Is that all?" Uncle Sandro asked, surprised by the brevity of the formula for the famous soft drink.

"That's all," the old man replied, "but I've already told you the main thing. If nature confers on a man love and talent, he will make soft drinks no worse than I do, and dance no worse than you do."

As Uncle Sandro told it, he could feel himself blushing under the mask: the old man had recognized him.

"Don't be offended," Uncle Sandro begged. "Politics . . ."

"I'm not offended," the old man said. "I'm used to it . . ."

Uncle Sandro left old man Logidze and delivered the formula for the famous beverage to Lakoba the next day. Lakoba sent the formula to Moscow or Tbilisi, Uncle Sandro doesn't know for sure which. The experts checked the formula and after a while informed Lakoba that the formula the old man had given him was no different from the formula for ordinary soft drinks. Lakoba gave up on it and did not harass the old man any more.

While Uncle Sandro was telling all this, the secretary brought in a tray of glasses. Abesalomon Nartovich opened the refrigerator and took out a carafe of poisonously yellow liquid.

"Old man Logidze tricked you, all the same, Sandro," Abesalomon Nartovich said in a voice filled with self-confidence, as he poured the glasses. "He carried the secret of his soft drinks to the grave . . . But I shall achieve a drink that will be no worse. Try this one, for now."

We reached for the glasses with a certain lack of confidence. I put my lips to the icy liquid and began to sip it slowly. It was on the bitter side, and my mouth puckered. The others, I noticed, also took cautious sips from their glasses. Only the cosmonaut, with his native decisiveness, tossed off the whole glass at once. Then he wiped his lips and said, "It tastes of pine needles."

His exactitude was disarming.

"Quite right," Abesalomon Nartovich said, unflustered. "There's feijoa juice in it, and that's what creates that original nuance of flavor."

The cosmonaut took a pear from the compote and juicily bit into it, obviously trying to wash out his mouth after that fantastic beverage. The others also took pieces of fruit.

"A magnificent pear," the cosmonaut said, chewing, and he slurped the excess juices noisily.

"A Duchess," Abesalomon Nartovich remarked, gratified. "Nadya, have them put a crate of pears in my trunk for our cosmonaut."

Smirking, Nadya walked to the door, still ridiculing us with her swaying hips. But after Abesalomon Nartovich's beverage, this ridicule was easy for us to endure. For me, at any rate.

"You're spoiling me," the cosmonaut said.

"The country loves its heroes," Abesalomon Nartovich replied. Turning once more to the subject of his latest passion, he added, "Our experiments with soft drinks are still in progress."

He went to the refrigerator and opened the door. We saw a dozen milk bottles filled with experimental samples of drinks, nearly every color of the rainbow.

"This is the most perfect in respect to taste, so far," Abesalomon Nartovich said, indicating the carafe from which we had drunk. "I recently served it to the Italian minister of agriculture; he was well pleased . . . if they translated his remark to me correctly."

I wanted to ask whether the poor Italian minister of agriculture had managed to get a bite of fruit, at least, but I didn't dare. We left the office.

"If anyone calls," Abesalomon Nartovich said over his shoulder to the secretary, "I've gone to the state farm."

"All right," the secretary said, and threw the cosmonaut a last sidelong look. She lowered her eyes to the book that lay before her, and on her lips trembled a wandering smile.

When we approached the cars, one of the institute staff was lugging a crate of pears to Abesalomon Nartovich's trunk. We got into the cars and drove off.

Finally, after long wanderings, I have emerged on the highway of my plot again. And so: We came rolling into this isolated Abkhazian village in three cars, for a reason that, as it turns out, has not completely slipped my mind. It has now become absolutely clear that there wasn't any reason. It was simply that one of our party had been invited to visit his relatives, he suggested out of politeness that we go with him, and we accepted the suggestion without thinking twice.

Three hours later we pulled up in a little hamlet, before an emerald Abkhazian yard. As we walked into the yard, a man of about thirty, with piercing, intensely blue eyes, came out of the house; behind him came a young woman, to all appearances his wife; and then there appeared a gray-headed patriarch, evidently the young host's father.

We were introduced. The hosts were obviously delighted that their long-awaited relative had arrived with a retinue headed by a former high official, the news of whose dismissal had probably not yet reached them, or if it had, it was still outweighed by his long and honorable career.

As it happened, Abesalomon Nartovich knew this house and this yard well, and he forthwith led us over to the fence, near which grew an old alder with a grapevine of unusual thickness twined around it. He began telling us the history of the vine, which he claimed was about a hundred and fifty years old.

I looked around the house and yard. The young host had already found time to slaughter a goat; he had hung it on a rope from the beam of the kitchen veranda and was quickly dressing the carcass. Smoke rose over the roof of the kitchen; they were probably already boiling the cornmeal mush there, preparing to receive us.

Drying on a rope stretched along the veranda of the house were fiery sheaves of pepper and dark crimson icicles of *churkhcheli*. By the steps leading to the main house a little garden had been laid out, in which bloomed dahlias, marigolds, languidly blazing cannas.

Two red calves, their tails switching, grazed in the yard. A procession of turkey hens walked past toward the kitchen, led by a large-cropped, gobbling turkey cock who looked like an open accordion. Beyond the fence that enclosed the yard shimmered the green of the corn, with strong ears already beginning to dry on every stalk. Through the leaves of the mulberry and cherry-plum trees that dotted the field, bunches of grapes glinted dark with the faraway sinful temptation of childhood.

Suddenly I had a feeling that soon I would never again see this smoke over an Abkhazian kitchen, nor this little yard gleaming with the green of its grass, nor this corn beyond the wattle fence, nor these trees, hushed under the sweet burden of ripened grapes. All this would end for me forever. A tormenting nostalgia gripped my soul.

(In the grown man's involuntary exhalation of "Lord help me!" at a moment of spiritual rebellion and in the child's cry of "Mama!" there is unquestionably a linking intonation, a single source. We feel that the child's cry is fully accounted for by the everyday reality of maternal protection. But doesn't the same reality, only unseen, stand behind the cry of the grown man? The same thought in inverted form—the holiness of motherhood. Think about it.)

I began listening to the words of the orating Abesalomon Nartovich. He was recounting the characteristics of local grape varieties, and the cosmonaut was jotting down the names of the varieties in his notebook. No, I couldn't listen to that now.

I glanced at Uncle Sandro and realized that he was the one to blame for my melancholy forebodings. I had an urge to unburden my heart to him. Taking him by the arm, I drew him apart from the company. We began to stroll around the yard.

"Has something happened?" he asked.

"I'm terrified, Uncle Sandro," I told him frankly.

"What are you afraid of?" he asked.

"I'm going to get it, Uncle Sandro, am I ever going to get it for describing your life!" I exclaimed.

"My life?" he repeated with touchy bewilderment. "My life is an open book for all Abkhazia. People are proud of me."

"I'm going to get it," I repeated, "if only for describing how Lakoba shot the egg off the cook's head with Stalin there. I'm going to get it for that."

"Nonsense," Uncle Sandro said with a shrug. "In the first place, there were a hundred people there besides me, and everybody saw it. In the second place, Lakoba was a wonderful marksman and he always hit the egg, he never hit the cook's head. Now if he'd hit the cook's head, then you couldn't have written about it . . ."

"That's not the problem," I explained. "They'll say why did I have to write about that. What's with the feudal diversions, they'll say, in the age of the building of socialism."

"What are feudal diversions?" Uncle Sandro asked me.

"That means old-time entertainments," I told him.

"How does the one interfere with the other?" Uncle Sandro asked in surprise. "Socialism takes place outside, and this was inside."

"What does outside mean and what does inside mean?" I asked, not quite understanding him.

"Very simple," Uncle Sandro said. "Socialism is when they build tea factories, mills, power plants. That always takes place outside, and Lakoba did his shooting inside, in the sanatorium hall. How does the one interfere with the other?"

"Oh, Uncle Sandro," I said, "they see it differently. Am I ever going to get it!"

"Still harping!" Uncle Sandro interrupted. "What, are you afraid of the KGB?"

"Yes," I confessed shyly.

"You're right, you should be afraid of the KGB," Uncle Sandro said, after considering a moment. "But keep in mind that it's a completely different setup there now. They've got other people there now. They don't decide anything for themselves. Before, they used to decide for themselves. Now they can detain a man for two or three days, but then—"

"Then *what*?" I said, breaking down.

"Then they ask the Party," Uncle Sandro replied. "The Party's got specialists on engineers, on doctors, and on people like you. On the different branches. So a man from the security organs asks them, 'We've detained so-and-so. What do we do with him?' And the Party man looks at the cards he has, on his branch. He finds this man's card, reads it, and already knows all about him. And he tells them, 'This is a very bad man, give him five years. And that man is dangerous too, but not so bad. Give him three years. And this man is just a fool! Give him a scare and let him go.' If they have to give a man a long term, they send over a certificate so that there'll be a document. But if it's a short term—two years, say—they can just do it over the phone."

"But it doesn't make me feel any better to hear how they decide," I said. "I'm terrified, Uncle Sandro—"

"Obey me in everything," Uncle Sandro replied, "and you'll never perish! You find me the phone number and the name of the man who takes care of your branch in the Party. We'll fix him a nice present and put everything right."

"Oh, Uncle Sandro!" I exclaimed. "This is ideology, they don't take bribes there!"

"Nonsense," Uncle Sandro replied. "They all eat. Ideology wants to eat too. Here's a fresh example for you. I got a call recently from a certain powerful person, whose name I won't tell you or else you'll be foolish enough to put it in somewhere. And he says to me, 'Uncle Sandro, you're a man respected by all. There's something you could do for the city, if you would, please. We're in terrible need of pipes, but we can't get them anywhere. Moscow promised us. Here's five hundred rubles pocket money, here are some parcels, here are the first names of the people you're to call up, remind about the pipes, and give the parcels to. Take the train to Moscow, we'll reserve a hotel room for you from here, you move into it and call up all these people, remind them about the pipes, and give out the parcels.' 'All right,' I say, and I take the money. And this man says, 'Now you see, Uncle Sandro, that I'm making efforts for the city, but people think I take bribes for myself.' 'Of course, I see,' I say.

"They load my whole compartment full of parcels, and I go to Moscow. And I don't know what's in the parcels. Since they didn't say, it's not nice to ask, or especially to open them myself. Every one of them looks to be about forty pounds. But it doesn't say on the parcel who it's for. All it says is the number of the parcel, and the same number stands opposite the man's first name on a paper. They were sly to think that up, so if an outsider came into the compartment he wouldn't read some big shot's name on the parcel.

"So I call from the hotel. Sometimes I get the man I need, sometimes I get the secretary, sometimes they say call tomorrow. I explain everything to them, about the pipes and about the parcels, and about the room I'm staying in. Now I'm curious to find out: The bosses I've brought the parcels for, are they very big or not very? The paper doesn't say their position—only the first name and phone number. Sly, but I'm even more sly. So they start coming. No, not a one of them came himself. They sent their chauffeurs. The chauffeur comes in, says which man he's from, I look at the paper and give him the parcel with the right number. But while I'm at it I talk with the chauffeur. I offer him a drink of *chacha*, a piece of *churkhcheli*. True, no one has a drink, but they all take *churkhcheli*. And when I get a chance I ask the chauffeur, 'What kind of car do you drive on the job?' 'A Chayka,' the first chauffeur answers.

"Aha, I think, they don't put small fry in a Chayka. That means he's no less than a deputy minister. And how did it come out? Out of six chauffeurs, four drove Chaykas on the job and only two drove Volgas. And you say it's ideology. The man who watches over *you* may not even ride in a Volga."

"Oh, Uncle Sandro, I don't know, I don't know," I said, but for some reason I felt a little better.

"But *I* know," Uncle Sandro replied. "I'll send him a present, and he'll say anything we want about you. But you haven't gone against the Party Line anywhere, have you?''

"Why, Uncle Sandro! What are you saying!"

"Never transgress the Line—the rest is rubbish!" Uncle Sandro said. "If you wrote something wrong, we'll suggest something for him to say. Like this, for example: 'Don't touch this man, he isn't quite right in the head. He doesn't even know what he's writing.' "

"Why, Uncle Sandro, what are you saying!" I said in fright. "That way they could put me in the insane asylum!"

"They could," Uncle Sandro agreed, after considering a moment. "Then we'll suggest something else. Like this, for example: 'He's silly, but he loves the government.' "

"That fits," I said, reassured by Uncle Sandro's invincible confidence that the world was just as he pictured it to himself.

"Remember, for the future," Uncle Sandro went on, "this regime sits firmly in place and no one will be able to budge it. Some foolish people think about that. You know the cobbler shop not far from my house? Six pathetic cobblers work there. And who's the manager over them? A Party man. He sees everything they say, everything they think, and which way they turn. No, he lets them eat. He eats himself, and he lets them eat. But he won't let anyone transgress the Line. And everything's been infiltrated that way, everything! Some fools don't understand that.

"Once I was sitting in an outdoor café drinking coffee and cognac. Taking my ease. Suddenly two young fellows sit down beside me, order coffee, and start talking. But you should hear what they're saying. One says, Under democracy we'll do this and this. But the other says No, under democracy we won't do this first, we'll do the other. And the first one argues with him—No, under democracy we'll do this first, and do the other later.

"They're talking right in front of me, they aren't afraid. They probably think, An illiterate old Abkhazian, he doesn't understand anything. But I know better than they do what democracy is. It means running a government like in foreign countries. But I know all about those foreign countries. I've met a lot of people who've been there. There, the countries are small and the roads are good. Here, the country is big and the roads are bad. And this means a completely different government setup. There, if someone rebels out in a district center—Whoa! The roads are good, the police arrive in an hour, they disperse everyone and pacify everyone. But with us? In Russia there are places where it's five hundred kilometers or more from a district center to the regional capital. If they rebelled out in the district, what wouldn't they do by the time the police arrived! They'd burn the club, trash the store, drink all the vodka. And the country is big, the roads are bad, the police wouldn't get there in time. And that's why the government's set up this way, so that people in the provinces sit in fear. So that before they rebel they'll consult among themselves for a whole week: Is it worth it or not! And that's what they do. One says, 'We'll burn the club, trash the store, drink all the vodka, and have the canned goods for hors d'oeuvres.'

"Another says, 'No, we shouldn't burn the club, we'd better trash the store first.'

"And a third says, 'No, we should burn the club, because it would be shameful to trash the store. People would think we did it to get the vodka.'

"While they're arguing, the police find out all about it, and although the roads are bad, there's time, they manage to get there.

"Well, these two young men sitting across from me didn't know anything about that. They kept saying, Democracy this, democracy that . . . Finally I couldn't take any more.

" 'You fools,' I said to them, 'you're a couple of babes in the woods. Hitler couldn't topple this regime with all his tanks, and what can you do with your blather? You'll just make your poor parents suffer.'

" 'Nuts,'' says one of them. 'They only look strong, we're going to win.'

"I got furious. I was talking sense to him and he was answering me back! Just at that moment a policeman I knew walked into the coffeehouse. 'Zhora,' I called to him, 'come over here!'

"These two looked around, they saw the policeman coming. They turned pale as death. I wasn't planning to inform on them, of course. I wasn't born in that kind of house, I'm not that kind of man. But I wanted to get it into their heads where they live, how they live. The policeman comes over, and he smiles and says, 'Hello, Uncle Sandro, what do you want?'

" 'Nothing,' I say. 'I'd like you to have a drink with me.'

" 'I'm sorry, Uncle Sandro,' he says, 'but I can't, I'm on duty.'

" 'Well then,' I say, 'good-bye, Zhora, that's all I had on my mind.'

"The policeman goes away, these fellows come back to life a little, and one of them says, 'Thanks, old chap, for not selling us out.'

" 'I wasn't about to sell you out,' I say, 'because I wasn't born in that kind of house, I'm not that kind of man. I wanted to teach you not to talk nonsense, especially in a café. In a place like this you'll find little old men with nodding heads who don't seem to understand anything, because they've got one foot in the grave; but they've got the other foot planted someplace else entirely. So you think before you go blabbing nonsense.'

"They didn't say anything, went away."

Uncle Sandro and I continued to stroll around the yard. While I struggled to comprehend the vast diagram of governmental organization he had drawn, his thought made a sudden leap to Golda Meir. He had mentioned her a couple of times before, in earlier conversations, with a certain veiled irritation. In the very idea of promoting a woman to the head of a government he apparently suspected a remote attempt—keenly detected by him, as a great tamada—on the principle of male authority at the Abkhazian table. He apparently reasoned thus: Today they've put a woman at the head of the government, tomorrow they'll put her at the head of the table. How could he understand this?

"Listen," he said, "is that old woman Golda Meir still running Israel? What is she, out of her mind? Why is she letting Russian Jews into her country? Doesn't she know they made a revolution in Russia, and they could do the same there?''

"Come on, Uncle Sandro," I said. "They won't make any trouble there. That was a completely different time."

"A different time," Uncle Sandro repeated. "You know it from books, but I remember it well. I actually went hunting with Trotsky—"

"How's that?" I asked in surprise, because he had never told me about that.

"Yes," Uncle Sandro said, "he was in Abkhazia in 1924. I happened to visit a house where he was a guest, and we all went hunting. He was very fond of hunting and was an excellent shot. He could turn and shoot a bird on the wing so adroitly that you'd think he'd spent his whole life hunting, not making revolutions. There was only one man who was a better shot—Lakoba. Trotsky was an excellent hunter, a learned man, and the best orator in the land. In those days they held All-Union competitions for orators, and he took first place every year. All the same, he was a stupid man. Why? I'll tell you.

"Nineteen twenty-four. The great Lenin is dying. Trotsky sits in Abkhazia and hunts. The leader is dead, but he sits in Abkhazia and hunts. Lenin is dead, go to Moscow, stand by the coffin like a close friend, maybe you can snatch a scrap of power from the Big Mustache, but he sits in Abkhazia and hunts. Later, when the Big Mustache has grabbed everything, he goes to Moscow and argues with him. Now is that a wise man? But he was an excellent marksman, the only one better was Lakoba . . . On the other hand, come to think of it, some marksmen! Beria poisoned one, and Big Mustache's man did in the other with a crowbar. If you're such a good shot, you should know what to shoot at . . .''

On this querulous note, my conversation with Uncle Sandro was interrupted. They summoned us to the table. The table had been set outdoors. I have described Abkhazian tables so many times that I'm frankly ashamed to return to the subject. The reader may think I'm some kind of glutton. Yes, I used to love to eat and drink, of course, but with the years one loses the appetite for a session at table, and for jokes, too. Anyway, the table was first-rate, and I'll give only a cursory description of what was on it, in no way revealing my own personal attitude toward the viands.

The main course, the meat of a young kid, lay steaming on several platters. Fresh cornmeal mush, smoked cheese, beans, *satsivi*, roast chickens, greens (the green onion is the vegetarian's love-arrow)—all this was crowded onto the table. As you see, not the smallest gastronomic delight.

Abesalomon Nartovich was seated at the middle of the table; to his right he seated the cosmonaut and to his left, Uncle Sandro. Perhaps he was still insisting on demonstrating the highest achievements of our past and present. And perhaps he was trying to impress on us without words the fact that he himself was the successor to Uncle Sandro's ideas, while the cosmonaut had been gemmated from his own ideas. The rest of us took our places.

Uncle Sandro was chosen tamada. But I will not describe how he conducted the table. That would seem to be altogether beyond description. All through the novel I have avoided this sort of scene, thereby creating in the reader's imagination a mythical image of the great tamada, as is only fitting for the grandeur of the Caucasian table's finest conductor. In this sphere he is a divinity, and by trying to fix the reality of a divinity in words, we invariably weaken his divine reality. A god combing his beard before our very eyes—that is already a small triumph of atheism, gentlemen!

To shield us from the sun, which still stood high in the sky, the young host cut a big armful of green branches in the alder thicket and stuck them into the ground, peering at us with morbid attention to be sure that the degree of thickness of the shade cast on our faces by the leaves would strictly correspond to each man's spiritual significance.

In many ways he was rather an odd person. His piercing, searching blue gaze seemed to elevate us to unfamiliar, though pleasant, heights; yet on the other hand it seemed to promise to punish us forthwith if we should prove unworthy of them. Therefore we were not quite sure how to behave.

At first he drove in the best, thickest-leaved branch opposite Abesalomon Nartovich, but then after some hesitation he realized that the cosmonaut was a more prominent figure. With a patriarchal straightforwardness, he pulled this best branch out of the ground and thrust it in opposite the cosmonaut. During this operation Abesalomon Nartovich nodded approvingly, indicating that the host was merely fulfilling a wish that had not had time to fall from Abesalomon Nartovich's lips.

The next thickest-leaved branch fell to the share of Abesalomon Nartovich, and the next to Uncle Sandro. The other branches the host divided among the rest of us, still peering searchingly at each of us, but no longer so morbidly. He seemed to be reassuring himself with the thought that nothing terrible would happen if he should make a little mistake at this point.

Since we were very long at table, and during this time the sun traveled quite some distance across the sky, the host transplanted the branches twice more so that their shade would fall on our faces. But the transplanting was far from an exercise in formality, it took into account a richer understanding of our spiritual essence as revealed to him in the course of the dinner conversation.

Independently of the smaller branches earmarked for us, there was a decisive reevaluation of the thickest-leaved branch after two pronouncements by the cosmonaut, though in our view they were innocent ones. At the last transplanting of his artificial grove, the young host again gave preference to Abesalomon Nartovich, as though returning to his first, intuitively correct, cordial impulse.

Everything at this table was good, but in all truth I must admit the wine was lousy. Wine spoils with time, or to put it more exactly, is corrupted along with my dear Abkhazians. Quite often now they add sugar and water to the wine, and the result is slop, quite strong, but unpalatable.

In the middle of the meal, the cosmonaut asked Uncle Sandro for the floor and Uncle Sandro yielded it to him.

"Dear friends," the cosmonaut said radiantly, "I propose that we at this excellent table drink a toast to the Komsomol that has nurtured us . . ."

When he heard that, the young host stopped dead as if struck by lightning. There was an awkward pause, which Abesalomon Nartovich tactfully covered by seconding the toast and saying that he himself had begun his career by working with the Komsomol.

The cosmonaut's toast did sound rather odd, of course, in this remote hamlet. But there was nothing remarkable about it. It was merely that the young host had made up his mind from the very beginning to accept nothing but pearls from us.

Fortunately, the cosmonaut himself noticed nothing. But the young host rested his piercing, searching gaze on him. Then he turned the same piercing, but still more searching, gaze on Uncle Sandro—on the tamada, who bears full responsibility for everthing said during a toast. After that, emerging from his torpor and regaining the gift of speech, he said in Abkhazian, with an expression of excruciating insight, "You don't suppose he's stupid?"

"No, that's what they teach them," Uncle Sandro corrected him severely in Abkhazian, as though alluding to a mysterious but unshakable connection between the cosmonaut's toast and the training for cosmic flights. With this explanation he was simultaneously brushing aside the impertinent, though ludicrous, suggestion that he could have erred as tamada in granting the floor to the cosmonaut.

They began to talk about my friend's case and then—not very tactfully, but without meaning to offend him—moved on to accounts of murders in general. At this point Abesalomon Nartovich produced what to my mind was a good short story. And it was particularly good in that it was told in a sustained realistic spirit, which testifies to the amazing versatility of Abesalomon Nartovich's talent as a storyteller; he was generally known among our intelligentsia as the author of tales of fantasy. I pass along what I heard, from memory, though I have undoubtedly lost many details and nuances.

In our village (Abesalomon Nartovich began), not far from our house, lived a shepherd by the name of Gedlach. He was small, like a young boy, with the burning eyes of an owl and a very unsociable disposition. It was considered very dangerous to tangle with him, although he had never done anything to anybody. But everyone understood he was capable of doing anything that entered his mind.

He was a shepherd, as I said, and an inveterate hunter. Every summer he disappeared in the alpine meadows and not only killed bear and ibex, but also was famous for having managed to sneak up on a live roebuck and catch it by the foot. It sounds unlikely, but that's what happened. The roebuck dragged him about a kilometer before he managed to inflict a fatal wound with his knife.

He had the nickname Iron Knee, bestowed on him for his indefatigability. On ibex-hunting expeditions, no one could keep up with him, and in the end he would leave everyone behind, while he scrambled up to the ibex's most inaccessible grazing spots on the very steepest slopes of the Caucasus.

Now, when I was a boy I had a flair for imitating the voices of people, animals, and birds. Hence my interest in songbirds. If I had developed that talent, I would probably be a National Artist by now. But I started working in the Komsomol, and my talent proved superfluous there.

When Iron Knee's father died, a comrade of mine with whom I grazed the family goats incited me to give Iron Knee a scare by imitating the voice of his father, whom I well remembered. So from time to time, when I found myself not far from Iron Knee's house, in their family burying ground, I began calling him in his father's voice.

"Oh, Gedlach," I would shout, "come over here, come here!"

Usually I would shout like that a few times toward evening, then stop and drive my flock home. My way took me past Iron Knee's house, and I sometimes saw him standing motionless on a rise in the middle of the yard and listening to something in amazement.

"Did you go past our graves?" he asked me.

"I did," I replied.

"You didn't see anyone?"

"No."

"Didn't hear anything?"

"No," I answered. "Why?"

"I heard my father's voice," he replied. "I don't see what he wants . . . We did the funeral right, we had a good fortieth-day memorial feast, the anniversary is coming and we'll mark the anniversary . . . I don't see what he's dissatisfied with . . ."

Soon the whole village learned that Iron Knee's father was calling him.

"Probably a bear's going to get you, or you're going to fall off a cliff," the villagers told him.

"Well, there's no help for it," he replied, his owl eyes glinting steadily. "If my time has come, I can't hide."

I didn't call every day, of course, more like once or twice a week. We were having fun making trouble for this wild unsociable man. Of course I had no way of knowing that in his wildness he possessed an animal cunning, which no one suspected at the time. As it turned out, he noticed a certain connection between his father's call and my appearing with my flock a little while later on the road that passed by his house.

Once I was standing near the graves in their family burying ground, I had just raised my hand to my mouth and cautiously called out, "Oh, Gedlach, come over here, come here!"

"So it's you, you son of a bitch!" I suddenly heard his voice, and I saw him jump out from behind a plane tree that grew in the graveyard. I cannot understand to this day how he could have concealed himself behind it.

At the first instant I froze in horror, seeing that face distorted with anger and the yellow eyes of an infuriated owl. He had a gun in his hands. The next instant I went tumbling down the precipitous slope, which was overgrown with sarsa-parilla bushes. A shot thundered after me, I heard the bullet whistle over my head. I jumped to my feet and ran all the way home. To this day I'm not clear whether he meant to kill me or just to put a scare into me.

That night my father brought home the flock I had abandoned, and reached an agreement with Iron Knee that he would punish me himself. But, knowing that Iron Knee had shot at me and it had frightened me to death, Father did not punish me.

One day soon after, when I was walking past Iron Knee's house on my way home with the flock of goats, he hailed me.

"Seems like Father's stopped calling to me," he said. "You don't know why?"

"I don't know," I said, hanging my head to avoid looking into his owl eyes.

"If the bullet hadn't missed your evil head," he said, "you'd have had a chance to ask my father if he wanted anything from me."

"I'm sorry, Iron Knee," I replied. "It was a joke."

"And I shot at you for a joke," he said, and turned back to the house.

Two years later Iron Knee got married. To everyone's surprise, he brought home a very pretty girl from a neighboring village. It was hard to see why she had consented to marry Iron Knee. He had never been attractive (he was almost a freak), nor did he have a particularly well-appointed house. Maybe she was seduced by his prowess as a hunter or something—I don't know.

Nevertheless, he married this beautiful girl, celebrated the wedding, but about two weeks after the marriage made ready to go to the mountains, because it was the beginning of summer. The villagers jokingly asked him how come he wasn't afraid to leave a little young wife without supervision when she was just getting a taste for it. His wife would be left alone in the house. But he didn't understand the jokes. He replied that he was too used to spending the summer in the alpine meadows, and there was no way he could stay in the hot and sweaty village. Anyway, he went off to the mountains. But it wasn't just in summer, he was also gone for long periods in winter, taking hunting trips that lasted many days.

God knows what kind of life he had there with his young wife, but they had no children. Two or three years later, people in the village began to say that Iron Knee's wife was sleeping with her neighbor. Next door lived a fellow of about thirty, a bachelor, tall and handsome. He lived alone with his nephew and worked in the village store. Well, they talked about it in whispers, of course, and it never occurred to anyone to open Iron Knee's eyes. Not among our relatives, in any case.

One day we were sitting in the kitchen in front of the fireplace fire. Mama was fixing dinner, and Father sat by the fire talking with Uncle Mikhel. From time to time he glanced out the open kitchen door, where he could see his horse, tethered by the bridle to a crowbar stuck in the ground. When the horse had eaten all the grass around the crowbar within the radius of the bridle, Father went out of the kitchen, walked over to the crowbar, and planted it in another spot so that the horse would have fresh grass to eat. He couldn't just let him graze, because there were seedling fruit trees growing in the yard.

So Father went outdoors for the third time to pull the crowbar out of the ground and plant it in a new spot. Suddenly he stopped in the middle of the yard, listening to something.

"Quiet!" he shouted into the kitchen, and stood still listening. Then he turned back to the kitchen and shouted to my uncle, "Come here, Mikhel. I keep hearing a spooky voice."

We all poured out into the yard and began to listen. At first it was impossible to make anything out, and then I heard the distant cry.

". . . Anyone . . . Trouble . . . Trouble . . ."

Uncle Mikhel's ears were keen as a deer's. He not only heard the words, he determined who was shouting.

"That's our storekeeper's nephew," he said, listening.

"Trouble, trouble . . . ," the barely audible voice rang out again in the silence. "Anyone, anyone . . ."

"Something terrible's happened over there!" Father shouted. Slipping the bridle from the crowbar, he climbed on the unsaddled horse and started for the storekeeper's house.

"Mikhel, call our brothers and come on over there," he said over his shoulder as he opened the gate and went out to the road.

About twenty minutes later we all walked up to the storekeeper's house. Several neighbors were already there, led by my father.

Everyone was crowded into the kitchen. I peered in the door and saw the storekeeper lying on his back near the kitchen couch. His head lay tipped back in a huge pool of blood, and I shuddered in horror when I saw the gaping black slit in his throat. One of his hands gripped a bloodied knife. His trousers were unbuttoned, for some reason, and the belt buckle lay in the blood. That's all I had time to see. The next moment Father looked back and drove us out. Several of us children had been standing in the doorway.

In a short time other neighbors began to arrive. We could hear people calling back and forth to each other all over the village, informing each other of the terrible news. More and more people kept coming to the storekeeper's yard, there was already a whole crowd standing in the yard, and his young nephew recounted over and over how he had come home and found his uncle in the kitchen in the pool of blood. About two hours went by. Suddenly a cry rang out from the direction of Iron Knee's house.

"Trouble, trouble!" he shouted. "Help!"

His voice was very clearly audible, and everyone was very surprised to hear it. Everyone knew he had left that day for the summer pastures in the mountains, and several people had seen him go by three hours before, with a heavily laden horse, and a gun slung across his back, walking in the direction of the mountains.

Many people rushed to his house, and we little boys ran over there too. His house was close by, about two hundred meters from the storekeeper's. When we walked into his yard, he was standing by the kitchen unpacking his horse. We went up to him. He lifted a sack off the horse, holding it in both hands, and jerked his chin toward the kitchen.

"My wife's hanged herself."

Everyone was stupefied, and he lugged the sack into the kitchen. When he had set it down and wiped the sweat from his brow, he nodded to us.

"Here . . ."

We went into the kitchen. She was hanging from a soot-covered kitchen beam, with her head bowed, ever so gently swaying. A little bench, which she had apparently kicked aside, lay upside down a few meters from her body.

"How come you're here?" one of the villagers asked. "Didn't I see you leave for the mountains?"

"That's it, I did leave," Iron Knee said. "But on the way I remembered that I'd forgotten salt. And what's a hunt without salt? Kill a roebuck and the meat will spoil without salt . . . So I came back and she was hanging here . . . But why are people running to the storekeeper's house, what's happened there?"

"He slit his throat," one of the neighbors said.

"Fatally?" Iron Knee asked.

"Yes, he's dead," they told him.

"That's odd," Iron Knee said suddenly. "This one hanged herself, and that one slit his throat . . . Like there was some quarrel between them . . ."

Everyone felt ill at ease. Even we children felt uncomfortable somehow. It was as if he knew something about them and was even jeering at their fate. That much I was aware of at the time, but nothing more.

"Think of it," Iron Knee said suddenly, his owl eyes blazing. "If I hadn't come back for the salt, I wouldn't have found out about their death till fall, till I came down from the mountains."

"Why not?" one of the neighbors said. "They'd have sent a messenger of woe for you—"

"Except for the messenger of woe," Iron Knee said. "But who knows if he would have found me in the shanty or not . . . After all, I go off and hunt for days at a time."

"Yes," my father said, "it's a good thing you forgot the salt."

"That's why I say," Iron Knee replied, "if I hadn't come back, she might have hung here till fall . . . No children crying, and the nearest neighbor, the only one who might have noticed that she wasn't to be seen or heard, had cut his own throat . . ."

I remember his words bothered me greatly at the time, but I didn't know why. It struck me that he seemed to be alluding to their intimate relationship, as though mocking the dead.

"Should we take her down or wait for the court officers?" Iron Knee asked, turning to Father, as the most senior man, one respected by all.

"We'll wait for the court officers," Father answered.

Then we all went home, the door to the kitchen where the storekeeper lived was shut, and two relatives stayed with the boy in the main house.

That evening Father's brothers gathered in our kitchen and discussed these two terrible deaths. The brothers would have set to guessing why they had committed suicide, but Father immediately interrupted them and said it was murder.

He said that Iron Knee must have suspected that she was betraying him with the storekeeper. Pretending that he was leaving for the mountains, he hid in the woods, tied his horse there, and stealthily returned to the storekeeper's house. When he caught them there, evidently at the very moment of intimacy, he sneaked up from behind and cut his throat. If he could sneak up on a roebuck, he could easily do it to these two, who were busy making love besides.

"But she hanged herself, didn't she?" said one of Father's brothers.

"Hanged herself," grinned Father, "and did you see the way the rope was tied to the beam? There isn't a woman in the world who knows that knot, only experienced shepherds tie knots like that. Perhaps she put her own head in the noose out of fear, but he tied the knot, and no one else. He killed them both, secretly went into the forest again, waited a couple of hours, and came back home. That's what happened, I think . . . Only you should all keep your mouths shut, there's no point in our tangling with this madman."

The next day the chief of the district police, the doctor, and some other people rode up from the city. The neighbors crowded into the storekeeper's yard, surrounding the police chief and his assistants. Iron Knee was there with them.

I stood on the kitchen veranda with a towel slung over my shoulder and a pitcher of water in my hands. They had told me that the doctor would need to wash his hands after examining the body, and I was to pour for him.

That was why I stood alone on the kitchen veranda and saw the doctor working over the body. First he seemed to me to be fingering the storekeeper's slit throat. Then he unclasped his hand, pulled out the bloody knife, examined it, and laid it on the kitchen table.

When the doctor laid the knife on the table and started to walk out of the kitchen, Iron Knee suddenly darted in. With his yellow owl eyes glittering, he impudently thrust something in the doctor's pocket. I don't know what it was—gold or bills. When he thrust whatever it was into the doctor's pocket, he glanced up at the doctor from below—the doctor was a big solid man—with a look that made me terrified for him. I'm sure the doctor also felt ill at ease. It all happened in a second, and an instant later Iron Knee was back in the crowd in front of the kitchen, listening to one of the neighbors say something to the police chief. Not a single person paid any attention that Iron Knee had gone into the kitchen and come out, although he did it openly. But you should have seen the way he looked at the doctor! It was a savage look, full of confidence that the doctor would not dare disobey him.

"Well?" the police chief asked, when the doctor appeared on the veranda with bloodied hands.

"Suicide," the doctor said.

He began washing his hands, and I poured for him. Then he took the towel from my shoulder and painstakingly dried his hands.

Anyway, it was simply decided that Iron Knee's wife and the storekeeper had committed suicide. The dead were given a proper burial and the incident was gradually forgotten in the village. Iron Knee did not marry again. A few years later, while hunting ibex, he fell off a cliff and drowned in a mountain lake.

Thus Abesalomon Nartovich ended his story. Everyone had listened to him with great interest. The cosmonaut was especially attentive. Unfortunately, after hearing Abesalomon Nartovich's story, he decided to make a correction in it, which was to have a telling effect on the fate of his thick-leaved alder branch.

"Abesalomon Nartovich," the cosmonaut said, "you know how much I respect you, and you've told us a wonderful story. But I'm sure our Soviet doctor couldn't have taken money or anything else to cover up a murder. That was just your imagination."

"I told it as I saw it," Abesalomon Nartovich replied pacifically, not completely renouncing his own version.

"Yes, yes," the cosmonaut repeated, "it was your imagination. The police chief was there too, so he had nothing to fear—"

"What is he, from another planet?" the young host exclaimed in Abkhazian, his searching gaze expressing incredible suffering.

"Well of course!" my comrade's friend remarked jokingly in Abkhazian. "He's a cosmonaut."

"That's what they're taught!" Uncle Sandro said with finality, still more sternly. Although as tamada he bore no responsibility at all for the cosmonaut's correction, to confess its absurdity could certainly have cast a shadow on the cosmonaut's toast, which Uncle Sandro had managed to neutralize earlier.

Despite Uncle Sandro's explanation, the young host adamantly set about transplanting his little grove, ostensibly blaming the sun's movement across the sky, but in fact with the obvious purpose of sticking the thickest-leaved alder branch into the ground in front of Abesalomon Nartovich again. It also looked a bit as if he were handing him the palm for the best dinner-table story. In any case, the sun's movement across the sky played no part at all; it was already so near setting that it wasn't bothering anyone.

After a while we got up from the table and scattered to stroll around the yard before departing.

I stood by the goat pen, which adjoined the yard, and watched the old man squatting on his haunches to milk the goats.

The sound of milk streaming into the pail, the sudden clank of the bell on a goat's neck when she scratched herself, the stamping and bleating of the kids in the neighboring pen, the gentleness of the setting sun, the green of the yard, Grandfather's house far away, the fading sadness of reconciliation.

We said good-bye to our hosts and drove away from the village. Half an hour later we were in the town where my comrade had once involuntarily committed murder. We stopped at a gas station to refuel, and I decided to get out and take a walk.

I headed toward the park across the street, where I hoped to find a toilet. When I got out of the car, my comrade's friend called jokingly that I was forgetting where I was, my life was in danger and he demanded my immediate return. I smiled and waved to let him know that I understood the total unlikelihood of such an encounter with the old man, especially since he had never met me face to face and could not recognize me for who I was.

So I thought, as I crossed the road and parted the clipped arborvitae bushes that hedged the park. When I got deeper into the park, along the sandy path lined with pampas grass, medlar saplings, and octopuslike agaves, it struck me that my comrade's friend's reminder was not all that ridiculous. Perhaps I was still under the impression of Abesalomon Nartovich's story about the terrible vengeance of Iron Knee.

I still had not come to the toilet, and I was getting farther and farther from our cars, and the park was amazingly empty. I was already thinking of disregarding propriety and taking advantage of this rather unpleasant absence of humanity, when I spotted the outlines of a public toilet, slightly concealed by bamboo thickets and in this concealment recalling a small neglected pagoda.

I went inside. Water was gushing into the sink from a faucet with a broken handle. The sink was apparently stopped up, because water was pouring over the edge and the whole floor was wet. There was no one in the toilet. The air smelled not only of bleach powder, but of an unintelligible anxiety, desolation, danger.

Having finished my uncomplicated business, I was about to turn around and leave when I suddenly heard the footsteps of a man approaching the building. Suddenly the footsteps ceased, and I sensed that the man had stopped at the doorway. He was obviously waiting for me.

All at once I was filled with a wild, inhuman terror that grew with every instant. Why should the ordinary visitor to a toilet stop in the doorway, when he could plainly see that there was only one man here, and many free places?

He's waiting for me! It's the old criminal himself, or one of his men! Like lightning, it came to me exactly how he could have learned about us. During dinner, when the talk got around to my comrade's involuntary murder, one of our host's neighbors had approached the table. He could have told others, they could have been relatives of the old man's, and they could have ridden to town and told him everything. I instantly remembered that a Pobeda had been standing not far from the corner where the gas station was located. Had it been waiting for us there?

Terrified to turn and face my mortal danger, I continued to stand with my back to the unknown man who was patiently waiting for me. The longer we remained in this strange position, the more terrified I became, because I became all the more sure that it was me he was waiting for, and this was the only reason he was standing in the doorway.

I badly wanted to turn around, but some instinct of self-preservation dictated that I must not; until I turned around he could still allow himself to delay, but as soon as I turned, he would have to shoot or come at me with a knife.

I can't say that it didn't occur to me to defend myself. I thought that if he had a knife, I must put up my arm at all costs, try to take the knife-blow on my arm, and then run, if possible. But I had no idea what I could do if he had a pistol in his hand. I imagined myself lying here with my cheek pressed to the wet, dirty, cold cement, and this was a form of death made additionally repulsive by its defilement. As it turns out, it does matter to a man where he becomes a corpse.

Perhaps partly for this reason, I decided to turn around and start walking. I say partly, because I had still another urgent thought. Aside from the fact that if I were wounded, or mortally wounded, it would be nicer to break free into the park and fall on the green lawn, rather than on the dirty, wet floor of a public toilet, I sensed that my further presence here seemed to affirm my consent to the impending retribution. My thought was that to display to a man who had come to execute me my readiness to be executed was to make his task morally easier. I wasn't worried about his morals, of course. I just thought that if he wasn't totally ready to murder, then my chances of living should be increased by my unreadiness to accept murder. But my readiness to accept murder would sanction his decision—perhaps not quite final—to murder. No one knows how many murders have been contemplated in this world, because statistics on planned but uncommitted murders do not exist.

All this flashed through my mind, and I decided it was too dangerous to stay in the toilet any longer. That is easy to say, but how hard it is to switch to another frame of mind, how hard to set in motion a benumbed body, to look into the eyes of a man who is planning to take your life! And I made a compromise decision.

I turned not to the door but to the sink, and began washing my hands, supposedly to imply a certain logical naturalness in my movements and camouflage my too-long presence here. As I washed my hands, I tried to lend my movements a cheerful carelessness. In effect I was shouting to him, "I'm completely unready to be murdered, because there's no reason to murder me!"

I won't prolong this passage by describing how I painstakingly dried my hands on my handkerchief and what I was thinking of at the time. The very fact that I'm writing about it testifies that I remained alive.

After putting the handkerchief in my pocket, I turned decisively—too decisively—to the door and seemed to look directly at the man standing in the doorway. I *seemed* to look directly at him. I saw the outlines of his figure, but I was conscious that my eyes did not want to look into his eyes. Fighting off my torpor, I walked past him, thinking about how if he whipped a knife out of his pocket now, I would have to fling my arm up at all costs.

I noticed with some relief that he was not hurrying to thrust his hand in his pocket and pull out a weapon. Trying to dart into this gap of hope, I slipped past him and at the same instant went cold with the awareness of my naked back.

Several encouraging instants went by. I strode down the garden path, treading on air. The longer I walked, the more obvious it became that I was safe, and I moved forward with exulting steps. Yet every nerve in my body had told me that he was standing in the doorway waiting for me—what had he wanted?

I realized that there was only one man in the world who could explain the mystery to me. Of course, that man was Uncle Sandro! I dashed to Abesalomon Nartovich's car, where Uncle Sandro was sitting. I got into the car, feeling within me an immoderate, shameful joy in life. I felt like cuddling up to someone and being quiet. For some reason I felt most like cuddling up to the cosmonaut, not only because he was a mighty spokesman for life, but also because the structure of his soul was palpably clear and uncomplicated. This was just the kind of soul I felt like cuddling up to now. After all, he was really an excellent fellow! Of course he pretended to be a little dumb, and I could see why. He had made it into the elite, he was happy, and he must have been terrified that he would find himself out of it because of some accidental piece of folly. So he cuddled up to ideology. I too felt like cuddling up to ideology, warming myself near it, purring a little.

I told Uncle Sandro about the terror I had suffered.

"You're a fool," Uncle Sandro smiled in reply. "You'll never learn. That man was a real Abkhazian, not yet corrupted. A real Abkhazian will never show his naked flesh to another man or look at another's naked flesh. That's considered an insult. So he waited for you to come out."

Yes! I suddenly saw the man's figure with uncommon clarity—the figure of an Abkhazian peasant, his shirt worn outside and belted with the narrow Caucasian belt, his wide breeches and Asiatic boots.

Abesalomon Nartovich, who was sitting next to the chauffeur, reclining grandly, had waited out my conversation with Uncle Sandro. Now he went on with the apparently endless topic he had begun back in the village, the characteristics of the local grape varieties.

"A young wine made from the Kachich grape, please remember," he told the cosmonaut, "is a very guileful drink."

The phrase struck me as uncommonly homely and endearing. Shudders of tenderness ran through me as I repeated it to myself: a guileful drink, a guileful drink. Grant, O Lord, that we may know no other guile!

The cars moved off on the homeward journey.

JAMKHOUKH, SON OF THE DEER OR THE GOSPEL ACCORDING TO CHEGEM

NOW WE WILL TELL about Jamkhoukh, Son of the Deer, a legend with the semblance of truth, or the truth about Jamkhoukh's life overgrown with legends. Think of it however you want. The Chegemians, for example, think of all this as real. If even now, they say, in our time, miracles sometimes happen, then in those far-off, forgiving times miracles took place nearly every day.

There's a grain of truth in this. Even in our time, when things rarely happen in the world, every once in a while something really will happen in Abkhazia.

The future Jamkhoukh was probably two or three months old, they say, when he turned up in a forest thicket not far from Chegem. He was found there by a doe. How he came there no one knows.

This is what the Chegemians said about it. They said that some family was probably walking down a forest road when they were set upon by bandits. The baby's mother managed to throw him into the thicket, before the bandits committed their bloody banditry or simply bound the travelers and sold them into slavery in other lands.

Slaves brought no money in Abkhazia then, because among the Abkhaz keeping slaves was considered a mark of bad taste. But even then a few contrived to keep slaves, because in all times there are people with bad taste and bad inclinations. Anyway, that's what the Chegemians think, but no one knows how it really was.

. . . The little boy, who had fortunately landed on soft grass in a fern thicket, grew hungry and began to cry. For a long time the little boy cried, until his voice was heard by a doe. She was grazing in these parts with her two fawns and had drawn near to the little boy as she cropped the grass.

Parting the fern stalks with her breast, the doe caught sight of the crying child. She realized that the baby was hungry, that he had somehow lost his own mother, and she began to offer him her udder. But the baby was so little that there was no way he could reach the udder, of course. Then the doe carefully lay down beside him and fitted her kind teats to the child's little face.

Now the baby guessed what to do. He caught the doe's kind teat in his mouth and began to suck the good warm milk from it, smacking his lips with sweet joy. Never mind, thought the doe, as she listened for her two fawns grazing nearby in the glade, we'll raise the baby, there's milk enough for three. Only we'll have to live in these parts, she thought, because the boy is too little and can't walk yet. The doe told all this to the boy when he learned deer language. Deer talk with their eyes, it seems. And the boy, later on when he began to live with the Chegemians, told them what he had learned from his mother deer.

So the doe began to raise the baby, who quickly grew and gained strength on the good deer's milk. The boy could walk now, and the doe no longer lay down to nurse him but merely knelt so that he could reach the udder. In the evenings, when the deer family lay down to sleep, the little boy always settled himself cozily on the doe's belly and fell asleep holding one of his mother's teats in his mouth, which was terribly funny to his foster brother and especially his little sister.

Before long the little boy began to run with the fawns and began to understand deer language, which requires remarkable sensitivity of soul and quickness of mind. Deer talk among themselves with their eyes, and it's only foolish people who think that animals merely moo and bleat. No, animals are a long way from mere mooing and bleating! They understand everything and talk among themselves with their eyes, and sometimes give signs with their heads or ears. Donkeys are especially good at talking with their ears.

Six years went by. The mother deer gave birth to new fawns, and the little boy nursed along with them. Although it was high time for him to switch to grass and leaves, he preferred milk. Or sometimes he pretended to be grazing near the bushes, when he was really eating buckthorn berries, blueberries, raspberries.

"I've spoiled him," the doe said sometimes, "but I can't help it, you know, he's an orphan."

In the evenings, when the mother deer lay down to sleep with her foundling and her new fawns, the little boy would ask her to tell how she had nursed him kneeling down. Each time, listening to her, he would choke with laughter and say, "Mama Deer, could I really have been so little?"

"Of course," the mother deer would reply, continuing to chew her cud, because they were talking with their eyes, "you were quite little then. Only don't cackle, for the love of God, or else the wolves will hear us."

"Think of it," the boy would say. "I was so little then that poor Mama had to kneel down for me to reach her udder. And now I'm so big that I kneel down myself, to be more comfortable nursing.''

"Spoiled child," the mother deer would grumble, "it's time you switched to grass.''

"But I ate lots of grass today," the little boy would reply. "I even have a bitter taste on my teeth from it.''

"That's not true!" his little fawn sister would pipe up at this point. "I saw how much grass you ate. You pretended to eat grass but you were picking strawberries.''

"It is true, it is," the little boy would assure her, "I ate lots of grass too. You just didn't notice.''

"Oh? I didn't notice?" his fawn sister would say hotly. "Then why don't you ever chew your cud?''

"I don't understand that myself," the future Jamkhoukh would reply. "For some reason I never get a cud from the grass I eat.''

"You can't make a cud from milk," his little sister would say doggedly.

"Milk turns to cheese in the stomach," the father deer would pronounce weightily at this point, "from the warmth of the entrails. I myself have seen shepherds place a kettle of milk on the fire and later take from it a big white lump, which they call cheese because it's cheesy. So the milk you drink can be chewed, too, if you return it to your mouth in time, when it has already turned to cheese but hasn't yet gone away into your body. And we'll say no more about it . . . But you, my little fawn daughter: never betray your brother. We deer don't do that, that's what bad people do.''

Thus or not very differently they conversed in the evenings, and then they lay down to sleep. The fawns would drift off with the little boy, nestled up to the mother deer's belly. Jamkhoukh had fond memories of these days and readily told his friends about them.

. . . Once the old hunter Beslan from the village of Chegem saw an amazing scene in a forest glade. He saw grazing there a stag, a doe, two fawns, and a naked, tanned little boy.

The hunter was so dumbfounded that at the first moment his trembling fingers could not pull the arrow from the quiver to shoot the stag, because in those far-off times a real hunter never killed a doe.

The next moment the stag scented him, the family bunched together, and by now it was impossible to shoot, because the hunter might hit the doe, the fawns, or the little boy.

An instant later the strange deer family had darted into the forest and the little boy was running after the fawns, almost keeping up. The hunter, though stunned by what he had seen, now seemed to collect his wits, and he rushed after the little boy. He would never have caught up, of course, but the boy tripped over a vine and fell to the ground. While he was freeing his foot from the vine the hunter ran up and seized him.

The little boy tried with all his might to break free from the hunter's grasp, he even bit him, but old Beslan held him tightly in his arms. And then, realizing that he was parting forever from the mother deer, the little boy cried out with inexpressible anguish, and this cry of parting was the first sound of his human voice. The mother deer replied to him from afar with a trumpeting sob, for she loved him as her own fawn, loved him even better, because she had nursed him longer than any of her fawns.

Old Beslan carried the little boy home, tied him tightly with a rope to a heavy kitchen bench so that he wouldn't run away, but close to the hearth so that he wouldn't be cold. It was fall, and the boy was naked, and old Beslan thought he might freeze to death.

People came from all over Chegem to admire the child who had lived with deer. The little boy missed his deer family terribly and ate nothing for five whole days. Old Beslan gave him bread, honey, cheese. He brought him some fresh grass, some millet straw, but the boy ate nothing, neither human food nor the food of the herbivores.

But people came, took seats on the benches around him, tried to guess where he came from, who he was, and what all this portended. Toward evening of the fifth day old Beslan brought him an armful of hazelnut branches, with a rustle of yellowing leaves, and threw them at the little boy's feet in the hope that he might be tempted by this goat treat. And now the little boy suddenly began to speak in a human voice, because a person gets used to everything, he even gets used to people.

"You might as well bring me an armful of ferns," he said to the old hunter. "Better give me some milk . . . goat's milk, if you don't have deer's . . ."

Now the Chegemians marveled greatly that the little boy had begun to speak like a human being, although to this point they hadn't tired of marveling that he said nothing in human language.

The old hunter gave him a big clay mug of milk, the little boy drank it down and began to talk with the people.

"First untie me," the boy said, "I won't run away now. It must be my fate to live with you, with people."

"Whose son are you?" the Chegemians asked. "Have you been in the forest long?"

"I don't know," the boy said, "I've never seen people. My mother deer found me in the bushes as a baby and raised me."

"What!" the Chegemians marveled. "You've never seen a person, but you're talking to us, and in our Abkhazian language at that? Who ever heard of such a thing?"

"You're hearing of it now," the boy said. "You kept buzzing at me here for five days. By the end of the second day I already understood all that you said. The reason is, deer speak with their eyes, and I understand the language of the eyes. When you—people—speak with your mouths, you speak with your eyes at the same time. Though not all that you say with your mouth coincides with what you say with your eyes, by comparing the one with the other I've learned to understand the meaning of the words you speak."

"Miracle child!" the Chegemians exclaimed. "Son of God!"

"I'll have to punish our Greek shepherd," one of the Chegemians said suddenly. "He's been my shepherd for a whole year, and to this day he can't speak Abkhazian!"

"Fool," the little boy said, looking at him with his big deer eyes. "He doesn't know the language of the eyes, that's why it's hard for him to start right out speaking someone else's language."

"How did you know he's a fool?" the Chegemians said, exchanging stunned glances. They did in fact consider this countryman of theirs the most foolish man in Chegem.

"First by his eyes," the little boy said with a shrug, "and then his words too."

Now the old hunter Beslan suddenly burst into tears.

"Chegemians," he said, "you know how my three sons perished. My wife died of grief, mourning them. Our God, the Great Weighmaster of Our Conscience, has sent me this little boy for consolation, so that I will have someone to gladden my old age and someone to close my eyes in the hour of death."

"Don't cry," the little boy said. He went over to the old hunter and nestled up to him, which made the old man cry still harder. "Last year," the little boy added, "when the wolf killed my fawn brother, my mama deer cried a long time. It hurts me terribly when anyone cries. I will comfort your old age, but pledge me your word never to hunt deer!"

"I swear by my perished sons," the old hunter exclaimed, "I will never again hunt deer!"

"All right," the little boy said, "I'll live with you always . . . Give me one of the human names, since you can't do without them."

"I name you Jamkhoukh," the old hunter declared, "in honor of my youngest son."

"Jamkhoukh, Son of the Deer," the Chegemians said. "That will be better."

They sat a good while longer at the old hunter's house and then went their ways, carrying the news of the little boy who had been raised by a doe and had mastered human speech in five days. Really he had mastered it in two days.

Thus Jamkhoukh, Son of the Deer, began to live in the old hunter's house, and never was a son more kind, nor any little boy quicker and brighter. In one month he mastered all the customs of the Abkhaz, and these customs are so many that the Abkhaz themselves sometimes mix them up.

At first he found it hard to get used to clothes and kept trying to run around naked, but then he grew accustomed to clothes too. He also loved to play with the calves and kids at first and didn't play with the children. He would start talking to them about various wise things that they didn't understand. But then when he realized that the children didn't understand him, he began to play with them as he did with the calves and kids.

The only thing that took the little boy a long while to get used to was the sight of a man sitting astride a horse. At first he took a horseman to be some outlandish animal, but then he gradually got used to this too.

Once when the Chegemians started fleeing in all directions before a rampaging she-buffalo, he calmly walked up to her and pulled from her eye the little piece of bark that had infuriated her.

"How did you know," the Chegemians asked, "that this was what had infuriated her?"

"The language of buffaloes is very similar to that of deer," the boy said, "much as the language of the Ubykhs is similar to Abkhazian."

Inside of ten years all Abkhazia knew about Jamkhoukh, Son of the Deer. He lived with his old father, was a good farmer, generously gave people wise advice, and rather accurately predicted the weather and various events. By this time he already knew, besides Abkhazian, the languages of the Greeks, the Kartveli, the Laz, the Circassians, the Scythians. He gave advice to all who consulted him, regardless of origin.

Although his advice sometimes proved to be not very correct, and his predictions occasionally did not come true, people weren't too disappointed. As they weighed and discussed Jamkhoukh's advice and prophecies, people always felt sure that the Son of the Deer's mistakes were the consequence of his excessive nobility.

If, for example, in calculating the actions of a villain, he predicted further villainies from him, they often turned out to be more villainous than Jamkhoukh had thought. And if he predicted the behavior of a good man, even the man's goodness, alas, fell short of the notch Jamkhoukh had hewed for him.

Gradually the people who came to Jamkhoukh for advice or a prediction began to amend his words.

"If the Son of the Deer," they said, "predicts the villainy a villain will commit, add a little villainy on your own and you'll hit it just right."

"If the Son of the Deer," others said, "predicts a good deed from a good man, take away some goodness on your own and you'll hit it just right."

But it soon became clear that this adding and taking away made Jamkhoukh's predictions come true still less often. The trouble was that in adding to the villainy of a villain and taking away from the goodness of a good man people were overzealous, and the result was utter confusion.

"This Jamkhoukh, Son of the Deer, has gotten us all mixed up," the stupidest said angrily. "He'd do better not to make us any predictions."

"No," said the more sensible ones, "we'll be better off doing as he says, adding nothing and taking away nothing."

Most people began adhering to the Son of the Deer's advice and predictions, though they felt it wouldn't hurt to add a little grief to his advice and predictions or take away some hope. For fear of getting confused, however, they hesitated to do it.

"Oof, this Jamkhoukh will be the ruin of me," some skinflint would say on receiving practical advice from him. Nevertheless he would do as Jamkhoukh ordered, for fear that things would otherwise go even worse.

Until he was twenty, despite all the small griefs caused by the chronic folly of many people, Jamkhoukh had a happy life. He was good-looking, strong, agile, had the light gait of a deer, and was as wise as a hundred wise men assembled in one place and all in agreement with one another. But since a hundred wise men assembled in one place begin to argue and contradict one another, Jamkhoukh was wiser than a hundred wise men.

Once in a while, when Jamkhoukh grew too weary of human folly and cruelty, he went away into the forest, sought out his mama deer, and sat down beside her, pressing himself to her breast and throwing his arms around her neck.

"Mama," Jamkhoukh would say, "I'm so weary of them. People make it hard to love them."

If he did not find his mama, he found other deer and asked how things were going for the mother deer and how she was. The others would tell him that the mother deer was alive and well, and Jamkhoukh would return to Chegem comforted.

By this time, in gratitude for Jamkhoukh's wisdom, the Chegemians had renounced deer-hunting, and the deer came very near the village. So if Jamkhoukh didn't encounter his mama when he started for the forest, he would encounter some other deer and give him news for her.

Jamkhoukh's father, old Beslan, could not be proud enough of his son, and the sunset days of his old age were illumined by a quiet happiness. But to everything there comes an end, and the end of life came to old Beslan.

He began to die. The Chegemians summoned a leech from Dioscurias, who said, after pompously examining the old man, that his blood had become too thick and he needed to have his veins opened.

"Fool," sighed old Beslan, "why open my veins? I'm dying of old age, not disease. Surely there's no medicine for old age?"

"Well, if you put it that way!" huffed the leech from Dioscurias, who in his time had opened veins for Constantinople merchants and was proud of it. "Then why did you summon me?"

"For the people," explained the Chegemians who were keeping watch by the sick man's bed. "People would say that Jamkhoukh had gotten uppish and wouldn't even summon a leech for his dying father. Better take the three sheep that are due you and drag them back to Dioscurias. Open veins for them there."

"Well, if you put it that way!" the leech repeated. Mounting his little donkey, however, he took the three sheep he had earned and dragged them back to Dioscurias on a rope.

Just before his death old Beslan ordered everyone out of the room. When he was left alone with Jamkhoukh, he said:

"My son, I must reveal a certain secret to you, because I am leaving this world, as must every man who has lived his time. I want to save you, my son, from a terrible danger. In our house there is a room locked with three locks. I never opened it and you never asked, knowing that I didn't want to tell you about it. Now the time has come to tell the secret of the locked room. Many years ago, to my misfortune, a wandering artist came to my house and began

dying of a fever. Before he died he said to me, 'I have painted the portrait of
the most beautiful girl ever to live in the world. She is the beauty Gunda, the
enchanted, eternally young sister of the seven famous giant brothers. They live
at the westernmost end of Abkhazia, not far from the village of Pshada. I beg
you, preserve this portrait and never show it to anyone, because every man who
sees the portrait will fall in love with the beauty and try to marry her. But the
fierce giant brothers promise each suitor they will give him their sister only in
the event that he meets all the tests of skill they have devised for mind and body.
If the suitor is not equal to all the tests, they kill him. Those are their conditions.
The skulls of unsuccessful suitors are cocked on the pickets of the fence around
the giants' courtyard. Two unsuccessful suitors perished while I was painting the
young beauty's portrait. I didn't fall in love with her because I transferred my
love to the portrait I was painting. This portrait must remain throughout the ages,
so that people may see how beautiful a girl can be and what a divine master I
was, the painter Nahar. Swear by our God, the Great Weighmaster of Our
Conscience, that you will forever preserve my portrait, so that it will go down
to posterity!' 'I swear!' I told him. And the artist died. I committed him to the
earth with all appropriate honors. Then, going through his meager belongings,
I found the portrait, rolled in a leopard skin. Without unrolling the skin, I carried
it to the room and locked the door with three locks. That was the beginning of
my misfortunes. By turns, it seems, all three of my sons stole the keys from
me, penetrated the locked room, looked at the portrait, fell in love with the
beauty, and secretly left the house to try their luck. My three sons were killed
in one week by the giant brothers. But I didn't know about it at the time, I
thought they had perished while hunting. I walked through all Abkhazia trying
to find their tracks. At last, by questioning people who had encountered them,
I realized they had all gone in the direction of the giant brothers' house. My
wife died of grief, mourning her children. But in my old age the Great Weighmaster of Our Conscience took pity on me and sent you to me. I entreat you
never to enter the room where the portrait of this beauty lies. After the death of
my sons I unrolled it and rolled it up again, this time in three skins. Let it lie
there until the giants die, or until a Dzhigit turns up who meets all their conditions
and she finally gets married.''

"Then you saw the portrait, Father?" Jamkhoukh asked. He was twenty years
old, and he was already dreaming about the remarkable girl.

"Yes," old Beslan replied.

"Well, what's she like?" Jamkhoukh could not resist asking.

"I don't know, son," the old hunter sighed, "I didn't notice her beauty,
because the blood of my sons was upon her."

Jamkhoukh pledged his word to his father that he would never enter the room
with the beauty's portrait, and the old man died. As one helps a woman in labor
Jamkhoukh helped ease the last spasms of his body, which was tormented by
the necessity of parting with the soul. When the soul had left the body, Jamkhoukh
closed the lids of his father's now-vacant eyes.

Jamkhoukh buried old Beslan with all honors and began to live alone in his house. Day and night he thought about the beauty's portrait, but he dared not open the room where it was kept.

Jamkhoukh's heart was torn. He burned with curiosity, but he could not break the pledge he had made to his father. Perhaps he might have broken his pledge, but he was afraid that if he fell in love, and if his attempt to marry the beauty Gunda ended in failure, he would not be able to observe the anniversary of his father's death. Jamkhoukh was a pious son and wanted his dead father to receive all that was due him by Abkhazian custom.

A year later, having observed the anniversary of his father's death, Jamkhoukh opened the room where the portrait lay. The smell of mold and rot from a badly cured hide struck his nostrils.

Rolled in a leopard skin, the portrait lay on a table in the empty room. Jamkhoukh unrolled the leopard skin and saw that under it was the skin of a wild pig. Jamkhoukh unrolled the wild pig skin and saw that under it was the skin of a donkey. Jamkhoukh unrolled the donkey skin and saw the portrait. He turned it toward the window. Transfixed by the gentle beauty of the golden-haired girl, he fainted and fell.

When he came to, he studied the girl's portrait again for a good while longer, still sitting on the floor and rubbing his bumped head. The pain in his bumped head softened the impression made by the girl's dizzying beauty.

At length he stood up, having seen his fill of the portrait. He rolled it carefully, this time in the leopard skin only, and put it on the table. Wondering at his father and not understanding why he had rolled the portrait in the three skins, Jamkhoukh took the skins of the donkey and the wild pig, locked the room with the three locks, and threw both skins in the fire on the hearth. Jamkhoukh was already in love.

"What is she like in real life?" he thought, watching the skins of the wild pig and the donkey twist, almost writhe, in the fire. "I will die," Jamkhoukh thought, "or free her from her monster brothers, who have been the ruin of so many innocent men."

Early the next morning Jamkhoukh went to the forest, intending to meet his mother deer and tell her he wanted to marry the beauty Gunda, who lived at the end of Abkhazia, not far from the village of Pshada, with her fierce giant brothers.

He did not find his mama anywhere around Chegem, but he encountered other deer and told them to tell his mother about his decision. When he returned home, he donned his best cherkeska, with the silver belt and dagger, and put soft moccasins on his feet. Over his shoulder he slung a tightly rolled burka, bound with a strap. Over the other shoulder he slung a *khurjin* containing a cheese, a slab of dried meat, and a dozen *churkhcheli*. After asking the neighbors to look after his livestock, he started on his journey without a word to anyone.

Toward noon on the second day of his journey, he emerged on a path that went past a plowed field. And this is the sight that met his eyes. The plowman had halted his oxen in the furrow and was stooping down to eat big slices of earth, saying now and again, "Very good earth, by God, very rich!"

Although the earth really was lush and rich, Jamkhoukh marveled greatly at this unusual sight, of course. He stood for a while staring at the plowman who was wolfing down earth, and then he couldn't resist hailing him.

"Good appetite to you, plowman!" Jamkhoukh called. "Though this is the first time I've seen a man eat earth!"

"Hello, traveler," the plowman replied, swallowing a big lump of earth. "As it happens, she on whose neck I'd like to be hanged, if I'm fated to be hanged, is late with my dinner. So I decided to fortify myself—"

"Who is it you're talking about?" Jamkhoukh asked blankly.

"Why, my sweet wife, of course," the plowman explained. "Who else!"

"Can you eat a lot of earth?" Jamkhoukh asked.

"Well, how shall I put it, traveler," the plowman replied, wiping his mouth on his sleeve. "I can eat about as much earth as you cast up when you dig a well a hundred cubits deep. Any deeper and I can't. Oh, maybe with great effort."

Jamkhoukh surveyed the plowman attentively. He was a stocky man, well nourished but not too fat.

"Good enough," Jamkhoukh said. "Though on the other hand, a man eats earth even so, because he feeds on her fruits. And then the earth eats the man, because she feeds on his corpse. But I never saw anyone do it directly."

"This is nothing," the plowman protested. "Now if you saw Jamkhoukh, Son of the Deer, you'd have someone to marvel at. He's the wisest man in Abkhazia, you might say the wisest in the whole world. Never once heard human speech, but when he did, he learned our language in five days! Who ever heard of such a thing!"

"I *am* Jamkhoukh, Son of the Deer," Jamkhoukh said, "and I really did learn Abkhazian, only in two days, not five, although that's of no importance. But I confess I couldn't eat a slice of earth."

"You're Jamkhoukh, Son of the Deer?" the plowman exclaimed. "Then take me with you! My name is Trencherman, chances are you'll find me useful somewhere!"

Jamkhoukh told him the purpose of his journey and warned him of the dangers it entailed.

"That's all right," Trencherman said. "With you, I'm ready for anything!"

"Well then, Trencherman, let's go," Jamkhoukh consented.

Trencherman lived not far off, and he shouted for his brother to come and finish plowing the field for him.

"Is everyone in your family like you?" Jamkhoukh wondered.

"No," Trencherman said, "I alone am Trencherman. But I can fill up like an ordinary man too—from chicken to lamb. And if I sometimes get hungry, like just now, I can fortify myself with a nice bit of earth. Traveling with me is no trouble."

"Well then, let's go," Jamkhoukh said, and they started out.

Toward noon the next day, they came out by a waterfall and saw a strange sight. Under the waterfall stood a man. He was catching the white-foamed stream

in his mouth, drinking it greedily, and whenever he stopped for breath he repeated, "Good Lord, what a thirst I've worked up! I can't possibly drink my
fill!"

Jamkhoukh and Trencherman watched for a long time as the man drank water,
standing on the bottom of the brook into which the waterfall flowed. Now the
brook had dropped so low that they could see a silvery, gold-speckled trout
flopping in the shallow backwaters.

"Damn it, man, you'll burst!" Jamkhoukh said finally, unable to contain
himself.

At this point the waterfall-drinker turned around to him and said proudly,
"Sooner a woodpecker will die of concussion than I, Tankerman, will get drunk
on this puny little waterfall. I'm sorry for the fishes, or else I'd drink some
more."

"It's the first time I've seen a man drink so much water," Jamkhoukh declared.
"I can't drink more than three tankards in the very hottest weather."

"This is child's play," Tankerman said, coming out on the bank. "Not for
nothing am I called Tankerman. Now if you saw Jamkhoukh, Son of the Deer,
you'd marvel at a real miracle! He gives everyone free advice and makes predictions that come to pass even before he predicted. He first heard human
speech—Abkhazian speech I mean, of course—when he was a six-year-old boy,
and he learned our language in five days! Now, there's a miracle!"

"I *am* Jamkhoukh, Son of the Deer," Jamkhoukh said. "There's considerable
truth in your words, although there are exaggerations too. But about the Abkhazian language—I learned it in two days, not five, although that's of no
importance."

"Thanks be to the Great Weighmaster," Tankerman exclaimed, "that he gave
me the idea of drinking from this waterfall! Take me with you, Jamkhoukh,
chances are you'll find me useful on the way."

"Well then, Tankerman, let's go," Jamkhoukh said, "only you should
know . . ."

And he told him the purpose of his journey and the many dangers it entailed.

"That's all right," Tankerman said reassuringly. "With you, I'm ready for
anything! And if it comes to a drinking match—sooner a woodpecker pecking
a tree will die of concussion than those giants will outdrink me!"

"Listen, but you look alike," Jamkhoukh said, surveying Tankerman's figure,
well-nourished but not too fat.

Tankerman and Trencherman really did look alike. Only Trencherman's hair
was black, like rich earth and Tankerman's hair was bright gold, like water at
dawn.

"Is that so," Tankerman said, shooting a jealous glance at Trencherman.
"Let *him* stand under the waterfall, and then we'll see what he's capable of."

"Is that so," Trencherman said. "May I be hanged on my wife's neck if
you're capable of eating even the little promontory we stand on. Eat it, and then
you can wash it down with the waterfall."

Tankerman was greatly astonished at such a suggestion, but now Jamkhoukh apprised him of Trencherman's capabilities, and the three of them walked on together.

They walked on down the road, and Jamkhoukh told them instructive stories so that they would grow wise on the way, and also made incidental observations about nature as he studied it around them.

At one point Trencherman said, "Here's something that surprises me, Son of the Deer. I once noticed an eagle flying high, high, *high!* in the sky, and suddenly he dropped to the ground like a stone. Now he'll grab a rabbit or a wild turkey, I thought; but he landed on a dead donkey and began pecking at it. I was amazed. Why should he fly so high, in order then to land on a dead donkey?"

"The higher a bird flies, the more likely he feeds on carrion," Jamkhoukh said. "The wiser a living creature, the more fetid his shit . . . Is my meaning clear, Trencherman?"

"The first part is clear," Trencherman declared, after a moment's thought, "but the second part isn't, quite."

"In my opinion, you're hinting at man," Tankerman said.

"That's right," Jamkhoukh remarked.

"But the pig has very bad-smelling dung too," Trencherman said, jealous that Tankerman had caught the hint but he hadn't.

"I'm sorry to say you're right," Jamkhoukh agreed. "That just goes to show that the pig bears a great resemblance to an evil man, or that man has much in common with a pig."

"But Jamkhoukh," good Trencherman exclaimed, "maybe in the future, at least, man will move away from the pig!"

"Let's hope so," Jamkhoukh smiled. "In a way, that's the point of your life and mine."

"Or the pig will move away from man," Tankerman joked.

"Friends, I can see you're profiting by our journey," Jamkhoukh said.

That night, when they had spread out the burka and eaten supper by the campfire, Jamkhoukh decided to acquaint his companions with poetry. It turned out that neither Trencherman nor Tankerman had ever heard real poems. True, they both loved folk songs. Tankerman especially knew a lot of drinking songs.

"No," Jamkhoukh said, "I mean something quite different. I'll recite a poem by an Old Abkhazian poet for you, and you guess what it's about." He recited these lines for them:

> *The scorpion*
> *Climbed on a white flower*
> *And died of surprise.*

Tankerman stared at Trencherman and pretended that he understood what the poem was about but didn't want to say. Trencherman stared back at Tankerman and pretended the same thing.

"What do you think?" Jamkhoukh asked.

"I can guess," said Tankerman, who was a bit more wily than Trencherman. "But if I tell, Trencherman will up and claim he thought the same thing."

"I have no such notion," Trencherman said, hurt. "Just think, the water-gulper knows it all! You can be sure I don't know what this parable's about, Jamkhoukh."

"Well, and you?" Jamkhoukh asked Tankerman.

"What I think," Tankerman declared, "is that the scorpion climbed on the white flower and the flower turned out to be poisonous! So he died!"

"No," Jamkhoukh said, "I see that you need to have the meaning of poetry explained to you for the time being. Here's what the poet meant. The scorpion was black himself, his thoughts were black, and his deeds were black. He thought everything in the world was black. Suddenly he saw the white flower and realized that his whole life was wrong, and he died of it."

"O-o-oh," Tankerman drawled, "you don't say! Clever idea!"

"But it's hard to get, at first," Trencherman added, pleased that Tankerman hadn't understood the poem any more than he had, it turned out.

"Never mind," Jamkhoukh said, "you'll get used to it gradually."

With that they lay down by the campfire on the outspread burka and went to sleep.

The next day Jamkhoukh and his friends walked through a flowering spring valley. Wild pears and cherry-plum trees scattered soft pink petals in the light breeze. Every little cherry-plum tree, bowed down by flowers and green leaves bursting with freshness, reminded Jamkhoukh of his beloved girl and the heroism of the feat whose reward would be the beautiful Gunda, sister of the fierce and wily giant brothers.

"I'm always telling you things," Jamkhoukh said, suddenly struck, "but now, friends, tell me something from your own lives. For instance, has either of you succeeded in performing a heroic feat? I'm sorry to say I haven't."

"Yes," Trencherman said, after a moment's thought, "there has been a heroic feat in my life."

"Of course," Tankerman affirmed. "If there's anything I'm good at it's a heroic feat."

"I want to be hanged on the neck of my beloved wife," Trencherman said, "if my heroic feat isn't better than yours."

"Sooner a woodpecker pecking a tree will die of concussion," Tankerman exclaimed, "than your heroic feat will prove better than mine!"

"Don't quarrel, friends," Jamkhoukh said. "You'd each better tell about your own heroic feat. You begin, Tankerman!"

Here is the story Tankerman told. In a certain Abkhazian village, it seems, there was a lake from which people took drinking water. In this lake there was a dragon. Almost every evening it grabbed one of the women who came there to get water or do laundry. No one could kill the dragon, because it hid in the depths of the lake, unexpectedly swooping up to catch a woman unawares.

When he learned of the dragon's outrageous behavior, Tankerman went to the village and offered his services. He ordered all the men of the village to stand around the lake with spears and arrows in their hands. He himself lay down by the water and began to drink, pausing to look from time to time lest the dragon swoop up on him. Tankerman drank the lake for four days and four nights in succession, and he drank up almost all the water, so that toward morning of the fifth day the dragon began thrashing in the shallows. Now the men who had surrounded the lake began showering it with arrows and spears. There was only one thing left for the dragon to do—die, which it did.

In honor of their deliverance from the dragon the villagers held a feast and invited Tankerman to it. Tankerman thanked them and said, "Sit down at the table, friends. I'll join you a little later. Since I've spent four days and four nights drinking the lake, I have to—excuse me for mentioning it, but I have to spend six days and six nights getting rid of the water. Then I'll join you and catch up."

"Fine," the villagers replied, "we'll sit down at the tables. Go to that brook over there, because we don't take water from it anyway, it's muddy. Then come back to us. No doubt you'll catch up."

"I expect I will," Tankerman said. Finding a secluded spot by the brook, he undertook to pour off water, as the Abkhaz say. The expression perhaps appeared among the Abkhaz at precisely this time.

Unfortunately, neither Tankerman himself nor the villagers, in their joy, took into account that he had drunk too much water. A whole lake, after all. By the end of the sixth day the brook had swollen and washed away a house that stood above it. Three goats who didn't have time to escape from their pen, as well as the owner of the house himself, were swept away by the flood.

They tried to save the owner, but failed, because he was too drunk.

"I was just getting ready to live!" he managed to shout at the last as he was swept away by the raging element, so to speak.

On the eve of Tankerman's arrival, it seems, the dragon had gobbled up the man's wife. With this serious excuse he had begun to drink, although it was unclear whether he was drinking from sorrow or joy. He drank without leaving the house, which was why they'd more or less forgotten him and hadn't invited him to the feast. And now, when the swollen brook swept the man away, everyone tried to guess what his last words might have meant: "I was just getting ready to live *without the dragon*," or "I was just getting ready to live *without the wife*."

"Without the dragon," said Jamkhoukh, as a man who had not yet grasped the complex diversity in the joys of family life.

"A pretty good feat," Trencherman agreed, after hearing Tankerman out, "but I must say, I've been to that village. What you called a lake would more properly be called a pond. Besides, you lost a man and three goats. A man's a man, but three goats are a pretty good snack."

"Tell about your heroic feat," Tankerman said, getting angry. "I suppose you ate half a mountain, but what good did it do anybody?"

"Here's what," Trencherman replied, and he told the story of his heroic feat.

It seems the Laz fell upon their village, killed many men, bound those who did not succeed in escaping, and drove them to their own village, along with the cattle. There they placed them (the people, that is, not the cattle) in a prison fortress, planning to sell them (the people, that is, not the cattle) into slavery.

Now Trencherman performed a heroic feat. With his fellow villagers he began to dig a tunnel in order to crawl out of the fortress. But the Laz were no fools either: they checked their prison fortress every day to see if there was any dug-up earth. But there wasn't any dug-up earth, for Trencherman was packing it all into his belly.

This was a very difficult feat, because the earth from under a prison is the most unpalatable earth in the world. Trencherman choked, but nevertheless he ate. Until now he had eaten the rich earth of the plowed field, the fragrant earth of vegetable gardens; he had eaten the sweet earth of river precipices, layered like *halva;* but the earth under the prison was the most unpalatable, the deadest, in the world.

Trencherman made the effort, however, and when the tunnel was done he escaped from the prison with his fellow villagers.

"Any fortress is always a prison," Jamkhoukh said, after hearing Trencherman out. "A certain Old Abkhazian poet of ours loved to repeat this simple maxim. And in fact, if those who besiege a fortress triumph, they make it into a prison for those who defended it. If those who defend a fortress triumph, they put into the fortress those who besieged it, as if to say: 'You were trying to get in? Then stay in.' "

Thus they walked along the road, talking of anything and everything.

The next day they found themselves on a broad mountain slope that gladdened their eyes with the kindly might of the spring flowering. Hawthorn bushes thickly studded with little white blossoms gave off a disturbing scent of bitter almond and reminded the love-smitten Jamkhoukh of bashful girls.

All the round curves of the grassy knolls, and all the round curves of the flowering shrubs, and all the round curves of the thickly leaved trees brought to Jamkhoukh's mind the festiveness of his encounter with his beloved Gunda.

Here on this flowering mountain slope Jamkhoukh and his comrades caught sight of a shepherd grazing a great many long-eared rabbits. The shepherd was a tall, trim young man. On his feet, right at the ankles, he wore a pair of smallish millstones. As soon as a rabbit started hopping away, the shepherd overtook it in a flash and turned it back.

"What a miracle!" Jamkhoukh marveled, after greeting him. "This is the first time I've seen a man graze rabbits, let alone run so nimbly with millstones on his feet."

"Oh, this is child's play!" the shepherd said with a wave of his hand. "Now if you saw Jamkhoukh, Son of the Deer—"

"That's me, *I'm* Jamkhoukh," Jamkhoukh said, "but not a word about my wisdom—"

"You're the Son of the Deer!" the shepherd said in amazement, and he jumped up and down with joy. "So you're the one who makes predictions that come true even before you predicted! You're the one who learned our language in just five days!"

"Yes, that's me," Jamkhoukh said, "only people have exaggerated some things and underrated some things. Thus, for example, I learned Abkhazian in two days, but that's beside the point—"

"Great Weighmaster of Our Conscience!" the shepherd exclaimed. "You have fulfilled my dream. I have seen the Son of the Deer! Jamkhoukh, take me with you. I am Highspeed. Chances are you'll need my speed somewhere!"

"But what about your rabbits?" Jamkhoukh asked.

"Well," said Highspeed, "they won't go any farther than this ridge. When the time comes, I'll take off the millstones and round them up."

Now Jamkhoukh explained to him the purpose of his expedition and the dangers it entailed. Highspeed listened to him and jumped up and down in anticipation of joy, so that sparks showered from the millstones as they bumped together.

They started on. The next day the friends emerged on the alpine meadows, where the grass was waist high, the mountain tops sparkled in the hot midday sun with fresh, appetizing snow, and the steep slopes were carved by majestic waterfalls.

"There's no greater pleasure," Tankerman said, "than to stand under a glacial waterfall in hot weather—stand steady, so the stream doesn't sweep you off your feet—open your mouth wide, and drink the mountain water for about two hours."

"And in my opinion," Trencherman said, "there's no greater pleasure than to climb to a snowy peak in hot weather and lick it all clean, till you feel its stony slopes rough under your tongue."

"Son of the Deer," Highspeed began, "I usually graze my rabbits in the mountains, and however much I feast my eyes on the alpine meadows and snowy peaks, I can never gaze my fill of them. Are the mountains the most beautiful place on earth, or does it seem so to me because I'm very sensitive?"

"I think this is the answer," Jamkhoukh said. "The mountains are the place that comes closest to the sky. The earth wants her best part to meet the eye first. And what's more, when God sends His angel to earth, it's better if he lands at the most beautiful place and then gradually gets used to certain uglinesses of earthly life."

"Exactly," Trencherman said. "In the same way, people in the village always receive a guest with bread and salt, though they're not kind and hospitable all the time."

They were walking along a mountain path, and around them on the slopes smoke was rising from shepherd shanties. Herds of horses and cows were grazing, flocks of sheep and goats.

In one place the little path passed a shepherd shanty where the shepherd was kneeling by an open hearth, fanning the fire.

"Notice this shepherd," Jamkhoukh said. "How beautiful his face is! A person's face is always beautiful when he fans the fire."

"Exactly!" Trencherman exclaimed. "I've oftened noticed this too. When she on whose neck I'd like to hanged, if I'm fated to be hanged, is fanning the fire, she strikes me as a very beautiful woman. When she's scolding me she strikes me as a dreadful freak. Then I don't want to be hanged on her neck, I don't want to be hanged at all—"

"Am I ever sick of hearing about your wife," Tankerman interrupted him. "May the both of you be hanged, you *and* your wife, on the same crossbeam."

"No," Trencherman said, "I don't consent to that. If we're both fated to be hanged, I'd like them to hang me first on my darling's neck, and then hang my darling on mine. That's how I'd like it!"

"But who's going to ask your consent, numskull?" Tankerman said hotly. "If the king orders the two of you hanged, they'll hang you on the same crossbeam!"

"I don't consent," Trencherman objected. "Only on my own conditions do I consent to be hanged."

"Jamkhoukh, he'll drive me crazy!" Tankerman ejaculated. "Who's going to ask you, you dolt, if the king himself orders it!"

"I'm sticking with my own opinion," Trencherman said, after a moment's thought, "and with that of her on whose neck—"

"Jamkhoukh," Tankerman implored, "I can't take any more!"

"Don't squabble, friends," Jamkhoukh said. "We'd better continue our conversation about the person who fans the fire. He who fans the fire always has a beautiful face, because fanning the fire is a thing pleasing to God. The soul of man is also a fire, which we are required to fan."

"Tankerman's soul went out long ago," Trencherman said suddenly, "it got doused with so much water and wine."

"What a simpleton!" Tankerman clapped his hands. "He thinks that when water and wine go down the throat they touch the soul. Certainly a man's soul is situated where the throat passes into the body, but it doesn't have an outlet to the gullet. It's located nearby, though. That's obvious, if only from the fact that if the soul is brought to great heat by anger, all you have to do is fill up on cold water and you calm down. But the gullet isn't directly connected to the soul. Otherwise, dirt-eater, you'd have buried your own soul long ago with the dirt you've eaten."

While they were talking, the shepherd fanned up the fire, put on some small logs, and glanced around at the travelers. He got partway to his feet and greeted them, inviting them into the shanty.

"No," Jamkhoukh said, "we have no time to stop. We're on a journey. But don't you think it's time to go down to the village and fetch lick-salt for your sheep and cows?"

"True," the shepherd agreed, "it's high time, but I've been too busy. I mean to go tomorrow. Stay a while. I'll climb up to my flock and be back in half an hour with a sheep. I'll slaughter it and treat you to young meat, we'll wash it down with koumiss from the skin bag."

"Thank you," Jamkhoukh said, "but we're in a hurry."

"And besides, you couldn't drive a sheep back here in half an hour," Highspeed joked, winking at his friends.

"And besides, the five of us couldn't get through a sheep," Trencherman said, taking up the joke.

"And besides, it's not worth opening a fresh skin of koumiss," Tankerman added. "We couldn't finish it up, and then it would start to ferment."

"No harm in that," said the openhearted shepherd, "if it started to ferment we'd pour it out for the dogs. Godspeed to you, if you're in a hurry."

"Good-bye!" The friends took their leave and started on.

"Wait!" The shepherd suddenly hailed them.

The friends looked back. The shepherd's face expressed perplexity and surprise.

"Traveler," he said, addressing Jamkhoukh, "how did you know my supply of lick-salt was gone? After all, you didn't even come into my shanty!"

"Very simple," Jamkhoukh said. "I saw your two cows and several sheep licking the white rocks."

"Of course!" The shepherd slapped his forehead. "You're almost as wise as Jamkhoukh, Son of the Deer."

"He is—"Trencherman began, but here Jamkhoukh inconspicuously nudged him, and Trencherman fell silent.

"How do you mean, 'He is'?" the shepherd asked.

"He is what he is," Tankerman said.

"Ah-h." The shepherd nodded his head and began threading dried meat on the spit.

Trencherman covertly licked his lips, and the friends started on.

In the evening Jamkhoukh and his companions built a campfire in a picturesque forest glade. They had a potluck supper and sat around the fire, talking of anything and everything.

"My friends," Jamkhoukh said, "I won't conceal from you that I'm nervous about my encounter with the beautiful Gunda. I have a feeling I'm very likely to overcome the giants, but I know nothing about the family life of men. I know how Mama Deer lived with her stag, but I came to my father when he was already a widower. Tell me about your wives. What their ways are like, how you're supposed to treat them. Let's start with you, Highspeed."

Highspeed, meanwhile, had taken the millstones off his feet and was greasing the openings with mutton fat so they wouldn't chafe his legs too much.

"With me, Jamkhoukh," he said, "as you begin, so shall you finish, because I'm terribly sensitive and therefore terribly susceptible to love. And because I'm susceptible, I can't possibly get married. The minute I want to marry a girl who's caught my fancy, or rather, the minute she wants me to marry her, I start to like another girl, and I turn tail and run from the first one. Once I even had to take off the millstones—one of them latched onto me that hard, almost got me. So, Son of the Deer, I have nothing to tell about family life."

"You're a light-minded man!" Jamkhoukh said.

"That's why I go around in millstones," Highspeed replied, not altogether to the point, continuing to grease the openings in his millstones with mutton fat.

"I'd better tell about her who—," Trencherman began eagerly, but here Tankerman interrupted him.

"Son of the Deer!" he implored. "If Trencherman now tells us about her on whose neck he'd like to be hanged, either I leave you or I clout him with a firebrand! Choose one!"

"All right," said the Son of the Deer, "he promises us not to talk that way."

"He's already said the whole thing," Trencherman put in pacifically. "Well," he went on after a short pause, "my wife, that is, she who—well, who is my wife, is a very good woman. I've lived with her for ten years now and acquired five children. I already miss them . . . Not to mention her on whose neck—"

"Jamkhoukh, he's at it again!" Tankerman exclaimed.

"—hang beads," Trencherman insisted, very pleased to have outwitted Tankerman. "Which beads I now envy. Our life is harmonious, peaceful, she knows how to do everything around the house. Sometimes if she gets busy in the vegetable garden or with the children . . . My, but she's a slowpoke . . . Well, anyway, if she gets busy and doesn't have time to fix supper, she shouts to me, 'Trencherman, I haven't had time to fix your supper! Get some salt and pepper in the kitchen and dig yourself some fresh dirt out back.' I go to the pasture, dig out a big solid chunk of turf, salt it heavily, pepper it heavily, and eat it. Meantime my children are dancing around me, laughing and shouting, 'Papa eats dirt! Papa eats dirt!' But otherwise everything's the same with me as with other people. In a word, I'm very content with her on whose—"

"Are you starting that again?" Tankerman said, flinching.

"I am very content," Trencherman went on firmly, "with her on whose neck—"

"Son of the Deer!" Tankerman cried.

"—on whose neck are beads . . . of carnelian," Trencherman concluded, elated that he had managed to tease Tankerman.

"Thank you, Trencherman," Jamkhoukh said, "I liked your family life very much. Now tell about yours, Tankerman."

"All right," Tankerman assented, and at the recollection of family life his Adam's apple positively worked. "Of course I'm a drinking man, which follows from my very name. That is, I drink, following my own name. Sooner a woodpecker—"

"Jamkhoukh, I beg you, stop him!" Trencherman exclaimed. "If he starts in about the woodpecker who'll die of concussion, I'll conk him on the head with this brand so hard that he'll die of concussion himself! And before he dies he'll see so many stars, not to mention the sparks that shower from the brand, that they'll eclipse the starry sky."

At this remark from Trencherman everyone looked at the brand, then at Tankerman's head, and then at the sky, as if trying to imagine whether the sparks from the brand and the stars in Tankerman's head could be so numerous as to eclipse the starry sky. Very likely they could, everyone decided, including Tankerman himself.

"Calm down, Trencherman," Jamkhoukh said. "Let's hope that Tankerman, like his famous woodpecker, will get by without a concussion."

"Well then," Tankerman began again, "you could say the woodpecker—"

"Jamkhoukh, he's at it again!" Trencherman cried.

"You could say the woodpecker," Tankerman continued stubbornly, "had gone off his rocker from his knocking, if they ever found anyone to outdrink me, the great Tankerman! But the woodpecker-knocker hasn't gone off his rocker, not yet! My family life is pretty good too. I have just three children, Trencherman has outdone me here. Why? Because I, Tankerman, am a great tamada, and the whole village invites me over, in order to have me drink the outsiders under the table. Which I do. And the feasts, as is usual with us, last far into the night. I rarely have any time left for family life, for which my wife scolds me, of course. She tells me that I drink away the night and snoozle away the day."

"So you're a freeloader?" Trencherman cried. "Who looks after your field and your livestock?"

"The neighbors," Tankerman confessed reluctantly. He added, "In my opinion, it's better to eat free, like me, than eat dirt, like you."

"No," Trencherman exclaimed, "it's a lot worse to be a freeloader! Right, Jamkhoukh?"

"Of course," Jamkhoukh agreed. "It's very bad to be a freeloader."

"Is that so?" Tankerman said caustically. "What about droughts?"

"What about them?" Trencherman said in amazement.

"Who, in time of drought," Tankerman asked, "drinks half the brook and then walks through all the fields of our village and sprinkles them—doing this, keep in mind, by mouth?"

"That's altogether different," Jamkhoukh said. "You're simply a people's hero."

"Yes," Tankerman agreed modestly, "people do say that about me . . . sometimes. My wife scolds me for drinking so much wine. But otherwise we have a good life. Sometimes on a sunny day I fill up on pure spring water, come to my children, and send the water spurting straight to the sky. By mouth, of course. If not the first time, then the second or third, I get a magnificent rainbow, and the children dance around me and squeal with delight. And I point to the rainbow and say to my children, 'What ho, a bow?' 'A rainbow! A rainbow!' my children shout. 'Papa, burp another rainbow!' And of course I burp rainbows as long as the water lasts. That's how life is with my wife and children."

"You have good lives," Jamkhoukh said, rejoicing for his friends. "I could dream of such a life!"

"But your life will be even better," Jamkhoukh's friends exclaimed. "After all, you're the wisest man in Abkhazia!"

"Really, I don't know," Jamkhoukh said. "I'm so nervous about my encounter with the golden-haired Gunda. One look at her portrait sent me crashing to the floor, you know! What will happen when I see her in real life?''

The friends comforted Jamkhoukh and settled down to sleep before the dying fire. Jamkhoukh lay for a long time, gazing at the vast starry sky and feeling in his breast a sweet sorrow.

The next day they started on and walked a long time through a beech forest. Suddenly, in a small glade, they saw a man lying with his ear to the ground, attentively listening to something.

''What are you doing?'' Tankerman asked.

The man merely waved a hand for them not to bother him. The friends watched him for a while, and then the man stood up, dusted off his clothes, and said with a smile, ''They've proclaimed the punishment.''

''What punishment?'' the friends asked in surprise.

''Such fun,'' the man said with another blissful smile. ''Two ants quarreled in the anthill. One said it was he who had dragged the dead one-winged wasp into the anthill. The second said it was he. The first one said, 'How could you have, if its wing got torn off when I was dragging it?' The second said, 'No, its wing got torn off when *I* was dragging it.' Then the first said, 'All right, name the spot where its wing got torn off.' The second said, 'I don't remember the spot, but I remember that its wing got torn off when I was dragging it.' Then the first said, 'Ah, but I remember well the spot where its wing got torn off.' The ant leader sent a courier to the spot, and he did indeed drag back a wasp wing. Scholar ants fitted the wing to the dead wasp and acknowledged that this wing was from this wasp. The second ant was shamed, and he confessed that he'd appropriated another's booty. The ant leader, in punishment for appropriating another's work, condemned the liar to hard labor dismembering three May-beetle corpses and carrying them to the anthill. That's the kind of thing that happens in an anthill.''

''What do you know,'' Jamkhoukh marveled. ''I can't make out people whispering two paces away, but you hear ants quarreling under the ground.''

''That's why I'm called Hear-All,'' Hear-All said. ''But I'm nothing! Now if you knew—''

''We know, we know,'' Jamkhoukh interrupted him.

''What do you know?'' Hear-All asked.

''We know that you mean the wisdom of Jamkhoukh, Son of the Deer,'' Trencherman said.

''How did you guess?'' Hear-All said, startled. Suddenly, peering intently at Trencherman, he exclaimed, ''May lightning strike me if you yourself aren't Jamkhoukh, Son of the Deer! Who else could have guessed my thoughts!''

When he heard this Trencherman blushed and hung his head.

''Oh, sure, the Son of the Deer,'' Tankerman remarked with great venom. ''You just can't tear him away from the grass. He breathes with his nose to the ground . . . Here's Jamkhoukh, Son of the Deer, standing beside you!''

''Travelers, is this the truth?! Travelers, you're not playing a trick on me, are you?!'' Hear-All exclaimed.

"Yes, I am Jamkhoukh, Son of the Deer," Jamkhoukh said.

"You are Jamkhoukh, Son of the Deer!" Hear-All exclaimed. "I didn't mishear you? But it would be strange if I, Hear-All, should mishear! So it's you? The very one? Our language in five days? Predictions! Even before predicted?"

"Why, no," Jamkhoukh said, "some things are exaggerated, and some things underrated. Thus, for example, I learned the Abkhazian language in two days, not five, although that's of no importance."

"Take me with you!" Hear-All begged. "I'll be sure not to miss a single one of your wise words."

Jamkhoukh explained to him the purpose of his journey and the dangers it entailed. Hear-All nodded joyfully, indicating his readiness to follow him, and at the same time stopped his ears with special cork plugs.

"Without jammers I'd die of the racket," he explained to the friends.

Jamkhoukh took Hear-All with him, and they started on.

"Jamkhoukh," Hear-All said on the way, "I've heard so much about your wisdom that my ears are dying of hunger, anticipating the treat of your wisdom."

"The rumors of my wisdom are exaggerated," Jamkhoukh said, "but I can tell you a few things. Listen to a parable. A certain man had in his house a loaf of bread. Another man came to him and said, 'Give me that bread, my children are dying of hunger.' And the owner of the bread gave his bread away to this man because he was sorry for his hungry children, although his very own children were left without bread that day. But in fact the man who asked for the bread had no children: he got the bread from him by deception. And another man had a loaf of bread. But a thief came to his house by night and quietly took the bread. And a third man had a loaf of bread, but a man came and killed him and took the loaf of bread. And now I ask you: Which of the three who took another's bread was worst of all?"

"The one who killed, of course, Jamkhoukh!" the friends chorused. "We're surprised you even ask!"

"No," Jamkhoukh said, "that's a mistake. Worst of all was the one who said his children were dying of hunger, the one who took another's bread by deception. He was unashamed to defile a man's soul and trample a man's trust!"

"But Jamkhoukh," Hear-All objected, "fouling a man's soul still isn't the same as killing a man!"

"I tell you truly, it's a hundred times worse than killing," Jamkhoukh replied. "A man capable of fouling a man's soul is even more capable of killing a man than the murderer is. It's merely that he doesn't need to kill for the time being; for the time being it's enough for him to deceive! Both the thief and the murderer, even though they were bandits, nevertheless committed their banditry because they had a drop of shame left in them! The one stole and the other killed, so as not to have anything to do with the soul of the man who owned the bread. But this man was not ashamed to deceive his soul!"

"Jamkhoukh is right!" Trencherman exclaimed. "I can feel that he's right, but I can't explain why!"

"Then lying is worse than killing?" Highspeed asked sadly, because, being a terribly sensitive man, he sometimes embroidered the truth, especially with girls.

"Not lying, but deceiving," Jamkhoukh said. "They're different."

"Then we can lie?" Highspeed said, cautiously, so as not to scare away his hope.

"No," Jamkhoukh said, "we can't, though in rare cases a man does have the right to a lie."

"Only in rare cases?" Highspeed asked. "Can't we increase their frequency?"

"We cannot," Jamkhoukh said. "Here's a parable for you about a justified lie. A certain wise man was riding through the forest on his mule. In the forest a bandit seized him and tied him to a tree in order to torture him and find out where he kept his money. There were a skin of wine and a roast haunch of mutton strapped to the mule's saddle—the wise man's victuals for the road. 'Why hurry,' the bandit decided. 'First I'll have a drink and a snack, and after that I'll start torturing the wise man to find out where he hides his money.' The bandit drank the skin of wine, snacking on the mutton haunch, and got drunk. When he got drunk he tossed his poleax into a blackberry patch and fell asleep. Three hours later he woke up sober and began asking the wise man, 'What did I do with my poleax?' The wise man, tied to the tree, answered, 'I don't know!'— although of course he'd seen where he threw his poleax. They quarreled a long time. And now, luckily for the wise man, some good men rode by in the vicinity On hearing the quarrel, they seized the bandit and bound him. And they untied the wise man. The wise man told them all about what had happened and fetched the bandit's poleax from the blackberry patch. The good men carried the bound bandit off to Dioscurias to imprison him in the fortress, and all the way there he kept shouting, 'There's no truth on earth! The wise man deceived me!' But the wise man, in his defenselessness, had the right to this deception. In cases like this, a lie is justified."

"Jamkhoukh is simply a miracle!" Hear-All exclaimed, and he neatly stopped his ears with the jammers as a sign that they had eaten their fill of wisdom and didn't want to overeat.

The friends walked and walked and walked, and before long they caught sight of a picturesque village, situated above the picturesque Gumista River. At the entrance to the village they were met by the worried elders.

The travelers greeted the elders, and the elders greeted the travelers.

"They say Jamkhoukh, Son of the Deer, is coming our way," one of the elders said to them. "You haven't met him on the road, by any chance?"

"I *am* Jamkhoukh," Jamkhoukh said. "What is worrying you, elders?"

"The Great Weighmaster of Our Conscience has sent you to us," one of the elders replied. "We've had an accident. A fly has flown into the ear of the eldest elder of our village. And he's already deaf in one ear as it is. So this fly managed to fly into the good ear, may lightning strike her! If she'd flown into the deaf one we wouldn't worry, he wouldn't hear her anyway. So this fly has been buzzing in his ear for a whole week, the hellcat, and torturing him. She refuses to die and she won't fly out. Our elder is tired to death, but we don't know how to lure her out. What trouble we have, Son of the Deer!''

"Never mind," Jamkhoukh said, smiling at the elders, "a thing like that isn't worth your worry. Catch a tiny spider, tie a horsehair to its leg, and let it into his ear. The spider will catch the fly and you'll pull them both out."

"Thank you, Son of the Deer!" the elders said jubilantly. "We shall immediately order it done as you have said."

Jamkhoukh and his friends were led to the home of one of the elders, the table was laid, and while they were drinking and snacking, a man came running with the good tidings.

"The spider got the fly on the very first try!" he shouted, to general joy.

"Let him stop his ears with corks, like me," said Hear-All. "No fly will get in then."

"Corks are a possibility, of course," the elders answered, "but he's deaf in one ear as it is, you know. What good would he be with corks—"

"But I hear fine even with corks," Hear-All boasted, for reasons completely unknown.

After packing their *khurjins* with provisions for the road, the friends started on.

That evening they made camp above a noisy little mountain stream and sat a long time by the fire. Now and again sparks soared up to the sky as if trying to become stars.

"Jamkhoukh," Highspeed said, lying on his back and gazing at the starry sky, "you know what a very sentimental man I am. The scholars of Dioscurias say that thousands or hundreds of thousands of years from now there won't be any people on earth. They'll die out. This thought makes me terribly melancholy. Will there really come a time, I wonder, when the sun rises in the sky just as ever, spring comes just as ever to the earth, cloudbursts roar just as ever in the leaves, but there isn't a single person on earth? Explain to me, for love of the Great Weighmaster: Do the scholars of Dioscurias speak the truth, or are they mistaken?''

"You've posed an interesting question, Highspeed," Jamkhoukh replied. He moved a brand to the middle of the campfire, and a fresh swarm of sparks flared up, rushing to the sky. "I've wondered about this, of course. But don't you listen to the cock-and-bull stories of phrasemongering scholars. It's no use arguing with them, they have chisels where their wisdom teeth should be. Since they know they're going to die, these egoists comfort themselves with the notion that sooner or later life on earth will come to an end anyway. But man's life on earth is eternal, and I'll prove it to you in just a moment. Only first, answer me this: Do you believe in the immortality of the soul?''

"What Abkhaz doesn't believe in the immortality of the soul!" Trencherman exclaimed.

"Correct," Jamkhoukh said, "our soul is immortal. Now think: Why did the Great Weighmaster create our immortal soul?''

"But there has to be something left of a man," Tankerman declared, glancing at the waterfall that streamed down the mountainside in a pale stripe. "A man has lived and lived and lived . . . It's happened he has drunk, and not just water . . . And suddenly he dies, and nothing's left of him. It hurts somehow, Son of the Deer, I tell you honestly. Oof, how it hurts!"

"That's right, in a general way," Jamkhoukh said, "but the Great Weighmaster does nothing by accident. He devised our immortal soul for our earthly life. Why? So that man should be horrified at the idea of his polluted soul forever stinking in eternity like burning dung."

"Great Weighmaster preserve us from such a fate!" Trencherman said in fright.

"And so," Jamkhoukh went on, "the Great Weighmaster of Our Conscience created our immortal soul so that living people should think about this all the time and their souls should get to eternity in the cleanest form. But if the soul is immortal for the benefit of earthly life, isn't it clear that earthly life is also immortal? Really, could our God, the Great Weighmaster of Our Conscience, create the senseless situation in which there were no longer any people on earth, while their immortal souls, created precisely for the support of earthly life, continued to abide in senseless immortality?"

"Oh, how wisely the Great Weighmaster has devised everything!" Highspeed exclaimed, jumping up from the burka and clapping his hands joyfully. "And how clearly Jamkhoukh has explained everything! Now I'm not worried for people, people will live on earth forever!"

"Happiness is drinking in the honey of wisdom with one's ears," Hear-All said, "and this honey pours daily into my ears from the lips of the Son of the Deer."

Having spoken these words, he stopped his ears with the jammers as a sign that he was full of the sweetness of wisdom and didn't want to be overfilled. Although Hear-All heard perfectly even with the corks in his ears, he always listened to Jamkhoukh's speeches with his ears open. "Wisdom," he loved to say, "must be heard in unfiltered form."

"You mustn't praise me, friends," Jamkhoukh said instructively, "or else you might corrupt me . . . After all, I'm a man too."

Now they settled down to sleep by the campfire, and Jamkhoukh lay for a long time with his eyes open, thinking of his golden-haired Gunda. Feeling the warmth of the campfire on his body, encompassing the starry sky in his gaze, he sensed with heart and soul that nothing so warms a man in the universal cold as the kind campfire of human friendship.

Therefore he listened tenderly to his friends' breathing.

From the breathing of each, one could tell how he lived when he was awake.

Hear-All slept quietly, as if listening for something even in his sleep.

Trencherman snored mightily and steadily, so that the overhanging branch of a chestnut tree swayed with his every breath.

Tankerman's throat emitted a sound as if someone were decanting wine from jug to jug and would never reach the end of it.

The next day the friends walked a long time through a chestnut forest, and by noon they found themselves in a vast green forest glade with a brook running through it, babbling over the stones.

Just as they reached the brook they saw a powerfully built man coming toward them, carrying a house on his shoulders. Not a large one, true, but nevertheless a house, with a veranda, steps, a henhouse tacked to the side wall, and a dozen hens' nests hung up around the house, with the hens sitting in them and cackling to make known that someone was keeping them from laying.

On the roof-peak sat a golden rooster, clucking loudly, reproaching the hens for their too noisy conduct. To crown all these oddities, a woman stood on the veranda clutching the railing in an attempt to peer under the house and locate the man who carried it. Judging by the words she was trying to hurl at him, she was the wife of the house-carrier.

"*Care*ful there, numskull!" she screamed. "You'll scare off the *chick*ens, booby! Walk softer! It's hard for the *chick*ens to *lay!*"

"There's a strongman!" Jamkhoukh said as the house-carrier crossed the brook and came up to them. "Never have I seen such a miracle."

After this remark of Jamkhoukh's, the house-carrier paused as if listening to see whether his scolding wife would stop. Convinced that she would not, he turned to Jamkhoukh:

"Yes, they do in fact call me Strongman. But surely this is no miracle! Now if you met the Son of the Deer, you'd marvel at a real miracle!"

"Why stand there like a tree, you simpleton!" his wife went on scolding. "Didn't you ever see a tramp before? Look, a convict, with the stocks on his feet! Escaped bandits, I daresay."

"I am Jamkhoukh, Son of the Deer," Jamkhoukh said.

"You are Jamkhoukh, Son of the Deer?" Strongman exclaimed. He banged the house down on the piling props—he really wasn't being very careful now— and came out from under it wiping his benumbed neck. "I'm going to give you a kiss, Jamkhoukh!" Strongman hugged Jamkhoukh tightly. "What a prince of a fellow! What a wise man!"

"Trusting nincompoop!" his wife was screaming meanwhile. "Let him show a royal certificate that he's the Son of the Deer! I daresay the only folks Jamkhoukh hobnobs with are princes and royal viziers! Would he tramp around with these ragtails and convicts? They'll steal the *chick*ens, the *chick*ens!"

"You're mistaken, woman," Jamkhoukh said. "I'm always with my people, not princes and viziers."

"I see what kind of people you're with, I see!" the woman cried, pointing at the totally guiltless Highspeed. Out of stupidity she took the millstones on his feet for a convict's stocks.

But now the rooster flew down from the roof with a loud cock-a-doodle-do, and after him came the rest of the chickens, flying down from the henhouse and the nests, and after them came four little children, charging out of the house with shouts of glee, their bare feet pounding, to surround Jamkhoukh and his comrades. Strongman's wife, too, came flying down the steps and dashed after her chickens with a loud wail.

"Jamkhoukh," said Trencherman, "don't you think that all this is a bad portent for your marriage?"

"I do not," Jamkhoukh replied, tenderly watching the sturdy little barefoot children. They had surrounded Highspeed and were pulling at him from all sides.

"Uncle!" they shouted. "What are you, a miller? Why do you have millstones on your feet?"

"No," Highspeed answered, "I'm Highspeed!"

"He's Highspeed!" the children cried ecstatically. "You highspeed, Uncle Highspeed, and we'll watch."

"All right," said Highspeed, and he carefully disentangled himself from the children. In a few bounds he overtook the chickens, which had scattered through the glade. He rounded them up in a flock and drove them to the house.

"Uncle Highspeed," the children squealed, "now highspeed without the millstones!"

"No," Highspeed protested, "without the millstones I get too light. I'm afraid I'd fly away!"

"Don't worry," the children clamored, trying to pull Highspeed's feet out of the millstones, "our papa will catch you!"

Strongman, meanwhile, conversing with Jamkhoukh, had learned where he was going and asked to go with him.

"What about your wife?" Jamkhoukh asked.

"She can just go to hell, and her chickens with her," Strongman replied. "I'm sick of dragging her and the house from village to village. She can't ever get along with the neighbors. Let her live in the middle of the forest for now, and I'll use the time to rest up from her scolding."

Now Strongman's wife, who had been chasing the chickens, came up to the house.

When she learned that her husband was leaving with Jamkhoukh, she consented to it with unexpected ease.

"Fine, go along," she said, "only let the convict stay here. Turns out he's good at rounding up chickens."

"Oh, no," Highspeed said indignantly. "If you leave me with her, I'll throw off the millstones and be back to my rabbits in half an hour."

"Listen, Trencherman," Tankerman said suddenly, "you should eat her up along with her chickens, and that'd be it! You'd set Strongman free from this witch!"

"What am I, a cannibal?" Trencherman said, hurt. His face darkened, and he turned away from Tankerman.

"Trencherman can't take a joke!" Tankerman laughed loudly.

"That kind of thing is no joke," Trencherman said. He gave Tankerman a look and turned away again.

"But this kind of thing is a joke!" Tankerman exclaimed. He prostrated himself by the brook and in a few minutes drank about five amphorae of water.

After that he straightened up, raised his head, and belched forth a long jet of water. Describing an arc the height of a good-sized tree, it turned into a rainbow, which slowly faded and fell to the ground in misty droplets.

Strongman's children started squealing with delight, hopping up and down and shouting, "Uncle, burp another rainbow!"

"What ho, a bow?" Tankerman asked, smiling.

"A rainbow, a rainbow!" the children chorused, hopping up and down in their impatience.

"You'll scare off the *chick*ens!" Strongman's wife said doggedly, and meanwhile Tankerman fountained several rainbows into the sky.

"Well, here goes," Highspeed shouted, removing the millstones from his feet. "I'm going to jump over the rainbow! Catch me, Strongman!"

He stationed Strongman at one side of the rainbow, took a running start from the other, and amid the children's gleeful squeals jumped over the rainbow.

After he had jumped over the rainbow several times, Highspeed put on his millstones.

Now, his hurt feelings finally forgotten, Trencherman too decided to amuse the children.

"Attention!" he said. "I will now eat grass pie!"

With these words he pulled a knife from the sheath that hung at his belt, cut two big slices of turf from the glade, stacked them together grass side in, and began to eat, to the delight of Strongman's children.

"Grass pie!" the children guffawed, surrounding Trencherman, who, though he pretended to be exaggerating his appetite as a joke, was really eating his pie with genuine pleasure.

"A child is a miracle!" Jamkhoukh said, gazing at Strongman's children's faces, which shone with joy. "The miracle of a child is that he is already a person but is still pure."

"The sweetest honey of wisdom have my ears drunk!" Hear-All exclaimed when he heard Jamkhoukh's words.

"Don't tell me I'm the only one who can't work a miracle!" Strongman said, spreading his hands helplessly.

"Strength, if it serves the good," Jamkhoukh said, "is the greatest miracle! You will accomplish one now. Do you have an egg on hand?"

"Certainly," Strongman said.

"Bring it out," Jamkhoukh requested.

Strongman mounted to the house, ignoring his wife's screams, and brought out a basket of eggs.

"Now you'll see a miracle!" Jamkhoukh said. Turning to Strongman, he added, "Throw the eggs up as close as you can to the sun. But careful—throw them underhand!"

Strongman began taking eggs from the basket and throwing them high in the sky, with a careful but powerful motion. Sparkling in the sun, they disappeared in the fathomless blue.

So high had Strongman thrown the eggs that they did not return for about fifteen minutes. In the ensuing stillness the only sounds were the howls of Strongman's wife and the astonished cackle of the hens, who had also seen the eggs being thrown into the sky and now kept swiveling their necks to look up.

And suddenly—a miracle!

A golden rain of chicks, flapping their weak little wings and palpitating in the air, showered onto the glade.

Not just the children but all Jamkhoukh's friends, too, now squealed with delight! And not just Jamkhoukh's friends, even the chickens set up a glad cackle and ran to the chicks. Before long, having resolved among themselves the problem of which ones had hatched from whose eggs, they spread out and began to teach their own cheeping babies to forage in the grass.

Only Strongman's wife was dissatisfied.

"An incorrect miracle! An incorrect miracle!" she screamed. "There were a hundred eggs, and only ninety chicks flew back!"

She had managed to count the chicks, it seems, as they landed in the glade.

"Ten eggs were rotten, then," Jamkhoukh said. "No miracle will make a chick hatch from a rotten egg."

"No miracle will make a chick hatch from a rotten egg!" Hear-All repeated ecstatically after Jamkhoukh, at the same time stopping his ears with the jammers. "Never have my ears drunk such a sherbet of wisdom."

Hear-All watched Jamkhoukh constantly, so that he could pull the corks out of his ears before Jamkhoukh opened his mouth: he had to muffle ordinary speeches, but he wanted to hear wisdom only in unfiltered form.

The friends made ready for the journey. Jolting the house a bit, Strongman placed stones under the piles so that it would stand nice and steady.

"Papa, bring us something good!" Strongman's children shouted in farewell.

An hour or two later, when they had gone deep into the forest, Tankerman winked at Hear-All.

"Come on, listen a minute—what's Strongman's wife saying, I wonder?"

"That we can do." Hear-All pulled the jammers out of his ears and rotated his head slightly in search of the requisite acoustic source. When he found it he stood still. " 'You'll scare off the chickens! You'll smother the chicks!' " he said. "That's what she's screaming."

"Listen a minute, Hear-All," Trencherman requested suddenly, looking shy, "find out what she on whose neck I'd like to be hanged, if I'm fated to be hanged, is saying."

"There he goes!" Tankerman said crossly.

Hear-All looked at Jamkhoukh in perplexity.

"You might as well ask me," he gritted through his teeth, "what the fish-mongers are quarreling about at the Constantinople bazaar. I am the famous Hear-All, I can hear human speech at twenty thousand paces, but there's a limit to everything."

Trencherman blushed for his blunder.

"I'm sorry, Hear-All," he said, "it's just that I was pining for her who—"

"Shut up!" Tankerman interrupted. "We know who you're pining for. We're family men ourselves, but we observe Abkhazian custom—we don't talk about our feeling for our wives."

"Don't quarrel, friends," Jamkhoukh said. "I'd better tell you the parable of the three pickpockets now."

"That's a different matter!" Hear-All exclaimed, hastily pulling the corks from his ears.

"At the Dioscurias bazaar," Jamkhoukh began, "where there are a great many people, especially when a Hindu fakir is doing his conjuring or a merchant has locked horns with a customer, the crowd simply crawls with pickpockets. I divide all pickpockets into three types. For simplicity I will speak of them as three pickpockets who have dipped into my pocket and whose thievish hand I have caught in my pocket. The first pickpocket, when caught with his hand in my pocket, says, 'Jamkhoukh, I swear by the Great Weighmaster, I'll never dip into pockets again! Don't call the constable!' You can take pity on him and not call the constable, but of course he'll break his vow and dip into somebody else's pocket another time. The second pickpocket, when caught with his hand in your pocket, turns white with anger and says, 'You have disgraced me today, Jamkhoukh, but tomorrow I will disgrace you!' And if he gets the chance, he'll disgrace you and take revenge. Such are the proud pickpockets. But there is yet another type of pickpocket, the most pernicious. When you catch hold of his hand in your pocket, he shouts, 'Shame on you, Jamkhoukh! Can't you see I dipped into your pocket by accident?' 'But how could you dip into somebody else's pocket by accident?' you ask him. 'Elementary, Jamkhoukh,' he assures you, 'we were standing there crushed by the crowd, I meant to reach into my own pocket and got into yours by accident.' Then, still gripping his hand in my pocket, I say to him, 'All right, you dipped into my pocket by accident. But why did you take from it the three silver coins that you now clench in your fist? You too had three silver coins in your pocket, I suppose, and you can show them?' Now he reflects for a moment and says, 'I don't have three silver coins in my pocket. But precisely for that reason, when I mistook your pocket for my own I was very surprised that there were coins in it. I thought, Let's look and see what these coins are that have turned up in my pocket!' And now he suddenly starts shouting to the whole bazaar, 'People of the city, hear what Jamkhoukh's saying! He's saying I dipped into his pocket like a thief! People of the city, come and hear what Jamkhoukh's saying!' At this point you can't take any more and you think probably he really did dip into your pocket by accident. He couldn't possibly have dipped into your pocket with ill intent and then summoned witnesses himself. You feel ashamed and try to escape from him quickly, you walk away, and he's still shouting after you: 'What, running away, Jamkhoukh? Ashamed you slandered a good man! What did I tell you!' Such things still happen in this world in our blessed land. All pickpockets are bad, but I tell you truly, fear this last above all others! He will both rob you and disgrace you before the whole world!"

"How disgusting," Strongman said. "I'd swat him like a mosquito!"

Thus they walked, talking of anything and everything, and toward evening they found themselves near a village whose inhabitants Jamkhoukh did not respect, because this was the only village in Abkhazia where people had sunk so low that they kept slaves without being ashamed before one another. Just at the entrance to the village Jamkhoukh and his friends turned off the road lest they even encounter the people of this village. But right near where they turned stood one of the villagers, whittling at a stick.

"Travelers!" he hailed them. "Why are you bypassing our village? You're not squeamish about us, are you?"

"We are," Jamkhoukh replied, "and you know why. There's nothing for the Weighmaster of Our Conscience to weigh when he works on the people of your village."

"But he needs somebody to rest up on," the villager retorted impertinently. "He rests at our expense. Because we're all afraid he'll strain himself weighing your consciences. Ha! Ha! Ha!"

"Jamkhoukh," said Strongman, rubbing his fists, "may I teach him a good lesson?"

"Don't," Jamkhoukh said, checking him. "They'll slaughter each other soon enough, for lack of anything better to do."

Thus they got past this village, which lay on the caravan route and had been corrupted by slave traders who transported slaves here on the way from North Caucasia to Rome and Byzantium.

Toward noon the next day, the friends came out at a large Abkhazian village by the name of Dal. It was a fine village in all respects, but a young prince lived here who traded in slaves on the side. He was the nephew of the childless Abkhazian king and had grown accustomed to his own impunity.

At the entrance to the village they were met by the elders.

"Well be you, travelers!" they said. "Who are you, and where are you bound for? You haven't encountered Jamkhoukh, Son of the Deer, have you? They say he's coming our way."

"I *am* Jamkhoukh, Son of the Deer," Jamkhoukh confessed. "I know your village is prosperous and hard-working. The best grapes in Abkhazia ripen in your vineyards. But I also know that your young prince trades in slaves on the side. That's a disgrace! Make him listen to reason before it's too late!"

Now the conscientious elders blushed and hung their heads.

"How right you are," the eldest of them said. "Our prince does trade in slaves secretly, at night. But the slaves he sells are from foreign nations. Well, except that his men occasionally catch an unwary Endursky."

"It doesn't matter whom he sells," Jamkhoukh decided. "An Abkhaz who sells a slave is already a corrupted Abkhaz. Today he sells an unwary Endursky, but tomorrow he'll lay hands on his fellow Abkhaz."

"O-ho," said Tankerman, "I don't even believe in an unwary Endursky. Sooner the whole world will be caught unawares than you'll find even one unwary Endursky."

"There is no worse contagion than slavery," Jamkhoukh went on. "Picture this: my shoe has gotten too dried out, let's say, and is pinching my foot. My foot is in slavery, you might say. Because my foot is in slavery, my whole body feels discomfort. Because my body feels discomfort, my mood is ruined, so my soul loses its equilibrium and its correct attitude toward people. It's exactly the same if the rot of slavery appears in a village: the soul of the inhabitants loses its equilibrium and its just attitude toward people.''

"You're right, Jamkhoukh," the elders said. "Your wisdom is our support. But for his nephew's sake our king has promised to build in our village a temple to the Great Weighmaster of Our Conscience. For the sake of the good that the temple will bring to the people of our village and to neighboring villages, we tolerate his indulging the prince in slave-trading.''

" 'Wise outside but empty inside,' as a certain Scythian used to say when he passed by!" Jamkhoukh answered. "A temple raised on guile is a money-changer's shop and nothing more. Can you really think the Weighmaster of Our Conscience doesn't know this? By the old laws, the highest authority of the village is the people's assembly. If the assembly censures the king he must submit to it. The people pay a tax to the king and give their sons for his army. The people owe nothing more to the king. The highest authority of the village is the people's assembly. If the Abkhaz forget this, they will be punished by Providence.''

"They've already been punished, it seems," said the eldest of the elders. "A strange miracle has happened in our village. Not a single soothsayer can guess its meaning. We are all saddened by it. A fish has appeared in a sixty-gallon jug belonging to our fellow villager, a respected wine merchant. It splashes in the jug and sometimes sticks its head up to sing the drinking song 'Many Summers.' Now, the fact that it sings is understandable. It's gotten drunk in the jug of wine, of course, and it sings. But what surprises and saddens us is how, *how,* could a fish get into a jug of wine? No Abkhaz ever heard of such a thing in his life.''

"All right," Jamkhoukh said. He had regained his composure somewhat. "Let's go have a look."

"Doesn't the fish, splashing in the jug," asked one of the elders as they walked to the wine merchant's house, "signify that the Endurskies are going to subdue us and throw us to the fishes in the sea?''

"It does not," Jamkhoukh said. "But who has heard it sing?''

"Somebody heard it sing," the elders answered. "But we ourselves, with our own eyes, have seen it splashing in the jug.''

They arrived at the home of the man who owned the richest vineyards in the village, and he led them to a barn, where he had his jugs sunk in the ground. The owner opened the lid of one of them, and Jamkhoukh and his friends peered in. The dark red surface of the wine was undulating. They could tell that some living creature was stirring in the jug.

"Maybe we should decant the wine from the jug," the owner said, "in order to catch the fish?''

"Why decant it," Tankerman said, throwing up his hands. "I'll go right to work and get down to the fish."

Before the owner could gather his wits, Tankerman prostrated himself before the jug. Poking his head into it, he began to drink the wine, gradually delving deeper and deeper into the jug. The owner was obviously displeased, although, like the elders, he was staggered at this talent of Tankerman's.

"Why did you have to drink it?" the owner grumbled, trying to peer into the jug from behind Tankerman's head. "We could have decanted it into an amphora."

Meanwhile, in his zeal, Tankerman had already crawled halfway into the jug, and it looked as though he would soon fall in.

"I think," said one of the elders, turning to Jamkhoukh, "that this man of yours will soon be splashing in the jug himself, singing a duet with the fish!"

"Why did he have to drink it at all," the owner said, no longer even trying to peer into the jug through Tankerman's head. "I have so many empty amphorae over there."

"It's all right," Jamkhoukh remarked, "he won't fall into the jug. Hold his feet, Strongman."

Strongman grabbed his feet. Tankerman continued to delve deeper into the meaning of the jug, mastering the meaning easily.

Suddenly, from the jug, came the sound of someone singing the drinking song "Many Summers."

"Who's singing?" they asked from above.

"The wine is," Tankerman replied enigmatically. He continued to delve deeper into the meaning of the jug.

"We could have decanted it," the owner said for the last time, and he waved a hand hopelessly.

"Done!" came Tankerman's voice at last from the depths of the jug.

"Catch the fish!" Strongman shouted, crouching in front of the jug.

He was holding both of Tankerman's ankles in one hand, stirring steadily so that Tankerman could reach all parts of the bottom of the jug.

"Got it!" Tankerman whooped, and Strongman pulled him up in a flash.

Flopping in Tankerman's hands was a large trout, rosy red from its sojourn in the wine.

"A trout?" they all said in surprise, as if they had been expecting some other fish entirely.

"Now *I'll* make it sing!" Trencherman exclaimed. He grabbed the trout away from Tankerman, bit off all but the tail, and for some reason offered the tail to Tankerman.

"I did the drinking, and you get the snack?" Tankerman said, slightly hurt, and for some reason he handed the tail to the owner of the wine.

"Why?" the owner asked. He did not understand at all, because he was still grieving over the emptied jug.

"Yes," Trencherman said with an expert air, as he finished chewing the trout, "trout is very good soaked in wine, it turns out. Even raw."

That, they say, was when connoisseurs of fine food began to soak their trout in wine before grilling it.

"It's all clear," Jamkhoukh said, turning to the owner. "The trout is a river fish. The only way it could get into the jug is along with river water. You're watering your wine. Most likely you do it at night. At night you ladled the trout into an amphora along with water from the river, and decanted it into the jug without noticing."

"Countrymen, don't be hard on me!" the wine merchant begged, still holding the trout tail in his hand. "I sell this wine only to the Dioscurians. I don't give it to our own folks—"

"That's how corruption begins," Jamkhoukh said. "Where one man trades by night in slaves, another starts watering the wine by night."

"Just prove that I've sold slaves!" the voice of the young prince rang out suddenly. He had approached them unnoticed, it seems, while Tankerman was getting to the bottom of the jug.

"Seems like the fish has started singing," Tankerman said, looking around. He turned a questioning gaze first on Trencherman, who had finished the trout, and then on the prince. Tankerman was obviously tipsy.

Jamkhoukh too glanced around and caught sight of the prince. He determined at once that the prince's face bore the imprint of youth, the imprint of beauty, but did not bear the imprint of wisdom.

After many years, time erased from his face the imprint of youth and the imprint of beauty, but did not succeed in furnishing it with the missing imprint of wisdom.

"I don't think I named the name of him who trades in slaves," Jamkhoukh said, looking around the gathering. "Or did I name the name of him who trades in slaves?"

"No, you didn't," the elders replied, looking first at Jamkhoukh and then at the prince.

"You were clearly alluding to me," the prince said. He added, "Everybody knows you learned Abkhazian in five days, not two as you claim. What kind of a righteous man does that make you, and what right have you to teach us?"

"You'd do better to deliver us from the Endurskies," the wine merchant said brightly, and at last he tossed aside the trout tail, "than to go peering into other people's jugs and bringing your freak tipplers around here."

"Phrasemongers," Jamkhoukh said. "Accuse them of one thing and they make excuses for another. He who sells a slave is himself the slave of power! He who sells impure wine is himself the slave of impurity! Remember, slavery is already bad in that it creates in the chained coward a sense of equality with the chained hero. And not merely a sense of equality! A sense of superiority! When both coward and hero are equally helpless, the coward ascribes to himself all that the hero might have done at liberty. Because both are helpless, but the hero is silent. The hero in chains is always silent, the coward in chains is always talking. When else could he talk about his heroic deeds, except in chains! But a caged lion is nonetheless a lion, not a jackal!''

With these words Jamkhoukh, Son of the Deer, and his friends abandoned the village, having tasted no bread and salt, and leaving the elders sadly bewildered.

The Son of the Deer was so enraged that he could not get over it for a long time and did not talk to his friends.

''A caged lion isn't the same thing as a caged jackal,'' Tankerman said to Trencherman in a whisper. ''What do *you* think, dirt-eater?''

''Don't bother me,'' Trencherman brushed him off. ''That's what I thought, too.''

''I know, I know what you thought.'' Tankerman wouldn't stop bothering him. ''You thought that once they were in a cage it didn't matter whether it was a jackal or a lion or a fox.''

''You're drunk, aren't you?'' Trencherman asked.

''Yes,'' Tankerman confessed, ''I'm a little bit tipsy. When you drink head down, it turns out, you get tipsy fast. The tipsiness runs straight to your head.''

''Really?'' Trencherman said, mollified.

''Really,'' Tankerman nodded. He added, ''Only don't make a habit of grabbing somebody else's fish out of his hands.''

''I thought you wouldn't be eating it raw,'' Trencherman said pacifically, ''but my stomach's used to it.''

''Somehow we'll figure out for ourselves,'' Tankerman replied, ''what to do with a fish caught at the bottom of a jug.''

With that they finally made peace. Now the path along which the friends were walking led them under the canopy of a walnut tree, where several men were sitting and eating, having tied their horses to the branches of a box tree that grew nearby. By their appearance they were city people. The men who had approached greeted those sitting on burkas. The latter stood up from their places and invited them to share their meal. The friends sat down.

''Travelers, where are you bound for?'' Jamkhoukh asked.

''We are from the city of Pityunt,'' the travelers replied. ''The city fathers have sent us to seek Jamkhoukh, Son of the Deer. We have very important business.''

''Consider him found,'' Jamkhoukh said, smiling at the travelers.

''And you won't be wrong,'' Trencherman added, lifting a roast chicken with his thumb and forefinger and directing it to his mouth with modest delicacy.

The travelers from Pityunt stared at Trencherman, marveling at this combination of mighty appetite and modest delicacy.

''If Jamkhoukh, Son of the Deer, is before us,'' said the eldest of the travelers, ''then we'll lay out our request immediately, and with it our supplies of food and drink. We brought enough for a week, in order to find you.''

''And you won't be wrong in laying them out,'' Tankerman agreed, when they set the wineskin beside him.

''Here it is, Son of the Deer,'' one of the travelers said. ''Our city has been famed from earliest times for its bazaars, baths, harbor, fort, temple to the Great Weighmaster, and many other works of man delightful to behold. There have always been Abkhaz, Ubykhs, Geniokhs, Kartveli, Mingrelians, Greeks, and people of many other tribes living here. Oh, and Endurskies, obviously. They have traded with Byzantium, with Rome, with the Scythians and the Khazars. They have caught fish, felled box trees, grown fruit, worked leather, minted coins, and engaged in all sorts of other trades. If they sometimes had occasion to quarrel, they did not quarrel for long. And now we don't know what's come over us all. Each tribe pulls in its own direction, whereas before, only Endurskies engaged in that. A man of one tribe now looks with suspicion on a man of another tribe, praises all that is his own and defames all that is someone else's. Life becomes more boring and dangerous with every day. The city fathers are alarmed. Explain to us, for love of the Great Weighmaster, what's come over us all and how to help the people of our city find peace and good will once more among the tribes."

"Corruption has come to you," Jamkhoukh said, "but not just to you, perhaps. People have lost sight of man's chief purpose—to be pleasing to our God, the Great Weighmaster of Our Conscience. Often there's nothing for him to weigh in his scales, and he grieves in the heavens. A people cannot live without holding some things sacred," Jamkhoukh argued. "Faith in a great thing engenders the many lesser ones necessary for daily life: the sacredness of motherhood, the sacredness of respect for elders, the sacredness of fidelity in friendship, the sacredness of fidelity to the pledged word, and things of that sort. When the chief sacred object is lost, gradually all the rest are lost as well, and corruption descends on the people. People begin to hate one another and to please only themselves—or to please those who are stronger than they, so as to please themselves still better. When a ship springs a leak at sea," Jamkhoukh went on, "the people on the ship behave in different ways. They may all be divided into three groups according to how they behave on the ship—"

"Jamkhoukh," Trencherman asked suddenly, "why is everything in your stories divided into threes?"

"Don't interrupt," Jamkhoukh replied, "I'll explain it all to you later. Well then, all the people on the ship may be divided into three groups according to how they behave when the ship has sprung a leak. Those spiritually blind in both eyes think only of how to save themselves, not knowing that it's impossible to save themselves far from shore without saving the ship. These are the worst. If they prove stronger than all the rest, the ship will sink and no one will be saved. Others, spiritually blind in one eye, think only of how to save themselves and their families. These are bad because, if they prove strongest of all, the ship will sink anyway. Only those spiritually sighted in both eyes think how to save everyone. These are the real men, beloved of the Great Weighmaster. If they prove strongest of all, the ship will be saved. Convey to the city fathers that they should draw these men close to them and appeal to the conscience of the rest."

"Thank you, Jamkhoukh," said the men from Pityunt, "we shall convey
your words to the city fathers. They must think and think about your words, as
about all wise words."

"Let them think," the Son of the Deer agreed. "It hasn't hurt anyone yet."
With that they parted.

The travelers mounted their horses and headed for Pityunt, and Jamkhoukh
and his friends went their own way. In the distance before their eyes rose a wall
of blue sea, dissolving at the horizon in the blue of the sky. At that time it was
called not the Black Sea, as it is now, but the Good Sea, or as the Greeks said,
the Pontus Euxinus.

"There is much of the barbaric in men," Jamkhoukh said, with a nod toward
the sea. "I won't be surprised if they rename our Good Sea one fine day and
call it something else. Men think that if they change the ancient names of
mountains, rivers, and seas they'll be powerful as gods. Pathetic egoists! A
nation must feel that their country did not begin yesterday and will not end
tomorrow. That way it's cozier for them to live in eternity, and easier to defend
their soil."

"Jamkhoukh," Trencherman reminded him, "you promised to explain why
you divide everything into threes."

"Yes," Jamkhoukh said, "now I'll explain it all to you. Three is a sacred
number, and I was not the one who invented it. Remember the folk tales, where
there are always three roads, three brothers, and much else. Three is a sacred
number and hints to us that a man has three lives. The first life is the life before
birth. The middle life is our life we live in this world. And the last life is the
life we will live after death. Of the first life, all we know is that a few people
arrive in the world with an inclination to good. Other people arrive in the world
with an inclination to evil. And still a third group—again three, you see—arrive
in this world slightly inclined to good and slightly inclined to evil. As one has
lived in the first life, so he arrives in this world. Our earthly life is the middle
one, and it is the most important for man. He who lived by the good in the first
life must try to preserve his goodness in this life. He who lived his first life in
evil has the chance to reform, and the sins of his first life will then be forgiven
him. And those who vacillated from good to evil in the first life have the chance
to be definitively shaped in good. That is why our middle life is the most important
for man. Never in eternity will there be another chance to rectify anything.
Severe is the Great Weighmaster, but his mercy too is vast! Seriously, a whole
life is given us for self-examination, and even if we have begun badly, there is
time to rectify all! Now is it clear to you why the number three is sacred, and
why the people so often speak of three roads, three brothers, three fates, and
the like? It is a hint from the Great Weighmaster."

"Yes," Trencherman said, "it's all clear to us now. But Jamkhoukh, why is
it that when you speak of something unclear, it immediately becomes simple
and clear? And then it becomes unclear why the thing that's clear now was
unclear before."

"It's because I learned to think before I learned to speak human language," Jamkhoukh answered. "Ever since, I have had the habit of clothing my thoughts in words, rather than molding words into a semblance of thought. Yes, I learned to talk late, and therefore speak more clearly than many. Thus a cat is born blind that it may later see in the dark."

"Oh, funnels of my ears!" Hear-All exclaimed. "Position yourselves always under the sweet stream of the speeches of the Son of the Deer. And may the flies of idle verbiage not congregate on the honey of his wisdom!"

As if hurrying to get ahead of those ravenous flies, he quickly pulled the jammers from his pocket and twisted them tightly into his ears.

Thus they walked along the road, and suddenly, at the edge of the forest, this is what they saw. On a limb of a wild persimmon tree, hiding behind its trunk, a man stood reaching toward three doves perched on a neighboring limb.

One dove was bluegray, the second dove was black, and the third was white. The man was plucking a feather from the plumage of one dove and promptly implanting it in the plumage of the second, and then a feather from the second in the plumage of the first. He was so slick about it that the doves noticed nothing and sat calmly on the branch, placidly turning their heads from side to side.

As Jamkhoukh and his friends watched in amazement, all three doves became black-bluegray-white.

Not only was the man remarkably slick at switching the feathers, he did it with taste, with a feel for color and proportion.

Only at the last, when the man was implanting a black feather in the formerly white dove, did the dove feel anything. It began preening the spot where he had put in the feather.

The man jumped down from the bottom limb of the persimmon tree. Now the doves noticed him and took flight to the sky, gleaming speckled in the sun and seeming to marvel at each other's new plumage.

The man watched from under his hand as the doves shot up into the sky.

One black feather came down, fluttering in the air, and fell slowly to the ground.

"You see," the man pronounced, turning around to Jamkhoukh and his friends, "the feather that came down is just the one that I implanted last. My hand was tired, even I slip up sometimes."

"A miracle," Jamkhoukh said. "How do you contrive to pluck the feather without the dove's noticing, and implant it in another dove?"

At this point, instead of marveling in his turn at Jamkhoukh's miracles, the man exclaimed suddenly, "Yes, just try and find another Slick like me!"

"I'm Jamkhoukh, Son of the Deer, for example," Jamkhoukh said, "but I can't even contemplate a thing like that."

"That's no surprise," Slick answered. "As I said, you won't find a second Slick like me in all Abkhazia!"

Now an awkward silence reigned. Trencherman tried to break it.

"You are speaking," he told Slick, "to that same famous Jamkhoukh, Son of the Deer."

"And you are speaking," Slick answered, not in the least embarrassed, "to that same famous Slick, son of Slick—"

"Surely you've heard of the famous Jamkhoukh, Son of the Deer?" Hear-All asked.

"Surely you've heard of the famous Slick, son of Slick?" Slick replied, answering a question with a question.

"Well, this is too much," Strongman said. Ominously rubbing his hands, he walked up to Slick.

"If Strongman's rubbing his hands," Highspeed remarked, turning to Slick, "you'd better be Highspeed, like me."

"Wait, friends!" Jamkhoukh said, stepping between Strongman and Slick. "I sense that fame is beginning to corrupt me. It's true, even though not quite true. Jamkhoukh is being corrupted by fame, obviously, but has not been completely corrupted, because he knows he's being corrupted. And because I sense that I'm beginning to be corrupted, I cease being corrupted. Having ceased being corrupted, however, I cease to watch myself and begin being corrupted anew. Such is life, unfortunately. Life is an endless inclination to corruption. But especially important, my friends, is that it's also an endless inclination to refrain from corruption."

"Oh boy, you said a mouthful," Slick said. Suddenly he thrust a quick hand into his shirtfront, caught a flea, and held it out to Strongman. "Here," he said.

"What do I want with a flea?" Strongman asked, disconcerted.

"They say you're Strongman, so kill it."

"Don't you laugh at me!" Strongman flared.

"A joke," Slick said. He flicked away the flea and asked Jamkhoukh, "Is it true that the Scythians know how to shoe a flea?"

"Yes," Jamkhoukh nodded, "rumors that the Scythians can shoe a flea have been corroborated over and over again by eyewitnesses. The Scythians are a surprising people. They know how to shoe a flea, but their horses often go unshod. They have no interest in shoeing horses."

"Listen, Jamkhoukh," Slick said, "I'll go with you. Turns out you're fun to be with."

"I should say so!" Jamkhoukh's friends chorused.

Jamkhoukh explained to him the purpose of his journey and warned of the dangers it entailed.

Slick gladly joined Jamkhoukh's friends, and they started on.

The next day they saw a hunter in a forest glade. Bow in hand, he was standing with his head tipped back, staring at the sky. Jamkhoukh and his companions also began to stare at the sky but noticed nothing there.

"What do you see, hunter?" Jamkhoukh asked.

"Don't you see?" the hunter answered, glancing at Jamkhoukh and his companions. "An eagle has chased three doves to the seventh heaven. Never have I seen doves with such unusual plumage. I took pity on them and shot the eagle with an arrow. He's falling now and has already dropped to the sixth heaven."

"Those are Slick's doves," Jamkhoukh said, "and this is a sign from the

Great Weighmaster that man can be a creator of nature, if he does it with good intentions. But what vision the hunter has! I can't see anything beyond the first heaven, and he sees what's happening in the seventh heaven!''

"Nothing special," the hunter shrugged. "All I am is Sharpsight. Now if you saw—"

"Not another word," Jamkhoukh said. "I *am* Jamkhoukh, Son of the Deer. For love of the Great Weighmaster, not a word about my wisdom."

"But at least the part about the five days, is that true?'' Sharpsight asked.

"Two, not five, but that's beside the point," Jamkhoukh said.

"I'll go with you, Jamkhoukh," Sharpsight declared. "I won't wait for the eagle to fall with my arrow. I have plenty of arrows in my quiver, chances are you'll find me useful."

Jamkhoukh told him the purpose of his journey, and Sharpsight joined Jamkhoukh's friends.

The next morning they walked out of the forest and found themselves not far from the giants' house.

The house was enclosed by a stockade with human skulls cocked on the pickets.

The friends halted in dismay at this grim sight. Suddenly, from inside the yard, someone's hand began busily taking skulls down from the fence pickets. After it had taken down eight skulls the hand did not reappear above the fence.

"Oh-oh," Trencherman said, "I don't like it that eight pickets have been freed up—exactly the number of our heads."

"And besides, that black feather the dove lost augurs no good for us," Tankerman added.

"If anything happens I'll handle three of them," Strongman said. "But what to do with the rest?''

Jamkhoukh realized that his companions were crushed by the giants' sly ruse.

"My friends!" Jamkhoukh exclaimed briskly. "They must be watching us from behind the fence. They're trying to scare us in advance. But if they're trying to scare us, it means they're not sure of themselves. Therefore be bold! The only thing I'm afraid of is keeling over at the sight of the beauty Gunda. Strongman, stand beside me and inconspicuously prop me up if I can't withstand Gunda's beauty. Forward—and may the Great Weighmaster of Our Conscience preserve us! Everyone on the alert! Hear-All, take the jammers out of your ears!''

Just as the friends approached, the gates flew open with a creak and out came the seven giant brothers. They were enormous, and in their fierce faces, for some reason, glittered the sly little eyes of evil dwarfs.

"Who are you?'' roared the eldest of the giants in a terrible voice. "Where are you bound for?''

"I am Jamkhoukh, Son of the Deer," Jamkhoukh said, "and these are my friends. I have come to court your sister, the beauty Gunda."

"Certainly you may court her," the eldest brother roared again, "but do you know the conditions?''

"We do, more or less," Jamkhoukh said.

"The conditions are these," the eldest brother continued. "Three questions on your mental skill. These questions were compiled for us by a Byzantine wise man. And then a trial of physical skill for you and your friends. You yourselves understand that it's not easy for us giant brothers to part with our beloved only sister. And besides, we want to know that she has married the most worthy of her suitors.''

"We will try to meet your conditions,'' Jamkhoukh said.

"Then welcome.'' The eldest brother pointed to the gate, in a gesture that also looked rather like an invitation to the stockade.

They entered a broad green yard. In the middle of it stood a tall smooth pole of unknown purpose. Not far from the pole lay a granite block. Otherwise the yard was just a yard, only very large.

Jamkhoukh was violently nervous, and yet at the same time his eyes greedily sought the beauty Gunda.

Suddenly a door of the house opened, and out came a girl of astounding beauty.

Smiling at Jamkhoukh, she descended the steps and sat down on a chair placed in the middle of the yard by one of the brothers, who had had time to go into the house. At his sister's feet he put a basket full of red Old Abkhazian tomatoes.

"Hello, Jamkhoukh, Son of the Deer!'' the fair Gunda said, smiling at Jamkhoukh. "I've heard a whole lot about you. I hope you'll be more successful in your courtship than the poor wretches who grin from our stockade. I know about your wisdom, but you have a beautiful gait, too. Not for nothing are you the Son of the Deer! And you look so nice, I could just hug you to me and eat you up, like a tomato!''

"Why a tomato?'' Jamkhoukh marveled joyfully. She was enchanting. Her beauty disturbed Jamkhoukh, yet not so violently as the portrait. In any case, he had no intention of fainting.

"Because I love our Old Abkhazian tomatoes more than anything in the world,'' the golden-haired Gunda answered. "My brothers feed me on nightingale brains and mermaid caviar, but I love tomatoes more than anything. You won't mind that, if you marry me?''

"No,'' Jamkhoukh exclaimed, enraptured by Gunda's sweet simplicity, "eat all the tomatoes you want.''

"Thank you, Son of the Deer,'' Gunda said. She reached a tomato from the basket and took a bite of it. "Because that suitor over there, the skull sticking up on the fourth picket to the right of the gate, he threatened me: 'I am a Khazar prince. As soon as I marry you, I shall break you of this vulgar habit.' I told him, 'Meet my brothers' conditions first, and then you'll order me around . . .' Son of the Deer, you're wise, they say, you're nice, and I want to marry you. Please try to do everything right. I'm so sick of living in perpetual maidenhood, surrounded by the skulls of my suitors!''

"For you, beloved Gunda, I will do all that I can,'' Jamkhoukh said. Turning to his friends, who were shifting from one foot to the other in embarrassment in the middle of the yard, he added: "An interesting observation. When I saw the fair Gunda's portrait I fainted. But when I saw the living, sweet-eyed Gunda

I did not, although she pleased me greatly. So art is more powerful than life. It must be. It shows a man in this life, and hints at his future and previous lives. When we look at a portrait of a man painted by a real artist, we seem to see him in all three lives. Therefore the impression made by the portrait must be more powerful than that of the living person himself—''

"Well, what about it?" the eldest giant interrupted at this point. "Are we going to listen to your sermons or begin the trials?"

"Let us begin," Jamkhoukh said, gazing at the golden-haired Gunda and reveling in her beauty.

"Before asking the questions," the eldest giant warned, "I want to give my brothers a few household instructions."

"Please do," Jamkhoukh said, gazing at Gunda, who was bashfully wolfing down a tomato and looking prettier than ever, "I am prepared to wait thus all my life."

"My brothers!" the eldest giant exclaimed. "I'll probably leave before the trials are over. An urgent piece of business awaits me. So listen to my instructions. Remember the order in which to cock the skulls on the fence. Hang Jamkhoukh's skull right by the gate: the wise head gets first place. The rest in the order in which they joined Jamkhoukh. That'll be fair. Put Highspeed's skull between his millstones. That'll be funny. But for the time being don't touch this marksman and his bow. We'll use him to scratch our backs with his arrows."

The brothers roared with friendly laughter, but Jamkhoukh's friends drooped noticeably.

"Heads up, my friends!" Jamkhoukh shouted. "Can't you see he's saying it on purpose to weaken our spirit!"

"That's as may be," Trencherman said, with a nod toward the stockade, "but there's something to corroborate his words, Jamkhoukh!"

"The trials of mental skill are about to begin!" the eldest giant shouted. "Which vice of the soul is most ignoble?"

A hush fell on everyone, and even the golden-haired Gunda stopped eating tomatoes.

"The most ignoble vice of the soul," Jamkhoukh said, "is uncleanliness of the soul, because in the presence of this vice all other vices are possible."

"Correct, correct!" Gunda started clapping. "I don't see why it's true, but I know all the answers ahead of time!"

"You stay out of it," the eldest giant remarked. "Yes, the answer is correct. All's fair and aboveboard here. Second question," the eldest giant said. "Which animal is the most bashful in the world?"

A tense silence reigned. Jamkhoukh's friends were dreadfully nervous for him.

"Of all the animals found in our parts, or in general?" Trencherman asked, unable to contain himself.

"Which animal is the most bashful in the world?" the giant reiterated, deeming Trencherman unworthy of notice and at the same time indicating that he was asking silly questions.

"The sheep," Jamkhoukh said at last, "is the most bashful animal. She veils her rump with the chador of her own fatty tail."

"Correct, Jamkhoukh!" Gunda exclaimed, and she started clapping again. "How wise you are! I could just smother you with kisses!"

"Gunda, behave yourself," the eldest giant said. He began to whisper with his brothers.

Jamkhoukh's companions brightened visibly. Strongman winked at his friends, rubbing his hands and darting warlike glances at the giant brothers: "I'll handle four of them."

"Which man should be counted bravest in the world?" came the third question at last. The giant brothers had rested their greatest hopes on the difficulty of this question.

But this was exactly the question that proved very easy for the Son of the Deer.

"The bravest man in the world," Jamkhoukh replied immediately, "is the man who has cast out of his life all manner of guile."

"Correct," the eldest of the giants agreed darkly, and it was obvious from his eyes that he himself was one of those who, if they'd cast anything out of their lives, it certainly wasn't guile. After whispering with his brothers for a while the eldest giant said, "We knew about the Son of the Deer's wisdom anyway . . . Let's turn to physical skill. Here before you is a granite block. Either Jamkhoukh hews it asunder with one blow of his dagger, or our daggers sunder your throats."

Fair Gunda stopped eating tomatoes in her agitation. She whispered with just her lips, "Poor Jamkhoukh, if you only knew, you have but to pass a hair from my braids over the dagger blade, and the rock will split apart at its touch."

Hear-All caught her whisper and instantly passed it on to Slick. Slick walked past Gunda. As if waving away a mosquito he imperceptibly tore a hair from her braid, then went over to Jamkhoukh and imperceptibly passed the hair over the dagger blade. Jamkhoukh walked up to the granite block and brought the dagger down with such inspired strength that sparks showered from the granite and the block split in two. Flecks of quartz sparkled at the cleft. Appalled at the strength of his own blow, Jamkhoukh stood frozen over the broken block. Then, sheathing the dagger, he said, "Evidently a man has incredible strength stored up within him that he doesn't suspect. I must think this over."

"Well then," the eldest giant said darkly, "evidently things are moving toward a wedding. Let's try you on trenchering and swilling."

"This we can do," Trencherman said, licking his lips.

"My throat's parched, I want a drink," Tankerman added.

Now the giant brothers slaughtered two oxen, built a fire in the middle of the yard, roasted the oxen whole on huge spits, brought out tables, and placed the roast oxen on them. The hosts sat on one side, the guests on the other. One ox they dressed and divided in equal parts for everyone, and the other they left in reserve. No sooner had everyone started on the food than Trencherman finished his helping and took a seat by the second ox. Slicing huge slabs of meat off the ox carcass with his knife, he ate the whole thing in an hour, and all that remained on the table was the ox's clean-picked skeleton. Peering at the giants through the bare ribs of the ox, Trencherman said, "Peek-a-boo! Aren't there any seconds?"

"Seconds!" the giants said in amazement, and began to exchange glances.

"You're all set on trenchering," the eldest giant announced. "Let's see how you are on swilling."

Two giant brothers carried out a ninety-gallon amphora from the wine cellar. They leaned it against the table and said, "Taste this, we'll drink the wine of your choice. This one's red. If you don't like it we'll carry out an amphora of white wine."

Trencherman walked over to the amphora and winked at Strongman: "Give me a hand, brother!"

Strongman picked up the amphora, tipped it cautiously, and began pouring wine into Tankerman's wide-open mouth. Fifteen minutes later, to the great amazement of the giants, Strongman tipped the amphora up, and the last driblet ran into Tankerman's mouth. Strongman rolled away the emptied amphora, and Tankerman, wiping himself off, looked at the giants and said, "Well? The red wine's not bad. Now let's taste the white."

"A ninety-gallon amphora for a taste?" the eldest giant exclaimed. "No, they're even better on swilling than trenchering."

"I protest!" Trencherman leaped up. "The trenchering yields in nothing to the swilling."

The giant brothers turned conspicuously glum and began to whisper back and forth about something. Jamkhoukh's friends were thoroughly invigorated.

"If anything goes wrong, friends," Strongman said loudly, "you can figure I've got five giants laid out in a row in the middle of the yard. I thought you were in a hurry," he reminded the giants' eldest brother. "Isn't it time for you to leave?"

"I'm postponing my business," the giant replied darkly.

He sent one of his brothers off somewhere, and a little while later the brother returned with an ancient old woman. The eldest giant introduced her to the friends.

"This is an old woman called Ostrich Leg," he said. "Now we'll test you on swiftness. Let your Highspeed run a race with our old woman."

"But where will we run the race?" Highspeed laughed, gazing good-naturedly at the old woman.

"There's the south gate," the eldest giant said. "It's open ground here right down to the sea. Twenty thousand paces each way."

"It's bad," Jamkhoukh objected, "to make an elderly woman run like a little girl."

"That's not your worry," the eldest giant replied, and everyone went to the south gate.

"I really feel sorry for this poor little old woman," said sentimental Highspeed when they walked out the gate. "She's like my grandmother, but I'm supposed to run a race with her."

At a signal from the eldest giant, old Ostrich Leg and Highspeed started off. Flailing her muscular legs shockingly, the old woman dashed after Highspeed. To the surprise of Jamkhoukh's friends, she wasn't lagging behind him by very much. Admittedly Highspeed kept turning around, unable to hide his smiles at the sight of a competitor so aged, though still very spry. The runners soon disappeared from sight, and those left behind settled down to wait for them, glancing occasionally at the sun. But somehow they were taking too long coming back.

Meanwhile, this is what happened to the runners.

When Highspeed reached the sea, he sat down on the sand to wait for the old woman. At last she galloped up and took a seat beside Highspeed. Panting hard, she declared, "I'm plumb tuckered out, sonny, have pity on me. You're the swifter, after all. We'd better sit here awhile on the nice warm sand, and I'll hunt in your hair. And then we'll run back."

"All right, Ostrich Leg," Highspeed said. "I wasn't wrong in remarking that you were like my grandmother. When I was a child, I did so love to lie on Grandma's lap while she hunted in my hair. But poor Grandma is dead . . ."

"Then lie here awhile," Ostrich Leg purred caressingly, edging closer to him, "and I'll hunt in your hair."

Highspeed stretched out on the sand, laying his head on the old woman's lap, and she began to hunt in his hair. Warmed by the sun, lulled by the rhythmic din of the waves, Highspeed fell asleep. This was just what Ostrich Leg needed. Hidden under her apron, it seems, she had a hen and some millet seed. She took a handful or two and sprinkled Highspeed's head thickly. Then she pulled out the hen, and the hen began to peck the seeds from his head. The old woman carefully shifted Highspeed's head to the sand. He just slept on. The hen kept pecking at the seeds on his head, and in his sleep it seemed to him that this was Ostrich Leg hunting in his hair.

Now Ostrich Leg started back faster than ever, flailing her shocking muscular legs, and still Highspeed slept, and now the old woman was so near the giants' house that they could plainly see her, and still Highspeed slept.

With loud, jubilant cheers and whistles the giants began to welcome and encourage her.

"Pour it on!" they bawled.

"Hear-All!" Jamkhoukh exclaimed. "Listen, what's happened there?"

Hear-All put his head to the ground.

"I hear snores, which are coming from the sea."

Sharpsight shaded his eyes with his hand and said, "Yes, he's lying on the shore, and there's a hen pecking something off his head. But I can't make out what."

"It's up to you!" Jamkhoukh shouted, seeing that the old woman was already quite near.

Sharpsight quickly pulled an arrow from his quiver, fitted it to the bowstring, drew the bowstring taut, took careful aim, and loosed the arrow. Flashing through the air, the arrow flew to the sea and pierced the hen. The hen began to flop, and the beating of her wings on Highspeed's head woke him up.

Highspeed leaped to his feet, not understanding where the old woman had gone, where the hen pierced by an arrow had come from, or why his head was sprinkled with millet seed. He wagged his head, shaking out the seeds and the remnants of sleep. Now he realized that Ostrich Leg had deceived him.

"*Khayt!*" he burst out, in an angry Abkhazian exclamation. He pulled the millstones off his feet, leaped up, and went dashing back with the speed of the wind.

He overtook the old woman in a few instants and gathered so much momentum that he nearly flew over the gate. But now Strongman grabbed him in midair, stood him on the ground, and said, "Friends, you can figure that five of them already lie in a row in the middle of the yard and the rest have fled."

Before long the old woman too arrived, panting hard.

"Well done, Ostrich Leg," the eldest giant hissed spitefully. "In a contest like this even second place is honorable."

"I did all I could," the old woman said, struggling to get her breath.

"You deceiving old woman!" Highspeed shouted. "Go and fetch my millstones this minute. It's your fault I had to leave them."

Now the old woman began to scold, saying that Highspeed didn't revere Abkhazian custom, according to which an old person must be respected and not be kept running errands. But the Son of the Deer intervened for Highspeed.

"The Abkhaz revere old age," he said, "because old age, in our understanding, is the age of wisdom, justice, freedom from vain scurrying. But old age that does not respect itself does not deserve the respect of others. Since you took advantage of our Highspeed's trusting sentimentality to scurry around and deceive him, scurry a little more and bring back his millstones."

The old woman looked at the giant brothers.

"Go along, go along," the eldest said, "you aren't fit to do anything else."

Old Ostrich Leg trudged grumbling off toward the sea.

"Where did you ever dig her up?" Trencherman asked.

"Oh, she lives here in the forest," one of the brothers said with a frown. "A local witch. Sometimes she helps us out with the housework, sometimes with witchery. But she's not good for much, her mind's completely gone."

The giant brothers went into the yard along with Jamkhoukh and his friends.

"All right," the eldest giant said, with a nod toward the tall pole that stood in the middle of the yard. "Now let Jamkhoukh show his own physical skill by way of conclusion. That pole is a hundred cubits tall. If Jamkhoukh climbs to the top of the pole holding a pot of boiling water on his head, and then climbs down the pole without spilling a drop—we'll give him our sister."

They boiled up the water, poured it into a clay pot, and carried it to Jamkhoukh, who was standing by the pole with his shoes off. Jamkhoukh spat on his hands, set the pot on his head on top of his felt cap, and began to shinny carefully up the pole. The giants huddled together under the pole and held their palms out, waiting for a drop to fall from above.

"Son of the Deer, don't spill boiling water on yourself!" the golden-haired Gunda called from below. "Or else my husband will have an ugly face! But on the other hand, if you spill the boiling water you can't be my husband, can you? Oh, Jamkhoukh, I'm mixed up somehow. Explain it to me—what's my mistake?"

"Dear Gunda," Jamkhoukh said, continuing to shinny carefully upward, "you don't mean to, but you're distracting me."

"Well then, I'll eat another tomato and wish you luck!" the enchanting Gunda exclaimed, and she sank her pearly teeth into the red flesh of a tomato.

"I swear by her on whose neck I'd like to be hanged," Trencherman whispered to his friends, "this Gunda is not conspicuous for great intellect."

"Great intellect!" Tankerman took him up sarcastically. "Why, sooner a woodpecker will knock himself into a concussion than our Jamkhoukh will knock her intellect awake!"

"Still, she's not a screamer like my wife," Strongman said pacifically, "and she's got a much prettier face!"

"And keep in mind," Sharpsight added, "she hasn't seen anything good in her life, except for the grinning skulls of these poor wretches."

"Even a great wise man, it seems," Hear-All sighed bitterly, "goes deaf from love. Any stupid thing Gunda comes out with, our Jamkhoukh thinks it's sweet."

"Never mind," Slick said, "if she turns out to be bad, I'll switch wives on him so slickly he won't even notice."

"My friends, you're being quite unfair!" Highspeed said excitedly. "Gunda's so pretty, so sweet, such a dear little enchantress that I'm happy for our Jamkhoukh! Intellect is merely to the detriment of a woman! Jamkhoukh has enough intellect for not only Gunda but the whole of our Abkhazia."

When Jamkhoukh reached the top of the pole, they suddenly heard his anguished cry. Another few instants and the giants, who were standing under the pole with their palms out, began to dance with joy.

"A drop! A drop!" they shouted. "And the sky is blue, so you can't blame it on a shower!"

Jamkhoukh's friends turned grim.

The Son of the Deer climbed down the pole and handed the pot back to the giants. Wordlessly, not looking at anyone, he began to put his shoes on.

"You spilled the water," the giant brothers said, holding out their palms to him.

"No," Jamkhoukh replied with a sorrow beyond belief, "I spilled nothing. It was only that from the top of the pole I saw the wolves tearing my mother deer to pieces. And I cried out and began to weep with pain."

The giants licked their palms and satisfied themselves that the moisture on them was salty.

"Yes," Jamkhoukh said, "tears are the blood of the soul, and therefore they are salty, like blood."

"It can't be helped, dear Jamkhoukh," the fair Gunda declared, biting into a tomato, "that's the fate of deer. Either the wolves get them or a hunter kills them."

"Yes, but this doe was my mama," Jamkhoukh said. "She brought me up in the forest. She used to kneel down when I was so little that I couldn't reach her udder . . . And you, beloved Gunda, might put aside your tomato for such a misfortune—"

"But my dear Jamkhoukh," exclaimed golden-haired Gunda, "what does the one have to do with the other? I'm sorry about your mama deer, but she won't come back to life if I stop eating tomatoes, will she?"

"Beloved Gunda, you are still so immature of soul . . . But never mind, I'll help you," Jamkhoukh declared. For a long moment he gazed at Gunda in sorrow.

Gunda gazed back at him in perplexity, as though asking if she might eat tomatoes now, and if not, until what time, exactly.

"No, my mother deer won't come back to life," Jamkhoukh said sadly. "You may eat your tomatoes, dear Gunda."

"Well then," the eldest giant announced, "you have met all the conditions. Our sister is yours. Now we must hold a feast for the occasion of parting with our only joy, our beloved sister."

The eldest giant, however, like all the others, was guileful and treacherous. He whispered to his brothers to serve Jamkhoukh and his friends poisoned dishes during the feast. No, the giant brothers had no wish to part with their beloved sister!

Hear-All, who hadn't stopped his ears with the jammers for a minute, heard it all and passed it on to Slick. Before the feast began Slick switched all the poisoned dishes to the giants' places and switched the giants' dishes to the friends' places.

When old Ostrich Leg brought back Highspeed's millstones she tried to help set the tables, but the giant brothers, angered by her unsuccessful race, chased her away.

Jamkhoukh sat sorrowfully beside his enchanting bride. Deep in thought, he noticed nothing of what was happening around him.

"One thing I simply can't understand," he said, thinking his own thoughts. "How could my mother deer have been here? She always grazed just around Chegem, you know."

Toward the middle of the festal dinner, the giant brothers began dropping dead. Some on their backs, others with their heads on the table.

Jamkhoukh surveyed them with sad eyes and understood all. Looking at Slick, he said, "A bit crude!"

"It's the best I could do!" Slick flared touchily, deciding that Jamkhoukh thought he hadn't been slick enough about switching the dishes.

Really Jamkhoukh had meant the very fact of reprisal against the giant brothers.

"Probably God punished my brothers," complained the golden-haired Gunda, who understood nothing at all, "for taking so long to marry me off."

"You mustn't speak of your brothers that way," Jamkhoukh said, "even though they were true evil-doers. The people themselves will judge them. It is not for a sister to judge her brothers, especially when they are dead. Nor is it fitting, my friends, for us to eat at this table! Let the dead be buried by the living, whom the dead wished dead while they themselves were living!"

Jamkhoukh's friends buried the giant brothers where the granite block lay split in two in the middle of the the yard.

The giants' house Jamkhoukh ordered destroyed. Strongman kicked two chestnut piles out from under it and the house collapsed, sending up a black cloud of dust.

The stockade with the suitors' skulls Jamkhoukh ordered left as an eternal memorial of human cruelty. After the passage of several centuries part of it caved in and rotted away, but part remained, and Byzantine scholars argued as to what vanished tribe had practiced this unusual method of burial.

But to get back to Jamkhoukh. The friends procured a horse at the nearest village, seated the golden-haired Gunda on it, and set out on the homeward journey.

Highspeed, of course, was a little bit in love with Gunda. He begged of Jamkhoukh the right to walk beside her horse and carry the basket of tomatoes. Each time she asked, he handed her a tomato, first wiping it on the horse's mane.

When they passed the village where the young prince and the celebrated wine merchant lived, Gunda flushed and said suddenly to Jamkhoukh, "But you know, dear Jamkhoukh, the prince almost courted me."

"Why almost?" Jamkhoukh asked, feeling a stab of jealousy and wondering at it.

"Because he rode up to our house on a camel, with his retinue," Gunda answered. "He rode on a camel so he could see me from behind the high stockade. My brothers invited him into the yard, they even said they'd ease the conditions of courtship for him, considering his lofty birth. But he just wouldn't ride in, though I pleased him greatly, and oh, he *is* handsome! 'I am the only nephew of the childless king,' he said. 'When I am king, I will take her anyway, by force!' 'We won't give her to you by force,' my brothers said, and he rode away. My brothers were very surprised he was so frank."

"Sometimes a man is very frank about one thing," Jamkhoukh declared, "to get the chance to be very secretive about something else."

"An Abkhaz who wasn't ashamed to mount a camel," Tankerman observed, "will not be ashamed to mount the throne by illegal means."

"I want to be hanged on the neck of her who is now at home pining for me," Trencherman said, "if Tankerman isn't right this time!"

"What's shameful about it?" Gunda interceded for the prince. "He did it to see me. You're just jealous of the camel, Tankerman, because it can drink more water than you!''

"A camel—more than me?" Tankerman choked with indignation. "Why, sooner a woodpecker pecking a tree—"

"Don't quarrel, friends," Jamkhoukh said, checking them. "But I must say that my friend Tankerman has displayed considerable insight into the soul of those who lust after power."

"Leave the prince alone," Gunda sighed. "He got married last year. His wife is distinguished, of course, but absolutely ugly. Everybody says so . . ."

Gunda's inappropriate mention of the prince's courtship grated terribly on Hear-All's delicate ears. He was indignant. After all, it was plain as day: had Jamkhoukh not arrived with his friends, Gunda would have been forever doomed to live without a husband!

"What is ingratitude, Jamkhoukh?" Hear-All asked, pointedly removing the jammers from his ears. He held firmly to his rule that wisdom must be heard in unfiltered form.

"Ingratitude," Jamkhoukh said, "is the luxury of a churlish man."

"Or a churlish woman," Hear-All added.

"Or a churlish woman," Jamkhoukh agreed, not catching the hint.

"And what is nobility?"

"Nobility," Jamkhoukh said, "is a flight to the summit of justice, bypassing the intermediate steps of prudence."

"The bird I was thinking of," Hear-All went on, "doesn't fly that high, if she flies at all."

"No," Jamkhoukh declared sadly, "nobility isn't encountered too often."

"And what is modesty, Jamkhoukh?" Hear-All persevered.

"Modesty," Jamkhoukh said after a moment's thought, "is a delineation of the bounds of virtue. When immodest people boast of the abundance of their virtues, as blatantly as barkers at a bazaar, we rightly suspect the absence of all virtue. Remember, friends, nonexistent virtues are easy to exaggerate . . . But modesty must be modest. Modesty that draws too much attention to itself is inverted brazenness."

"And now what's rudeness, Jamkhoukh?" Trencherman asked suddenly, with a meaningful sidelong glance at Tankerman.

"Rudeness is the neglect of eternity," Jamkhoukh said. He fell silent, as though plunged into that same eternity.

"Oh, my ears!" Hear-All exclaimed. "You sniff at Jamkhoukh's speeches as at the roses of Khorosan, and in so doing you yourselves bloom like roses!"

As if afraid that the rose oil of wisdom would run out of his ears, he cautiously and painstakingly stopped them with the jammers.

"At last I see," Trencherman said reproachfully, "why you're so often rude to me, Tankerman. You neglect eternity, and that's extremely ugly of you."

"*I* neglect eternity?" Tankerman exclaimed, thunderstruck. He even came to a standstill, he was so indignant. "Why, if you must know, thinking about eternity is my very favorite pastime. And after a good drinking bout I really do feel I have eternity inside me. I make no secret of it—it's a nice, bracing feeling.''

This familiar, hail-fellow-well-met attitude toward eternity enraged even good-natured Trencherman.

"Just hear him talk!" he shouted, clapping his hands. "You're supposed to be inside eternity, eternity's not supposed to be inside you! Right, Jamkhoukh?''

"You're right," the Son of the Deer replied. "Tankerman is joking, of course. But many of the strong of this world do indeed give themselves airs as if they'd swallowed eternity and eternity weren't about to swallow them.''

"Dirt-eater missed the joke again!" Tankerman exclaimed, almost toppling over with laughter. "I sure got you!"

"You were not joking!" Trencherman protested excitedly. "I know for sure you weren't! I swear—''

But here Tankerman interrupted him and covered his ears in mock horror.

"Hear-All," he begged, "give me your jammers, quick! Or else he'll swear by her on whose neck I too will die on the spot. Then you'll all get to Jamkhoukh's wedding with a fine little present!''

"No, now—we don't need presents like that," the fair Gunda said suddenly. Looking down at Highspeed from the horse, she added, "Pick me out a nice big tomato. May the Great Weighmaster strike me dead if I see what they're quarreling about . . .''

Highspeed took a big tomato from the basket, wiped it on the horse's mane, and presented it to Gunda.

"That's exactly what I meant to swear by, too—the Great Weighmaster, not my sweet wife," Trencherman said, addressing his tormenter. "So your mockery of me was extremely foolish. Foolish and off the mark!''

"Aha," Tankerman persisted, "this time you wanted to be hanged on the neck of the Great Weighmaster! As if he didn't have enough of the ungodly hanging on his neck! You're the only one missing!''

"The way I figure it," Strongman intervened suddenly, "the Great Weighmaster's neck is much stronger than mine. You think I'm Strongman? No! He's the one—the real Strongman!''

A week later the friends arrived in Chegem, where a splendid wedding lasting three days and three nights was held for Jamkhoukh. All the Chegemians feasted, sang, and danced at the wedding. By the end of the third night even Trencherman couldn't eat another scrap of meat, and Tankerman was just plain drunk.

Jamkhoukh gave his friends presents and put all sorts of sweets in their traveling *khurdjins* for those who had children.

Now it came time to part. The Son of the Deer and his friends had tears in their eyes. Highspeed sobbed openly. Jamkhoukh hugged his friends tightly and kissed each of them three times (again, for some reason, three times!). First he kissed Trencherman, then Tankerman, then Highspeed, then Strongman, then Hear-All, then Slick, and then finally Sharpsight.

"Enough of kissing your friends!" the Chegemians shouted. "Or you won't have any kisses left for your wife!''

"This is altogether different," answered Jamkhoukh, Son of the Deer. "I think the days of the journey to my beloved Gunda have been the happiest of my life with people. Good-bye, friends!"

"Good-bye, Son of the Deer," the friends answered. "May your life be happy with the golden-haired Gunda! If anything comes up, let us know! We'll help any way we can!"

"Jamkhoukh!" Highspeed shouted at the last. "May I visit you? I'm quick, you know—one foot here, the other there! I'll bring tomatoes for sweet Gunda. Tomatoes go with her red-gold hair!"

"Of course. Come whenever you can," Jamkhoukh answered. With an occasional backward glance and a wave, the friends disappeared on the upper Chegem road.

And so, Jamkhoukh began to live with fair golden-haired Gunda.

Jamkhoukh loved his wife passionately, and his happiness seemed cloudless. During the first year of their life in Chegem, Highspeed came to see them every week bringing a big basket full of ruddy Old Abkhazian tomatoes. So Gunda didn't notice that tomatoes would not ripen in the mountain village of Chegem.

After a year, sentimental Highspeed fell in love with a Circassian girl who lived beyond the Caucasian crest, and he began coming less and less often with tomatoes. Gunda took to grumbling.

"My brothers fed me on mermaid caviar and nightingale brains," she would say to Jamkhoukh, "and you can't even provide me with tomatoes."

"But there's no help for it, dear Gunda," Jamkhoukh would answer, "if tomatoes won't ripen here in Chegem."

"Then let's live in a lowland village," Gunda would say.

"No." Jamkhoukh would not consent. "I don't want to leave the house of my father Beslan. Besides, the people who come for advice and predictions are used to seeing me here."

Before very long, however, Gunda developed the knack of taking gifts, in the form of baskets of tomatoes, from the people who came to Jamkhoukh for wise advice. As is usually the case, everyone knew about this but Jamkhoukh himself. He thought people were bringing the tomatoes out of admiration for Gunda's beauty.

Jamkhoukh very much loved children, but for some reason Gunda could not have a baby.

"You're the wise man," she would say, "how come you don't understand that the most beautiful woman and the wisest man can't have children? Nature can't join your intellect and my beauty in one child. It's beyond her strength."

"But I'd like ordinary children," Jamkhoukh would answer thoughtfully, "the kind I saw at my Strongman's house . . ."

"There are plenty of things we'd like," Gunda would say querulously. "We have to resign ourselves to being unique."

Jamkhoukh had no choice but to resign himself. Nevertheless, he loved his golden-haired Gunda very much.

Many people came to Jamkhoukh, sometimes with comical requests, sometimes in woeful perplexity, sometimes for wise advice, and sometimes goodness only knows why. With the years, Gunda grew sick and tired of Jamkhoukh's never-ending visitors.

"What the hell is it this time?" she would say to the petitioners, when Jamkhoukh wasn't home.

"Our mule has foaled," the petitioners might say. "Why should this be?"

"Great Weighmaster!" Gunda would cry. "They'll drive me stark staring mad! She foaled—fine and dandy!"

"No, it's not fine," one of the petitioners would say with restraint, but firmly. "It's not supposed to happen in nature. We want to find out what it portends."

"Great Weighmaster!" Gunda would yell at the top of her lungs. "Petitioners have tortured me to death! Leave the basket of tomatoes and get out of here. He's down in Sabid's Hollow grazing the goats!"

But since the number of people who came to Jamkhoukh far exceeded her need for tomatoes, Gunda quite often nagged Jamkhoukh for not spending enough time with her.

Once when she was scolding him for this, a man came to seek advice on what to do about a swarm of bees that had flown from the hive and clustered on a branch high in a walnut tree.

After hearing out the petitioner, Jamkhoukh said to him confidingly, "A woman wants the time of love to exceed the space of life. But that's absurd, isn't it?"

"Most absurd thing you could think of," the visitor agreed hastily, and he left, deciding that Jamkhoukh was a little off his rocker.

"Where's my swarm, and where's the woman who wants love?" he said wonderingly, conversing with his fellow villagers. They shrugged their shoulders and expressed various thoughts on the subject.

Thus they lived for four years and four months, and now all of a sudden an extraordinary event occurred. The king of Abkhazia, who had arrived in the village of Dal to celebrate the opening of the Temple to the Great Weighmaster of Our Conscience, suddenly passed away in his nephew's house, where he was a guest.

The young prince mounted the throne. Although he had been called by the Abkhazian name Kobzach, he named himself Theodore the Fair in imitation of the Byzantine emperors.

For two years the people kept a close eye on him, calling him now by the old name, now by the new. Then they dubbed him the Pumpkinhead Prettyboy and no longer referred to him by name at all.

One fine day a dozen courtiers, led by a vizier, rode up to Jamkhoukh's house. One of the courtiers held the reins of a horse with an opulent saddle for a lady. Jamkhoukh immediately understood all, his soul contracted with pain, but there was no help for it. The guests dismounted and walked into the house.

"Jamkhoukh," the vizier said, "our king, Theodore the Fair, has long loved the golden-haired Gunda. Only the necessity of keeping himself safe for the

Abkhazian throne prevented him from joining battle with the giant brothers. Now his hour has come. You must give the king the fair Gunda, otherwise the king will make war on Chegem. Surely, you who have forever summoned all to peace will not contribute to the shedding of our Abkhazian blood?''

"But the king is married," Jamkhoukh said in astonishment. "Haven't I even heard that a son was recently born to him?"

"Yes," the vizier said. "A son was born to him, and he is named George. But what does that matter? Don't you know that the Byzantine emperors take as many wives as they please? We must learn from our great neighbor Byzantium, the most civilized state in the world.''

Jamkhoukh became thoughtful. Then for a long moment he gazed at Gunda. He saw that she wanted to go to the king. Jamkhoukh's soul bled. But he was proud, the Son of the Deer, and wanted Gunda herself to choose him over the king.

"Ah well," Jamkhoukh said. "Take her, since she wants it so."

"But I didn't say I wanted to leave you, did I, Jamkhoukh?" Gunda exclaimed, and she flushed all pink.

"Dear Gunda," Jamkhoukh said, "you forget that I am the Son of the Deer, I know the language of eyes. Your mellifluous eyes told me all . . ."

"In the interests of Chegem," Gunda whispered, and she hung her lovely little head.

"Yes," the vizier affirmed, "the interests of the people are highest of all."

"My portrait will be left to you," Gunda said, "you'll live with my portrait."

"Yes," the vizier agreed, "you may leave the portrait. We have lots of court painters.''

"All right," Jamkhoukh said, "I'll live with your portrait."

Gunda kissed Jamkhoukh good-bye, and never was a kiss more bitter, because Jamkhoukh felt its grateful tenderness.

Gunda was led over to a purebred Arabian racehorse. When the vizier held the stirrup for her foot he could not resist a nod toward the stirrup: "Pure gold."

"Son of the Deer, don't pine," Gunda said, settling herself comfortably in the saddle. "Look at my portrait often."

The courtiers disappeared with Gunda on the lower Chegem road. Jamkhoukh stood there a while in the middle of the yard, then sighed and went into the house.

The Chegemians long discussed this event, pitying Jamkhoukh and expressing various hypotheses.

"In general," they said, "bringing a redheaded woman into the house is the same as setting fire to it. You'd do better to just stick a burning brand up under the roof than bring in a redheaded woman.''

"We should have gone to war with the Pumpkinhead," said others, "our Jamkhoukh shouldn't have yielded her."

"But how could we go to war," said still others, "when Jamkhoukh himself strapped the tomato basket to her saddle."

This was a gross fabrication. Jamkhoukh had strapped no tomato basket to

Gunda's saddle. He missed his Gunda, of course, but not a single man ever heard a single complaint from him.

Only once, sitting before the fireplace fire in a circle of Chegemians, did he suddenly think aloud: "It turns out an empty soul can't be filled by anything. Emptiness of the spirit is a substance that is unknown to us. If the substance of emptiness fills the soul, the soul is filled. And what is filled can no longer be filled with anything."

"Don't grieve, Son of the Deer," said an old Chegemian. "You're still quite young, you have everything ahead of you."

"I feel bad about Mama Deer," Jamkhoukh replied. "She wanted to catch up with me and stop me, but she forgot to be careful, and perished . . ." He remembered his foster father, the old hunter Beslan, and added with a sigh, "When all that we love is in the other world, time is on our side: we are drawing nearer to our loved ones."

Jamkhoukh never again let slip a word of what was in his heart. Certainly time is a great healer, but it heals by bloodletting, like the Dioscurian who was summoned to Jamkhoukh's father.

For three years the Son of the Deer lived with the portrait of the golden-haired Gunda. But as everyone knows, the portrait of even the most beautiful girl bears no children.

One fine day Jamkhoukh called the Chegemians together, built a bonfire in the middle of the yard, and threw the fair Gunda's portrait into the flames.

"Beauty of face," Jamkhoukh said, "must be equally matched by beauty of soul, otherwise beauty is a lie and art is vanity."

"He's talking like this," the shrewdest Chegemian spoke up, "because he wants to get married."

Six months later Jamkhoukh really did marry an ordinary Chegem girl, and in time three children were born to him. First two little boys were born to him and then a girl. The elder boy was named Esnat, the younger Gid. And then the laughing little Tata came into the world, Jamkhoukh's dearly beloved comforter in moments of sadness.

With the years Jamkhoukh's fame kept on growing and growing. He not only gave advice and made prophecies, but sometimes pacified warring clans and even tribes. He could do by force of wisdom what the king could not do by force of arms.

King Theodore was exasperated with him, of course, but at first concealed the fact that he could envy a simple shepherd. He decided to bring glory on himself by a military feat and outfitted a great fleet to make war on Lazia. The fleet did not reach the shores of Lazia, however; it was destroyed by a storm on the open sea.

When he learned that the fleet had been lost, King Theodore the Fair flew into a great rage. He rushed around the palace screaming loudly, "And they call this sea Good? It's a bad sea! A cursed sea! Henceforth I will change its name! It shall be called the Black Sea! Let the heralds ride through all Abkhazia and order the people henceforth to call this sea Black!"

The heralds rode through all Abkhazia, and in all the cities and villages announced the sea's new name to the people. But the people made fun of the king.

"The Pumpkinhead's gone completely off his rocker!" they said, laughing out loud. "Can you really change the name of the sea? Then let him change the name of the sky, too!"

The sea's new name was absurd, because everyone saw that the sea was blue, and he was calling it Black. At first the people who lived on the coast made fun of the Pumpkinhead, repeating as a joke, "Well, how's that Black Sea—turned blue, hasn't it? About time to go out fishing, don't you think?"

People laughed and laughed, joked and joked, and joked to the point where they got used to it and started calling the sea Black themselves, by now in earnest. Such is the basis of many triumphs of folly.

King Theodore was very pleased that the sea's new name had been accepted by the people.

"Not a single king," he said, "has succeeded in renaming a sea before. Only the god Poseidon was capable of such a thing, and that in ancient Greek times."

Meanwhile, at the other end of the sea—where Byzantium lay—they continued to call it the Pontus Euxinus, that is, the Good Sea. Byzantium interpreted the sea's new name as a blow at its own prestige and nursed its anger against King Theodore the Fair. But he didn't realize this, and he sent his son, as was the custom among Abkhazian kings, to be educated at the court of the Byzantine emperor.

The fame of Jamkhoukh, Son of the Deer, was growing and growing, and this poisoned the Pumpkinhead's life. He sought a way to disgrace the Son of the Deer, and finally he had an idea. He called the courtiers together and said:

"The people count the Son of the Deer a wise and righteous man. But can a man be counted wise who wakes up every morning and starts chewing his cud, in keeping with his wild deer habit? We learned about this from our beloved queen, who left him because she loved me but also because she couldn't break him of this habit. Send the heralds through all Abkhazia, that people may know how the false wise man occupies himself when he wakes up in the morning."

All the heralds, except the chief herald, scattered through all Abkhazia. The chief herald at this time was Highspeed. He had been drawn to the court by the golden-haired Gunda. Since Highspeed knew perfectly well that Jamkhoukh chewed no cud in the morning, and he loved Jamkhoukh, he couldn't spread such a lie. But he dared not speak the truth either. Therefore he pretended that the millstone on his right foot had chafed his ankle and he couldn't leave the palace.

The heralds who had been sent through all the cities and villages of Abkhazia told the people that Jamkhoukh, Son of the Deer, chewed his cud when he woke up in the morning. But the people took this news in stride.

"Oh, she's always telling lies," some said when they heard the heralds. "Some queen! *We* remember how she took bribes of tomatoes."

Others said when they heard the heralds, "We know wise men have their foibles. He learned Abkhazian in five days, he says it was two. But how does that bear on his wisdom? Let him chew his cud, and welcome to it, so long as he helps us with advice and predictions.''

One day Highspeed came to Jamkhoukh and said, "Son of the Deer, Gunda swears by all that's sacred that she never said such nonsense to the king.''

"I'm glad that Gunda now holds something sacred," Jamkhoukh replied, "and I believe her. But the rumors the Pumpkinhead is putting out don't disturb me a bit. Tell the king's court: 'Those who chew their cud are a thousand times better than those who chew over their own folly.' ''

"All the way to the king?" Highspeed asked.

"Starting with the king," Jamkhoukh corrected him.

"Oh, I'm afraid for you," Highspeed sighed. "I won't say that.''

"Fear and love of the truth are incompatible," Jamkhoukh said. "A sign of maturity in the thinker is the readiness to sacrifice life for the sake of his thoughts. A sign of immaturity in the ruler is the readiness to accept that sacrifice. And don't say that cowardice is bravery in maidenhood. Such a maiden will be an old maid. My dear Highspeed, I still love you, and that's why I warn you: a man too much in fear of the constables unwittingly becomes a constable himself.''

Highspeed ran to the palace, flashing his gilded millstones, which many took for pure gold. He was thinking how to keep from saying too much at the palace and thereby harming the Son of the Deer.

Ah, Jamkhoukh, Son of the Deer! Certainly fear and love of the truth are incompatible. But in real life, love of the truth is not uncommonly incompatible with life itself.

A year later King Theodore decided to dispatch Jamkhoukh. For a long time he wondered how to do it without causing a murmur among the people, and finally he had an idea. Despite his folly, or rather thanks to his folly, King Theodore was sly, for slyness is the only form of intellect available to fools. But precisely because it's the only form, fools are tireless in perfecting it.

He secretly summoned to the palace one of his most experienced warriors. On such men King Theodore conferred the title of Warrior of Lightweight Field-Type Conscience. It had been observed that a fighting man who has spent his whole life killing foreigners ends by developing the natural desire to try his own people. Especially in times of truce with hostile tribes.

Just such a warrior had the king summoned to his presence.

"For the security of the motherland you will have to kill Jamkhoukh, Son of the Deer," the king said.

"How's that?" the warrior asked in surprise. "Haven't I heard he's a wise man, he's our pride and joy?''

"That's true," King Theodore replied, "and we have always hailed him for his wisdom. But he preaches that all nations are equal before the Great Weighmaster of Our Conscience. And this is ruinous for our nation.''

"How's that?" the warrior again asked in surprise.

"What lands have you fought in?" the king asked.

"I have fought," the warrior replied, "in the west, on the Khazar steppes, where in the summer noonday there is no shade but the shade of your own horse. I have fought in the east, where from under the rocks, instead of water, spurts the blood of the earth, which burns like brushwood. And I have fought in the north, where in winter the rivers die of the cold and you can cross the dead water on horseback. I have fought everywhere.''

"So have you seen a land anywhere more beautiful than our motherland?" the king asked.

"No." The warrior shook his head. "I haven't seen such a land. I even think there's no land on earth better than our land."

"That's just our trouble," the king said. "Jamkhoukh preaches that all nations are equal. But if all nations are equal, that means they're equally pleasing to the Great Weighmaster, and if they're equally pleasing to the Great Weighmaster, that means all the best lands must be divided equally among the nations."

"How's that?" the warrior again asked in surprise.

"That's how it works out," the king said. "Imagine that the Great Weighmaster of Our Conscience is our master. And we, the nations of the earth, are his workers. If the master is equally pleased with all the workers, is he or is he not supposed to feed them equally?"

"That's most important," the warrior agreed. "Myself, when I go off to war, I always order my wife to see to the workers she hires. See to it that they work equally well and that she feeds them equally well."

"That's just my point," the king nodded. "And several nations are already telling us: Move over in your fair land, give us a little bit of it too. Your wise man himself, Jamkhoukh, Son of the Deer, preaches that all nations are equal."

"So that's what they're after!" the warrior cried out. After a moment's thought he added, "Then order Jamkhoukh not to preach that any more."

"You're a good warrior," the king answered, "but too kind and plain a man. I've warned Jamkhoukh over and over again, but he doesn't listen to me. It will end with all nations making war on us and annihilating our people or turning them all into slaves. Choose. Either you kill Jamkhoukh and thereby preserve our nation, which will give us a new wise man in the future; or you don't kill Jamkhoukh, and in the end our enemies will annihilate our nation and Jamkhoukh with it."

"It works out it's better to kill Jamkhoukh," the warrior said.

"It does," the king agreed. He held out to him an arrow with a forked tip. "Here's the arrow you'll kill him with. This arrow was invented by a certain top-secret Persian. But our spies stole it from the Persians. You're the first warrior in the Caucasus to try it. To keep the people calm, it will be sounder to let them decide that Jamkhoukh has been killed by the foreign arrow of a foreigner. So you can leave the arrow in the body; we've already begun to manufacture arrows like it. Your king has a few ideas up his sleeve to make his warriors happy. But this is a secret for now."

Taking the arrow in hand, the warrior zestfully tried its clawed tip with his fingers. Then he suddenly became thoughtful and scratched the back of his head with that clawed tip.

"Why are you thoughtful, my warrior?" the king asked. "Isn't it all clear to you?"

"Oh, it's clear enough," the warrior answered, still thinking his own thoughts, "but for some reason I don't like the idea of killing Jamkhoukh, even though I'm very curious to try out the new arrow . . . Double strike—this is certainly a miracle . . . But all the same I feel sorry for Jamkhoukh somehow."

"Listen here," the king said, peering at him closely, "aren't you a Warrior of Lightweight Field-Type Conscience?"

"I do hold that title," the warrior sighed, "but all the same I don't like this somehow . . ."

"Do you suppose I like giving you this charge?" the king said. "But it's necessary for the preservation of our people. I don't even promise you a reward. You're exerting yourself for the motherland, not for me."

"I wouldn't kill Jamkhoukh for a reward, myself," the warrior declared. "I just don't like killing him, for some reason, even though I'm very curious to try out the new arrow."

"But you drink medicine when you're sick, don't you," the king said, "even though you don't like the bitterness of it?"

"Yes," the warrior agreed.

"As with medicine," the king said, "so with this: you don't like it, but you must."

"If I must, I must." Bidding the king farewell, the warrior left the palace.

Three days later the Son of the Deer met his end.

In the morning he set out as usual to graze his goats in Sabid's Hollow, and in the evening the goats came home without him. He was found in the forest with an arrow sticking out of his back. Jamkhoukh was still alive. When they carried him into the house, a Chegem witch doctor warily pulled from his back a fork-tipped arrow, unprecedented in this part of the world. But they were too late to save Jamkhoukh. Not long before his death he said suddenly:

"He who comes in time always comes too early . . ."

Then he sank into a reverie, and after a while he said, in a fitful, failing voice:

" . . . The cold of life . . . A common campfire . . . Or hand out firewood . . . I can't understand . . ."

His voice faded, as if the speaker, thinking aloud, had disappeared around a bend in the path. Jamkhoukh, Son of the Deer, was dead.

The yard was already thronged with saddened and murmuring Chegemians. Some said that Jamkhoukh had been killed by an unknown foreigner, others said that the murderer had very much wanted to be thought a foreigner.

Nearly half of Abkhazia gathered to mourn the Son of the Deer. And his faithful friends came, of course—Trencherman, Tankerman, Hear-All, Strongman, Sharpsight, Slick, and Highspeed. They sobbed more than anyone else by Jamkhoukh's coffin. Highspeed especially carried on. People noticed them.

"What relatives are those?" they asked. "We thought the Son of the Deer didn't have any relatives."

"Those are his comrades," older Chegemians answered. "They helped

Jamkhoukh marry his first wife, the present queen. That one in the golden millstones used to run up here every week. Used to lug tomatoes for Gunda, and now he's the chief royal herald.''

After Jamkhoukh's funeral, Highspeed, whose sobbing rent the soul, suddenly took the gilded royal millstones off his feet, in front of everyone, and hurled them away with such force that they rolled down into Sabid's Hollow.

The friends of Jamkhoukh, Son of the Deer, sat for a while at the funeral table, telling each other of their life and times. Tankerman complained about his elder son, who, it seems, was excessively enamored of drink.

"We drank in our day too," he said, "but we knew moderation. Today's young people don't know moderation in anything."

"Very well taken," said Hear-All, who by now had become a little hard of hearing, even without jammers. "I used to understand ant language. But now-adays young people talk such gibberish that you can't make anything out of it. The other day some friends came to see my son, and he said to them: 'How about it, mellaroos, shall we whoop up the amph?' 'Let's whoop it up!' they answered gleefully. And I didn't understand at all. Later they explained to me what was what. 'Mellaroos' are people out to get mellow, it seems. 'Amph' is what they call our amphora. How lazy can they get, eh? Can't say 'amphora' any more! Quicker to say 'amph'! Whoop up the amph—that means drain it dry so it whoops if you shout in it . . . Suit yourselves, friends, but on account of this gibberish I sense a wrong, wrong slant of thought. In our day everything was simple, noble. The way it used to be—ah, the dear old days!—friends would drop in to visit, and you'd say to them, 'Fellow jugslingers, shall we honor my vine?' 'Let's do the honors,' they'd reply, sitting down in a friendly way. 'Oh, will we do the honors!' At once everything was clear, beautiful. You weren't drinking, you were rendering a tribute of gratitude to the god of winegrowing and fertility. Of course that's a completely different slant of thought. But these fellows: 'Mellaroos, let's whoop up the amph!' Whoop it up! Why whoop, I ask you, why? Well, they drank, fooled around a bit, and home they went! If the amphora's been emptied you can whoop or not whoop—you won't whoop anything out of it!''

"Friends," Strongman said, "we have to face the truth. We've grown old. And honestly, sometimes now I find it hard to believe that I once could lay five giants out in a row in the middle of the yard."

"What a time that was," the friends sighed, remembering their expedition. "How young we were, and how happy to walk beside Jamkhoukh."

Old Chegemians, who remembered how Tankerman used to drink, set a jug of wine before him, but he ordered it taken away, though he did drink a couple of tankards. Trencherman too had trouble finishing his helping of cornmeal mush.

"Oh, the time we stand in . . . ," said the oldtimers of Chegem, as they told the young people about Tankerman and Trencherman's heroic dinner-table feats at Jamkhoukh's long-ago wedding.

The friends sat for a while at the table, felt sweetly sad remembering the past, and then rode off to their homes. It's good when you still have someone with whom to feel sweetly sad, remembering the years of youth. Worse can happen, my friends, it can happen you have no one with whom to feel sweetly sad, remembering the years of youth.

Highspeed was never again seen in the royal court, they say. Rumor has it that he went away beyond the Caucasian crest and there married his Circassian girl at last.

After Jamkhoukh's death there was widespread popular unrest in Abkhazia. Many felt that the king had been involved in the murder of Jamkhoukh.

"Ugh, we should shake the Pumpkinhead till the pumpkin seeds pop out of his ears!" said some. "Then he'd confess who killed our Jamkhoukh!"

"Oh sure," others said sarcastically, apropos of this. "All we have to do is find the man who'll shake him."

"Jamkhoukh was such a man," the wisest claimed, "but we didn't protect him."

But the king knew how to calm the people. The heralds broadcast his words in all the cities and villages.

These were his words:

"The greatness of the king who changed the name of the sea is equal to the greatness of the people's wise man, our beloved Jamkhoukh. Henceforth and forever we give our chief court wise man the title of 'Son of the Deer.' And our beloved queen, in token of mourning, renounces the eating of tomatoes for forty days."

The heralds gradually calmed the people. Laugh though they might at the Pumpkinhead Prettyboy, the people did not suspect him of being so guileful as to kill the Son of the Deer and then give the court wise man his title.

But King Theodore himself did not have long to reign. His twenty-year-old son George returned from Byzantium. Having secured the support of the Byzantine emperor, he formed a conspiracy, burst into his father's bedroom one night, and poleaxed him. "Greetings from Grandpa," he remarked as he did it, they say.

Not only did he mount the throne of the father he had killed; a year later he married the golden-haired Gunda, whose face still preserved some considerable trace of her erstwhile beauty. According to the well-known doctrine, having killed his father he should have married his own mother, but all Byzantine sources confirm that it was Gunda he married, his father's second wife.

In the years of the reign of George the Fierce—so the nation dubbed him—people were mowed down by cruel wars, harvest failures, and smallpox. Things reached a point where ordinary goatmeat became accessible only to families close to the court.

At the height of all these innumerable misfortunes, Gunda suddenly became pregnant and bore a son. After the first son she had a baby every year for nine years, sometimes two babies at once. There were even three years out of the nine when she managed to have four babies.

"They're the same breed," the Abkhaz said, but more softly by far than under the Pumpkinhead.

Meanwhile, despite all the calamities that had befallen Abkhazia, its international prestige grew stronger.

Abkhazia's prestige was especially enhanced after Byzantium, in token of eternal friendship with Abkhazia, copied the name of the Black Sea and forbade its subjects to pronounce the old name, Pontus Euxinus.

Appalled by the calamities that had befallen their land, the people often said, "It's because the Great Weighmaster of Our Conscience was wroth with us for not protecting the Son of the Deer."

Ah, well. Perhaps the people were right in their belated penitence. The duty of a wise man is to help his people honor the things they hold sacred, and not let them dissolve into an unthinking mob. The duty of a people is to protect its wise man. Jamkhoukh, Son of the Deer, fulfilled his duty.

That is what I heard in childhood about Jamkhoukh, Son of the Deer, and have retold here in my own words. This legend, or perhaps truth overgrown with legends, is known through all Abkhazia.

But the Chegemians in particular loved to tell about the Son of the Deer. They were proud of their countryman, especially since Chegem still preserved a green little mound that everyone called the grave of Jamkhoukh, Son of the Deer.

It is situated on a magical meadow, a level grassy hilltop not far from our settlement's tobacco shed. The little path that leads to Sabid's Hollow begins on the left, and the upper Chegem road goes by on the right.

The hill ended in a precipice overgrown with clumps of Christ's thorn, privet, blackberry. At the brink of the hill grew an enormous chestnut tree, slightly tilted toward the precipice.

Our family burial ground is there now. But I still remember a time, I was quite little then, when this meadow held—it's hard to believe!—not a single grave.

Early in summer we used to gather wild strawberries here, and occasionally I picked the red berries right from the grave of the Son of the Deer.

Sometimes the village games were held here. Teenage boys and more grown-up youths, knife in hand, would run at top speed to gather momentum and go leaping up the slightly tilted trunk of the chestnut tree. Taking several insane steps up the trunk, trying to reach as high as possible, they would stab the knife into the trunk with all their might. Then with a sort of animal grace they would manage to turn, push off, and leap down to the brink of the precipice.

Later they would race each other from the tobacco shed to the chestnut tree and back. Both the boys and the girls ran, and we youngsters sometimes chased shouting after them.

Among the girls of our settlement there was one who easily outdistanced all the girls and nearly all the boys. Even now she runs, runs, runs before my eyes, and the tall grass lashes her bare legs and feet with its sky-blue bellflowers, blue-gray wormwood, fanlike ferns, and still she runs, with a peculiar, smoothly lunging stride, as though she might go even faster if she took a notion to. And on her pure face, on her immortal (as I now already know) face, there is no grimace of effort, only the radiance of joy, as though her very speed is turning to the radiance of joy, and her very joy gratefully whipping up speed.

In my soul, back then as a ten-year-old boy, I secretly guessed that she was a distant descendant of the Son of the Deer. But I didn't tell anyone, out of shame that they might laugh at me.

One time when she was running I suddenly felt a piercing, throat-chilling ecstasy, a desire to seize her with newly preying fingers and sculpt her afresh, perhaps giving her stride a definitive stability. This was probably a first, as yet unrecognized, impulse toward creation.

But once in a while these days, strangely, as in a dream, the times come together in my memory. I see the runners running from the tobacco shed to the chestnut tree and back, and at the same time I see the sad and modest graves in which several of the runners already lie—fiery-eyed Adgur and his sister, the proud, modest Lyuba, and dear little Sofya.

They run past their own graves without noticing them, brake lightly at the chestnut tree, slap the trunk with flashing hand, and back they run, back in a rush of excitement, heads joyously up, again without noticing their own graves, running farther and farther away from them now, triumphantly, irretrievably!

THE TREE
OF CHILDHOOD

I LOVE TREES. It seems to me the tree is one of nature's noblest creations. Sometimes I think a tree is more than just a noble design of nature, it's a design intended to intimate to us desirable form for our souls, that is, a form that permits us, while holding tightly to the ground, to rise boldly to the heavens.

The peaceable might of a tree teaches us goodness and selflessness. If the tree does not bear fruit, if it belongs, so to speak, to the bachelor clan, then at least it gives us its shade in the heat of summer. The very concept of the fruitfulness of trees is tied to our own egotistical considerations. In point of fact, all trees bear fruit, it's just that not every fruit is edible for man.

Many trees have given me pleasure in my lifetime, and as a grown man I carry with me very affectionate memories of them.

I well remember the trees of our city yard, part vegetable garden, part orchard, hemmed in by houses. I remember a big, slowly withering pear tree (there were enough pears for my childhood), from which I once fell. I went flying down the length of the trunk, grabbing at the branches. Even though they snapped off, they broke my fall enough so that before I hit the ground I caught a strong branch and hung on.

I remember a large wild persimmon tree that grew in that same garden; I remember a quince tree, strong, small, gnarled, like a muscular old man; I remember a peach sapling, with a trunk as slight and lithe as a girlish figure; I remember a fig tree with lop-eared leaves and fruit as sweet as original sin.

But I loved above all others the walnut tree that grew in Sabid's Hollow. This was a huge tree with a huge hollow trunk, charred at the base by the naive rural Komsomol members of the thirties. They had wanted to destroy it, but they did a rather sloppy job, or perhaps the tree was just too hardy and vigorous to be susceptible to fire.

Long before that, incidentally, it had been struck by lightning. Some of the branches, those facing east, were charred and dead, but to make up for it, the other branches flourished as before and bore fruit—not only nuts, but also Isabella grapes. The vine climbed straight to the first limb and then ran in mighty coils toward the top, along the way putting out branches with dense clusters of grapes drooping from them.

Neither earth nor heaven, it seemed, could kill this mighty walnut tree. It continued to live and bear fruit, and the peasants who lived in the vicinity called it the Prayer Tree and brought sacrifices to it. They would slaughter a kid or a ram at the foot of the tree; after dressing the hide, they would cook the meat and eat it on the spot, the whole family, sometimes sharing it with travelers who chanced along the lower Chegem road.

In the prewar years I spent every summer at my grandfather's house. Every time we left the village at the end of August, the Chegem grapes were only just beginning to redden, and this was enough to bring tears to my eyes. What particularly hurt was that on the way down from Chegem we saw the grapes becoming riper and riper with practically every step, and below, near the River Kodor, they became completely black.

When the grapes began to turn pink on the Chegem trees, I used to walk around with my head tipped back, peering at the just-pink bunches, searching among them for ripe ones until I almost began to hallucinate. Sometimes I mistook a withered leaf from last year, lodged by chance in the interlacing of the branches and the vine, for a blackly ripe cluster of grapes. My heart skipped a beat for joy, but it lasted only a few instants, because when I looked again, I invariably discovered my mistake.

Nevertheless, I kept on tirelessly inspecting the trees on which the grapes twined, as a youth ready to fall in love inspects the girls streaming past him.

At last one time I noticed that the grapes hanging from one of the upper branches of the Prayer Tree were almost ripe. The rosy-black clusters stood out with gleaming allure in the thick green foliage of the mighty tree.

At that instant I felt a surge of inspiration, perhaps the strongest of my entire life. I went to the foot of the tree and began to climb up the vine, like a rope. There was no other way. It was quite impossible to clasp the tree with my arms or legs.

With great difficulty I made it to the first branch. Perched astride it, I paused for breath and began to consider what to do next. I could climb no farther on the vine, because here it began to wind around the trunk. The trunk itself was still too thick to climb.

I inspected the branch I was sitting on and noticed that its tip almost rested against the next branch, which grew five meters higher. Sitting astride the lower branch, I inched my way out to the point where it came near the next one. Half-rising on my branch, I grasped the upper one and began bending it down as hard as I could, to feel whether it would break when I hung from it. It felt as if it would hold me, although I was still afraid it would snap.

Still experiencing intense fear, I clung to the branch with my hands and legs and managed to haul myself up and sit on it. Out here the branch bounced and swayed, and its every motion brought on a wave of nauseating fear. But the nearer I crept to the trunk, the less it swayed, and gradually the fear passed. When I reached the crotch, I settled down to rest, leaning back against the trunk.

Suddenly, with a flash of wings and a splintery scream, a jay flew into the crown of the walnut tree and perched near me on the same branch.

Noticing me, she sat there a little while longer, probably to show that she wasn't afraid of me. Then, with another ugly scream, she shot up out of the crown, grazing the foliage with her wings, and flew away.

From here the vine rose straight to the next limb, and when I had rested I began to climb it. Although the vine was a little less thick here and therefore easier to grasp, and the distance I had to travel was less than what I had covered the first time, still, my muscles were fettered by fear of the height and I had a hard time creeping up to the next branch. Once there, I took a long rest, shaking out of my shirtfront the dry debris that my hands had peeled off the vine.

The higher I climbed, the fewer were the gaps between branches through which I could see the ground. Finally, the ground vanished completely, screened by the thick greenery of the branches, and I almost got over being scared. My sense of how far I might fall had vanished.

Suddenly I heard somewhere above my head a familiar creaking sound: *krr* . . . I had heard this sound many times in the forest and could never understand where it came from. I had finally decided that the sound resulted from dry branch rubbing against dry branch. Sometimes when I heard the sound, I tried to associate it with gusts of wind swishing through the leaves of the trees. Occasionally it did in fact coincide with gusts of wind, but most often it did not. Yet since I could find no other explanation, I continued to assume that it was a branch rubbing a branch.

Again came the familiar, close sound: *krrr!* I looked up and saw a redheaded woodpecker clinging to the trunk. It was hard to believe that this little bird could produce the loud, far-reaching sound of creaking wood. I froze, trying to remain unnoticed. The woodpecker, after glancing from side to side several times, struck the trunk of the tree with his beak again, and the familiar sound rang out: *krrr* . . . After his beak first struck the trunk, it seemed to keep on striking out of inertia. Apparently after the first blow the woodpecker simply could not stop his vibrating head, and while it vibrated, his beak chiseled at the trunk several more times.

This sound has nothing in common with the businesslike tap that one usually hears when the woodpecker is chiseling at the bark of a tree in search of food. He obviously wasn't searching for food now, and the sound may have stood for some sort of signal call or a song of triumph.

When he noticed me, he observed my behavior for a while. Finding it safe enough, he elicited the strange sound several times from a withered part of the trunk.

It occurred to me that when birds see a man in a tree, they fear him less than when they see him on the ground. It's as though he has become a denizen of their milieu, and part of their fear is probably lost in their heightened curiosity. In the same way, I used to notice when diving in the sea that the fish will sometimes scrutinize you with curiosity, with no particular fear.

But now the redheaded woodpecker flew away, and I continued my journey up the trunk. At last I made it to the branch at whose tip hung the bunches of grapes that had begun to ripen. What a spell those grapes cast over my eyes: the pink, the red, especially the violet-black ones, on the point of ripening!

But they were still hard to reach. I would have to get to the tip of the branch, and once I was there, I would have to catch hold of the vine and haul up the grapes.

I sat down astride the base of the branch, by the trunk, and began moving slowly nearer to the tip. My progress wasn't too terrifying because the ground was completely hidden by the green of the lower branches.

When I had almost reached the tip of the branch, I carefully stood up a little and grabbed the branch above, which out here was fairly close to my hand. My stance felt steady enough; my bare feet were braced against the slightly springy lower branch, and my hands clung to the upper one. In the faith that my body was sufficiently stable, I stretched one hand toward a bunch of grapes and got hold of it with great difficulty. It was resistant and springy. At moments I thought that the hand with which I was clinging to the upper branch was on the point of giving out, and I would be torn loose and go flying after the grapevine, which was bent like a drawn bow. In the end, I pulled it to me, and now, before my very face, swayed the mouth-watering bunches of grapes that I had admired from the ground.

But now a new obstacle developed: both my hands were full. One hand continued to cling to the upper branch, while the other tensely gripped the grapevine, which was still trying to pull away.

In desperation I leaned over and began biting the ripest grapes out of the bunches, although this was very awkward, and sometimes I got completely green grapes in my mouth instead of ripe ones.

At last I thought to haul the grapevine up to the upper branch. Passing my right arm through it (an instant of wild fear), I grabbed the branch again, and my left hand was now free.

I plucked the ripest grapes out of the juicy bunches and put them in my mouth. I hurried, aware that my feet were already trembling a little from tension. My right hand, clinging to the branch, was also beginning to tire from the pull of the tightly stretched grapevine still held in the crook of my elbow.

But what bliss it was to eat a just-ripe grape, fragrant as only an Isabella can be; to feel its tart pulp slide sweetly down my throat; to hear the spat-out grape skins plop sonorously on the leaves of the walnut tree; to listen to the faraway tinkle of bells in a herd of cows, the resonant beating of my own heart in the silence. I don't know how long my bliss lasted, but it was suddenly cut short by a harsh bellow.

"What are you doing up there? Come down right now!"

At the top of the ridge, where Sabid's Hollow began, stood Uncle Kyazym.

To this day I can't understand why I was so frightened by his voice. Horrified that I had been caught in the tree, I rushed to climb down. When I let go of the grapevine it broke loose from my grip with a swoosh, and a rain of grapes showered down, splatting on the leaves.

My swift, panicky return trip was accompanied by several shouts from him, which I couldn't make out over the noise of my descent. Apparently he was shouting for me to take it easy coming down, but I didn't catch what he said.

That night, I heard from my uncle the pleasantest praise I have ever heard come my way. He was sitting in the kitchen in front of the fire. With a nod at me, he told Mama, "This boy of yours climbed a tree today that no city boy would have dared to climb, even if there was a gang of them gathered under the walnut tree . . ."

Mama began to scold me, of course, but I was happy that Uncle Kyazym, usually so mocking, had praised me.

I remember a rainy evening in 1942. We are sitting having supper by the flaming hearth. My uncle is not there, he has been mobilized to cut firewood. Far away from the house, right on the slope overhanging Sabid's Hollow, the dogs are barking—our dogs, the neighbors'. But we pay no attention, there are plenty of things a dog might scent in Sabid's Hollow.

"Sh-h-h," my aunt says suddenly. She stops eating and cocks her ear to the night darkness, to the open kitchen door.

We stop chewing and listen along with her, but we hear nothing, nothing except the din of the rain, the distant barking of the dogs, and the still more distant artillery barrage, somewhere out beyond the pass. Auntie stands in the open door, tense and motionless, and listens to something.

"I thought I heard something," she says. Returning to the kitchen, she sits down at our little low table.

Everyone goes on eating.

"Sh-h-h," she says suddenly, stopping us again, and now she goes out on the open veranda. "I think I hear a voice . . ."

We stop chewing again and listen to the night. But we can distinguish nothing except the din of the rain, the barking of the dogs, and the distant artillery from the pass.

"I think someone's cow is bellowing," Auntie says, but we do not hear anything. Auntie has very sharp ears.

All of us, the four children, go out on the veranda and listen. Only Grandpa stays in the kitchen.

At first we hear nothing, but after a while, when the barking of the dogs becomes barely distinguishable—they have run down into Sabid's Hollow—we hear it, the plaintive bellowing reaches our ears.

"M-moo-oooo!"

"Someone's cow is lost in the forest," Auntie says. "The broadpaw must be tearing her to pieces . . ."

We listen again. Through the gusting wind the din of the rain now intensifies, now diminishes. In a flash of lightning I notice the solitary figure of our cousin Lilisha next door. She too is standing on the veranda and listening to the night. Her mother and father are long dead; her only brother, Chunka, serving somewhere on the western border, has evidently perished, there has been neither a letter nor any news of him since the beginning of the war.

Again we listen to the night. And now we hear it, suddenly distinct, plaintive, as if calling for people: "M-moo-oooo!"

"Give me back my youth, just for the day," Grandpa says from the kitchen, "and I'd show the broadpaw . . ."

"Be quiet a minute!" Auntie brushes him aside, and again we listen to the night, to the din of the rain, through which we hear again: "M-moo-oooo!"

"She's done for, poor thing," Auntie says. "What a shame the master's gone . . ."

She has in mind not the cow's owner but her own husband, Uncle Kyazym. He would certainly have gone down with his gun and most likely would have killed the bear, but he isn't home now, he's cutting wood in the village of Atara. I picture my uncle going down into Sabid's Hollow with his gun in this eerie dark, this rain, and I become uncomfortable. I am aware that I wouldn't dare do it for anything: the night, the eerie rain, the steep little path leading into the hollow, and somewhere there in the depths an infuriated bear is killing the cow . . .

From the goat pen—we can't see it from here—comes the clank of a bell and a muffled din. Has someone attacked the goats?

"They're worried, they scent it," Auntie says, peering into the darkness.

"Eh-hey, Adgur," Auntie shouts into the darkness. "Do you hear anything?"

She is shouting in the direction of Isa's house. Isa was one of her husband's brothers; now only his son and daughter live there. The rest—the father, mother, elder sister—have all died of tuberculosis. Adgur has it, too, and only Zarifa, his sister, is untouched by the disease.

"We hear it, we hear it!" Zarifa shouts from over there. "A cow in Sabid's Hollow."

"Are your cattle home?" Auntie shouts into the darkness.

"All home, all home!" comes Zarifa's voice.

"Hey, everybody, what happened?" Aunt Masha shouts, hearing the voices calling back and forth.

Aunt Masha and her family live in the little dip near the spring, and the sounds from Sabid's Hollow do not carry there.

"The broadpaw is tearing someone's cow apart," Auntie Noutsa shouts. "Are your cattle home?"

"All home! All home!" Aunt Masha and her daughters chorus in answer.

For several minutes everyone is silent, and all we can hear is the din of the rain and the distant artillery from the pass. Then, from the goat pen, again comes the feverish clanking of a bell and the noise of the anxious flock.

"They're afraid . . . they scent it," Auntie says.

Then the goats are silent, and from Sabid's Hollow again comes the agonizing bellow: "M-moo-oooo!"

"Why is he taking so long with her?" says Remzik, the youngest of us.

"It means the cow is fighting back," his sister tells him.

"A cow couldn't fight back to a bear, could she?" Remzik asks. "Could she, Grandpa?"

"Sure she's fighting back," Grandpa says from the kitchen. "Give me back my youth for one little hour, and I'd show that broadpaw . . ."

"Quiet, everyone," Aunt Noutsa shouts at us. "I'm having enough trouble hearing as it is."

A violet flare of lightning illumines the slanting streams of rain, the huge crown of a walnut tree, and the solitary figure of Lilisha on the veranda of her house.

There is a sharp clap of thunder, like a blow punching new holes in the sky; fresh torrents of rain pour down from them.

"It's completely burst," Auntie says, jerking her chin toward the sky. "I hate this."

"Meat—it's raining meat," Grandpa says, as if in answer, meaning that the fields and vegetable gardens badly need the rain.

Now, through the din of the rain, comes the distant voice of a man. The voice rises from the low-lying spot where the family settlement's nearest neighbors live. Someone over there is calling, but here where we are it's impossible to make out the words. Aunt Masha lives closest to him, she's the one who answers.

"A bear is tearing someone's cow to pieces, a bear!" Aunt Masha shouts to him.

"A cow can't fight back to a bear," Remzik says softly. "Only a buffalo can fight back to a bear."

"A buffalo can't," his sister replies. "Maybe a buffalo-cow, but only if she has a baby buffalo-calf."

"Noutsa!" comes Lilisha's voice from next door. "I'm afraid to spend the night alone, I'm coming over to your house."

"Of course, come on over," Auntie answers her.

Everyone loves Lilisha, because she is a kind, obliging girl, and besides she's completely without family. She does not believe that her brother has perished, she thinks he's in a Partisan detachment or, at worst, he's been taken prisoner.

In a flash of lightning we can see Lilisha running across the yard, her head covered with a piece of burlap. The thunder catches her right by the house, and with a loud cry of fright she runs up on the veranda, where everyone but Grandpa stands listening to the moans of the cow carrying from Sabid's Hollow.

"Let's go have supper," Auntie says. "There's no way we can help."

"I've already had supper," Lilisha says. Leaving her burlap on the veranda, she comes into the kitchen with everyone.

"You won't burst," Auntie Noutsa tells her. "At least have some mush and yogurt with us . . ."

"No, no," Lilisha answers. "I'm not hungry at all."

"Well, all right, if you're sure," Auntie says, and gives everyone yogurt in iron bowls. I immediately put the last of my cornmeal mush in the bowl and stir it with a bone spoon, turning the mixture into an incredibly tasty soup. Despite my anxiety and pity for the unknown cow being torn to pieces by the bear, I feel a traitorous appetite and eat the cornmeal soup with gusto. The other children, too, eat mush and yogurt, and with just as good appetite. No one leaves so much as a crumb, because our helpings of mush have been cut back: it's wartime, corn is short.

"Come with me," Auntie says to me. "Let's look at the goats."

"All right," I answer.

Auntie lights a kerosene lantern, throws on my uncle's old raincoat, I put on my uncle's quilted jacket, and we go outdoors. Up ahead of me the lantern glimmers dimly, partly hidden by the wide raincoat. We walk out of the yard, and on the way to the goat pen we inspect the foot of the walnut tree, where the cows usually station themselves at night. It is almost dry here. All three cows are standing at the foot of the tree, and it is obvious that they are listening to what is happening in Sabid's Hollow. Not one of them is chewing her cud. Usually at this hour they lie at the foot of the walnut tree and chew their cuds.

We pass the cows and approach a structure made of woven rhododendron branches. This is the pen for the goats, built about a meter and a half off the ground. The goats live here almost year round, with the exception of the few very cold winter months, when they are kept in the barn. From the sound of the bells and the racket coming from the pen, it is obvious that the goats are restless.

By a sloping ladder made from the same woven rhododendron we climb to the door of the pen, and Auntie holds up the lantern. Seeing us, the goats stop fretting and stare motionlessly in our direction. All the goats are standing up, they look distraught, and it is clear they are troubled by what is happening in Sabid's Hollow. In the lantern light, which picks out of the darkness first one group of goats and then another, they look at us with a sort of timid hope. Auntie checks that the door is shut tight, reassures the goats with a few caressing words— Don't be afraid, silly things, nothing can get you—and goes down, and I follow her.

When we reach the veranda, she extinguishes the lantern, shakes the raindrops off the raincoat, and hangs it in the kitchen. I, too, hang up my uncle's quilted jacket and settle down on a bench by the fire. The table has already been put away, and all the children and Lilisha are sitting by the hearth. Grandpa is lying on his bunk. Auntie sets a pitcher of water beside the fire, then fetches a basin, sets it at our feet, and orders, "All right now, wash your feet!"

We take turns washing our feet, tuck them up on the bench and dry them. The older girl, Riziko, who is my age, tends to us: pours water into the basin, pours it out, warms the pitcher. She washes her own feet last. After putting on any kind of footgear we can find, we walk over to the clean half of the house. Remzik is carried in his mother's arms.

We pause on the veranda and listen again to the night. After a while, through the din of the rain, the cow's moan comes again. We continue to listen, and again, through the din of the rain, through the far-off hysterical barking of the dogs, through the muffled din of the artillery, comes the moan of the cow. I had noticed that the interval between her moans was slowly getting longer. Just now, it was not less than ten minutes.

We leave the cold veranda and go into the house. Remzik and his sister are put in the same room with me. The older sister and Lilisha go to bed in the room where my uncle and aunt usually sleep. My aunt will sleep in the big room, the hall. Anyone else would be terrified to sleep there: there are portraits of dead relatives on the walls, once in a while the walls themselves make cracking sounds for some reason, and now the bear is out there somewhere, tearing the cow to pieces . . .

The rain beats on the roof, now and again the thunder rumbles. Under the blanket it is cozy and a little scary. Remzik and Zina, lying head to foot, will not settle down; their covers rustle, they squabble softly.

"I'm going to put you to bed out here in the hall!" their mother threatens from the next room.

"She keeps pulling the covers off me," he complains.

"That's a lie, you shameless thing!" his sister says.

Gradually they settle down, fall silent. I can hear Lilisha and Riziko whispering in the little room. I hear Auntie blow on the lamp several times out in the hall, and the stripe of light in the crack of the door disappears. I still hear Riziko and Lilisha's whispers coming from the little room.

The rain beats on the roof, a gust of wind now brings the sound of the rain near, now carries it away. Under the covers it is unusually cozy and warm; drowsiness comes over me.

The next morning the sun sparkles on the wet leaves of the trees, on the grass, on the cornstalks revived by the abundant moisture. We children go down into Sabid's Hollow. Of course the grown-ups have already been here before us. On the hooks driven into the trunk of the Prayer Tree hang several pieces of meat, evidently all that is left of the cow.

From up here we can see a large flat area trampled out among the fern thickets. He must have attacked her there, and she tried to break free, but he dragged her and tore her to pieces.

The cows are grazing on this same slope. From time to time a cow draws apart from the herd and comes over to the Prayer Tree; craning her neck, she moos plaintively at the suspended remains of the cow, and walks on. Then she begins to graze. She seems to be tearing off the clumps of grass with reluctance, but then, as if caught up in her habitual activity, she begins tearing off the grass with steady zeal. Meanwhile, another cow draws apart from the herd and comes over to the Prayer Tree to crane her neck and moo with the grief of farewell over the remains of the perished cow . . . Astounded at this strange spectacle, we stand and watch for a long time.

A vague suspicion that I'm getting malaria comes to me while I am under the Prayer Tree, knocking down green walnuts with a stick. Inside the thick green husks is a soft, unripe kernel, and today the kernels taste flat, even bitter.

Trying to convince myself that I do not have malaria after all, I crawl into a blackberry patch and begin eating the ripe, inky berries, but they too seem tasteless to me, they smell of some mysterious insect.

Moreover I am beginning to shiver with cold, although I stand in the full blaze of the summer noonday sun. I am still trying to make myself believe that it isn't malaria, that I'm only imagining I'm getting an attack.

To restore full sensation of the taste of ripe blackberries, I gather a whole handful and shake them into my mouth. This time I do taste the sweetness of the berries, yet even so they still have an unbearable smell, as if some kind of insect had sat on them.

Down beyond the Prayer Tree, a bell sounds in the copse in the gully. The goats are grazing there. I realize that if I really am coming down with malaria the best thing is for me to be at home. I decide to drive the flock out of the copse and return home.

I go down and begin rounding up the goats, who have scattered in the blackberry and hazelnut bushes, in the thickets of dogwood, cherry-laurel, and fern. *"Kheyt! Kheyt!"* I shout, sometimes tossing stones into the most impassable thickets, from which the goats stubbornly refuse to come out, knowing that I can't get at them.

At the very bottom of the hollow babbles a waterfall, which flows down a wooden trough from a rocky crevice. The water here is ice-cold. Coming upon the waterfall now, I recall a tale told by a certain shepherd, who says that if you wash yourself in spring water at the very beginning of a malaria attack, the malaria may leave your body.

I drop my ax and strip naked. After some hesitation, clenching my teeth, I step under the icy stream, which beats hard on my back, my neck, my head, battering me with the pain of cold. The unbearable cold takes my breath away, the air sticks in my chest, and I jump out from under the stream.

After I catch my breath, I climb under the waterfall again, and again jump out. With each try my body feels more and more at home with the icy stream, and on the fourth or fifth try the water doesn't seem all that cold to me.

In fact, the spring water is so bracing that I begin to have faith the malaria has left my body. I decide not to go home but to stay here with the goats until evening. Someone is supposed to bring my dinner to me here.

I feel such a surge of strength that I decide to cut down a small beech sapling that is growing nearby. I decide to treat the goats to fresh beech leaves. I take my ax in hand and begin to chop at the sapling. When they hear the sound of the ax, the goats begin to gather around me, glancing up at the sapling and waiting impatiently for it to fall. After a while the trunk creaks and falls. The goats throng around it on all sides, greedily devouring the leaves.

I get dressed and stand near the goats, watching with satisfaction as they greedily devour the fresh beech leaves. Presently I feel another chill. Choosing a spot where the sun penetrates the forest canopy, I sit down to get warm.

"Hey, you!" I hear the voice of my little cousin Zina, the younger of the two girls. "I've brought your dinner."

I can tell from her voice that she is standing at the foot of the Prayer Tree.

"Come on down, here I am!" I shout in reply.

"I'm scared," she shouts. "You'll hide!"

I often did hide from her in the forest to frighten her, and she would always be terrified.

"Don't be scared, I won't!" I call back.

"Swear!" she shouts from above.

I sense that she won't let me alone till I swear.

"I swear by everyone!" I shout.

"Even the ones at the front?" she specifies, after a moment's thought.

"Even the ones at the front!" I shout back.

Hailing me from time to time to be sure that I haven't moved, she comes down. Although I am shaking with chill, I'm sorry to miss the chance to frighten her, but I can't bring myself to do it, I have no wish to move from my place, abandon the patch of sunlight. She emerges from the bushes, looking over her shoulder, warily turning her round, rosy face.

She has brought me a slice of boiled pumpkin and a small bottle of milk. I see that she has not been able to resist taking a good big bite out of my pumpkin along the way. She has obviously had a sip of milk as well.

She looks into my eyes to determine whether or not I can tell that she has eaten some of my dinner. But just now I have absolutely no desire to eat, and I pretend not to notice anything. I begin eating the pumpkin, and I tip up the bottle and take several sips from it. The milk does not taste good, and the pumpkin is bitter. I force myself to eat. My cousin watches me and guesses that I don't feel like eating.

"If you don't like it, let me finish it for you," she says.

I try for a while longer, knowing that I must eat to keep my strength up. But in the end I don't have the will power.

"Here," I say to her, and give her the rest of the milk and the pumpkin.

"But why don't you want it?" she says, first taking the bottle of milk from me and then the unfinished slice of pumpkin.

"I probably have malaria," I say. "I feel shivery."

"True," she agrees, taking a bite of pumpkin and washing it down with milk. "You're as yellow as the pumpkin."

For some reason I find her remark disagreeable, especially when I mentally compare her rosy, pretty little face and her whole healthy, strong, barefoot figure with my own, probably pathetic, appearance.

"Look, your nails have even turned blue!" she says suddenly, pointing to my fingers. Indeed, my nails have turned blue with the chill.

"I'll go home," I say, "and you stay here with the goats."

"I wouldn't stay here alone for anything!" she says, looking quickly over her shoulder and moving close to me. I glance behind me and nod significantly, as if to certain otherworldly forces with which I am in cahoots and which can deal with her.

"I know there isn't anything there!" she says, quickly following my glance. "I know you're doing it on purpose to scare me!"

She moves still closer to me and looks into my eyes, trying to catch the instant when I will exchange glances with these beings so hateful to her, although perhaps invented by me.

But I feel so rotten that I don't have it in me to tease her. I stand up, take my ax in hand, and begin to drive the goats up. The goats climb up slowly, straggling a little from time to time. My little cousin, although she tries to stick close to me, picks blackberries along the way and stuffs some of them into the bottle. There are so many blackberries that by the time we get to the foot of the Prayer Tree she has a full bottle of them. She shakes it with all her might to make the juice flow from the berries, then tips up the bottle and drinks blackberry juice from it.

"Want some?" she offers, catching her breath with difficulty. Her lips are stained with blackberry juice.

"No," I say, and drive the goats on. Everything that she is doing now strikes me as an expression of strength and health. As a matter of fact, that is so. It's nice to see, and at the same time enviable, because I seem pathetic and impotent to myself.

Half an hour later, arriving at the house with the goats, I walk into the yard and see Auntie coming out of the kitchen. The clank of the bells has caught her ear. She doesn't know what to think when she sees me.

"He's coming down with malaria!" Zina blurts, trying to beat me out and be first to tell the news.

"Malaria? Oh, you poor thing!" she says, and I sense the instant division in her attention: she pities me, but at the same time she is thinking, What will I do with the goats, someone has to graze them till evening.

Auntie puts me to bed in the big hall, covers me with two blankets at once. I continue to shake with the chill, but gradually I get warm. I become hotter and hotter, and by now my head is filling with an oppressive fire, and I'm afraid to move it because the pain grows more intense, flames up with every movement.

I throw off the heavy blankets, and someone puts a sheet over me. They give me a thermometer, I stick it under my arm. Presently it develops that I have a temperature of forty-one and five tenths.

I am a little proud of my temperature, especially since Auntie and all the others are frightened by it. They don't know that I always have a very high temperature when I have malaria. They think that with a temperature of forty-two degrees a person dies. I am confident that I wouldn't die even with that temperature, but I find it pleasant that they are so distressed by my proximity to the fatal mark.

They put a wet towel on my head and change it every ten or fifteen minutes. Noutsa's older girl, Riziko, the one who is my age, sits beside me and waves an apple branch over me, makes it easier for me to breathe, fans away the stuffy heat.

Two hours later I am in a semidelirious state and sometimes confuse the people who come and go from the room where I lie. Through the open door I see a person enter our yard and approach the house, then climb the steps, cross the veranda, and enter the room. While he is doing all this, I watch him and see his appearance change several times. Now he resembles one person, now another, then a third, and very likely it's not until he enters the room where I lie that his appearance is finally fixed. This happens only in dreams, and though my eyes are open I am in a dreamlike state.

In the night I sweat heavily, and I feel better. My temperature is thirty-nine. I hear voices on the veranda and recognize among them the honeyed voice of the witch doctor. She suggests that they have me drink the urine of a goat without a single black hair. According to her, the urine will destroy the nesting place of the malaria in my stomach.

They let me change my shorts and undershirt, they change the thoroughly soaked bed linen; I drink a big mug of yogurt and water (after looking closely to be sure they aren't slipping me anything), and fall into a heavy sleep.

The attack is not renewed the next day, but I am thoroughly spent; with leaden head I lie under the apple tree on a cowhide. Auntie suggests that I drink the urine of a goat without a single black spot (almost all our goats are like that), but I refuse.

The next day another attack begins, and Auntie finally persuades me to drink the urine of a white goat. Strictly speaking, she doesn't really have to persuade me. Dreading a return of the horror I suffered the day before yesterday, I am ready to do anything to ease my lot.

For some reason my mind is preoccupied with the technique of obtaining the urine, and I correctly guess that this is most easily done in the narrow pen, where the goats stand close to one another, bunched together. Most likely the urine is taken from the nanny goats, because they are used to being milked and will let a person get near them.

Auntie brings me about half of a half-liter jar, and I hold my breath and take several big gulps. A basin stands ready by my bed. As soon as I set the jar on the chair, a spasm of nausea rises from my stomach with terrible force. I lean over the basin and the contents of my stomach spurt out of me.

"Come on, do it again! Again!" Auntie says joyfully, apparently sure that I am vomiting up my disease. After being turned inside out three or four times, my obviously emptied stomach begins to send up a sort of blood-flecked slime.

"Aha," Auntie says with satisfaction, even with gloating, "we've finally got you, you she-devil! Look at that! So that's what she looks like! Here now, you have to take one more drink . . ."

She presents me with the jar. Again I go through it, holding my breath. Again the spasm of vomiting. I have no strength left at all. My empty stomach squeezes up some sort of slime in drops of blood, and everyone thinks that this is a poisonous liquid pouring from the destroyed nesting place of the malaria itself.

Then they give me some pure water. I spend a long time rinsing my mouth and drink the pure, cold, spring water. I feel it pass down my throat, and farther, touching my stomach with purifying cold.

Despite the fact that we have destroyed the menacing citadel of malaria in my stomach, this same day everything is repeated as in the first attack, only I have a much harder time because I have gotten weaker.

At the height of the attack I hear my aunt and uncle talking in the next room. She says he should ride to the village where my mother is staying and fetch her. Uncle says that's unnecessary, there's no point alarming my mother. Auntie protests and says what if I died on their hands. Although things are very bad, I cannot believe that I'm going to die.

The next day my uncle rides to a village where there is a doctor and a hospital and brings me back some quinine tablets. Even so, a day later I have a third attack, and then the malaria leaves me for another six months . . .

The day after the third attack, when I hobbled to the shade of the apple tree to lie in the cool breeze, several kolkhoz women were sitting there, resting during their dinner break. Among them was my cousin Zarifa, the very picture of health. Seeing me, she said with a smile, "Look at him, he's a sight. His head weighs more than his body."

It was true, every attack of malaria turned me into a walking shadow. I always lost strength terribly fast, though I gained it all back afterward with almost the same rapidity.

The funny thing is that the hurt lingers to this day: why did she say it, anyway? Well, okay, she thought it; but after all, she didn't have to say it . . .

Autumn. Around the end of September. Uncle Kyazym and I are going down into Sabid's Hollow. In my hand is a large basket, and slung on his shoulder is a hook-blade ax, called in our part of the world a *tsalda*. We are on our way to gather nuts from the Prayer Tree.

We come to the foot of the tree. My uncle looks it over attentively, evidently searching out the branches richest in walnuts. Then he goes downhill, crawls into a brambly thicket, and chops out a good-sized hazelnut stalk, about four meters long. He is preparing a stick to knock the walnuts down with. I see him strip the branches from it, then shake it in his hand, testing it for elasticity and strength. When he comes back up to the foot of the walnut tree, he suddenly pulls from his pocket a piece of paper about the size of the blotter in a school notebook.

"Here, read this," he says, and holds the sheet out to me.

"Where did you get it?" I ask, already guessing what it is.

"It was hanging there in the bushes," he answers.

I read the German leaflet. It says that the Germans have already won the war anyway, and the Caucasian peoples, who are oppressed by the Soviet regime, must cease to struggle against the Germans. At the end there is a drawing of a gun, its bayonet stuck in the ground, graphically illustrating what must be done, for the benefit of any illiterates who happen to find the leaflet.

"So what do they say there?" he asks.

"They say for us not to fight against them," I translate from the leaflet, which is written in Russian.

"Ha!" he grins. He takes the leaflet from my hands and fingers it. Evidently deciding that it's no good for cigarette papers, he tears it to bits and throws it away.

I am curious to see how he will climb the Prayer Tree. He walks up to it, grasps the vine, but, in contrast to me, he does not wrap his legs around it. He braces them against the trunk and reaches the first branch amazingly fast. Here he asks me to hand him the stick. I reach it up to him and have trouble getting it as far as his feet. He catches it by clasping it between the soles of his feet, then pulls up his legs and gets the stick in his hands.

He climbs the tree with an extraordinary, giantlike swiftness, and after a few minutes I hear the stick beating the walnut-studded branches.

The first nuts fall to the ground. Some have already shed their husks; others pop from the husk when they strike the ground, their shells flashing. Despite the grass on the slope where the Prayer Tree stands, some of the nuts roll on down into the depths of Sabid's Hollow. I try to stand downhill from where the nuts are falling so that I can stop at least some of the ones that roll down.

Whenever my uncle finishes knocking the nuts down from one branch and climbs to another, I take advantage of the interval to savor the fruit of the mighty tree. I choose from the basket the nuts most beautiful in form, with the cleanest shell, still wet from the husk; I crack them open, pick out the tender nutmeats covered with a creamy membrane, and eat them. It is hard to convey how delicious they are, especially in those hungry times!

I have already gathered almost a basketful when suddenly I hear a voice right above me.

"Good labors to you!"

Next to me, just up the slope, stands a lieutenant I do not know, with two privates from the Destroyer Battalion, the local militia. They are standing just a little apart from him and dressed in ordinary peasant clothes. All three have carbines slung over their shoulders.

One of the peasants, a man of about fifty or a little over, is a distant relative of ours. He used to live in Chegem but later moved to another village.

"Hello," I reply to the lieutenant's slightly derisive greeting. It is the greeting we use here when we come upon people at work. What I am doing can hardly be called work, especially since my mouth is full of nuts, and his greeting sounds as if it refers to the working of my jaws.

"How's life, how's your mother?" the former Chegemian asks me.

"All right," I answer. Opening the basket, I add, "Have some . . ."

The men from the Destroyer Battalion make no response to my invitation, they even sit down on the grass, but the lieutenant comes over and takes several handfuls of nuts, putting them in his pocket. Then he takes two nuts from his pocket and squeezes them between his palms, crushing one of them without difficulty. He picks out the tender kernel, puts it in his mouth, and looks up, trying to make out through the branches who is up there.

"That's not Sandro, is it?" he calls up.

"Just try and get Sandro up a tree," Uncle answers with a grin. "Is that you, Rasim?"

"It's me, while I last," the lieutenant answers. He crushes another nut between his palms. "So it's you I didn't recognize, Kyazym! Aren't you afraid the deity will shake you down from the branch?"

"No," Uncle laughs, "our deity doesn't touch its own. Now if you were to climb up—"

"I'd fall out of a tree like that, deity or no deity," the lieutenant answers with a chuckle, still eating nuts.

I have a feeling that as soon as we finish gathering nuts, Uncle will take the men home and give them potluck. Whatever it is, the dinner will be much more bountiful than usual . . . That is clear—they will eat at our house, and we children will get some of the company dinner.

This thought fills me with extraordinary cheer, and my mouth is already watering in anticipation of chicken with walnut sauce, or dried meat browning on the spit, dripping fat into the coals.

"What brings you to our parts?" comes my unseen uncle's voice from above. He is moving to the next higher branch now.

"Nothing special," the lieutenant replies. "It's a bad time . . . All sorts of people roaming the mountains."

"Take cover," my uncle says, and he begins beating a branch with the stick. In a few seconds the walnuts start hitting the ground, just where the lieutenant and I are standing. He cowers in mock fright and mutters, "God help us! God help us!"

I had liked this lieutenant from the moment he first appeared. I liked him for his gallant air, the medals clinking on his chest, and his joking ways.

When he began lamenting as though frightened by the nuts falling from above, I smiled and looked up to show that I understood and appreciated his joke.

As I raised my head, I also looked at the men from the Destroyer Battalion, who were sitting uphill from the spot where the falling nuts might land. Both of them were smiling, looking at their commander. The vague smile of benevolence on their faces showed that they, too, had registered the possibility of an imminent session at table.

Suddenly I saw that above them, on top of the ridge, to the right and left of which were the two hollows, one Sabid's and the other nameless, at least to us—on top of that ridge, twenty or thirty paces from us, two men in soldier's uniforms were walking along with submachine guns over their shoulders.

They were walking very fast, and the strange thing was that they didn't notice us, or didn't want to look in our direction. But the strangest thing—I sensed it immediately, although I didn't recognize it consciously (I recognized it much later, but sensed it immediately)—was that they were not walking in a direction soldiers might have been walking. They were walking up the path that led into the forest, the backwoods. No one but the shepherds went there, and a military man definitely had no business there unless he meant to hide from someone. That is what I sensed, even though I didn't consciously recognize it, when I caught sight of the two on the path, walking past us along the top of the ridge.

Evidently something of what I had sensed was reflected in my eyes, because the lieutenant suddenly turned and froze. He watched the soldiers walking up the path for several seconds. His hand, holding a partly eaten nut, unclenched and let go of it, and the carbine, as if by itself, without any effort on his part, slowly slid down from his shoulder and ended up in his hands.

Up above, my uncle was beating the branches with the stick, and the nuts were falling, but I was no longer gathering them. Looking at their commander, still sitting down, the two men from the Destroyer Battalion also turned around. At first they didn't see anything because they were sitting down, but then when they stood up they saw, and they too unslung their carbines.

The lieutenant quickly stepped forward and gestured for his men to follow him as he went up the slope. By the time they all came out on top of the ridge, the others were no longer visible from where I stood. They had obviously taken the path that led into the forest. There was nowhere else they could have disappeared to.

"Hey, halt!" the lieutenant's loud voice rang out. Now the nuts stopped falling, my uncle must have finally noticed that something had happened down below.

The already invisible soldiers probably made no reply. The lieutenant and the men from the Destroyer Battalion, who were lagging somewhat behind him, strode quickly along the top of the ridge. Even over this relatively short stretch it was obvious that the men from the Destroyer Battalion were lagging farther and farther behind their commander.

"Hey, halt!" the lieutenant's voice rang out again. By now no one was visible.

Suddenly—*tra-ta-ta-ta!*—distinct and wild, came a burst of submachine gun fire. In reply came several single shots from a carbine. Once more, *tra-ta-ta-ta!* Once more, several single shots from a carbine. And again, immediately, two long bursts of submachine gun fire.

Then all was still . . . still. The terrible stillness lasted several minutes, but it seemed to me that half an hour had gone by, maybe more. Piercing the foliage with a swish, my uncle's stick flew down from above and landed on its tip, like a spear. My uncle quickly descended from the tree. In a moment he was on the ground.

"Wait here!" he told me, and he started quickly up the slope, taking his hook-blade ax with him.

He climbed to the crest and stopped. For some time he stared in the direction everyone had gone. It seemed to me that he was taking forever. Then he suddenly turned to me, pale in the face, and signaled for me to climb up.

I didn't know whether or not to bring the basket. I picked it up anyway, although it was rather heavy for me, being filled with green walnuts, and lugged it uphill. When I made it to the top and came to stand beside my uncle, I saw the two men from the Destroyer Battalion lugging something in a tarpaulin. Where's the lieutenant, I thought, could he have gone after those soldiers? Not until the next instant, when I saw two carbines over the shoulder of one of the men from the Destroyer Battalion, did I understand that it was he they were carrying.

"Is he alive?" my uncle asked when they walked up to us. One of them shook his head mournfully, and the other said, "May your enemies be as alive as he is . . ."

They were both very pale. I did not see the slain lieutenant's face. It was covered with his service cap. I only noticed how heavily the tarpaulin sagged where the lieutenant's body lay. Death seemed to have added an extra weight to his body.

We climbed uphill. My uncle was in the lead with his light ax on his shoulder, behind him walked the two soldiers from the Destroyer Battalion with their sad burden, and I brought up the rear with my basket, which weighed down first my right shoulder, then my left. Although no one had ordered me to keep up with the others, I walked and walked, drenched in hot sweat and occasionally glancing with irritation at my uncle, who didn't even think to help me.

Just before we emerged from Sabid's Hollow, where the rise was steepest and the walking especially hard, I suddenly noticed a walnut come from somewhere ahead of me on the path and roll downhill. Then a second, and a third . . . And suddenly I guessed that they were falling out of the dead lieutenant's pocket.

Above, at the very brim of the hollow, stood Auntie with all her children and several other peasants who happened to be nearby. They had heard the shots, of course.

"What happened?" Auntie asked in a thick voice.

"The Germans killed our commander," one of the soldiers answered. They carefully laid their burden on the ground.

"The Germans or some other plague," my uncle corrected him. "Now no one will ever know."

"They were parachutists, of course," the second soldier remarked. "Experienced saboteurs—"

"Yes, they had plenty of experience," my uncle said, as if jeering at the soldiers from the Destroyer Battalion.

"His poor mother, his poor, poor mother," my aunt keened.

"Go with them to the village soviet," my uncle told Kunta and another peasant. They nodded, and helped the soldiers from the Destroyer Battalion lift the tarpaulin with the lieutenant's body. Taking a shortcut, they started toward the upper Chegem road.

"Why didn't you invite them in?" my aunt said. "At least for a drink of water."

"They'll manage," my uncle cut her off harshly. "I saw it all."

They had both been cowards, according to him, while the criminals had indeed proved to be experienced men. The reason they didn't stop when the lieutenant first hailed them, according to my uncle, was that there was a pit ten paces ahead. They headed for the pit, and when the lieutenant hailed them the second time, they both instantly leaped into it and began firing their submachine guns. First one of them fired, then both.

As soon as they leaped into the pit, the lieutenant also flung himself on the ground and began firing, but he was in a disadvantageous position relative to them, and they got him with the last burst of submachine gun fire. Seeing that the lieutenant had been killed, and that both the other soldiers had hit the dirt and hadn't raised their heads once, these two got out of the pit and walked backwards along the path about ten paces, until it disappeared into deep forest. Only when convinced that the criminals had gone into the forest did the soldiers from the Destroyer Battalion go to their slain commander.

We were already approaching the house. Auntie was carrying my basket.

"Uncle," I asked, "there's something I can't understand. Why didn't he hail them right off? He let them get away."

I remembered how distinctly visible they were on top of the ridge and how hard it would have been for them to fight the lieutenant if he had lain down by the Prayer Tree.

"I think it was because of you," Uncle answered.

"Why?" I asked blankly.

"Just in case," Uncle said. "He didn't want to risk any extra lives."

"What will happen to those two now?" I asked, meaning the soldiers from the Destroyer Battalion.

"Nothing," Uncle answered. "I expect they'll throw away a dozen cartridges along the road."

"Why?" I asked.

"Why, to make it look as if they'd fought," Uncle said scornfully.

"Leave those poor men alone," Auntie interrupted him, shifting her grip on the basket. "How could they fight? They've never held anything but a hoe in their hands in their whole lives."

"That's just what I mean," Uncle answered, taking a sheet of newspaper from his pocket and tearing off a piece for a cigarette. "What did you think I meant?"

"For God's sake leave them alone," Auntie said.

A bale of tobacco had disappeared from the kolkhoz tobacco shed. The general opinion was that the shepherd Kunta had taken it. Although no one had seen him do it, everyone decided that only he was capable of such a stupid theft.

In the first place, he had stolen tobacco of the very lowest grade, which the Chegemians called by the old-fashioned name of *dip*. This grade of tobacco is obtained from the bottom leaves of the tobacco plant. They are always under-developed, have little juice in them, which is probably why, after drying, they have little of the aroma or other virtues of tobacco.

Then again, they have one indisputable virtue: the priming and drying of the tobacco begins with them, they are the first. So those who have used up last's year's supply of tobacco can start smoking this.

Usually the peasants stocked up on tobacco while it was still drying on the frames. They took a little at a time so that it would not be noticed. But to steal tobacco when it had been baled and inventoried was senseless and foolish. Only Kunta was capable of such folly. So the Chegemians presumed.

Tomorrow or the day after, a cart would arrive from the kolkhoz management and the tobacco would have to be turned over—the deficit would be discovered on the spot. In those menacing war years, people were sent to prison without formality for this kind of thing.

That day, Uncle Kyazym, who was foreman of the field brigade, decided he must expose Kunta at all costs and force him to return the tobacco before the investigative agencies got involved. Uncle Kyazym was not afraid for himself. Any fool could see that he had no reason to steal a lousy bale of this lousy tobacco, which was hardly better than alder leaves. But those wiseacres from Kengur (our family ties with the city give us the right to call it sometimes by its full name of Kengursk, sometimes by the truncated common name, Kengur)— well, the wiseacres from the city (who, incidentally, never truncated its name) were quite capable of putting a man in prison just for the hell of it.

Apart from the simple human pity that Uncle Kyazym felt for the poor shepherd, the wiseacres from the district center did not understand that if they arrested Kunta, there would be no one to take over those mangy goats.

The wiseacres in tussah tunics would neither get a raise for this nor take a cut in pay. Or maybe they would get a raise, who knows. Maybe they too had a plan that they must fulfill and overfulfill. No, Uncle Kyazym decided, do it any way you want, but I won't give you our Kunta.

So thought Uncle Kyazym, walking up to the shepherd's house. A tall, spare man, he walked with care not to brush his legs against the wet grass that hung swollen and heavy over the path.

He did not know yet what he would say or how he would make Kunta return the tobacco before the case got to the kolkhoz management, but he knew that the tobacco had to be returned, and therefore he would find a way to return it.

Yesterday he had talked to him nicely about it, then threatened him; but Kunta dug his heels in and kept saying the same thing over and over: I didn't take it, and if anyone saw, let him prove it. He repeated it over and over intentionally, because he sensed that if he didn't stick to his story Uncle Kyazym would confuse and outwit him.

Uncle Kyazym loved to make fun of Kunta's foolish and ridiculous eccentricities over a good session at table, and sometimes it was hard to tell how much was Kyazym's imagination and how much was the real truth. In any case, Kunta provided so much solid food for the imagination that it was quite impossible to make out where the truth ended and fiction began.

Thus Uncle Kyazym claimed that one time when he was going to the city and inquired whether he could bring Kunta anything, Kunta asked Uncle Kyazym to bring him a photograph. Now, could you invent something like that?

One of Uncle Kyazym's favorite stories was about the time Kunta was working as a postman and got lost during a winter snowstorm, a stone's throw from his own house. He wandered into a barn where Uncle Kyazym kept *chala*—that is, corn straw—and buried himself in it, then lay there for almost twenty-four hours waiting for the storm to blow over.

When Uncle Kyazym came the next morning to get some sheaves of *chala* for the stock, he was very surprised to see Kunta buried in the dry cornstalks. Kunta was even more surprised to see Uncle Kyazym.

"What are you doing here?" Uncle Kyazym asked Kunta.

"Why, are you lost too?" Kunta said, answering a question with a question.

"Like hell I'm lost," Uncle Kyazym replied. "I'm in my own barn . . ."

Uncle Kyazym knew many such stories from Kunta's life. But here is another sadly comic story, which we did not learn by way of Uncle Kyazym.

On the tenth anniversary of the Soviet regime in Abkhazia, certificates and medals were conferred on many men who had been in the Civil War. Poor Kunta went to the village soviet and requested recognition for his son, who had died in the war.

Through other participants in the famous Battle of the Kodor, the village soviet easily established that his son had died fighting against the Bolsheviks, not with them, as poor Kunta thought.

To all appearances, his train of thought was this: Stalin stands at the head of the government. Stalin is a Georgian. Kunta's son fought alongside those who attacked from the direction of Georgia. Since Stalin himself and all the men in power with him call themselves Bolsheviks, those who attacked from the direction of Georgia must have been Bolsheviks too.

The village soviet made an effort to instruct him in the more complex dialectics of the Civil War, but he understood nothing and they finally sent him home, ridiculing his ignorance but not punishing him.

. . . Uncle Kyazym walked up to Kunta's house, opened the gate, and went into the yard. The smoke rose wispy and slow over the kitchen roof, as if reluctant to crawl out of the warm building into this wet, drizzly fall day. It was a long time since Uncle Kyazym had dropped in on Kunta, and he would not soon have done so if this matter hadn't come up.

The dog ran barking to meet him, but he did not even glance its way. It gave another few barks and crawled under the house.

The shepherd's wife, hearing the dog bark, came out of the kitchen and stood in the doorway, shading her eyes with her hand as if trying to make out who it was. She did not call the dog, did not make even a symbolic effort to drive it off, as the mistress has done from time immemorial, and Uncle Kyazym realized that Kunta had told her about yesterday's skirmish.

Still, Kunta's wife did not want to quarrel openly with Uncle Kyazym or show him that she was angry at him, and that was why she continued to peer at him from under her hand as if she didn't recognize him, without quieting the dog, as though wary of a stranger, an outsider. Uncle Kyazym saw through this naive stratagem at once and grinned to himself.

"Where's the master?" he asked when they went into the kitchen. Uncle Kyazym settled down on a low bench by the fire.

"He should be here soon," Kunta's wife answered, standing on the far side of the fire. With a wooden spatula she stirred the cornmeal mixture in the kettle that hung over the flames.

Ignoring the mistress's hostile silence, Uncle Kyazym looked around the kitchen.

In the corner lay a mound of corn, as yet unshucked. Next to the mound stood a large basket of beans, still in the pod. Near it stood a sack of shelled corn. The kitchen was littered with scraped corncobs and empty bean pods. At the head of the open hearth stood a wet and dirty calf, swaying and squinting in the smoke.

Maybe he hid it in the attic, Uncle Kyazym thought, glancing around the kitchen; doesn't look like there's any place else. He could not have hidden anything in the single room adjoining the kitchen, because it was all open and there was nothing in it but two beds and a chest. Either the attic or an inaccessible spot somewhere in the forest, Uncle Kyazym thought. But where?

Behind the house the sound of bells rang out, the bustling commotion of goats being driven home.

"Where do you think you're going? May you be mobilized to cut firewood!" came Kunta's voice, shouting at a goat.

"Hey, I don't see the calf," he shouted to his wife, without changing his tone of voice, "damn your eyes—you've gone running to the cows again!"

"He's in here! Waiting for your funeral!" his wife sang out, unruffled, but she tossed some corncobs on the fire to make the mush boil harder.

It occurred to Uncle Kyazym that Kunta needn't have driven the flock home for dinner, because the fields had all been harvested and there was no fear of the goats' doing any damage. But Kunta did everything out of habit; he drove the flock home in summer when it came time for dinner, and he drove them home now.

Dumping a bundle of firewood by the threshold, Kunta appeared in the doorway. He stood in the doorway for several seconds, small, long-armed, long-legged, holding an ax on his humped shoulder and sucking at his everlasting stinking pipe.

Seeing Uncle Kyazym, he hesitated at the door as if about to walk away. But then he entered the kitchen, leaned the ax against the wall, and, sucking wetly at his pipe, sat down across from Uncle Kyazym. He sat down, spread his hands to the fire, and stared at it in silence, blinking his watery, pale blue eyes.

It occurred to Uncle Kyazym that the weak color of his eyes had something to do with the weakness of his mind. His wet clothes began giving off thick clouds of steam because he was sitting too close to the fire. But Kunta did not think to change his position. He sat as motionless as ever, blinking his little birdlike eyelids, sucking at his squelching pipe. As if made bashful by the big blaze on the hearth, the pipe showed every intention of going out, which Kunta prevented by his tireless pulling and squelching. Finally he took the pipe and scooped an ember out of the fire, whereupon it gave off a thick smoke and the stink of the lowest grade tobacco, *dip*.

"I came to find out if you were planning to go to the mill," Uncle Kyazym said, recalling the sack of corn and letting the shepherd know that he did not intend to pursue yesterday's conversation.

To tell the truth, Uncle Kyazym had just concocted a plan: First choice— return the stolen tobacco and send the shepherd to the mill. Second choice— merely send the shepherd to the mill.

"I should," Kunta said slowly. He glanced at Uncle Kyazym with his weak eyes, trying to figure out what he was driving at.

"You can take my donkey, and my corn too, while you're at it," Uncle Kyazym said.

"All right," the shepherd replied submissively, not even rejoicing that he wouldn't have to lug his corn on his own hump. Although the mill was three kilometers from the village at the bottom of a ravine, he did not see much difference—lug it himself, tramp beside a donkey, either way he would have to walk.

In the past Kunta had lived next door to his brother Omar, who, exercising his rights as a forest warden and a member of the Wild Division, not only made Kunta work for him but also used his wife from time to time, according to the observations of the Chegemians.

Several times in his life Kunta had moved out, meaning to set up on his own for good, but then fate always swept him off his feet and dragged him back to his brother's house, and everything began all over again.

This time, as Uncle Kyazym pointed out, Kunta had set up housekeeping half a kilometer from their settlement in order to be closer to the mill, while forgetting that this put him too far from the spring, the only source of pure water.

Thus, in making his monthly trip to the mill shorter, he made his wife's daily trip for water several times longer. The curses she directed at her husband were several times longer, too, especially when she was returning from the spring, the jug on her shoulder cushioned by a protruding clump of fern.

. . . Now Kunta was waiting alertly to see whether Uncle Kyazym would start asking about the tobacco, but he held his peace, and finally Kunta decided that things had turned out all right somehow, although nothing could turn out all right.

Actually, Uncle Kyazym had decided to eat dinner with the shepherd first and talk later. He sensed that a wet, hungry, and therefore stubborn shepherd would be much harder to deal with. Uncle Kyazym felt there were things he needed to think through before beginning the conversation.

Kunta's wife, a thin, hooknosed woman, was now straining every muscle to stir the stiff cornmeal mixture with the spatula. Uncle Kyazym himself had married them, once upon a time, but both of them had long since forgotten that. Evidently there was too little good in their lives to make it worth remembering.

Any other time, Uncle Kyazym would not likely have sat down to table in this house, because Kunta's wife was a slob and a terrible cook. But now the situation made it necessary, and he had decided to eat dinner with Kunta.

After washing their hands, they sat down at a low table set right by the fire. They ate the cornmeal mush, dipping it in a lima bean sauce. Uncle Kyazym noticed at once that the mush had not been kept on the fire long enough and the beans were slightly scorched.

The hungry Kunta ate with placid greed. Almost without chewing, he swallowed huge chunks of mush with slow, difficult enjoyment. The very fact that the food went down his throat with difficulty clearly added to his enjoyment.

"You might bring some wine," he suddenly remembered in the middle of dinner, glancing uncertainly at his wife. The wife silently went out and brought back some wine in a grimy teapot. Then she found two glasses—also rather dirty, although she did have the sense to put the cleaner one by Uncle Kyazym— and poured the wine.

Does it take much intelligence, Uncle Kyazym thought coldly, to wash glasses? Everything depends on whether a person is from good stock . . . No, that's not all.

Uncle Kyazym sensed that he was not quite right; even though a lot depended on being from good stock, there was something else here. They were accustomed to looking at themselves this way, because it was the way other people looked at them.

He did not let himself finish this thought, because it kept him from thinking of the main issue. He took his glass in hand, trying not to think how bitter it was going to be.

"Abundance to your house!" he said—the usual first toast in such circumstances.

"Thank you," Kunta said, trying to play the experienced host. He waited for Uncle Kyazym to drink, then drank himself.

The wine proved even more bitter than Uncle Kyazym expected. No new regime, no equality, will force Kunta to make good wine, as my father or some of the other peasants do, Uncle Kyazym thought, setting his glass on the table. And if some one person makes it for all? Then it will be better than Kunta's, but worse than good wine, and in the end people will forget good wine. So thought Uncle Kyazym.

"What's the news on your boy?" he asked, taking a languid bite.

"Nothing, so far," Kunta answered with a sigh. His back humped dolefully.

"The time isn't up yet," his wife put in.

Except for the one son who died in the Civil War, Kunta had no children of his own. Twice he had taken in a foster child to bring up, both times unsuccessfully. The first boy, while still a minor, had stolen his cow and vanished forever. The last seven or eight years he had been raising a boy who was a relative of his wife's.

About a month ago the boy had run away from home, making off with some money that Kunta had received from the sale of pigs. When he learned about the theft, Kunta was shaken. He had hidden the money in his mattress. What distressed him most was that he had planned to hide it in the forest but then changed his mind, somehow, and stuck it in his mattress. He had always trusted the forest more than his own house. But here he'd relented toward his house and lost his money.

Kunta had long since cooled toward his foster son, because the boy often made fun of him in front of others, to show them that he did not regard Kunta as his own father: since he himself was laughing at him, he didn't mind when others laughed.

Of course if I'd given the kid a good licking, Kunta thought, I probably could've made a man out of him, but who could lick a bruiser like that.

And now he had run away from home, taking eight hundred rubles that Kunta had hidden in the mattress.

For two weeks Kunta had waited for news from him, but when there wasn't any, he set out for the neighboring village to see the mullah, who had been almost without work for a long time now. At first he wanted to go to Kengursk and bring suit in court. But then he remembered what a lot of papers one needed for the court, remembered that the trip there was many times longer than to the neighboring village, and set out for the mullah's.

Since his wife was from the village where the mullah lived, she went along to make it easier to bargain with him.

After haggling with him a while, they reached an agreement that the mullah would put a curse on the former foster son in return for a hundred pounds of corn from the new harvest.

The terms of the curse were as follows: If the boy did not bring back the money within two months, or at least send it by mail, the hand that had extracted the money from the mattress would wither. The mullah suggested adding another sack of corn and making the oath harsher by having both hands wither.

But Kunta didn't consent to that, and not because he begrudged the corn. He felt it would be too much to deprive the lad of two hands. Kunta was not malicious, he merely wanted justice.

The mullah laid his hand on a sacred stone, similar to an ordinary whetstone, and muttered an incantation in Arabic. Kunta wanted him to translate the incantation into Abkhazian, but then guessed that he couldn't do it, because if he did everyone would penetrate the secrets of his trade.

Still, Kunta would have liked the incantation to be longer. He felt dimly that it did not amount to a hundred pounds of corn. Still, he kept his mouth shut about this, too, and on the way back his wife completely reassured him. The mullah was from her village, and she considered it her duty to praise everything connected with her village.

"Don't give him the corn unless the curse comes true," Uncle Kyazym said, pretending to believe in this venture.

"He's already sent someone to remind us," Kunta sighed.

"How many days to go?" Uncle Kyazym asked, still pretending to believe in the venture.

"It's still two weeks from Monday," Kunta's wife answered at once. She was obviously counting the days.

"How will you learn that the curse has caught up with him, if you don't know where he is?" Uncle Kyazym asked.

"Here's what I think," Kunta said. "He'll come back as soon as his hand starts to wither. Who needs him with a withered hand?"

"You can't say that," Uncle Kyazym remarked. "Bad Hand, there, shouts his way through life even with a withered hand."

"All is in the hands of Allah," Kunta sighed.

"It's a while yet, be patient," Uncle Kyazym said.

He felt suddenly cheerful. He had just realized that after an incident like that the shepherd would not keep the tobacco in his house, he must have hidden it somewhere in the forest. But where could he have hidden it? Of course— somewhere around where he grazed the goats. Most likely in Sabid's Hollow, in some inaccessible spot.

He sensed that he was getting at some point, some thought, most likely a question, by means of which he would trap the shepherd and force him to reveal the spot.

On the rocky summit of the mountain beyond Sabid's Hollow there were many caves. That was probably where he had stuck the bale, in one of the caves. Or was it in the attic after all? One way or the other, he was keeping the tobacco in a dry, inaccessible place . . . In a dry, inaccessible . . . Uncle Kyazym sensed that all it would take was one more shove, the trap would snap shut on this simple fool.

Uncle Kyazym became still more cheerful, and they each drank another two glasses of wine, which didn't seem all that bitter to him now.

Kunta also became cheerful. He had grown warm by the fire, the wine had started his blood moving easily and freely in his body. He decided that if the curse did not come true, he really did not have to give the mullah the corn.

Kunta's wife put the table away and threw the leftover mush to the dog, which had been standing in the doorway, patiently and silently waiting its hour.

Kunta got his pipe from his pocket, where he had stuck it before dinner. He went and sat in his old place, knocked the ashes from the pipe, filled it with tobacco, then took a smoldering brand and lighted up.

Uncle Kyazym wanted to smoke too. He got a sheet of newspaper from his pocket, neatly tore off a piece big enough for a cigarette, worked the paper in his fingers to make it softer, and held it out for Kunta to sprinkle some tobacco on. Kunta took a pinch from his pocket and sprinkled it for Uncle Kyazym to roll a cigarette. Uncle Kyazym had never smoked this kind of tobacco, but he sensed that he'd better do it now. Kunta must interpret his action to mean: Since he's asking me for tobacco, it means he's reconciled to the loss and isn't going to keep on about it or try to persuade me any more.

Sprinkling the tobacco for him, Kunta covertly watched his eyes: Was Uncle Kyazym laughing at him? But no, he didn't seem to be laughing.

The two of them smoked, sitting across from each other, separated by the cozy fire on the domestic hearth and united by the one tobacco they were smoking.

Kunta felt thoroughly reassured. He had been waiting for Uncle Kyazym to start talking the same as yesterday, but he still hadn't started and evidently didn't intend to. Kunta decided that everything had worked itself out, and now he wanted to know how.

"Well now, did you find the tobacco?" he asked, after an especially good, reassuring pull at his pipe.

"Yes, we did," Uncle Kyazym answered unexpectedly, and he looked at Kunta with laughing eyes.

"Where did you find it?" Kunta asked weakly, and he realized that he could never in all his life outwit Uncle Kyazym.

"Where you put it," Uncle Kyazym answered pensively, as if recalling the spot where he had found the hidden tobacco. "The only thing I can't understand is how you ever got it up there without falling . . ."

"I went up the vine," Kunta answered, sighing submissively.

Uncle Kyazym understood instantly what Kunta meant. Of course—he had scrambled up the Prayer Tree and stuck the tobacco in its hollow. Kunta's father had climbed up to gather wild honey in that hollow, once upon a time, and had died there. And now Kunta had hidden his tobacco there.

"That tree has a fatal fascination for your clan," Uncle Kyazym said with a grin. "But how did you lift it up there?"

"With a rope," Kunta answered, sighing bitterly.

He remembered how long it had taken him to get up the vine, how hard it had been to pull the bale of tobacco up, because it kept swinging and getting caught on the boughs. And all in vain. Plainly, he would never outwit this Kyazym. It never entered his head that he had given himself away.

Uncle Kyazym sat a little while longer and then got up. On the way out, he said simply, as a foreman giving a task to a kolkhoz worker, "Bring the tobacco to the shed . . . Watch out you don't get it wet when you let it down."

"Should I bring it now or later?" Kunta asked, getting up and seeing him to the door.

"Late in the day, or someone will see."

Uncle Kyazym snapped out these words without turning around, so as to hide his smile. He was thinking how he would tell his friends about this affair after the dust had settled. He was pleased with himself. It seemed to him that he had outwitted not only Kunta but also the people who would have been glad to throw Kunta in prison.

Late in the day, after he had taken the goats to the kolkhoz pen, Kunta walked to the mill, driving a donkey laden with two sacks of corn—one his, one Uncle Kyazym's.

He had returned the tobacco to the kolkhoz shed, pinching a little from the bale on the way. And now he thought no more about it. He was thinking what to do about the corn that he owed the mullah. He wondered whether there might be some ill effect on the execution of the curse from the fact that he had decided not to give him the corn if the curse didn't come true. He mentally tried to impress on the executor of the curse that he wasn't refusing to give the corn outright, he was refusing to give it only if the curse didn't happen. He tried to make his thoughts about this as distinct as possible, so that He who was in charge, or whoever had been entrusted with executing the curse, would understand him right.

But if the curse didn't come true, Kunta decided, not only wouldn't he give the mullah the corn, he'd file a complaint against him with the village soviet.

Kunta knew that the village soviet had no love for such men; he had only to file a complaint and they would act on it. He did not know exactly why the village soviet had no love for them, but he vaguely sensed that the village soviet didn't want to share with them its power over people.

Kunta filled his pipe with tobacco. With a steel he struck a spark from his flint, raised the smoldering tinder to the tobacco, and puffed at his pipe. The pipe smoked, but he pulled and pulled, inhaling the stinking *dip* tobacco in voluptuous gasps, until he was sure the pipe wouldn't go out.

He quickened his steps, because the donkey had gone on ahead while he was lighting up.

Thirty years after the events I have been describing, Uncle Sandro and I rode into Chegem on horses that we had procured in the neighboring village of Dzhgerdy, which we had reached by bus.

I knew that none of my close friends or relatives were here any more: some had died, some had moved to the city, some to more prosperous lowland villages.

Where the forest path along which we rode entered Chegem, there stood a tractor. Near it lay a huge log, a monstrous section cut from a beech trunk. Slightly downhill from here—actually within the boundaries of our family settlement—in the top of an old alder tree with a grapevine twined around it, two men sat eating grapes. The grapeskins were plopping on the leaves as they fell.

"Who are you?" I asked, riding up to the foot of the tree.

"We're loggers," they answered from the tree.

"Where from?" Uncle Sandro asked.

"We're Huzuls," was the reply.

Uncle Sandro did not understand what Huzuls were. When I explained to him, he marveled at the remoteness of the region the loggers came from, and he asked me, "Did they really have to come all the way to Chegem to find logs?"

"Apparently so," I answered.

We were already near my grandfather's house, and I felt my excitement rising. There it was, the old apple tree, already visible from the road . . . There were the two gigantic walnut trees—the higher one stood on the rise behind Grandfather's house, and the lower one right by the barnyard.

But neither the barnyard nor Grandfather's house was there; all that remained was a green vacant lot with someone's cows grazing on it. We rode over to the apple tree, dismounted, and tied the horses to the thick grapevine that climbed up the tree.

Of Grandfather's house there remained not a scrap, not a trace. Where the house had stood, as everywhere, was a level carpet of grass. But in one spot the grass was a little thicker and brighter, and we could guess that this was where the kitchen hearth had been.

After Uncle Kyazym's death, none of our people were left in this part of Chegem. His wife, Aunt Noutsa, moved to the city to be with her sons.

When the doctors in Mukhus suspected that Uncle Kyazym had cancer, I took him to Moscow. There they spent several days giving him every imaginable test, taking X-rays, and finally a woman professor received us in her office. Leafing through pages of test results, she said there was nothing to worry about, their worst suspicions had not been confirmed.

Joyfully I translated everything she said for Uncle Kyazym, but his handsome, stern face showed nothing. He was pleased at her words, of course, but he considered it unworthy to rejoice openly over his own life.

When we were walking out of the office, a second woman doctor, who had sat silently beside the professor, inconspicuously crowded me aside. My uncle walked out, and I remained in the office.

"Unfortunately, it was all confirmed," the professor said. "He has no more than six months to live."

Staggered by this plunge from hope to a death sentence, I walked out of the office and rejoined my uncle. I don't know whether he guessed. At all events, I pretended nothing had happened.

We walked by a kiosk where they were selling watermelons. We bought one and stopped in a public park to eat it, cutting it with my uncle's knife.

In Moscow, with characteristic reserve, my uncle was surprised at nothing, accepted everything as fitting; he was surprised only at the complete absence of mountains and patiently awaited our departure.

In six months he was gone. I loved this man and had admired him since childhood, without especially understanding the nature of my admiration. I saw him at home in the village, in his native milieu; saw him in the city among strangers; and everywhere he was himself—never ingratiating, always benevolently derisive. Now, trying to find the words to capture the essence of the man, I can only say that one felt in him an extraordinary spiritual importance.

At table in the city, among people he hardly knew, he did not feel conspicuous and awkward, as peasants often do; on the contrary, he seemed to be a disguised King Lear, sitting among beggarly Philistines.

Where did it come from, this perpetual easy scorn for food (any food); this ability to listen to his companion without anticipating his thought and butting in; the nobility with which he let his companion's commonplaces pass, while seizing on and developing the fragments of wit, of keen observation, in other people's speech; and the gentle urgency with which he always asserted what he considered right.

I was there once when he was making some repairs in the tobacco shed, and an airplane came out of the pass with a terrible roar, flying very low directly overhead.

"How come the pilot doesn't go deaf," said a peasant standing nearby, "when he even deafens us?"

"Evidently the plane outstrips its own sound," Uncle said, after thinking a moment. "That's why the pilot doesn't hear it so loud."

Although there were no planes that outstripped their own sound in those days, this was said by an illiterate man who signed his name with an *X*, who had never known iron in any form more complex than an ordinary plow.

"Every blade of grass is cattle, you know," he said another time, with piercing sorrow. It was because of that piercing sorrow that I remembered the phrase. And now, recalling it as an adult, I can guess at the reason he said it, guess how much suffering and reflection lay behind it.

. . . Uncle Sandro and I went down to our famous spring. The stream of water that once beat from under the cliff as thick as a man's arm had become a barely discernible rivulet. To drink from it, we had to touch our lips to the pebbles at the bottom. And the water! Was it really that same icy crystal stream?

We might have expected that the spring would decline, become choked, with no one to tend it, but why the water had grown warm I cannot understand.

It was because of this spring, which my grandfather discovered, that he had chosen this spot to live and had begun a new life here.

We climbed back up and decided to go down to Sabid's Hollow, looking in on our family burial ground on the way. But we did not succeed in doing that, because the burial ground was overgrown with an impenetrable wall of brambles. With what rapacious swiftness nature reclaims lands once won from her!

From where we stood, we could clearly see an ivy-covered segment of a fortress, a remnant of the Great Wall of Abkhazia. As children, playing by that fortress wall, we had dug up the bones of people buried there in ancient times.

And who knows who will arrive in Chegem some day, as our grandfather did once, to clear a piece of land where our graves lie now. By that time there will be no trace of them, and only the man's children, playing as we did once, will dig up from the tilth the bones of our loved ones, marveling and wondering what kind of people once lived here.

We went down into Sabid's Hollow. The grassy slope where the Prayer Tree had stood in the old days was now overgrown almost to the top with a stand of young alder. The Prayer Tree had fallen, probably from old age. Its gigantic trunk stretched downward to the very bottom of the hollow, into the gloom of the Caucasian jungle.

I clambered up on the trunk and began walking down it, in some places bending its thick branches back. I walked about fifty meters like this, and the farther I went, the harder it got, because the brambles swarmed over the tree on all sides.

Around me the trunks of chestnuts, beeches, hornbeams, wild persimmons rose like a dense wall, entwined with lianas and brambly blackberries. In the air hung the twitter of birds and the powerful twin smells of flourishing and rotting wood-flesh.

Somewhere quite close sounded the roebuck's short bark of alarm. I unslung my carbine and peered into the impenetrable green gloom, where the roebuck's voice had come from. Several times more the roebuck barked in alarm, his voice spooky, but it looked impossible to get down from the trunk and force my way through the entangling, hobbling growth. I turned around and climbed back up the trunk to the foot of the Prayer Tree, where Uncle Sandro was waiting for me.

We went back up to Grandfather's yard. In the middle of the yard the unfamiliar cows were still grazing. A cowbell tinkled—the biblical sound of life and desolation.

I unslung my carbine, laid it on the ground, took off my shoes, and climbed the apple tree to pick grapes. Uncle Sandro went to the spring to water the horses. Presently I heard someone hail me from below. It was Kunta. He didn't recognize me, of course. A small flock of goats came pouring into the yard.

His voice none too confident, Kunta asked me not to touch the grapes, since the kolkhoz had granted him the right to pick them here on this former private allotment. I told him that the grapes wouldn't be diminished by my eating a few bunches, and he said there'd be nothing left of the grapes if every passing traveler picked them.

We argued peaceably for a while, and in the end, when I had eaten my fill of grapes, I climbed down from the tree. Kunta was sitting at the foot of the tree. Next to him stood a charming little boy in picturesque rags, a dark-eyed little eastern Christ figure.

"Don't you know me, Kunta?" I asked him.

"Pardon me, I didn't recognize you," Kunta answered, peering at me with his weak, pale blue eyes.

I gave my name. Recognizing me, he was somewhat embarrassed that he had forbidden me to pick my grandfather's grapes. Surprisingly, he had not changed over the last fifteen years; if anything, he looked better. The angular leanness had disappeared, and his face had filled out a little and become more agreeable to the eye.

"How old are you?" I asked Kunta.

"A hundred and three," he answered me.

"And is your brother still living?" I asked him.

"Still living," Kunta answered. "What could happen to him?"

"How old is he?" I asked.

"Brother's a hundred and six," he answered.

"Do you live with him?" I asked.

"No," he answered, not without pride. "I've been on my own for ten years now."

"Whose boy is that?" I asked, looking at the little boy, who was hiding behind Kunta's back and watching me with big dark eyes.

"I've taken him on as a foster child," Kunta answered. "A relative of my wife's."

I beckoned the child to me, but he shook his head, keeping behind Kunta's back. Then I took a five-ruble bill from my pocket and held it out to him, following the local custom of giving children money.

The boy sensibly roused himself. His lips, bright enough already, blazed; breathing heavily, he slowly came near me, snatched the money in his grubby little hand, and disappeared behind his guardian's back again.

"You might at least say thank you," Kunta remarked to him, but the boy said nothing, his big dark eyes peeping out from behind Kunta's back.

"What's the news?" Kunta asked shyly after a short silence. "The One That Meant to Do Good but Didn't Have Time—have they committed him to the earth?"

"No," I said.

Uncle Sandro came uphill with the horses. Kunta greeted him and said for us to go down to his brother's house; he himself would drive his goats there, he wouldn't be long.

Half an hour later Uncle Sandro and I rode up to the former forest warden's house. Dismounting by the gate, I noticed a magnificent chestnut horse in a little pen, his tail for some reason clipped like a lion's little broom.

At the dog's bark, the master came out of the house and approached us, shading his eyes with his hand.

"Is that you, Sandro?" he said in a shrill voice from about ten paces away.

"Yes, it's me," Uncle Sandro answered.

"And who's that with you?" he asked in the same shrill voice, although by now he was quite close to us.

"My nephew," Uncle Sandro answered.

"Not the one that settled in Moscow?" he asked, peering at me sharply and taking the reins from us.

"The very one," Uncle Sandro answered.

Omar tied our horses to the side of the house. Behind the house we saw a whole city of beehives. There were a great many, no fewer than a hundred of the hollowed-out logs.

I looked at Omar. Just like Kunta, he had not grown old over the last thirty

years but had even come to be better-looking. His face had even filled out a
little, although he still looked to be spare of build.

Long ago, very early in my childhood, I had visited their house when his first
wife was still alive. A soldier in the World War, he had brought his bride from
Poland as a sixteen-year-old girl. She spoke Abkhazian with an impenetrable
accent and whitewashed her kitchen like a Ukrainian hut. The Chegemians
chuckled good-naturedly at her accent and her white kitchen.

After the death of his first wife, he did not remarry for a long time; only when
he had reached a ripe old age did he take a second wife. But recently, unable
to bear his cranky ways, his wife had left him to go back to her village. Kunta
had told us about this.

"Come on up," our host suggested, and let us go ahead. My glance fell on
the stone steps and my heart contracted. They were the steps from my grandfather's house, and every hollow and crack in those white stones was familiar
as the wrinkles on a beloved face. The person who bought the house must have
taken away everything but the steps, and then the indefatigable Omar had carried
them off and fitted them to his own house.

"Folly climbs our steps," Uncle Sandro said to me quietly, nodding toward
the stairs.

"There's a little favor you could do for me, Sandro," our host said when we
had settled down on the veranda.

"What is it?" Uncle Sandro asked.

"Give me time, I'll tell you," the host answered. He went to the kitchen to
fix us something to eat.

Having driven his goats up to the gate, Kunta appeared with his foster son.
Our host put his brother to work turning the dried meat on the spit over the fire,
while he himself made the cornmeal mush.

They brought the steaming plates of mush to the veranda, along with the
sizzling meat, and put them on the table. Then our host brought from the
storeroom a big plate of honey still in the comb, *churkhcheli*, and a decanter of
fiendishly strong *chacha*.

Kunta waited on table, pouring *chacha* for us and serving pieces of meat,
very salty and very good. The little boy, his big dark eyes flashing, put in his
mouth now a chunk of honeycomb, now a chunk of roast meat. Uncle Sandro
appealed to Kunta several times to sit down at the table, but Kunta was too
modest and continued to wait on us.

"Leave him alone," the master of the house shouted. "He'll gorge himself
yet, don't worry!"

The favor that Omar had requested concerned his runaway wife. He began in
a roundabout way, saying that he was no longer a boy, to eat any old thing fixed
any old way; he was a man getting on in years, he needed a person who could
prepare and serve his food for him. He had a wife, but he must have failed to
gain the upper hand over her, and she had gone home to the village of Atary.
Despite the fact that he had secretly dispatched men of substance to her relatives

to shame them into sending her back, she had not returned. All this was causing him a lot of trouble and incalculable losses. Uncle Sandro promised to find a diplomatic way to the hearts of his runaway wife and her relatives.

Somewhat reassured as to the future of his family life, the old man cheered up and began recounting his military exploits during the First World War. He had served in the Wild Division, and as he told it, they had fought on many fronts, inspiring terror in their enemies. As he told it, they had fought well in all countries; only in Hungary, he said, had they become very angry and refused to fight, because there they were promised feed for the horses but it wasn't issued. To make this more convincing, he fetched his saber, unsheathed it, and rather unceremoniously brandished it over our heads, demonstrating how the men of the Wild Division, and he himself, had sliced their enemies in half.

I asked him how he had managed to make the young Polish girl fall so deeply in love with him that she forever abandoned her native land and came to Abkhazia. He got angry at me for some reason and answered, How could she have fallen in love with him, when he was forty and she sixteen: he had taken her by force!

After a while we finished the *chacha* in the decanter, and the old man sent me to the back room, explaining that I would find a cask and a tube there. The natural thing would have been for him to send Kunta to get the brandy, but he sent me. I realized that he did not admit Kunta to the key positions in his household.

The cask of brandy rested on a squat bench. I got down on my haunches, pulled the bung from the cask, stuck the tube in, and made several efforts to draw a stream from it, but the stream wouldn't start. I understood that I was supposed to suck the brandy out in several big swallows and then set the decanter under it. But the brandy was too strong, and I managed to choke before the liquid got flowing. The little stream that I drew out proved too feeble and quickly ran dry.

Omar finally came himself and said, "You poor fool!" He squatted down to the keg, took the tube in his mouth, sucked the brandy into him with several strong swallows, and a steady stream began flowing into the decanter. I felt myself shamed.

Two hours later we mounted our sorry nags. Omar opened the gate and let us out, calling to Uncle Sandro, "That favor—don't forget that little favor!"

As we rode out of Chegem and started up the forest path, Uncle Sandro turned and looked back. Thinking of all those who had died or had left Chegem, as well as all who remained there, he said, "The cow shed has gone to the worst cow . . ."

Well, that's how it is, I thought. When all that we have loved slips away from us, all that has shone to us with the light of hope, courage, tenderness, nobility, when all of that slips away from us, I am ready to clasp even folly to my breast, because folly, too, is a part of man. More than that, I am ready to fall down before her with filial sorrow. She has seen with her own eyes, heard with her own ears all those whom we have lost, and it is not for me to disparage the last witness of our life.

So ended our last trip to Chegem. We will not soon remember it now, but if we do, we will not likely speak of it.

ABKHAZIA:
A SELECTIVE
HISTORICAL OUTLINE

Sixth century B.C.

The Greeks colonize Abkhazia, a Caucasian land then known as Colchis, at the eastern end of the Black Sea. Their cities—especially Dioscurias, modern Sukhum—grow to be prosperous trade centers.

First century B.C.

The Romans build fortifications at Sukhum. Roman writers comment on the longevity of the indigenous hunters and shepherds.

Third century A.D.

Abkhazia begins to develop a form of feudalism based on the patriarchal clan system.

523 A.D.

Abkhazia becomes a vassal of the Byzantine Empire, accepts Christianity. The city of Pityunt (modern Pitsunda) becomes a bishopric.

780–978

The Kingdom of Abkhazia enjoys a brief flowering before being absorbed by its powerful neighbor to the east, Georgia.

1578

Abkhazia falls to the Ottoman Empire, accepts Islam, although traces of Christianity and paganism endure. The country enters a period of economic decay, since the Turks use it primarily as a source of cattle and slaves.

Eighteenth century

In alliance with Georgia, Abkhazia makes repeated efforts to drive out the Turks.

1810	The prince of Abkhazia seeks and receives formal Russian protection, although the highland tribesmen resist "infidel" czarist rule.
1840s	After a series of revolts, Abkhazian peasants begin emigrating, deluded by promises of wealth and religious tolerance in Turkey.
1860s	Abkhazia is annexed outright by the Russian Empire; a major rebellion is crushed; the ancient fortress at Sukhum is converted to a prison. Mass emigrations reach their peak.
1880s	Emigrants begin returning in small numbers to reclaim deserted Abkhazian villages.
1905	The abortive revolution in Russia sparks a wave of violence in the Caucasus; many socialists are imprisoned at Sukhum.
February 1917	Following the February Revolution in Russia, a Menshevik government takes over in Transcaucasia (the area including Abkhazia, Georgia, Azerbaidzhan, and Armenia).
October 1917	Lenin and the Bolsheviks take over the Soviet government in Leningrad.
April 1918	The Menshevik government in Transcaucasia declares its independence from the U.S.S.R.
May 1918	The Battle of the Kodor ends in victory for the Mensheviks, a major success in their struggle for control of Transcaucasia.
1921	The Red Army regains Transcaucasia after heavy fighting; Abkhazia is now a republic of the U.S.S.R., headed by Nestor Lakoba.
1922–23	Lenin, gravely weakened by a stroke, writes a secret "Testament" warning of the dangers of a split between Trotsky and Stalin. In his last year of life he opposes certain of Stalin's policies, including his treatment of national minorities.
1924	Lenin dies. Trotsky, on the Black Sea coast recuperating from a fever, is not informed of the funeral arrangements. Stalin moves to seize power.
1929	The collectivization of agriculture begins, over widespread resistance in Abkhazia.
1931	Abkhazia is reduced to the status of an administrative unit within Georgia, although Lakoba remains president of its Central Executive Committee until his death in 1936.

1936–38	Stalin's purge is carried out in the Transcaucasus by Beria.
1942–43	The Germans invade Abkhazia, aiming for the North Caucasian oil fields.
1948	Tito's revolt against Stalin and a rise in nationalist sentiments among other ethnic groups lead to a renewed period of terror in the U.S.S.R., with many groups being resettled to areas remote from their traditional homelands.
1953	Stalin dies, Khrushchev takes over.
1956	At the Twentieth Party Congress, Khrushchev denounces the cult of personality surrounding Stalin and inaugurates a period of liberalization.
c. 1960	To curb profiteering in bay leaves by private growers, Khrushchev advises the chief of the Party in Georgia to buy only from state farms.
1964	Khrushchev is ousted, succeeded by Brezhnev and Kosygin.
October 1972	Shevarnadze, newly appointed Party chief in Georgia, begins a severe crackdown on corruption in commerce, construction, and government.

GLOSSARY

NOTE: Foreign words, except where otherwise indicated, are common to several Caucasian or Middle Eastern Languages.

The surnames of the various ethnic groups living in Abkhazia have distinctive endings: Abkhazian, *-ba;* Armenian, *-ian, -yan;* Georgian, *-dze, -iani, -shvili;* Mingrelian *-aya, -ia, -ua;* Russian, *-in, -ov, -sky.* (The ending *-ovich* occurs not in surnames but in patronymics, which people use in combination with the first name as a polite form of address when speaking Russian.)

Although place names have been omitted from the glossary, the places mentioned in the text are (or were) real. The exceptions are the districts of Kenguria and Enduria, with their respective central cities, Kengursk and Endursk. The latter name derives from the Russian root *dur-,* "fool." The name Mukhus is an anagram for Sukhum, the capital of Abkhazia.

The spelling *kh* represents a gritty *h*-sound, something like the *ch* in "loch" or "chutzpah."

ABREK A rebel outlaw; originally, a member of one of the guerrilla bands formed by Caucasian highlanders to resist the rule of czarist Russia in the nineteenth century.

AJIKA A very hot condiment made of ground walnuts, garlic, red pepper, and other spices.

ALLAVERDY To your health!

AMAUSOLEUM Local Abkhazian pronunciation of *mausoleum.*

ANASINI (Turkish) Literally, "his/her mother"; used as a general term of abuse.

ANDREEVNA, SOFYA Wife of Leo Tolstoy (q.v.).

ANTI-PARTY GROUP   A loose coalition of old Stalinist leaders who tried to unseat Khrushchev (q.v.) and were dismissed in 1957.

ARAKI   A strong liquor distilled from various fruits, used as an aperitif.

ASHIPKA   (Russian; properly spelled *oshibka*) Mistake. The word passed easily into the Abkhazian language because the initial *o* is pronounced *a*, and all Abkhazian nouns begin with an *a*.

AYRAN   A mixture of yogurt and water.

BERIA, LAVRENTY (1899–1953)   Chief of security in Georgia, 1921–31; first secretary of the Party in the Transcaucasus, 1931–38; became head of the Soviet secret police, then minister for internal affairs; executed for conspiracy in 1953.

BOLSHEVIKS   After 1903, the majority wing of the Russian Communist party, led by Lenin.

BORZHOM   Sparkling mineral water from Borzhomi, in Georgia.

BUNIN, IVAN (1870–1953)   Russian poet and novelist, Nobel laureate (1933); his greatness is recognized in the U.S.S.R. despite his hostility to the revolution of 1917.

BURKA   The Russian name for the long felt cloak traditionally worn by Caucasian men. The Abkhazian version is usually black, very full, with broad boxy shoulders.

CHACHA   A strong liquor distilled from grape pressings.

CHADOR   The long dark veil worn by some Muslim women.

CHAYKA   An eight-cylinder Soviet car, the social equivalent of a Cadillac.

CHEKA   (Russian) Acronym for a notorious special unit of the Soviet secret police, 1917–22.

CHERKESKA   The Russian name for the coat traditionally worn by Caucasian highlanders. It is usually calf-length, collarless, closely fitted to the waist, with a row of polished cartridge cases stitched across the chest. The usual color was black, although other colors—especially red—are now used by folk ensembles.

CHOCHMEH   (Yiddish) Joke, wise remark.

CHUREK   Unleavened bread, baked in flat rounds.

CHURKHCHELI   A snack made by stringing walnut meats, candying them in grape syrup, and hanging them to dry.

CIRCASSIANS   A people of the Northern Caucasus.

COUNCIL OF MINISTERS   Since 1946, the appointed executive and administrative body of the U.S.S.R., or of one of its member republics.

COUNCIL OF PEOPLE'S COMMISSARS   From 1917 to 1946, the appointed governing body of the U.S.S.R., or of one of its member republics.

DEPUTY   An elected representative of the people to a Soviet of Workers' Deputies, the local governmental unit of the U.S.S.R.

DESTROYER BATTALION   A civilian militia raised to help repel the German invasion of Abkhazia during World War II.

DIABOLOS   (Greek) Devil.

-DJAN   (Armenian) An affectionate term of address: "dear."

DYNAMO   A Soviet government-run athletic association, with about a thousand sports facilities nationwide.

DZHIGIT   A type of Caucasian horseman, noted for a daring, showy riding style.

ENGELS, FRIEDRICH (1820–1895)   German socialist, Marx's collaborator.

GENIOKHS The medieval name for a group of small ethnic and tribal units on the northeast shore of the Black Sea.

GMADLOB (Georgian) Thank you.

GOGOL, NIKOLAI (1809–1852) Russian author, famous especially for his novel *Dead Souls*, which features the characters Nozdrev, Plyushkin, and Sobakevich.

GORKY, MAXIM (1868–1936) Russian novelist, playwright, biographer.

GÖTFERAN (Turkish) Homosexual.

GREAT WALL OF ABKHAZIA Built in the sixth century A.D. to keep out marauding northern tribes.

GULIA, DMITRY (1874–1960) Educator, historian, national poet of Abkhazia, founder of Abkhazian literature.

HALVA A sweet made of nuts or sesame seeds and honey.

HUZULS Ukrainian inhabitants of the Carpathians, in eastern Europe.

JEZVE A small, narrow-necked, long-handled Turkish coffeepot made of brass or enamel.

KARTVELI A collective name for the ancient group of tribes—Karts, Mingrelians, Svans, and Laz—who made up the Georgian nation.

KATSO (Georgian) Man; as form of address, "friend."

KAVKAZISCH (German; properly, *Kaukasisch*) Caucasian. The misspelling represents a natural mistake for a Russian speaker, because the Russian name for the Caucasus is *Kavkaz*.

KEN DREPESE (Greek, evidently a dialectical variant, equivalent to Modern Greek *den drepese*) Shame on you!

KGB State Security Committee, the contemporary Soviet secret police agency.

KHACHAPURI Caucasian cheese-filled pastry made for special occasions.

KHAZARS A Turkic people who from the eighth to tenth centuries controlled a great empire in the Volga region, stretching from Kiev to the Urals, and south to the Black and Caspian seas.

KHRUSHCHEV, N.S. (1894–1971) First secretary of the Communist party, 1953–64; premier of the U.S.S.R., 1958–64; presided over a period of liberalization in internal politics; was ousted in 1964.

KHRUSHCHIT Local Abkhazian pronunciation of Khrushchev's name.

KHURJIN A Middle Eastern saddlebag.

KOLKHOZ (Russian) Collective farm.

KOMSOMOL (Russian) Young Communists' League, for ages fourteen to twenty-five.

KOSYGIN, A.N. (1904–1980) Succeeded Khrushchev as Soviet premier in 1964; attempted economic reforms to increase the efficiency of industry and raise the people's standard of living.

KOUMISS A fermented beverage usually made from mare's milk.

KUMKHOZ Local Abkhazian pronunciation of *kolkhoz* (q.v.).

KVASS (Russian) A fermented and slightly alcoholic Russian beverage made from bread.

LAKOBA, NESTOR APOLLONOVICH (1893–1936) President of the Abkhazian Council of People's Commissars from 1922, president of the Abkhazian Central Executive Committee 1930–36.

LAZ An ancient Caucasian tribe, eastern neighbors of the Abkhazians.

LENIN See ULYANOV.

LEZGINKA   A Caucasian dance.

LOMONOSOV-LAVOISIER LAW   The law of the conservation of matter, credited in the West to the French chemist Lavoisier (1743–1794), and in the U.S.S.R. to M.V. Lomonosov (1711–1765), a Russian scientist and man of letters.

LONGO, LUIGI (1900–80)   President of the Italian Communist party from 1972.

LUCULLUS (c.110 B.C.–56 B.C.)   Roman general; forced Mithridates the Great to retreat into Armenia, then besieged and took the Armenian capital, Tigrankert.

LUMUMBA, PATRICE (1925–1961)   Led the Belgian Congo (now Zaire) to independence; served as its first president; was murdered in the chaos following a mutiny and Belgian intervention.

MARX, KARL (1818–1883)   German socialist; author, with Engels (q.v.), of *Communist Manifesto* and *Das Kapital*.

MEIR, GOLDA (1898–1978)   Prime minister of Israel, 1969–74.

MENSHEVIKS   After 1903, the minority wing of the Russian Communist party; opposed to Lenin; held power in Transcaucasia, 1917–21.

MIKOYAN, A. I. (1895–1978)   Soviet statesman of Armenian descent; served in various offices from 1924 to 1976, holding positions of power under both Stalin and Khrushchev.

MINGRELIANS   An ethnic group living in Abkhazia and western Georgia.

MOROZOVA, F. P. (d. 1675)   A Russian *Boyarynya*, or noblewoman, who represented the spirit of the people in opposing a set of seemingly alien church reforms; in a famous painting by Surikov (q.v.), she is shown making the sign of the cross as she is dragged off to prison.

MZHAVANADZE, V. P. (b. 1902)   First secretary of the Georgian Communist party, 1953–72.

NARZAN   A sparkling mineral water found in the Caucasus.

NICHOLAS II (1868–1918)   Emperor of Russia, 1894–1917; executed with his family in 1918.

NKVD   People's Commissariat of Internal Affairs, the Soviet security agency, 1934–41; predecessor to the KGB.

OLDENBURGSKY, ALEXANDER PETROVICH   A Russian nobleman descended from the German house of Oldenburg; opened a health resort at Gagra on the Black Sea coast in 1903.

PARTISANS   Communist guerrilla bands, especially those active in the Revolution of 1917 and in German-occupied territories during World War II.

PARTY SCHOOL   One of the special schools of higher education designed to train Communist party leaders.

PEOPLE'S COMMISSAR   See COUNCIL OF PEOPLE'S COMMISSARS.

PETER I (the Great, 1672–1725)   Czar of Russia from 1682, emperor 1721–25; famous for his attempts to westernize Russian government and culture. Among his favorites was a black Abyssinian prince, Ibrahim Hannibal, who had been purchased as a slave at the Constantinople bazaar and sent to the court as a gift; Peter eventually made him a general.

PETROSIAN, TIGRAN (b. 1929)   Soviet chess master of Armenian descent; lost the world crown to Boris Spassky in 1969.

POBEDA   A medium-sized 52-horsepower Soviet car, produced between 1946 and 1958.

PRIESTLEY, J. B. (b. 1894)   English novelist, playwright, social critic.

RAYKIN, ARKADY (b. 1911)   A gifted Leningrad actor specializing in satirical character sketches.

ROYSON, ROY   This character suggests the distinguished black American singer Paul Robeson (1898–1976), a Communist, whose interest in visiting Abkhazian blacks was reported in the Soviet press in 1958.

RUSTAVELI, SHOTA   Twelfth-century Georgian statesman, author of the epic poem "Knight in the Tigerskin."

SATSIVI   A spicy walnut sauce.

SCYTHIANS   A nomadic Iranian people famed for their skill in metalworking who in the first millennium B.C. dominated most of what is now southern Russia. The Russians are sometimes thought of as heirs to the Scythian civilization.

SERGO (G. K. ORDZHONIKIDZE, 1886–1937)   Georgian Communist, hero of the revolutions of 1905 and 1917 in the Caucasus; tried to halt Stalin's purges in the late 1930s. He is said to have committed suicide in disillusionment.

SHASHLYK   Meat chunks (usually lamb), skewered with onion and broiled.

SHEVARNADZE, E. A. (b. 1928)   First secretary of the Georgian Communist party since 1972.

SOĞUK-SU (Turkish)   Ice-cold water.

SOVIET (Russian)   An elected council.

STALIN (Iosif V. Dzhugashvili, 1879–1953)   A Georgian, active in revolutionary politics from the 1890s; people's commissar for nationalities, 1921–23; seized power after Lenin's death in 1924, making himself a dictator.

STENDHAL (1783–1842)   Great French novelist; also the author of a psychological study of love (1822).

SURIKOV, V. I. (1848–1916)   Russian painter of historical subjects, especially famous for his moving depiction of the dissident noblewoman Morozova (q.v.).

SVANKA   The Russian name for a small round felt cap with decorative stitching, originally Svanian, now often worn by Abkhazian men.

SVANS   An isolated tribe of the high mountain valleys of the Caucasus. Their remarkable tower-houses, which kept them from being buried in the deep snow of winter, also gave them a reputation as being always on the watch for enemies. Their language, still unwritten, is related to Georgian.

TABAKA   Spicy Georgian fried chicken. The dish requires a very young chicken, flattened and fried under a weight.

TAMADA   Head of the table, toastmaster. Always a skillful speaker, a master of ritual, an indefatigable drinker, and an expert in human nature.

TIGRAN II (the Great, c. 140–55 B.C.)   King of Armenia, c. 95–55 B.C.; founded a new royal city, Tigrankert, which was besieged and taken by the Romans under Lucullus in 69–68 B.C. Tigran surrendered to Pompey in 66 B.C. and thereafter ruled as a vassal of Rome.

TOLSTOY, LEO (1828–1910)   Great Russian novelist, whose idealistic beliefs made him the object of a cult. For reasons that are not entirely clear, his last act was to flee from his home, and he died in a railroad station.

TROTSKY, LEON (1879–1940)   Russian revolutionary, held several positions of power after 1917. He was in the Caucasus at the time of Lenin's death and lost out to Stalin in the struggle for control. Banished in 1929 for "anti-Party activities," he was assassinated in Mexico.

TSALDA   Caucasian long-handled light ax with a hooked blade, used for clearing thickets.

TSHOMBE, MOISE (1919–1969)   Led the province of Katanga in its brief secession from the Congo Republic (now Zaire) in 1960; seen as a pawn of European commercial interests; implicated in the death of Lumumba (q.v.).

TWENTIETH CONGRESS   The 1956 Party congress at which Khrushchev gave his "secret speech" denouncing Stalin and the cult of personality.

TWENTY-SECOND CONGRESS   The 1961 Party congress, at which Khrushchev denounced many of the Anti-Party Group (q.v.).

UBYKHS   An ethnic group related in language and culture to the Abkhazians. They lived on the Black Sea near Sochi until 1864, when they were moved to Turkey.

ULYANOV, A. I. (1866–1887)   Older brother of Lenin; member of a Marxist-oriented terrorist group. His plot to assassinate the reactionary Czar Alexander III was discovered, and he was hanged with his co-conspirators.

ULYANOV, V. I. (LENIN, 1870–1924)   Russian Communist; son of a teacher; twice banished to Siberia for revolutionary activities; went into exile in Switzerland, 1900; became leader of the Bolsheviks, 1903; returned in 1917 to assume leadership of the revolution.

VOLGA   A medium-sized, 98-horsepower Soviet car, manufactured since 1957.

VOROSHILOV, KLIMENTY (1881–1969)   Fought alongside Stalin in the revolution; commanded Leningrad front in World War II; president of the U.S.S.R., 1953–60.

WILD DIVISION   World War I Russian army unit drawn from warlike southern tribesmen.

YASNAYA POLYANA   Tolstoy's estate, near Tula.

YESENIN, S. A. (1895–1925)   Russian lyric poet of peasant origin. Turned against the revolution; married Isadora Duncan; separated from her; committed suicide.

ZHIGULI   A light, four-cylinder Soviet car manufactured since 1970.

ABOUT THE AUTHOR

FAZIL ISKANDER, who was born in 1929, is one of the Soviet Union's most popular writers. A native of Abkhazia, an autonomous republic in the Caucasus, he has lived and worked in Moscow for over two decades, though he returns frequently to his homeland. He is widely considered the preeminent example of a non-Russian writing in Russian and making a permanent contribution to Soviet multinational literature.

Iskander began his career as a poet, but it is his fiction that has won him fame. *The Goatibex Constellation*, the best known of his novels published in the U.S.S.R., was brought out in the United States by Ardis in 1975. *Sandro of Chegem*, the series of interconnected tales that is Iskander's major work, has been published by Vintage Books in two volumes, titled *Sandro of Chegem* and *The Gospel According to Chegem*.

ABOUT THE TRANSLATOR

SUSAN BROWNSBERGER holds degrees from Radcliffe and from Boston College. She has also translated work by the nineteenth-century novelist Mikhail Saltykov-Shchedrin and by Vassily Aksyonov.